50 GREATEST SHORT STORIES

50 GREATEST SHORT STORIES

Selection and Introduction by
TERRY O'BRIEN

RUPA

Published by
Rupa Publications India Pvt. Ltd 2015
7/16, Ansari Road, Daryaganj
New Delhi 110002

Sales centres:
Allahabad Bengaluru Chennai
Hyderabad Jaipur Kathmandu
Kolkata Mumbai

This is a work of fiction. Names, characters, places and incidents are either the product of the author's imagination or are used fictitiously and any resemblance to any actual person, living or dead, events or locales is entirely coincidental.

ISBN: 978-81-291-3725-8

Thirteenth impression 2019

20 19 18 17 16 15 14 13

Printed at HT Media Ltd, Gr. Noida

CONTENTS

INTRODUCTION

A short story must be short! By short, we mean must have brevity. ABC is the essence of a short story: Accuracy, Brevity, Conciseness. Thus, it must have a single leit-motif, like a lyric, almost 'a moment's monument'. The action in the story has connected happenings and their result. There are four major components of a short story: plot, setting, characters and theme. There is, however, a subtle difference between a plot and a story. A story is 'life in time'; a plot is 'life in values'. The story cannot diverge from the main plot. It leaves behind a single impression or effect. Great short-story writers have the art of excellence. These writers 'carve on an inch of ivory'. This book has some of the timeless gems of the short-story genre.

Terry O'Brien

1

THE MODEL MILLIONAIRE

Oscar Wilde

Unless one is wealthy there is no use in being a charming fellow. Romance is the privilege of the rich, not the profession of the unemployed. The poor should be practical and prosaic. It is better to have a permanent income than to be fascinating. These are the great truths of modern life which Hughie Erskine never realised. Poor Hughie! Intellectually, we must admit, he was not of much importance. He never said a brilliant or even an ill-natured thing in his life. But then he was wonderfully good-looking, with his crisp brown hair, his clear-cut profile, and his grey eyes. He was as popular with men as he was with women, and he had every accomplishment except that of making money. His father had bequeathed him his cavalry sword, and a History of the Peninsular War in fifteen volumes. Hughie hung the first over his looking-glass, put the second on a shelf between Ruff's Guide and Bailey's Magazine, and lived on two hundred a year that an old aunt allowed him. He had tried everything. He had gone on the Stock Exchange for six months; but what was a butterfly to do among bulls and bears? He had been a tea-merchant for a little longer, but had soon tired of pekoe and souchong. Then he had tried selling dry sherry. That did not answer; the sherry was a little too dry. Ultimately he became nothing, a delightful, ineffectual young man with a perfect profile and no profession.

To make matters worse, he was in love. The girl he loved was Laura Merton, the daughter of a retired Colonel who had lost his temper and his digestion in India, and had never found either of them again. Laura adored him, and he was ready to kiss her shoe-strings. They were the handsomest couple in London, and had not a penny-piece between them. The Colonel was very fond of Hughie, but would not hear of any engagement.

'Come to me, my boy, when you have got ten thousand pounds of your own, and we will see about it,' he used to say; and Hughie looked very glum on those days, and had to go to Laura for consolation.

One morning, as he was on his way to Holland Park, where the Mertons lived, he dropped in to see a great friend of his, Alan Trevor. Trevor was a painter. Indeed, few people escape that nowadays. But he was also an artist, and artists are rather rare. Personally he was a strange rough fellow, with a freckled face and a red ragged beard. However, when he took up the brush he was a real master, and his pictures were eagerly sought after. He had been very much attracted by Hughie at first, it must be acknowledged, entirely on account of his personal charm. 'The only people a painter should know,' he used to say, 'are people who are bête and beautiful, people who are an artistic pleasure to look at and an intellectual repose to talk to. Men who are dandies and women who are darlings rule the world, at least they should do so.' However, after he got to know Hughie better, he liked him quite as much for his bright buoyant spirits and his generous reckless nature, and had given him the permanent entrée to his studio.

When Hughie came in he found Trevor putting the finishing touches to a wonderful life-size picture of a beggar-man. The beggar himself was standing on a raised platform in a corner of the studio. He was a wizened old man, with a face like wrinkled parchment, and a most piteous expression. Over his shoulders was flung a coarse brown cloak, all tears and tatters; his thick boots were patched and cobbled, and with one hand he leant on a rough stick, while with the other he held out his battered hat for alms.

'What an amazing model!' whispered Hughie, as he shook hands with his friend.

'An amazing model?' shouted Trevor at the top of his voice; 'I should think so! Such beggars as he are not to be met with every day. A trouvaille, mon cher; a living Velasquez! My stars! what an etching Rembrandt would have made of him!'

'Poor old chap!' said Hughie, 'how miserable he looks! But I suppose, to you painters, his face is his fortune?'

'Certainly,' replied Trevor, 'you don't want a beggar to look happy, do you?'

'How much does a model get for sitting?' asked Hughie, as he found himself a comfortable seat on a divan.

'A shilling an hour.'

'And how much do you get for your picture, Alan?'

'Oh, for this I get two thousand!'

'Pounds?'

'Guineas. Painters, poets, and physicians always get guineas.'

'Well, I think the model should have a percentage,' cried Hughie, laughing; 'they work quite as hard as you do.'

'Nonsense, nonsense! Why, look at the trouble of laying on the paint alone, and standing all day long at one's easel! It's all very well, Hughie, for you to talk, but I assure you that there are moments when Art almost attains to the dignity of manual labour. But you mustn't chatter; I'm very busy. Smoke a cigarette, and keep quiet.'

After some time the servant came in, and told Trevor that the frame-maker wanted to speak to him.

'Don't run away, Hughie,' he said, as he went out, 'I will be back in a moment.'

The old beggar-man took advantage of Trevor's absence to rest for a moment on a wooden bench that was behind him. He looked so forlorn and wretched that Hughie could not help pitying him, and felt in his pockets to see what money he had. All he could find was a sovereign and some coppers. 'Poor old fellow,' he thought to himself, 'he wants it more than I do, but it means no hansoms for a fortnight'; and he walked across the studio and slipped the sovereign into the beggar's hand.

The old man started, and a faint smile flitted across his withered lips. 'Thank you, sir,' he said, 'thank you.'

Then Trevor arrived, and Hughie took his leave, blushing a

little at what he had done. He spent the day with Laura, got a charming scolding for his extravagance, and had to walk home.

That night he strolled into the Palette Club about eleven o'clock, and found Trevor sitting by himself in the smoking-room drinking hock and seltzer.

'Well, Alan, did you get the picture finished all right?' he said, as he lit his cigarette.

'Finished and framed, my boy!' answered Trevor; 'and, by-the-bye, you have made a conquest. That old model you saw is quite devoted to you. I had to tell him all about you—who you are, where you live, what your income is, what prospects you have—'

'My dear Alan,' cried Hughie, 'I shall probably find him waiting for me when I go home. But of course you are only joking. Poor old wretch! I wish I could do something for him. I think it is dreadful that any one should be so miserable. I have got heaps of old clothes at home—do you think he would care for any of them? Why, his rags were falling to bits.'

'But he looks splendid in them,' said Trevor. 'I wouldn't paint him in a frock-coat for anything. What you call rags I call romance. What seems poverty to you is picturesqueness to me. However, I'll tell him of your offer.'

'Alan,' said Hughie seriously, 'you painters are a heartless lot.'

'An artist's heart is his head,' replied Trevor; 'and besides, our business is to realise the world as we see it, not to reform it as we know it. À chacun son métier. And now tell me how Laura is. The old model was quite interested in her.'

'You don't mean to say you talked to him about her?' said Hughie.

'Certainly I did. He knows all about the relentless colonel, the lovely Laura, and the £10,000.'

'You told that old beggar all my private affairs?' cried Hughie, looking very red and angry.

'My dear boy,' said Trevor, smiling, 'that old beggar, as you call him, is one of the richest men in Europe. He could buy all London to-morrow without overdrawing his account. He has a house in every capital, dines off gold plate, and can prevent Russia going to war when he chooses.'

'What on earth do you mean?' exclaimed Hughie.

'What I say,' said Trevor. 'The old man you saw to-day in the studio was Baron Hausberg. He is a great friend of mine, buys all my pictures and that sort of thing, and gave me a commission a month ago to paint him as a beggar. Que voulez-vous? La fantaisie d'un millionnaire! And I must say he made a magnificent figure in his rags, or perhaps I should say in my rags; they are an old suit I got in Spain.'

'Baron Hausberg!' cried Hughie. 'Good heavens! I gave him a sovereign!' and he sank into an armchair the picture of dismay.

'Gave him a sovereign!' shouted Trevor, and he burst into a roar of laughter. 'My dear boy, you'll never see it again. Son affaire c'est l'argent des autres.'

'I think you might have told me, Alan,' said Hughie sulkily, 'and not have let me make such a fool of myself.'

'Well, to begin with, Hughie,' said Trevor, 'it never entered my mind that you went about distributing alms in that reckless way. I can understand your kissing a pretty model, but your giving a sovereign to an ugly one—by Jove, no! Besides, the fact is that I really was not at home to-day to any one; and when you came in I didn't know whether Hausberg would like his name mentioned. You know he wasn't in full dress.'

'What a duffer he must think me!' said Hughie.

'Not at all. He was in the highest spirits after you left; kept chuckling to himself and rubbing his old wrinkled hands together. I couldn't make out why he was so interested to know all about you; but I see it all now. He'll invest your sovereign for you, Hughie, pay you the interest every six months, and have a capital story to tell after dinner.'

'I am an unlucky devil,' growled Hughie. 'The best thing I can do is to go to bed; and, my dear Alan, you mustn't tell any one. I shouldn't dare show my face in the Row.'

'Nonsense! It reflects the highest credit on your philanthropic spirit, Hughie. And don't run away. Have another cigarette, and you can talk about Laura as much as you like.'

However, Hughie wouldn't stop, but walked home, feeling very unhappy, and leaving Alan Trevor in fits of laughter.

The next morning, as he was at breakfast, the servant brought him up a card on which was written, Monsieur Gustave Naudin, de la part de M. le Baron Hausberg."

'I suppose he has come for an apology,' said Hughie to himself; and he told the servant to show the visitor up.

An old gentleman with gold spectacles and grey hair came into the room, and said, in a slight French accent, 'Have I the honour of addressing Monsieur Erskine?'

Hughie bowed.

'I have come from Baron Hausberg,' he continued. 'The Baron—'

'I beg, sir, that you will offer him my sincerest apologies,' stammered Hughie.

'The Baron,' said the old gentleman, with a smile, 'has commissioned me to bring you this letter;' and he extended a sealed envelope.

On the outside was written, 'A wedding present to Hugh Erskine and Laura Merton, from an old beggar,' and inside was a cheque for £10,000.

When they were married Alan Trevor was the best-man, and the Baron made a speech at the wedding-breakfast.

'Millionaire models,' remarked Alan, 'are rare enough; but, by Jove, model millionaires are rarer still!'

2

THE FLY

Katherine Mansfield

'Y'are very snug in here,' piped old Mr. Woodifield, and peered out of the great, green-leather armchair by his friend the boss's desk as a baby peers out of its pram. His talk was over; it was time for him to be off. But he did not want to go. Since he had retired, since his...stroke, the wife and the girls kept him boxed up in the house every day of the week except Tuesday. On Tuesday he was dressed and brushed and allowed to cut back to the City for the day. Though what he did there the wife and girls couldn't imagine. Made a nuisance of himself to his friends, they supposed...Well, perhaps so. All the same, we cling to our last pleasures as the tree clings to its last leaves. So there sat old Woodifield, smoking a cigar and staring almost greedily at the boss, who rolled in his office chair, stout, rosy, five years older than he, and still going strong, still at the helm. It did one good to see him.

Wistfully, admiringly, the old voice added, 'It's snug in here, upon my word!'

'Yes, it's comfortable enough,' agreed the boss, and he flipped the Financial Times with a paper-knife. As a matter of fact he was proud of his room; he liked to have it admired, especially by old Woodifield. It gave him a feeling of deep, solid satisfaction to be planted there in the midst of it in full view of that frail old figure in the muffler.

'I've had it done up lately,' he explained, as he had explained for the past—how many!—weeks. 'New carpet,' and he pointed to the bright red carpet with a pattern of large white rings. 'New furniture,' and he nodded towards the massive bookcase and the table with legs like twisted treacle. 'Electric heating!'

He waved almost exultantly towards the five transparent, pearly sausages glowing so softly in the tilted copper pan.

But he did not draw old Woodifield's attention to the photograph over the table of a grave-looking boy in uniform standing in one of those spectral photographers' parks with photographers' storm-clouds behind him. It was not new. It had been there for over six years.

'There was something I wanted to tell you,' said old Woodifield, and his eyes grew dim remembering. 'Now what was it? I had it in my mind when I started out this morning.' His hands began to tremble, and patches of red showed above his beard.

Poor old chap, he's on his last pins, thought the boss. And, feeling kindly, he winked at the old man, and said jokingly, 'I tell you what. I've got a little drop of something here that'll do you good before you go out into the cold again. It's beautiful stuff. It wouldn't hurt a child.' He took a key off his watch-chain, unlocked a cupboard below his desk, and drew forth a dark, squat bottle. 'That's the medicine,' said he. 'And the man from whom I got it told me on the strict Q.T. it came from the cellars at Windsor Castle.'

Old Woodifield's mouth fell open at the sight. He couldn't have looked more surprised if the boss had produced a rabbit. 'It's whisky, ain't it?' he piped feebly.

The boss turned the bottle and lovingly showed him the label. Whisky it was.

'D'you know,' said he, peering up at the boss wonderingly, 'they won't let me touch it at home.' And he looked as though he was going to cry.

'Ah, that's where we know a bit more than the ladies,' cried the boss, swooping across for two tumblers that stood on the table with the water-bottle, and pouring a generous finger into each. 'Drink it down. It'll do you good. And don't put any water with it. It's sacrilege to tamper with stuff like this. Ah!' He tossed off his, pulled out his handkerchief, hastily wiped his moustaches, and cocked an eye at old Woodifield, who was rolling his in his chaps.

The old man swallowed, was silent a moment, and then said faintly, 'It's nutty!'

But it warmed him; it crept into his chill old brain—he remembered.

'That was it,' he said, heaving himself out of his chair. 'I thought you'd like to know. The girls were in Belgium last week having a look at poor Reggie's grave, and they happened to come across your boy's. They're quite near each other, it seems.

Old Woodifield paused, but the boss made no reply. Only a quiver in his eyelids showed that he heard.

'The girls were delighted with the way the place is kept,' piped the old voice. 'Beautifully looked after. Couldn't be better if they were at home. You've not been across, have yer?'

'No, no!' For various reasons the boss had not been across.

'There's miles of it,' quavered old Woodifield, 'and it's all as neat as a garden. Flowers growing on all the graves. Nice broad paths.' It was plain from his voice how much he liked a nice broad path.

The pause came again. Then the old man brightened wonderfully.

'D'you know what the hotel made the girls pay for a pot of jam?' he piped. 'Ten francs! Robbery, I call it. It was a little pot, so Gertrude says, no bigger than a half-crown. And she hadn't taken more than a spoonful when they charged her ten francs. Gertrude brought the pot away with her to teach 'em a lesson. Quite right, too; it's trading on our feelings. They think because we're over there having a look round we're ready to pay anything. That's what it is.' And he turned towards the door.

'Quite right, quite right!' cried the boss, though what was quite right he hadn't the least idea. He came round by his desk, followed the shuffling footsteps to the door, and saw the old fellow out. Woodifield was gone.

For a long moment the boss stayed, staring at nothing, while the grey-haired office messenger, watching him, dodged in and out of his cubby-hole like a dog that expects to be taken for a run. Then, 'I'll see nobody for half an hour, Macey,' said the boss. 'Understand! Nobody at all.'

'Very good, sir.'

The door shut, the firm heavy steps recrossed the bright carpet, the fat body plumped down in the spring chair, and leaning forward, the boss covered his face with his hands. He wanted, he intended, he had arranged to weep...

It had been a terrible shock to him when old Woodifield sprang that remark upon him about the boy's grave. It was exactly as though the earth had opened and he had seen the boy lying there with Woodifield's girls staring down at him. For it was strange. Although over six years had passed away, the boss never thought of the boy except as lying unchanged, unblemished in his uniform, asleep for ever. 'My son!' groaned the boss. But no tears came yet. In the past, in the first months and even years after the boy's death, he had only to say those words to be overcome by such grief that nothing short of a violent fit of weeping could relieve him. Time, he had declared then, he had told everybody, could make no difference. Other men perhaps might recover, might live their loss down, but not he. How was it possible! His boy was an only son. Ever since his birth the boss had worked at building up this business for him; it had no other meaning if it was not for the boy. Life itself had come to have no other meaning. How on earth could he have slaved, denied himself, kept going all those years without the promise for ever before him of the boy's stepping into his shoes and carrying on where he left off?

And that promise had been so near being fulfilled. The boy had been in the office learning the ropes for a year before the war. Every morning they had started off together; they had come back by the same train. And what congratulations he had received as the boy's father! No wonder; he had taken to it marvellously. As to his popularity with the staff, every man jack of them down to old Macey couldn't make enough of the boy. And he wasn't in the least spoilt. No, he was just his bright natural self, with the right word for everybody, with that boyish look and his habit of saying, 'Simply splendid!'

But all that was over and done with as though it never had been. The day had come when Macey had handed him the telegram that brought the whole place crashing about his head. 'Deeply regret to inform you...' And he had left the office a broken man, with his life in ruins.

Six years ago, six years... How quickly time passed! It might have happened yesterday. The boss took his hands from his face; he was puzzled. Something seemed to be wrong with him. He wasn't feeling as he wanted to feel. He decided to get up and have a look at the boy's photograph. But it wasn't a favourite photograph of his; the expression was unnatural. It was cold, even stern-looking. The boy had never looked like that.

At that moment the boss noticed that a fly had fallen into his broad inkpot, and was trying feebly but desperately to clamber out again. Help! Help! said those struggling legs. But the sides of the inkpot were wet and slippery; it fell back again and began to swim. The boss took up a pen, picked the fly out of the ink, and shook it on to a piece of blotting-paper. For a fraction of a second it lay still on the dark patch that oozed round it. Then the front legs waved, took hold, and, pulling its small, sodden body up, it began the immense task of cleaning the ink from its wings. Over and under, over and under, went a leg along a wing as the stone goes over and under the scythe. Then there was a pause, while the fly, seeming to stand on the tips of its toes, tried to expand first one wing and then the other. It succeeded at last, and, sitting down, it began, like a minute cat, to clean its face. Now one could Imagine that the little front legs rubbed against each other lightly, joyfully. The horrible danger was over; it had escaped; it was ready for life again.

But just then the boss had an idea. He plunged his pen back into the ink, leaned his thick wrist on the blotting-paper, and as the fly tried its wings down came a great heavy blot. What would it make of that! What indeed! The little beggar seemed absolutely cowed, stunned, and afraid to move because of what would happen next. But then, as if painfully, it dragged itself forward. The front legs waved, caught hold, and, more slowly this time, the task began from the beginning.

He's a plucky little devil, thought the boss, and he felt a real admiration for the fly's courage. That was the way to tackle things; that was the right spirit. Never say die; it was only a question of... But the fly had again finished its laborious task, and the boss had just time to refill his pen, to shake fair and square on the new-cleaned body yet another dark drop. What about it this time? A painful moment of suspense followed. But behold, the front legs were again waving; the boss felt a rush of relief. He leaned over the fly and said to it tenderly, 'You artful little b...' And he actually had the brilliant notion of breathing on it to help the drying process. All the same, there was something timid and weak about its efforts now, and the boss decided that this time should be the last, as he dipped the pen deep into the inkpot.

It was. The last blot fell on the soaked blotting-paper, and the draggled fly lay in it and did not stir. The back legs were stuck to the body; the front legs were not to be seen.

'Come on,' said the boss. 'Look sharp!' And he stirred it with his pen—in vain. Nothing happened or was likely to happen. The fly was dead.

The boss lifted the corpse on the end of the paper-knife and flung it into the waste-paper basket. But such a grinding feeling of wretchedness seized him that he felt positively frightened. He started forward and pressed the bell for Macey.

'Bring me some fresh blotting-paper,' he said sternly, 'and look sharp about it.' And while the old dog padded away he fell to wondering what it was he had been thinking about before. What was it? It was... He took out his handkerchief and passed it inside his collar. For the life of him he could not remember.

3

AN OCCURRENCE AT OWL CREEK BRIDGE

Ambrose Bierce

A man stood upon a railroad bridge in northern Alabama, looking down into the swift water twenty feet below. The man's hands were behind his back, the wrists bound with a cord. A rope closely encircled his neck. It was attached to a stout cross-timber above his head and the slack fell to the level of his knees. Some loose boards laid upon the ties supporting the rails of the railway supplied a footing for him and his executioners—two private soldiers of the Federal army, directed by a sergeant who in civil life may have been a deputy sheriff. At a short remove upon the same temporary platform was an officer in the uniform of his rank, armed. He was a captain. A sentinel at each end of the bridge stood with his rifle in the position known as 'support,' that is to say, vertical in front of the left shoulder, the hammer resting on the forearm thrown straight across the chest—a formal and unnatural position, enforcing an erect carriage of the body. It did not appear to be the duty of these two men to know what was occurring at the center of the bridge; they merely blockaded the two ends of the foot planking that traversed it.

Beyond one of the sentinels nobody was in sight; the railroad ran straight away into a forest for a hundred yards, then, curving, was lost to view. Doubtless there was an outpost farther along. The other bank of the stream was open ground—a gentle slope topped with a stockade of vertical tree trunks, loopholed for rifles, with a single embrasure through which protruded the muzzle of a brass cannon commanding the bridge. Midway up the slope between the bridge and fort were the spectators—a single company of infantry in line, at 'parade rest,' the butts of their rifles on the ground, the barrels inclining slightly backward against the right shoulder, the hands crossed upon the stock. A lieutenant stood at the right of the line, the point of his sword upon the ground, his left hand resting upon his right. Excepting the group of four at the center of the bridge, not a man moved. The company faced the bridge, staring stonily, motionless. The sentinels, facing the banks of the stream, might have been statues to adorn the bridge. The captain stood with folded arms, silent, observing the work of his subordinates, but making no sign. Death is a dignitary who when he comes announced is to be received with formal manifestations of respect, even by those most familiar with him. In the code of military etiquette silence and fixity are forms of deference.

The man who was engaged in being hanged was apparently about thirty-five years of age. He was a civilian, if one might judge from his habit, which was that of a planter. His features were good—a straight nose, firm mouth, broad forehead, from which his long, dark hair was combed straight back, falling behind his ears to the collar of his well fitting frock coat. He wore a moustache and pointed beard, but no whiskers; his eyes were large and dark gray, and had a kindly expression which one would hardly have expected in one whose neck was in the hemp. Evidently this was no vulgar assassin. The liberal military code makes provision for hanging many kinds of persons, and gentlemen are not excluded.

The preparations being complete, the two private soldiers stepped aside and each drew away the plank upon which he had been standing. The sergeant turned to the captain, saluted and placed himself immediately behind that officer, who in turn moved apart one pace. These movements left the condemned man and the sergeant standing on the two ends of the same plank, which spanned three of the cross-ties of the bridge. The end upon which the civilian stood almost, but not quite, reached a fourth. This plank had been held in place by the weight of the captain; it was now held by that of the sergeant. At a signal from the former the latter would step aside, the plank would tilt and the condemned man go down between two ties. The arrangement commended itself to his judgement as simple and effective. His face had not been covered nor his eyes bandaged. He looked a moment at his 'unsteadfast footing,' then let his gaze wander to the swirling water of the stream racing madly beneath his feet. A piece of dancing driftwood caught his attention and his eyes followed it down the current. How slowly it appeared to move! What a sluggish stream!

He closed his eyes in order to fix his last thoughts upon his wife and children. The water, touched to gold by the early sun, the brooding mists under the banks at some distance down the stream, the fort, the soldiers, the piece of drift—all had distracted him. And now he became conscious of a new disturbance. Striking through the thought of his dear ones was sound which he could neither ignore nor understand, a sharp, distinct, metallic percussion like the stroke of a blacksmith's hammer upon the anvil; it had the same ringing quality. He wondered what it was, and whether immeasurably distant or near by—it seemed both. Its recurrence was regular, but as slow as the tolling of a death knell. He awaited each new stroke with impatience and—he knew not why—apprehension. The intervals of silence grew progressively longer; the delays became maddening. With their greater infrequency the sounds increased in strength and sharpness. They hurt his ear like the trust of a knife; he feared he would shriek. What he heard was the ticking of his watch.

He unclosed his eyes and saw again the water below him. 'If I could free my hands,' he thought, 'I might throw off the noose and spring into the stream. By diving I could evade the bullets and, swimming vigorously, reach the bank, take to the woods and get away home. My home, thank God, is as yet outside their lines; my wife and little ones are still beyond the invader's farthest advance.'

As these thoughts, which have here to be set down in words, were flashed into the doomed man's brain rather than evolved from it the captain nodded to the sergeant. The sergeant stepped aside.

Peyton Farquhar was a well to do planter, of an old and highly respected Alabama family. Being a slave owner and like other slave owners a politician, he was naturally an original secessionist and ardently devoted to the Southern cause. Circumstances of an imperious nature, which it is unnecessary to relate here, had prevented him from taking service with that gallant army which had fought the disastrous campaigns ending with the fall of Corinth, and he chafed under the inglorious restraint, longing for the release of his energies, the larger life of the soldier, the opportunity for distinction. That opportunity, he felt, would come, as it comes to all in wartime. Meanwhile he did what he could. No service was too humble for him to perform in the aid of the South, no adventure too perilous for him to undertake if consistent with the character of a civilian who was at heart a soldier, and who in good faith and without too much qualification assented to at least a part of the frankly villainous dictum that all is fair in love and war.

One evening while Farquhar and his wife were sitting on a rustic bench near the entrance to his grounds, a gray-clad soldier rode up to the gate and asked for a drink of water. Mrs. Farquhar was only too happy to serve him with her own white hands. While she was fetching the water her husband approached the dusty horseman and inquired eagerly for news from the front.

'The Yanks are repairing the railroads,' said the man, 'and are getting ready for another advance. They have reached the Owl Creek bridge, put it in order and built a stockade on the north bank. The commandant has issued an order, which is posted everywhere, declaring that any civilian caught interfering with the railroad, its bridges, tunnels, or trains will be summarily hanged. I saw the order.'

'How far is it to the Owl Creek bridge?' Farquhar asked.

'About thirty miles.'

'Is there no force on this side of the creek?'

'Only a picket post half a mile out, on the railroad, and a single sentinel at this end of the bridge.'

'Suppose a man—a civilian and student of hanging—should elude the picket post and perhaps get the better of the sentinel,' said Farquhar, smiling, 'what could he accomplish?'

The soldier reflected. 'I was there a month ago,' he replied. 'I observed that the flood of last winter had lodged a great quantity of driftwood against the wooden pier at this end of the bridge. It is now dry and would burn like tinder.'

The lady had now brought the water, which the soldier drank. He thanked her ceremoniously, bowed to her husband and rode away. An hour later, after nightfall, he repassed the plantation, going northward in the direction from which he had come. He was a Federal scout.

As Peyton Farquhar fell straight downward through the bridge he lost consciousness and was as one already dead. From this state he was awakened—ages later, it seemed to him—by the pain of a sharp pressure upon his throat, followed by a sense of suffocation. Keen, poignant agonies seemed to shoot from his neck downward through every fiber of his body and limbs. These pains appeared to flash along well defined lines of ramification and to beat with an inconceivably rapid periodicity. They seemed like streams of pulsating fire heating him to an intolerable temperature. As to his head, he was conscious of nothing but a feeling of fullness—of congestion. These sensations were unaccompanied by thought. The intellectual part of his nature was already effaced; he had power only to feel, and feeling was torment. He was conscious of motion. Encompassed in a luminous cloud, of which he was now merely the fiery heart, without material substance, he swung through unthinkable arcs of oscillation, like a vast pendulum. Then all at once, with terrible suddenness, the light about him shot upward with the noise of a loud splash; a frightful roaring was in his ears, and all was cold and dark. The power of thought was restored; he knew that the rope had broken and he had fallen into the stream. There was no additional strangulation;

the noose about his neck was already suffocating him and kept the water from his lungs. To die of hanging at the bottom of a river!—the idea seemed to him ludicrous. He opened his eyes in the darkness and saw above him a gleam of light, but how distant, how inaccessible! He was still sinking, for the light became fainter and fainter until it was a mere glimmer. Then it began to grow and brighten, and he knew that he was rising toward the surface—knew it with reluctance, for he was now very comfortable. 'To be hanged and drowned,' he thought, 'that is not so bad; but I do not wish to be shot. No; I will not be shot; that is not fair.'

He was not conscious of an effort, but a sharp pain in his wrist apprised him that he was trying to free his hands. He gave the struggle his attention, as an idler might observe the feat of a juggler, without interest in the outcome. What splendid effort!—what magnificent, what superhuman strength! Ah, that was a fine endeavor! Bravo! The cord fell away; his arms parted and floated upward, the hands dimly seen on each side in the growing light. He watched them with a new interest as first one and then the other pounced upon the noose at his neck. They tore it away and thrust it fiercely aside, its undulations resembling those of a water snake. 'Put it back, put it back!' He thought he shouted these words to his hands, for the undoing of the noose had been succeeded by the direst pang that he had yet experienced. His neck ached horribly; his brain was on fire, his heart, which had been fluttering faintly, gave a great leap, trying to force itself out at his mouth. His whole body was racked and wrenched with an insupportable anguish! But his disobedient hands gave no heed to the command. They beat the water vigorously with quick, downward strokes, forcing him to the surface. He felt his head emerge; his eyes were blinded by the sunlight; his chest expanded convulsively, and with a supreme and crowning agony his lungs engulfed a great draught of air, which instantly he expelled in a shriek!

He was now in full possession of his physical senses. They were, indeed, preternaturally keen and alert. Something in the awful disturbance of his organic system had so exalted and refined them that they made record of things never before perceived. He felt the ripples upon his face and heard their separate sounds as they struck. He looked at the forest on the bank of the stream, saw the individual trees, the leaves and the veining of each leaf—he saw the very insects upon them: the locusts, the brilliant bodied flies, the gray spiders stretching their webs from twig to twig. He noted the prismatic colors in all the dewdrops upon a million blades of grass. The humming of the gnats that danced above the eddies of the stream, the beating of the dragon flies' wings, the strokes of the water spiders' legs, like oars which had lifted their boat—all these made audible music. A fish slid along beneath his eyes and he heard the rush of its body parting the water.

He had come to the surface facing down the stream; in a moment the visible world seemed to wheel slowly round, himself the pivotal point, and he saw the bridge, the fort, the soldiers upon the bridge, the captain, the sergeant, the two privates, his executioners. They were in silhouette against the blue sky. They shouted and gesticulated, pointing at him. The captain had drawn his pistol, but did not fire; the others were unarmed. Their movements were grotesque and horrible, their forms gigantic.

Suddenly he heard a sharp report and something struck the water smartly within a few inches of his head, spattering his face with spray. He heard a second report, and saw one of the sentinels with his rifle at his shoulder, a light cloud of blue smoke rising from the muzzle. The man in the water saw the eye of the man on the bridge gazing into his own through the sights of the rifle. He observed that it was a gray eye and remembered having read that gray eyes were keenest, and that all famous marksmen had them. Nevertheless, this one had missed.

A counter-swirl had caught Farquhar and turned him half round; he was again looking at the forest on the bank opposite the fort. The sound of a clear, high voice in a monotonous singsong now rang out behind him and came across the water with a distinctness that pierced and subdued all other sounds, even the beating of the ripples in his ears. Although no soldier, he had frequented camps enough to know the dread significance of that deliberate, drawling, aspirated chant; the lieutenant on shore was taking a part in the morning's work. How coldly and pitilessly—with what an even, calm intonation, presaging, and enforcing tranquility in the men—with what accurately measured interval fell those cruel words:

'Company!...Attention!...Shoulder arms!...Ready!...Aim!... Fire!'

Farquhar dived—dived as deeply as he could. The water roared in his ears like the voice of Niagara, yet he heard the dull thunder of the volley and, rising again toward the surface, met shining bits of metal, singularly flattened, oscillating slowly downward. Some of them touched him on the face and hands, then fell away, continuing their descent. One lodged between his collar and neck; it was uncomfortably warm and he snatched it out.

As he rose to the surface, gasping for breath, he saw that he had been a long time under water; he was perceptibly farther downstream—nearer to safety. The soldiers had almost finished reloading; the metal ramrods flashed all at once in the sunshine as they were drawn from the barrels, turned in the air, and thrust into their sockets. The two sentinels fired again, independently and ineffectually.

The hunted man saw all this over his shoulder; he was now swimming vigorously with the current. His brain was as energetic as his arms and legs; he thought with the rapidity of lightning:

'The officer,' he reasoned, 'will not make that martinet's error a second time. It is as easy to dodge a volley as a single shot. He has probably already given the command to fire at will. God help me, I cannot dodge them all!'

An appalling splash within two yards of him was followed by a loud, rushing sound, DIMINUENDO, which seemed to travel back through the air to the fort and died in an explosion which stirred the very river to its deeps! A rising sheet of water curved over him, fell down upon him, blinded him, strangled him! The cannon had taken an hand in the game. As he shook his head free from the commotion of the smitten water he heard the deflected shot humming through the air ahead, and in an instant it was cracking and smashing the branches in the forest beyond.

'They will not do that again,' he thought; 'the next time they will use a charge of grape. I must keep my eye upon the gun; the smoke will apprise me—the report arrives too late; it lags behind the missile. That is a good gun.'

Suddenly he felt himself whirled round and round—spinning like a top. The water, the banks, the forests, the now distant bridge, fort and men, all were commingled and blurred. Objects were represented by their colors only; circular horizontal streaks of color—that was all he saw. He had been caught in a vortex and was being whirled on with a velocity of advance and gyration that made him giddy and sick. In few moments he was flung upon the gravel at the foot of the left bank of the stream—the southern bank—and behind a projecting point which concealed him from his enemies. The sudden arrest of his motion, the abrasion of one of his hands on the gravel, restored him, and he wept with delight. He dug his fingers into the sand, threw it over himself in handfuls and audibly blessed it. It looked like diamonds, rubies, emeralds; he could think of nothing beautiful which it did not resemble. The trees upon the bank were giant garden plants; he noted a definite order in their arrangement, inhaled the fragrance of their blooms. A strange roseate light shone through the spaces among their trunks and the wind made in their branches the music of AEolian harps. He had not wish to perfect his escape—he was content to remain in that enchanting spot until retaken.

A whiz and a rattle of grapeshot among the branches high above his head roused him from his dream. The baffled cannoneer had fired him a random farewell. He sprang to his feet, rushed up the sloping bank, and plunged into the forest.

All that day he traveled, laying his course by the rounding sun. The forest seemed interminable; nowhere did he discover a break in it, not even a woodman's road. He had not known that he lived in so wild a region. There was something uncanny in the revelation.

By nightfall he was fatigued, footsore, famished. The thought of his wife and children urged him on. At last he found a road which led him in what he knew to be the right direction. It was as wide and straight as a city street, yet it seemed untraveled. No fields bordered it, no dwelling anywhere. Not so much as the barking of a dog suggested human habitation. The black bodies of the trees formed a straight wall on both sides, terminating on the horizon in a point, like a diagram in a lesson in perspective. Overhead, as he looked up through this rift in the wood, shone great golden stars looking unfamiliar and grouped in strange constellations. He was sure they were arranged in some order which had a secret and malign significance. The wood on either side was full of singular noises, among which—once, twice, and again—he distinctly heard whispers in an unknown tongue.

His neck was in pain and lifting his hand to it found it horribly swollen. He knew that it had a circle of black where the rope had bruised it. His eyes felt congested; he could no longer close them. His tongue was swollen with thirst; he relieved its fever by thrusting it forward from between his teeth into the cold air. How softly the turf had carpeted the untraveled avenue—he could no longer feel the roadway beneath his feet!

Doubtless, despite his suffering, he had fallen asleep while walking, for now he sees another scene—perhaps he has merely recovered from a delirium. He stands at the gate of his own home. All is as he left it, and all bright and beautiful in the morning sunshine. He must have traveled the entire night. As he pushes open the gate and passes up the wide white walk, he sees a flutter of female garments; his wife, looking fresh and cool and sweet, steps down from the veranda to meet him. At the bottom of the steps she stands waiting, with a smile of ineffable joy, an attitude of matchless grace and dignity. Ah, how beautiful she is! He springs forwards with extended arms. As he is about to clasp her he feels a stunning blow upon the back of the neck; a blinding white light blazes all about him with a sound like the shock of a cannon—then all is darkness and silence!

Peyton Farquhar was dead; his body, with a broken neck, swung gently from side to side beneath the timbers of the Owl Creek bridge.

4

THE LAST LEAF

O. Henry

In a little district west of Washington Square the streets have run crazy and broken themselves into small strips called 'places.' These 'places' make strange angles and curves. One street crosses itself a time or two. An artist once discovered a valuable possibility in this street. Suppose a collector with a bill for paints, paper and canvas should, in traversing this route, suddenly meet himself coming back, without a cent having been paid on account!

So, to quaint old Greenwich Village the art people soon came prowling, hunting for north windows and eighteenth-century gables and Dutch attics and low rents. Then they imported some pewter mugs and a chafing dish or two from Sixth Avenue, and became a 'colony.'

At the top of a squatty, three story brick Sue and Johnsy had their studio. 'Johnsy' was familiar for Joanna. One was from Maine; the other from California. They had met at the *table d'hote* of an Eighth Street 'Delmonico's,' and found their tastes in art, chicory salad and bishop sleeves so congenial that the studio resulted.

That was in May. In November a cold, unseen stranger, whom the doctors called Pneumonia, stalked about the colony, touching one here and there with his icy fingers. Over on the east side this ravager strode boldly, smiting his victims by scores, but his feet trod slowly through the maze of the narrow and moss-grown 'places.'

Mr. Pneumonia was not what you would call a chivalric old gentleman. A mite of a little woman with blood thinned by California zephyrs was hardly fair game for the red-fisted, short breathed old duffer. But Johnsy he smote; and she lay scarcely moving, on her painted iron bedstead, looking through the small Dutch window-panes at the blank side of the next brick house.

One morning the busy doctor invited Sue into the hallway with a shaggy, gray eyebrow.

'She has one chance in—let us say, ten,' he said, as he shook down the mercury in his clinical thermometer. 'And that chance is for her to want to live. This way people have of lining—up on the side of the undertaker makes the entire pharmacopoeia look silly. Your little lady has made up her mind that she's not going to get well. Has she anything on her mind?'

'She-she wanted to paint the Bay of Naples some day,' said Sue.

'Paint?—bosh! Has she anything on her mind worth thinking about twice—a man, for instance?'

'A man?' said Sue, with a jew's-harp twang in her voice. 'Is a man worth—but, no, doctor; there is nothing of the kind.'

'Well, it is the weakness, then,' said the doctor. 'I will do all that science, so far as it may filter through my efforts, can accomplish. But whenever my patient begins to count the carriages in her funeral procession I subtract 50 per cent from the curative power of medicines. If you will get her to ask one question about the new winter styles in cloak sleeves I will promise you a one-in-five chance for her, instead of ten.'

After the doctor had gone Sue went into the workroom and cried a Japanese napkin to a pulp. Then she swaggered into Johnsy's room with her drawing board, whistling ragtime.

Johnsy, lay, scarcely making a ripple under the bedclothes, with her face toward the window. Sue stopped whistling, thinking she was asleep.

She arranged her board and began a pen and ink drawing to illustrate a magazine story. Young artists must pave their way to Art by drawing pictures for magazine stories that young authors write to pave their way to literature.

As Sue was sketching a pair of elegant horseshow riding

trousers, a monocle on the figure of the hero, an Idaho cowboy, she heard a low sound, several times repeated. She went quickly to the bedside.

Johnsy's eyes were open wide. She was looking out the window and counting-counting backward.

'Twelve,' she said, and a little later 'eleven'; and then 'ten,' and 'nine'; and then 'eight' and 'seven,' almost together.

Sue looked solicitously out the window. What was there to count? There was only a bare, dreary yard to be seen, and the blank side of the brick house twenty feet away. An old, old ivy vine, gnarled and decayed at the roots, climbed half way up the brick wall. The cold breath of autumn had stricken its leaves from the vine until its skeleton branches clung, almost bare, to the crumbling bricks.

'What is it, dear? Tell your Sudie.'

'Leaves. On the ivy vine. When the last one falls I must go, too. I've known that for three days. Didn't the doctor tell you?'

'Oh, I never heard of such nonsense,' complained Sue, with magnificent scorn. 'What have old ivy leaves to do with your getting well? And you used to love that vine, so, you naughty girl. Don't be a goosey. Why, the doctor told me this morning that your chances for getting well real soon were—let's see exactly what he said—he said the chances were ten to one! Why that's almost as good a chance as we have in New York when we ride on the street cars or walk past a new building. Try to take some broth now, and let Sudie go back to her drawing, so she can sell the editor man with it, and buy port wine for her sick child, and pork chops for her greedy self.'

'You needn't get any more wine,' said Johnsy, keeping her eyes fixed on the window. 'There goes another. No, I don't want any broth. That leaves just four. I want to see the last one fall before it gets dark. Then I'll go too.'

'Johnsy, dear,' said Sue, bending over her, 'will you promise me to keep your eyes closed, and not look out the window until I am done working? I must hand those drawings in by to-morrow. I need the light, or I could draw the shade down.'

'Couldn't you draw in the other room?' asked Johnsy, coldly.

'I'd rather be here by you,' said Sue. 'Besides, I don't want you to keep looking at those silly ivy leaves.'

'Tell me as soon as you have finished,' said Johnsy, closing her eyes, and lying white and still as a fallen statue, 'because I want to see the last one fall. I'm tired of waiting. I'm tired of thinking. I want to turn loose my hold on everything, and go sailing down, down, just like one of those poor, tired leaves.'

'Try to sleep,' said Sue. 'I must call Behrman up to be my model for the old hermit miner. I'll not be gone a minute. Don't try to move 'til I come back.'

Old Behrman was a painter who lived on the ground floor beneath them. He was past sixty and had a Michelangelo's Moses beard curling down from the head of a satyr along the body of an imp. Behrman was a failure in art. Forty years he had wielded the brush without getting near enough to touch the hem of his Mistress's robe. He had been always about to paint a masterpiece, but had never yet begun it. For several years he had painted nothing except now and then a daub in the line of commerce or advertising. He earned a little by serving as a model to those young artists in the colony who could not pay the price of a professional. He drank gin to excess, and still talked of his coming masterpiece. For the rest he was a fierce little old man, who scoffed terribly at the softness in any one, and who regarded himself as especial mastiff-in-waiting to protect the two young artists in the studio above.

Sue found Behrman smelling strongly of juniper berries in his dimly lighted den below. In one corner was a blank canvas on an easel that had been waiting there for twenty-five years to receive the first line of the masterpiece. She told him of Johnsy's fancy, and how she feared she would, indeed light and fragile as a leaf herself, float away, when her slight hold upon the world grew weaker.

Old Behrman, with his red eyes plainly streaming, shouted his contempt and derision for such idiotic imaginings.

'Vass!' he cried. 'Is dere people in de world mit der

foolishness to die because leafs dey drop off from a confounded vine? I haf not heard of such a thing. No, I will not bose as a model for you fool hermit-dunder-head. Vy do you allow dot silly pusiness to come in der brain aof her? Ach, dot poor lettle Miss Yohnsy.'

'She is very ill and weak,' said Sue, 'and the fever has left her mind morbid and full of strange fancies. Very well, Mr. Behrman, if you do not care to pose for me, you needn't. But I think you are a horrid old—old flibbertigibbet.'

'You are just like a woman!' yelled Behrman. 'Who said I will not bose? Go on. I come mit you. For half and hour I haf peen trying to say dot I am ready to bose. Gott! Dis is not any blace in which one so gooot as Miss Yohnsy shall lie sick. Some day I vill baint a masterpiece, and ve shall all go away. Gott! Yes.'

Johnsy was sleeping when they went upstairs. She pulled the shade down to the window-sill, and motioned Behrman into the other room. In there they peered out the window fearfully at the ivy vine. Then they looked at each other for a moment with out speaking. A persistent, cold rain was falling, mingled with snow. Behrman, in his old blue shirt, took his seat as the hermit miner on an upturned kettle for a rock.

When Sue awoke from an hour's sleep the next morning she found Johnsy with dull, wide-open eyes staring at the drawn green shade.

'Pull it up; I want to see,' she ordered, in a whisper.

Wearily Sue obeyed.

But lo! after the beating rain and fierce gusts of wind that had endured through the livelong night, there yet stood out against the brick wall one ivy leaf. It was the last on the vine. Still dark green near its stem, but with its serrated edges tinted with the yellow of dissolution and decay, it hung bravely from a branch some twenty feet above the ground.

'It is the last one,' said Johnsy. 'I thought it would surely fall during the night. I heard the wind. It will fall to-day, and I shall die at the same time.'

'Dear, dear!' said Sue, leaning her worn face down to the pillow, 'think of me, if you won't think of yourself. What would I do?'

But Johnsy did not answer. The lonesomest thing in all the world is a soul when it is making ready to go on its mysterious, far journey. The fancy seemed to possess her more strongly as one by one the ties that bound her to friendship and to earth were loosed.

The day wore away, and even through the twilight they could see the lone ivy leaf clinging to its stem against the wall. And then, with the coming of the night the north wind was again down from the low Dutch eaves.

When it was light enough Johnsy, the merciless, commanded that the shade be raised.

The ivy leaf was still there.

Johnsy lay for a long time looking at it. And then she called to Sue, who was stirring her chicken broth over the gas stove.

'I've been a bad girl, Sudie,' said Johnsy. 'Something has made that last leaf stay there to show me how wicked I was. It is a sin to want to die. You may bring me a little broth now, and some milk with a little port in it, and—no; bring me a hand-mirror first, and then pack some pillows about me, and I will sit up and watch you cook.'

An hour later she said:

'Sudie, some day I hope to paint the Bay of Naples.'

The doctor came in the afternoon, and Sue had an excuse to go into the hallway as he left.

'Even chances,' said the doctor, taking Sue's thin shaking hand in his. 'With good nursing you'll win. And now I must see another case I have downstairs. Behrman, his name is—some kind of artist, I believe. Pneumonia, too. He is an old, weak man, and the attack is acute. There is no hope for him; but he goes to the hospital to-day to be made more comfortable.'

The next day the doctor said to Sue, 'She's out of danger. You've won. Nutrition and care now—that's all.'

And that afternoon Sue came to the bed where Johnsy

lay, contentedly knitting a very blue and very useless woollen shoulder scarf, and put one arm around her, pillows and all.

'I have something to tell you, white mouse,' she said. 'Mr. Behrman died of pneumonia to-day in the hospital. He was ill only two days. The janitor found him on the morning of the first day in his room downstairs helpless with pain. His shoes and clothing were wet through and icy cold. They couldn't imagine where he had been on such a dreadful night. And then they found a lantern, still lighted, and a ladder that had been dragged from its place, and some scattered brushes, and a palette with green and yellow colors mixed on it, and—look out the window, dear, at the last ivy leaf on the wall. Didn't you wonder why it never fluttered or moved when the wind blew? Ah, darling, it's Behrman's masterpiece—he painted it there the night the last leaf fell.'

5

THE LOTTERY TICKET

Anton Chekov

Ivan Dmitritch, a middle-class man who lived with his family on an income of twelve hundred a year and was very well satisfied with his lot, sat down on the sofa after supper and began reading the newspaper.

'I forgot to look at the newspaper to-day,' his wife said to him as she cleared the table. 'Look and see whether the list of drawings is there.'

'Yes, it is,' said Ivan Dmitritch; 'but hasn't your ticket lapsed?'

'No; I took the interest on Tuesday.'

'What is the number?'

'Series 9,499, number 26.'

'All right...we will look...9,499 and 26.'

Ivan Dmitritch had no faith in lottery luck, and would not, as a rule, have consented to look at the lists of winning numbers, but now, as he had nothing else to do and as the newspaper was before his eyes, he passed his finger downwards along the column of numbers. And immediately, as though in mockery of his scepticism, no further than the second line from the top, his eye was caught by the figure 9,499! Unable to believe his eyes, he hurriedly dropped the paper on his knees without looking to see the number of the ticket, and, just as though some one had given him a douche of cold water, he felt an agreeable chill in the pit of the stomach; tingling and terrible and sweet!

'Masha, 9,499 is there!' he said in a hollow voice.

His wife looked at his astonished and panic-stricken face, and realized that he was not joking.

'9,499?' she asked, turning pale and dropping the folded

tablecloth on the table.

'Yes, yes...it really is there!'

'And the number of the ticket?'

'Oh yes! There's the number of the ticket too. But stay... wait! No, I say! Anyway, the number of our series is there! Anyway, you understand...'

Looking at his wife, Ivan Dmitritch gave a broad, senseless smile, like a baby when a bright object is shown it. His wife smiled too; it was as pleasant to her as to him that he only mentioned the series, and did not try to find out the number of the winning ticket. To torment and tantalize oneself with hopes of possible fortune is so sweet, so thrilling!

'It is our series,' said Ivan Dmitritch, after a long silence. 'So there is a probability that we have won. It's only a probability, but there it is!'

'Well, now look!'

'Wait a little. We have plenty of time to be disappointed. It's on the second line from the top, so the prize is seventy-five thousand. That's not money, but power, capital! And in a minute I shall look at the list, and there—26! Eh? I say, what if we really have won?'

The husband and wife began laughing and staring at one another in silence. The possibility of winning bewildered them; they could not have said, could not have dreamed, what they both needed that seventy-five thousand for, what they would buy, where they would go. They thought only of the figures 9,499 and 75,000 and pictured them in their imagination, while somehow they could not think of the happiness itself which was so possible.

Ivan Dmitritch, holding the paper in his hand, walked several times from corner to corner, and only when he had recovered from the first impression began dreaming a little.

'And if we have won,' he said—'why, it will be a new life, it will be a transformation! The ticket is yours, but if it were mine I should, first of all, of course, spend twenty-five thousand on real property in the shape of an estate; ten thousand on immediate expenses, new furnishing...travelling...paying debts, and so on...The other forty thousand I would put in the bank and get interest on it.'

'Yes, an estate, that would be nice,' said his wife, sitting down and dropping her hands in her lap.

'Somewhere in the Tula or Oryol provinces...In the first place we shouldn't need a summer villa, and besides, it would always bring in an income.'

And pictures came crowding on his imagination, each more gracious and poetical than the last. And in all these pictures he saw himself well-fed, serene, healthy, felt warm, even hot! Here, after eating a summer soup, cold as ice, he lay on his back on the burning sand close to a stream or in the garden under a lime-tree...It is hot...His little boy and girl are crawling about near him, digging in the sand or catching ladybirds in the grass. He dozes sweetly, thinking of nothing, and feeling all over that he need not go to the office to-day, to-morrow, or the day after. Or, tired of lying still, he goes to the hayfield, or to the forest for mushrooms, or watches the peasants catching fish with a net. When the sun sets he takes a towel and soap and saunters to the bathing shed, where he undresses at his leisure, slowly rubs his bare chest with his hands, and goes into the water. And in the water, near the opaque soapy circles, little fish flit to and fro and green water-weeds nod their heads. After bathing there is tea with cream and milk rolls...In the evening a walk or vint with the neighbors.

'Yes, it would be nice to buy an estate,' said his wife, also dreaming, and from her face it was evident that she was enchanted by her thoughts.

Ivan Dmitritch pictured to himself autumn with its rains, its cold evenings, and its St. Martin's summer. At that season he would have to take longer walks about the garden and beside the river, so as to get thoroughly chilled, and then drink a big glass of vodka and eat a salted mushroom or a soused cucumber, and then—drink another...The children would come running from the kitchen-garden, bringing a carrot and a radish smelling of fresh earth...And then, he would lie stretched full length on the sofa, and in leisurely fashion turn over the pages of some illustrated magazine, or, covering his face with it and unbuttoning his waistcoat, give himself up to slumber.

The St. Martin's summer is followed by cloudy, gloomy weather. It rains day and night, the bare trees weep, the wind is damp and cold. The dogs, the horses, the fowls—all are wet, depressed, downcast. There is nowhere to walk; one can't go out for days together; one has to pace up and down the room, looking despondently at the grey window. It is dreary!

Ivan Dmitritch stopped and looked at his wife.

'I should go abroad, you know, Masha,' he said.

And he began thinking how nice it would be in late autumn to go abroad somewhere to the South of France...to Italy...to India!

'I should certainly go abroad too,' his wife said. 'But look at the number of the ticket!'

'Wait, wait!...'

He walked about the room and went on thinking. It occurred to him: what if his wife really did go abroad? It is pleasant to travel alone, or in the society of light, careless women who live in the present, and not such as think and talk all the journey about nothing but their children, sigh, and tremble with dismay over every farthing. Ivan Dmitritch imagined his wife in the train with a multitude of parcels, baskets, and bags; she would be sighing over something, complaining that the train made her head ache, that she had spent so much money.... At the stations he would continually be having to run for boiling water, bread and butter... She wouldn't have dinner because of its being too dear...

'She would begrudge me every farthing,' he thought, with a glance at his wife. 'The lottery ticket is hers, not mine! Besides, what is the use of her going abroad? What does she want there? She would shut herself up in the hotel, and not let me out of her sight... I know!'

And for the first time in his life his mind dwelt on the fact that his wife had grown elderly and plain, and that she was saturated through and through with the smell of cooking, while he was still young, fresh, and healthy, and might well have got married again.

'Of course, all that is silly nonsense,' he thought; 'but... why should she go abroad? What would she make of it? And yet she would go, of course... I can fancy... In reality it is all one to her, whether it is Naples or Klin. She would only be in my way. I should be dependent upon her. I can fancy how, like a regular woman, she will lock the money up as soon as she gets it... She will look after her relations and grudge me every farthing.'

Ivan Dmitritch thought of her relations. All those wretched brothers and sisters and aunts and uncles would come crawling about as soon as they heard of the winning ticket, would begin whining like beggars, and fawning upon them with oily, hypocritical smiles. Wretched, detestable people! If they were given anything, they would ask for more; while if they were refused, they would swear at them, slander them, and wish them every kind of misfortune.

Ivan Dmitritch remembered his own relations, and their faces, at which he had looked impartially in the past, struck him now as repulsive and hateful.

'They are such reptiles!' he thought.

And his wife's face, too, struck him as repulsive and hateful. Anger surged up in his heart against her, and he thought malignantly:

'She knows nothing about money, and so she is stingy. If she won it she would give me a hundred roubles, and put the rest away under lock and key.'

And he looked at his wife, not with a smile now, but with hatred. She glanced at him too, and also with hatred and anger. She had her own daydreams, her own plans, her own reflections; she understood perfectly well what her husband's dreams were. She knew who would be the first to try to grab her winnings.

'It's very nice making daydreams at other people's expense!' is what her eyes expressed. 'No, don't you dare!'

Her husband understood her look; hatred began stirring again in his breast, and in order to annoy his wife he glanced quickly, to spite her at the fourth page on the newspaper and read out triumphantly:

'Series 9,499, number 46! Not 26!'

Hatred and hope both disappeared at once, and it began immediately to seem to Ivan Dmitritch and his wife that their rooms were dark and small and low-pitched, that the supper they had been eating was not doing them good, but lying heavy on their stomachs, that the evenings were long and wearisome.

'What the devil's the meaning of it?' said Ivan Dmitritch, beginning to be ill-humoured. 'Wherever one steps there are bits of paper under one's feet, crumbs, husks. The rooms are never swept! One is simply forced to go out. Damnation take my soul entirely! I shall go and hang myself on the first aspen-tree!'

6

A PAIR OF SILK STOCKINGS

Kate Chopin

Little Mrs. Sommers one day found herself the unexpected possessor of fifteen dollars. It seemed to her a very large amount of money, and the way in which it stuffed and bulged her worn old porte-monnaie gave her a feeling of importance such as she had not enjoyed for years.

The question of investment was one that occupied her greatly. For a day or two she walked about apparently in a dreamy state, but really absorbed in speculation and calculation. She did not wish to act hastily, to do anything she might afterward regret. But it was during the still hours of the night when she lay awake revolving plans in her mind that she seemed to see her way clearly toward a proper and judicious use of the money.

A dollar or two should be added to the price usually paid for Janie's shoes, which would insure their lasting an appreciable time longer than they usually did. She would buy so and so many yards of percale for new shirt waists for the boys and Janie and Mag. She had intended to make the old ones do by skilful patching. Mag should have another gown. She had seen some beautiful patterns, veritable bargains in the shop windows. And still there would be left enough for new stockings—two pairs apiece—and what darning that would save for a while! She would get caps for the boys and sailor-hats for the girls. The vision of her little brood looking fresh and dainty and new for once in their lives excited her and made her restless and wakeful with anticipation.

The neighbors sometimes talked of certain 'better days' that little Mrs. Sommers had known before she had ever thought of being Mrs. Sommers. She herself indulged in no such morbid retrospection. She had no time—no second of time to devote to the past. The needs of the present absorbed her every faculty. A vision of the future like some dim, gaunt monster sometimes appalled her, but luckily to-morrow never comes.

Mrs. Sommers was one who knew the value of bargains; who could stand for hours making her way inch by inch toward the desired object that was selling below cost. She could elbow her way if need be; she had learned to clutch a piece of goods and hold it and stick to it with persistence and determination till her turn came to be served, no matter when it came.

But that day she was a little faint and tired. She had swallowed a light luncheon—no! when she came to think of it, between getting the children fed and the place righted, and preparing herself for the shopping bout, she had actually forgotten to eat any luncheon at all!

She sat herself upon a revolving stool before a counter that was comparatively deserted, trying to gather strength and courage to charge through an eager multitude that was besieging breastworks of shirting and figured lawn. An all-gone limp feeling had come over her and she rested her hand aimlessly upon the counter. She wore no gloves. By degrees she grew aware that her hand had encountered something very soothing, very pleasant to touch. She looked down to see that her hand lay upon a pile of silk stockings. A placard near by announced that they had been reduced in price from two dollars and fifty cents to one dollar and ninety-eight cents; and a young girl who stood behind the counter asked her if she wished to examine their line of silk hosiery. She smiled, just as if she had been asked to inspect a tiara of diamonds with the ultimate view of purchasing it. But she went on feeling the soft, sheeny luxurious things—with both hands now, holding them up to see them glisten, and to feel them glide serpent-like through her fingers.

Two hectic blotches came suddenly into her pale cheeks. She looked up at the girl.

'Do you think there are any eights-and-a-half among these?'

There were any number of eights-and-a-half. In fact, there

were more of that size than any other. Here was a light-blue pair; there were some lavender, some all black and various shades of tan and gray. Mrs. Sommers selected a black pair and looked at them very long and closely. She pretended to be examining their texture, which the clerk assured her was excellent.

'A dollar and ninety-eight cents,' she mused aloud. 'Well, I'll take this pair.' She handed the girl a five-dollar bill and waited for her change and for her parcel. What a very small parcel it was! It seemed lost in the depths of her shabby old shopping-bag.

Mrs. Sommers after that did not move in the direction of the bargain counter. She took the elevator, which carried her to an upper floor into the region of the ladies' waiting-rooms. Here, in a retired corner, she exchanged her cotton stockings for the new silk ones which she had just bought. She was not going through any acute mental process or reasoning with herself, nor was she striving to explain to her satisfaction the motive of her action. She was not thinking at all. She seemed for the time to be taking a rest from that laborious and fatiguing function and to have abandoned herself to some mechanical impulse that directed her actions and freed her of responsibility.

How good was the touch of the raw silk to her flesh! She felt like lying back in the cushioned chair and reveling for a while in the luxury of it. She did for a little while. Then she replaced her shoes, rolled the cotton stockings together and thrust them into her bag. After doing this she crossed straight over to the shoe department and took her seat to be fitted.

She was fastidious. The clerk could not make her out; he could not reconcile her shoes with her stockings, and she was not too easily pleased. She held back her skirts and turned her feet one way and her head another way as she glanced down at the polished, pointed-tipped boots. Her foot and ankle looked very pretty. She could not realize that they belonged to her and were a part of herself. She wanted an excellent and stylish fit, she told the young fellow who served her, and she did not mind the difference of a dollar or two more in the price so long as she got what she desired.

It was a long time since Mrs. Sommers had been fitted with gloves. On rare occasions when she had bought a pair they were always 'bargains,' so cheap that it would have been preposterous and unreasonable to have expected them to be fitted to the hand.

Now she rested her elbow on the cushion of the glove counter, and a pretty, pleasant young creature, delicate and deft of touch, drew a long-wristed 'kid' over Mrs. Sommers's hand. She smoothed it down over the wrist and buttoned it neatly, and both lost themselves for a second or two in admiring contemplation of the little symmetrical gloved hand. But there were other places where money might be spent.

There were books and magazines piled up in the window of a stall a few paces down the street. Mrs. Sommers bought two high-priced magazines such as she had been accustomed to read in the days when she had been accustomed to other pleasant things. She carried them without wrapping. As well as she could she lifted her skirts at the crossings. Her stockings and boots and well fitting gloves had worked marvels in her bearing—had given her a feeling of assurance, a sense of belonging to the well-dressed multitude.

She was very hungry. Another time she would have stilled the cravings for food until reaching her own home, where she would have brewed herself a cup of tea and taken a snack of anything that was available. But the impulse that was guiding her would not suffer her to entertain any such thought.

There was a restaurant at the corner. She had never entered its doors; from the outside she had sometimes caught glimpses of spotless damask and shining crystal, and soft-stepping waiters serving people of fashion.

When she entered her appearance created no surprise, no consternation, as she had half feared it might. She seated herself at a small table alone, and an attentive waiter at once approached to take her order. She did not want a profusion; she craved a nice and tasty bite—a half dozen blue-points, a plump chop with cress, a something sweet—a creme-frappee, for instance; a glass of Rhine wine, and after all a small cup of black coffee.

While waiting to be served she removed her gloves very leisurely and laid them beside her. Then she picked up a magazine and glanced through it, cutting the pages with a blunt edge of her knife. It was all very agreeable. The damask was even more spotless than it had seemed through the window, and the crystal more sparkling. There were quiet ladies and gentlemen, who did not notice her, lunching at the small tables like her own. A soft, pleasing strain of music could be heard, and a gentle breeze was blowing through the window. She tasted a bite, and she read a word or two, and she sipped the amber wine and wiggled her toes in the silk stockings. The price of it made no difference. She counted the money out to the waiter and left an extra coin on his tray, whereupon he bowed before her as before a princess of royal blood.

There was still money in her purse, and her next temptation presented itself in the shape of a matinee poster.

It was a little later when she entered the theatre, the play had begun and the house seemed to her to be packed. But there were vacant seats here and there, and into one of them she was ushered, between brilliantly dressed women who had gone there to kill time and eat candy and display their gaudy attire. There were many others who were there solely for the play and acting. It is safe to say there was no one present who bore quite the attitude which Mrs. Sommers did to her surroundings. She gathered in the whole—stage and players and people in one wide impression, and absorbed it and enjoyed it. She laughed at the comedy and wept—she and the gaudy woman next to her wept over the tragedy. And they talked a little together over it. And the gaudy woman wiped her eyes and sniffled on a tiny square of filmy, perfumed lace and passed little Mrs. Sommers her box of candy.

The play was over, the music ceased, the crowd filed out. It was like a dream ended. People scattered in all directions.

Mrs. Sommers went to the corner and waited for the cable car.

A man with keen eyes, who sat opposite to her, seemed to like the study of her small, pale face. It puzzled him to decipher what he saw there. In truth, he saw nothing—unless he were wizard enough to detect a poignant wish, a powerful longing that the cable car would never stop anywhere, but go on and on with her forever.

7

HOW THE LEOPARD GOT HIS SPOTS

Rudyard Kipling

In the days when everybody started fair, Best Beloved, the Leopard lived in a place called the High Veldt. 'Member it wasn't the Low Veldt, or the Bush Veldt, or the Sour Veldt, but the 'sclusively bare, hot shiny High Veldt, where there was sand and sandy-coloured rock and 'sclusively tufts of sandy-yellowish grass. The Giraffe and the Zebra and the Eland and the Koodoo and the Hartebeest lived there: and they were 'sclusively sandy-yellow-brownish all over; but the Leopard, he was the 'sclusivest sandiest-yellowest-brownest of them all—a greyish-yellowish catty-shaped kind of beast, and he matched the 'sclusively yellowish-greyish-brownish colour of the High Veldt to one hair. This was very bad for the Giraffe and the Zebra and the rest of them: for he would lie down by a 'sclusively yellowish-greyish-brownish stone or clump of grass, and when the Giraffe or the Zebra or the Eland or the Koodoo or the Bush-Buck or the Bonte-Buck came by he would surprise them out of their jumpsome lives. He would indeed! And, also, there was an Ethiopian with bows and arrows (a 'sclusively greyish-brownish-yellowish man he was then), who lived on the High Veldt with the Leopard: and the two used to hunt together—the Ethiopian with his bows and arrows, and the Leopard 'sclusively with his teeth and claws—till the Giraffe and the Eland and the Koodoo and the Quagga and all the rest of them didn't know which way to jump, Best Beloved. They didn't indeed!

After a long time—things lived for ever so long in those days—they learned to avoid anything that looked like a Leopard or an Ethiopian: and bit by bit—the Giraffe began it, because his legs were the longest—they went away from the High Veldt. They scuttled for days and days till they came to a great forest, 'sclusively full of trees and bushes and stripy, speckly, patchy-blatchy shadows, and there they hid: and after another long time, what with standing half in the shade and half out of it, and what with the slippery-slidy shadows of the trees falling on them, the Giraffe grew blotchy, and the Zebra grew stripy, and the Eland and the Koodoo grew darker, with little wavy grey lines on their backs like bark on a tree-trunk: and so, though you could hear them and smell them, you could very seldom see them, and then only when you knew precisely where to look. They had a beautiful time in the 'sclusively speckly-spickly shadows of the forest, while the Leopard and the Ethiopian ran about over the 'sclusively greyish-yellowish-reddish High Veldt outside, wondering where all their breakfasts and their dinners and their teas had gone. At last they were so hungry that they ate rats and beetles and rock-rabbits, the Leopard and the Ethiopian, and then they had the Big Tummy-ache, both together: and then they met Baviaan—the dog-headed, barking baboon, who is Quite the Wisest Animal in All South Africa.

Said the Leopard to Baviaan (and it was a very hot day), 'Where has all the game gone?'

And Baviaan winked. He knew.

Said Ethiopian to Baviaan, 'Can you tell me the present habitat of the aboriginal Fauna?' (That meant just the same thing, but the Ethiopian always used long words. He was a grown-up.)

And Baviaan winked. He knew.

Then said Baviaan, 'The game has gone into other spots: and my advice to you, Leopard, is to go into other spots as soon as you can.'

And the Ethiopian said, 'That is all very fine, but I wish to know whither the aboriginal Fauna has migrated.'

Then said Baviaan, 'The aboriginal Fauna has joined the aboriginal Flora because it was high time for a change; and my advice to you, Ethiopian, is to change as soon as you can.'

That puzzled the Leopard and the Ethiopian, but they set off to look for the aboriginal Flora, and presently, after ever so many days, they saw a great, high, tall forest full of tree-trunks all 'sclusively speckled and sprottled and spottled, dotted and splashed and slashed and hatched and cross-hatched with shadows. (Say that quickly aloud, and you will see how very shadowy the forest must have been.)

'What is this,' said the Leopard, 'that is so 'sclusively dark, and yet so full of little pieces of light?'

'I don't know,' said the Ethiopian, 'but it ought to be the aboriginal Flora. I can smell Giraffe, and I can hear Giraffe, but I can't see Giraffe.'

'That's curious,' said the Leopard. 'I suppose it is because we have just come in out of the sunshine. I can smell Zebra, and I can hear Zebra, but I can't see Zebra.'

'Wait a bit,' said the Ethiopian. 'It's a long time since we've hunted 'em. Perhaps we've forgotten what they were like.'

'Fiddle!' said the Leopard. 'I remember them perfectly on the High Veldt, especially their marrow-bones. Giraffe is about seventeen feet high, of a 'sclusively fulvous golden-yellow from head to heel: and Zebra is about four and a half feet high, of a 'sclusively grey-fawn colour from head to heel.'

'Umm,' said the Ethiopian, looking into the speckly-spickly shadows of the aboriginal Flora-forest. 'Then they ought to show up in this dark place like ripe bananas in a smoke-house.'

But they didn't. The Leopard and the Ethiopian hunted all day; and though they could smell them and hear them, they never saw one of them.

'For goodness' sake,' said the Leopard at tea-time, 'let us wait till it gets dark. This daylight hunting is a perfect scandal.'

So they waited till dark, and then the Leopard heard something breathing sniffily in the starlight that fell all stripy through the branches, and he jumped at the noise, and it smelt like Zebra, and it felt like Zebra, and when he knocked it down it kicked like Zebra, but he couldn't see it. So he said, 'Be quiet, O you person without any form. I am going to sit on your head till morning, because there is something about you that I don't understand.'

Presently he heard a grunt and a crash and a scramble, and the Ethiopian called out, 'I've caught a thing that I can't see. It smells like Giraffe, and it kicks like Giraffe, but it hasn't any form.'

'Don't you trust it, said the Leopard. 'Sit on its head till the morning—same as me. They haven't any form—any of 'em.'

So they sat down on them hard till bright morning-time, and then Leopard said, 'What have you at your end of the table, Brother?'

The Ethiopian scratched his head and said, 'It ought to be 'sclusively a rich fulvous orange-tawny from head to heel, and it ought to be Giraffe; but it is covered all over with chestnut blotches. What have you at your end of the table, Brother?'

And the Leopard scratched his head and said, 'It ought to be 'sclusively a delicate greyish-fawn, and it ought to be Zebra; but it is covered all over with black and purple stripes. What in the world have you been doing to yourself, Zebra? Don't you know that if you were on the High Veldt I could see you ten miles off? You haven't any form.'

'Yes,' said the Zebra, 'but this isn't the High Veldt. Can't you see?'

'I can now,' said the Leopard, 'But I couldn't all yesterday. How is it done?'

'Let us up,' said the Zebra, 'and we will show you.'

They let the Zebra and the Giraffe get up; and Zebra moved away to some little thorn-bushes where the sunlight fell all stripy, and the Giraffe moved off to some tallish trees where the shadows fell all blotchy.

'Now watch,' said the Zebra and the Giraffe. 'This is the way it's done. One—two—three! And where's your breakfast?'

Leopard stared, and Ethiopian stared, but all they could see were stripy shadows and blotched shadows in the forest, but never a sign of Zebra and Giraffe. They had just walked off and hidden themselves in the shadowy forest.

'Hi! Hi!' said the Ethiopian. 'That's a trick worth learning. Take a lesson by it, Leopard. You show up in this dark place like a bar of soap in a coal-scuttle.'

'Ho! Ho!' said the Leopard. 'Would it surprise you very much to know that you show up in this dark place like a mustard-plaster on a sack of coals?'

'Well, calling names won't catch dinner,' said the Ethiopian. 'The long and the little of it is that we don't match our backgrounds. I'm going to take Baviaan's advice. He told me I ought to change: and as I've nothing to change except my skin I'm going to change that.'

'What to?' said the Leopard, tremendously excited.

'To a nice working blackish-brownish colour, with a little purple in it, and touches of slaty-blue. It will be the very thing for hiding in hollows and behind trees.'

So he changed his skin then and there, and the Leopard was more excited than ever: he had never seen a man change his skin before.

'But what about me?' She said, when the Ethiopian had worked his last little finger into his fine new black skin.

'You take Baviaan's advice too. He told you to go into spots.'

'So I did,' said the Leopard. 'I went into other spots as fast as I could. I went into this spot with you, and a lot of good it has done me.'

'Oh,' said the Ethiopian. 'Baviaan didn't mean spots in South Africa. He meant spots on your skin.'

'What's the use of that?' said the Leopard.

'Think of Giraffe,' said the Ethiopian. 'Or if you prefer stripes, think of Zebra. They find their spots and stripes give them per-fect satisfaction.'

'Umm,' said the Leopard. 'I wouldn't look like Zebra—not for ever so.'

'Well, make up your mind,' said the Ethiopian, 'because I'd hate to go hunting without you, but I must if you insist on looking like a sunflower against a tarred fence.'

'I'll take spots, then,' said the Leopard; 'but don't make 'em too vulgar-big. I wouldn't look like Giraffe—not for ever so.'

'I'll make 'em with the tips of my fingers,' said the Ethiopian. 'There's plenty of black left on my skin still. Stand over!'

Then the Ethiopian put his five fingers close together (there was plenty of black left on his new skin still) and pressed them all over the Leopard, and wherever the five fingers touched they left five little black marks, all close together. You can see them on any Leopard's skin you like, Best Beloved. Sometimes the fingers slipped and the marks got a little blurred; but if you look closely at any Leopard now you will see that there are always five spots—of five black finger-tips.

'Now you are a beauty!' said the Ethiopian. 'You can lie out on the bare ground and look like a heap of pebbles. You can lie out on the naked rocks and look like a piece of pudding-stone. You can lie out on a leafy branch and look like sunshine sifting through the leaves; and you can lie right across the centre of a path and look like nothing in particular. Think of that and purr!'

'But if I'm all this,' said the Leopard, 'why didn't you go spotty too?'

'Oh, plain black's best,' said the Ethiopian. 'Now come along and we'll see if we can't get even with Mr One-Two-Three-Where's-your-Breakfast!'

So they went away and lived happily ever afterwards, Best Beloved. That is all.

Oh, now and then you will hear grown-ups say, 'Can the Ethiopian change his skin or the Leopard his spots?' I don't think even grown-ups would keep on saying such a silly thing if the Leopard and the Ethiopian hadn't done it once—do you? But they will never do it again, Best Beloved. They are quite contented as they are.

8

THE BLIND MAN

D.H. Lawrence

Isabel Pervin was listening for two sounds—for the sound of wheels on the drive outside and for the noise of her husband's footsteps in the hall. Her dearest and oldest friend, a man who seemed almost indispensable to her living, would drive up in the rainy dusk of the closing November day. The trap had gone to fetch him from the station. And her husband, who had been blinded in Flanders, and who had a disfiguring mark on his brow, would be coming in from the outhouses.

He had been home for a year now. He was totally blind. Yet they had been very happy. The Grange was Maurice's own place. The back was a farmstead, and the Wernhams, who occupied the rear premises, acted as farmers. Isabel lived with her husband in the handsome rooms in front. She and he had been almost entirely alone together since he was wounded. They talked and sang and read together in a wonderful and unspeakable intimacy. Then she reviewed books for a Scottish newspaper, carrying on her old interest, and he occupied himself a good deal with the farm. Sightless, he could still discuss everything with Wernham, and he could also do a good deal of work about the place—menial work, it is true, but it gave him satisfaction. He milked the cows, carried in the pails, turned the separator, attended to the pigs and horses. Life was still very full and strangely serene for the blind man, peaceful with the almost incomprehensible peace of immediate contact in darkness. With his wife he had a whole world, rich and real and invisible.

They were newly and remotely happy. He did not even regret the loss of his sight in these times of dark, palpable joy. A certain exultance swelled his soul.

But as time wore on, sometimes the rich glamour would leave them. Sometimes, after months of this intensity, a sense of burden overcame Isabel, a weariness, a terrible *ennui*, in that silent house approached between a colonnade of tall-shafted pines. Then she felt she would go mad, for she could not bear it. And sometimes he had devastating fits of depression, which seemed to lay waste his whole being. It was worse than depression—a black misery, when his own life was a torture to him, and when his presence was unbearable to his wife. The dread went down to the roots of her soul as these black days recurred. In a kind of panic she tried to wrap herself up still further in her husband. She forced the old spontaneous cheerfulness and joy to continue. But the effort it cost her was almost too much. She knew she could not keep it up. She felt she would scream with the strain, and would give anything, anything, to escape. She longed to possess her husband utterly; it gave her inordinate joy to have him entirely to herself. And yet, when again he was gone in a black and massive misery, she could not bear him, she could not bear herself; she wished she could be snatched away off the earth altogether, anything rather than live at this cost.

Dazed, she schemed for a way out. She invited friends, she tried to give him some further connexion with the outer world. But it was no good. After all their joy and suffering, after their dark, great year of blindness and solitude and unspeakable nearness, other people seemed to them both shallow, prattling, rather impertinent. Shallow prattle seemed presumptuous. He became impatient and irritated, she was wearied. And so they lapsed into their solitude again. For they preferred it.

But now, in a few weeks' time, her second baby would be born. The first had died, an infant, when her husband first went out to France. She looked with joy and relief to the coming of the second. It would be her salvation. But also she felt some anxiety. She was thirty years old, her husband was a year younger. They both wanted the child very much. Yet she could not help feeling afraid. She had her husband on her hands, a terrible joy to her, and a terrifying burden. The child would occupy her love and attention. And then, what of Maurice? What would he do? If only she could feel that he, too, would be at peace and happy when the child came! She did so want to luxuriate in a rich, physical satisfaction of maternity. But the man, what would he do? How could she provide for him, how avert those shattering black moods of his, which destroyed them both?

She sighed with fear. But at this time Bertie Reid wrote to Isabel. He was her old friend, a second or third cousin, a Scotchman, as she was a Scotchwoman. They had been brought up near to one another, and all her life he had been her friend, like a brother, but better than her own brothers. She loved him—though not in the marrying sense. There was a sort of kinship between them, an affinity. They understood one another instinctively. But Isabel would never have thought of marrying Bertie. It would have seemed like marrying in her own family.

Bertie was a barrister and a man of letters, a Scotchman of the intellectual type, quick, ironical, sentimental, and on his knees before the woman he adored but did not want to marry. Maurice Pervin was different. He came of a good old country family—the Grange was not a very great distance from Oxford. He was passionate, sensitive, perhaps over-sensitive, wincing—a big fellow with heavy limbs and a forehead that flushed painfully. For his mind was slow, as if drugged by the strong provincial blood that beat in his veins. He was very sensitive to his own mental slowness, his feelings being quick and acute. So that he was just the opposite to Bertie, whose mind was much quicker than his emotions, which were not so very fine.

From the first the two men did not like each other. Isabel felt that they *ought* to get on together. But they did not. She felt that if only each could have the clue to the other there would be such a rare understanding between them. It did not come off, however. Bertie adopted a slightly ironical attitude, very offensive to Maurice, who returned the Scotch irony with English resentment, a resentment which deepened sometimes into stupid hatred.

This was a little puzzling to Isabel. However, she accepted it in the course of things. Men were made freakish and unreasonable. Therefore, when Maurice was going out to France for the second time, she felt that, for her husband's sake, she must discontinue her friendship with Bertie. She wrote to the barrister to this effect. Bertram Reid simply replied that in this, as in all other matters, he must obey her wishes, if these were indeed her wishes.

For nearly two years nothing had passed between the two friends. Isabel rather gloried in the fact; she had no compunction. She had one great article of faith, which was, that husband and wife should be so important to one another, that the rest of the world simply did not count. She and Maurice were husband and wife. They loved one another. They would have children. Then let everybody and everything else fade into insignificance outside this connubial felicity. She professed herself quite happy and ready to receive Maurice's friends. She was happy and ready: the happy wife, the ready woman in possession. Without knowing why, the friends retired abashed and came no more. Maurice, of course, took as much satisfaction in this connubial absorption as Isabel did.

He shared in Isabel's literary activities, she cultivated a real interest in agriculture and cattle-raising. For she, being at heart perhaps an emotional enthusiast, always cultivated the practical side of life, and prided herself on her mastery of practical affairs. Thus the husband and wife had spent the five years of their married life. The last had been one of blindness and unspeakable intimacy. And now Isabel felt a great indifference coming over her, a sort of lethargy. She wanted to be allowed to bear her child in peace, to nod by the fire and drift vaguely, physically, from day to day. Maurice was like an ominous thunder-cloud. She had to keep waking up to remember him.

When a little note came from Bertie, asking if he were to put up a tombstone to their dead friendship, and speaking of the real pain he felt on account of her husband's loss of sight, she felt a pang, a fluttering agitation of re-awakening. And she read the letter to Maurice.

'Ask him to come down,' he said.

'Ask Bertie to come here!' she re-echoed.

'Yes—if he wants to.'

Isabel paused for a few moments.

'I know he wants to—he'd only be too glad,' she replied. 'But what about you, Maurice? How would you like it?'

'I should like it.'

'Well—in that case—But I thought you didn't care for him—'

'Oh, I don't know. I might think differently of him now,' the blind man replied. It was rather abstruse to Isabel.

'Well, dear,' she said, 'if you're quite sure—'

'I'm sure enough. Let him come,' said Maurice.

So Bertie was coming, coming this evening, in the November rain and darkness. Isabel was agitated, racked with her old restlessness and indecision. She had always suffered from this pain of doubt, just an agonizing sense of uncertainty. It had begun to pass off, in the lethargy of maternity. Now it returned, and she resented it. She struggled as usual to maintain her calm, composed, friendly bearing, a sort of mask she wore over all her body.

A woman had lighted a tall lamp beside the table, and spread the cloth. The long dining-room was dim, with its elegant but rather severe pieces of old furniture. Only the round table glowed softly under the light. It had a rich, beautiful effect. The white cloth glistened and dropped its heavy, pointed lace corners almost to the carpet, the china was old and handsome, creamy-yellow, with a blotched pattern of harsh red and deep blue, the cups large and bell-shaped, the teapot gallant. Isabel looked at it with superficial appreciation.

Her nerves were hurting her. She looked automatically again at the high, uncurtained windows. In the last dusk she could just perceive outside a huge fir-tree swaying its boughs: it was as if she thought it rather than saw it. The rain came flying on the window panes. Ah, why had she no peace? These two men, why did they tear at her? Why did they not come—why was there this suspense?

She sat in a lassitude that was really suspense and irritation. Maurice, at least, might come in—there was nothing to keep him out. She rose to her feet. Catching sight of her reflection in a mirror, she glanced at herself with a slight smile of recognition, as if she were an old friend to herself. Her face was oval and calm, her nose a little arched. Her neck made a beautiful line down to her shoulder. With hair knotted loosely behind, she had something of a warm, maternal look. Thinking this of herself, she arched her eyebrows and her rather heavy eyelids, with a little flicker of a smile, and for a moment her grey eyes looked amused and wicked, a little sardonic, out of her transfigured Madonna face.

Then, resuming her air of womanly patience—she was really fatally self-determined—she went with a little jerk towards the door. Her eyes were slightly reddened.

She passed down the wide hall, and through a door at the end. Then she was in the farm premises. The scent of dairy, and of farm-kitchen, and of farm-yard and of leather almost overcame her: but particularly the scent of dairy. They had been scalding out the pans. The flagged passage in front of her was dark, puddled and wet. Light came out from the open kitchen door. She went forward and stood in the doorway. The farm-people were at tea, seated at a little distance from her, round a long, narrow table, in the centre of which stood a white lamp. Ruddy faces, ruddy hands holding food, red mouths working, heads bent over the tea-cups: men, land-girls, boys: it was tea-time, feeding-time. Some faces caught sight of her. Mrs. Wernham, going round behind the chairs with a large black teapot, halting slightly in her walk, was not aware of her for a moment. Then she turned suddenly.

'Oh, is it Madam!' she exclaimed. 'Come in, then, come in! We're at tea.' And she dragged forward a chair.

'No, I won't come in,' said Isabel, 'I'm afraid I interrupt your meal.'

'No—no—not likely, Madam, not likely.'

'Hasn't Mr. Pervin come in, do you know?'

'I'm sure I couldn't say! Missed him, have you, Madam?'

'No, I only wanted him to come in,' laughed Isabel, as if shyly.

'Wanted him, did ye? Get you, boy—get up, now—'

Mrs. Wernham knocked one of the boys on the shoulder. He began to scrape to his feet, chewing largely.

'I believe he's in top stable,' said another face from the table.

'Ah! No, don't get up. I'm going myself,' said Isabel.

'Don't you go out of a dirty night like this. Let the lad go. Get along wi' ye, boy,' said Mrs. Wernham.

'No, no,' said Isabel, with a decision that was always obeyed. 'Go on with your tea, Tom. I'd like to go across to the stable, Mrs. Wernham.'

'Did ever you hear tell!' exclaimed the woman.

'Isn't the trap late?' asked Isabel.

'Why, no,' said Mrs. Wernham, peering into the distance at the tall, dim clock. 'No, Madam—we can give it another quarter or twenty minutes yet, good—yes, every bit of a quarter.'

'Ah! It seems late when darkness falls so early,' said Isabel.

'It do, that it do. Bother the days, that they draw in so,' answered Mrs. Wernham. 'Proper miserable!'

'They are,' said Isabel, withdrawing.

She pulled on her overshoes, wrapped a large tartan shawl around her, put on a man's felt hat, and ventured out along the causeways of the first yard. It was very dark. The wind was roaring in the great elms behind the outhouses. When she came to the second yard the darkness seemed deeper. She was unsure of her footing. She wished she had brought a lantern. Rain blew against her. Half she liked it, half she felt unwilling to battle.

She reached at last the just visible door of the stable. There was no sign of a light anywhere. Opening the upper half, she looked in: into a simple well of darkness. The smell of horses, and ammonia, and of warmth was startling to her, in that full night. She listened with all her ears, but could hear nothing save the night, and the stirring of a horse.

'Maurice!' she called, softly and musically, though she was afraid. 'Maurice—are you there?'

Nothing came from the darkness. She knew the rain and wind blew in upon the horses, the hot animal life. Feeling it wrong, she entered the stable, and drew the lower half of the door shut, holding the upper part close. She did not stir, because she was aware of the presence of the dark hindquarters of the horses, though she could not see them, and she was afraid. Something wild stirred in her heart.

She listened intensely. Then she heard a small noise in the distance—far away, it seemed—the chink of a pan, and a man's voice speaking a brief word. It would be Maurice, in the other part of the stable. She stood motionless, waiting for him to come through the partition door. The horses were so terrifyingly near to her, in the invisible.

The loud jarring of the inner door-latch made her start; the door was opened. She could hear and feel her husband entering and invisibly passing among the horses near to her, in darkness as they were, actively intermingled. The rather low sound of his voice as he spoke to the horses came velvety to her nerves. How near he was, and how invisible! The darkness seemed to be in a strange swirl of violent life, just upon her. She turned giddy.

Her presence of mind made her call, quietly and musically:

'Maurice! Maurice—dea-ar!'

'Yes,' he answered. 'Isabel?'

She saw nothing, and the sound of his voice seemed to touch her.

'Hello!' she answered cheerfully, straining her eyes to see him. He was still busy, attending to the horses near her, but she saw only darkness. It made her almost desperate.

'Won't you come in, dear?' she said.

'Yes, I'm coming. Just half a minute. *Stand over—now*! Trap's not come, has it?'

'Not yet,' said Isabel.

His voice was pleasant and ordinary, but it had a slight suggestion of the stable to her. She wished he would come away. Whilst he was so utterly invisible she was afraid of him.

'How's the time?' he asked.

'Not yet six,' she replied. She disliked to answer into the dark. Presently he came very near to her, and she retreated out of doors.

'The weather blows in here,' he said, coming steadily forward, feeling for the doors. She shrank away. At last she could dimly see him.

'Bertie won't have much of a drive,' he said, as he closed the doors.

'He won't indeed!' said Isabel calmly, watching the dark shape at the door.

'Give me your arm, dear,' she said.

She pressed his arm close to her, as she went. But she longed to see him, to look at him. She was nervous. He walked erect, with face rather lifted, but with a curious tentative movement of his powerful, muscular legs. She could feel the clever, careful, strong contact of his feet with the earth, as she balanced against him. For a moment he was a tower of darkness to her, as if he rose out of the earth.

In the house-passage he wavered, and went cautiously, with a curious look of silence about him as he felt for the bench. Then he sat down heavily. He was a man with rather sloping shoulders, but with heavy limbs, powerful legs that seemed to know the earth. His head was small, usually carried high and light. As he bent down to unfasten his gaiters and boots he did not look blind. His hair was brown and crisp, his hands were large, reddish, intelligent, the veins stood out in the wrists; and his thighs and knees seemed massive. When he stood up his face and neck were surcharged with blood, the veins stood out on his temples. She did not look at his blindness.

Isabel was always glad when they had passed through the dividing door into their own regions of repose and beauty. She was a little afraid of him, out there in the animal grossness of the back. His bearing also changed, as he smelt the familiar, indefinable odour that pervaded his wife's surroundings, a delicate, refined scent, very faintly spicy. Perhaps it came from the pot-pourri bowls.

He stood at the foot of the stairs, arrested, listening. She watched him, and her heart sickened. He seemed to be listening to fate.

'He's not here yet,' he said. 'I'll go up and change.'

'Maurice,' she said, 'you're not wishing he wouldn't come, are you?'

'I couldn't quite say,' he answered. 'I feel myself rather on the *qui vive*.'

'I can see you are,' she answered. And she reached up and kissed his cheek. She saw his mouth relax into a slow smile.

'What are you laughing at?' she said roguishly.

'You consoling me,' he answered.

'Nay,' she answered. 'Why should I console you? You know we love each other—you know *how* married we are! What does anything else matter?'

'Nothing at all, my dear.'

He felt for her face, and touched it, smiling.

'*You're* all right, aren't you?' he asked, anxiously.

'I'm wonderfully all right, love,' she answered. 'It's you I am a little troubled about, at times.'

'Why me?' he said, touching her cheeks delicately with the tips of his fingers. The touch had an almost hypnotizing effect on her.

He went away upstairs. She saw him mount into the darkness, unseeing and unchanging. He did not know that the lamps on the upper corridor were unlighted. He went on into the darkness with unchanging step. She heard him in the bathroom.

Pervin moved about almost unconsciously in his familiar surroundings, dark though everything was. He seemed to know the presence of objects before he touched them. It was a pleasure to him to rock thus through a world of things, carried on the flood in a sort of blood-prescience. He did not think much or trouble much. So long as he kept this sheer immediacy of blood-contact with the substantial world he was happy, he wanted no intervention of visual consciousness. In this state there was a certain rich positivity, bordering sometimes on rapture. Life seemed to move in him like a tide lapping, and advancing, enveloping all things darkly. It was a pleasure to stretch forth the hand and meet the unseen object, clasp it, and possess it in pure contact. He did not try to remember, to visualize. He did not want to. The new way of consciousness substituted itself in him.

The rich suffusion of this state generally kept him happy, reaching its culmination in the consuming passion for his wife. But at times the flow would seem to be checked and thrown back. Then it would beat inside him like a tangled sea, and he was tortured in the shattered chaos of his own blood. He grew to dread this arrest, this throw-back, this chaos inside himself, when he seemed merely at the mercy of his own powerful and conflicting elements. How to get some measure of control or surety, this was the question. And when the question rose maddening in him, he would clench his fists as if he would *compel* the whole universe to submit to him. But it was in vain. He could not even compel himself.

Tonight, however, he was still serene, though little tremors of unreasonable exasperation ran through him. He had to handle the razor very carefully, as he shaved, for it was not at one with him, he was afraid of it. His hearing also was too much sharpened. He heard the woman lighting the lamps on the corridor, and attending to the fire in the visitor's room. And then, as he went to his room he heard the trap arrive. Then came Isabel's voice, lifted and calling, like a bell ringing:

'Is it you, Bertie? Have you come?'

And a man's voice answered out of the wind:

'Hello, Isabel. There you are.'

'Have you had a miserable drive? I'm so sorry we couldn't send a closed carriage. I can't see you at all, you know.'

'I'm coming. No, I liked the drive—it was like Perthshire. Well, how are you? You're looking fit as ever, as far as I can see.'

'Oh, yes,' said Isabel. 'I'm wonderfully well. How are you? Rather thin, I think—'

'Worked to death—everybody's old cry. But I'm all right, Ciss. How's Pervin?—isn't he here?'

'Oh, yes, he's upstairs changing. Yes, he's awfully well. Take off your wet things; I'll send them to be dried.'

'And how are you both, in spirits? He doesn't fret?'

'No—no, not at all. No, on the contrary, really. We've been wonderfully happy, incredibly. It's more than I can understand—so wonderful: the nearness, and the peace—'

'Ah! Well, that's awfully good news—'

They moved away. Pervin heard no more. But a childish sense of desolation had come over him, as he heard their brisk voices. He seemed shut out—like a child that is left out. He was aimless and excluded, he did not know what to do with himself. The helpless desolation came over him. He fumbled nervously as he dressed himself, in a state almost of childishness. He disliked the Scotch accent in Bertie's speech, and the slight response it found on Isabel's tongue. He disliked the slight purr of complacency in the Scottish speech. He disliked intensely the glib way in which Isabel spoke of their happiness and nearness. It made him recoil. He was fretful and beside himself like a child, he had almost a childish nostalgia to be included in the life circle. And at the same time he was a man, dark and powerful and infuriated by his own weakness. By some fatal flaw, he could not be by himself, he had to depend on the support of another. And this very dependence enraged him. He hated Bertie Reid, and at the same time he knew the hatred was nonsense, he knew it was the outcome of his own weakness.

He went downstairs. Isabel was alone in the dining-room. She watched him enter, head erect, his feet tentative. He looked so strong-blooded and healthy, and, at the same time, cancelled. Cancelled—that was the word that flew across her mind. Perhaps it was his scars suggested it.

'You heard Bertie come, Maurice?' she said.

'Yes—isn't he here?'

'He's in his room. He looks very thin and worn.'

'I suppose he works himself to death.'

A woman came in with a tray—and after a few minutes Bertie came down. He was a little dark man, with a very big forehead, thin, wispy hair, and sad, large eyes. His expression was inordinately sad—almost funny. He had odd, short legs.

Isabel watched him hesitate under the door, and glance nervously at her husband. Pervin heard him and turned.

'Here you are, now,' said Isabel. 'Come, let us eat.'

Bertie went across to Maurice.

'How are you, Pervin,' he said, as he advanced.

The blind man stuck his hand out into space, and Bertie took it.

'Very fit. Glad you've come,' said Maurice.

Isabel glanced at them, and glanced away, as if she could not bear to see them.

'Come,' she said. 'Come to table. Aren't you both awfully hungry? I am, tremendously.'

'I'm afraid you waited for me,' said Bertie, as they sat down.

Maurice had a curious monolithic way of sitting in a chair, erect and distant. Isabel's heart always beat when she caught sight of him thus.

'No,' she replied to Bertie. 'We're very little later than usual. We're having a sort of high tea, not dinner. Do you mind? It gives us such a nice long evening, uninterrupted.'

'I like it,' said Bertie.

Maurice was feeling, with curious little movements, almost like a cat kneading her bed, for his place, his knife and fork, his napkin. He was getting the whole geography of his cover into his consciousness. He sat erect and inscrutable, remote-seeming Bertie watched the static figure of the blind man, the delicate tactile discernment of the large, ruddy hands, and the curious mindless silence of the brow, above the scar. With difficulty he looked away, and without knowing what he did, picked up a little crystal bowl of violets from the table, and held them to his nose.

'They are sweet-scented,' he said. 'Where do they come from?'

'From the garden—under the windows,' said Isabel.

'So late in the year—and so fragrant! Do you remember the violets under Aunt Bell's south wall?'

The two friends looked at each other and exchanged a smile, Isabel's eyes lighting up.

'Don't I?' she replied. '*Wasn't* she queer!'

'A curious old girl,' laughed Bertie. 'There's a streak of freakishness in the family, Isabel.'

'Ah—but not in you and me, Bertie,' said Isabel. 'Give them to Maurice, will you?' she added, as Bertie was putting down the flowers. 'Have you smelled the violets, dear? Do!—they are so scented.'

Maurice held out his hand, and Bertie placed the tiny bowl against his large, warm-looking fingers. Maurice's hand closed over the thin white fingers of the barrister. Bertie carefully extricated himself. Then the two watched the blind man smelling the violets. He bent his head and seemed to be thinking. Isabel waited.

'Aren't they sweet, Maurice?' she said at last, anxiously.

'Very,' he said. And he held out the bowl. Bertie took it. Both he and Isabel were a little afraid, and deeply disturbed.

The meal continued. Isabel and Bertie chatted spasmodically. The blind man was silent. He touched his food repeatedly, with quick, delicate touches of his knife-point, then cut irregular bits. He could not bear to be helped. Both Isabel and Bertie suffered: Isabel wondered why. She did not suffer when she was alone with Maurice. Bertie made her conscious of a strangeness.

After the meal the three drew their chairs to the fire, and sat down to talk. The decanters were put on a table near at hand. Isabel knocked the logs on the fire, and clouds of brilliant sparks went up the chimney. Bertie noticed a slight weariness in her bearing.

'You will be glad when your child comes now, Isabel?' he said.

She looked up to him with a quick wan smile.

'Yes, I shall be glad,' she answered. 'It begins to seem long. Yes, I shall be very glad. So will you, Maurice, won't you?' she added.

'Yes, I shall,' replied her husband.

'We are both looking forward so much to having it,' she said.

'Yes, of course,' said Bertie.

He was a bachelor, three or four years older than Isabel. He lived in beautiful rooms overlooking the river, guarded by a faithful Scottish man-servant. And he had his friends among the fair sex—not lovers, friends. So long as he could avoid any danger of courtship or marriage, he adored a few good women with constant and unfailing homage, and he was chivalrously fond of quite a number. But if they seemed to encroach on him, he withdrew and detested them.

Isabel knew him very well, knew his beautiful constancy, and kindness, also his incurable weakness, which made him unable ever to enter into close contact of any sort. He was ashamed of himself, because he could not marry, could not approach women physically. He wanted to do so. But he could not. At the centre of him he was afraid, helplessly and even brutally afraid. He had given up hope, had ceased to expect any more that he could escape his own weakness. Hence he was a brilliant and successful barrister, also *litterateur* of high repute, a rich man, and a great social success. At the centre he felt himself neuter, nothing.

Isabel knew him well. She despised him even while she admired him. She looked at his sad face, his little short legs, and felt contempt of him. She looked at his dark grey eyes, with their uncanny, almost childlike intuition, and she loved him. He understood amazingly—but she had no fear of his understanding. As a man she patronized him.

And she turned to the impassive, silent figure of her husband. He sat leaning back, with folded arms, and face a little uptilted. His knees were straight and massive. She sighed, picked up the poker, and again began to prod the fire, to rouse the clouds of soft, brilliant sparks.

'Isabel tells me,' Bertie began suddenly, 'that you have not suffered unbearably from the loss of sight.'

Maurice straightened himself to attend, but kept his arms folded.

'No,' he said, 'not unbearably. Now and again one struggles against it, you know. But there are compensations.'

'They say it is much worse to be stone deaf,' said Isabel.

'I believe it is,' said Bertie. 'Are there compensations?' he added, to Maurice.

'Yes. You cease to bother about a great many things.' Again Maurice stretched his figure, stretched the strong muscles of his back, and leaned backwards, with uplifted face.

'And that is a relief,' said Bertie. 'But what is there in place of the bothering? What replaces the activity?'

There was a pause. At length the blind man replied, as out of a negligent, unattentive thinking:

'Oh, I don't know. There's a good deal when you're not active.'

'Is there?' said Bertie. 'What, exactly? It always seems to me that when there is no thought and no action, there is nothing.'

Again Maurice was slow in replying.

'There is something,' he replied. 'I couldn't tell you what it is.'

And the talk lapsed once more, Isabel and Bertie chatting gossip and reminiscence, the blind man silent.

At length Maurice rose restlessly, a big, obtrusive figure. He felt tight and hampered. He wanted to go away.

'Do you mind,' he said, 'if I go and speak to Wernham?'

'No—go along, dear,' said Isabel.

And he went out. A silence came over the two friends. At length Bertie said:

'Nevertheless, it is a great deprivation, Cissie.'

'It is, Bertie. I know it is.'

'Something lacking all the time,' said Bertie.

'Yes, I know. And yet—and yet—Maurice is right. There is something else, something *there*, which you never knew was there, and which you can't express.'

'What is there?' asked Bertie.

'I don't know—it's awfully hard to define it—but something strong and immediate. There's something strange in Maurice's presence—indefinable—but I couldn't do without it. I agree that it seems to put one's mind to sleep. But when we're alone I miss nothing; it seems awfully rich, almost splendid, you know.'

'I'm afraid I don't follow,' said Bertie.

They talked desultorily. The wind blew loudly outside, rain chattered on the window-panes, making a sharp, drum-sound, because of the closed, mellow-golden shutters inside. The logs burned slowly, with hot, almost invisible small flames. Bertie seemed uneasy, there were dark circles round his eyes. Isabel, rich with her approaching maternity, leaned looking into the fire. Her hair curled in odd, loose strands, very pleasing to the man. But she had a curious feeling of old woe in her heart, old, timeless night-woe.

'I suppose we're all deficient somewhere,' said Bertie.

'I suppose so,' said Isabel wearily.

'Damned, sooner or later.'

'I don't know,' she said, rousing herself. 'I feel quite all right, you know. The child coming seems to make me indifferent to everything, just placid. I can't feel that there's anything to trouble about, you know.'

'A good thing, I should say,' he replied slowly.

'Well, there it is. I suppose it's just Nature. If only I felt I needn't trouble about Maurice, I should be perfectly content—'

'But you feel you must trouble about him?'

'Well—I don't know—' She even resented this much effort.

The evening passed slowly. Isabel looked at the clock. 'I say,' she said. 'It's nearly ten o'clock. Where can Maurice be? I'm sure they're all in bed at the back. Excuse me a moment.'

She went out, returning almost immediately.

'It's all shut up and in darkness,' she said. 'I wonder where he is. He must have gone out to the farm—'

Bertie looked at her.

'I suppose he'll come in,' he said.

'I suppose so,' she said. 'But it's unusual for him to be out now.'

'Would you like me to go out and see?'

'Well—if you wouldn't mind. I'd go, but—' She did not want to make the physical effort.

Bertie put on an old overcoat and took a lantern. He went out from the side door. He shrank from the wet and roaring night. Such weather had a nervous effect on him: too much moisture everywhere made him feel almost imbecile. Unwilling, he went through it all. A dog barked violently at him. He peered in all the buildings. At last, as he opened the upper door of a sort of intermediate barn, he heard a grinding noise, and looking in, holding up his lantern, saw Maurice, in his shirt-sleeves, standing listening, holding the handle of a turnip-pulper. He had been pulping sweet roots, a pile of which lay dimly heaped in a corner behind him.

'That you, Wernham?' said Maurice, listening.

'No, it's me,' said Bertie.

A large, half-wild grey cat was rubbing at Maurice's leg. The blind man stooped to rub its sides. Bertie watched the scene, then unconsciously entered and shut the door behind him, He was in a high sort of barn-place, from which, right and left, ran off the corridors in front of the stalled cattle. He watched the slow, stooping motion of the other man, as he caressed the great cat.

Maurice straightened himself.

'You came to look for me?' he said.

'Isabel was a little uneasy,' said Bertie.

'I'll come in. I like messing about doing these jobs.'

The cat had reared her sinister, feline length against his leg, clawing at his thigh affectionately. He lifted her claws out of his flesh.

'I hope I'm not in your way at all at the Grange here,' said

Bertie, rather shy and stiff.

'My way? No, not a bit. I'm glad Isabel has somebody to talk to. I'm afraid it's I who am in the way. I know I'm not very lively company. Isabel's all right, don't you think? She's not unhappy, is she?'

'I don't think so.'

'What does she say?'

'She says she's very content—only a little troubled about you.'

'Why me?'

'Perhaps afraid that you might brood,' said Bertie, cautiously.

'She needn't be afraid of that.' He continued to caress the flattened grey head of the cat with his fingers. 'What I am a bit afraid of,' he resumed, 'is that she'll find me a dead weight, always alone with me down here.'

'I don't think you need think that,' said Bertie, though this was what he feared himself.

'I don't know,' said Maurice. 'Sometimes I feel it isn't fair that she's saddled with me.' Then he dropped his voice curiously. 'I say,' he asked, secretly struggling, 'is my face much disfigured? Do you mind telling me?'

'There is the scar,' said Bertie, wondering. 'Yes, it is a disfigurement. But more pitiable than shocking.'

'A pretty bad scar, though,' said Maurice.

'Oh, yes.'

There was a pause.

'Sometimes I feel I am horrible,' said Maurice, in a low voice, talking as if to himself. And Bertie actually felt a quiver of horror.

'That's nonsense,' he said.

Maurice again straightened himself, leaving the cat.

'There's no telling,' he said. Then again, in an odd tone, he added: 'I don't really know you, do I?'

'Probably not,' said Bertie.

'Do you mind if I touch you?'

The lawyer shrank away instinctively. And yet, out of very philanthropy, he said, in a small voice: 'Not at all.'

But he suffered as the blind man stretched out a strong, naked hand to him. Maurice accidentally knocked off Bertie's hat.

'I thought you were taller,' he said, starting. Then he laid his hand on Bertie Reid's head, closing the dome of the skull in a soft, firm grasp, gathering it, as it were; then, shifting his grasp and softly closing again, with a fine, close pressure, till he had covered the skull and the face of the smaller man, tracing the brows, and touching the full, closed eyes, touching the small nose and the nostrils, the rough, short moustache, the mouth, the rather strong chin. The hand of the blind man grasped the shoulder, the arm, the hand of the other man. He seemed to take him, in the soft, travelling grasp.

'You seem young,' he said quietly, at last.

The lawyer stood almost annihilated, unable to answer.

'Your head seems tender, as if you were young,' Maurice repeated. 'So do your hands. Touch my eyes, will you?—touch my scar.'

Now Bertie quivered with revulsion. Yet he was under the power of the blind man, as if hypnotized. He lifted his hand, and laid the fingers on the scar, on the scarred eyes. Maurice suddenly covered them with his own hand, pressed the fingers of the other man upon his disfigured eye-sockets, trembling in every fibre, and rocking slightly, slowly, from side to side. He remained thus for a minute or more, whilst Bertie stood as if in a swoon, unconscious, imprisoned.

Then suddenly Maurice removed the hand of the other man from his brow, and stood holding it in his own.

'Oh, my God,' he said, 'we shall know each other now, shan't we? We shall know each other now.'

Bertie could not answer. He gazed mute and terror-struck, overcome by his own weakness. He knew he could not answer. He had an unreasonable fear, lest the other man should suddenly destroy him. Whereas Maurice was actually filled with hot, poignant love, the passion of friendship. Perhaps it was this very passion of friendship which Bertie shrank from most.

'We're all right together now, aren't we?' said Maurice. 'It's all right now, as long as we live, so far as we're concerned?'

'Yes,' said Bertie, trying by any means to escape.

Maurice stood with head lifted, as if listening. The new delicate fulfilment of mortal friendship had come as a revelation and surprise to him, something exquisite and unhoped-for. He seemed to be listening to hear if it were real.

Then he turned for his coat.

'Come,' he said, 'we'll go to Isabel.'

Bertie took the lantern and opened the door. The cat disappeared. The two men went in silence along the causeways. Isabel, as they came, thought their footsteps sounded strange. She looked up pathetically and anxiously for their entrance. There seemed a curious elation about Maurice. Bertie was haggard, with sunken eyes.

'What is it?' she asked.

'We've become friends,' said Maurice, standing with his feet apart, like a strange colossus.

'Friends!' re-echoed Isabel. And she looked again at Bertie. He met her eyes with a furtive, haggard look; his eyes were as if glazed with misery.

'I'm so glad,' she said, in sheer perplexity.

'Yes,' said Maurice.

He was indeed so glad. Isabel took his hand with both hers, and held it fast.

'You'll be happier now, dear,' she said.

But she was watching Bertie. She knew that he had one desire—to escape from this intimacy, this friendship, which had been thrust upon him. He could not bear it that he had been touched by the blind man, his insane reserve broken in. He was like a mollusk whose shell is broken.

9

THE VALLEY OF SPIDERS

H.G. Wells

Towards mid-day the three pursuers came abruptly round a bend in the torrent bed upon the sight of a very broad and spacious valley. The difficult and winding trench of pebbles along which they had tracked the fugitives for so long, expanded to a broad slope, and with a common impulse the three men left the trail, and rode to a little eminence set with olive-dun trees, and there halted, the two others, as became them, a little behind the man with the silver-studded bridle.

For a space they scanned the great expanse below them with eager eyes.

It spread remoter and remoter, with only a few clusters of sere thorn bushes here and there, and the dim suggestions of some now waterless ravine, to break its desolation of yellow grass. Its purple distances melted at last into the bluish slopes of the further hills—hills it might be of a greener kind—and above them invisibly supported, and seeming indeed to hang in the blue, were the snowclad summits of mountains that grew larger and bolder to the north-westward as the sides of the valley drew together. And westward the valley opened until a distant darkness under the sky told where the forests began. But the three men looked neither east nor west, but only steadfastly across the valley.

The gaunt man with the scarred lip was the first to speak. 'Nowhere,' he said, with a sigh of disappointment in his voice. 'But after all, they had a full day's start.'

'They don't know we are after them,' said the little man on the white horse.

'SHE would know,' said the leader bitterly, as if speaking

to himself.

'Even then they can't go fast. They've got no beast but the mule, and all to-day the girl's foot has been bleeding—'

The man with the silver bridle flashed a quick intensity of rage on him. 'Do you think I haven't seen that?' he snarled.

'It helps, anyhow,' whispered the little man to himself.

The gaunt man with the scarred lip stared impassively. 'They can't be over the valley,' he said. 'If we ride hard—'

He glanced at the white horse and paused.

'Curse all white horses!' said the man with the silver bridle, and turned to scan the beast his curse included.

The little man looked down between the melancholy ears of his steed.

'I did my best,' he said.

The two others stared again across the valley for a space. The gaunt man passed the back of his hand across the scarred lip.

'Come up!' said the man who owned the silver bridle, suddenly.

The little man started and jerked his rein, and the horse hoofs of the three made a multitudinous faint pattering upon the withered grass as they turned back towards the trail...

They rode cautiously down the long slope before them, and so came through a waste of prickly, twisted bushes and strange dry shapes of horny branches that grew amongst the rocks, into the levels below.

And there the trail grew faint, for the soil was scanty, and the only herbage was this scorched dead straw that lay upon the ground. Still, by hard scanning, by leaning beside the horses' necks and pausing ever and again, even these white men could contrive to follow after their prey.

There were trodden places, bent and broken blades of the coarse grass, and ever and again the sufficient intimation of a footmark. And once the leader saw a brown smear of blood where the half-caste girl may have trod. And at that under his breath he cursed her for a fool.

The gaunt man checked his leader's tracking, and the little

man on the white horse rode behind, a man lost in a dream. They rode one after another, the man with the silver bridle led the way, and they spoke never a word. After a time it came to the little man on the white horse that the world was very still. He started out of his dream. Besides the little noises of their horses and equipment, the whole great valley kept the brooding quiet of a painted scene.

Before him went his master and his fellow, each intently leaning forward to the left, each impassively moving with the paces of his horse; their shadows went before them—still, noiseless, tapering attendants; and nearer a crouched cool shape was his own. He looked about him. What was it had gone? Then he remembered the reverberation from the banks of the gorge and the perpetual accompaniment of shifting, jostling pebbles. And, moreover—? There was no breeze.

That was it! What a vast, still place it was, a monotonous afternoon slumber. And the sky open and blank, except for a sombre veil of haze that had gathered in the upper valley.

He straightened his back, fretted with his bridle, puckered his lips to whistle, and simply sighed. He turned in his saddle for a time, and stared at the throat of the mountain gorge out of which they had come. Blank! Blank slopes on either side, with never a sign of a decent beast or tree—much less a man. What a land it was!

What a wilderness! He dropped again into his former pose.

It filled him with a momentary pleasure to see a wry stick of purple black flash out into the form of a snake, and vanish amidst the brown.

After all, the infernal valley *was* alive. And then, to rejoice him still more, came a little breath across his face, a whisper that came and went, the faintest inclination of a stiff black-antlered bush upon a little crest, the first intimations of a possible breeze.

Idly he wetted his finger, and held it up.

He pulled up sharply to avoid a collision with the gaunt man, who had stopped at fault upon the trail. Just at that guilty moment he caught his master's eye looking towards him.

For a time he forced an interest in the tracking. Then, as they rode on again, he studied his master's shadow and hat and shoulder, appearing and disappearing behind the gaunt man's nearer contours.

They had ridden four days out of the very limits of the world into this desolate place, short of water, with nothing but a strip of dried meat under their saddles, over rocks and mountains, where surely none but these fugitives had ever been before—for *that*!

And all this was for a girl, a mere willful child! And the man had whole cityfulls of people to do his basest bidding—girls, women!

Why in the name of passionate folly THIS one in particular? asked the little man, and scowled at the world, and licked his parched lips with a blackened tongue. It was the way of the master, and that was all he knew. Just because she sought to evade him...

His eye caught a whole row of high plumed canes bending in unison, and then the tails of silk that hung before his neck flapped and fell.

The breeze was growing stronger. Somehow it took the stiff stillness out of things—and that was well.

'Hullo!' said the gaunt man.

All three stopped abruptly.

'What?' asked the master. 'What?'

'Over there,' said the gaunt man, pointing up the valley.

'What?'

'Something coming towards us.'

And as he spoke a yellow animal crested a rise and came bearing down upon them. It was a big wild dog, coming before the wind, tongue out, at a steady pace, and running with such an intensity of purpose that he did not seem to see the horsemen he approached.

He ran with his nose up, following, it was plain, neither scent nor quarry. As he drew nearer the little man felt for his sword.

'He's mad,' said the gaunt rider.

'Shout!' said the little man, and shouted.

The dog came on. Then when the little man's blade was already out, it swerved aside and went panting by them and past. The eyes of the little man followed its flight. 'There was no foam,' he said.

For a space the man with the silver-studded bridle stared up the valley. 'Oh, come on!' he cried at last. 'What does it matter?' and jerked his horse into movement again.

The little man left the insoluble mystery of a dog that fled from nothing but the wind, and lapsed into profound musings on human character. 'Come on!' he whispered to himself. 'Why should it be given to one man to say "Come on!" with that stupendous violence of effect. Always, all his life, the man with the silver bridle has been saying that. If *I* said it—!' thought the little man. But people marvelled when the master was disobeyed even in the wildest things. This half-caste girl seemed to him, seemed to every one, mad—blasphemous almost. The little man, by way of comparison, reflected on the gaunt rider with the scarred lip, as stalwart as his master, as brave and, indeed, perhaps braver, and yet for him there was obedience, nothing but to give obedience duly and stoutly...

Certain sensations of the hands and knees called the little man back to more immediate things. He became aware of something. He rode up beside his gaunt fellow. 'Do you notice the horses?' he said in an undertone.

The gaunt face looked interrogation.

'They don't like this wind,' said the little man, and dropped behind as the man with the silver bridle turned upon him.

'It's all right,' said the gaunt-faced man.

They rode on again for a space in silence. The foremost two rode downcast upon the trail, the hindmost man watched the haze that crept down the vastness of the valley, nearer and nearer, and noted how the wind grew in strength moment by moment. Far away on the left he saw a line of dark bulks—wild hog perhaps, galloping down the valley, but of that he said nothing, nor did he remark again upon the uneasiness of the horses.

And then he saw first one and then a second great white ball, a great shining white ball like a gigantic head of thistle-down, that drove before the wind athwart the path. These balls soared high in the air, and dropped and rose again and caught for a moment, and hurried on and passed, but at the sight of them the restlessness of the horses increased.

Then presently he saw that more of these drifting globes—and then soon very many more—were hurrying towards him down the valley.

They became aware of a squealing. Athwart the path a huge boar rushed, turning his head but for one instant to glance at them, and then hurling on down the valley again. And at that, all three stopped and sat in their saddles, staring into the thickening haze that was coming upon them.

'If it were not for this thistle-down—' began the leader.

But now a big globe came drifting past within a score of yards of them. It was really not an even sphere at all, but a vast, soft, ragged, filmy thing, a sheet gathered by the corners, an aerial jelly-fish, as it were, but rolling over and over as it advanced, and trailing long, cobwebby threads and streamers that floated in its wake.

'It isn't thistle-down,' said the little man.

'I don't like the stuff,' said the gaunt man.

And they looked at one another.

'Curse it!' cried the leader. 'The air's full of it up there. If it keeps on at this pace long, it will stop us altogether.'

An instinctive feeling, such as lines out a herd of deer at the approach of some ambiguous thing, prompted them to turn their horses to the wind, ride forward for a few paces, and stare at that advancing multitude of floating masses. They came on before the wind with a sort of smooth swiftness, rising and falling noiselessly, sinking to earth, rebounding high, soaring—all with a perfect unanimity, with a still, deliberate assurance.

Right and left of the horsemen the pioneers of this strange

army passed. At one that rolled along the ground, breaking shapelessly and trailing out reluctantly into long grappling ribbons and bands, all three horses began to shy and dance. The master was seized with a sudden unreasonable impatience. He cursed the drifting globes roundly. 'Get on!' he cried; 'get on! What do these things matter? How *can* they matter? Back to the trail!' He fell swearing at his horse and sawed the bit across its mouth.

He shouted aloud with rage. 'I will follow that trail, I tell you!' he cried. 'Where is the trail?'

He gripped the bridle of his prancing horse and searched amidst the grass. A long and clinging thread fell across his face, a grey streamer dropped about his bridle-arm, some big, active thing with many legs ran down the back of his head. He looked up to discover one of those grey masses anchored as it were above him by these things and flapping out ends as a sail flaps when a boat comes, about—but noiselessly.

He had an impression of many eyes, of a dense crew of squat bodies, of long, many-jointed limbs hauling at their mooring ropes to bring the thing down upon him. For a space he stared up, reining in his prancing horse with the instinct born of years of horsemanship. Then the flat of a sword smote his back, and a blade flashed overhead and cut the drifting balloon of spider-web free, and the whole mass lifted softly and drove clear and away.

'Spiders!' cried the voice of the gaunt man. 'The things are full of big spiders! Look, my lord!'

The man with the silver bridle still followed the mass that drove away.

'Look, my lord!'

The master found himself staring down at a red, smashed thing on the ground that, in spite of partial obliteration, could still wriggle unavailing legs. Then when the gaunt man pointed to another mass that bore down upon them, he drew his sword hastily. Up the valley now it was like a fog bank torn to rags. He tried to grasp the situation.

'Ride for it!' the little man was shouting. 'Ride for it down the valley.'

What happened then was like the confusion of a battle. The man with the silver bridle saw the little man go past him slashing furiously at imaginary cobwebs, saw him cannon into the horse of the gaunt man and hurl it and its rider to earth. His own horse went a dozen paces before he could rein it in. Then he looked up to avoid imaginary dangers, and then back again to see a horse rolling on the ground, the gaunt man standing and slashing over it at a rent and fluttering mass of grey that streamed and wrapped about them both. And thick and fast as thistle-down on waste land on a windy day in July, the cobweb masses were coming on.

The little man had dismounted, but he dared not release his horse. He was endeavouring to lug the struggling brute back with the strength of one arm, while with the other he slashed aimlessly, The tentacles of a second grey mass had entangled themselves with the struggle, and this second grey mass came to its moorings, and slowly sank.

The master set his teeth, gripped his bridle, lowered his head, and spurred his horse forward. The horse on the ground rolled over, there were blood and moving shapes upon the flanks, and the gaunt man, suddenly leaving it, ran forward towards his master, perhaps ten paces. His legs were swathed and encumbered with grey; he made ineffectual movements with his sword. Grey streamers waved from him; there was a thin veil of grey across his face. With his left hand he beat at something on his body, and suddenly he stumbled and fell. He struggled to rise, and fell again, and suddenly, horribly, began to howl, 'Oh—ohoo, ohooh!'

The master could see the great spiders upon him, and others upon the ground.

As he strove to force his horse nearer to this gesticulating, screaming grey object that struggled up and down, there came a clatter of hoofs, and the little man, in act of mounting, swordless, balanced on his belly athwart the white horse, and clutching its mane, whirled past. And again a clinging thread of grey gossamer swept across the master's face. All about him, and over him, it seemed this drifting, noiseless cobweb circled and drew nearer him...

To the day of his death he never knew just how the event of that moment happened. Did he, indeed, turn his horse, or did it really of its own accord stampede after its fellow? Suffice it that in another second he was galloping full tilt down the valley with his sword whirling furiously overhead. And all about him on the quickening breeze, the spiders' airships, their air bundles and air sheets, seemed to him to hurry in a conscious pursuit.

Clatter, clatter, thud, thud—the man with the silver bridle rode, heedless of his direction, with his fearful face looking up now right, now left, and his sword arm ready to slash. And a few hundred yards ahead of him, with a tail of torn cobweb trailing behind him, rode the little man on the white horse, still but imperfectly in the saddle. The reeds bent before them, the wind blew fresh and strong, over his shoulder the master could see the webs hurrying to overtake...

He was so intent to escape the spiders' webs that only as his horse gathered together for a leap did he realise the ravine ahead. And then he realised it only to misunderstand and interfere. He was leaning forward on his horse's neck and sat up and back all too late.

But if in his excitement he had failed to leap, at any rate he had not forgotten how to fall. He was horseman again in mid-air. He came off clear with a mere bruise upon his shoulder, and his horse rolled, kicking spasmodic legs, and lay still. But the master's sword drove its point into the hard soil, and snapped clean across, as though Chance refused him any longer as her Knight, and the splintered end missed his face by an inch or so.

He was on his feet in a moment, breathlessly scanning the onrushing spider-webs. For a moment he was minded to run, and then thought of the ravine, and turned back. He ran aside once to dodge one drifting terror, and then he was swiftly clambering down the precipitous sides, and out of the touch of the gale.

There under the lee of the dry torrent's steeper banks he might crouch, and watch these strange, grey masses pass and pass in safety till the wind fell, and it became possible to escape. And there for a long time he crouched, watching the strange, grey, ragged masses trail their streamers across his narrowed sky.

Once a stray spider fell into the ravine close beside him—a full foot it measured from leg to leg, and its body was half a man's hand—and after he had watched its monstrous alacrity of search and escape for a little while, and tempted it to bite his broken sword, he lifted up his iron-heeled boot and smashed it into a pulp. He swore as he did so, and for a time sought up and down for another.

Then presently, when he was surer these spider swarms could not drop into the ravine, he found a place where he could sit down, and sat and fell into deep thought and began after his manner to gnaw his knuckles and bite his nails. And from this he was moved by the coming of the man with the white horse.

He heard him long before he saw him, as a clattering of hoofs, stumbling footsteps, and a reassuring voice. Then the little man appeared, a rueful figure, still with a tail of white cobweb trailing behind him. They approached each other without speaking, without a salutation. The little man was fatigued and shamed to the pitch of hopeless bitterness, and came to a stop at last, face to face with his seated master. The latter winced a little under his dependant's eye. 'Well?' he said at last, with no pretence of authority.

'You left him?'

'My horse bolted.'

'I know. So did mine.'

He laughed at his master mirthlessly.

'I say my horse bolted,' said the man who once had a silver-studded bridle.

'Cowards both,' said the little man.

The other gnawed his knuckle through some meditative

moments, with his eye on his inferior.

'Don't call me a coward,' he said at length.

'You are a coward like myself.'

'A coward possibly. There is a limit beyond which every man must fear. That I have learnt at last. But not like yourself. That is where the difference comes in.'

'I never could have dreamt you would have left him. He saved your life two minutes before... Why are you our lord?'

The master gnawed his knuckles again, and his countenance was dark.

'No man calls me a coward,' he said. 'No. A broken sword is better than none... One spavined white horse cannot be expected to carry two men a four days' journey. I hate white horses, but this time it cannot be helped. You begin to understand me?... I perceive that you are minded, on the strength of what you have seen and fancy, to taint my reputation. It is men of your sort who unmake kings. Besides which—I never liked you.'

'My lord!' said the little man.

'No,' said the master. 'NO!'

He stood up sharply as the little man moved. For a minute perhaps they faced one another. Overhead the spiders' balls went driving. There was a quick movement among the pebbles; a running of feet, a cry of despair, a gasp and a blow...

Towards nightfall the wind fell. The sun set in a calm serenity, and the man who had once possessed the silver bridle came at last very cautiously and by an easy slope out of the ravine again; but now he led the white horse that once belonged to the little man. He would have gone back to his horse to get his silver-mounted bridle again, but he feared night and a quickening breeze might still find him in the valley, and besides he disliked greatly to think he might discover his horse all swathed in cobwebs and perhaps unpleasantly eaten.

And as he thought of those cobwebs and of all the dangers he had been through, and the manner in which he had been preserved that day, his hand sought a little reliquary that hung about his neck, and he clasped it for a moment with heartfelt gratitude. As he did so his eyes went across the valley.

'I was hot with passion,' he said, 'and now she has met her reward. They also, no doubt—'

And behold! Far away out of the wooded slopes across the valley, but in the clearness of the sunset distinct and unmistakable, he saw a little spire of smoke.

At that his expression of serene resignation changed to an amazed anger. Smoke? He turned the head of the white horse about, and hesitated. And as he did so a little rustle of air went through the grass about him. Far away upon some reeds swayed a tattered sheet of grey. He looked at the cobwebs; he looked at the smoke.

'Perhaps, after all, it is not them,' he said at last.

But he knew better.

After he had stared at the smoke for some time, he mounted the white horse.

As he rode, he picked his way amidst stranded masses of web. For some reason there were many dead spiders on the ground, and those that lived feasted guiltily on their fellows. At the sound of his horse's hoofs they fled.

Their time had passed. From the ground without either a wind to carry them or a winding sheet ready, these things, for all their poison, could do him little evil. He flicked with his belt at those he fancied came too near. Once, where a number ran together over a bare place, he was minded to dismount and trample them with his boots, but this impulse he overcame. Ever and again he turned in his saddle, and looked back at the smoke. 'Spiders,' he muttered over and over again. 'Spiders! Well, well...

The next time I must spin a web.'

10

THE MUSIC ON THE HILL

Saki

Sylvia Seltoun ate her breakfast in the morning-room at Yessney with a pleasant sense of ultimate victory, such as a fervent Ironside might have permitted himself on the morrow of Worcester fight. She was scarcely pugnacious by temperament, but belonged to that more successful class of fighters who are pugnacious by circumstance. Fate had willed that her life should be occupied with a series of small struggles, usually with the odds slightly against her, and usually she had just managed to come through winning. And now she felt that she had brought her hardest and certainly her most important struggle to a successful issue. To have married Mortimer Seltoun, 'Dead Mortimer' as his more intimate enemies called him, in the teeth of the cold hostility of his family, and in spite of his unaffected indifference to women, was indeed an achievement that had needed some determination and adroitness to carry through; yesterday she had brought her victory to its concluding stage by wrenching her husband away from Town and its group of satellite watering-places and 'settling him down,' in the vocabulary of her kind, in this remote wood-girt manor farm which was his country house.

'You will never get Mortimer to go,' his mother had said carpingly, 'but if he once goes he'll stay; Yessney throws almost as much a spell over him as Town does. One can understand what holds him to Town, but Yessney—,' and the dowager had shrugged her shoulders.

There was a sombre almost savage wildness about Yessney that was certainly not likely to appeal to town-bred tastes, and Sylvia, notwithstanding her name, was accustomed to nothing much more sylvan than 'leafy Kensington.' She looked on the country as something excellent and wholesome in its way, which was apt to become troublesome if you encouraged it overmuch. Distrust of townlife had been a new thing with her, born of her marriage with Mortimer, and she had watched with satisfaction the gradual fading of what she called 'the Jermyn-Street-look' in his eyes as the woods and heather of Yessney had closed in on them yesternight. Her will-power and strategy had prevailed; Mortimer would stay. Outside the morning-room windows was a triangular slope of turf, which the indulgent might call a lawn, and beyond its low hedge of neglected fuschia bushes a steeper slope of heather and bracken dropped down into cavernous combes overgrown with oak and yew. In its wild open savagery there seemed a stealthy linking of the joy of life with the terror of unseen things. Sylvia smiled complacently as she gazed with a School-of-Art appreciation at the landscape, and then of a sudden she almost shuddered.

'It is very wild,' she said to Mortimer, who had joined her; 'one could almost think that in such a place the worship of Pan had never quite died out.'

'The worship of Pan never has died out,' said Mortimer. 'Other newer gods have drawn aside his votaries from time to time, but he is the Nature-God to whom all must come back at last. He has been called the Father of all the Gods, but most of his children have been stillborn.'

Sylvia was religious in an honest, vaguely devotional kind of way, and did not like to hear her beliefs spoken of as mere aftergrowths, but it was at least something new and hopeful to hear Dead Mortimer speak with such energy and conviction on any subject.

'You don't really believe in Pan?' she asked incredulously.

'I've been a fool in most things,' said Mortimer quietly, 'but I'm not such a fool as not to believe in Pan when I'm down here. And if you're wise you won't disbelieve in him too boastfully while you're in his country.'

It was not till a week later, when Sylvia had exhausted

the attractions of the woodland walks round Yessney, that she ventured on a tour of inspection of the farm buildings. A farmyard suggested in her mind a scene of cheerful bustle, with churns and flails and smiling dairymaids, and teams of horses drinking knee-deep in duck-crowded ponds. As she wandered among the gaunt grey buildings of Yessney manor farm her first impression was one of crushing stillness and desolation, as though she had happened on some lone deserted homestead long given over to owls and cobwebs; then came a sense of furtive watchful hostility, the same shadow of unseen things that seemed to lurk in the wooded combes and coppices. From behind heavy doors and shuttered windows came the restless stamp of hoof or rasp of chain halter, and at times a muffled bellow from some stalled beast. From a distant comer a shaggy dog watched her with intent unfriendly eyes; as she drew near it slipped quietly into its kennel, and slipped out again as noiselessly when she had passed by. A few hens, questing for food under a rick, stole away under a gate at her approach. Sylvia felt that if she had come across any human beings in this wilderness of barn and byre they would have fled wraith-like from her gaze. At last, turning a corner quickly, she came upon a living thing that did not fly from her. Astretch in a pool of mud was an enormous sow, gigantic beyond the town-woman's wildest computation of swine-flesh, and speedily alert to resent and if necessary repel the unwonted intrusion. It was Sylvia's turn to make an unobtrusive retreat. As she threaded her way past rickyards and cowsheds and long blank walls, she started suddenly at a strange sound—the echo of a boy's laughter, golden and equivocal. Jan, the only boy employed on the farm, a tow-headed, wizen-faced yokel, was visibly at work on a potato clearing half-way up the nearest hill-side, and Mortimer, when questioned, knew of no other probable or possible begetter of the hidden mockery that had ambushed Sylvia's retreat. The memory of that untraceable echo was added to her other impressions of a furtive sinister 'something' that hung around Yessney.

Of Mortimer she saw very little; farm and woods and trout-streams seemed to swallow him up from dawn till dusk. Once, following the direction she had seen him take in the morning, she came to an open space in a nut copse, further shut in by huge yew trees, in the centre of which stood a stone pedestal surmounted by a small bronze figure of a youthful Pan. It was a beautiful piece of workmanship, but her attention was chiefly held by the fact that a newly cut bunch of grapes had been placed as an offering at its feet. Grapes were none too plentiful at the manor house, and Sylvia snatched the bunch angrily from the pedestal. Contemptuous annoyance dominated her thoughts as she strolled slowly homeward, and then gave way to a sharp feeling of something that was very near fright; across a thick tangle of undergrowth a boy's face was scowling at her, brown and beautiful, with unutterably evil eyes. It was a lonely pathway, all pathways round Yessney were lonely for the matter of that, and she sped forward without waiting to give a closer scrutiny to this sudden apparition. It was not till she had reached the house that she discovered that she had dropped the bunch of grapes in her flight.

'I saw a youth in the wood to-day,' she told Mortimer that evening, 'brown-faced and rather handsome, but a scoundrel to look at. A gipsy lad, I suppose.'

'A reasonable theory,' said Mortimer, 'only there aren't any gipsies in these parts at present.'

'Then who was he?' asked Sylvia, and as Mortimer appeared to have no theory of his own she passed on to recount her finding of the votive offering.

'I suppose it was your doing,' she observed; 'it's a harmless piece of lunacy, but people would think you dreadfully silly if they knew of it.'

'Did you meddle with it in any way?' asked Mortimer.

'I—I threw the grapes away. It seemed so silly,' said Sylvia, watching Mortimer's impassive face for a sign of annoyance.

'I don't think you were wise to do that,' he said reflectively. 'I've heard it said that the Wood Gods are rather horrible to those who molest them.'

'Horrible perhaps to those that believe in them, but you see I don't,' retorted Sylvia.

'All the same,' said Mortimer in his even, dispassionate tone, 'I should avoid the woods and orchards if I were you, and give a wide berth to the horned beasts on the farm.'

It was all nonsense, of course, but in that lonely wood-girt spot nonsense seemed able to rear a bastard brood of uneasiness.

'Mortimer,' said Sylvia suddenly, 'I think we will go back to Town some time soon.'

Her victory had not been so complete as she had supposed; it had carried her on to ground that she was already anxious to quit.

'I don't think you will ever go back to Town,' said Mortimer. He seemed to be paraphrasing his mother's prediction as to himself.

Sylvia noted with dissatisfaction and some self-contempt that the course of her next afternoon's ramble took her instinctively clear of the network of woods. As to the horned cattle, Mortimer's warning was scarcely needed, for she had always regarded them as of doubtful neutrality at the best: her imagination unsexed the most matronly dairy cows and turned them into bulls liable to 'see red' at any moment. The ram who fed in the narrow paddock below the orchards she had adjudged, after ample and cautious probation, to be of docile temper; to-day, however, she decided to leave his docility untested, for the usually tranquil beast was roaming with every sign of restlessness from corner to corner of his meadow. A low, fitful piping, as of some reedy flute, was coming from the depth of a neighbouring copse, and there seemed to be some subtle connection between the animal's restless pacing and the wild music from the wood. Sylvia turned her steps in an upward direction and climbed the heather-clad slopes that stretched in rolling shoulders high above Yessney. She had left the piping notes behind her, but across the wooded combes at her feet the wind brought her another kind of music, the straining bay of hounds in full chase. Yessney was just on the outskirts of the Devon-and-Somerset country, and the hunted deer sometimes came that way. Sylvia could presently see a dark body, breasting hill after hill, and sinking again and again out of sight as he crossed the combes, while behind him steadily swelled that relentless chorus, and she grew tense with the excited sympathy that one feels for any hunted thing in whose capture one is not directly interested. And at last he broke through the outermost line of oak scrub and fern and stood panting in the open, a fat September stag carrying a well-furnished head. His obvious course was to drop down to the brown pools of Undercombe, and thence make his way towards the red deer's favoured sanctuary, the sea. To Sylvia's surprise, however, he turned his head to the upland slope and came lumbering resolutely onward over the heather. 'It will be dreadful,' she thought, 'the hounds will pull him down under my very eyes.' But the music of the pack seemed to have died away for a moment, and in its place she heard again that wild piping, which rose now on this side, now on that, as though urging the failing stag to a final effort. Sylvia stood well aside from his path, half hidden in a thick growth of whortle bushes, and watched him swing stiffly upward, his flanks dark with sweat, the coarse hair on his neck showing light by contrast. The pipe music shrilled suddenly around her, seeming to come from the bushes at her very feet, and at the same moment the great beast slewed round and bore directly down upon her. In an instant her pity for the hunted animal was changed to wild terror at her own danger; the thick heather roots mocked her scrambling efforts at flight, and she looked frantically downward for a glimpse of oncoming hounds. The huge antler spikes were within a few yards of her, and in a flash of numbing fear she remembered Mortimer's warning, to beware of horned beasts on the farm. And then with a quick throb of joy she saw that she was not alone; a human figure stood a few paces aside, knee-deep in the whortle bushes.

'Drive it off!' she shrieked. But the figure made no answering movement.

The antlers drove straight at her breast, the acrid smell of the hunted animal was in her nostrils, but her eyes were filled with the horror of something she saw other than her oncoming death. And in her ears rang the echo of a boy's laughter, golden and equivocal.

11

THE ROCKING-HORSE WINNER

D.H. Lawrence

There was a woman who was beautiful, who started with all the advantages, yet she had no luck. She married for love, and the love turned to dust. She had bonny children, yet she felt they had been thrust upon her, and she could not love them. They looked at her coldly, as if they were finding fault with her. And hurriedly she felt she must cover up some fault in herself. Yet what it was that she must cover up she never knew. Nevertheless, when her children were present, she always felt the centre of her heart go hard. This troubled her, and in her manner she was all the more gentle and anxious for her children, as if she loved them very much. Only she herself knew that at the centre of her heart was a hard little place that could not feel love, no, not for anybody. Everybody else said of her: 'She is such a good mother. She adores her children.' Only she herself, and her children themselves, knew it was not so. They read it in each other's eyes.

There were a boy and two little girls. They lived in a pleasant house, with a garden, and they had discreet servants, and felt themselves superior to anyone in the neighbourhood.

Although they lived in style, they felt always an anxiety in the house. There was never enough money. The mother had a small income, and the father had a small income, but not nearly enough for the social position which they had to keep up. The father went into town to some office. But though he had good prospects, these prospects never materialised. There was always the grinding sense of the shortage of money, though the style was always kept up.

At last the mother said: 'I will see if I can't make something.'

But she did not know where to begin. She racked her brains, and tried this thing and the other, but could not find anything successful. The failure made deep lines come into her face. Her children were growing up, they would have to go to school. There must be more money, there must be more money. The father, who was always very handsome and expensive in his tastes, seemed as if he never would be able to do anything worth doing. And the mother, who had a great belief in herself, did not succeed any better, and her tastes were just as expensive.

And so the house came to be haunted by the unspoken phrase: There must be more money! There must be more money! The children could hear it all the time though nobody said it aloud. They heard it at Christmas, when the expensive and splendid toys filled the nursery. Behind the shining modern rocking-horse, behind the smart doll's house, a voice would start whispering: 'There must be more money! There must be more money!' And the children would stop playing, to listen for a moment. They would look into each other's eyes, to see if they had all heard. And each one saw in the eyes of the other two that they too had heard. 'There must be more money! There must be more money!'

It came whispering from the springs of the still-swaying rocking-horse, and even the horse, bending his wooden, champing head, heard it. The big doll, sitting so pink and smirking in her new pram, could hear it quite plainly, and seemed to be smirking all the more self-consciously because of it. The foolish puppy, too, that took the place of the teddy-bear, he was looking so extraordinarily foolish for no other reason but that he heard the secret whisper all over the house: 'There must be more money!'

Yet nobody ever said it aloud. The whisper was everywhere, and therefore no one spoke it. Just as no one ever says: 'We are breathing!' in spite of the fact that breath is coming and going all the time.

'Mother,' said the boy Paul one day, 'why don't we keep a car of our own? Why do we always use uncle's, or else a taxi?'

'Because we're the poor members of the family,' said the mother.

'But why are we, mother?'

'Well—I suppose,' she said slowly and bitterly, 'it's because your father has no luck.'

The boy was silent for some time.

'Is luck money, mother?' he asked, rather timidly.

'No, Paul. Not quite. It's what causes you to have money.'

'Oh!' said Paul vaguely. 'I thought when Uncle Oscar said filthy lucker, it meant money.'

'Filthy lucre does mean money,' said the mother. 'But it's lucre, not luck.'

'Oh!' said the boy. 'Then what is luck, mother?'

'It's what causes you to have money. If you're lucky you have money. That's why it's better to be born lucky than rich. If you're rich, you may lose your money. But if you're lucky, you will always get more money.'

'Oh! Will you? And is father not lucky?'

'Very unlucky, I should say,' she said bitterly.

The boy watched her with unsure eyes.

'Why?' he asked.

'I don't know. Nobody ever knows why one person is lucky and another unlucky.'

'Don't they? Nobody at all? Does nobody know?'

'Perhaps God. But He never tells.'

'He ought to, then. And aren't you lucky either, mother?'

'I can't be, if I married an unlucky husband.'

'But by yourself, aren't you?'

'I used to think I was, before I married. Now I think I am very unlucky indeed.'

'Why?'

'Well—never mind! Perhaps I'm not really,' she said.

The child looked at her to see if she meant it. But he saw, by the lines of her mouth, that she was only trying to hide something from him.

'Well, anyhow,' he said stoutly, 'I'm a lucky person.'

'Why?' said his mother, with a sudden laugh.

He stared at her. He didn't even know why he had said it.

'God told me,' he asserted, brazening it out.

'I hope he did, dear!' she said, again with a laugh, but rather bitter.

'He did, mother!'

'Excellent!' said the mother, using one of her husband's exclamations.

The boy saw she did not believe him; or rather, that she paid no attention to his assertion. This angered him somewhere, and made him want to compel her attention.

He went off by himself, vaguely, in a childish way, seeking for the clue to 'luck'. Absorbed, taking no heed of other people, he went about with a sort of stealth, seeking inwardly for luck. He wanted luck, he wanted it, he wanted it. When the two girls were playing dolls in the nursery, he would sit on his big rocking-horse, charging madly into space, with a frenzy that made the little girls peer at him uneasily. Wildly the horse careered, the waving dark hair of the boy tossed, his eyes had a strange glare in them. The little girls dared not speak to him.

When he had ridden to the end of his mad little journey, he climbed down and stood in front of his rocking-horse, staring fixedly into its lowered face. Its red mouth was slightly open, its big eye was wide and glassy-bright.

'Now!' he would silently command the snorting steed. 'Now take me to where there is luck! Now take me!'

And he would slash the horse on the neck with the little whip he had asked Uncle Oscar for. He knew the horse could take him to where there was luck, if only he forced it. So he would mount again and start on his furious ride, hoping at last to get there.

'You'll break your horse, Paul!' said the nurse.

'He's always riding like that! I wish he'd leave off!' said his elder sister Joan.

But he only glared down on them in silence. Nurse gave him up. She could make nothing of him. Anyhow, he was growing beyond her.

One day his mother and his Uncle Oscar came in when he was on one of his furious rides. He did not speak to them.

'Hallo, you young jockey! Riding a winner?' said his uncle.

'Aren't you growing too big for a rocking-horse? You're not a very little boy any longer, you know,' said his mother.

But Paul only gave a blue glare from his big, rather close-set eyes. He would speak to nobody when he was in full tilt. His mother watched him with an anxious expression on her face.

At last he suddenly stopped forcing his horse into the mechanical gallop and slid down.

'Well, I got there!' he announced fiercely, his blue eyes still flaring, and his sturdy long legs straddling apart.

'Where did you get to?' asked his mother.

'Where I wanted to go,' he flared back at her.

'That's right, son!' said Uncle Oscar. 'Don't you stop till you get there. What's the horse's name?'

'He doesn't have a name,' said the boy.

'Get's on without all right?' asked the uncle.

'Well, he has different names. He was called Sansovino last week.'

'Sansovino, eh? Won the Ascot. How did you know this name?'

'He always talks about horse-races with Bassett,' said Joan.

The uncle was delighted to find that his small nephew was posted with all the racing news. Bassett, the young gardener, who had been wounded in the left foot in the war and had got his present job through Oscar Cresswell, whose batman he had been, was a perfect blade of the 'turf'. He lived in the racing events, and the small boy lived with him.

Oscar Cresswell got it all from Bassett.

'Master Paul comes and asks me, so I can't do more than tell him, sir,' said Bassett, his face terribly serious, as if he were speaking of religious matters.

'And does he ever put anything on a horse he fancies?'

'Well—I don't want to give him away—he's a young sport,

a fine sport, sir. Would you mind asking him himself? He sort of takes a pleasure in it, and perhaps he'd feel I was giving him away, sir, if you don't mind.

Bassett was serious as a church.

The uncle went back to his nephew and took him off for a ride in the car.

'Say, Paul, old man, do you ever put anything on a horse?' the uncle asked.

The boy watched the handsome man closely.

'Why, do you think I oughtn't to?' he parried.

'Not a bit of it! I thought perhaps you might give me a tip for the Lincoln.'

The car sped on into the country, going down to Uncle Oscar's place in Hampshire.

'Honour bright?' said the nephew.

'Honour bright, son!' said the uncle.

'Well, then, Daffodil.'

'Daffodil! I doubt it, sonny. What about Mirza?'

'I only know the winner,' said the boy. 'That's Daffodil.'

'Daffodil, eh?'

There was a pause. Daffodil was an obscure horse comparatively.

'Uncle!'

'Yes, son?'

'You won't let it go any further, will you? I promised Bassett.'

'Bassett be damned, old man! What's he got to do with it?'

'We're partners. We've been partners from the first. Uncle, he lent me my first five shillings, which I lost. I promised him, honour bright, it was only between me and him; only you gave me that ten-shilling note I started winning with, so I thought you were lucky. You won't let it go any further, will you?'

The boy gazed at his uncle from those big, hot, blue eyes, set rather close together. The uncle stirred and laughed uneasily.

'Right you are, son! I'll keep your tip private. How much are you putting on him?'

'All except twenty pounds,' said the boy. 'I keep that in reserve.'

The uncle thought it a good joke.

'You keep twenty pounds in reserve, do you, you young romancer? What are you betting, then?'

'I'm betting three hundred,' said the boy gravely. 'But it's between you and me, Uncle Oscar! Honour bright?'

'It's between you and me all right, you young Nat Gould,' he said, laughing. 'But where's your three hundred?'

'Bassett keeps it for me. We're partners.'

'You are, are you! And what is Bassett putting on Daffodil?'

'He won't go quite as high as I do, I expect. Perhaps he'll go a hundred and fifty.'

'What, pennies?' laughed the uncle.

'Pounds,' said the child, with a surprised look at his uncle. 'Bassett keeps a bigger reserve than I do.'

Between wonder and amusement Uncle Oscar was silent. He pursued the matter no further, but he determined to take his nephew with him to the Lincoln races.

'Now, son,' he said, 'I'm putting twenty on Mirza, and I'll put five on for you on any horse you fancy. What's your pick?'

'Daffodil, uncle.'

'No, not the fiver on Daffodil!'

'I should if it was my own fiver,' said the child.

'Good! Good! Right you are! A fiver for me and a fiver for you on Daffodil.'

The child had never been to a race-meeting before, and his eyes were blue fire. He pursed his mouth tight and watched. A Frenchman just in front had put his money on Lancelot. Wild with excitement, he flayed his arms up and down, yelling 'Lancelot! Lancelot!' in his French accent.

Daffodil came in first, Lancelot second, Mirza third. The child, flushed and with eyes blazing, was curiously serene. His uncle brought him four five-pound notes, four to one.

'What am I to do with these?' he cried, waving them before the boy's eyes.

'I suppose we'll talk to Bassett,' said the boy. 'I expect I have fifteen hundred now; and twenty in reserve; and this twenty.'

His uncle studied him for some moments.

'Look here, son!' he said. 'You're not serious about Bassett and that fifteen hundred, are you?'

'Yes, I am. But it's between you and me, uncle. Honour bright?'

'Honour bright all right, son! But I must talk to Bassett.'

'If you'd like to be a partner, uncle, with Bassett and me, we could all be partners. Only, you'd have to promise, honour bright, uncle, not to let it go beyond us three. Bassett and I are lucky, and you must be lucky, because it was your ten shillings I started winning with...'

Uncle Oscar took both Bassett and Paul into Richmond Park for an afternoon, and there they talked.

'It's like this, you see, sir,' Bassett said. 'Master Paul would get me talking about racing events, spinning yarns, you know, sir. And he was always keen on knowing if I'd made or if I'd lost. It's about a year since, now, that I put five shillings on Blush of Dawn for him: and we lost. Then the luck turned, with that ten shillings he had from you: that we put on Singhalese. And since that time, it's been pretty steady, all things considering. What do you say, Master Paul?'

'We're all right when we're sure,' said Paul. 'It's when we're not quite sure that we go down.'

'Oh, but we're careful then,' said Bassett.

'But when are you sure?' smiled Uncle Oscar.

'It's Master Paul, sir,' said Bassett in a secret, religious voice. 'It's as if he had it from heaven. Like Daffodil, now, for the Lincoln. That was as sure as eggs.'

'Did you put anything on Daffodil?' asked Oscar Cresswell.

'Yes, sir, I made my bit.'

'And my nephew?'

Bassett was obstinately silent, looking at Paul.

'I made twelve hundred, didn't I, Bassett? I told uncle I was putting three hundred on Daffodil.'

'That's right,' said Bassett, nodding.

'But where's the money?' asked the uncle.

'I keep it safe locked up, sir. Master Paul he can have it any minute he likes to ask for it.'

'What, fifteen hundred pounds?'

'And twenty! And forty, that is, with the twenty he made on the course.'

'It's amazing!' said the uncle.

'If Master Paul offers you to be partners, sir, I would, if I were you: if you'll excuse me,' said Bassett.

Oscar Cresswell thought about it.

'I'll see the money,' he said.

They drove home again, and, sure enough, Bassett came round to the garden-house with fifteen hundred pounds in notes. The twenty pounds reserve was left with Joe Glee, in the Turf Commission deposit.

'You see, it's all right, uncle, when I'm sure! Then we go strong, for all we're worth, don't we, Bassett?'

'We do that, Master Paul.'

'And when are you sure?' said the uncle, laughing.

'Oh, well, sometimes I'm absolutely sure, like about Daffodil,' said the boy; 'and sometimes I have an idea; and sometimes I haven't even an idea, have I, Bassett? Then we're careful, because we mostly go down.'

'You do, do you! And when you're sure, like about Daffodil, what makes you sure, sonny?'

'Oh, well, I don't know,' said the boy uneasily. 'I'm sure, you know, uncle; that's all.'

'It's as if he had it from heaven, sir,' Bassett reiterated.

'I should say so!' said the uncle.

But he became a partner. And when the Leger was coming on Paul was 'sure' about Lively Spark, which was a quite inconsiderable horse. The boy insisted on putting a thousand on the horse, Bassett went for five hundred, and Oscar Cresswell two hundred. Lively Spark came in first, and the betting had been ten to one against him. Paul had made ten thousand.

'You see,' he said. 'I was absolutely sure of him.'

Even Oscar Cresswell had cleared two thousand.

'Look here, son,' he said, 'this sort of thing makes me nervous.'

'It needn't, uncle! Perhaps I shan't be sure again for a long time.'

'But what are you going to do with your money?' asked the uncle.

'Of course,' said the boy, 'I started it for mother. She said she had no luck, because father is unlucky, so I thought if I was lucky, it might stop whispering.'

'What might stop whispering?'

'Our house. I hate our house for whispering.'

'What does it whisper?'

'Why—why'—the boy fidgeted—'why, I don't know. But it's always short of money, you know, uncle.'

'I know it, son, I know it.'

'You know people send mother writs, don't you, uncle?'

'I'm afraid I do,' said the uncle.

'And then the house whispers, like people laughing at you behind your back. It's awful, that is! I thought if I was lucky—'

'You might stop it,' added the uncle.

The boy watched him with big blue eyes, that had an uncanny cold fire in them, and he said never a word.

'Well, then!' said the uncle. 'What are we doing?'

'I shouldn't like mother to know I was lucky,' said the boy.

'Why not, son?'

'She'd stop me.'

'I don't think she would.'

'Oh!'—and the boy writhed in an odd way—'I don't want her to know, uncle.'

'All right, son! We'll manage it without her knowing.'

They managed it very easily. Paul, at the other's suggestion, handed over five thousand pounds to his uncle, who deposited it with the family lawyer, who was then to inform Paul's mother that a relative had put five thousand pounds into his hands, which sum was to be paid out a thousand pounds at a time, on the mother's birthday, for the next five years.

'So she'll have a birthday present of a thousand pounds for five successive years,' said Uncle Oscar. 'I hope it won't make it all the harder for her later.'

Paul's mother had her birthday in November. The house had been 'whispering' worse than ever lately, and, even in spite of his luck, Paul could not bear up against it. He was very anxious to see the effect of the birthday letter, telling his mother about the thousand pounds.

When there were no visitors, Paul now took his meals with his parents, as he was beyond the nursery control. His mother went into town nearly every day. She had discovered that she had an odd knack of sketching furs and dress materials, so she worked secretly in the studio of a friend who was the chief 'artist' for the leading drapers. She drew the figures of ladies in furs and ladies in silk and sequins for the newspaper advertisements. This young woman artist earned several thousand pounds a year, but Paul's mother only made several hundreds, and she was again dissatisfied. She so wanted to be first in something, and she did not succeed, even in making sketches for drapery advertisements.

She was down to breakfast on the morning of her birthday. Paul watched her face as she read her letters. He knew the lawyer's letter. As his mother read it, her face hardened and became more expressionless. Then a cold, determined look came on her mouth. She hid the letter under the pile of others, and said not a word about it.

'Didn't you have anything nice in the post for your birthday, mother?' said Paul.

'Quite moderately nice,' she said, her voice cold and hard and absent.

She went away to town without saying more.

But in the afternoon Uncle Oscar appeared. He said Paul's mother had had a long interview with the lawyer, asking if the whole five thousand could not be advanced at once, as she was in debt.

'What do you think, uncle?' said the boy.

'I leave it to you, son.'

'Oh, let her have it, then! We can get some more with the other,' said the boy.

'A bird in the hand is worth two in the bush, laddie!' said Uncle Oscar.

'But I'm sure to know for the Grand National; or the Lincolnshire; or else the Derby. I'm sure to know for one of them,' said Paul.

So Uncle Oscar signed the agreement, and Paul's mother touched the whole five thousand. Then something very curious happened. The voices in the house suddenly went mad, like a chorus of frogs on a spring evening. There were certain new furnishings, and Paul had a tutor. He was really going to Eton, his father's school, in the following autumn. There were flowers in the winter, and a blossoming of the luxury Paul's mother had been used to. And yet the voices in the house, behind the sprays of mimosa and almond-blossom, and from under the piles of iridescent cushions, simply trilled and screamed in a sort of ecstasy: 'There must be more money! Oh-h-h; there must be more money. Oh, now, now-w! Now-w-w—there must be more money!—more than ever! More than ever!'

It frightened Paul terribly. He studied away at his Latin and Greek with his tutor. But his intense hours were spent with Bassett. The Grand National had gone by: he had not 'known', and had lost a hundred pounds. Summer was at hand. He was in agony for the Lincoln. But even for the Lincoln he didn't 'know', and he lost fifty pounds. He became wild-eyed and strange, as if something were going to explode in him.

'Let it alone, son! Don't you bother about it!' urged Uncle Oscar. But it was as if the boy couldn't really hear what his uncle was saying.

'I've got to know for the Derby! I've got to know for the Derby!' the child reiterated, his big blue eyes blazing with a sort of madness.

His mother noticed how overwrought he was.

'You'd better go to the seaside. Wouldn't you like to go now to the seaside, instead of waiting? I think you'd better,' she said, looking down at him anxiously, her heart curiously heavy because of him.

But the child lifted his uncanny blue eyes.

'I couldn't possibly go before the Derby, mother!' he said. 'I couldn't possibly!'

'Why not?' she said, her voice becoming heavy when she was opposed. 'Why not? You can still go from the seaside to see the Derby with your Uncle Oscar, if that that's what you wish. No need for you to wait here. Besides, I think you care too much about these races. It's a bad sign. My family has been a gambling family, and you won't know till you grow up how much damage it has done. But it has done damage. I shall have to send Bassett away, and ask Uncle Oscar not to talk racing to you, unless you promise to be reasonable about it: go away to the seaside and forget it. You're all nerves!'

'I'll do what you like, mother, so long as you don't send me away till after the Derby,' the boy said.

'Send you away from where? Just from this house?'

'Yes,' he said, gazing at her.

'Why, you curious child, what makes you care about this house so much, suddenly? I never knew you loved it.'

He gazed at her without speaking. He had a secret within a secret, something he had not divulged, even to Bassett or to his Uncle Oscar.

But his mother, after standing undecided and a little bit sullen for some moments, said: 'Very well, then! Don't go to the seaside till after the Derby, if you don't wish it. But promise me you won't think so much about horse-racing and events as you call them!'

'Oh no,' said the boy casually. 'I won't think much about them, mother. You needn't worry. I wouldn't worry, mother, if I were you.'

'If you were me and I were you,' said his mother, 'I wonder

what we should do!'

'But you know you needn't worry, mother, don't you?' the boy repeated.

'I should be awfully glad to know it,' she said wearily.

'Oh, well, you can, you know. I mean, you ought to know you needn't worry,' he insisted.

'Ought I? Then I'll see about it,' she said.

Paul's secret of secrets was his wooden horse, that which had no name. Since he was emancipated from a nurse and a nursery-governess, he had had his rocking-horse removed to his own bedroom at the top of the house.

'Surely you're too big for a rocking-horse!' his mother had remonstrated.

'Well, you see, mother, till I can have a real horse, I like to have some sort of animal about,' had been his quaint answer.

'Do you feel he keeps you company?' she laughed.

'Oh yes! He's very good, he always keeps me company, when I'm there,' said Paul.

So the horse, rather shabby, stood in an arrested prance in the boy's bedroom.

The Derby was drawing near, and the boy grew more and more tense. He hardly heard what was spoken to him, he was very frail, and his eyes were really uncanny. His mother had sudden strange seizures of uneasiness about him. Sometimes, for half an hour, she would feel a sudden anxiety about him that was almost anguish. She wanted to rush to him at once, and know he was safe.

Two nights before the Derby, she was at a big party in town, when one of her rushes of anxiety about her boy, her first-born, gripped her heart till she could hardly speak. She fought with the feeling, might and main, for she believed in common sense. But it was too strong. She had to leave the dance and go downstairs to telephone to the country. The children's nursery-governess was terribly surprised and startled at being rung up in the night.

'Are the children all right, Miss Wilmot?'

'Oh yes, they are quite all right.'

'Master Paul? Is he all right?'

'He went to bed as right as a trivet. Shall I run up and look at him?'

'No,' said Paul's mother reluctantly. 'No! Don't trouble. It's all right. Don't sit up. We shall be home fairly soon.' She did not want her son's privacy intruded upon.

'Very good,' said the governess.

It was about one o'clock when Paul's mother and father drove up to their house. All was still. Paul's mother went to her room and slipped off her white fur cloak. She had told her maid not to wait up for her. She heard her husband downstairs, mixing a whisky and soda.

And then, because of the strange anxiety at her heart, she stole upstairs to her son's room. Noiselessly she went along the upper corridor. Was there a faint noise? What was it?

She stood, with arrested muscles, outside his door, listening. There was a strange, heavy, and yet not loud noise. Her heart stood still. It was a soundless noise, yet rushing and powerful. Something huge, in violent, hushed motion. What was it? What in God's name was it? She ought to know. She felt that she knew the noise. She knew what it was.

Yet she could not place it. She couldn't say what it was. And on and on it went, like a madness.

Softly, frozen with anxiety and fear, she turned the door-handle.

The room was dark. Yet in the space near the window, she heard and saw something plunging to and fro. She gazed in fear and amazement.

Then suddenly she switched on the light, and saw her son, in his green pyjamas, madly surging on the rocking-horse. The blaze of light suddenly lit him up, as he urged the wooden horse, and lit her up, as she stood, blonde, in her dress of pale green and crystal, in the doorway.

'Paul!' she cried. 'Whatever are you doing?'

'It's Malabar!' he screamed in a powerful, strange voice.

'It's Malabar!'

His eyes blazed at her for one strange and senseless second, as he ceased urging his wooden horse. Then he fell with a crash to the ground, and she, all her tormented motherhood flooding upon her, rushed to gather him up.

But he was unconscious, and unconscious he remained, with some brain-fever. He talked and tossed, and his mother sat stonily by his side.

'Malabar! It's Malabar! Bassett, Bassett, I know! It's Malabar!'

So the child cried, trying to get up and urge the rocking-horse that gave him his inspiration.

'What does he mean by Malabar?' asked the heart-frozen mother.

'I don't know,' said the father stonily.

'What does he mean by Malabar?' she asked her brother Oscar.

'It's one of the horses running for the Derby,' was the answer.

And, in spite of himself, Oscar Cresswell spoke to Bassett, and himself put a thousand on Malabar: at fourteen to one.

The third day of the illness was critical: they were waiting for a change. The boy, with his rather long, curly hair, was tossing ceaselessly on the pillow. He neither slept nor regained consciousness, and his eyes were like blue stones. His mother sat, feeling her heart had gone, turned actually into a stone.

In the evening Oscar Cresswell did not come, but Bassett sent a message, saying could he come up for one moment, just one moment? Paul's mother was very angry at the intrusion, but on second thoughts she agreed. The boy was the same. Perhaps Bassett might bring him to consciousness.

The gardener, a shortish fellow with a little brown moustache and sharp little brown eyes, tiptoed into the room, touched his imaginary cap to Paul's mother, and stole to the bedside, staring with glittering, smallish eyes at the tossing, dying child.

'Master Paul!' he whispered. 'Master Paul! Malabar came in first all right, a clean win. I did as you told me. You've made over seventy thousand pounds, you have; you've got over eighty thousand. Malabar came in all right, Master Paul.'

'Malabar! Malabar! Did I say Malabar, mother? Did I say Malabar? Do you think I'm lucky, mother? I knew Malabar, didn't I? Over eighty thousand pounds! I call that lucky, don't you, mother? Over eighty thousand pounds! I knew, didn't I know I knew? Malabar came in all right. If I ride my horse till I'm sure, then I tell you, Bassett, you can go as high as you like. Did you go for all you were worth, Bassett?'

'I went a thousand on it, Master Paul.'

'I never told you, mother, that if I can ride my horse, and get there, then I'm absolutely sure—oh, absolutely! Mother, did I ever tell you? I am lucky!'

'No, you never did,' said his mother.

But the boy died in the night.

And even as he lay dead, his mother heard her brother's voice saying to her, 'My God, Hester, you're eighty-odd thousand to the good, and a poor devil of a son to the bad. But, poor devil, poor devil, he's best gone out of a life where he rides his rocking-horse to find a winner.'

12

THE LADY WITH THE DOG

Anton Chekov

IT was said that a new person had appeared on the sea-front: a lady with a little dog. Dmitri Dmitritch Gurov, who had by then been a fortnight at Yalta, and so was fairly at home there, had begun to take an interest in new arrivals. Sitting in Verney's pavilion, he saw, walking on the sea-front, a fair-haired young lady of medium height, wearing a béret; a white Pomeranian dog was running behind her.

And afterwards he met her in the public gardens and in the square several times a day. She was walking alone, always wearing the same béret, and always with the same white dog; no one knew who she was, and every one called her simply 'the lady with the dog.'

'If she is here alone without a husband or friends, it wouldn't be amiss to make her acquaintance,' Gurov reflected.

He was under forty, but he had a daughter already twelve years old, and two sons at school. He had been married young, when he was a student in his second year, and by now his wife seemed half as old again as he. She was a tall, erect woman with dark eyebrows, staid and dignified, and, as she said of herself, intellectual. She read a great deal, used phonetic spelling, called her husband, not Dmitri, but Dimitri, and he secretly considered her unintelligent, narrow, inelegant, was afraid of her, and did not like to be at home. He had begun being unfaithful to her long ago—had been unfaithful to her often, and, probably on that account, almost always spoke ill of women, and when they were talked about in his presence, used to call them 'the lower race.'

It seemed to him that he had been so schooled by bitter

experience that he might call them what he liked, and yet he could not get on for two days together without 'the lower race.' In the society of men he was bored and not himself, with them he was cold and uncommunicative; but when he was in the company of women he felt free, and knew what to say to them and how to behave; and he was at ease with them even when he was silent. In his appearance, in his character, in his whole nature, there was something attractive and elusive which allured women and disposed them in his favour; he knew that, and some force seemed to draw him, too, to them.

Experience often repeated, truly bitter experience, had taught him long ago that with decent people, especially Moscow people—always slow to move and irresolute—every intimacy, which at first so agreeably diversifies life and appears a light and charming adventure, inevitably grows into a regular problem of extreme intricacy, and in the long run the situation becomes unbearable. But at every fresh meeting with an interesting woman this experience seemed to slip out of his memory, and he was eager for life, and everything seemed simple and amusing.

One evening he was dining in the gardens, and the lady in the béret came up slowly to take the next table. Her expression, her gait, her dress, and the way she did her hair told him that she was a lady, that she was married, that she was in Yalta for the first time and alone, and that she was dull there...The stories told of the immorality in such places as Yalta are to a great extent untrue; he despised them, and knew that such stories were for the most part made up by persons who would themselves have been glad to sin if they had been able; but when the lady sat down at the next table three paces from him, he remembered these tales of easy conquests, of trips to the mountains, and the tempting thought of a swift, fleeting love affair, a romance with an unknown woman, whose name he did not know, suddenly took possession of him.

He beckoned coaxingly to the Pomeranian, and when the dog came up to him he shook his finger at it. The Pomeranian growled: Gurov shook his finger at it again.

The lady looked at him and at once dropped her eyes.

'He doesn't bite,' she said, and blushed.

'May I give him a bone?' he asked; and when she nodded he asked courteously, 'Have you been long in Yalta?'

'Five days.'

'And I have already dragged out a fortnight here.'

There was a brief silence.

'Time goes fast, and yet it is so dull here!' she said, not looking at him.

'That's only the fashion to say it is dull here. A provincial will live in Belyov or Zhidra and not be dull, and when he comes here it's "Oh, the dulness! Oh, the dust!" One would think he came from Grenada.'

She laughed. Then both continued eating in silence, like strangers, but after dinner they walked side by side; and there sprang up between them the light jesting conversation of people who are free and satisfied, to whom it does not matter where they go or what they talk about. They walked and talked of the strange light on the sea: the water was of a soft warm lilac hue, and there was a golden streak from the moon upon it. They talked of how sultry it was after a hot day. Gurov told her that he came from Moscow, that he had taken his degree in Arts, but had a post in a bank; that he had trained as an opera-singer, but had given it up, that he owned two houses in Moscow...And from her he learnt that she had grown up in Petersburg, but had lived in S— since her marriage two years before, that she was staying another month in Yalta, and that her husband, who needed a holiday too, might perhaps come and fetch her. She was not sure whether her husband had a post in a Crown Department or under the Provincial Council—and was amused by her own ignorance. And Gurov learnt, too, that she was called Anna Sergeyevna.

Afterwards he thought about her in his room at the hotel—thought she would certainly meet him next day; it would be sure to happen. As he got into bed he thought how lately she had been a girl at school, doing lessons like his own daughter;

he recalled the diffidence, the angularity, that was still manifest in her laugh and her manner of talking with a stranger. This must have been the first time in her life she had been alone in surroundings in which she was followed, looked at, and spoken to merely from a secret motive which she could hardly fail to guess. He recalled her slender, delicate neck, her lovely grey eyes.

'There's something pathetic about her, anyway,' he thought, and fell asleep.

A week had passed since they had made acquaintance. It was a holiday. It was sultry indoors, while in the street the wind whirled the dust round and round, and blew people's hats off. It was a thirsty day, and Gurov often went into the pavilion, and pressed Anna Sergeyevna to have syrup and water or an ice. One did not know what to do with oneself.

In the evening when the wind had dropped a little, they went out on the groyne to see the steamer come in. There were a great many people walking about the harbour; they had gathered to welcome some one, bringing bouquets. And two peculiarities of a well-dressed Yalta crowd were very conspicuous: the elderly ladies were dressed like young ones, and there were great numbers of generals.

Owing to the roughness of the sea, the steamer arrived late, after the sun had set, and it was a long time turning about before it reached the groyne. Anna Sergeyevna looked through her lorgnette at the steamer and the passengers as though looking for acquaintances, and when she turned to Gurov her eyes were shining. She talked a great deal and asked disconnected questions, forgetting next moment what she had asked; then she dropped her lorgnette in the crush.

The festive crowd began to disperse; it was too dark to see people's faces. The wind had completely dropped, but Gurov and Anna Sergeyevna still stood as though waiting to see some one else come from the steamer. Anna Sergeyevna was silent now, and sniffed the flowers without looking at Gurov.

'The weather is better this evening,' he said. 'Where shall we go now? Shall we drive somewhere?'

She made no answer.

Then he looked at her intently, and all at once put his arm round her and kissed her on the lips, and breathed in the moisture and the fragrance of the flowers; and he immediately looked round him, anxiously wondering whether any one had seen them.

'Let us go to your hotel,' he said softly. And both walked quickly.

The room was close and smelt of the scent she had bought at the Japanese shop. Gurov looked at her and thought: 'What different people one meets in the world!' From the past he preserved memories of careless, good-natured women, who loved cheerfully and were grateful to him for the happiness he gave them, however brief it might be; and of women like his wife who loved without any genuine feeling, with superfluous phrases, affectedly, hysterically, with an expression that suggested that it was not love nor passion, but something more significant; and of two or three others, very beautiful, cold women, on whose faces he had caught a glimpse of a rapacious expression—an obstinate desire to snatch from life more than it could give, and these were capricious, unreflecting, domineering, unintelligent women not in their first youth, and when Gurov grew cold to them their beauty excited his hatred, and the lace on their linen seemed to him like scales.

But in this case there was still the diffidence, the angularity of inexperienced youth, an awkward feeling; and there was a sense of consternation as though some one had suddenly knocked at the door. The attitude of Anna Sergeyevna—'the lady with the dog'—to what had happened was somehow peculiar, very grave, as though it were her fall—so it seemed, and it was strange and inappropriate. Her face dropped and faded, and on both sides of it her long hair hung down mournfully; she mused in a dejected attitude like 'the woman who was a sinner' in an old-fashioned picture.

'It's wrong,' she said. 'You will be the first to despise me now.'

There was a water-melon on the table. Gurov cut himself a slice and began eating it without haste. There followed at least half an hour of silence.

Anna Sergeyevna was touching; there was about her the purity of a good, simple woman who had seen little of life. The solitary candle burning on the table threw a faint light on her face, yet it was clear that she was very unhappy.

'How could I despise you?' asked Gurov. 'You don't know what you are saying.'

'God forgive me,' she said, and her eyes filled with tears. 'It's awful.'

'You seem to feel you need to be forgiven.'

'Forgiven? No. I am a bad, low woman; I despise myself and don't attempt to justify myself. It's not my husband but myself I have deceived. And not only just now; I have been deceiving myself for a long time. My husband may be a good, honest man, but he is a flunkey! I don't know what he does there, what his work is, but I know he is a flunkey! I was twenty when I was married to him. I have been tormented by curiosity; I wanted something better. "There must be a different sort of life," I said to myself. I wanted to live! To live, to live!...I was fired by curiosity...you don't understand it, but, I swear to God, I could not control myself; something happened to me: I could not be restrained. I told my husband I was ill, and came here...And here I have been walking about as though I were dazed, like a mad creature;...and now I have become a vulgar, contemptible woman whom any one may despise.'

Gurov felt bored already, listening to her. He was irritated by the naïve tone, by this remorse, so unexpected and inopportune; but for the tears in her eyes, he might have thought she was jesting or playing a part.

'I don't understand,' he said softly. 'What is it you want?'

She hid her face on his breast and pressed close to him.

'Believe me, believe me, I beseech you...,' she said. 'I love a pure, honest life, and sin is loathsome to me. I don't know what I am doing. Simple people say: "The Evil One has beguiled me." And I may say of myself now that the Evil One has beguiled me.'

'Hush, hush!...' he muttered.

He looked at her fixed, scared eyes, kissed her, talked softly and affectionately, and by degrees she was comforted, and her gaiety returned; they both began laughing.

Afterwards when they went out there was not a soul on the sea-front. The town with its cypresses had quite a deathlike air, but the sea still broke noisily on the shore; a single barge was rocking on the waves, and a lantern was blinking sleepily on it.

They found a cab and drove to Oreanda.

'I found out your surname in the hall just now: it was written on the board—Von Diderits,' said Gurov. 'Is your husband a German?'

'No; I believe his grandfather was a German, but he is an Orthodox Russian himself.'

At Oreanda they sat on a seat not far from the church, looked down at the sea, and were silent. Yalta was hardly visible through the morning mist; white clouds stood motionless on the mountain-tops. The leaves did not stir on the trees, grasshoppers chirruped, and the monotonous hollow sound of the sea rising up from below, spoke of the peace, of the eternal sleep awaiting us. So it must have sounded when there was no Yalta, no Oreanda here; so it sounds now, and it will sound as indifferently and monotonously when we are all no more. And in this constancy, in this complete indifference to the life and death of each of us, there lies hid, perhaps, a pledge of our eternal salvation, of the unceasing movement of life upon earth, of unceasing progress towards perfection. Sitting beside a young woman who in the dawn seemed so lovely, soothed and spellbound in these magical surroundings—the sea, mountains, clouds, the open sky—Gurov thought how in reality everything is beautiful in this world when one reflects: everything except what we think or do ourselves when we forget our human dignity and the higher aims of our existence.

A man walked up to them—probably a keeper—looked at

them and walked away. And this detail seemed mysterious and beautiful, too. They saw a steamer come from Theodosia, with its lights out in the glow of dawn.

'There is dew on the grass,' said Anna Sergeyevna, after a silence.

'Yes. It's time to go home.'

They went back to the town.

Then they met every day at twelve o'clock on the sea-front, lunched and dined together, went for walks, admired the sea. She complained that she slept badly, that her heart throbbed violently; asked the same questions, troubled now by jealousy and now by the fear that he did not respect her sufficiently. And often in the square or gardens, when there was no one near them, he suddenly drew her to him and kissed her passionately. Complete idleness, these kisses in broad daylight while he looked round in dread of some one's seeing them, the heat, the smell of the sea, and the continual passing to and fro before him of idle, well-dressed, well-fed people, made a new man of him; he told Anna Sergeyevna how beautiful she was, how fascinating. He was impatiently passionate, he would not move a step away from her, while she was often pensive and continually urged him to confess that he did not respect her, did not love her in the least, and thought of her as nothing but a common woman. Rather late almost every evening they drove somewhere out of town, to Oreanda or to the waterfall; and the expedition was always a success, the scenery invariably impressed them as grand and beautiful.

They were expecting her husband to come, but a letter came from him, saying that there was something wrong with his eyes, and he entreated his wife to come home as quickly as possible. Anna Sergeyevna made haste to go.

'It's a good thing I am going away,' she said to Gurov. 'It's the finger of destiny!'

She went by coach and he went with her. They were driving the whole day. When she had got into a compartment of the express, and when the second bell had rung, she said:

'Let me look at you once more...look at you once again. That's right.'

She did not shed tears, but was so sad that she seemed ill, and her face was quivering.

'I shall remember you...think of you,' she said. 'God be with you; be happy. Don't remember evil against me. We are parting forever—it must be so, for we ought never to have met. Well, God be with you.'

The train moved off rapidly, its lights soon vanished from sight, and a minute later there was no sound of it, as though everything had conspired together to end as quickly as possible that sweet delirium, that madness. Left alone on the platform, and gazing into the dark distance, Gurov listened to the chirrup of the grasshoppers and the hum of the telegraph wires, feeling as though he had only just waked up. And he thought, musing, that there had been another episode or adventure in his life, and it, too, was at an end, and nothing was left of it but a memory...He was moved, sad, and conscious of a slight remorse. This young woman whom he would never meet again had not been happy with him; he was genuinely warm and affectionate with her, but yet in his manner, his tone, and his caresses there had been a shade of light irony, the coarse condescension of a happy man who was, besides, almost twice her age. All the time she had called him kind, exceptional, lofty; obviously he had seemed to her different from what he really was, so he had unintentionally deceived her...

Here at the station was already a scent of autumn; it was a cold evening.

'It's time for me to go north,' thought Gurov as he left the platform. 'High time!'

At home in Moscow everything was in its winter routine; the stoves were heated, and in the morning it was still dark when the children were having breakfast and getting ready for school, and the nurse would light the lamp for a short time. The frosts had begun already. When the first snow has fallen, on the first day of sledge-driving it is pleasant to see the white earth, the white roofs, to draw soft, delicious breath, and the season brings back the days of one's youth. The old limes and birches, white with hoar-frost, have a good-natured expression; they are nearer to one's heart than cypresses and palms, and near them one doesn't want to be thinking of the sea and the mountains.

Gurov was Moscow born; he arrived in Moscow on a fine frosty day, and when he put on his fur coat and warm gloves, and walked along Petrovka, and when on Saturday evening he heard the ringing of the bells, his recent trip and the places he had seen lost all charm for him. Little by little he became absorbed in Moscow life, greedily read three newspapers a day, and declared he did not read the Moscow papers on principle! He already felt a longing to go to restaurants, clubs, dinner-parties, anniversary celebrations, and he felt flattered at entertaining distinguished lawyers and artists, and at playing cards with a professor at the doctors' club. He could already eat a whole plateful of salt fish and cabbage.

In another month, he fancied, the image of Anna Sergeyevna would be shrouded in a mist in his memory, and only from time to time would visit him in his dreams with a touching smile as others did. But more than a month passed, real winter had come, and everything was still clear in his memory as though he had parted with Anna Sergeyevna only the day before. And his memories glowed more and more vividly. When in the evening stillness he heard from his study the voices of his children, preparing their lessons, or when he listened to a song or the organ at the restaurant, or the storm howled in the chimney, suddenly everything would rise up in his memory: what had happened on the groyne, and the early morning with the mist on the mountains, and the steamer coming from Theodosia, and the kisses. He would pace a long time about his room, remembering it all and smiling; then his memories passed into dreams, and in his fancy the past was mingled with what was to come. Anna Sergeyevna did not visit him in dreams, but followed him about everywhere like a shadow and haunted him. When he shut his eyes he saw her as though she were living before him, and she seemed to him lovelier, younger, tenderer than she was; and he imagined himself finer than he had been in Yalta. In the evenings she peeped out at him from the bookcase, from the fireplace, from the corner—he heard her breathing, the caressing rustle of her dress. In the street he watched the women, looking for some one like her.

He was tormented by an intense desire to confide his memories to some one. But in his home it was impossible to talk of his love, and he had no one outside; he could not talk to his tenants nor to any one at the bank. And what had he to talk of? Had he been in love, then? Had there been anything beautiful, poetical, or edifying or simply interesting in his relations with Anna Sergeyevna? And there was nothing for him but to talk vaguely of love, of woman, and no one guessed what it meant; only his wife twitched her black eyebrows, and said:

'The part of a lady-killer does not suit you at all, Dimitri.'

One evening, coming out of the doctors' club with an official with whom he had been playing cards, he could not resist saying:

'If only you knew what a fascinating woman I made the acquaintance of in Yalta!'

The official got into his sledge and was driving away, but turned suddenly and shouted:

'Dmitri Dmitritch!'

'What?'

'You were right this evening: the sturgeon was a bit too strong!'

These words, so ordinary, for some reason moved Gurov to indignation, and struck him as degrading and unclean. What savage manners, what people! What senseless nights, what uninteresting, uneventful days! The rage for card-playing, the gluttony, the drunkenness, the continual talk always about the same thing. Useless pursuits and conversations always about the same things absorb the better part of one's time, the better part of one's strength, and in the end there is left a life grovelling and curtailed, worthless and trivial, and there is no escaping or getting away from it—just as though one were in a madhouse or a prison.

Gurov did not sleep all night, and was filled with indignation. And he had a headache all next day. And the next night he slept badly; he sat up in bed, thinking, or paced up and down his room. He was sick of his children, sick of the bank; he had no desire to go anywhere or to talk of anything.

In the holidays in December he prepared for a journey, and told his wife he was going to Petersburg to do something in the interests of a young friend—and he set off for S—. What for? He did not very well know himself. He wanted to see Anna Sergeyevna and to talk with her—to arrange a meeting, if possible.

He reached S— in the morning, and took the best room at the hotel, in which the floor was covered with grey army cloth, and on the table was an inkstand, grey with dust and adorned with a figure on horseback, with its hat in its hand and its head broken off. The hotel porter gave him the necessary information; Von Diderits lived in a house of his own in Old Gontcharny Street—it was not far from the hotel: he was rich and lived in good style, and had his own horses; every one in the town knew him. The porter pronounced the name 'Dridirits.'

Gurov went without haste to Old Gontcharny Street and found the house. Just opposite the house stretched a long grey fence adorned with nails.

'One would run away from a fence like that,' thought Gurov, looking from the fence to the windows of the house and back again.

He considered: to-day was a holiday, and the husband would probably be at home. And in any case it would be tactless to go into the house and upset her. If he were to send her a note it might fall into her husband's hands, and then it might ruin everything. The best thing was to trust to chance. And he kept walking up and down the street by the fence, waiting for the chance. He saw a beggar go in at the gate and dogs fly at him;

then an hour later he heard a piano, and the sounds were faint and indistinct. Probably it was Anna Sergeyevna playing. The front door suddenly opened, and an old woman came out, followed by the familiar white Pomeranian. Gurov was on the point of calling to the dog, but his heart began beating violently, and in his excitement he could not remember the dog's name.

He walked up and down, and loathed the grey fence more and more, and by now he thought irritably that Anna Sergeyevna had forgotten him, and was perhaps already amusing herself with some one else, and that that was very natural in a young woman who had nothing to look at from morning till night but that confounded fence. He went back to his hotel room and sat for a long while on the sofa, not knowing what to do, then he had dinner and a long nap.

'How stupid and worrying it is!' he thought when he woke and looked at the dark windows: it was already evening. 'Here I've had a good sleep for some reason. What shall I do in the night?'

He sat on the bed, which was covered by a cheap grey blanket, such as one sees in hospitals, and he taunted himself in his vexation:

'So much for the lady with the dog...so much for the adventure... You're in a nice fix...'

That morning at the station a poster in large letters had caught his eye. 'The Geisha' was to be performed for the first time. He thought of this and went to the theatre.

'It's quite possible she may go to the first performance,' he thought.

The theatre was full. As in all provincial theatres, there was a fog above the chandelier, the gallery was noisy and restless; in the front row the local dandies were standing up before the beginning of the performance, with their hands behind them; in the Governor's box the Governor's daughter, wearing a boa, was sitting in the front seat, while the Governor himself lurked modestly behind the curtain with only his hands visible; the orchestra was a long time tuning up; the stage curtain swayed.

All the time the audience were coming in and taking their seats Gurov looked at them eagerly.

Anna Sergeyevna, too, came in. She sat down in the third row, and when Gurov looked at her his heart contracted, and he understood clearly that for him there was in the whole world no creature so near, so precious, and so important to him; she, this little woman, in no way remarkable, lost in a provincial crowd, with a vulgar lorgnette in her hand, filled his whole life now, was his sorrow and his joy, the one happiness that he now desired for himself, and to the sounds of the inferior orchestra, of the wretched provincial violins, he thought how lovely she was. He thought and dreamed.

A young man with small side-whiskers, tall and stooping, came in with Anna Sergeyevna and sat down beside her; he bent his head at every step and seemed to be continually bowing. Most likely this was the husband whom at Yalta, in a rush of bitter feeling, she had called a flunkey. And there really was in his long figure, his side-whiskers, and the small bald patch on his head, something of the flunkey's obsequiousness; his smile was sugary, and in his buttonhole there was some badge of distinction like the number on a waiter.

During the first interval the husband went away to smoke; she remained alone in her stall. Gurov, who was sitting in the stalls, too, went up to her and said in a trembling voice, with a forced smile:

'Good-evening.'

She glanced at him and turned pale, then glanced again with horror, unable to believe her eyes, and tightly gripped the fan and the lorgnette in her hands, evidently struggling with herself not to faint. Both were silent. She was sitting, he was standing, frightened by her confusion and not venturing to sit down beside her. The violins and the flute began tuning up. He felt suddenly frightened; it seemed as though all the people in the boxes were looking at them. She got up and went quickly to the door; he followed her, and both walked senselessly along passages, and up and down stairs, and figures in legal, scholastic, and civil service uniforms, all wearing badges, flitted before their eyes. They caught glimpses of ladies, of fur coats hanging on pegs; the draughts blew on them, bringing a smell of stale tobacco. And Gurov, whose heart was beating violently, thought:

'Oh, heavens! Why are these people here and this orchestra!...'

And at that instant he recalled how when he had seen Anna Sergeyevna off at the station he had thought that everything was over and they would never meet again. But how far they were still from the end!

On the narrow, gloomy staircase over which was written 'To the Amphitheatre,' she stopped.

'How you have frightened me!' she said, breathing hard, still pale and overwhelmed. 'Oh, how you have frightened me! I am half dead. Why have you come? Why?'

'But do understand, Anna, do understand...' he said hastily in a low voice. 'I entreat you to understand...'

She looked at him with dread, with entreaty, with love; she looked at him intently, to keep his features more distinctly in her memory.

'I am so unhappy,' she went on, not heeding him. 'I have thought of nothing but you all the time; I live only in the thought of you. And I wanted to forget, to forget you; but why, oh, why, have you come?'

On the landing above them two schoolboys were smoking and looking down, but that was nothing to Gurov; he drew Anna Sergeyevna to him, and began kissing her face, her cheeks, and her hands.

'What are you doing, what are you doing!' she cried in horror, pushing him away. 'We are mad. Go away to-day; go away at once...I beseech you by all that is sacred, I implore you...There are people coming this way!'

Some one was coming up the stairs.

'You must go away,' Anna Sergeyevna went on in a whisper. 'Do you hear, Dmitri Dmitritch? I will come and see you in Moscow. I have never been happy; I am miserable now, and I never, never shall be happy, never! Don't make me suffer still more! I swear I'll come to Moscow. But now let us part. My precious, good, dear one, we must part!'

She pressed his hand and began rapidly going downstairs, looking round at him, and from her eyes he could see that she really was unhappy. Gurov stood for a little while, listened, then, when all sound had died away, he found his coat and left the theatre.

And Anna Sergeyevna began coming to see him in Moscow. Once in two or three months she left S—, telling her husband that she was going to consult a doctor about an internal complaint—and her husband believed her, and did not believe her. In Moscow she stayed at the Slaviansky Bazaar hotel, and at once sent a man in a red cap to Gurov. Gurov went to see her, and no one in Moscow knew of it.

Once he was going to see her in this way on a winter morning (the messenger had come the evening before when he was out). With him walked his daughter, whom he wanted to take to school: it was on the way. Snow was falling in big wet flakes.

'It's three degrees above freezing-point, and yet it is snowing,' said Gurov to his daughter. 'The thaw is only on the surface of the earth; there is quite a different temperature at a greater height in the atmosphere.'

'And why are there no thunderstorms in the winter, father?'

He explained that, too. He talked, thinking all the while that he was going to see her, and no living soul knew of it, and probably never would know. He had two lives: one, open, seen and known by all who cared to know, full of relative truth and of relative falsehood, exactly like the lives of his friends and acquaintances; and another life running its course in secret. And through some strange, perhaps accidental, conjunction of circumstances, everything that was essential, of interest and of value to him, everything in which he was sincere and did not deceive himself, everything that made the kernel of his life, was hidden from other people; and all that was false in him, the sheath in which he hid himself to conceal the truth—such, for instance, as his work in the bank, his discussions at the club, his 'lower race,' his presence with his wife at anniversary festivities—all that was open. And he judged of others by himself, not believing in what he saw, and always believing that every man had his real, most interesting life under the cover of secrecy and under the cover of night. All personal life rested on secrecy, and possibly it was partly on that account that civilised man was so nervously anxious that personal privacy should be respected.

After leaving his daughter at school, Gurov went on to the Slaviansky Bazaar. He took off his fur coat below, went upstairs, and softly knocked at the door. Anna Sergeyevna, wearing his favourite grey dress, exhausted by the journey and the suspense, had been expecting him since the evening before. She was pale; she looked at him, and did not smile, and he had hardly come in when she fell on his breast. Their kiss was slow and prolonged, as though they had not met for two years.

'Well, how are you getting on there?' he asked. 'What news?'

'Wait; I'll tell you directly... I can't talk.'

She could not speak; she was crying. She turned away from him, and pressed her handkerchief to her eyes.

'Let her have her cry out. I'll sit down and wait,' he thought, and he sat down in an arm-chair.

Then he rang and asked for tea to be brought him, and while he drank his tea she remained standing at the window with her back to him. She was crying from emotion, from the miserable consciousness that their life was so hard for them; they could only meet in secret, hiding themselves from people, like thieves! Was not their life shattered?

'Come, do stop!' he said.

It was evident to him that this love of theirs would not soon be over, that he could not see the end of it. Anna Sergeyevna grew more and more attached to him. She adored him, and it was unthinkable to say to her that it was bound to have an end some day; besides, she would not have believed it!

He went up to her and took her by the shoulders to say

something affectionate and cheering, and at that moment he saw himself in the looking-glass.

His hair was already beginning to turn grey. And it seemed strange to him that he had grown so much older, so much plainer during the last few years. The shoulders on which his hands rested were warm and quivering. He felt compassion for this life, still so warm and lovely, but probably already not far from beginning to fade and wither like his own. Why did she love him so much? He always seemed to women different from what he was, and they loved in him not himself, but the man created by their imagination, whom they had been eagerly seeking all their lives; and afterwards, when they noticed their mistake, they loved him all the same. And not one of them had been happy with him. Time passed, he had made their acquaintance, got on with them, parted, but he had never once loved; it was anything you like, but not love.

And only now when his head was grey he had fallen properly, really in love—for the first time in his life.

Anna Sergeyevna and he loved each other like people very close and akin, like husband and wife, like tender friends; it seemed to them that fate itself had meant them for one another, and they could not understand why he had a wife and she a husband; and it was as though they were a pair of birds of passage, caught and forced to live in different cages. They forgave each other for what they were ashamed of in their past, they forgave everything in the present, and felt that this love of theirs had changed them both.

In moments of depression in the past he had comforted himself with any arguments that came into his mind, but now he no longer cared for arguments; he felt profound compassion, he wanted to be sincere and tender...

'Don't cry, my darling,' he said. 'You've had your cry; that's enough... Let us talk now, let us think of some plan.'

Then they spent a long while taking counsel together, talked of how to avoid the necessity for secrecy, for deception, for living in different towns and not seeing each other for long at a time. How could they be free from this intolerable bondage?

'How? How?' he asked, clutching his head. 'How?'

And it seemed as though in a little while the solution would be found, and then a new and splendid life would begin; and it was clear to both of them that they had still a long, long road before them, and that the most complicated and difficult part of it was only just beginning.

13

THE COP AND THE ANTHEM

O. Henry

On his bench in Madison Square Soapy moved uneasily. When wild geese honk high of nights, and when women without sealskin coats grow kind to their husbands, and when Soapy moves uneasily on his bench in the park, you may know that winter is near at hand.

A dead leaf fell in Soapy's lap. That was Jack Frost's card. Jack is kind to the regular denizens of Madison Square, and gives fair warning of his annual call. At the corners of four streets he hands his pasteboard to the North Wind, footman of the mansion of All Outdoors, so that the inhabitants thereof may make ready.

Soapy's mind became cognisant of the fact that the time had come for him to resolve himself into a singular Committee of Ways and Means to provide against the coming rigour. And therefore he moved uneasily on his bench.

The hibernatorial ambitions of Soapy were not of the highest. In them there were no considerations of Mediterranean cruises, of soporific Southern skies drifting in the Vesuvian Bay. Three months on the Island was what his soul craved. Three months of assured board and bed and congenial company, safe from Boreas and bluecoats, seemed to Soapy the essence of things desirable.

For years the hospitable Blackwell's had been his winter quarters. Just as his more fortunate fellow New Yorkers had bought their tickets to Palm Beach and the Riviera each winter, so Soapy had made his humble arrangements for his annual hegira to the Island. And now the time was come. On the previous night three Sabbath newspapers, distributed beneath his coat, about his ankles and over his lap, had failed to repulse the cold as he slept on his bench near the spurting fountain in the ancient square. So the Island loomed big and timely in Soapy's mind. He scorned the provisions made in the name of charity for the city's dependents. In Soapy's opinion the Law was more benign than Philanthropy. There was an endless round of institutions, municipal and eleemosynary, on which he might set out and receive lodging and food accordant with the simple life. But to one of Soapy's proud spirit the gifts of charity are encumbered. If not in coin you must pay in humiliation of spirit for every benefit received at the hands of philanthropy. As Caesar had his Brutus, every bed of charity must have its toll of a bath, every loaf of bread its compensation of a private and personal inquisition. Wherefore it is better to be a guest of the law, which though conducted by rules, does not meddle unduly with a gentleman's private affairs.

Soapy, having decided to go to the Island, at once set about accomplishing his desire. There were many easy ways of doing this. The pleasantest was to dine luxuriously at some expensive restaurant; and then, after declaring insolvency, be handed over quietly and without uproar to a policeman. An accommodating magistrate would do the rest.

Soapy left his bench and strolled out of the square and across the level sea of asphalt, where Broadway and Fifth Avenue flow together. Up Broadway he turned, and halted at a glittering cafe, where are gathered together nightly the choicest products of the grape, the silkworm and the protoplasm.

Soapy had confidence in himself from the lowest button of his vest upward. He was shaven, and his coat was decent and his neat black, ready-tied four-in-hand had been presented to him by a lady missionary on Thanksgiving Day. If he could reach a table in the restaurant unsuspected success would be his. The portion of him that would show above the table would raise no doubt in the waiter's mind. A roasted mallard duck, thought Soapy, would be about the thing—with a bottle of Chablis, and then Camembert, a demi-tasse and a cigar. One dollar for the cigar would be enough. The total would not be so high as to call forth any supreme manifestation of revenge from the cafe management; and yet the meat would leave him filled and happy for the journey to his winter refuge.

But as Soapy set foot inside the restaurant door the head waiter's eye fell upon his frayed trousers and decadent shoes. Strong and ready hands turned him about and conveyed him in silence and haste to the sidewalk and averted the ignoble fate of the menaced mallard.

Soapy turned off Broadway. It seemed that his route to the coveted island was not to be an epicurean one. Some other way of entering limbo must be thought of.

At a corner of Sixth Avenue electric lights and cunningly displayed wares behind plate-glass made a shop window conspicuous. Soapy took a cobblestone and dashed it through the glass. People came running around the corner, a policeman in the lead. Soapy stood still, with his hands in his pockets, and smiled at the sight of brass buttons.

'Where's the man that done that?' inquired the officer excitedly.

'Don't you figure out that I might have had something to do with it?' said Soapy, not without sarcasm, but friendly, as one greets good fortune.

The policeman's mind refused to accept Soapy even as a clue. Men who smash windows do not remain to parley with the law's minions. They take to their heels. The policeman saw a man half way down the block running to catch a car. With drawn club he joined in the pursuit. Soapy, with disgust in his heart, loafed along, twice unsuccessful.

On the opposite side of the street was a restaurant of no great pretensions. It catered to large appetites and modest purses. Its crockery and atmosphere were thick; its soup and napery thin. Into this place Soapy took his accusive shoes and telltale trousers without challenge. At a table he sat and consumed beefsteak, flapjacks, doughnuts and pie. And then to the waiter be betrayed the fact that the minutest coin and himself were strangers.

'Now, get busy and call a cop,' said Soapy. 'And don't keep a gentleman waiting.'

'No cop for youse,' said the waiter, with a voice like butter cakes and an eye like the cherry in a Manhattan cocktail. 'Hey, Con!'

Neatly upon his left ear on the callous pavement two waiters pitched Soapy. He arose, joint by joint, as a carpenter's rule opens, and beat the dust from his clothes. Arrest seemed but a rosy dream. The Island seemed very far away. A policeman who stood before a drug store two doors away laughed and walked down the street.

Five blocks Soapy travelled before his courage permitted him to woo capture again. This time the opportunity presented what he fatuously termed to himself a 'cinch.' A young woman of a modest and pleasing guise was standing before a show window gazing with sprightly interest at its display of shaving mugs and inkstands, and two yards from the window a large policeman of severe demeanour leaned against a water plug.

It was Soapy's design to assume the role of the despicable and execrated 'masher.' The refined and elegant appearance of his victim and the contiguity of the conscientious cop encouraged him to believe that he would soon feel the pleasant official clutch upon his arm that would insure his winter quarters on the right little, tight little isle.

Soapy straightened the lady missionary's readymade tie, dragged his shrinking cuffs into the open, set his hat at a killing cant and sidled toward the young woman. He made eyes at her, was taken with sudden coughs and 'hems,' smiled, smirked and went brazenly through the impudent and contemptible litany of the 'masher.' With half an eye Soapy saw that the policeman was watching him fixedly. The young woman moved away a few steps, and again bestowed her absorbed attention upon the shaving mugs. Soapy followed, boldly stepping to her side, raised his hat and said:

'Ah there, Bedelia! Don't you want to come and play in

my yard?'

The policeman was still looking. The persecuted young woman had but to beckon a finger and Soapy would be practically en route for his insular haven. Already he imagined he could feel the cozy warmth of the station-house. The young woman faced him and, stretching out a hand, caught Soapy's coat sleeve.

Sure, Mike,' she said joyfully, 'if you'll blow me to a pail of suds. I'd have spoke to you sooner, but the cop was watching.'

With the young woman playing the clinging ivy to his oak Soapy walked past the policeman overcome with gloom. He seemed doomed to liberty.

At the next corner he shook off his companion and ran. He halted in the district where by night are found the lightest streets, hearts, vows and librettos.

Women in furs and men in greatcoats moved gaily in the wintry air. A sudden fear seized Soapy that some dreadful enchantment had rendered him immune to arrest. The thought brought a little of panic upon it, and when he came upon another policeman lounging grandly in front of a transplendent theatre he caught at the immediate straw of 'disorderly conduct.'

On the sidewalk Soapy began to yell drunken gibberish at the top of his harsh voice. He danced, howled, raved and otherwise disturbed the welkin.

The policeman twirled his club, turned his back to Soapy and remarked to a citizen.

''Tis one of them Yale lads celebratin' the goose egg they give to the Hartford College. Noisy; but no harm. We've instructions to lave them be.'

Disconsolate, Soapy ceased his unavailing racket. Would never a policeman lay hands on him? In his fancy the Island seemed an unattainable Arcadia. He buttoned his thin coat against the chilling wind.

In a cigar store he saw a well-dressed man lighting a cigar at a swinging light. His silk umbrella he had set by the door on entering. Soapy stepped inside, secured the umbrella and sauntered off with it slowly. The man at the cigar light followed hastily.

'My umbrella,' he said, sternly.

'Oh, is it?' sneered Soapy, adding insult to petit larceny. 'Well, why don't you call a policeman? I took it. Your umbrella! Why don't you call a cop? There stands one on the corner.'

The umbrella owner slowed his steps. Soapy did likewise, with a presentiment that luck would again run against him. The policeman looked at the two curiously.

'Of course,' said the umbrella man—'that is—well, you know how these mistakes occur—I—if it's your umbrella I hope you'll excuse me—I picked it up this morning in a restaurant—If you recognise it as yours, why—I hope you'll—'

'Of course it's mine,' said Soapy, viciously.

The ex-umbrella man retreated. The policeman hurried to assist a tall blonde in an opera cloak across the street in front of a street car that was approaching two blocks away.

Soapy walked eastward through a street damaged by improvements. He hurled the umbrella wrathfully into an excavation. He muttered against the men who wear helmets and carry clubs. Because he wanted to fall into their clutches, they seemed to regard him as a king who could do no wrong.

At length Soapy reached one of the avenues to the east where the glitter and turmoil was but faint. He set his face down this toward Madison Square, for the homing instinct survives even when the home is a park bench.

But on an unusually quiet corner Soapy came to a standstill. Here was an old church, quaint and rambling and gabled. Through one violet-stained window a soft light glowed, where, no doubt, the organist loitered over the keys, making sure of his mastery of the coming Sabbath anthem. For there drifted out to Soapy's ears sweet music that caught and held him transfixed against the convolutions of the iron fence.

The moon was above, lustrous and serene; vehicles and pedestrians were few; sparrows twittered sleepily in the eaves—for a little while the scene might have been a country churchyard. And the anthem that the organist played cemented

Soapy to the iron fence, for he had known it well in the days when his life contained such things as mothers and roses and ambitions and friends and immaculate thoughts and collars.

The conjunction of Soapy's receptive state of mind and the influences about the old church wrought a sudden and wonderful change in his soul. He viewed with swift horror the pit into which he had tumbled, the degraded days, unworthy desires, dead hopes, wrecked faculties and base motives that made up his existence.

And also in a moment his heart responded thrillingly to this novel mood. An instantaneous and strong impulse moved him to battle with his desperate fate. He would pull himself out of the mire; he would make a man of himself again; he would conquer the evil that had taken possession of him. There was time; he was comparatively young yet; he would resurrect his old eager ambitions and pursue them without faltering. Those solemn but sweet organ notes had set up a revolution in him. To-morrow he would go into the roaring downtown district and find work. A fur importer had once offered him a place as driver. He would find him to-morrow and ask for the position. He would be somebody in the world. He would—

Soapy felt a hand laid on his arm. He looked quickly around into the broad face of a policeman.

'What are you doin' here?' asked the officer.

'Nothin',' said Soapy.

'Then come along,' said the policeman.

'Three months on the Island,' said the Magistrate in the Police Court the next morning.

14

A CHAMELEON

Anton Chekov

The police superintendent Otchumyelov is walking across the market square wearing a new overcoat and carrying a parcel under his arm. A red-haired policeman strides after him with a sieve full of confiscated gooseberries in his hands. There is silence all around. Not a soul in the square...The open doors of the shops and taverns look out upon God's world disconsolately, like hungry mouths; there is not even a beggar near them.

'So you bite, you damned brute?' Otchumyelov hears suddenly. 'Lads, don't let him go! Biting is prohibited nowadays! Hold him! ah...ah!'

There is the sound of a dog yelping. Otchumyelov looks in the direction of the sound and sees a dog, hopping on three legs and looking about her, run out of Pitchugin's timber-yard. A man in a starched cotton shirt, with his waistcoat unbuttoned, is chasing her. He runs after her, and throwing his body forward falls down and seizes the dog by her hind legs. Once more there is a yelping and a shout of 'Don't let go!' Sleepy countenances are protruded from the shops, and soon a crowd, which seems to have sprung out of the earth, is gathered round the timber-yard.

'It looks like a row, your honour...,' says the policeman.

Otchumyelov makes a half turn to the left and strides towards the crowd.

He sees the aforementioned man in the unbuttoned waistcoat standing close by the gate of the timber-yard, holding his right hand in the air and displaying a bleeding finger to the crowd. On his half-drunken face there is plainly written: 'I'll pay you out, you rogue!' and indeed the very finger has the look of a flag of victory. In this man Otchumyelov recognises Hryukin, the goldsmith. The culprit who has caused the sensation, a white borzoy puppy with a sharp muzzle and a yellow patch on her back, is sitting on the ground with her fore-paws outstretched in the middle of the crowd, trembling all over. There is an expression of misery and terror in her tearful eyes.

'What's it all about?' Otchumyelov inquires, pushing his way through the crowd. 'What are you here for? Why are you waving your finger...? Who was it shouted?'

'I was walking along here, not interfering with anyone, your honour,' Hryukin begins, coughing into his fist. 'I was talking about firewood to Mitry Mitritch, when this low brute for no rhyme or reason bit my finger...You must excuse me, I am a working man...Mine is fine work. I must have damages, for I shan't be able to use this finger for a week, may be...It's not even the law, your honour, that one should put up with it from a beast...If everyone is going to be bitten, life won't be worth living...'

'H'm. Very good,' says Otchumyelov sternly, coughing and raising his eyebrows. 'Very good. Whose dog is it? I won't let this pass! I'll teach them to let their dogs run all over the place! It's time these gentry were looked after, if they won't obey the regulations! When he's fined, the blackguard, I'll teach him what it means to keep dogs and such stray cattle! I'll give him a lesson!...Yeldyrin,' cries the superintendent, addressing the policeman, 'find out whose dog this is and draw up a report! And the dog must be strangled. Without delay! It's sure to be mad...Whose dog is it, I ask?'

'I fancy it's General Zhigalov's,' says someone in the crowd.

'General Zhigalov's, h'm...Help me off with my coat, Yeldyrin...it's frightfully hot! It must be a sign of rain... There's one thing I can't make out, how it came to bite you?' Otchumyelov turns to Hryukin. 'Surely it couldn't reach your finger. It's a little dog, and you are a great hulking fellow! You must have scratched your finger with a nail, and then the idea struck you to get damages for it. We all know...your sort! I know you devils!'

'He put a cigarette in her face, your honour, for a joke, and she had the sense to snap at him...He is a nonsensical fellow, your honour!'

'That's a lie, Squinteye! You didn't see, so why tell lies about it? His honour is a wise gentleman, and will see who is telling lies and who is telling the truth, as in God's sight...And if I am lying let the court decide. It's written in the law...We are all equal nowadays. My own brother is in the gendarmes... let me tell you...'

'Don't argue!'

'No, that's not the General's dog,' says the policeman, with profound conviction, 'the General hasn't got one like that. His are mostly setters.'

'Do you know that for a fact?'

'Yes, your honour.'

'I know it, too. The General has valuable dogs, thoroughbred, and this is goodness knows what! No coat, no shape...A low creature. And to keep a dog like that!...where's the sense of it. If a dog like that were to turn up in Petersburg or Moscow, do you know what would happen? They would not worry about the law, they would strangle it in a twinkling! You've been injured, Hryukin, and we can't let the matter drop...We must give them a lesson! It is high time...!'

'Yet maybe it is the General's,' says the policeman, thinking aloud. 'It's not written on its face...I saw one like it the other day in his yard.'

'It is the General's, that's certain!' says a voice in the crowd.

'H'm, help me on with my overcoat, Yeldyrin, my lad... the wind's getting up...I am cold...You take it to the General's, and inquire there. Say I found it and sent it. And tell them not to let it out into the street...It may be a valuable dog, and if every swine goes sticking a cigar in its mouth, it will soon be ruined. A dog is a delicate animal...And you put your hand down, you blockhead. It's no use your displaying your fool of a finger. It's your own fault...'

'Here comes the General's cook, ask him...Hi, Prohor! Come here, my dear man! Look at this dog...Is it one of yours?'

'What an idea! We have never had one like that!'

'There's no need to waste time asking,' says Otchumyelov. 'It's a stray dog! There's no need to waste time talking about it...Since he says it's a stray dog, a stray dog it is...It must be destroyed, that's all about it.'

'It is not our dog,' Prohor goes on. 'It belongs to the General's brother, who arrived the other day. Our master does not care for hounds. But his honour is fond of them...'

'You don't say his Excellency's brother is here? Vladimir Ivanitch?' inquires Otchumyelov, and his whole face beams with an ecstatic smile. 'Well, I never! And I didn't know! Has he come on a visit?'

'Yes.'

'Well, I never...He couldn't stay away from his brother...And there I didn't know! So this is his honour's dog? Delighted to hear it...Take it. It's not a bad pup...A lively creature...Snapped at this fellow's finger! Ha-ha-ha...Come, why are you shivering? Rrr...Rrrr...The rogue's angry...a nice little pup.'

Prohor calls the dog, and walks away from the timber-yard with her. The crowd laughs at Hryukin.

'I'll make you smart yet!' Otchumyelov threatens him, and wrapping himself in his greatcoat, goes on his way across the square.

15

THE LADY OR THE TIGER?

Frank Stockton

In the very olden time there lived a semi-barbaric king, whose ideas, though somewhat polished and sharpened by the progressiveness of distant Latin neighbors, were still large, florid, and untrammeled, as became the half of him which was barbaric. He was a man of exuberant fancy, and, withal, of an authority so irresistible that, at his will, he turned his varied fancies into facts. He was greatly given to self-communing, and, when he and himself agreed upon anything, the thing was done. When every member of his domestic and political systems moved smoothly in its appointed course, his nature was bland and genial; but, whenever there was a little hitch, and some of his orbs got out of their orbits, he was blander and more genial still, for nothing pleased him so much as to make the crooked straight and crush down uneven places.

Among the borrowed notions by which his barbarism had become semified was that of the public arena, in which, by exhibitions of manly and beastly valor, the minds of his subjects were refined and cultured.

But even here the exuberant and barbaric fancy asserted itself. The arena of the king was built, not to give the people an opportunity of hearing the rhapsodies of dying gladiators, nor to enable them to view the inevitable conclusion of a conflict between religious opinions and hungry jaws, but for purposes far better adapted to widen and develop the mental energies of the people. This vast amphitheater, with its encircling galleries, its mysterious vaults, and its unseen passages, was an agent of poetic justice, in which crime was punished, or virtue rewarded, by the decrees of an impartial and incorruptible chance.

When a subject was accused of a crime of sufficient importance to interest the king, public notice was given that on an appointed day the fate of the accused person would be decided in the king's arena, a structure which well deserved its name, for, although its form and plan were borrowed from afar, its purpose emanated solely from the brain of this man, who, every barleycorn a king, knew no tradition to which he owed more allegiance than pleased his fancy, and who ingrafted on every adopted form of human thought and action the rich growth of his barbaric idealism.

When all the people had assembled in the galleries, and the king, surrounded by his court, sat high up on his throne of royal state on one side of the arena, he gave a signal, a door beneath him opened, and the accused subject stepped out into the amphitheater. Directly opposite him, on the other side of the enclosed space, were two doors, exactly alike and side by side. It was the duty and the privilege of the person on trial to walk directly to these doors and open one of them. He could open either door he pleased; he was subject to no guidance or influence but that of the aforementioned impartial and incorruptible chance. If he opened the one, there came out of it a hungry tiger, the fiercest and most cruel that could be procured, which immediately sprang upon him and tore him to pieces as a punishment for his guilt. The moment that the case of the criminal was thus decided, doleful iron bells were clanged, great wails went up from the hired mourners posted on the outer rim of the arena, and the vast audience, with bowed heads and downcast hearts, wended slowly their homeward way, mourning greatly that one so young and fair, or so old and respected, should have merited so dire a fate.

But, if the accused person opened the other door, there came forth from it a lady, the most suitable to his years and station that his majesty could select among his fair subjects, and to this lady he was immediately married, as a reward of his innocence. It mattered not that he might already possess a wife and family, or that his affections might be engaged upon an object of his own selection; the king allowed no such subordinate arrangements to interfere with his great scheme of retribution and reward. The exercises, as in the other instance, took place immediately, and in the arena. Another door opened beneath the king, and a priest, followed by a band of choristers, and dancing maidens blowing joyous airs on golden horns and treading an epithalamic measure, advanced to where the pair stood, side by side, and the wedding was promptly and cheerily solemnized. Then the gay brass bells rang forth their merry peals, the people shouted glad hurrahs, and the innocent man, preceded by children strewing flowers on his path, led his bride to his home.

This was the king's semi-barbaric method of administering justice. Its perfect fairness is obvious. The criminal could not know out of which door would come the lady; he opened either he pleased, without having the slightest idea whether, in the next instant, he was to be devoured or married. On some occasions the tiger came out of one door, and on some out of the other. The decisions of this tribunal were not only fair, they were positively determinate: the accused person was instantly punished if he found himself guilty, and, if innocent, he was rewarded on the spot, whether he liked it or not. There was no escape from the judgments of the king's arena.

The institution was a very popular one. When the people gathered together on one of the great trial days, they never knew whether they were to witness a bloody slaughter or a hilarious wedding. This element of uncertainty lent an interest to the occasion which it could not otherwise have attained. Thus, the masses were entertained and pleased, and the thinking part of the community could bring no charge of unfairness against this plan, for did not the accused person have the whole matter in his own hands?

This semi-barbaric king had a daughter as blooming as his most florid fancies, and with a soul as fervent and imperious as his own. As is usual in such cases, she was the apple of his eye, and was loved by him above all humanity. Among his courtiers was a young man of that fineness of blood and lowness of station common to the conventional heroes of romance who love royal maidens. This royal maiden was well satisfied with her lover, for he was handsome and brave to a degree unsurpassed in all this kingdom, and she loved him with an ardor that had enough of barbarism in it to make it exceedingly warm and strong. This love affair moved on happily for many months, until one day the king happened to discover its existence. He did not hesitate nor waver in regard to his duty in the premises. The youth was immediately cast into prison, and a day was appointed for his trial in the king's arena. This, of course, was an especially important occasion, and his majesty, as well as all the people, was greatly interested in the workings and development of this trial. Never before had such a case occurred; never before had a subject dared to love the daughter of the king. In after years such things became commonplace enough, but then they were in no slight degree novel and startling.

The tiger-cages of the kingdom were searched for the most savage and relentless beasts, from which the fiercest monster might be selected for the arena; and the ranks of maiden youth and beauty throughout the land were carefully surveyed by competent judges in order that the young man might have a fitting bride in case fate did not determine for him a different destiny. Of course, everybody knew that the deed with which the accused was charged had been done. He had loved the princess, and neither he, she, nor any one else, thought of denying the fact; but the king would not think of allowing any fact of this kind to interfere with the workings of the tribunal, in which he took such great delight and satisfaction. No matter how the affair turned out, the youth would be disposed of, and the king would take an aesthetic pleasure in watching the course of events, which would determine whether or not the young man had done wrong in allowing himself to love the princess.

The appointed day arrived. From far and near the people gathered, and thronged the great galleries of the arena, and crowds, unable to gain admittance, massed themselves against its outside walls. The king and his court were in their places, opposite the twin doors, those fateful portals, so terrible in their similarity.

All was ready. The signal was given. A door beneath the royal party opened, and the lover of the princess walked into the arena. Tall, beautiful, fair, his appearance was greeted with a low hum of admiration and anxiety. Half the audience had not known so grand a youth had lived among them. No wonder the princess loved him! What a terrible thing for him to be there!

As the youth advanced into the arena he turned, as the custom was, to bow to the king, but he did not think at all of that royal personage. His eyes were fixed upon the princess, who sat to the right of her father. Had it not been for the moiety of barbarism in her nature it is probable that lady would not have been there, but her intense and fervid soul would not allow her to be absent on an occasion in which she was so terribly interested. From the moment that the decree had gone forth that her lover should decide his fate in the king's arena, she had thought of nothing, night or day, but this great event and the various subjects connected with it. Possessed of more power, influence, and force of character than any one who had ever before been interested in such a case, she had done what no other person had done—she had possessed herself of the secret of the doors. She knew in which of the two rooms, that lay behind those doors, stood the cage of the tiger, with its open front, and in which waited the lady. Through these thick doors, heavily curtained with skins on the inside, it was impossible that any noise or suggestion should come from within to the person who should approach to raise the latch of one of them. But gold, and the power of a woman's will, had brought the secret to the princess.

And not only did she know in which room stood the lady ready to emerge, all blushing and radiant, should her door be opened, but she knew who the lady was. It was one of the fairest and loveliest of the damsels of the court who had been selected as the reward of the accused youth, should he be proved innocent of the crime of aspiring to one so far above him; and the princess hated her. Often had she seen, or imagined that she had seen, this fair creature throwing glances of admiration upon the person of her lover, and sometimes she thought these glances were perceived, and even returned. Now and then she had seen them talking together; it was but for a moment or two, but much can be said in a brief space; it may have been on most unimportant topics, but how could she know that? The girl was lovely, but she had dared to raise her eyes to the loved one of the princess; and, with all the intensity of the savage blood transmitted to her through long lines of wholly barbaric ancestors, she hated the woman who blushed and trembled behind that silent door.

When her lover turned and looked at her, and his eye met hers as she sat there, paler and whiter than any one in the vast ocean of anxious faces about her, he saw, by that power of quick perception which is given to those whose souls are one, that she knew behind which door crouched the tiger, and behind which stood the lady. He had expected her to know it. He understood her nature, and his soul was assured that she would never rest until she had made plain to herself this thing, hidden to all other lookers-on, even to the king. The only hope for the youth in which there was any element of certainty was based upon the success of the princess in discovering this mystery; and the moment he looked upon her, he saw she had succeeded, as in his soul he knew she would succeed.

Then it was that his quick and anxious glance asked the question: 'Which?' It was as plain to her as if he shouted it from where he stood. There was not an instant to be lost. The question was asked in a flash; it must be answered in another.

Her right arm lay on the cushioned parapet before her. She raised her hand, and made a slight, quick movement toward the right. No one but her lover saw her. Every eye but his was fixed on the man in the arena.

He turned, and with a firm and rapid step he walked across the empty space. Every heart stopped beating, every breath was held, every eye was fixed immovably upon that man. Without the slightest hesitation, he went to the door on the right, and opened it.

Now, the point of the story is this: Did the tiger come out of that door, or did the lady ?

The more we reflect upon this question, the harder it is to answer. It involves a study of the human heart which leads us through devious mazes of passion, out of which it is difficult to find our way. Think of it, fair reader, not as if the decision of the question depended upon yourself, but upon that hot-blooded, semi-barbaric princess, her soul at a white heat beneath the combined fires of despair and jealousy. She had lost him, but who should have him?

How often, in her waking hours and in her dreams, had she started in wild horror, and covered her face with her hands as she thought of her lover opening the door on the other side of which waited the cruel fangs of the tiger!

But how much oftener had she seen him at the other door! How in her grievous reveries had she gnashed her teeth, and torn her hair, when she saw his start of rapturous delight as he opened the door of the lady! How her soul had burned in agony when she had seen him rush to meet that woman, with her flushing cheek and sparkling eye of triumph; when she had seen him lead her forth, his whole frame kindled with the joy of recovered life; when she had heard the glad shouts from the multitude, and the wild ringing of the happy bells; when she had seen the priest, with his joyous followers, advance to the couple, and make them man and wife before her very eyes; and when she had seen them walk away together upon their path of flowers, followed by the tremendous shouts of the hilarious multitude, in which her one despairing shriek was lost and drowned!

Would it not be better for him to die at once, and go to wait for her in the blessed regions of semi-barbaric futurity?

And yet, that awful tiger, those shrieks, that blood!

Her decision had been indicated in an instant, but it had

been made after days and nights of anguished deliberation. She had known she would be asked, she had decided what she would answer, and, without the slightest hesitation, she had moved her hand to the right.

The question of her decision is one not to be lightly considered, and it is not for me to presume to set myself up as the one person able to answer it. And so I leave it with all of you: Which came out of the opened door—the lady, or the tiger?

16

THE MONKEY'S PAW

W.W. Jacobs

Without, the night was cold and wet, but in the small parlour of Laburnam Villa the blinds were drawn and the fire burned brightly. Father and son were at chess, the former, who possessed ideas about the game involving radical changes, putting his king into such sharp and unnecessary perils that it even provoked comment from the white-haired old lady knitting placidly by the fire.

'Hark at the wind,' said Mr. White, who, having seen a fatal mistake after it was too late, was amiably desirous of preventing his son from seeing it.

'I'm listening,' said the latter, grimly surveying the board as he stretched out his hand. 'Check.'

'I should hardly think that he'd come to-night,' said his father, with his hand poised over the board.

'Mate,' replied the son.

'That's the worst of living so far out,' bawled Mr. White, with sudden and unlooked-for violence; 'of all the beastly, slushy, out-of-the-way places to live in, this is the worst. Pathway's a bog, and the road's a torrent. I don't know what people are thinking about. I suppose because only two houses in the road are let, they think it doesn't matter.'

'Never mind, dear,' said his wife, soothingly; 'perhaps you'll win the next one.'

Mr. White looked up sharply, just in time to intercept a knowing glance between mother and son. The words died away on his lips, and he hid a guilty grin in his thin grey beard.

'There he is,' said Herbert White, as the gate banged to loudly and heavy footsteps came toward the door.

The old man rose with hospitable haste, and opening the door, was heard condoling with the new arrival. The new arrival also condoled with himself, so that Mrs. White said, 'Tut, tut!' and coughed gently as her husband entered the room, followed by a tall, burly man, beady of eye and rubicund of visage.

'Sergeant-Major Morris,' he said, introducing him.

The sergeant-major shook hands, and taking the proffered seat by the fire, watched contentedly while his host got out whiskey and tumblers and stood a small copper kettle on the fire.

At the third glass his eyes got brighter, and he began to talk, the little family circle regarding with eager interest this visitor from distant parts, as he squared his broad shoulders in the chair and spoke of wild scenes and doughty deeds; of wars and plagues and strange peoples.

'Twenty-one years of it,' said Mr. White, nodding at his wife and son. 'When he went away he was a slip of a youth in the warehouse. Now look at him.'

'He don't look to have taken much harm,' said Mrs. White, politely.

'I'd like to go to India myself,' said the old man, 'just to look round a bit, you know.'

'Better where you are,' said the sergeant-major, shaking his head. He put down the empty glass, and sighing softly, shook it again.

'I should like to see those old temples and fakirs and jugglers,' said the old man. 'What was that you started telling me the other day about a monkey's paw or something, Morris?'

'Nothing,' said the soldier, hastily. 'Leastways nothing worth hearing.'

'Monkey's paw?' said Mrs. White, curiously.

'Well, it's just a bit of what you might call magic, perhaps,' said the sergeant-major, offhandedly.

His three listeners leaned forward eagerly. The visitor absent-mindedly put his empty glass to his lips and then set it down again. His host filled it for him.

'To look at,' said the sergeant-major, fumbling in his pocket, 'it's just an ordinary little paw, dried to a mummy.'

He took something out of his pocket and proffered it. Mrs. White drew back with a grimace, but her son, taking it, examined it curiously.

'And what is there special about it?' inquired Mr. White as he took it from his son, and having examined it, placed it upon the table.

'It had a spell put on it by an old fakir,' said the sergeant-major, 'a very holy man. He wanted to show that fate ruled people's lives, and that those who interfered with it did so to their sorrow. He put a spell on it so that three separate men could each have three wishes from it.'

His manner was so impressive that his hearers were conscious that their light laughter jarred somewhat.

'Well, why don't you have three, sir?' said Herbert White, cleverly.

The soldier regarded him in the way that middle age is wont to regard presumptuous youth. 'I have,' he said, quietly, and his blotchy face whitened.

'And did you really have the three wishes granted?' asked Mrs. White.

'I did,' said the sergeant-major, and his glass tapped against his strong teeth.

'And has anybody else wished?' persisted the old lady.

'The first man had his three wishes. Yes,' was the reply; 'I don't know what the first two were, but the third was for death. That's how I got the paw.'

His tones were so grave that a hush fell upon the group.

'If you've had your three wishes, it's no good to you now, then, Morris,' said the old man at last. 'What do you keep it for?'

The soldier shook his head. 'Fancy, I suppose,' he said, slowly. 'I did have some idea of selling it, but I don't think I will. It has caused enough mischief already. Besides, people won't buy. They think it's a fairy tale; some of them, and those who do think anything of it want to try it first and pay me afterward.'

'If you could have another three wishes,' said the old man,

eyeing him keenly, 'would you have them?'

'I don't know,' said the other. 'I don't know.'

He took the paw, and dangling it between his forefinger and thumb, suddenly threw it upon the fire. White, with a slight cry, stooped down and snatched it off.

'Better let it burn,' said the soldier, solemnly.

'If you don't want it, Morris,' said the other, 'give it to me.'

'I won't,' said his friend, doggedly. 'I threw it on the fire. If you keep it, don't blame me for what happens. Pitch it on the fire again like a sensible man.'

The other shook his head and examined his new possession closely. 'How do you do it?' he inquired.

'Hold it up in your right hand and wish aloud,' said the sergeant-major, 'but I warn you of the consequences.'

'Sounds like the Arabian Nights,' said Mrs. White, as she rose and began to set the supper. 'Don't you think you might wish for four pairs of hands for me?'

Her husband drew the talisman from pocket, and then all three burst into laughter as the sergeant-major, with a look of alarm on his face, caught him by the arm.

'If you must wish,' he said, gruffly, 'wish for something sensible.'

Mr. White dropped it back in his pocket, and placing chairs, motioned his friend to the table. In the business of supper the talisman was partly forgotten, and afterward the three sat listening in an enthralled fashion to a second instalment of the soldier's adventures in India.

'If the tale about the monkey's paw is not more truthful than those he has been telling us,' said Herbert, as the door closed behind their guest, just in time for him to catch the last train, 'we sha'nt make much out of it.'

'Did you give him anything for it, father?' inquired Mrs. White, regarding her husband closely.

'A trifle,' said he, colouring slightly. 'He didn't want it, but I made him take it. And he pressed me again to throw it away.'

'Likely,' said Herbert, with pretended horror. 'Why, we're

going to be rich, and famous and happy. Wish to be an emperor, father, to begin with; then you can't be henpecked.'

He darted round the table, pursued by the maligned Mrs. White armed with an antimacassar.

Mr. White took the paw from his pocket and eyed it dubiously. 'I don't know what to wish for, and that's a fact,' he said, slowly. 'It seems to me I've got all I want.'

'If you only cleared the house, you'd be quite happy, wouldn't you?' said Herbert, with his hand on his shoulder. 'Well, wish for two hundred pounds, then; that'll just do it.'

His father, smiling shamefacedly at his own credulity, held up the talisman, as his son, with a solemn face, somewhat marred by a wink at his mother, sat down at the piano and struck a few impressive chords.

'I wish for two hundred pounds,' said the old man distinctly.

A fine crash from the piano greeted the words, interrupted by a shuddering cry from the old man. His wife and son ran toward him.

'It moved,' he cried, with a glance of disgust at the object as it lay on the floor.

'As I wished, it twisted in my hand like a snake.'

'Well, I don't see the money,' said his son as he picked it up and placed it on the table, 'and I bet I never shall.'

'It must have been your fancy, father,' said his wife, regarding him anxiously.

He shook his head. 'Never mind, though; there's no harm done, but it gave me a shock all the same.'

They sat down by the fire again while the two men finished their pipes. Outside, the wind was higher than ever, and the old man started nervously at the sound of a door banging upstairs. A silence unusual and depressing settled upon all three, which lasted until the old couple rose to retire for the night.

'I expect you'll find the cash tied up in a big bag in the middle of your bed,' said Herbert, as he bade them good-night, 'and something horrible squatting up on top of the wardrobe watching you as you pocket your ill-gotten gains.'

He sat alone in the darkness, gazing at the dying fire, and seeing faces in it. The last face was so horrible and so simian that he gazed at it in amazement. It got so vivid that, with a little uneasy laugh, he felt on the table for a glass containing a little water to throw over it. His hand grasped the monkey's paw, and with a little shiver he wiped his hand on his coat and went up to bed.

In the brightness of the wintry sun next morning as it streamed over the breakfast table he laughed at his fears. There was an air of prosaic wholesomeness about the room which it had lacked on the previous night, and the dirty, shrivelled little paw was pitched on the sideboard with a carelessness which betokened no great belief in its virtues.

'I suppose all old soldiers are the same,' said Mrs. White. 'The idea of our listening to such nonsense! How could wishes be granted in these days? And if they could, how could two hundred pounds hurt you, father?'

'Might drop on his head from the sky,' said the frivolous Herbert.

'Morris said the things happened so naturally,' said his father, 'that you might if you so wished attribute it to coincidence.'

'Well, don't break into the money before I come back,' said Herbert as he rose from the table. 'I'm afraid it'll turn you into a mean, avaricious man, and we shall have to disown you.'

His mother laughed, and following him to the door, watched him down the road; and returning to the breakfast table, was very happy at the expense of her husband's credulity. All of which did not prevent her from scurrying to the door at the postman's knock, nor prevent her from referring somewhat shortly to retired sergeant-majors of bibulous habits when she found that the post brought a tailor's bill.

'Herbert will have some more of his funny remarks, I expect, when he comes home,' she said, as they sat at dinner.

'I dare say,' said Mr. White, pouring himself out some beer; 'but for all that, the thing moved in my hand; that I'll swear to.'

'You thought it did,' said the old lady soothingly.

'I say it did,' replied the other. 'There was no thought about it; I had just—What's the matter?'

His wife made no reply. She was watching the mysterious movements of a man outside, who, peering in an undecided fashion at the house, appeared to be trying to make up his mind to enter. In mental connection with the two hundred pounds, she noticed that the stranger was well dressed, and wore a silk hat of glossy newness. Three times he paused at the gate, and then walked on again. The fourth time he stood with his hand upon it, and then with sudden resolution flung it open and walked up the path. Mrs. White at the same moment placed her hands behind her, and hurriedly unfastening the strings of her apron, put that useful article of apparel beneath the cushion of her chair.

She brought the stranger, who seemed ill at ease, into the room. He gazed at her furtively, and listened in a preoccupied fashion as the old lady apologized for the appearance of the room, and her husband's coat, a garment which he usually reserved for the garden. She then waited as patiently as her sex would permit, for him to broach his business, but he was at first strangely silent.

'I—was asked to call,' he said at last, and stooped and picked a piece of cotton from his trousers. 'I come from "Maw and Meggins".'

The old lady started. 'Is anything the matter?' she asked, breathlessly. 'Has anything happened to Herbert? What is it? What is it?'

Her husband interposed. 'There, there, mother,' he said, hastily. 'Sit down, and don't jump to conclusions. You've not brought bad news, I'm sure, sir;' and he eyed the other wistfully.

'I'm sorry—', began the visitor.

'Is he hurt?' demanded the mother, wildly.

The visitor bowed in assent. 'Badly hurt,' he said, quietly, 'but he is not in any pain.'

'Oh, thank God!' said the old woman, clasping her hands. 'Thank God for that! Thank—'

She broke off suddenly as the sinister meaning of the assurance dawned upon her and she saw the awful confirmation of her fears in the other's averted face. She caught her breath, and turning to her slower-witted husband, laid her trembling old hand upon his. There was a long silence.

'He was caught in the machinery,' said the visitor at length in a low voice.

'Caught in the machinery,' repeated Mr. White, in a dazed fashion, 'yes.'

He sat staring blankly out at the window, and taking his wife's hand between his own, pressed it as he had been wont to do in their old courting-days nearly forty years before.

'He was the only one left to us,' he said, turning gently to the visitor. 'It is hard.'

The other coughed, and rising, walked slowly to the window. 'The firm wished me to convey their sincere sympathy with you in your great loss,' he said, without looking round. 'I beg that you will understand I am only their servant and merely obeying orders.'

There was no reply; the old woman's face was white, her eyes staring, and her breath inaudible; on the husband's face was a look such as his friend the sergeant might have carried into his first action.

'I was to say that "Maw and Meggins" disclaim all responsibility,' continued the other. 'They admit no liability at all, but in consideration of your son's services, they wish to present you with a certain sum as compensation.'

Mr. White dropped his wife's hand, and rising to his feet, gazed with a look of horror at his visitor. His dry lips shaped the words, 'How much?'

'Two hundred pounds,' was the answer.

Unconscious of his wife's shriek, the old man smiled faintly, put out his hands like a sightless man, and dropped, a senseless heap, to the floor.

In the huge new cemetery, some two miles distant, the old people buried their dead, and came back to a house steeped in shadow and silence. It was all over so quickly that at first they could hardly realize it, and remained in a state of expectation as though of something else to happen—something else which was to lighten this load, too heavy for old hearts to bear.

But the days passed, and expectation gave place to resignation—the hopeless resignation of the old, sometimes miscalled, apathy. Sometimes they hardly exchanged a word, for now they had nothing to talk about, and their days were long to weariness.

It was about a week after that the old man, waking suddenly in the night, stretched out his hand and found himself alone. The room was in darkness, and the sound of subdued weeping came from the window. He raised himself in bed and listened.

'Come back,' he said, tenderly. 'You will be cold.'

'It is colder for my son,' said the old woman, and wept afresh.

The sound of her sobs died away on his ears. The bed was warm, and his eyes heavy with sleep. He dozed fitfully, and then slept until a sudden wild cry from his wife awoke him with a start.

'The paw!' she cried wildly. 'The monkey's paw!'

He started up in alarm. 'Where? Where is it? What's the matter?'

She came stumbling across the room toward him. 'I want it,' she said, quietly. 'You've not destroyed it?'

'It's in the parlour, on the bracket,' he replied, marvelling. 'Why?'

She cried and laughed together, and bending over, kissed his cheek.

'I only just thought of it,' she said, hysterically. 'Why didn't I think of it before? Why didn't you think of it?'

'Think of what?' he questioned.

'The other two wishes,' she replied, rapidly. 'We've only had one.'

'Was not that enough?' he demanded, fiercely.

'No,' she cried, triumphantly; 'we'll have one more. Go down and get it quickly, and wish our boy alive again.'

The man sat up in bed and flung the bedclothes from his quaking limbs. 'Good God, you are mad!' he cried, aghast.

'Get it,' she panted; 'get it quickly, and wish—Oh, my boy, my boy!'

Her husband struck a match and lit the candle. 'Get back to bed,' he said, unsteadily. 'You don't know what you are saying.'

'We had the first wish granted,' said the old woman, feverishly; 'why not the second?'

'A coincidence,' stammered the old man.

'Go and get it and wish,' cried his wife, quivering with excitement.

The old man turned and regarded her, and his voice shook. 'He has been dead ten days, and besides he—I would not tell you else, but—I could only recognize him by his clothing. If he was too terrible for you to see then, how now?'

'Bring him back,' cried the old woman, and dragged him toward the door. 'Do you think I fear the child I have nursed?'

He went down in the darkness, and felt his way to the parlour, and then to the mantelpiece. The talisman was in its place, and a horrible fear that the unspoken wish might bring his mutilated son before him ere he could escape from the room seized upon him, and he caught his breath as he found that he had lost the direction of the door. His brow cold with sweat, he felt his way round the table, and groped along the wall until he found himself in the small passage with the unwholesome thing in his hand.

Even his wife's face seemed changed as he entered the room. It was white and expectant, and to his fears seemed to have an unnatural look upon it. He was afraid of her.

'Wish!' she cried, in a strong voice.

'It is foolish and wicked,' he faltered.

'Wish!' repeated his wife.

He raised his hand. 'I wish my son alive again.'

The talisman fell to the floor, and he regarded it fearfully. Then he sank trembling into a chair as the old woman, with burning eyes, walked to the window and raised the blind.

He sat until he was chilled with the cold, glancing occasionally at the figure of the old woman peering through the window. The candle-end, which had burned below the rim of the china candlestick, was throwing pulsating shadows on the ceiling and walls, until, with a flicker larger than the rest, it expired. The old man, with an unspeakable sense of relief at the failure of the talisman, crept back to his bed, and a minute or two afterward the old woman came silently and apathetically beside him.

Neither spoke, but lay silently listening to the ticking of the clock. A stair creaked, and a squeaky mouse scurried noisily through the wall. The darkness was oppressive, and after lying for some time screwing up his courage, he took the box of matches, and striking one, went downstairs for a candle.

At the foot of the stairs the match went out, and he paused to strike another; and at the same moment a knock, so quiet and stealthy as to be scarcely audible, sounded on the front door.

The matches fell from his hand and spilled in the passage. He stood motionless, his breath suspended until the knock was repeated. Then he turned and fled swiftly back to his room, and closed the door behind him. A third knock sounded through the house.

'What's that?' cried the old woman, starting up.

'A rat,' said the old man in shaking tones—'a rat. It passed me on the stairs.'

His wife sat up in bed listening. A loud knock resounded through the house.

'It's Herbert!' she screamed. 'It's Herbert!'

She ran to the door, but her husband was before her, and catching her by the arm, held her tightly.

'What are you going to do?' he whispered hoarsely.

'It's my boy; it's Herbert!' she cried, struggling mechanically. 'I forgot it was two miles away. What are you holding me for? Let go. I must open the door.'

'For God's sake don't let it in,' cried the old man, trembling.

'You're afraid of your own son,' she cried, struggling. 'Let me go. I'm coming, Herbert; I'm coming.'

There was another knock, and another. The old woman with a sudden wrench broke free and ran from the room. Her husband followed to the landing, and called after her appealingly as she hurried downstairs. He heard the chain rattle back and the bottom bolt drawn slowly and stiffly from the socket. Then the old woman's voice, strained and panting.

'The bolt,' she cried, loudly. 'Come down. I can't reach it.'

But her husband was on his hands and knees groping wildly on the floor in search of the paw. If he could only find it before the thing outside got in. A perfect fusillade of knocks reverberated through the house, and he heard the scraping of a chair as his wife put it down in the passage against the door. He heard the creaking of the bolt as it came slowly back, and at the same moment he found the monkey's paw, and frantically breathed his third and last wish.

The knocking ceased suddenly, although the echoes of it were still in the house. He heard the chair drawn back, and the door opened. A cold wind rushed up the staircase, and a long loud wail of disappointment and misery from his wife gave him courage to run down to her side, and then to the gate beyond. The street lamp flickering opposite shone on a quiet and deserted road.

17

THE STORY OF AN HOUR

Kate Chopin

Knowing that Mrs. Mallard was afflicted with a heart trouble, great care was taken to break to her as gently as possible the news of her husband's death.

It was her sister Josephine who told her, in broken sentences; veiled hints that revealed in half concealing. Her husband's friend Richards was there, too, near her. It was he who had been in the newspaper office when intelligence of the railroad disaster was received, with Brently Mallard's name leading the list of 'killed.' He had only taken the time to assure himself of its truth by a second telegram, and had hastened to forestall any less careful, less tender friend in bearing the sad message.

She did not hear the story as many women have heard the same, with a paralyzed inability to accept its significance. She wept at once, with sudden, wild abandonment, in her sister's arms. When the storm of grief had spent itself she went away to her room alone. She would have no one follow her.

There stood, facing the open window, a comfortable, roomy armchair. Into this she sank, pressed down by a physical exhaustion that haunted her body and seemed to reach into her soul.

She could see in the open square before her house the tops of trees that were all aquiver with the new spring life. The delicious breath of rain was in the air. In the street below a peddler was crying his wares. The notes of a distant song which some one was singing reached her faintly, and countless sparrows were twittering in the eaves.

There were patches of blue sky showing here and there through the clouds that had met and piled one above the other in the west facing her window.

She sat with her head thrown back upon the cushion of the chair, quite motionless, except when a sob came up into her throat and shook her, as a child who has cried itself to sleep continues to sob in its dreams.

She was young, with a fair, calm face, whose lines bespoke repression and even a certain strength. But now there was a dull stare in her eyes, whose gaze was fixed away off yonder on one of those patches of blue sky. It was not a glance of reflection, but rather indicated a suspension of intelligent thought.

There was something coming to her and she was waiting for it, fearfully. What was it? She did not know; it was too subtle and elusive to name. But she felt it, creeping out of the sky, reaching toward her through the sounds, the scents, the color that filled the air.

Now her bosom rose and fell tumultuously. She was beginning to recognize this thing that was approaching to possess her, and she was striving to beat it back with her will—as powerless as her two white slender hands would have been. When she abandoned herself a little whispered word escaped her slightly parted lips. She said it over and over under her breath: 'free, free, free!' The vacant stare and the look of terror that had followed it went from her eyes. They stayed keen and bright. Her pulses beat fast, and the coursing blood warmed and relaxed every inch of her body.

She did not stop to ask if it were or were not a monstrous joy that held her. A clear and exalted perception enabled her to dismiss the suggestion as trivial. She knew that she would weep again when she saw the kind, tender hands folded in death; the face that had never looked save with love upon her, fixed and gray and dead. But she saw beyond that bitter moment a long procession of years to come that would belong to her absolutely. And she opened and spread her arms out to them in welcome.

There would be no one to live for during those coming years; she would live for herself. There would be no powerful will bending hers in that blind persistence with which men and women believe they have a right to impose a private will upon a fellow-creature. A kind intention or a cruel intention made the act seem no less a crime as she looked upon it in that brief moment of illumination.

And yet she had loved him—sometimes. Often she had not. What did it matter! What could love, the unsolved mystery, count for in the face of this possession of self-assertion which she suddenly recognized as the strongest impulse of her being!

'Free! Body and soul free!' she kept whispering.

Josephine was kneeling before the closed door with her lips to the keyhold, imploring for admission. 'Louise, open the door! I beg; open the door—you will make yourself ill. What are you doing, Louise? For heaven's sake open the door.'

'Go away. I am not making myself ill.' No; she was drinking in a very elixir of life through that open window.

Her fancy was running riot along those days ahead of her. Spring days, and summer days, and all sorts of days that would be her own. She breathed a quick prayer that life might be long. It was only yesterday she had thought with a shudder that life might be long.

She arose at length and opened the door to her sister's importunities. There was a feverish triumph in her eyes, and she carried herself unwittingly like a goddess of Victory. She clasped her sister's waist, and together they descended the stairs. Richards stood waiting for them at the bottom.

Some one was opening the front door with a latchkey. It was Brently Mallard who entered, a little travel-stained, composedly carrying his grip-sack and umbrella. He had been far from the scene of the accident, and did not even know there had been one. He stood amazed at Josephine's piercing cry; at Richards' quick motion to screen him from the view of his wife.

When the doctors came they said she had died of heart disease—of the joy that kills.

18

THE CACTUS

O. Henry

The most notable thing about Time is that it is so purely relative. A large amount of reminiscence is, by common consent, conceded to the drowning man; and it is not past belief that one may review an entire courtship while removing one's gloves.

That is what Trysdale was doing, standing by a table in his bachelor apartments. On the table stood a singular-looking green plant in a red earthen jar. The plant was one of the species of cacti, and was provided with long, tentacular leaves that perpetually swayed with the slightest breeze with a peculiar beckoning motion.

Trysdale's friend, the brother of the bride, stood at a sideboard complaining at being allowed to drink alone. Both men were in evening dress. White favors like stars upon their coats shone through the gloom of the apartment.

As he slowly unbuttoned his gloves, there passed through Trysdale's mind a swift, scarifying retrospect of the last few hours. It seemed that in his nostrils was still the scent of the flowers that had been banked in odorous masses about the church, and in his ears the lowpitched hum of a thousand well-bred voices, the rustle of crisp garments, and, most insistently recurring, the drawling words of the minister irrevocably binding her to another.

From this last hopeless point of view he still strove, as if it had become a habit of his mind, to reach some conjecture as to why and how he had lost her. Shaken rudely by the uncompromising fact, he had suddenly found himself confronted by a thing he had never before faced—his own innermost, unmitigated, arid unbedecked self. He saw all the garbs of pretence and egoism that he had worn now turn to rags of folly. He shuddered at the thought that to others, before now, the garments of his soul must have appeared sorry and threadbare. Vanity and conceit? These were the joints in his armor. And how free from either she had always been—But why—

As she had slowly moved up the aisle toward the altar he had felt an unworthy, sullen exultation that had served to support him. He had told himself that her paleness was from thoughts of another than the man to whom she was about to give herself. But even that poor consolation had been wrenched from him. For, when he saw that swift, limpid, upward look that she gave the man when he took her hand, he knew himself to be forgotten. Once that same look had been raised to him, and he had gauged its meaning. Indeed, his conceit had crumbled; its last prop was gone. Why had it ended thus? There had been no quarrel between them, nothing—

For the thousandth time he remarshalled in his mind the events of those last few days before the tide had so suddenly turned.

She had always insisted upon placing him upon a pedestal, and he had accepted her homage with royal grandeur. It had been a very sweet incense that she had burned before him; so modest (he told himself); so childlike and worshipful, and (he would once have sworn) so sincere. She had invested him with an almost supernatural number of high attributes and excellencies and talents, and he had absorbed the oblation as a desert drinks the rain that can coax from it no promise of blossom or fruit.

As Trysdale grimly wrenched apart the seam of his last glove, the crowning instance of his fatuous and tardily mourned egoism came vividly back to him. The scene was the night when he had asked her to come up on his pedestal with him and share his greatness. He could not, now, for the pain of it, allow his mind to dwell upon the memory of her convincing beauty that night—the careless wave of her hair, the tenderness and virginal charm of her looks and words. But they had been enough, and they had brought him to speak. During their conversation she had said:

'And Captain Carruthers tells me that you speak the Spanish language like a native. Why have you hidden this accomplishment from me? Is there anything you do not know?'

Now, Carruthers was an idiot. No doubt he (Trysdale) had been guilty (he sometimes did such things) of airing at the club some old, canting Castilian proverb dug from the hotchpotch at the back of dictionaries. Carruthers, who was one of his incontinent admirers, was the very man to have magnified this exhibition of doubtful erudition.

But, alas! the incense of her admiration had been so sweet and flattering. He allowed the imputation to pass without denial. Without protest, he allowed her to twine about his brow this spurious bay of Spanish scholarship. He let it grace his conquering head, and, among its soft convolutions, he did not feel the prick of the thorn that was to pierce him later.

How glad, how shy, how tremulous she was! How she fluttered like a snared bird when he laid his mightiness at her feet! He could have sworn, and he could swear now, that unmistakable consent was in her eyes, but, coyly, she would give him no direct answer. 'I will send you my answer to-morrow,' she said; and he, the indulgent, confident victor, smilingly granted the delay. The next day he waited, impatient, in his rooms for the word. At noon her groom came to the door and left the strange cactus in the red earthen jar. There was no note, no message, merely a tag upon the plant bearing a barbarous foreign or botanical name. He waited until night, but her answer did not come. His large pride and hurt vanity kept him from seeking her. Two evenings later they met at a dinner. Their greetings were conventional, but she looked at him, breathless, wondering, eager. He was courteous, adamant, waiting her explanation. With womanly swiftness she took her cue from his manner, and turned to snow and ice. Thus, and wider from this on, they had drifted apart. Where was his fault? Who had been to blame? Humbled now, he sought the answer amid the ruins of his self-conceit. If—

The voice of the other man in the room, querulously intruding upon his thoughts, aroused him.

'I say, Trysdale, what the deuce is the matter with you? You look unhappy as if you yourself had been married instead of having acted merely as an accomplice. Look at me, another accessory, come two thousand miles on a garlicky, cockroachy banana steamer all the way from South America to connive at the sacrifice—please to observe how lightly my guilt rests upon my shoulders. Only little sister I had, too, and now she's gone. Come now! take something to ease your conscience.'

'I don't drink just now, thanks,' said Trysdale.

'Your brandy,' resumed the other, coming over and joining him, 'is abominable. Run down to see me some time at Punta Redonda, and try some of our stuff that old Garcia smuggles in. It's worth the trip. Hallo! here's an old acquaintance. Wherever did you rake up this cactus, Trysdale?'

'A present,' said Trysdale, 'from a friend. Know the species?'

'Very well. It's a tropical concern. See hundreds of 'em around Punta every day. Here's the name on this tag tied to it. Know any Spanish, Trysdale?'

'No,' said Trysdale, with the bitter wraith of a smile—'Is it Spanish?'

'Yes. The natives imagine the leaves are reaching out and beckoning to you. They call it by this name—Ventomarme. Name means in English, "Come and take me."'

19

THE PIT AND THE PENDULUM

Edgar Allan Poe

I was sick—sick unto death with that long agony; and when they at length unbound me, and I was permitted to sit, I felt that my senses were leaving me. The sentence—the dread sentence of death—was the last of distinct accentuation which reached my ears. After that, the sound of the inquisitorial voices seemed merged in one dreamy indeterminate hum. It conveyed to my soul the idea of revolution—perhaps from its association in fancy with the burr of a mill wheel. This only for a brief period; for presently I heard no more. Yet, for a while, I saw; but with how terrible an exaggeration! I saw the lips of the black-robed judges. They appeared to me white—whiter than the sheet upon which I trace these words—and thin even to grotesqueness; thin with the intensity of their expression of firmness—of immoveable resolution—of stern contempt of human torture. I saw that the decrees of what to me was Fate, were still issuing from those lips. I saw them writhe with a deadly locution. I saw them fashion the syllables of my name; and I shuddered because no sound succeeded. I saw, too, for a few moments of delirious horror, the soft and nearly imperceptible waving of the sable draperies which enwrapped the walls of the apartment. And then my vision fell upon the seven tall candles upon the table. At first they wore the aspect of charity, and seemed white and slender angels who would save me; but then, all at once, there came a most deadly nausea over my spirit, and I felt every fibre in my frame thrill as if I had touched the wire of a galvanic battery, while the angel forms became meaningless spectres, with heads of flame, and I saw that from them there would be no help. And then there stole into my fancy, like a rich musical note, the thought of what sweet rest there must be in the grave. The thought came gently and stealthily, and it seemed long before it attained full appreciation; but just as my spirit came at length properly to feel and entertain it, the figures of the judges vanished, as if magically, from before me; the tall candles sank into nothingness; their flames went out utterly; the blackness of darkness supervened; all sensations appeared swallowed up in a mad rushing descent as of the soul into Hades. Then silence, and stillness, night were the universe.

I had swooned; but still will not say that all of consciousness was lost. What of it there remained I will not attempt to define, or even to describe; yet all was not lost. In the deepest slumber—no! In delirium—no! In a swoon—no! In death—no! even in the grave all is not lost. Else there is no immortality for man. Arousing from the most profound of slumbers, we break the gossamer web of some dream. Yet in a second afterward, (so frail may that web have been) we remember not that we have dreamed. In the return to life from the swoon there are two stages; first, that of the sense of mental or spiritual; secondly, that of the sense of physical, existence. It seems probable that if, upon reaching the second stage, we could recall the impressions of the first, we should find these impressions eloquent in memories of the gulf beyond. And that gulf is—what? How at least shall we distinguish its shadows from those of the tomb? But if the impressions of what I have termed the first stage, are not, at will, recalled, yet, after long interval, do they not come unbidden, while we marvel whence they come? He who has never swooned, is not he who finds strange palaces and wildly familiar faces in coals that glow; is not he who beholds floating in mid-air the sad visions that the many may not view; is not he who ponders over the perfume of some novel flower—is not he whose brain grows bewildered with the meaning of some musical cadence which has never before arrested his attention.

Amid frequent and thoughtful endeavors to remember; amid earnest struggles to regather some token of the state of seeming nothingness into which my soul had lapsed, there have been moments when I have dreamed of success; there have been brief, very brief periods when I have conjured up remembrances which the lucid reason of a later epoch assures me could have had reference only to that condition of seeming unconsciousness. These shadows of memory tell, indistinctly, of tall figures that lifted and bore me in silence down—down—still down—till a hideous dizziness oppressed me at the mere idea of the interminableness of the descent. They tell also of a vague horror at my heart, on account of that heart's unnatural stillness. Then comes a sense of sudden motionlessness throughout all things; as if those who bore me (a ghastly train!) had outrun, in their descent, the limits of the limitless, and paused from the wearisomeness of their toil. After this I call to mind flatness and dampness; and then all is madness—the madness of a memory which busies itself among forbidden things.

Very suddenly there came back to my soul motion and sound—the tumultuous motion of the heart, and, in my ears, the sound of its beating. Then a pause in which all is blank. Then again sound, and motion, and touch—a tingling sensation pervading my frame. Then the mere consciousness of existence, without thought—a condition which lasted long. Then, very suddenly, thought, and shuddering terror, and earnest endeavor to comprehend my true state. Then a strong desire to lapse into insensibility. Then a rushing revival of soul and a successful effort to move. And now a full memory of the trial, of the judges, of the sable draperies, of the sentence, of the sickness, of the swoon. Then entire forgetfulness of all that followed; of all that a later day and much earnestness of endeavor have enabled me vaguely to recall.

So far, I had not opened my eyes. I felt that I lay upon my back, unbound. I reached out my hand, and it fell heavily upon something damp and hard. There I suffered it to remain for many minutes, while I strove to imagine where and what I could be. I longed, yet dared not to employ my vision. I dreaded the first glance at objects around me. It was not that I feared to look upon things horrible, but that I grew aghast lest there should be nothing to see. At length, with a wild desperation at heart, I quickly unclosed my eyes. My worst thoughts, then, were confirmed. The blackness of eternal night encompassed me. I struggled for breath. The intensity of the darkness seemed to oppress and stifle me. The atmosphere was intolerably close. I still lay quietly, and made effort to exercise my reason. I brought to mind the inquisitorial proceedings, and attempted from that point to deduce my real condition. The sentence had passed; and it appeared to me that a very long interval of time had since elapsed. Yet not for a moment did I suppose myself actually dead. Such a supposition, notwithstanding what we read in fiction, is altogether inconsistent with real existence;—but where and in what state was I? The condemned to death, I knew, perished usually at the autos-da-fe, and one of these had been held on the very night of the day of my trial. Had I been remanded to my dungeon, to await the next sacrifice, which would not take place for many months? This I at once saw could not be. Victims had been in immediate demand. Moreover, my dungeon, as well as all the condemned cells at Toledo, had stone floors, and light was not altogether excluded.

A fearful idea now suddenly drove the blood in torrents upon my heart, and for a brief period, I once more relapsed into insensibility. Upon recovering, I at once started to my feet, trembling convulsively in every fibre. I thrust my arms wildly above and around me in all directions. I felt nothing; yet dreaded to move a step, lest I should be impeded by the walls of a tomb. Perspiration burst from every pore, and stood in cold big beads upon my forehead. The agony of suspense grew at length intolerable, and I cautiously moved forward, with my arms extended, and my eyes straining from their sockets, in the hope of catching some faint ray of light. I proceeded for many paces; but still all was blackness and vacancy. I breathed more freely. It seemed evident that mine was not, at least, the most hideous of fates.

And now, as I still continued to step cautiously onward, there came thronging upon my recollection a thousand vague rumors of the horrors of Toledo. Of the dungeons there had been strange things narrated—fables I had always deemed them—but yet strange, and too ghastly to repeat, save in a whisper. Was I left to perish of starvation in this subterranean world of darkness; or what fate, perhaps even more fearful, awaited me? That the result would be death, and a death of more than customary bitterness, I knew too well the character of my judges to doubt. The mode and the hour were all that occupied or distracted me.

My outstretched hands at length encountered some solid obstruction. It was a wall, seemingly of stone masonry—very smooth, slimy, and cold. I followed it up; stepping with all the careful distrust with which certain antique narratives had inspired me. This process, however, afforded me no means of ascertaining the dimensions of my dungeon; as I might make its circuit, and return to the point whence I set out, without being aware of the fact; so perfectly uniform seemed the wall. I therefore sought the knife which had been in my pocket, when led into the inquisitorial chamber; but it was gone; my clothes had been exchanged for a wrapper of coarse serge. I had thought of forcing the blade in some minute crevice of the masonry, so as to identify my point of departure. The difficulty, nevertheless, was but trivial; although, in the disorder of my fancy, it seemed at first insuperable. I tore a part of the hem from the robe and placed the fragment at full length, and at right angles to the wall. In groping my way around the prison, I could not fail to encounter this rag upon completing the circuit. So, at least I thought: but I had not counted upon the extent of the dungeon, or upon my own weakness. The ground was moist and slippery. I staggered onward for some time, when I stumbled and fell. My excessive fatigue induced me to remain prostrate; and sleep soon overtook me as I lay.

Upon awaking, and stretching forth an arm, I found beside me a loaf and a pitcher with water. I was too much exhausted to reflect upon this circumstance, but ate and drank with avidity. Shortly afterward, I resumed my tour around the prison, and with much toil came at last upon the fragment of the serge. Up to the period when I fell I had counted fifty-two paces, and upon resuming my walk, I had counted forty-eight more;—when I arrived at the rag. There were in all, then, a hundred paces; and, admitting two paces to the yard, I presumed the dungeon to be fifty yards in circuit. I had met, however, with many angles in the wall, and thus I could form no guess at the shape of the vault; for vault I could not help supposing it to be.

I had little object—certainly no hope—in these researches; but a vague curiosity prompted me to continue them. Quitting the wall, I resolved to cross the area of the enclosure. At first I proceeded with extreme caution, for the floor, although seemingly of solid material, was treacherous with slime. At length, however, I took courage, and did not hesitate to step firmly; endeavoring to cross in as direct a line as possible. I had advanced some ten or twelve paces in this manner, when the remnant of the torn hem of my robe became entangled between my legs. I stepped on it, and fell violently on my face.

In the confusion attending my fall, I did not immediately apprehend a somewhat startling circumstance, which yet, in a few seconds afterward, and while I still lay prostrate, arrested my attention. It was this—my chin rested upon the floor of the prison, but my lips and the upper portion of my head, although seemingly at a less elevation than the chin, touched nothing. At the same time my forehead seemed bathed in a clammy vapor, and the peculiar smell of decayed fungus arose to my nostrils. I put forward my arm, and shuddered to find that I had fallen at the very brink of a circular pit, whose extent, of course, I had no means of ascertaining at the moment. Groping about the masonry just below the margin, I succeeded in dislodging a small fragment, and let it fall into the abyss. For many seconds I hearkened to its reverberations as it dashed against the sides of the chasm in its descent; at length there was a sullen plunge into water, succeeded by loud echoes. At the same moment there came a sound resembling the quick opening, and as rapid closing of a door overhead, while a faint gleam of light flashed suddenly through the gloom, and as suddenly faded away.

I saw clearly the doom which had been prepared for me, and congratulated myself upon the timely accident by which I had escaped. Another step before my fall, and the world had seen me no more. And the death just avoided, was of that very character which I had regarded as fabulous and frivolous in the tales respecting the Inquisition. To the victims of its tyranny, there was the choice of death with its direst physical agonies, or death with its most hideous moral horrors. I had been reserved for the latter. By long suffering my nerves had been unstrung, until I trembled at the sound of my own voice, and had become in every respect a fitting subject for the species of torture which awaited me.

Shaking in every limb, I groped my way back to the wall; resolving there to perish rather than risk the terrors of the wells, of which my imagination now pictured many in various positions about the dungeon. In other conditions of mind I might have had courage to end my misery at once by a plunge into one of these abysses; but now I was the veriest of cowards. Neither could I forget what I had read of these pits—that the sudden extinction of life formed no part of their most horrible plan.

Agitation of spirit kept me awake for many long hours; but at length I again slumbered. Upon arousing, I found by my side, as before, a loaf and a pitcher of water. A burning thirst consumed me, and I emptied the vessel at a draught. It must have been drugged; for scarcely had I drunk, before I became irresistibly drowsy. A deep sleep fell upon me—a sleep like that of death. How long it lasted of course, I know not; but when, once again, I unclosed my eyes, the objects around me were visible. By a wild sulphurous lustre, the origin of which I could not at first determine, I was enabled to see the extent and aspect of the prison.

In its size I had been greatly mistaken. The whole circuit of its walls did not exceed twenty-five yards. For some minutes this fact occasioned me a world of vain trouble; vain indeed! for what could be of less importance, under the terrible circumstances which environed me, then the mere dimensions of my dungeon? But my soul took a wild interest in trifles, and I busied myself in endeavors to account for the error I had committed in my measurement. The truth at length flashed upon me. In my first attempt at exploration I had counted fifty-two paces, up to the period when I fell; I must then have been within a pace or two of the fragment of serge; in fact, I had nearly performed the circuit of the vault. I then slept, and upon awaking, I must have returned upon my steps—thus supposing the circuit nearly double what it actually was. My confusion of mind prevented me from observing that I began my tour with the wall to the left, and ended it with the wall to the right.

I had been deceived, too, in respect to the shape of the enclosure. In feeling my way I had found many angles, and thus deduced an idea of great irregularity; so potent is the effect of total darkness upon one arousing from lethargy or sleep! The angles were simply those of a few slight depressions, or niches, at odd intervals. The general shape of the prison was square. What I had taken for masonry seemed now to be iron, or some other metal, in huge plates, whose sutures or joints occasioned the depression. The entire surface of this metallic enclosure was rudely daubed in all the hideous and repulsive devices to which the charnel superstition of the monks has given rise. The figures of fiends in aspects of menace, with skeleton forms, and other more really fearful images, overspread and disfigured the walls. I observed that the outlines of these monstrosities were sufficiently distinct, but that the colors seemed faded and blurred, as if from the effects of a damp atmosphere. I now noticed the floor, too, which was of stone. In the centre yawned the circular pit from whose jaws I had escaped; but it was the only one in the dungeon.

All this I saw indistinctly and by much effort: for my personal condition had been greatly changed during slumber. I now lay upon my back, and at full length, on a species of low framework of wood. To this I was securely bound by a long strap resembling a surcingle. It passed in many convolutions about my limbs and body, leaving at liberty only my head, and my left arm to such extent that I could, by dint of much exertion, supply myself with food from an earthen dish which lay by my side on the floor. I saw, to my horror, that the pitcher had been removed. I say to my horror; for I was consumed with intolerable thirst. This thirst it appeared to be the design of my persecutors to stimulate: for the food in the dish was meat pungently seasoned.

Looking upward, I surveyed the ceiling of my prison. It was some thirty or forty feet overhead, and constructed much as the side walls. In one of its panels a very singular figure riveted my whole attention. It was the painted figure of Time as he is commonly represented, save that, in lieu of a scythe, he held what, at a casual glance, I supposed to be the pictured image of a huge pendulum such as we see on antique clocks. There was something, however, in the appearance of this machine which caused me to regard it more attentively. While I gazed directly upward at it (for its position was immediately over my own) I fancied that I saw it in motion. In an instant afterward the fancy was confirmed. Its sweep was brief, and of course slow. I watched it for some minutes, somewhat in fear, but more in wonder. Wearied at length with observing its dull movement, I turned my eyes upon the other objects in the cell.

A slight noise attracted my notice, and, looking to the floor, I saw several enormous rats traversing it. They had issued from the well, which lay just within view to my right. Even then, while I gazed, they came up in troops, hurriedly, with ravenous eyes, allured by the scent of the meat. From this it required much effort and attention to scare them away.

It might have been half an hour, perhaps even an hour, (for in cast my I could take but imperfect note of time) before I again cast my eyes upward. What I then saw confounded and amazed me. The sweep of the pendulum had increased in extent by nearly a yard. As a natural consequence, its velocity was also much greater. But what mainly disturbed me was the idea that had perceptibly descended. I now observed—with what horror it is needless to say—that its nether extremity was formed of a crescent of glittering steel, about a foot in length from horn to horn; the horns upward, and the under edge evidently as keen as that of a razor. Like a razor also, it seemed massy and heavy, tapering from the edge into a solid and broad structure above. It was appended to a weighty rod of brass, and the whole hissed as it swung through the air.

I could no longer doubt the doom prepared for me by monkish ingenuity in torture. My cognizance of the pit had become known to the inquisitorial agents—the pit whose horrors had been destined for so bold a recusant as myself—the pit, typical of hell, and regarded by rumor as the Ultima Thule of all their punishments. The plunge into this pit I had avoided by the merest of accidents, I knew that surprise, or entrapment into torment, formed an important portion of all the grotesquerie of these dungeon deaths. Having failed to fall, it was no part of the demon plan to hurl me into the abyss; and thus (there being no alternative) a different and a milder destruction awaited me. Milder! I half smiled in my agony as I thought of such application of such a term.

What boots it to tell of the long, long hours of horror more than mortal, during which I counted the rushing vibrations of the steel! Inch by inch—line by line—with a descent only appreciable at intervals that seemed ages—down and still down it came! Days passed—it might have been that many days passed—ere it swept so closely over me as to fan me with its acrid breath. The odor of the sharp steel forced itself into my nostrils. I prayed—I wearied heaven with my prayer for its more speedy descent. I grew frantically mad, and struggled to force myself upward against the sweep of the fearful scimitar. And then I fell suddenly calm, and lay smiling at the glittering death, as a child at some rare bauble.

There was another interval of utter insensibility; it was brief; for, upon again lapsing into life there had been no perceptible descent in the pendulum. But it might have been long; for I knew there were demons who took note of my swoon, and who could have arrested the vibration at pleasure. Upon my recovery, too, I felt very—oh, inexpressibly sick and weak, as if through long inanition. Even amid the agonies of that period, the human nature craved food. With painful effort I outstretched my left arm as far as my bonds permitted, and took possession of the small remnant which had been spared me by the rats. As I put a portion of it within my lips, there rushed to my mind a half formed thought of joy—of hope. Yet what business had I with hope? It was, as I say, a half formed thought—man has many such which are never completed. I felt that it was of joy—of hope; but felt also that it had perished in its formation. In vain I struggled to perfect—to regain it. Long suffering had nearly annihilated all my ordinary powers of mind. I was an imbecile—an idiot.

The vibration of the pendulum was at right angles to my length. I saw that the crescent was designed to cross the region of the heart. It would fray the serge of my robe—it would return and repeat its operations—again—and again. Notwithstanding terrifically wide sweep (some thirty feet or more) and the hissing vigor of its descent, sufficient to sunder these very walls of iron, still the fraying of my robe would be all that, for several minutes, it would accomplish. And at this thought I paused. I dared not go farther than this reflection. I dwelt upon it with a pertinacity of attention—as if, in so dwelling, I could arrest here the descent of the steel. I forced myself to ponder upon the sound of the crescent as it should pass across the garment—upon the peculiar thrilling sensation which the friction of cloth produces on the nerves. I pondered upon all this frivolity until my teeth were on edge.

Down—steadily down it crept. I took a frenzied pleasure in contrasting its downward with its lateral velocity. To the right—to the left—far and wide—with the shriek of a damned spirit; to my heart with the stealthy pace of the tiger! I alternately laughed and howled as the one or the other idea grew predominant.

Down—certainly, relentlessly down! It vibrated within three inches of my bosom! I struggled violently, furiously, to free my left arm. This was free only from the elbow to the hand. I could reach the latter, from the platter beside me, to my mouth, with great effort, but no farther. Could I have broken the fastenings above the elbow, I would have seized and attempted to arrest the pendulum. I might as well have attempted to arrest an avalanche!

Down—still unceasingly—still inevitably down! I gasped and struggled at each vibration. I shrunk convulsively at its every sweep. My eyes followed its outward or upward whirls with the eagerness of the most unmeaning despair; they closed themselves spasmodically at the descent, although death would have been a relief, oh! how unspeakable! Still I quivered in every nerve to think how slight a sinking of the machinery would precipitate that keen, glistening axe upon my bosom. It was hope that prompted the nerve to quiver—the frame to shrink. It was hope—the hope that triumphs on the rack—that whispers to the death-condemned even in the dungeons of the Inquisition.

I saw that some ten or twelve vibrations would bring the steel in actual contact with my robe, and with this observation there suddenly came over my spirit all the keen, collected calmness of despair. For the first time during many hours—or perhaps days—I thought. It now occurred to me that the bandage, or surcingle, which enveloped me, was unique. I was tied by no separate cord. The first stroke of the razorlike crescent athwart any portion of the band, would so detach it that it might be unwound from my person by means of my left hand. But how fearful, in that case, the proximity of the steel! The result of the slightest struggle how deadly! Was it likely, moreover, that the minions of the torturer had not foreseen and provided for this possibility! Was it probable that the bandage crossed my bosom in the track of the pendulum? Dreading to find my faint, and, as it seemed, in last hope frustrated, I so far elevated my head as to obtain a distinct view of my breast. The surcingle enveloped my limbs and body close in all directions—save in the path of the destroying crescent.

Scarcely had I dropped my head back into its original position, when there flashed upon my mind what I cannot better describe than as the unformed half of that idea of deliverance to which I have previously alluded, and of which a moiety only floated indeterminately through my brain when I raised food to my burning lips. The whole thought was now present—feeble, scarcely sane, scarcely definite—but still entire. I proceeded at once, with the nervous energy of despair, to attempt its execution.

For many hours the immediate vicinity of the low framework upon which I lay, had been literally swarming with rats. They were wild, bold, ravenous; their red eyes glaring upon me as if they waited but for motionlessness on my part to make me their prey. 'To what food,' I thought, 'have they been accustomed in the well?'

They had devoured, in spite of all my efforts to prevent them, all but a small remnant of the contents of the dish. I had fallen into an habitual see-saw, or wave of the hand about the platter: and, at length, the unconscious uniformity of the movement deprived it of effect. In their voracity the vermin frequently fastened their sharp fangs in my fingers. With the particles of the oily and spicy viand which now remained, I thoroughly rubbed the bandage wherever I could reach it; then, raising my hand from the floor, I lay breathlessly still.

At first the ravenous animals were startled and terrified at the change—at the cessation of movement. They shrank alarmedly back; many sought the well. But this was only for a moment. I had not counted in vain upon their voracity. Observing that I remained without motion, one or two of the boldest leaped upon the frame-work, and smelt at the surcingle. This seemed the signal for a general rush. Forth from the well they hurried in fresh troops. They clung to the wood—they overran it, and leaped in hundreds upon my person. The measured movement of the pendulum disturbed them not at all. Avoiding its strokes they busied themselves with the anointed bandage. They pressed—they swarmed upon me in ever accumulating heaps. They writhed upon my throat; their cold lips sought my own; I was half stifled by their thronging pressure; disgust, for which the world has no name, swelled my bosom, and chilled, with a heavy clamminess, my heart. Yet one minute, and I felt that the struggle would be over. Plainly I perceived the loosening of the bandage. I knew that in more than one place it must be already severed. With a more than human resolution I lay still.

Nor had I erred in my calculations—nor had I endured in vain. I at length felt that I was free. The surcingle hung in ribands from my body. But the stroke of the pendulum already pressed upon my bosom. It had divided the serge of the robe. It had cut through the linen beneath. Twice again it swung, and a sharp sense of pain shot through every nerve. But the moment of escape had arrived. At a wave of my hand my deliverers hurried tumultuously away. With a steady movement—cautious, sidelong, shrinking, and slow—I slid from the embrace of the bandage and beyond the reach of the scimitar. For the moment, at least, I was free.

Free!—and in the grasp of the Inquisition! I had scarcely stepped from my wooden bed of horror upon the stone floor of the prison, when the motion of the hellish machine ceased and I beheld it drawn up, by some invisible force, through the ceiling. This was a lesson which I took desperately to heart. My every motion was undoubtedly watched. Free!—I had but escaped death in one form of agony, to be delivered unto worse than death in some other. With that thought I rolled my eves nervously around on the barriers of iron that hemmed me in. Something unusual—some change which, at first, I could not appreciate distinctly—it was obvious, had taken place in the apartment. For many minutes of a dreamy and trembling abstraction, I busied myself in vain, unconnected conjecture. During this period, I became aware, for the first time, of the origin of the sulphurous light which illumined the cell. It proceeded from a fissure, about half an inch in width, extending entirely around the prison at the base of the walls, which thus appeared, and were, completely separated from the floor. I endeavored, but of course in vain, to look through the aperture.

As I arose from the attempt, the mystery of the alteration in the chamber broke at once upon my understanding. I have observed that, although the outlines of the figures upon the walls were sufficiently distinct, yet the colors seemed blurred and indefinite. These colors had now assumed, and were momentarily assuming, a startling and most intense brilliancy, that gave to the spectral and fiendish portraitures an aspect that might have thrilled even firmer nerves than my own. Demon eyes, of a wild and ghastly vivacity, glared upon me in a thousand directions, where none had been visible before, and gleamed with the lurid lustre of a fire that I could not force my imagination to regard as unreal.

Unreal!—Even while I breathed there came to my nostrils the breath of the vapour of heated iron! A suffocating odour pervaded the prison! A deeper glow settled each moment in the eyes that glared at my agonies! A richer tint of crimson diffused itself over the pictured horrors of blood. I panted! I gasped for breath! There could be no doubt of the design of my tormentors—oh! most unrelenting! oh! most demoniac of men! I shrank from the glowing metal to the centre of the cell. Amid the thought of the fiery destruction that impended, the idea of the coolness of the well came over my soul like balm. I rushed to its deadly brink. I threw my straining vision below. The glare from the enkindled roof illumined its inmost recesses. Yet, for a wild moment, did my spirit refuse to comprehend the meaning of what I saw. At length it forced—it wrestled its way into my soul—it burned itself in upon my shuddering reason.—Oh! for a voice to speak!—oh! horror!—oh! any horror but this! With a shriek, I rushed from the margin, and buried my face in my hands—weeping bitterly.

The heat rapidly increased, and once again I looked up, shuddering as with a fit of the ague. There had been a second change in the cell—and now the change was obviously in the form. As before, it was in vain that I, at first, endeavoured to appreciate or understand what was taking place. But not long was I left in doubt. The Inquisitorial vengeance had been hurried by my two-fold escape, and there was to be no more dallying with the King of Terrors. The room had been square. I saw that two of its iron angles were now acute—two, consequently, obtuse. The fearful difference quickly increased with a low rumbling or moaning sound. In an instant the apartment had shifted its form into that of a lozenge. But the alteration stopped not here—I neither hoped nor desired it to stop. I could have clasped the red walls to my bosom as a garment of eternal peace. 'Death,' I said, 'any death but that of the pit!' Fool! might I have not known that into the pit it was the object of the burning iron to urge me? Could I resist its glow? or, if even that, could I withstand its pressure And now, flatter and flatter grew the lozenge, with a rapidity that left me no time for contemplation. Its centre, and of course, its greatest width, came just over the yawning gulf. I shrank back—but the closing walls pressed me resistlessly onward. At length for my seared and writhing body there was no longer an inch of foothold on the firm floor of the prison. I struggled no more, but the agony of my soul found vent in one loud, long, and final scream of despair. I felt that I tottered upon the brink—I averted my eyes—

There was a discordant hum of human voices! There was a loud blast as of many trumpets! There was a harsh grating as of a thousand thunders! The fiery walls rushed back! An outstretched arm caught my own as I fell, fainting, into the abyss. It was that of General Lasalle. The French army had entered Toledo. The Inquisition was in the hands of its enemies.

20

TO BUILD A FIRE

Jack London

Day had broken cold and gray when the man turned aside from the main Yukon trail. He climbed the high earth-bank where a little-traveled trail led east through the pine forest.

It was a high bank, and he paused to breathe at the top. He excused the act to himself by looking at his watch. It was nine o'clock in the morning. There was no sun or promise of sun, although there was not a cloud in the sky. It was a clear day. However, there seemed to be an indescribable darkness over the face of things. That was because the sun was absent from the sky. This fact did not worry the man. He was not alarmed by the lack of sun. It had been days since he had seen the sun.

The man looked along the way he had come. The Yukon lay a mile wide and hidden under three feet of ice. On top of this ice were as many feet of snow. It was all pure white. North and south, as far as his eye could see, it was unbroken white. The one thing that relieved the whiteness was a thin dark line that curved from the pine-covered island to the south. It curved into the north, where it disappeared behind another pine-covered island. This dark line was the trail—the main trail. It led south 500 miles to the Chilcoot Pass, and salt water. It led north 75 miles to Dawson, and still farther on to the north a thousand miles to Nulato, and finally to St. Michael, on Bering Sea, a thousand miles and half a thousand more. But all this—the distant trail, no sun in the sky, the great cold, and the strangeness of it all—had no effect on the man. It was not because he was long familiar with it. He was a newcomer in the land, and this was his first winter.

The trouble with him was that he was not able to imagine.

He was quick and ready in the things of life, but only in the things, and not in their meanings. Fifty degrees below zero meant 80 degrees of frost. Such facts told him that it was cold and uncomfortable, and that was all. It did not lead him to consider his weaknesses as a creature affected by temperature. Nor did he think about man's general weakness, able to live only within narrow limits of heat and cold. From there, it did not lead him to thoughts of heaven and the meaning of a man's life. 50 degrees below zero meant a bite of frost that hurt and that must be guarded against by the use of mittens, ear coverings, warm moccasins, and thick socks. 50 degrees below zero was to him nothing more than 50 degrees below zero. That it should be more important than that was a thought that never entered his head.

As he turned to go, he forced some water from his mouth as an experiment. There was a sudden noise that surprised him. He tried it again. And again, in the air, before they could fall to the snow, the drops of water became ice that broke with a noise. He knew that at 50 below zero water from the mouth made a noise when it hit the snow. But this had done that in the air. Undoubtedly it was colder than 50 below. But exactly how much colder he did not know. But the temperature did not matter.

He was headed for the old camp on Henderson Creek, where the boys were already. They had come across the mountain from the Indian Creek country. He had taken the long trail to look at the possibility of floating logs from the islands in the Yukon down the river when the ice melted. He would be in camp by six o'clock that evening. It would be a little after dark, but the boys would be there, a fire would be burning, and a hot supper would be ready. As he thought of lunch, he pressed his hand against the package under his jacket. It was also under his shirt, wrapped in a handkerchief, and lying for warmth against the naked skin. Otherwise, the bread would freeze. He smiled contentedly to himself as he thought of those pieces of bread, each of which enclosed a generous portion of cooked meat.

He plunged among the big pine trees. The trail was not well marked here. Several inches of snow had fallen since the last sled had passed. He was glad he was without a sled. Actually, he carried nothing but the lunch wrapped in the handkerchief. He was surprised, however, at the cold. It certainly was cold, he decided, as he rubbed his nose and face with his mittened hand. He had a good growth of hair on his face, but that did not protect his nose or the upper part of his face from the frosty air.

Following at the man's heels was a big native dog. It was a wolf dog, gray-coated and not noticeably different from its brother, the wild wolf. The animal was worried by the great cold. It knew that this was no time for traveling. Its own feeling was closer to the truth than the man's judgment. In reality, it was not merely colder than 50 below zero; it was colder than 60 below, than 70 below. It was 75 below zero. Because the freezing point is 32 above zero, it meant that there were 107 degrees of frost.

The dog did not know anything about temperatures. Possibly in its brain there was no understanding of a condition of very cold, such as was in the man's brain. But the animal sensed the danger. Its fear made it question eagerly every movement of the man as if expecting him to go into camp or to seek shelter somewhere and build a fire. The dog had learned about fire, and it wanted fire. Otherwise, it would dig itself into the snow and find shelter from the cold air.

The frozen moistness of its breathing had settled on its fur in a fine powder of frost. The hair on the man's face was similarly frosted, but more solidly. It took the form of ice and increased with every warm, moist breath from his mouth. Also, the man had tobacco in his mouth. The ice held his lips so tightly together that he could not empty the juice from his mouth. The result was a long piece of yellow ice hanging from his lips. If he fell down it would break, like glass, into many pieces. He expected the ice formed by the tobacco juice, having been out twice before when it was very cold. But it had not been as cold as this, he knew.

He continued through the level forest for several miles. Then he went down a bank to the frozen path of a small stream. This was Henderson Creek and he knew he was ten miles from where the stream divided. He looked at his watch. It was ten o'clock. He was traveling at the rate of four miles an hour. Thus, he figured that he would arrive where the stream divided at half-past twelve. He decided he would eat his lunch when he arrived there.

The dog followed again at his heels, with its tail hanging low, as the man started to walk along the frozen stream. The old sled trail could be seen, but a dozen inches of snow covered the marks of the last sleds. In a month no man had traveled up or down that silent creek. The man went steadily ahead. He was not much of a thinker. At that moment he had nothing to think about except that he would eat lunch at the stream's divide and that at six o'clock he would be in camp with the boys. There was nobody to talk to; and, had there been, speech would not have been possible because of the ice around his mouth. Once in a while the thought repeated itself that it was very cold and that he had never experienced such cold. As he walked along he rubbed his face and nose with the back of his mittened hand. He did this without thinking, frequently changing hands. But, with all his rubbing, the instant he stopped, his face and nose became numb. His face would surely be frozen. He knew that and he was sorry that he had not worn the sort of nose guard Bud wore when it was cold. Such a guard passed across the nose and covered the entire face. But it did not matter much, he decided. What was a little frost? A bit painful, that was all. It was never serious.

Empty as the man's mind was of thoughts, he was most observant. He noticed the changes in the creek, the curves and the bends. And always he noted where he placed his feet. Once, coming around a bend, he moved suddenly to the side, like a frightened horse. He curved away from the place where he had been walking and retraced his steps several feet along the trail. He knew the creek was frozen to the bottom. No creek could contain water in that winter. But he knew also that there were streams of water that came out from the hillsides and ran along under the snow and on top of the ice of the creek. He knew that even in the coldest weather these streams were never frozen, and he also knew their danger. They hid pools of water under the snow that might be three inches deep, or three feet. Sometimes a skin of ice half an inch thick covered them, and in turn was covered by the snow. Sometimes there was both water and thin ice, and when a man broke through he could get very wet.

That was why he had jumped away so suddenly. He had felt the ice move under his feet. He had also heard the noise of the snow-covered ice skin breaking. And to get his feet wet in such a temperature meant trouble and danger. At the very least it meant delay, because he would be forced to stop and build a fire. Only under its protection could he bare his feet while he dried his socks and moccasins. He stood and studied the creek bottom and its banks. He decided that the flowing stream of water came from the right side. He thought a while, rubbing his nose and face. Then he walked to the left. He stepped carefully and tested the ice at each step. Once away from the danger, he continued at his four-mile pace.

During the next two hours he came to several similar dangers. Usually the snow above the pools had a sunken appearance. However, once again he came near to falling through the ice. Once, sensing danger, he made the dog go ahead. The dog did not want to go. It hesitated until the man pushed it forward. Then it went quickly across the white, unbroken surface. Suddenly it fell through the ice, but climbed out on the other side, which was firm. It had wet its feet and legs. Almost immediately the water on them turned to ice. The dog made quick efforts to get the ice off its legs. Then it lay down in the snow and began to bite out the ice that had formed between the toes. The animal knew enough to do this. To permit the ice to remain would mean sore feet. It did not know this. It merely obeyed the commands that arose from the deepest part of its being.

But the man knew these things, having learned them from experience. He removed the mitten from his right hand and helped the dog tear out the pieces of ice. He did not bare his fingers more than a minute, and was surprised to find that they were numb. It certainly was cold. He pulled on the mitten quickly and beat the hand across his breast. At twelve o'clock the day was at its brightest. Yet the sun did not appear in the sky. At half-past twelve, on the minute, he arrived at the divide of the creek. He was pleased at his rate of speed. If he continued, he would certainly be with the boys by six o'clock that evening. He unbuttoned his jacket and shirt and pulled forth his lunch. The action took no more than a quarter of a minute, yet in that brief moment the numbness touched his bare fingers. He did not put the mitten on, but instead, struck the fingers against his leg. Then he sat down on a snow-covered log to eat. The pain that followed the striking of his fingers against his leg ceased so quickly that he was frightened. He had not had time to take a bite of his lunch. He struck the fingers repeatedly and returned them to the mitten. Then he bared the other hand for the purpose of eating. He tried to take a mouthful, but the ice around his mouth prevented him.

Then he knew what was wrong. He had forgotten to build a fire and warm himself. He laughed at his own foolishness. As he laughed, he noted the numbness in his bare fingers. Also, he noted that the feeling which had first come to his toes when he sat down was already passing away. He wondered whether the toes were warm or whether they were numb. He moved them inside the moccasins and decided that they were numb.

He pulled the mitten on hurriedly and stood up. He was somewhat frightened. He stamped forcefully until the feeling returned to his feet. It certainly was cold, was his thought. That man from Sulphur Creek had spoken the truth when telling how cold it sometimes got in this country. And he had laughed at him at the time! That showed one must not be too sure of things. There was no mistake about it, it was cold. He walked a few steps, stamping his feet and waving his arms, until reassured by the returning warmth. Then he took some matches and proceeded to make a fire. In the bushes, the high water had left a supply of sticks. From here he got wood for his fire. Working carefully from a small beginning, he soon had a roaring fire. Bending over the fire, he first melted the ice from his face. With the protection of the fire's warmth he ate his lunch. For the moment, the cold had been forced away. The dog took comfort in the fire, lying at full length close enough for warmth and far enough away to escape being burned. When the man had finished eating, he filled his pipe with tobacco and had a comfortable time with a smoke. Then he pulled on his mittens, settled his cap firmly about his ears, and started along the creek trail toward the left.

The dog was sorry to leave and looked toward the fire. This man did not know cold. Possibly none of his ancestors had known cold, real cold. But the dog knew and all of its family knew. And it knew that it was not good to walk outside in such fearful cold. It was the time to lie in a hole in the snow and to wait for this awful cold to stop. There was no real bond between the dog and the man. The one was the slave of the other. The dog made no effort to indicate its fears to the man. It was not concerned with the well-being of the man. It was for its own sake that it looked toward the fire. But the man whistled, and spoke to it with the sound of the whip in his voice. So the dog started walking close to the man's heels and followed him along the trail.

The man put more tobacco in his mouth and started a new growth of yellow ice on his face. Again his moist breath quickly powdered the hair on his face with white. He looked around him. There did not seem to be so many pools of water under the snow on the left side of Henderson Creek, and for half an hour the man saw no signs of any. And then it happened. At a place where there were no signs, the man broke through. It was not deep. He was wet to the knees before he got out of the water to the firm snow.

He was angry and cursed his luck aloud. He had hoped

to get into camp with the boys at six o'clock, and this would delay him an hour. Now he would have to build a fire and dry his moccasins and socks. This was most important at that low temperature. He knew that much. So he turned aside to the bank, which he climbed. On top, under several small pine trees, he found some firewood which had been carried there by the high water of last year. There were some sticks, but also larger branches, and some dry grasses. He threw several large branches on top of the snow. This served for a foundation and prevented the young flame from dying in the wet snow. He made a flame by touching a match to a small piece of tree bark that he took from his pocket. This burned even better than paper. Placing it on the foundation, he fed the young flame with pieces of dry grass and with the smallest dry sticks.

He worked slowly and carefully, realizing his danger. Gradually, as the flame grew stronger, he increased the size of the sticks with which he fed it. He sat in the snow, pulling the sticks from the bushes under the trees and feeding them directly to the flame. He knew he must not fail. When it is 75 below zero, a man must not fail in his first attempt to build a fire. This is especially true if his feet are wet. If his feet are dry, and he fails, he can run along the trail for half a mile to keep his blood moving. But the blood in wet and freezing feet cannot be kept moving by running when it is 75 degrees below. No matter how fast he runs, the wet feet will freeze even harder.

All this the man knew. The old man on Sulphur Creek had told him about it, and now he was grateful for the advice. Already all feeling had gone from his feet. To build the fire he had been forced to remove his mittens, and the fingers had quickly become numb. His pace of four miles an hour had kept his heart pushing the blood to all parts of his body. But the instant he stopped, the action of the heart slowed down. He now received the full force of the cold. The blood of his body drew back from it. The blood was alive, like the dog. Like the dog, it wanted to hide and seek cover, away from the fearful cold. As long as he walked four miles an hour, the blood rose to the surface. But now it sank down into the lowest depths of his body. His feet and hands were the first to feel its absence. His wet feet froze first. His bare fingers were numb, although they had not yet begun to freeze. Nose and face were already freezing, while the skin of all his body became cold as it lost its blood.

But he was safe. Toes and nose and face would be only touched by the frost, because the fire was beginning to burn with strength. He was feeding it with sticks the size of his finger. In another minute he would be able to feed it with larger branches. Then he could remove his wet moccasins and socks. While they dried, he could keep his naked feet warm by the fire, rubbing them first with snow. The fire was a success. He was safe.

He remembered the advice of the old man on Sulphur Creek, and smiled. The man had been very serious when he said that no man should travel alone in that country after 50 below zero. Well, here he was; he had had the accident; he was alone; and he had saved himself. Those old men were rather womanish, he thought. All a man must do was to keep his head, and he was all right. Any man who was a man could travel alone. But it was surprising, the rapidity with which his face and nose were freezing. And he had not thought his fingers could lose their feeling in so short a time. Without feeling they were, because he found it very difficult to make them move together to grasp a stick. They seemed far from his body and from him. When he touched a stick, he had to look to see whether or not he was holding it. All of which mattered little. There was the fire, promising life with every dancing flame. He started to untie his moccasins. They were coated with ice. The thick socks were like iron almost to the knees. The moccasin's strings were like ropes of steel. For a moment he pulled them with his unfeeling fingers. Then, realizing the foolishness of it, he grasped his knife.

But before he could cut the strings, it happened. It was his own fault, or instead, his mistake. He should not have built the fire under the pine tree. He should have built it in an open space. But it had been easier to pull the sticks from the bushes and drop them directly on the fire. Now the tree under which he had done this carried a weight of snow on its branches. No wind had been blowing for weeks and each branch was heavy with snow. Each time he pulled a stick he shook the tree slightly. There had been just enough movement to cause the awful thing to happen. High up in the tree one branch dropped its load of snow. This fell on the branches beneath. This process continued, spreading through the whole tree. The snow fell without warning upon the man and the fire, and the fire was dead. Where it had burned was a pile of fresh snow.

The man was shocked. It was like hearing his own judgment of death. For a moment he sat and stared at the spot where the fire had been. Then he grew very calm. Perhaps the old man on Sulphur Creek was right. If he had a companion on the trail he would be in no danger now. The companion could have built the fire. Now, he must build the fire again, and this second time he must not fail. Even if he succeeded, he would be likely to lose some toes. His feet must be badly frozen by now, and there would be some time before the second fire was ready. Such were his thoughts, but he did not sit and think them. He was busy all the time they were passing through his mind. He made a new foundation for a fire, this time in the open space, where no tree would be above it. Next, he gathered dry grasses and tiny sticks. He could not bring his fingers together to pull them out of the ground, but he was able to gather them by the handful. In this way he also got many pieces that were undesirable, but it was the best he could do. He worked carefully, even collecting an armful of the larger branches to be used later when the fire gathered strength. And all the while the dog sat and watched him. There was an anxious look in its eyes, because it depended upon him as the fire provider, and the fire was slow in coming. When all was ready, the man reached in his pocket for the second piece of tree bark. He knew the bark was there, although he could not feel it with his fingers. He tried again and again, but he could not grasp it. And all the time, in his mind, he knew that each instant his feet were freezing. This thought alarmed him, but he fought against it and kept calm.

He pulled on his mittens with his teeth, and began swinging his arms. Then he beat his hands with all his strength against his sides. He did this while he was sitting down. Then he stood up to do it. All the while the dog sat in the snow, its tail curled warmly over its feet and its sharp wolf ears bent forward as it looked at the man. And the man, as he waved his arms and hands, looked with longing at the creature that was warm and secure in the covering provided by nature. After a time, he began to notice some feeling in his beaten fingers. The feeling grew stronger until it became very painful, but the man welcomed the pain. He pulled the mitten from his right hand and grasped the tree bark from his pocket. The bare fingers were quickly numb again. Next, he brought out his pack of matches. But the awful cold had already driven the life out of his fingers. In his effort to separate one match from the others, the whole pack fell in the snow. He tried to pick it out of the snow, but failed. The dead fingers could neither touch nor hold.

Now he was very careful. He drove the thought of his freezing feet, and nose, and face, from his mind. He devoted his whole soul to picking up the matches. He followed the movement of his fingers with his eyes, using his sense of sight instead of that of touch. When he saw his fingers on each side of the pack, he closed them. That is, he willed to close them, because the fingers did not obey. He put the mitten on the right hand again, and beat it fiercely against his knee. Then, with both mittened hands, he lifted up the pack of matches, along with much snow, to the front of his jacket. But he had gained nothing. After some struggling he managed to get the pack between his mittened hands. In this manner he carried it to his mouth. The ice broke as he opened his mouth with a fierce effort. He used his upper teeth to rub across the pack in order to separate a single match. He succeeded in getting one, which he dropped on his jacket. His condition was no better. He could not pick up the match. Then he thought how he might do it. He picked up the match in his teeth and drew it across his leg. Twenty times he did this before he succeeded in lighting it. As it flamed he held it with his teeth to the tree bark. But the burning smell went up his nose, causing him to cough. The match fell into the snow and the flame died.

The old man on Sulphur Creek was right, he thought in the moment of controlled despair that followed. After 50 below zero, a man should travel with a companion. He beat his hands, but failed to produce any feeling in them. Suddenly he bared both hands, removing the mittens with his teeth. He caught the whole pack of matches between his hands. His arm muscles were not frozen and he was able to press the hands tightly against the matches. Then he drew the whole pack along his leg. It burst into flame, 70 matches at once!

There was no wind to blow them out. He kept his head to one side to escape the burning smell, and held the flaming pack to the tree bark. As he so held it, he noticed some feeling in his hand. His flesh was burning. He could smell it. The feeling developed into pain. He continued to endure it. He held the flame of the matches to the bark that would not light readily because his own burning hands were taking most of the flame.

Finally, when he could endure no more, he pulled his hands apart. The flaming matches fell into the snow, but the tree bark was burning. He began laying dry grasses and the tiniest sticks on the flame. He could not choose carefully because they must be pieces that could be lifted between his hands. Small pieces of green grass stayed on the sticks, and he bit them off as well as he could with his teeth. He treated the flame carefully. It meant life, and it must not cease.

The blood had left the surface of his body and he now began to shake from the cold. A large piece of a wet plant fell on the little fire. He tried to push it out with his fingers. His shaking body made him push it too far and he scattered the little fire over a wide space. He tried to push the burning grasses and sticks together again. Even with the strong effort that he made, his trembling fingers would not obey and the sticks were hopelessly scattered. Each stick smoked a little and died. The fire provider had failed. As he looked about him, his eyes noticed the dog sitting across the ruins of the fire from him. It was making uneasy movements, slightly lifting one foot and then the other.

The sight of the dog put a wild idea into his head. He remembered the story of the man, caught in a storm, who killed an animal and sheltered himself inside the dead body and thus was saved. He would kill the dog and bury his hands in the warm body until feeling returned to them. Then he could build another fire.

He spoke to the dog, calling it to him. But in his voice was a strange note of fear that frightened the animal. It had never known the man to speak in such a tone before. Something was wrong and it sensed danger. It knew not what danger, but somewhere in its brain arose a fear of the man. It flattened its ears at the sound of the man's voice; its uneasy movements and the liftings of its feet became more noticeable. But it would not come to the man. He got down on his hands and knees and went toward the dog. But this unusual position again excited fear and the animal moved away.

The man sat in the snow for a moment and struggled for calmness. Then he pulled on his mittens, using his teeth, and then stood on his feet. He glanced down to assure himself that he was really standing, because lack of feeling in his feet gave him no relation to the earth. His position, however, removed the fear from the dog's mind. When he commanded the dog with his usual voice, the dog obeyed and came to him. As it came within his reach, the man lost control. His arms stretched out to hold the dog and he experienced real surprise when he discovered that his hands could not grasp. There was neither bend nor feeling in the fingers. He had forgotten for the moment that they were frozen and that they were freezing more and more. All this happened quickly and before the animal could escape, he encircled its body with his arms. He sat down in the snow, and in this fashion held the dog, while it barked and struggled.

But it was all he could do: hold its body encircled in his arms and sit there. He realized that he could not kill the dog. There was no way to do it. With his frozen hands he could neither draw nor hold his knife. Nor could he grasp the dog around the throat. He freed it and it dashed wildly away, still barking. It stopped 40 feet away and observed him curiously, with ears sharply bent forward. The man looked down at his hands to locate them and found them hanging on the ends of his arms. He thought it curious that it was necessary to use his eyes to discover where his hands were. He began waving his arms, beating the mittened hands against his sides. He did this for five minutes. His heart produced enough blood to stop his shaking. But no feeling was created in his hands.

A certain fear of death came upon him. He realized that it was no longer a mere problem of freezing his fingers and toes, or of losing his hands and feet. Now it was a problem of life and death with the circumstances against him. The fear made him lose control of himself and he turned and ran along the creek bed on the old trail. The dog joined him and followed closely behind. The man ran blindly in fear such as he had never known in his life. Slowly, as he struggled through the snow, he began to see things again—the banks of the creek, the bare trees, and the sky. The running made him feel better. He did not shake any more.

Maybe, if he continued to run, his feet would stop freezing. Maybe if he ran far enough, he would find the camp and the boys. Without doubt, he would lose some fingers and toes and some of his face. But the boys would take care of him and save the rest of him when he got there. And at the same time, there was another thought in his mind that said he would never get to the camp and the boys. It told him that it was too many miles away, that the freezing had too great a start and that he would soon be dead. He pushed this thought to the back of his mind and refused to consider it. Sometimes it came forward and demanded to be heard. But he pushed it away and tried to think of other things. It seemed strange to him that he could run on feet so frozen that he could not feel them when they struck the earth and took the weight of his body. He seemed to be flying along above the surface and to have no connection with the earth.

His idea of running until he arrived at the camp and the boys presented one problem: he lacked the endurance. Several times he caught himself as he was falling. Finally, he dropped to the ground, unable to stop his fall. When he tried to rise, he failed. He must sit and rest, he decided. Next time he would merely walk and keep going. As he sat and regained his breath, he noted that he was feeling warm and comfortable. He was not shaking, and it even seemed that a warm glow had come to his body. And yet, when he touched his nose or face, there was no feeling. Running would not bring life to them. Nor would it help his hands and feet. Then the thought came to him that the frozen portions of his body must be increasing. He tried to keep this thought out of his mind and to forget it. He knew that such thoughts caused a feeling of fright in him and he was afraid of such feelings. But the thought returned and continued, until he could picture his body totally frozen. This was too much, and again he ran wildly along the trail. Once he slowed to a walk, but the thought that the freezing of his body was increasing made him run again.

And all the time the dog ran with him, at his heels. When he fell a second time, the dog curled its tail over its feet and sat in front of him, facing him, curiously eager. The warmth and security of the animal angered him. He cursed it until it flattened its ears. This time the shaking because of the cold began more quickly. He was losing his battle with the frost. It was moving into his body from all sides. This thought drove him forward. But he ran no more than 100 feet, when he fell head first.

It was his last moment of fear. When he had recovered his breath and his control, he sat and thought about meeting death with dignity. However, the idea did not come to him in exactly this manner. His idea was that he had been acting like a fool. He had been running around like a chicken with its head cut off. He was certain to freeze in his present circumstances, and he should accept it calmly. With this newfound peace of mind came the first sleepiness. A good idea, he thought, to sleep his way to death. Freezing was not as bad as people thought. There were many worse ways to die.

He pictured the boys finding his body the next day. Suddenly he saw himself with them, coming along the trail and looking for himself. And, still with them, he came around a turn in the trail and found himself lying in the snow. He did not belong with himself any more. Even then he was outside of himself, standing with the boys and looking at himself in the snow. It certainly was cold, was his thought. When he returned to the United States he could tell the folks what real cold was. His mind went from this to the thought of the old man of Sulphur Creek. He could see him quite clearly, warm and comfortable, and smoking a pipe.

'You were right, old fellow. You were right,' he murmured to the old man of Sulphur Creek.

Then the man dropped into what seemed to him the most comfortable and satisfying sleep he had ever known. The dog sat facing him and waiting. The brief day ended in a long evening. There were no signs of a fire to be made. Never in the dog's experience had it known a man to sit like that in the snow and make no fire. As the evening grew darker, its eager longing for the fire mastered it. With much lifting of its feet, it cried softly. Then it flattened its ears, expecting the man's curse. But the man remained silent. Later, the dog howled loudly. And still later it moved close to the man and caught the smell of death. This made the animal back away. A little longer it delayed, howling under the stars that leaped and danced and shone brightly in the cold sky. Then it turned and ran along the trail toward the camp it knew, where there were the other food providers and fire providers.

21

THE GIFT OF THE MAGI

O. Henry

One dollar and eighty-seven cents. That was all. And sixty cents of it was in pennies. Pennies saved one and two at a time by bulldozing the grocer and the vegetable man and the butcher until one's cheeks burned with the silent imputation of parsimony that such close dealing implied. Three times Della counted it. One dollar and eighty-seven cents. And the next day would be Christmas.

There was clearly nothing to do but flop down on the shabby little couch and howl. So Della did it. Which instigates the moral reflection that life is made up of sobs, sniffles, and smiles, with sniffles predominating.

While the mistress of the home is gradually subsiding from the first stage to the second, take a look at the home. A furnished flat at $8 per week. It did not exactly beggar description, but it certainly had that word on the lookout for the mendicancy squad.

In the vestibule below was a letter-box into which no letter would go, and an electric button from which no mortal finger could coax a ring. Also appertaining thereunto was a card bearing the name 'Mr. James Dillingham Young.'

The 'Dillingham' had been flung to the breeze during a former period of prosperity when its possessor was being paid $30 per week. Now, when the income was shrunk to $20, though, they were thinking seriously of contracting to a modest and unassuming D. But whenever Mr. James Dillingham Young came home and reached his flat above he was called 'Jim' and greatly hugged by Mrs. James Dillingham Young, already introduced to you as Della. Which is all very good.

Della finished her cry and attended to her cheeks with the powder rag. She stood by the window and looked out dully at a gray cat walking a gray fence in a gray backyard. To-morrow would be Christmas Day, and she had only $1.87 with which to buy Jim a present. She had been saving every penny she could for months, with this result. Twenty dollars a week doesn't go far. Expenses had been greater than she had calculated. They always are. Only $1.87 to buy a present for Jim. Her Jim. Many a happy hour she had spent planning for something nice for him. Something fine and rare and sterling—something just a little bit near to being worthy of the honor of being owned by Jim.

There was a pier-glass between the windows of the room. Perhaps you have seen a pier-glass in an $8 flat. A very thin and very agile person may, by observing his reflection in a rapid sequence of longitudinal strips, obtain a fairly accurate conception of his looks. Della, being slender, had mastered the art.

Suddenly she whirled from the window and stood before the glass. Her eyes were shining brilliantly, but her face had lost its color within twenty seconds. Rapidly she pulled down her hair and let it fall to its full length.

Now, there were two possessions of the James Dillingham Youngs in which they both took a mighty pride. One was Jim's gold watch that had been his father's and his grandfather's. The other was Della's hair. Had the queen of Sheba lived in the flat across the airshaft, Della would have let her hair hang out the window some day to dry just to depreciate Her Majesty's jewels and gifts. Had King Solomon been the janitor, with all his treasures piled up in the basement, Jim would have pulled out his watch every time he passed, just to see him pluck at his beard from envy.

So now Della's beautiful hair fell about her rippling and shining like a cascade of brown waters. It reached below her knee and made itself almost a garment for her. And then she did it up again nervously and quickly. Once she faltered for a minute and stood still while a tear or two splashed on the worn red carpet.

On went her old brown jacket; on went her old brown hat. With a whirl of skirts and with the brilliant sparkle still in her eyes, she fluttered out the door and down the stairs to the street.

Where she stopped the sign read: 'Mne. Sofronie. Hair Goods of All Kinds.' One flight up Della ran, and collected herself, panting. Madame, large, too white, chilly, hardly looked the 'Sofronie.'

'Will you buy my hair?' asked Della.

'I buy hair,' said Madame. 'Take yer hat off and let's have a sight at the looks of it.'

Down rippled the brown cascade.

'Twenty dollars,' said Madame, lifting the mass with a practiced hand.

'Give it to me quick,' said Della.

Oh, and the next two hours tripped by on rosy wings. Forget the hashed metaphor. She was ransacking the stores for Jim's present.

She found it at last. It surely had been made for Jim and no one else. There was no other like it in any of the stores, and she had turned all of them inside out. It was a platinum fob chain simple and chaste in design, properly proclaiming its value by substance alone and not by meretricious ornamentation—as all good things should do. It was even worthy of The Watch. As soon as she saw it she knew that it must be Jim's. It was like him. Quietness and value—the description applied to both. Twenty-one dollars they took from her for it, and she hurried home with the 87 cents. With that chain on his watch Jim might be properly anxious about the time in any company. Grand as the watch was, he sometimes looked at it on the sly on account of the old leather strap that he used in place of a chain.

When Della reached home her intoxication gave way a little to prudence and reason. She got out her curling irons and lighted the gas and went to work repairing the ravages made by generosity added to love. Which is always a tremendous task, dear friends—a mammoth task.

Within forty minutes her head was covered with tiny, close-lying curls that made her look wonderfully like a truant schoolboy. She looked at her reflection in the mirror long, carefully, and critically.

'If Jim doesn't kill me,' she said to herself, 'before he takes a second look at me, he'll say I look like a Coney Island chorus girl. But what could I do—oh! what could I do with a dollar and eighty seven cents?'

At 7 o'clock the coffee was made and the frying-pan was on the back of the stove hot and ready to cook the chops.

Jim was never late. Della doubled the fob chain in her hand and sat on the corner of the table near the door that he always entered. Then she heard his step on the stair away down on the first flight, and she turned white for just a moment. She had a habit for saying little silent prayer about the simplest everyday things, and now she whispered: 'Please God, make him think I am still pretty.'

The door opened and Jim stepped in and closed it. He looked thin and very serious. Poor fellow, he was only twenty-two—and to be burdened with a family! He needed a new overcoat and he was without gloves.

Jim stopped inside the door, as immovable as a setter at the scent of quail. His eyes were fixed upon Della, and there was an expression in them that she could not read, and it terrified her. It was not anger, nor surprise, nor disapproval, nor horror, nor any of the sentiments that she had been prepared for. He simply stared at her fixedly with that peculiar expression on his face.

Della wriggled off the table and went for him.

'Jim, darling,' she cried, 'don't look at me that way. I had my hair cut off and sold because I couldn't have lived through Christmas without giving you a present. It'll grow out again—you won't mind, will you? I just had to do it. My hair grows awfully fast. Say "Merry Christmas!" Jim, and let's be happy. You don't know what a nice—what a beautiful, nice gift I've got for you.'

'You've cut off your hair?' asked Jim, laboriously, as if he had not arrived at that patent fact yet even after the hardest mental labor.

'Cut it off and sold it,' said Della. 'Don't you like me just as well, anyhow? I'm me without my hair, ain't I?'

Jim looked about the room curiously.

'You say your hair is gone?' he said, with an air almost of idiocy.

'You needn't look for it,' said Della. 'It's sold, I tell you—sold and gone, too. It's Christmas Eve, boy. Be good to me, for it went for you. Maybe the hairs of my head were numbered,' she went on with sudden serious sweetness, 'but nobody could ever count my love for you. Shall I put the chops on, Jim?'

Out of his trance Jim seemed quickly to wake. He enfolded his Della. For ten seconds let us regard with discreet scrutiny some inconsequential object in the other direction. Eight dollars a week or a million a year—what is the difference? A mathematician or a wit would give you the wrong answer. The magi brought valuable gifts, but that was not among them. This dark assertion will be illuminated later on.

Jim drew a package from his overcoat pocket and threw it upon the table.

'Don't make any mistake, Dell,' he said, 'about me. I don't think there's anything in the way of a haircut or a shave or a shampoo that could make me like my girl any less. But if you'll unwrap that package you may see why you had me going a while at first.'

White fingers and nimble tore at the string and paper. And then an ecstatic scream of joy; and then, alas! a quick feminine change to hysterical tears and wails, necessitating the immediate employment of all the comforting powers of the lord of the flat.

For there lay The Combs—the set of combs, side and back, that Della had worshipped long in a Broadway window. Beautiful combs, pure tortoise shell, with jeweled rims—just the shade to wear in the beautiful vanished hair. They were expensive combs, she knew, and her heart had simply craved and yearned over them without the least hope of possession. And now, they were hers, but the tresses that should have adorned the coveted adornments were gone.

But she hugged them to her bosom, and at length she was able to look up with dim eyes and a smile and say: 'My hair grows so fast, Jim!'

And then Della leaped up like a little singed cat and cried, 'Oh, oh!'

Jim had not yet seen his beautiful present. She held it out to him eagerly upon her open palm. The dull precious metal seemed to flash with a reflection of her bright and ardent spirit.

'Isn't it a dandy, Jim? I hunted all over town to find it. You'll have to look at the time a hundred times a day now. Give me your watch. I want to see how it looks on it.'

Instead of obeying, Jim tumbled down on the couch and put his hands under the back of his head and smiled.

'Dell,' said he, 'let's put our Christmas presents away and keep 'em a while. They're too nice to use just at present. I sold the watch to get the money to buy your combs. And now suppose you put the chops on.'

The magi, as you know, were wise men—wonderfully wise men—who brought gifts to the Babe in the manger. They invented the art of giving Christmas presents. Being wise, their gifts were no doubt wise ones, possibly bearing the privilege of exchange in case of duplication. And here I have lamely related to you the uneventful chronicle of two foolish children in a flat who most unwisely sacrificed for each other the greatest treasures of their house. But in a last word to the wise of these days let it be said that of all who give gifts these two were the wisest. O all who give and receive gifts, such as they are wisest. Everywhere they are wisest. They are the magi.

22
MY FINANCIAL CAREER

Stephen Leacock

My salary had been raised to fifty dollars a month and I felt that the bank was the only place for it. So I walked in and looked round at the clerks. I had an idea that a person who was about to open an account must necessarily speak to the manager.

'Can I see the manager?' I asked the clerk and added 'alone.' I don't know why I said 'alone'.

'Certainly,' said the clerk, and brought him.

The manager was a calm, serious man. While talking to him I held my fifty-six dollars in my pocket.

'Are you the manager?' I said. God knows I didn't doubt it.

'Yes,' he said.

'Can I see you,' I asked, 'alone?' I didn't want to say 'alone' again, but without this word the question seemed useless.

'Come in here,' he said, and led the way to a private room.

'We're safe from interruption here,' he said. 'Sit down.'

We both sat down and looked at each other. I found no voice to speak.

'You're one of Pinkerton's detectives, I suppose,' he said.

The expression in my eyes had made him think that I was a detective, and he looked worried.

'To speak the truth,' I began. 'I'm not a detective at all. I've come to open an account. I intend to keep all my money in this bank.'

The manager looked serious, he felt sure now that I was a very rich man, probably a son of Baron Rothschild.

'A large account, I suppose,' he said. 'Rather a large one,' I whispered. 'I intend to place in this bank the sum of fifty-six dollars now, and fifty dollars a month regularly.'

The manager got up and opened the door. He called out to the clerk.

'Mr Montgomery,' he said loudly, 'this gentleman is opening an account. He will place fifty-six dollars in it. Good morning.'

'Good morning,' I said, standing up, and walked through a big door into a safe.

'Come out,' said the manager coldly and showed me the other way.

I went up to the clerk and pushed the money to him. My face was terribly pale.

'Here,' I said, 'put it on my account.' The sound of my voice seemed to mean, 'Let's do this painful thing while we feel that we want to do it.'

When the operation had been performed, I remembered that I hadn't left any money for present use. My idea was to draw out six dollars. Someone gave me a chequebook and someone else began telling me how to write it out. The people in the bank seemed to think that I was a man who owned millions of dollars, but was not feeling very well. I wrote something on the cheque and pushed it towards the clerk. He looked at it.

'What, are you drawing it all out again?' he asked in surprise.

Then I realized that I had written fifty-six dollars instead of six. I was too upset to think clearly now. I had a feeling that it was impossible to explain the thing. All the clerks stopped writing to look at me. One of them prepared to pay the money.

'How will you have it?' he said.

'What?'

'How will you have it?'

'Oh,' I caught his meaning and answered without even trying to think,—'in fifty-dollar notes.' He gave me a fifty-dollar note.

'And the six?' he asked coldly.

'In six-dollar notes', I said.

He gave me six dollars, and I ran out. As the big door closed behind me, I heard a sound of laughter that went up to the roof of the bank. Since then I use a bank no more. I keep my money in my pocket and my savings in silver dollars in a sock.

23

MRS. PACKLETIDE'S TIGER

Saki

It was Mrs. Packletide's pleasure and intention that she should shoot a tiger. Not that the lust to kill had suddenly descended on her, or that she felt that she would leave India safer and more wholesome than she had found it, with one fraction less of wild beast per million of inhabitants. The compelling motive for her sudden deviation towards the footsteps of Nimrod was the fact that Loona Bimberton had recently been carried eleven miles in an aeroplane by an Algerian aviator, and talked of nothing else; only a personally procured tiger-skin and a heavy harvest of Press photographs could successfully counter that sort of thing. Mrs. Packletide had already arranged in her mind the lunch she would give at her house in Curzon Street, ostensibly in Loona Bimberton's honour, with a tiger-skin rug occupying most of the foreground and all of the conversation. She had also already designed in her mind the tiger-claw broach that she was going to give Loona Bimberton on her next birthday. In a world that is supposed to be chiefly swayed by hunger and by love Mrs. Packletide was an exception; her movements and motives were largely governed by dislike of Loona Bimberton.

Circumstances proved propitious. Mrs. Packletide had offered a thousand rupees for the opportunity of shooting a tiger without over-much risk or exertion, and it so happened that a neighbouring village could boast of being the favoured rendezvous of an animal of respectable antecedents, which had been driven by the increasing infirmities of age to abandon game-killing and confine its appetite to the smaller domestic animals. The prospect of earning the thousand rupees had stimulated the sporting and commercial instinct of the villagers; children were posted night and day on the outskirts of the local jungle to head the tiger back in the unlikely event of his attempting to roam away to fresh hunting-grounds, and the cheaper kinds of goats were left about with elaborate carelessness to keep him satisfied with his present quarters. The one great anxiety was lest he should die of old age before the date appointed for the memsahib's shoot. Mothers carrying their babies home through the jungle after the day's work in the fields hushed their singing lest they might curtail the restful sleep of the venerable herd-robber.

2

The great night duly arrived, moonlit and cloudless. A platform had been constructed in a comfortable and conveniently placed tree, and thereon crouched Mrs. Packletide and her paid companion, Miss Mebbin. A goat, gifted with a particularly persistent bleat, such as even a partially deaf tiger might be reasonably expected to hear on a still night, was tethered at the correct distance. With an accurately sighted rifle and a thumb-nail pack of patience cards the sportswoman awaited the coming of the quarry.

'I suppose we are in some danger?' said Miss Mebbin.

She was not actually nervous about the wild beast, but she had a morbid dread of performing an atom more service than she had been paid for.

'Nonsense,' said Mrs. Packletide; 'it's a very old tiger. It couldn't spring up here even if it wanted to.'

'If it's an old tiger I think you ought to get it cheaper. A thousand rupees is a lot of money.'

Louisa Mebbin adopted a protective elder-sister attitude towards money in general, irrespective of nationality or denomination. Her energetic intervention had saved many a rouble from dissipating itself in tips in some Moscow hotel, and francs and centimes clung to her instinctively under circumstances which would have driven them headlong from less sympathetic hands. Her speculations as to the market depreciation of tiger remnants were cut short by the appearance on the scene of the animal itself. As soon as it caught sight of the tethered goat it lay flat on the earth, seemingly less from a desire to take advantage of all available cover than for the purpose of snatching a short rest before commencing the grand attack.

'I believe it's ill,' said Louisa Mebbin, loudly in Hindustani, for the benefit of the village headman, who was in ambush in a neighbouring tree.

'Hush!' said Mrs. Packletide, and at that moment the tiger commenced ambling towards his victim.

'Now, now!' urged Miss Mebbin with some excitement; 'if he doesn't touch the goat we needn't pay for it.' (The bait was an extra.)

3

The rifle flashed out with a loud report, and the great tawny beast sprang to one side and then rolled over in the stillness of death. In a moment a crowd of excited natives had swarmed on to the scene, and their shouting speedily carried the glad news to the village, where a thumping of tom-toms took up the chorus of triumph. And their triumph and rejoicing found a ready echo in the heart of Mrs. Packletide; already that luncheon-party in Curzon Street seemed immeasurably nearer.

It was Louisa Mebbin who drew attention to the fact that the goat was in death-throes from a mortal bullet-wound, while no trace of the rifle's deadly work could be found on the tiger. Evidently the wrong animal had been hit, and the beast of prey had succumbed to heart-failure, caused by the sudden report of the rifle, accelerated by senile decay. Mrs. Packletide was pardonably annoyed at the discovery; but, at any rate, she was the possessor of a dead tiger, and the villagers, anxious for their thousand rupees, gladly connived at the fiction that she had shot the beast. And Miss Mebbin was a paid companion. Therefore did Mrs. Packletide face the cameras with a light heart, and her pictured fame reached from the pages of the

Texas Weekly Snapshot to the illustrated Monday supplement of the Novoe Vremya. As for Loona Bimberton, she refused to look at an illustrated paper for weeks, and her letter of thanks for the gift of a tiger-claw brooch was a model of repressed emotions. The luncheon-party she declined; there are limits beyond which repressed emotions become dangerous.

From Curzon Street the tiger-skin rug travelled down to the Manor House, and was duly inspected and admired by the county, and it seemed a fitting and appropriate thing when Mrs. Packletide went to the County Costume Ball in the character of Diana. She refused to fall in, however, with Clovis's tempting suggestion of a primeval dance party, at which every one should wear the skins of beasts they had recently slain. 'I should be in rather a Baby Bunting condition,' confessed Clovis, 'with a miserable rabbit-skin or two to wrap up in, but then,' he added, with a rather malicious glance at Diana's proportions, 'my figure is quite as good as that Russian dancing boy's.'

4

'How amused every one would be if they knew what really happened,' said Louisa Mebbin a few days after the ball.

'What do you mean?' asked Mrs. Packletide quickly.

'How you shot the goat and frightened the tiger to death,' said Miss Mebbin, with her disagreeably pleasant laugh.

'No one would believe it,' said Mrs. Packletide, her face changing colour as rapidly as though it were going through a book of patterns before post-time.

'Loona Bimberton would,' said Miss Mebbin. Mrs. Packletide's face settled on an unbecoming shade of greenish white.

'You surely wouldn't give me away?' she asked.

'I've seen a week-end cottage near Darking that I should rather like to buy,' said Miss Mebbin with seeming irrelevance. 'Six hundred and eighty, freehold. Quite a bargain, only I don't happen to have the money.'

Louisa Mebbin's pretty week-end cottage, christened by her

'Les Fauves,' and gay in summer-time with its garden borders of tiger-lilies, is the wonder and admiration of her friends.

'It is a marvel how Louisa manages to do it,' is the general verdict.

Mrs. Packletide indulges in no more big-game shooting.

'The incidental expenses are so heavy,' she confides to inquiring friends.

24

HUNTER QUATERMAIN'S STORY

H. Rider Haggard

Sir Henry Curtis, as everybody acquainted with him knows, is one of the most hospitable men on earth. It was in the course of the enjoyment of his hospitality at his place in Yorkshire the other day that I heard the hunting story which I am now about to transcribe. Many of those who read it will no doubt have heard some of the strange rumours that are flying about to the effect that Sir Henry Curtis and his friend Captain Good, R.N., recently found a vast treasure of diamonds out in the heart of Africa, supposed to have been hidden by the Egyptians, or King Solomon, or some other antique people. I first saw the matter alluded to in a paragraph in one of the society papers the day before I started for Yorkshire to pay my visit to Curtis, and arrived, needless to say, burning with curiosity; for there is something very fascinating to the mind in the idea of hidden treasure. When I reached the Hall, I at once asked Curtis about it, and he did not deny the truth of the story; but on my pressing him to tell it he would not, nor would Captain Good, who was also staying in the house.

'You would not believe me if I did,' Sir Henry said, with one of the hearty laughs which seem to come right out of his great lungs. 'You must wait till Hunter Quatermain comes; he will arrive here from Africa to-night, and I am not going to say a word about the matter, or Good either, until he turns up. Quatermain was with us all through; he has known about the business for years and years, and if it had not been for him we should not have been here to-day. I am going to meet him presently.'

I could not get a word more out of him, nor could anybody

else, though we were all dying of curiosity, especially some of the ladies. I shall never forget how they looked in the drawing-room before dinner when Captain Good produced a great rough diamond, weighing fifty carats or more, and told them that he had many larger than that. If ever I saw curiosity and envy printed on fair faces, I saw them then.

It was just at this moment that the door was opened, and Mr. Allan Quatermain announced, whereupon Good put the diamond into his pocket, and sprang at a little man who limped shyly into the room, convoyed by Sir Henry Curtis himself.

'Here he is, Good, safe and sound,' said Sir Henry, gleefully. 'Ladies and gentlemen, let me introduce you to one of the oldest hunters and the very best shot in Africa, who has killed more elephants and lions than any other man alive.'

Everybody turned and stared politely at the curious-looking little lame man, and though his size was insignificant, he was quite worth staring at. He had short grizzled hair, which stood about an inch above his head like the bristles of a brush, gentle brown eyes, that seemed to notice everything, and a withered face, tanned to the colour of mahogany from exposure to the weather. He spoke, too, when he returned Good's enthusiastic greeting, with a curious little accent, which made his speech noticeable.

It so happened that I sat next to Mr. Allan Quatermain at dinner, and, of course, did my best to draw him; but he was not to be drawn. He admitted that he had recently been a long journey into the interior of Africa with Sir Henry Curtis and Captain Good, and that they had found treasure, and then politely turned the subject and began to ask me questions about England, where he had never been before—that is, since he came to years of discretion. Of course, I did not find this very interesting, and so cast about for some means to bring the conversation round again.

Now, we were dining in an oak-panelled vestibule, and on the wall opposite to me were fixed two gigantic elephant tusks, and under them a pair of buffalo horns, very rough and knotted, showing that they came off an old bull, and having the tip of one horn split and chipped. I noticed that Hunter Quatermain's eyes kept glancing at these trophies, and took an occasion to ask him if he knew anything about them.

'I ought to,' he answered, with a little laugh; 'the elephant to which those tusks belonged tore one of our party right in two about eighteen months ago, and as for the buffalo horns, they were nearly my death, and were the end of a servant of mine to whom I was much attached. I gave them to Sir Henry when he left Natal some months ago;' and Mr. Quatermain sighed and turned to answer a question from the lady whom he had taken down to dinner, and who, needless to say, was also employed in trying to pump him about the diamonds.

Indeed, all round the table there was a simmer of scarcely suppressed excitement, which, when the servants had left the room, could no longer be restrained.

'Now, Mr. Quatermain,' said the lady next him, 'we have been kept in an agony of suspense by Sir Henry and Captain Good, who have persistently refused to tell us a word of this story about the hidden treasure till you came, and we simply can bear it no longer; so, please, begin at once.'

'Yes,' said everybody, 'go on, please.'

Hunter Quatermain glanced round the table apprehensively; he did not seem to appreciate finding himself the object of so much curiosity.

'Ladies and gentlemen,' he said at last, with a shake of his grizzled head, 'I am very sorry to disappoint you, but I cannot do it. It is this way. At the request of Sir Henry and Captain Good I have written down a true and plain account of King Solomon's Mines and how we found them, so you will soon be able to learn all about that wonderful adventure for yourselves; but until then I will say nothing about it, not from any wish to disappoint your curiosity, or to make myself important, but simply because the whole story partakes so much of the marvellous, that I am afraid to tell it in a piecemeal, hasty fashion, for fear I should be set down as one of those common fellows of whom there are so many in my profession, who are not ashamed to narrate things they have not seen, and even to tell wonderful stories about wild animals they have never killed. And I think that my companions in adventure, Sir Henry Curtis and Captain Good, will bear me out in what I say.'

'Yes, Quatermain, I think you are quite right,' said Sir Henry. 'Precisely the same considerations have forced Good and myself to hold our tongues. We did not wish to be bracketed with—well, with other famous travellers.'

There was a murmur of disappointment at these announcements.

'I believe you are all hoaxing us,' said the young lady next Mr. Quatermain, rather sharply.

'Believe me,' answered the old hunter, with a quaint courtesy and a little bow of his grizzled head; 'though I have lived all my life in the wilderness, and amongst savages, I have neither the heart, nor the want of manners, to wish to deceive one so lovely.'

Whereat the young lady, who was pretty, looked appeased.

'This is very dreadful,' I broke in. 'We ask for bread and you give us a stone, Mr. Quatermain. The least that you can do is to tell us the story of the tusks opposite and the buffalo horns underneath. We won't let you off with less.'

'I am but a poor story-teller,' put in the old hunter, 'but if you will forgive my want of skill, I shall be happy to tell you, not the story of the tusks, for that is part of the history of our journey to King Solomon's Mines, but that of the buffalo horns beneath them, which is now ten years old.'

'Bravo, Quatermain!' said Sir Henry. 'We shall all be delighted. Fire away! Fill up your glass first.'

The little man did as he was bid, took a sip of claret, and began:—'About ten years ago I was hunting up in the far interior of Africa, at a place called Gatgarra, not a great way from the Chobe River. I had with me four native servants, namely, a driver and voorlooper, or leader, who were natives of Matabeleland, a Hottentot named Hans, who had once been the slave of a Transvaal Boer, and a Zulu hunter, who for five years had accompanied me upon my trips, and whose name was Mashune. Now near Gatgarra I found a fine piece of healthy, park-like country, where the grass was very good, considering the time of year; and here I made a little camp or head-quarter settlement, from whence I went expeditions on all sides in search of game, especially elephant. My luck, however, was bad; I got but little ivory. I was therefore very glad when some natives brought me news that a large herd of elephants were feeding in a valley about thirty miles away. At first I thought of trekking down to the valley, waggon and all, but gave up the idea on hearing that it was infested with the deadly "tsetse" fly, which is certain death to all animals, except men, donkeys, and wild game. So I reluctantly determined to leave the waggon in the charge of the Matabele leader and driver, and to start on a trip into the thorn country, accompanied only by the Hottentot Hans, and Mashune.

'Accordingly on the following morning we started, and on the evening of the next day reached the spot where the elephants were reported to be. But here again we were met by ill luck. That the elephants had been there was evident enough, for their spoor was plentiful, and so were other traces of their presence in the shape of mimosa trees torn out of the ground, and placed topsy-turvy on their flat crowns, in order to enable the great beasts to feed on their sweet roots; but the elephants themselves were conspicuous by their absence. They had elected to move on. This being so, there was only one thing to do, and that was to move after them, which we did, and a pretty hunt they led us. For a fortnight or more we dodged about after those elephants, coming up with them on two occasions, and a splendid herd they were—only, however, to lose them again. At length we came up with them a third time, and I managed to shoot one bull, and then they started off again, where it was useless to try and follow them. After this I gave it up in disgust, and we made the best of our way back to the camp, not in the sweetest of tempers, carrying the tusks of the elephant I had shot.

'It was on the afternoon of the fifth day of our tramp that we reached the little koppie overlooking the spot where the waggon stood, and I confess that I climbed it with a pleasurable sense of home-coming, for his waggon is the hunter's home, as much as his house is that of the civilized person. I reached the top of the koppie, and looked in the direction where the friendly white tent of the waggon should be, but there was no waggon, only a black burnt plain stretching away as far as the eye could reach. I rubbed my eyes, looked again, and made out on the spot of the camp, not my waggon, but some charred beams of wood. Half wild with grief and anxiety, followed by Hans and Mashune, I ran at full speed down the slope of the koppie, and across the space of plain below to the spring of water, where my camp had been. I was soon there, only to find that my worst suspicions were confirmed.

'The waggon and all its contents, including my spare guns and ammunition, had been destroyed by a grass fire.

'Now before I started, I had left orders with the driver to burn off the grass round the camp, in order to guard against accidents of this nature, and here was the reward of my folly: a very proper illustration of the necessity, especially where natives are concerned, of doing a thing one's self if one wants it done at all. Evidently the lazy rascals had not burnt round the waggon; most probably, indeed, they had themselves carelessly fired the tall and resinous tambouki grass near by; the wind had driven the flames on to the waggon tent, and there was quickly an end of the matter. As for the driver and leader, I know not what became of them: probably fearing my anger, they bolted, taking the oxen with them. I have never seen them from that hour to this.

'I sat down on the black veldt by the spring, and gazed at the charred axles and disselboom of my waggon, and I can assure you, ladies and gentlemen, I felt inclined to weep. As for Mashune and Hans they cursed away vigorously, one in Zulu and the other in Dutch. Ours was a pretty position. We were nearly 300 miles away from Bamangwato, the capital of Khama's country, which was the nearest spot where we could get any help, and our ammunition, spare guns, clothing, food, and everything else, were all totally destroyed. I had just what I stood in, which was a flannel shirt, a pair of "veldt-schoons," or shoes of raw hide, my eight-bore rifle, and a few cartridges. Hans and Mashune had also each a Martini rifle and some cartridges, not many. And it was with this equipment that we had to undertake a journey of 300 miles through a desolate and almost uninhabited region. I can assure you that I have rarely been in a worse position, and I have been in some queer ones. However, these things are the natural incidents of a hunter's life, and the only thing to do was to make the best of them.

'Accordingly, after passing a comfortless night by the remains of my waggon, we started next morning on our long journey towards civilization. Now if I were to set to work to tell you all the troubles and incidents of that dreadful journey I should keep you listening here till midnight; so I will, with your permission, pass on to the particular adventure of which the pair of buffalo horns opposite are the melancholy memento.

'We had been travelling for about a month, living and getting along as best we could, when one evening we camped some forty miles from Bamangwato. By this time we were indeed in a melancholy plight, footsore, half starved, and utterly worn out; and, in addition, I was suffering from a sharp attack of fever, which half blinded me and made me weak as a babe. Our ammunition, too, was exhausted; I had only one cartridge left for my eight-bore rifle, and Hans and Mashune, who were armed with Martini Henrys, had three between them. It was about an hour from sundown when we halted and lit a fire—for luckily we had still a few matches. It was a charming spot to camp, I remember. Just off the game track we were following was a little hollow, fringed about with flat-crowned mimosa trees, and at the bottom of the hollow, a spring of clear water welled up out of the earth, and formed a pool, round the edges of which grew an abundance of watercresses of an exactly similar kind to those which were handed round the table just now. Now we had no food of any kind left, having that morning devoured the last remains of a little oribé antelope, which I had shot two days previously. Accordingly Hans, who was a better shot than Mashune, took two of the three remaining Martini cartridges, and started out to see if he could not kill a buck for supper. I was too weak to go myself.

'Meanwhile Mashune employed himself in dragging together some dead boughs from the mimosa trees to make a sort of "skerm," or shelter for us to sleep in, about forty yards from the edge of the pool of water. We had been greatly troubled with lions in the course of our long tramp, and only on the previous night have very nearly been attacked by them, which made me nervous, especially in my weak state. Just as we had finished the skerm, or rather something which did duty for one, Mashune and I heard a shot apparently fired about a mile away.

'"Hark to it!" sung out Mashune in Zulu, more, I fancy, by way of keeping his spirits up than for any other reason—for he was a sort of black Mark Tapley, and very cheerful under difficulties. "Hark to the wonderful sound with which the 'Maboona' (the Boers) shook our fathers to the ground at the Battle of the Blood River. We are hungry now, my father; our stomachs are small and withered up like a dried ox's paunch, but they will soon be full of good meat. Hans is a Hottentot, and an 'umfagozan,' that is, a low fellow, but he shoots straight—ah! he certainly shoots straight. Be of a good heart, my father, there will soon be meat upon the fire, and we shall rise up men."

'And so he went on talking nonsense till I told him to stop, because he made my head ache with his empty words.

'Shortly after we heard the shot the sun sank in his red splendour, and there fell upon earth and sky the great hush of the African wilderness. The lions were not up as yet, they would probably wait for the moon, and the birds and beasts were all at rest. I cannot describe the intensity of the quiet of the night: to me in my weak state, and fretting as I was over the non-return of the Hottentot Hans, it seemed almost ominous—as though Nature were brooding over some tragedy which was being enacted in her sight.

'It was quiet—quiet as death, and lonely as the grave.

'"Mashune," I said at last, "where is Hans? my heart is heavy for him."

'"Nay, my father, I know not; mayhap he is weary, and sleeps, or mayhap he has lost his way."

'"Mashune, art thou a boy to talk folly to me?" I answered. "Tell me, in all the years thou hast hunted by my side, didst thou ever know a Hottentot to lose his path or to sleep upon the way to camp?"

'"Nay, Macumazahn" (that, ladies, is my native name, and means the man who "gets up by night," or who "is always awake"), "I know not where he is."

'But though we talked thus, we neither of us liked to hint at what was in both our minds, namely, that misfortunate had overtaken the poor Hottentot.

'"Mashune," I said at last, "go down to the water and bring me of those green herbs that grow there. I am hungered, and must eat something."

'"Nay, my father; surely the ghosts are there; they come out of the water at night, and sit upon the banks to dry themselves. An Isanusi* told it me."

'Mashune was, I think, one of the bravest men I ever knew in the daytime, but he had a more than civilized dread of the supernatural.

'"Must I go myself, thou fool?" I said, sternly.

'"Nay, Macumazahn, if thy heart yearns for strange things like a sick woman, I go, even if the ghosts devour me."

'And accordingly he went, and soon returned with a large bundle of watercresses, of which I ate greedily.

'"Art thou not hungry?" I asked the great Zulu presently, as he sat eyeing me eating.

'"Never was I hungrier, my father."

*Isanusi, witch-finder.

'"Then eat," and I pointed to the watercresses.

'"Nay, Macumazahn, I cannot eat those herbs."

'"If thou dost not eat thou wilt starve: eat, Mashune."

'He stared at the watercresses doubtfully for a while, and at last seized a handful and crammed them into his mouth, crying out as he did so, "Oh, why was I born that I should live to feed on green weeds like an ox? Surely if my mother could have known it she would have killed me when I was born!" and so he went on lamenting between each fistful of watercresses till all were finished, when he declared that he was full indeed of stuff, but it lay very cold on his stomach, "like snow upon a mountain." At any other time I should have laughed, for it must be admitted he had a ludicrous way of putting things. Zulus do not like green food.

'Just after Mashune had finished his watercress, we heard the loud "woof! woof!" of a lion, who was evidently promenading much nearer to our little skerm than was pleasant. Indeed, on looking into the darkness and listening intently, I could hear his snoring breath, and catch the light of his great yellow eyes. We shouted loudly, and Mashune threw some sticks on the fire to frighten him, which apparently had the desired effect, for we saw no more of him for a while.

'Just after we had had this fright from the lion, the moon rose in her fullest splendour, throwing a robe of silver light over all the earth. I have rarely seen a more beautiful moonrise. I remember that sitting in the skerm I could with ease read faint pencil notes in my pocket-book. As soon as the moon was up game began to trek down to the water just below us. I could, from where I sat, see all sorts of them passing along a little ridge that ran to our right, on their way to the drinking place. Indeed, one buck—a large eland—came within twenty yards of the skerm, and stood at gaze, staring at it suspiciously, his beautiful head and twisted horns standing out clearly against the sky. I had, I recollect, every mind to have a pull at him on the chance of providing ourselves with a good supply of beef; but remembering that we had but two cartridges left, and the extreme uncertainty of a shot by moonlight, I at length decided to refrain. The eland presently moved on to the water, and a minute or two afterwards there arose a great sound of splashing, followed by the quick fall of galloping hoofs.

'"What's that, Mashune?"' I asked.

'"That dam lion; buck smell him,"' replied the Zulu in English, of which he had a very superficial knowledge.

'Scarcely were the words out of his mouth before we heard a sort of whine over the other side of the pool, which was instantly answered by a loud coughing roar close to us.

'"By Jove!" I said, "there are two of them. They have lost the buck; we must look out they don't catch us." And again we made up the fire, and shouted, with the result that the lions moved off.

'"Mashune," I said, "do you watch till the moon gets over that tree, when it will be the middle of the night. Then wake me. Watch well, now, or the lions will be picking those worthless bones of yours before you are three hours older. I must rest a little, or I shall die."'

'"Koos!" (chief), answered the Zulu. "Sleep, my father, sleep in peace; my eyes shall be open as the stars; and like the stars watch over you."'

'Although I was so weak, I could not at once follow his advice. To begin with, my head ached with fever, and I was torn with anxiety as to the fate of the Hottentot Hans; and, indeed, as to our own fate, left with sore feet, empty stomachs, and two cartridges, to find our way to Bamangwato, forty miles off. Then the mere sensation of knowing that there are one or more hungry lions prowling round you somewhere in the dark is disquieting, however well one may be used to it, and, by keeping the attention on the stretch, tends to prevent one from sleeping. In addition to all these troubles, too, I was, I remember, seized with a dreadful longing for a pipe of tobacco, whereas, under the circumstances, I might as well have longed for the moon.

'At last, however, I fell into an uneasy sleep as full of bad dreams as a prickly pear is of points, one of which, I recollect, was that I was setting my naked foot upon a cobra which rose upon its tail and hissed my name, "Macumazahn," into my ear. Indeed, the cobra hissed with such persistency that at last I roused myself.

'"*Macumazahn, nanzia, nanzia*!" (there, there!) whispered Mashune's voice into my drowsy ears. Raising myself, I opened my eyes, and I saw Mashune kneeling by my side and pointing towards the water. Following the line of his outstretched hand, my eyes fell upon a sight that made me jump, old hunter as I was even in those days. About twenty paces from the little skerm was a large ant-heap, and on the summit of the ant-heap, her four feet rather close together, so as to find standing space, stood the massive form of a big lioness. Her head was towards the skerm, and in the bright moonlight I saw her lower it and lick her paws.

'Mashune thrust the Martini rifle into my hands, whispering that it was loaded. I lifted it and covered the lioness, but found that even in that light I could not make out the foresight of the Martini. As it would be madness to fire without doing so, for the result would probably be that I should wound the lioness, if, indeed, I did not miss her altogether, I lowered the rifle; and, hastily tearing a fragment of paper from one of the leaves of my pocket-book, which I had been consulting just before I went to sleep, I proceeded to fix it on to the front sight. But all this took a little time, and before the paper was satisfactorily arranged, Mashune again gripped me by the arm, and pointed to a dark heap under the shade of a small mimosa tree which grew not more than ten paces from the skerm.

'"Well, what is it?" I whispered; "I can see nothing."

'"It is another lion," he answered.

'"Nonsense! thy heart is dead with fear, thou seest double;" and I bent forward over the edge of the surrounding fence, and stared at the heap.

'Even as I said the words, the dark mass rose and stalked out into the moonlight. It was a magnificent, black-maned lion, one of the largest I had ever seen. When he had gone two or three steps he caught sight of me, halted, and stood there gazing straight towards us;—he was so close that I could see the firelight reflected in his wicked, greenish eyes.

'"Shoot, shoot!" said Mashune. "The devil is coming—he is going to spring!"

'I raised the rifle, and got the bit of paper on the foresight, straight on to a little path of white hair just where the throat is set into the chest and shoulders. As I did so, the lion glanced back over his shoulder, as, according to my experience, a lion nearly always does before he springs. Then he dropped his body a little, and I saw his big paws spread out upon the ground as he put his weight on them to gather purchase. In haste I pressed the trigger of the Martini, and not a moment too soon; for, as I did so, he was in the act of springing. The report of the rifle rang out sharp and clear on the intense silence of the night, and in another second the great brute had landed on his head within four feet of us, and rolling over and over towards us, was sending the bushes which composed our little fence flying with convulsive strokes of his great paws. We sprang out of the other side of the "skerm," and he rolled on to it and into it and then right through the fire. Next he raised himself and sat upon his haunches like a great dog, and began to roar. Heavens! how he roared! I never heard anything like it before or since. He kept filling his lungs with air, and then emitting it in the most heart-shaking volumes of sound. Suddenly, in the middle of one of the loudest roars, he rolled over on to his side and lay still, and I knew that he was dead. A lion generally dies upon his side.

'With a sigh of relief I looked up towards his mate upon the ant-heap. She was standing there apparently petrified with astonishment, looking over her shoulder, and lashing her tail; but to our intense joy, when the dying beast ceased roaring, she turned, and, with one enormous bound, vanished into the night.

'Then we advanced cautiously towards the prostrate brute, Mashune droning an improvised Zulu song as he went, about how Macumazahn, the hunter of hunters, whose eyes are open by night as well as by day, put his hand down the lion's stomach when it came to devour him and pulled out his heart by the roots, &c., &c., by way of expressing his satisfaction, in his hyperbolical Zulu way, at the turn events had taken.

'There was no need for caution; the lion was as dead as though he had already been stuffed with straw. The Martini bullet had entered within an inch of the white spot I had aimed at, and travelled right through him, passing out at the right buttock, near the root of the tail. The Martini has wonderful driving power, though the shock it gives to the system is, comparatively speaking, slight, owing to the smallness of the hole it makes. But fortunately the lion is an easy beast to kill.

'I passed the rest of that night in a profound slumber, my head reposing upon the deceased lion's flank, a position that had, I thought, a beautiful touch of irony about it, though the smell of his singed hair was disagreeable. When I woke again the faint primrose lights of dawn were flushing in the eastern sky. For a moment I could not understand the chill sense of anxiety that lay like a lump of ice at my heart, till the feel and smell of the skin of the dead lion beneath my head recalled the circumstances in which we were placed. I rose, and eagerly looked round to see if I could discover any signs of Hans, who, if he had escaped accident, would surely return to us at dawn, but there were none. Then hope grew faint, and I felt that it was not well with the poor fellow. Setting Mashune to build up the fire I hastily removed the hide from the flank of the lion, which was indeed a splendid beast, and cutting off some lumps of flesh, we toasted and ate them greedily. Lions' flesh, strange as it may seem, is very good eating, and tastes more like veal than anything else.

'By the time we had finished our much-needed meal the sun was getting up, and after a drink of water and a wash at the pool, we started to try and find Hans, leaving the dead lion to the tender mercies of the hyænas. Both Mashune and myself were, by constant practice, pretty good hands at tracking, and we had not much difficulty in following the Hottentot's spoor, faint as it was. We had gone on in this way for half-an-hour or so, and were, perhaps, a mile or more from the site of our camping-place, when we discovered the spoor of a solitary bull buffalo mixed up with the spoor of Hans, and were able, from various indications, to make out that he had been tracking the buffalo. At length we reached a little glade in which there grew a stunted old mimosa thorn, with a peculiar and overhanging formation of root, under which a porcupine, or an ant-bear, or some such animal, had hollowed out a wide-lipped hole. About ten or fifteen paces from this thorn-tree there was a thick patch of bush.

'"See, Macumazahn! see!" said Mashune, excitedly, as we drew near the thorn; "the buffalo has charged him. Look, here he stood to fire at him; see how firmly he planted his feet upon the earth; there is the mark of his crooked toe (Hans had one bent toe). Look! here the bull came like a boulder down the hill, his hoofs turning up the earth like a hoe. Hans had hit him: he bled as he came; there are the blood spots. It is all written down there, my father—there upon the earth."

'"Yes," I said; "yes; *but where is Hans*?"

'Even as I said it Mashune clutched my arm, and pointed to the stunted thorn just by us. Even now, gentlemen, it makes me feel sick when I think of what I saw.

'For fixed in a stout fork of the tree some eight feet from the ground was Hans himself, or rather his dead body, evidently tossed there by the furious buffalo. One leg was twisted round the fork, probably in a dying convulsion. In the side, just beneath the ribs, was a great hole, from which the entrails protruded. But this was not all. The other leg hung down to within five feet of the ground. The skin and most of the flesh were gone from it. For a moment we stood aghast, and gazed at this horrifying sight. Then I understood what had happened. The buffalo, with that devilish cruelty which distinguishes the animal, had, after his enemy was dead, stood underneath his body, and licked the flesh off the pendant leg with his file-like tongue. I had heard of such a thing before, but had always treated the stories as hunters' yarns; but I had no doubt about it now. Poor Hans' skeleton foot and ankle were an ample proof.

'We stood aghast under the tree, and stared and stared at this awful sight, when suddenly our cogitations were interrupted in a painful manner. The thick bush about fifteen paces off burst asunder with a crashing sound, and uttering a series of ferocious pig-like grunts, the bull buffalo himself came charging out straight at us. Even as he came I saw the blood mark on his side where poor Hans' bullet had struck him, and also, as is often the case with particularly savage buffaloes, that his flanks had recently been terribly torn in an encounter with a lion.

'On he came, his head well up (a buffalo does not generally lower his head till he does so to strike); those great black horns—as I look at them before me, gentlemen, I seem to see them come charging at me as I did ten years ago, silhouetted against the green bush behind;—on, on!

'With a shout Mashune bolted off sideways towards the bush. I had instinctively lifted my eight-bore, which I had in my hand. It would have been useless to fire at the buffalo's head, for the dense horns must have turned the bullet; but as Mashune bolted, the bull slewed a little, with the momentary idea of following him, and as this gave me a ghost of a chance, I let drive my only cartridge at his shoulder. The bullet struck the shoulder-blade and smashed it up, and then travelled on under the skin into his flank; but it did not stop him, though for a second he staggered.

'Throwing myself on to the ground with the energy of despair, I rolled under the shelter of the projecting root of the thorn, crushing myself as far into the mouth of the ant-bear hole as I could. In a single instant the buffalo was after me. Kneeling down on his uninjured knee—for one leg, that of which I had broken the shoulder, was swinging helplessly to and fro—he set to work to try and hook me out of the hole with his crooked horn. At first he struck at me furiously, and it was one of the blows against the base of the tree which splintered the tip of the horn in the way that you see. Then he grew more cunning, and pushed his head as far under the root as possible, made long semicircular sweeps at me, grunting furiously, and blowing saliva and hot steamy breath all over me. I was just out of reach of the horn, though every stroke, by widening the hole and making more room for his head, brought it closer to me, but every now and again I received heavy blows in the ribs from his muzzle. Feeling that I was being knocked silly, I made an effort and seizing his rough tongue, which was hanging from his jaws, I twisted it with all my force. The great brute bellowed with pain and fury, and jerked himself backwards so strongly, that he dragged me some inches further from the mouth of the hole, and again made a sweep at me, catching me this time round the shoulder-joint in the hook of his horn.

'I felt that it was all up now, and began to holloa.

'"He has got me!" I shouted in mortal terror. "*Gwasa, Mashune, gwasa*!" ("Stab, Mashune, stab!").

'One hoist of the great head, and out of the hole I came like a periwinkle out of his shell. But even as I did so, I caught sight of Mashune's stalwart form advancing with his "bangwan," or broad stabbing assegai, raised above his head. In another quarter of a second I had fallen from the horn, and heard the blow of the spear, followed by the indescribable sound of steel shearing its way through flesh. I had fallen on my back, and, looking up, I saw that the gallant Mashune had driven the assegai a foot or more into the carcass of the buffalo, and was turning to fly.

'Alas! it was too late. Bellowing madly, and spouting blood from mouth and nostrils, the devilish brute was on him, and had thrown him up like a feather, and then gored him twice as he lay. I struggled up with some wild idea of affording help, but before I had gone a step the buffalo gave one long sighing bellow, and rolled over dead by the side of his victim.

'Mashune was still living, but a single glance at him told me that his hour had come. The buffalo's horn had driven a great hole in his right lung, and inflicted other injuries.

'I knelt down beside him in the uttermost distress, and took his hand.

'"Is he dead, Macumazahn?" he whispered. "My eyes are blind; I cannot see."

'"Yes, he is dead."

'"Did the black devil hurt thee, Macumazahn?"

'"No, my poor fellow, I am not much hurt."

'"Ow! I am glad."

'Then came a long silence, broken only by the sound of the air whistling through the hole in his lung as he breathed.

'"Macumazahn, art thou there? I cannot feel thee."

'"I am here, Mashune."

'"I die, Macumazahn—the world flies round and round. I go—I go out into the dark! Surely, my father, at times in days to come—thou wilt think of Mashune who stood by thy side—when thou killest elephants, as we used—as we used—"

'They were his last words, his brave spirit passed with him. I dragged his body to the hole under the tree, and pushed it in, placing his broad assegai by him, according to the custom of his people, that he might not go defenceless on his long journey; and then, ladies—I am not ashamed to confess—I stood alone there before it, and wept like a woman.'

25

THE NECKLACE

Guy de Maupassant

She was one of those pretty and charming girls born, as though fate had blundered over her, into a family of artisans. She had no marriage portion, no expectations, no means of getting known, understood, loved, and wedded by a man of wealth and distinction; and she let herself be married off to a little clerk in the Ministry of Education. Her tastes were simple because she had never been able to afford any other, but she was as unhappy as though she had married beneath her; for women have no caste or class, their beauty, grace, and charm serving them for birth or family, their natural delicacy, their instinctive elegance, their nimbleness of wit, are their only mark of rank, and put the slum girl on a level with the highest lady in the land.

She suffered endlessly, feeling herself born for every delicacy and luxury. She suffered from the poorness of her house, from its mean walls, worn chairs, and ugly curtains. All these things, of which other women of her class would not even have been aware, tormented and insulted her. The sight of the little Breton girl who came to do the work in her little house aroused heart-broken regrets and hopeless dreams in her mind. She imagined silent antechambers, heavy with Oriental tapestries, lit by torches in lofty bronze sockets, with two tall footmen in knee-breeches sleeping in large arm-chairs, overcome by the heavy warmth of the stove. She imagined vast saloons hung with antique silks, exquisite pieces of furniture supporting priceless ornaments, and small, charming, perfumed rooms, created just for little parties of intimate friends, men who were famous and sought after, whose homage roused every other woman's envious longings.

When she sat down for dinner at the round table covered with a three-days-old cloth, opposite her husband, who took the cover off the soup-tureen, exclaiming delightedly: 'Aha! Scotch broth! What could be better?' she imagined delicate meals, gleaming silver, tapestries peopling the walls with folk of a past age and strange birds in faery forests; she imagined delicate food served in marvellous dishes, murmured gallantries, listened to with an inscrutable smile as one trifled with the rosy flesh of trout or wings of asparagus chicken.

She had no clothes, no jewels, nothing. And these were the only things she loved; she felt that she was made for them. She had longed so eagerly to charm, to be desired, to be wildly attractive and sought after.

She had a rich friend, an old school friend whom she refused to visit, because she suffered so keenly when she returned home. She would weep whole days, with grief, regret, despair, and misery.

One evening her husband came home with an exultant air, holding a large envelope in his hand.

'Here's something for you,' he said.

Swiftly she tore the paper and drew out a printed card on which were these words:

'The Minister of Education and Madame Ramponneau request the pleasure of the company of Monsieur and Madame Loisel at the Ministry on the evening of Monday, January the 18th.'

Instead of being delighted, as her husband hoped, she flung the invitation petulantly across the table, murmuring:

'What do you want me to do with this?'

'Why, darling, I thought you'd be pleased. You never go out, and this is a great occasion. I had tremendous trouble to get it. Every one wants one; it's very select, and very few go to the clerks. You'll see all the really big people there.'

She looked at him out of furious eyes, and said impatiently: 'And what do you suppose I am to wear at such an affair?'

He had not thought about it; he stammered:

'Why, the dress you go to the theatre in. It looks very

nice, to me...'

He stopped, stupefied and utterly at a loss when he saw that his wife was beginning to cry. Two large tears ran slowly down from the corners of her eyes towards the corners of her mouth.

'What's the matter with you? What's the matter with you?' he faltered.

But with a violent effort she overcame her grief and replied in a calm voice, wiping her wet cheeks:

'Nothing. Only I haven't a dress and so I can't go to this party. Give your invitation to some friend of yours whose wife will be turned out better than I shall.'

He was heart-broken.

'Look here, Mathilde,' he persisted. 'What would be the cost of a suitable dress, which you could use on other occasions as well, something very simple?'

She thought for several seconds, reckoning up prices and also wondering for how large a sum she could ask without bringing upon herself an immediate refusal and an exclamation of horror from the careful-minded clerk.

At last she replied with some hesitation:

'I don't know exactly, but I think I could do it on four hundred francs.'

He grew slightly pale, for this was exactly the amount he had been saving for a gun, intending to get a little shooting next summer on the plain of Nanterre with some friends who went lark-shooting there on Sundays.

Nevertheless he said: 'Very well. I'll give you four hundred francs. But try and get a really nice dress with the money.'

The day of the party drew near, and Madame Loisel seemed sad, uneasy and anxious. Her dress was ready, however. One evening her husband said to her:

'What's the matter with you? You've been very odd for the last three days.'

'I'm utterly miserable at not having any jewels, not a single stone, to wear,' she replied. 'I shall look absolutely no one. I would almost rather not go to the party.'

'Wear flowers,' he said. 'They're very smart at this time of the year. For ten francs you could get two or three gorgeous roses.'

She was not convinced.

'No...there's nothing so humiliating as looking poor in the middle of a lot of rich women.'

'How stupid you are!' exclaimed her husband. 'Go and see Madame Forestier and ask her to lend you some jewels. You know her quite well enough for that.'

She uttered a cry of delight.

'That's true. I never thought of it.'

Next day she went to see her friend and told her her trouble.

Madame Forestier went to her dressing-table, took up a large box, brought it to Madame Loisel, opened it, and said:

'Choose, my dear.'

First she saw some bracelets, then a pearl necklace, then a Venetian cross in gold and gems, of exquisite workmanship. She tried the effect of the jewels before the mirror, hesitating, unable to make up her mind to leave them, to give them up. She kept on asking:

'Haven't you anything else?'

'Yes. Look for yourself. I don't know what you would like best.'

Suddenly she discovered, in a black satin case, a superb diamond necklace; her heart began to beat covetously. Her hands trembled as she lifted it. She fastened it round her neck, upon her high dress, and remained in ecstasy at sight of herself.

Then, with hesitation, she asked in anguish:

'Could you lend me this, just this alone?'

'Yes, of course.'

She flung herself on her friend's breast, embraced her frenziedly, and went away with her treasure. The day of the party arrived. Madame Loisel was a success. She was the prettiest woman present, elegant, graceful, smiling, and quite above herself with happiness. All the men stared at her, inquired her name, and asked to be introduced to her. All the Under-Secretaries of

State were eager to waltz with her. The Minister noticed her.

She danced madly, ecstatically, drunk with pleasure, with no thought for anything, in the triumph of her beauty, in the pride of her success, in a cloud of happiness made up of this universal homage and admiration, of the desires she had aroused, of the completeness of a victory so dear to her feminine heart.

She left about four o'clock in the morning. Since midnight her husband had been dozing in a deserted little room, in company with three other men whose wives were having a good time. He threw over her shoulders the garments he had brought for them to go home in, modest everyday clothes, whose poverty clashed with the beauty of the ball-dress. She was conscious of this and was anxious to hurry away, so that she should not be noticed by the other women putting on their costly furs.

Loisel restrained her.

'Wait a little. You'll catch cold in the open. I'm going to fetch a cab.'

But she did not listen to him and rapidly descended the staircase. When they were out in the street they could not find a cab; they began to look for one, shouting at the drivers whom they saw passing in the distance.

They walked down towards the Seine, desperate and shivering. At last they found on the quay one of those old nightprowling carriages which are only to be seen in Paris after dark, as though they were ashamed of their shabbiness in the daylight.

It brought them to their door in the Rue des Martyrs, and sadly they walked up to their own apartment. It was the end, for her. As for him, he was thinking that he must be at the office at ten.

She took off the garments in which she had wrapped her shoulders, so as to see herself in all her glory before the mirror. But suddenly she uttered a cry. The necklace was no longer round her neck!

'What's the matter with you?' asked her husband, already half undressed.

She turned towards him in the utmost distress.

'I...I...I've no longer got Madame Forestier's necklace...'

He started with astonishment.

'What!...Impossible!'

They searched in the folds of her dress, in the folds of the coat, in the pockets, everywhere. They could not find it.

'Are you sure that you still had it on when you came away from the ball?' he asked.

'Yes, I touched it in the hall at the Ministry.'

'But if you had lost it in the street, we should have heard it fall.'

'Yes. Probably we should. Did you take the number of the cab?'

'No. You didn't notice it, did you?'

'No.'

They stared at one another, dumbfounded. At last Loisel put on his clothes again.

'I'll go over all the ground we walked,' he said, 'and see if I can't find it.'

And he went out. She remained in her evening clothes, lacking strength to get into bed, huddled on a chair, without volition or power of thought.

Her husband returned about seven. He had found nothing.

He went to the police station, to the newspapers, to offer a reward, to the cab companies, everywhere that a ray of hope impelled him.

She waited all day long, in the same state of bewilderment at this fearful catastrophe.

Loisel came home at night, his face lined and pale; he had discovered nothing.

'You must write to your friend,' he said, 'and tell her that you've broken the clasp of her necklace and are getting it mended. That will give us time to look about us.'

She wrote at his dictation.

By the end of a week they had lost all hope.

Loisel, who had aged five years, declared:

'We must see about replacing the diamonds.'

Next day they took the box which had held the necklace and went to the jewellers whose name was inside. He consulted his books.

'It was not I who sold this necklace, Madame; I must have merely supplied the clasp.'

Then they went from jeweller to jeweller, searching for another necklace like the first, consulting their memories, both ill with remorse and anguish of mind.

In a shop at the Palais-Royal they found a string of diamonds which seemed to them exactly like the one they were looking for. It was worth forty thousand francs. They were allowed to have it for thirty-six thousand.

They begged the jeweller not to sell it for three days. And they arranged matters on the understanding that it would be taken back for thirty-four thousand francs, if the first one were found before the end of February.

Loisel possessed eighteen thousand francs left to him by his father. He intended to borrow the rest.

He did borrow it, getting a thousand from one man, five hundred from another, five louis here, three louis there. He gave notes of hand, entered into ruinous agreements, did business with usurers and the whole tribe of money-lenders. He mortgaged the whole remaining years of his existence, risked his signature without even knowing if he could honour it, and, appalled at the agonising face of the future, at the black misery about to fall upon him, at the prospect of every possible physical privation and moral torture, he went to get the new necklace and put down upon the jeweller's counter thirty-six thousand francs.

When Madame Loisel took back the necklace to Madame Forestier, the latter said to her in a chilly voice:

'You ought to have brought it back sooner; I might have needed it.'

She did not, as her friend had feared, open the case. If she had noticed the substitution, what would she have thought? What would she have said? Would she not have taken her for a thief?

Madame Loisel came to know the ghastly life of abject poverty. From the very first she played her part heroically. This fearful debt must be paid off. She would pay it. The servant was dismissed. They changed their flat; they took a garret under the roof.

She came to know the heavy work of the house, the hateful duties of the kitchen. She washed the plates, wearing out her pink nails on the coarse pottery and the bottoms of pans. She washed the dirty linen, the shirts and dish-cloths, and hung them out to dry on a string; every morning she took the dustbin down into the street and carried up the water, stopping on each landing to get her breath. And, clad like a poor woman, she went to the fruiterer, to the grocer, to the butcher, a basket on her arm, haggling, insulted, fighting for every wretched halfpenny of her money.

Every month notes had to be paid off, others renewed, time gained.

Her husband worked in the evenings at putting straight a merchant's accounts, and often at night he did copying at twopence-halfpenny a page.

And this life lasted ten years.

At the end of ten years everything was paid off, everything, the usurer's charges and the accumulation of superimposed interest.

Madame Loisel looked old now. She had become like all the other strong, hard, coarse women of poor households. Her hair was badly done, her skirts were awry, her hands were red. She spoke in a shrill voice, and the water slopped all over the floor when she scrubbed it. But sometimes, when her husband was at the office, she sat down by the window and thought of that evening long ago, of the ball at which she had been so beautiful and so much admired.

What would have happened if she had never lost those jewels. Who knows? Who knows? How strange life is, how fickle! How little is needed to ruin or to save!

One Sunday, as she had gone for a walk along the Champs-Elysees to freshen herself after the labours of the week, she caught sight suddenly of a woman who was taking a child out for a walk. It was Madame Forestier, still young, still beautiful, still attractive.

Madame Loisel was conscious of some emotion. Should she speak to her? Yes, certainly. And now that she had paid, she would tell her all. Why not?

She went up to her.

'Good morning, Jeanne.'

The other did not recognize her, and was surprised at being thus familiarly addressed by a poor woman.

'But...Madame...,' she stammered. 'I don't know...you must be making a mistake.'

'No...I am Mathilde Loisel.'

Her friend uttered a cry.

'Oh!...my poor Mathilde, how you have changed!...'

'Yes, I've had some hard times since I saw you last; and many sorrows...and all on your account.'

'On my account!...How was that?'

'You remember the diamond necklace you lent me for the ball at the Ministry?'

'Yes. Well?'

'Well, I lost it.'

'How could you? Why, you brought it back.'

'I brought you another one just like it. And for the last ten years we have been paying for it. You realize it wasn't easy for us; we had no money...Well, it's paid for at last, and I'm glad indeed.'

Madame Forestier had halted.

'You say you bought a diamond necklace to replace mine?'

'Yes. You hadn't noticed it? They were very much alike.'

And she smiled in proud and innocent happiness.

Madame Forestier, deeply moved, took her two hands.

'Oh, my poor Mathilde! But mine was imitation. It was worth at the very most five hundred francs!...'

26

THE TELL-TALE HEART

Edgar Allan Poe

TRUE!—nervous—very, very dreadfully nervous I had been and am; but why will you say that I am mad? The disease had sharpened my senses—not destroyed—not dulled them. Above all was the sense of hearing acute. I heard all things in the heaven and in the earth. I heard many things in hell. How, then, am I mad? Hearken! and observe how healthily—how calmly I can tell you the whole story.

It is impossible to say how first the idea entered my brain; but once conceived, it haunted me day and night. Object there was none. Passion there was none. I loved the old man. He had never wronged me. He had never given me insult. For his gold I had no desire. I think it was his eye! yes, it was this! He had the eye of a vulture—a pale blue eye, with a film over it. Whenever it fell upon me, my blood ran cold; and so by degrees—very gradually—I made up my mind to take the life of the old man, and thus rid myself of the eye forever.

Now this is the point. You fancy me mad. Madmen know nothing. But you should have seen me. You should have seen how wisely I proceeded—with what caution—with what foresight—with what dissimulation I went to work! I was never kinder to the old man than during the whole week before I killed him. And every night, about midnight, I turned the latch of his door and opened it—oh so gently! And then, when I had made an opening sufficient for my head, I put in a dark lantern, all closed, closed, that no light shone out, and then I thrust in my head. Oh, you would have laughed to see how cunningly I thrust it in! I moved it slowly—very, very slowly, so that I might not disturb the old man's sleep. It took me an hour to place my whole head within the opening so far that I could see him as he lay upon his bed. Ha! would a madman have been so wise as this, And then, when my head was well in the room, I undid the lantern cautiously—oh, so cautiously—cautiously (for the hinges creaked)—I undid it just so much that a single thin ray fell upon the vulture eye. And this I did for seven long nights—every night just at midnight—but I found the eye always closed; and so it was impossible to do the work; for it was not the old man who vexed me, but his Evil Eye. And every morning, when the day broke, I went boldly into the chamber, and spoke courageously to him, calling him by name in a hearty tone, and inquiring how he has passed the night. So you see he would have been a very profound old man, indeed, to suspect that every night, just at twelve, I looked in upon him while he slept.

Upon the eighth night I was more than usually cautious in opening the door. A watch's minute hand moves more quickly than did mine. Never before that night had I felt the extent of my own powers—of my sagacity. I could scarcely contain my feelings of triumph. To think that there I was, opening the door, little by little, and he not even to dream of my secret deeds or thoughts. I fairly chuckled at the idea; and perhaps he heard me; for he moved on the bed suddenly, as if startled. Now you may think that I drew back—but no. His room was as black as pitch with the thick darkness, (for the shutters were close fastened, through fear of robbers,) and so I knew that he could not see the opening of the door, and I kept pushing it on steadily, steadily.

I had my head in, and was about to open the lantern, when my thumb slipped upon the tin fastening, and the old man sprang up in bed, crying out—'Who's there?'

I kept quite still and said nothing. For a whole hour I did not move a muscle, and in the meantime I did not hear him lie down. He was still sitting up in the bed listening;—just as I have done, night after night, hearkening to the death watches in the wall.

Presently I heard a slight groan, and I knew it was the groan of mortal terror. It was not a groan of pain or of grief—oh, no!—it was the low stifled sound that arises from the bottom of the soul when overcharged with awe. I knew the sound well. Many a night, just at midnight, when all the world slept, it has welled up from my own bosom, deepening, with its dreadful echo, the terrors that distracted me. I say I knew it well. I knew what the old man felt, and pitied him, although I chuckled at heart. I knew that he had been lying awake ever since the first slight noise, when he had turned in the bed. His fears had been ever since growing upon him. He had been trying to fancy them causeless, but could not. He had been saying to himself—'It is nothing but the wind in the chimney—it is only a mouse crossing the floor,' or 'It is merely a cricket which has made a single chirp.' Yes, he had been trying to comfort himself with these suppositions: but he had found all in vain. All in vain; because Death, in approaching him had stalked with his black shadow before him, and enveloped the victim. And it was the mournful influence of the unperceived shadow that caused him to feel—although he neither saw nor heard—to feel the presence of my head within the room.

When I had waited a long time, very patiently, without hearing him lie down, I resolved to open a little—a very, very little crevice in the lantern. So I opened it—you cannot imagine how stealthily, stealthily—until, at length a simple dim ray, like the thread of the spider, shot from out the crevice and fell full upon the vulture eye.

It was open—wide, wide open—and I grew furious as I gazed upon it. I saw it with perfect distinctness—all a dull blue, with a hideous veil over it that chilled the very marrow in my bones; but I could see nothing else of the old man's face or person: for I had directed the ray as if by instinct, precisely upon the damned spot.

And have I not told you that what you mistake for madness is but over-acuteness of the sense?—now, I say, there came to my ears a low, dull, quick sound, such as a watch makes when enveloped in cotton. I knew that sound well, too. It was the beating of the old man's heart. It increased my fury, as the beating of a drum stimulates the soldier into courage.

But even yet I refrained and kept still. I scarcely breathed. I held the lantern motionless. I tried how steadily I could maintain the ray upon the eye. Meantime the hellish tattoo of the heart increased. It grew quicker and quicker, and louder and louder every instant. The old man's terror must have been extreme! It grew louder, I say, louder every moment!—do you mark me well I have told you that I am nervous: so I am. And now at the dead hour of the night, amid the dreadful silence of that old house, so strange a noise as this excited me to uncontrollable terror. Yet, for some minutes longer I refrained and stood still. But the beating grew louder, louder! I thought the heart must burst. And now a new anxiety seized me—the sound would be heard by a neighbour! The old man's hour had come! With a loud yell, I threw open the lantern and leaped into the room. He shrieked once—once only. In an instant I dragged him to the floor, and pulled the heavy bed over him. I then smiled gaily, to find the deed so far done. But, for many minutes, the heart beat on with a muffled sound. This, however, did not vex me; it would not be heard through the wall. At length it ceased. The old man was dead. I removed the bed and examined the corpse. Yes, he was stone, stone dead. I placed my hand upon the heart and held it there many minutes. There was no pulsation. He was stone dead. His eye would trouble me no more.

If still you think me mad, you will think so no longer when I describe the wise precautions I took for the concealment of the body. The night waned, and I worked hastily, but in silence. First of all I dismembered the corpse. I cut off the head and the arms and the legs.

I then took up three planks from the flooring of the chamber, and deposited all between the scantlings. I then replaced the boards so cleverly, so cunningly, that no human eye—not even his—could have detected any thing wrong. There was nothing to wash out—no stain of any kind—no blood-spot whatever. I had been too wary for that. A tub had caught all—ha! ha!

When I had made an end of these labors, it was four o'clock—still dark as midnight. As the bell sounded the hour, there came a knocking at the street door. I went down to open it with a light heart,—for what had I now to fear? There entered three men, who introduced themselves, with perfect suavity, as officers of the police. A shriek had been heard by a neighbour during the night; suspicion of foul play had been aroused; information had been lodged at the police office, and they (the officers) had been deputed to search the premises.

I smiled,—for what had I to fear? I bade the gentlemen welcome. The shriek, I said, was my own in a dream. The old man, I mentioned, was absent in the country. I took my visitors all over the house. I bade them search—search well. I led them, at length, to his chamber. I showed them his treasures, secure, undisturbed. In the enthusiasm of my confidence, I brought chairs into the room, and desired them here to rest from their fatigues, while I myself, in the wild audacity of my perfect triumph, placed my own seat upon the very spot beneath which reposed the corpse of the victim.

The officers were satisfied. My manner had convinced them. I was singularly at ease. They sat, and while I answered cheerily, they chatted of familiar things. But, ere long, I felt myself getting pale and wished them gone. My head ached, and I fancied a ringing in my ears: but still they sat and still chatted. The ringing became more distinct:—It continued and became more distinct: I talked more freely to get rid of the feeling: but it continued and gained definiteness—until, at length, I found that the noise was not within my ears.

No doubt I now grew very pale;—but I talked more fluently, and with a heightened voice. Yet the sound increased—and what could I do? It was a low, dull, quick sound—much such a sound as a watch makes when enveloped in cotton. I gasped for breath—and yet the officers heard it not. I talked more quickly—more vehemently; but the noise steadily increased. I arose and argued about trifles, in a high key and with violent gesticulations; but the noise steadily increased. Why would they not be gone? I paced the floor to and fro with heavy strides, as if excited to fury by the observations of the men—but the noise steadily increased. Oh God! what could I do? I foamed—I raved—I swore! I swung the chair upon which I had been sitting, and grated it upon the boards, but the noise arose over all and continually increased. It grew louder—louder—louder! And still the men chatted pleasantly, and smiled. Was it possible they heard not? Almighty God!—no, no! They heard!—they suspected!—they knew!—they were making a mockery of my horror!—this I thought, and this I think. But anything was better than this agony! Anything was more tolerable than this derision! I could bear those hypocritical smiles no longer! I felt that I must scream or die! and now—again!—hark! louder! louder! louder! louder!

'Villains!' I shrieked, 'dissemble no more! I admit the deed!—tear up the planks! here, here!—It is the beating of his hideous heart!'

27

THE FIDDLER

Herman Melville

So my poem is damned, and immortal fame is not for me! I am nobody forever and ever. Intolerable fate!

Snatching my hat, I dashed down the criticism, and rushed out into Broadway, where enthusiastic throngs were crowding to a circus in a side-street near by, very recently started, and famous for a capital clown.

Presently my old friend Standard rather boisterously accosted me.

'Well met, Helmstone, my boy! Ah! what's the matter? Haven't been committing murder? Ain't flying justice? You look wild!'

'You have seen it then?' said I, of course referring to the critism.

'Oh yes; I was there at the morning performance. Great clown, I assure you. But here comes Hautboy. Hautboy—Helmstone.'

Without having time or inclination to resent so mortifying a mistake, I was instantly soothed as I gazed on the face of the new acquaintance so unceremoniously introduced. His person was short and full, with a juvenile, animated cast to it. His complexion rurally ruddy; his eye sincere, cheery, and gray. His hair alone betrayed that he was not an overgrown boy. From his hair I set him down as forty or more.

'Come, Standard,' he gleefully cried to my friend, 'are you not going to the circus? The clown is inimitable, they say. Come; Mr. Helmstone, too—come both; and circus over, we'll take a nice stew and punch at Taylor's.'

The sterling content, good humor, and extraordinary ruddy, sincere expression of this most singular new acquaintance acted upon me like magic. It seemed mere loyalty to human nature to accept an invitation from so unmistakably kind and honest a heart.

During the circus performance I kept my eye more on Hautboy than on the celebrated clown. Hautboy was the sight for me. Such genuine enjoyment as his struck me to the soul with a sense of the reality of the thing called happiness. The jokes of the clown he seemed to roll under his tongue as ripe magnum bonums. Now the foot, now the hand, was employed to attest his grateful applause. At any hit more than ordinary, he turned upon Standard and me to see if his rare pleasure was shared. In a man of forty I saw a boy of twelve; and this too without the slightest abatement of my respect. Because all was so honest and natural, every expression and attitude so graceful with genuine good-nature, that the marvelous juvenility of Hautboy assumed a sort of divine and immortal air, like that of some forever youthful god of Greece.

But much as I gazed upon Hautboy, and as much as I admired his air, yet that desperate mood in which I had first rushed from the house had not so entirely departed as not to molest me with momentary returns. But from these relapses I would rouse myself, and swiftly glance round the broad amphitheatre of eagerly interested and all-applauding human faces. Hark! claps, thumps, deafening huzzas; the vast assembly seemed frantic, with acclamation; and what, mused I, has caused all this? Why, the clown only comically grinned with one of his extra grins.

Then I repeated in my mind that sublime passage in my poem, in which Cleothemes the Argive vindicates the justice of the war. Aye, aye, thought I to myself, did I now leap into the ring there, and repeat that identical passage, nay, enact the whole tragic poem before them, would they applaud the poet as they applaud the clown? No! They would hoot me, and call me doting or mad. Then what does this prove? Your infatuation or their insensibility? Perhaps both; but indubitably the first. But why wail? Do you seek admiration from the admirers of a buffoon? Call to mind the saying of the Athenian, who when the people vociferously applauded in the forum, asked his friend in a whisper, what foolish thing had he said?

Again my eye swept the circus, and fell on the ruddy radiance of the countenance of Hautboy. But its clear honest cheeriness disdained my disdain. My intolerant pride was rebuked. And yet Hautboy dreamed not what magic reproof to a soul like mine sat on his laughing brow. At the very instant I felt the dart of the censure, his eye twinkled, his hand waved, his voice was lifted in jubilant delight at another joke of the inexhaustible clown.

Circus over, we went to Taylor's. Among crowds of others, we sat down to our stews and punches at one of the small marble tables. Hautboy sat opposite to me. Though greatly subdued from its former hilarity, his face still shone with gladness. But added to this was a quality not so prominent before: a certain serene expression of leisurely, deep good sense. Good sense and good humor in him joined hands. As the conversation proceeded between the brisk Standard and him—for I said little or nothing—I was more and more struck with the excellent judgment he evinced. In most of his remarks upon a variety of topics Hautboy seemed intuitively to hit the exact line between enthusiasm and apathy. It was plain that while Hautboy saw the world pretty much as it was, yet he did not theoretically espouse its bright side nor its dark side. Rejecting all solutions, he but acknowledged facts. What was sad in the world he did not superficially gainsay; what was glad in it he did not cynically slur; and all which was to him personally enjoyable, he gratefully took to his heart. It was plain, then—so it seemed at that moment, at least—that his extraordinary cheerfulness did not arise either from deficiency of feeling or thought.

Suddenly remembering an engagement, he took up his hat, bowed pleasantly, and left us.

'Well, Helmstone,' said Standard, inaudibly drumming on the slab, 'what do you think of your new acquaintance?'

The two last words tingled with a peculiar and novel

significance.

'New acquaintance indeed,' echoed I. 'Standard, I owe you a thousand thanks for introducing me to one of the most singular men I have ever seen. It needed the optical sight of such a man to believe in the possibility of his existence.'

'You rather like him, then,' said Standard, with ironical dryness.

'I hugely love and admire him, Standard. I wish I were Hautboy.'

'Ah? That's a pity, now. There's only one Hautboy in the world.'

This last remark set me to pondering again, and somehow it revived my dark mood.

'His wonderful cheerfulness, I suppose,' said I, sneering with spleen, 'originates not less in a felicitous fortune than in a felicitous temper. His great good sense is apparent; but great good sense may exist without sublime endowments. Nay, I take it, in certain cases, that good sense is simply owing to the absence of those. Much more, cheerfulness. Unpossessed of genius, Hautboy is eternally blessed.'

'Ah? You would not think him an extraordinary genius, then?'

'Genius? What! such a short, fat fellow a genius! Genius, like Cassius, is lank.'

'Ah? But could you not fancy that Hautboy might formerly have had genius, but luckily getting rid of it, at last fatted up?'

'For a genius to get rid of his genius is as impossible as for a man in the galloping consumption to get rid of that.'

'Ah? You speak very decidedly.'

'Yes, Standard,' cried I, increasing in spleen, 'your cheery Hautboy, after all, is no pattern, no lesson for you and me. With average abilities; opinions clear, because circumscribed; passions docile, because they are feeble; a temper hilarious, because he was born to it—how can your Hautboy be made a reasonable example to a handy fellow like you, or an ambitious dreamer like me? Nothing tempts him beyond common limit; in himself he has nothing to restrain. By constitution he is exempted from all moral harm. Could ambition but prick him; had he but once heard applause, or endured contempt, a very different man would your Hautboy be. Acquiescent and calm from the cradle to the grave, he obviously slides through the crowd.'

'Ah?'

'Why do you say Ah to me so strangely whenever I speak?'

'Did you ever hear of Master Betty?'

'The great English prodigy, who long ago ousted the Siddons and the Kembles from Drury Lane, and made the whole town run mad with acclamation?

'The same,' said Standard, once more inaudibly drumming on the slab.

I looked at him perplexed. He seemed to be holding the master-key of our theme in mysterious reserve; seemed to be throwing out his Master Betty, too, to puzzle me only the more.

'What under heaven can Master Betty, the great genius and prodigy, and English boy twelve years old, have to do with the poor commonplace plodder, Hautboy, an American of forty?'

'Oh, nothing in the least. I don't imagine that they ever saw each other. Besides, Master Betty must be dead and buried long ere this.'

'Then why cross the ocean, and rifle the grave to drag his remains into this living discussion?'

'Absent-mindedness, I suppose. I humbly beg pardon. Proceed with your observations on Hautboy. You think he never had genius, quite too contented, and happy and fat for that—ah? You think him no pattern for men in general? affording no lesson of value to neglected merit, genius ignored, or impotent presumption rebuked?—all of which three amount to much the same thing. You admire his cheerfulness, while scorning his commonplace soul. Poor Hautboy, how sad that your very cheerfulness should, by a by-blow, bring you despite!'

'I don't say I scorn him; you are unjust. I simply declare that he is no pattern for me.'

A sudden noise at my side attracted my ear. Turning, I saw Hautboy again, who very blithely reseated himself on the chair he had left.

'I was behind time with my engagement,' said Hautboy, 'so thought I would run back and rejoin you. But come, you have sat long enough here. Let us go to my rooms. It is only a five minutes' walk.'

'If you will promise to fiddle for us, we will,' said Standard.

Fiddle! thought I—he's a jiggumbob fiddler, then? No wonder genius declines to measure its pace to a fiddler's bow. My spleen was very strong on me now.

'I will gladly fiddle you your fill,' replied Hautboy to Standard. 'Come on.'

In a few minutes we found ourselves in the fifth story of a sort of storehouse, in a lateral street to Broadway. It was curiously furnished with all sorts of odd furniture which seemed to have been obtained, piece by piece, at auctions of old-fashioned household stuff. But all was charmingly clean and cozy.

Pressed by Standard, Hautboy forthwith got out his dented old fiddle and, sitting down on a tall rickety stool, played away right merrily at 'Yankee Doodle' and other off-handed, dashing, and disdainfully care-free airs. But common as were the tunes, I was transfixed by something miraculously superior in the style. Sitting there on the old stool, his rusty hat sidways cocked on his head, one foot dangling adrift, he plied the bow of an enchanter. All my moody discontent, every vestige of peevishness, fled. My whole splenetic soul capitulated to the magical fiddle.

'Something of an Orpheus, ah?' said Standard, archly nudging me beneath the left rib.

'And I, the charmed Briun,' murmured I.

The fiddle ceased. Once more, with redoubled curiosity, I gazed upon the easy, indifferent Hautboy. But he entirely baffled inquisition.

When, leaving him, Standard and I were in the street once more, I earnestly conjured him to tell me who, in sober truth, this marvelous Hautboy was.

'Why, haven't you seen him? And didn't you yourself lay his whole anatomy open on the marble slab at Taylor's? What more can you possibly learn? Doubtless, your own masterly insight has already put you in possession of all.'

'You mock me, Standard. There is some mystery here. Tell me, I entreat you, who is Hautboy?'

'An extraordinary genius, Helmstone,' said Standard, with sudden ardor, 'who in boyhood drained the whole flagon of glory; whose going from city to city was a going from triumph to triumph. One who has been an object of wonder to the wisest, been caressed by the loveliest, received the open homage of thousands on thousands of the rabble. But to-day he walks Broadway and no man knows him. With you and me, the elbow of the hurrying clerk, and the pole of the remorseless omnibus, shove him. He who has a hundred times been crowned with laurels, now wears, as you see, a bunged beaver. Once fortune poured showers of gold into his lap, as showers of laurel leaves upon his brow. To-day, from house to house he hies, teaching fiddling for a living. Crammed once with fame, he is now hilarious without it. With genius and without fame, he is happier than a king. More a prodigy now than ever.'

'His true name?'

'Let me whisper it in your ear.'

'What! Oh, Standard, myself, as a child, have shouted myself hoarse applauding that very name in the theatre.'

'I have heard your poem was not very handsomely received,' said Standard, now suddenly shifting the subject.

'Not a word of that, for Heaven's sake!' cried I. 'If Cicero, traveling in the East, found sympathetic solace for his grief in beholding the arid overthrow of a once gorgeous city, shall not my petty affair be as nothing, when I behold in Hautboy the vine and the rose climbing the shattered shafts of his tumbled temple of Fame?'

Next day I tore all my manuscripts, bought me a fiddle, and went to take regular lessons of Hautboy.

28

A HORSEMAN IN THE SKY

Ambrose Bierce

One sunny afternoon in the autumn of the year 1861 a soldier lay in clump of laurel by the side of a road in western Virginia. He lay at full length upon his stomach, his feet resting upon the toes, his head upon the left forearm. His extended right hand loosely grasped his rifle. But for the somewhat methodical disposition of his limbs and a slight rhythmic movement of the cartridge-box at the back of his belt, he might have been thought to be dead. He was asleep at his post of duty. But if detected he would be dead shortly afterward, death being the just and legal penalty of his crime.

The clump of laurel in which the criminal lay was in the angle of a road which after ascending southward a steep acclivity to that point turned sharply to the west, running along the summit for perhaps one hundred yards. There it turned southward again and went zigzagging downward through the forest. At the salient of that second angle was a large flat rock, jutting out northward, overlooking the deep valley from which the road ascended. The rock capped a high cliff; a stone dropped from its outer edge would have fallen sheer downward one thousand feet to the tops of the pines. The angle where the soldier lay was on another spur of the same cliff. Had he been awake he would have commanded a view, not only of the short arm of the road and the jutting rock, but of the entire profile of the cliff below it. It might well have made him giddy to look.

The country was wooded everywhere except at the bottom of the valley to the northward, where there was a small natural meadow, through which flowed a stream scarcely visible from the valley's rim. This open ground looked hardly larger than an ordinary door-yard, but was really several acres in extent. Its green was more vivid than that of the enclosing forest. Away beyond it rose a line of giant cliffs similar to those upon which we are supposed to stand in our survey of the savage scene, and through which the road had somehow made its climb to the summit. The configuration of the valley, indeed, was such that from our point of observation it seemed entirely shut in, and one could but have wondered how the road which found a way out of it had found a way into it, and whence came and whither went the waters of the stream that parted the meadow more than a thousand feet below.

No country is so wild and difficult but men will make it a theatre of war; concealed in the forest at the bottom of that military rat-trap, in which half a hundred men in possession of the exits might have starved an army to submission, lay five regiments of Federal infantry. They had marched all the previous day and night and were resting. At nightfall they would take to the road again, climb to the place where their unfaithful sentinel now slept, and descending the other slope of the ridge fall upon a camp of the enemy at about midnight. Their hope was to surprise it, for the road led to the rear of it. In case of failure, their position would be perilous in the extreme; and fall they surely would should accident or vigilance apprise the enemy of the movement.

The sleeping sentinel in the clump of laurel was a young Virginian named Carter Druse. He was the son of wealthy parents, an only child, and had known such ease and cultivation and high living as wealth and taste were able to command in the mountain country of western Virginia. His home was but a few miles from where he now lay. One morning he had risen from the breakfast-table and said, quietly but gravely: 'Father, a Union regiment has arrived at Grafton. I am going to join it.'

The father lifted his leonine head, looked at the son a moment in silence, and replied: 'Go, Carter, and whatever may occur, do what you conceive to be your duty. Virginia, to which you are a traitor, must get on without you. Should we both live to the end of the war, we will speak further of the matter. Your mother, as the physician has informed you, is in a most critical condition; at the best she cannot be with us longer than a few weeks, but that time is precious. It would be better not to disturb her.'

So Carter Druse, bowing reverently to his father, who returned the salute with a stately courtesy that masked a breaking heart, left the home of his childhood to go soldiering. By conscience and courage, by deeds of devotion and daring, he soon commended himself to his fellows and his officers; and it was to these qualities and to some knowledge of the country that he owed his selection for his present perilous duty at the extreme outpost. Nevertheless, fatigue had been stronger than resolution and he had fallen asleep. What good or bad angel came in a dream to rouse him from his state of crime, who shall say? Without a movement, without a sound, in the profound silence and the languor of the late afternoon, some invisible messenger of fate touched with unsealing finger the eyes of his consciousness—whispered into the ear of his spirit the mysterious awakening word which no human lips ever have spoken, no human memory ever has recalled. He quietly raised his forehead from his arm and looked between the masking stems of the laurels, instinctively closing his right hand about the stock of his rifle.

His first feeling was a keen artistic delight. On a colossal pedestal, the cliff, motionless at the extreme edge of the capping rock and sharply outlined against the sky, was an equestrian statue of impressive dignity. The figure of the man sat the figure of the horse, straight and soldierly, but with the repose of a Grecian god carved in the marble which limits the suggestion of activity. The gray costume harmonized with its aerial background; the metal of accoutrement and caparison was softened and subdued by the shadow; the animal's skin had no points of high light. A carbine strikingly foreshortened lay across the pommel of the saddle, kept in place by the right hand grasping it at the 'grip;' the left hand, holding the bridle rein, was invisible. In silhouette against the sky the profile of the horse was cut with the sharpness of a cameo; it looked across the heights of air to the confronting cliffs beyond. The face of the rider, turned slightly away, showed only an outline of temple and beard; he was looking downward to the bottom of the valley. Magnified by its lift against the sky and by the soldier's testifying sense of the formidableness of a near enemy the group appeared of heroic, almost colossal, size.

For an instant Druse had a strange, half-defined feeling that he had slept to the end of the war and was looking upon a noble work of art reared upon that eminence to commemorate the deeds of an heroic past of which he had been an inglorious part. The feeling was dispelled by a slight movement of the group: the horse, without moving its feet, had drawn its body slightly backward from the verge; the man remained immobile as before. Broad awake and keenly alive to the significance of the situation, Druse now brought the butt of his rifle against his cheek by cautiously pushing the barrel forward through the bushes, cocked the piece, and glancing through the sights covered a vital spot of the horseman's breast. A touch upon the trigger and all would have been well with Carter Druse. At that instant the horseman turned his head and looked in the direction of his concealed foeman—seemed to look into his very face, into his eyes, into his brave, compassionate heart.

Is it then so terrible to kill an enemy in war—an enemy who has surprised a secret vital to the safety of one's self and comrades—an enemy more formidable for his knowledge than all his army for its numbers? Carter Druse grew pale; he shook in every limb, turned faint, and saw the statuesque group before him as black figures, rising, falling, moving unsteadily in arcs of circles in a fiery sky. His hand fell away from his weapon, his head slowly dropped until his face rested on the leaves in which he lay. This courageous gentleman and hardy soldier was near swooning from intensity of emotion.

It was not for long; in another moment his face was raised from earth, his hands resumed their places on the rifle, his forefinger sought the trigger; mind, heart, and eyes were clear, conscience and reason sound. He could not hope to capture that enemy; to alarm him would but send him dashing to his camp with his fatal news. The duty of the soldier was plain: the man must be shot dead from ambush—without warning, without a moment's spiritual preparation, with never so much as an unspoken prayer, he must be sent to his account. But no—there is a hope; he may have discovered nothing—perhaps he is but admiring the sublimity of the landscape. If permitted, he may turn and ride carelessly away in the direction whence he came. Surely it will be possible to judge at the instant of his withdrawing whether he knows. It may well be that his fixity of attention—Druse turned his head and looked through the deeps of air downward, as from the surface to the bottom of a translucent sea. He saw creeping across the green meadow a sinuous line of figures of men and horses—some foolish commander was permitting the soldiers of his escort to water their beasts in the open, in plain view from a dozen summits!

Druse withdrew his eyes from the valley and fixed them again upon the group of man and horse in the sky, and again it was through the sights of his rifle. But this time his aim was at the horse. In his memory, as if they were a divine mandate, rang the words of his father at their parting: 'Whatever may occur, do what you conceive to be your duty.' He was calm now. His teeth were firmly but not rigidly closed; his nerves were as tranquil as a sleeping babe's—not a tremor affected any muscle of his body; his breathing, until suspended in the act of taking aim, was regular and slow. Duty had conquered; the spirit had said to the body: 'Peace, be still.' He fired.

An officer of the Federal force, who in a spirit of adventure or in quest of knowledge had left the hidden bivouac in the valley, and with aimless feet had made his way to the lower edge of a small open space near the foot of the cliff, was considering what he had to gain by pushing his exploration further. At a distance of a quarter-mile before him, but apparently at a stone's throw, rose from its fringe of pines the gigantic face of rock, towering to so great a height above him that it made him giddy to look up to where its edge cut a sharp, rugged line against the sky. It presented a clean, vertical profile against a background of blue sky to a point half the way down, and of distant hills, hardly less blue, thence to the tops of the trees at its base. Lifting his eyes to the dizzy altitude of its summit the officer saw an astonishing sight—a man on horseback riding down into the valley through the air!

Straight upright sat the rider, in military fashion, with a firm seat in the saddle, a strong clutch upon the rein to hold his charger from too impetuous a plunge. From his bare head his long hair streamed upward, waving like a plume. His hands were concealed in the cloud of the horse's lifted mane. The animal's body was as level as if every hoof-stroke encountered the resistant earth. Its motions were those of a wild gallop, but even as the officer looked they ceased, with all the legs thrown sharply forward as in the act of alighting from a leap. But this was a flight!

Filled with amazement and terror by this apparition of a horseman in the sky—half believing himself the chosen scribe of some new Apocalypse, the officer was overcome by the intensity of his emotions; his legs failed him and he fell. Almost at the same instant he heard a crashing sound in the trees—a sound that died without an echo, and all was still.

The officer rose to his feet, trembling. The familiar sensation of an abraded shin recalled his dazed faculties. Pulling himself together he ran rapidly obliquely away from the cliff to a point distant from its foot; thereabout he expected to find his man; and thereabout he naturally failed. In the fleeting instant of his vision his imagination had been so wrought upon by the apparent grace and ease and intention of the marvelous performance that it did not occur to him that the line of march of aerial cavalry is directly downward, and that he could find the objects of his search at the very foot of the cliff. A half-hour later he returned to camp.

This officer was a wise man; he knew better than to tell

an incredible truth. He said nothing of what he had seen. But when the commander asked him if in his scout he had learned anything of advantage to the expedition he answered:

'Yes, sir; there is no road leading down into this valley from the southward.'

The commander, knowing better, smiled.

After firing his shot, Private Carter Druse reloaded his rifle and resumed his watch. Ten minutes had hardly passed when a Federal sergeant crept cautiously to him on hands and knees. Druse neither turned his head nor looked at him, but lay without motion or sign of recognition.

'Did you fire?' the sergeant whispered.

'Yes.'

'At what?'

'A horse. It was standing on yonder rock—pretty far out. You see it is no longer there. It went over the cliff.'

The man's face was white, but he showed no other sign of emotion. Having answered, he turned away his eyes and said no more. The sergeant did not understand.

'See here, Druse,' he said, after a moment's silence, 'it's no use making a mystery. I order you to report. Was there anybody on the horse?'

'Yes.'

'Well?'

'My father.'

The sergeant rose to his feet and walked away. 'Good God!' he said.

29

THE BEGGING-LETTER WRITER

Charles Dickens

The amount of money he annually diverts from wholesome and useful purposes in the United Kingdom, would be a set-off against the Window Tax. He is one of the most shameless frauds and impositions of this time. In his idleness, his mendacity, and the immeasurable harm he does to the deserving, dirtying the stream of true benevolence, and muddling the brains of foolish justices, with inability to distinguish between the base coin of distress, and the true currency we have always among us,—he is more worthy of Norfolk Island than three-fourths of the worst characters who are sent there. Under any rational system, he would have been sent there long ago.

I, the writer of this paper, have been, for some time, a chosen receiver of Begging Letters. For fourteen years, my house has been made as regular a Receiving House for such communications as any one of the great branch Post-Offices is for general correspondence. I ought to know something of the Begging-Letter Writer. He has besieged my door at all hours of the day and night; he has fought my servant; he has lain in ambush for me, going out and coming in; he has followed me out of town into the country; he has appeared at provincial hotels, where I have been staying for only a few hours; he has written to me from immense distances, when I have been out of England. He has fallen sick; he has died and been buried; he has come to life again, and again departed from this transitory scene: he has been his own son, his own mother, his own baby, his idiot brother, his uncle, his aunt, his aged grandfather. He has wanted a greatcoat, to go to India in; a pound to set him up in life for ever; a pair of boots to take him to the coast of China; a hat to get him into a permanent situation under Government. He has frequently been exactly seven-and-sixpence short of independence. He has had such openings at Liverpool—posts of great trust and confidence in merchants' houses, which nothing but seven-and-sixpence was wanting to him to secure—that I wonder he is not Mayor of that flourishing town at the present moment.

The natural phenomena of which he has been the victim, are of a most astounding nature. He has had two children who have never grown up; who have never had anything to cover them at night; who have been continually driving him mad, by asking in vain for food; who have never come out of fevers and measles (which, I suppose, has accounted for his fuming his letters with tobacco smoke, as a disinfectant); who have never changed in the least degree through fourteen long revolving years. As to his wife, what that suffering woman has undergone, nobody knows. She has always been in an interesting situation through the same long period, and has never been confined yet. His devotion to her has been unceasing. He has never cared for himself; *he* could have perished—he would rather, in short—but was it not his Christian duty as a man, a husband, and a father,—to write begging letters when he looked at her? (He has usually remarked that he would call in the evening for an answer to this question.)

He has been the sport of the strangest misfortunes. What his brother has done to him would have broken anybody else's heart. His brother went into business with him, and ran away with the money; his brother got him to be security for an immense sum and left him to pay it; his brother would have given him employment to the tune of hundreds a-year, if he would have consented to write letters on a Sunday; his brother enunciated principles incompatible with his religious views, and he could not (in consequence) permit his brother to provide for him. His landlord has never shown a spark of human feeling. When he put in that execution I don't know, but he has never taken it out. The broker's man has grown grey in possession.

They will have to bury him some day.

He has been attached to every conceivable pursuit. He has been in the army, in the navy, in the church, in the law; connected with the press, the fine arts, public institutions, every description and grade of business. He has been brought up as a gentleman; he has been at every college in Oxford and Cambridge; he can quote Latin in his letters (but generally misspells some minor English word); he can tell you what Shakespeare says about begging, better than you know it. It is to be observed, that in the midst of his afflictions he always reads the newspapers; and rounds off his appeal with some allusion, that may be supposed to be in my way, to the popular subject of the hour.

His life presents a series of inconsistencies. Sometimes he has never written such a letter before. He blushes with shame. That is the first time; that shall be the last. Don't answer it, and let it be understood that, then, he will kill himself quietly. Sometimes (and more frequently) he *has* written a few such letters. Then he encloses the answers, with an intimation that they are of inestimable value to him, and a request that they may be carefully returned. He is fond of enclosing something—verses, letters, pawnbrokers' duplicates, anything to necessitate an answer. He is very severe upon 'the pampered minion of fortune,' who refused him the half-sovereign referred to in the enclosure number two—but he knows me better.

He writes in a variety of styles; sometimes in low spirits; sometimes quite jocosely. When he is in low spirits he writes down-hill and repeats words—these little indications being expressive of the perturbation of his mind. When he is more vivacious, he is frank with me; he is quite the agreeable rattle. I know what human nature is,—who better? Well! He had a little money once, and he ran through it—as many men have done before him. He finds his old friends turn away from him now—many men have done that before him too! Shall he tell me why he writes to me? Because he has no kind of claim upon me. He puts it on that ground plainly; and begs to ask for the loan (as I know human nature) of two sovereigns, to be repaid next Tuesday six weeks, before twelve at noon.

Sometimes, when he is sure that I have found him out, and that there is no chance of money, he writes to inform me that I have got rid of him at last. He has enlisted into the Company's service, and is off directly—but he wants a cheese. He is informed by the serjeant that it is essential to his prospects in the regiment that he should take out a single Gloucester cheese, weighing from twelve to fifteen pounds. Eight or nine shillings would buy it. He does not ask for money, after what has passed; but if he calls at nine, to-morrow morning may he hope to find a cheese? And is there anything he can do to show his gratitude in Bengal?

Once he wrote me rather a special letter, proposing relief in kind. He had got into a little trouble by leaving parcels of mud done up in brown paper, at people's houses, on pretence of being a Railway-Porter, in which character he received carriage money. This sportive fancy he expiated in the House of Correction. Not long after his release, and on a Sunday morning, he called with a letter (having first dusted himself all over), in which he gave me to understand that, being resolved to earn an honest livelihood, he had been travelling about the country with a cart of crockery. That he had been doing pretty well until the day before, when his horse had dropped down dead near Chatham, in Kent. That this had reduced him to the unpleasant necessity of getting into the shafts himself, and drawing the cart of crockery to London—a somewhat exhausting pull of thirty miles. That he did not venture to ask again for money; but that if I would have the goodness *to leave him out a donkey*, he would call for the animal before breakfast!

At another time my friend (I am describing actual experiences) introduced himself as a literary gentleman in the last extremity of distress. He had had a play accepted at a certain Theatre—which was really open; its representation was delayed by the indisposition of a leading actor—who was really ill; and he and his were in a state of absolute starvation. If he made his necessities known to the Manager of the Theatre, he put it to me to say what kind of treatment he might expect? Well! we got over that difficulty to our mutual satisfaction. A little while afterwards he was in some other strait. I think Mrs. Southcote, his wife, was in extremity—and we adjusted that point too. A little while afterwards he had taken a new house, and was going headlong to ruin for want of a water-butt. I had my misgivings about the water-butt, and did not reply to that epistle. But a little while afterwards, I had reason to feel penitent for my neglect. He wrote me a few broken-hearted lines, informing me that the dear partner of his sorrows died in his arms last night at nine o'clock!

I despatched a trusty messenger to comfort the bereaved mourner and his poor children; but the messenger went so soon, that the play was not ready to be played out; my friend was not at home, and his wife was in a most delightful state of health. He was taken up by the Mendicity Society (informally it afterwards appeared), and I presented myself at a London Police-Office with my testimony against him. The Magistrate was wonderfully struck by his educational acquirements, deeply impressed by the excellence of his letters, exceedingly sorry to see a man of his attainments there, complimented him highly on his powers of composition, and was quite charmed to have the agreeable duty of discharging him. A collection was made for the 'poor fellow,' as he was called in the reports, and I left the court with a comfortable sense of being universally regarded as a sort of monster. Next day comes to me a friend of mine, the governor of a large prison. 'Why did you ever go to the Police-Office against that man,' says he, 'without coming to me first? I know all about him and his frauds. He lodged in the house of one of my warders, at the very time when he first wrote to you; and then he was eating spring-lamb at eighteen-pence a pound, and early asparagus at I don't know how much a bundle!' On that very same day, and in that very same hour, my injured gentleman wrote a solemn address to me, demanding to know what compensation I proposed to make him for his having passed the night in a 'loathsome dungeon.' And next morning an Irish gentleman, a member of the same fraternity, who had read the case, and was very well persuaded I should be chary of going to that Police-Office again, positively refused to leave my door for less than a sovereign, and, resolved to besiege me into compliance, literally 'sat down' before it for ten mortal hours. The garrison being well provisioned, I remained within the walls; and he raised the siege at midnight with a prodigious alarum on the bell.

The Begging-Letter Writer often has an extensive circle of acquaintance. Whole pages of the 'Court Guide' are ready to be references for him. Noblemen and gentlemen write to say there never was such a man for probity and virtue. They have known him time out of mind, and there is nothing they wouldn't do for him. Somehow, they don't give him that one pound ten he stands in need of; but perhaps it is not enough—they want to do more, and his modesty will not allow it. It is to be remarked of his trade that it is a very fascinating one. He never leaves it; and those who are near to him become smitten with a love of it, too, and sooner or later set up for themselves. He employs a messenger—man, woman, or child. That messenger is certain ultimately to become an independent Begging-Letter Writer. His sons and daughters succeed to his calling, and write begging-letters when he is no more. He throws off the infection of begging-letter writing, like the contagion of disease. What Sydney Smith so happily called 'the dangerous luxury of dishonesty' is more tempting, and more catching, it would seem, in this instance than in any other.

He always belongs to a Corresponding-Society of Begging-Letter Writers. Any one who will, may ascertain this fact. Give money to-day in recognition of a begging-letter,—no matter how unlike a common begging-letter,—and for the next fortnight you will have a rush of such communications. Steadily refuse to give; and the begging-letters become Angels' visits, until the Society is from some cause or other in a dull way of business, and may as well try you as anybody else. It is of little use inquiring into the Begging-Letter Writer's circumstances. He may be sometimes accidentally found out, as in the case already mentioned (though that was not the first inquiry made); but apparent misery is always a part of his trade, and real misery very often is, in the intervals of spring-lamb and early asparagus. It is naturally an incident of his dissipated and dishonest life.

That the calling is a successful one, and that large sums of money are gained by it, must be evident to anybody who reads the Police Reports of such cases. But, prosecutions are of rare occurrence, relatively to the extent to which the trade is carried on. The cause of this is to be found (as no one knows better than the Begging-Letter Writer, for it is a part of his speculation) in the aversion people feel to exhibit themselves as having been imposed upon, or as having weakly gratified their consciences with a lazy, flimsy substitute for the noblest of all virtues. There is a man at large, at the moment when this paper is preparing for the press (on the 29th of April, 1850), and never once taken up yet, who, within these twelvemonths, has been probably the most audacious and the most successful swindler that even this trade has ever known. There has been something singularly base in this fellow's proceedings; it has been his business to write to all sorts and conditions of people, in the names of persons of high reputation and unblemished honour, professing to be in distress—the general admiration and respect for whom has ensured a ready and generous reply.

Now, in the hope that the results of the real experience of a real person may do something more to induce reflection on this subject than any abstract treatise—and with a personal knowledge of the extent to which the Begging-Letter Trade has been carried on for some time, and has been for some time constantly increasing—the writer of this paper entreats the attention of his readers to a few concluding words. His experience is a type of the experience of many; some on a smaller, some on an infinitely larger scale. All may judge of the soundness or unsoundness of his conclusions from it.

Long doubtful of the efficacy of such assistance in any case whatever, and able to recall but one, within his whole individual knowledge, in which he had the least after-reason to suppose that any good was done by it, he was led, last autumn, into some serious considerations. The begging-letters flying about by every post, made it perfectly manifest that a set of lazy vagabonds were interposed between the general desire to do something to relieve the sickness and misery under which the poor were suffering, and the suffering poor themselves. That many who sought to do some little to repair the social wrongs, inflicted in the way of preventible sickness and death upon the poor, were strengthening those wrongs, however innocently, by wasting money on pestilent knaves cumbering society. That imagination,—soberly following one of these knaves into his life of punishment in jail, and comparing it with the life of one of these poor in a cholera-stricken alley, or one of the children of one of these poor, soothed in its dying hour by the late lamented Mr. Drouet,—contemplated a grim farce, impossible to be presented very much longer before God or man. That the crowning miracle of all the miracles summed up in the New Testament, after the miracle of the blind seeing, and the lame walking, and the restoration of the dead to life, was the miracle that the poor had the Gospel preached to them. That while the poor were unnaturally and unnecessarily cut off by the thousand, in the prematurity of their age, or in the rottenness of their youth—for of flower or blossom such youth has none—the Gospel was *not* preached to them, saving in hollow and unmeaning voices. That of all wrongs, this was the first mighty wrong the Pestilence warned us to set right. And that no Post-Office Order to any amount, given to a Begging-Letter Writer for the quieting of an uneasy breast, would be presentable on the Last Great Day as anything towards it.

The poor never write these letters. Nothing could be more unlike their habits. The writers are public robbers; and we who support them are parties to their depredations. They trade upon every circumstance within their knowledge that affects us, public or private, joyful or sorrowful; they pervert the lessons of our lives; they change what ought to be our strength and virtue into weakness, and encouragement of vice. There is a plain remedy, and it is in our own hands. We must resolve, at any sacrifice of feeling, to be deaf to such appeals, and crush the trade.

There are degrees in murder. Life must be held sacred among us in more ways than one—sacred, not merely from the murderous weapon, or the subtle poison, or the cruel blow, but sacred from preventible diseases, distortions, and pains. That is the first great end we have to set against this miserable imposition. Physical life respected, moral life comes next. What will not content a Begging-Letter Writer for a week, would educate a score of children for a year. Let us give all we can; let us give more than ever. Let us do all we can; let us do more than ever. But let us give, and do, with a high purpose; not to endow the scum of the earth, to its own greater corruption, with the offals of our duty.

30

THE BLACK CAT

Edgar Allan Poe

For the most wild, yet most homely narrative which I am about to pen, I neither expect nor solicit belief. Mad indeed would I be to expect it, in a case where my very senses reject their own evidence. Yet, mad am I not—and very surely do I not dream. But to-morrow I die, and to-day I would unburthen my soul. My immediate purpose is to place before the world, plainly, succinctly, and without comment, a series of mere household events. In their consequences, these events have terrified—have tortured—have destroyed me. Yet I will not attempt to expound them. To me, they have presented little but Horror—to many they will seem less terrible than barroques. Hereafter, perhaps, some intellect may be found which will reduce my phantasm to the common-place—some intellect more calm, more logical, and far less excitable than my own, which will perceive, in the circumstances I detail with awe, nothing more than an ordinary succession of very natural causes and effects.

From my infancy I was noted for the docility and humanity of my disposition. My tenderness of heart was even so conspicuous as to make me the jest of my companions. I was especially fond of animals, and was indulged by my parents with a great variety of pets. With these I spent most of my time, and never was so happy as when feeding and caressing them. This peculiarity of character grew with my growth, and, in my manhood, I derived from it one of my principal sources of pleasure. To those who have cherished an affection for a faithful and sagacious dog, I need hardly be at the trouble of explaining the nature or the intensity of the gratification thus derivable. There is something in the unselfish and self-sacrificing love of a brute, which goes directly to the heart of him who has had frequent occasion to test the paltry friendship and gossamer fidelity of mere Man.

I married early, and was happy to find in my wife a disposition not uncongenial with my own. Observing my partiality for domestic pets, she lost no opportunity of procuring those of the most agreeable kind. We had birds, gold-fish, a fine dog, rabbits, a small monkey, and a cat.

This latter was a remarkably large and beautiful animal, entirely black, and sagacious to an astonishing degree. In speaking of his intelligence, my wife, who at heart was not a little tinctured with superstition, made frequent allusion to the ancient popular notion, which regarded all black cats as witches in disguise. Not that she was ever serious upon this point—and I mention the matter at all for no better reason than that it happens, just now, to be remembered.

Pluto—this was the cat's name—was my favorite pet and playmate. I alone fed him, and he attended me wherever I went about the house. It was even with difficulty that I could prevent him from following me through the streets.

Our friendship lasted, in this manner, for several years, during which my general temperament and character—through the instrumentality of the Fiend Intemperance—had (I blush to confess it) experienced a radical alteration for the worse. I grew, day by day, more moody, more irritable, more regardless of the feelings of others. I suffered myself to use intemperate language to my wife. At length, I even offered her personal violence. My pets, of course, were made to feel the change in my disposition. I not only neglected, but ill-used them. For Pluto, however, I still retained sufficient regard to restrain me from maltreating him, as I made no scruple of maltreating the rabbits, the monkey, or even the dog, when by accident, or through affection, they came in my way. But my disease grew upon me—for what disease is like Alcohol!—and at length even Pluto, who was now becoming old, and consequently somewhat peevish—even Pluto began to experience the effects of my ill temper.

One night, returning home, much intoxicated, from one of my haunts about town, I fancied that the cat avoided my presence. I seized him; when, in his fright at my violence, he inflicted a slight wound upon my hand with his teeth. The fury of a demon instantly possessed me. I knew myself no longer. My original soul seemed, at once, to take its flight from my body; and a more than fiendish malevolence, gin-nurtured, thrilled every fibre of my frame. I took from my waistcoat-pocket a pen-knife, opened it, grasped the poor beast by the throat, and deliberately cut one of its eyes from the socket! I blush, I burn, I shudder, while I pen the damnable atrocity.

When reason returned with the morning—when I had slept off the fumes of the night's debauch—I experienced a sentiment half of horror, half of remorse, for the crime of which I had been guilty; but it was, at best, a feeble and equivocal feeling, and the soul remained untouched. I again plunged into excess, and soon drowned in wine all memory of the deed.

In the meantime the cat slowly recovered. The socket of the lost eye presented, it is true, a frightful appearance, but he no longer appeared to suffer any pain. He went about the house as usual, but, as might be expected, fled in extreme terror at my approach. I had so much of my old heart left, as to be at first grieved by this evident dislike on the part of a creature which had once so loved me. But this feeling soon gave place to irritation. And then came, as if to my final and irrevocable overthrow, the spirit of *perverseness*. Of this spirit philosophy takes no account. Yet I am not more sure that my soul lives, than I am that perverseness is one of the primitive impulses of the human heart—one of the indivisible primary faculties, or sentiments, which give direction to the character of Man. Who has not, a hundred times, found himself committing a vile or a silly action, for no other reason than because he knows he should not? Have we not a perpetual inclination, in the teeth of our best judgment, to violate that which is Law, merely because we understand it to be such? This spirit of perverseness, I say, came to my final overthrow. It was this unfathomable longing of the soul to vex itself—to offer violence to its own nature—to do wrong for the wrong's sake only—that urged me to continue and finally to consummate the injury I had inflicted upon the unoffending brute. One morning, in cool blood, I slipped a noose about its neck and hung it to the limb of a tree;—hung it with the tears streaming from my eyes, and with the bitterest remorse at my heart;—hung it because I knew that it had loved me, and because I felt it had given me no reason of offence;—hung it because I knew that in so doing I was committing a sin—a deadly sin that would so jeopardize my immortal soul as to place it—if such a thing were possible—even beyond the reach of the infinite mercy of the Most Merciful and Most Terrible God.

On the night of the day on which this cruel deed was done, I was aroused from sleep by the cry of fire. The curtains of my bed were in flames. The whole house was blazing. It was with great difficulty that my wife, a servant, and myself, made our escape from the conflagration. The destruction was complete. My entire worldly wealth was swallowed up, and I resigned myself thenceforward to despair.

I am above the weakness of seeking to establish a sequence of cause and effect, between the disaster and the atrocity. But I am detailing a chain of facts—and wish not to leave even a possible link imperfect. On the day succeeding the fire, I visited the ruins. The walls, with one exception, had fallen in. This exception was found in a compartment wall, not very thick, which stood about the middle of the house, and against which had rested the head of my bed. The plastering had here, in great measure, resisted the action of the fire—a fact which I attributed to its having been recently spread. About this wall a dense crowd were collected, and many persons seemed to be examining a particular portion of it with very minute and eager attention. The words 'strange!' 'singular!' and other similar expressions, excited my curiosity. I approached and saw, as if graven in bas relief upon the white surface, the figure of a gigantic cat. The impression was given with an accuracy truly marvellous. There was a rope about the animal's neck.

When I first beheld this apparition—for I could scarcely regard it as less—my wonder and my terror were extreme. But at length reflection came to my aid. The cat, I remembered, had been hung in a garden adjacent to the house. Upon the alarm of fire, this garden had been immediately filled by the crowd—by some one of whom the animal must have been cut from the tree and thrown, through an open window, into my chamber. This had probably been done with the view of arousing me from sleep. The falling of other walls had compressed the victim of my cruelty into the substance of the freshly-spread plaster; the lime of which, with the flames, and the ammonia from the carcass, had then accomplished the portraiture as I saw it.

Although I thus readily accounted to my reason, if not altogether to my conscience, for the startling fact just detailed, it did not the less fail to make a deep impression upon my fancy. For months I could not rid myself of the phantasm of the cat; and, during this period, there came back into my spirit a half-sentiment that seemed, but was not, remorse. I went so far as to regret the loss of the animal, and to look about me, among the vile haunts which I now habitually frequented, for another pet of the same species, and of somewhat similar appearance, with which to supply its place.

One night as I sat, half stupified, in a den of more than infamy, my attention was suddenly drawn to some black object, reposing upon the head of one of the immense hogsheads of Gin, or of Rum, which constituted the chief furniture of the apartment. I had been looking steadily at the top of this hogshead for some minutes, and what now caused me surprise was the fact that I had not sooner perceived the object thereupon. I approached it, and touched it with my hand. It was a black cat—a very large one—fully as large as Pluto, and closely resembling him in every respect but one. Pluto had not a white hair upon any portion of his body; but this cat had a large, although indefinite splotch of white, covering nearly the whole region of the breast.

Upon my touching him, he immediately arose, purred loudly, rubbed against my hand, and appeared delighted with my notice. This, then, was the very creature of which I was in search. I at once offered to purchase it of the landlord; but this person made no claim to it—knew nothing of it—had never seen it before.

I continued my caresses, and, when I prepared to go home, the animal evinced a disposition to accompany me. I permitted it to do so; occasionally stooping and patting it as I proceeded. When it reached the house it domesticated itself at once, and became immediately a great favorite with my wife.

For my own part, I soon found a dislike to it arising within me. This was just the reverse of what I had anticipated; but—I know not how or why it was—its evident fondness for myself rather disgusted and annoyed. By slow degrees, these feelings of disgust and annoyance rose into the bitterness of hatred. I avoided the creature; a certain sense of shame, and the remembrance of my former deed of cruelty, preventing me from physically abusing it. I did not, for some weeks, strike, or otherwise violently ill use it; but gradually—very gradually—I came to look upon it with unutterable loathing, and to flee silently from its odious presence, as from the breath of a pestilence.

What added, no doubt, to my hatred of the beast, was the discovery, on the morning after I brought it home, that, like Pluto, it also had been deprived of one of its eyes. This circumstance, however, only endeared it to my wife, who, as I have already said, possessed, in a high degree, that humanity of feeling which had once been my distinguishing trait, and the source of many of my simplest and purest pleasures.

With my aversion to this cat, however, its partiality for myself seemed to increase. It followed my footsteps with a pertinacity which it would be difficult to make the reader comprehend. Whenever I sat, it would crouch beneath my chair, or spring upon my knees, covering me with its loathsome caresses. If I arose to walk it would get between my feet and thus nearly throw me down, or, fastening its long and sharp claws in my dress, clamber, in this manner, to my breast. At such times, although I longed to destroy it with a blow, I was yet withheld from so doing, partly by a memory of my former crime, but chiefly—let me confess it at once—by absolute dread of the beast.

This dread was not exactly a dread of physical evil—and yet I should be at a loss how otherwise to define it. I am almost ashamed to own—yes, even in this felon's cell, I am almost ashamed to own—that the terror and horror with which the animal inspired me, had been heightened by one of the merest chimæras it would be possible to conceive. My wife had called my attention, more than once, to the character of the mark of white hair, of which I have spoken, and which constituted the sole visible difference between the strange beast and the one I had destroyed. The reader will remember that this mark, although large, had been originally very indefinite; but, by slow degrees—degrees nearly imperceptible, and which for a long time my Reason struggled to reject as fanciful—it had, at length, assumed a rigorous distinctness of outline. It was now the representation of an object that I shudder to name—and for this, above all, I loathed, and dreaded, and would have rid myself of the monster had I dared—it was now, I say, the image of a hideous—of a ghastly thing—of the *gallows*!—oh, mournful and terrible engine of Horror and of Crime—of Agony and of Death!

And now was I indeed wretched beyond the wretchedness of mere Humanity. And a brute beast—whose fellow I had contemptuously destroyed—a brute beast to work out for me—for me a man, fashioned in the image of the High God—so much of insufferable woe! Alas! neither by day nor by night knew I the blessing of Rest any more! During the former the creature left me no moment alone; and, in the latter, I started, hourly, from dreams of unutterable fear, to find the hot breath of the thing upon my face, and its vast weight—an incarnate Night-Mare that I had no power to shake off—incumbent eternally upon my heart!

Beneath the pressure of torments such as these, the feeble remnant of the good within me succumbed. Evil thoughts became my sole intimates—the darkest and most evil of thoughts. The moodiness of my usual temper increased to hatred of all things and of all mankind; while, from the sudden, frequent, and ungovernable outbursts of a fury to which I now blindly abandoned myself, my uncomplaining wife, alas! was the most usual and the most patient of sufferers.

One day she accompanied me, upon some household errand, into the cellar of the old building which our poverty compelled us to inhabit. The cat followed me down the steep stairs, and, nearly throwing me headlong, exasperated me to madness. Uplifting an axe, and forgetting, in my wrath, the childish dread which had hitherto stayed my hand, I aimed a blow at the animal which, of course, would have proved instantly fatal had it descended as I wished. But this blow was arrested by the hand of my wife. Goaded, by the interference, into a rage more than demoniacal, I withdrew my arm from her grasp and buried the axe in her brain. She fell dead upon the spot, without a groan.

This hideous murder accomplished, I set myself forthwith, and with entire deliberation, to the task of concealing the body. I knew that I could not remove it from the house, either by day or by night, without the risk of being observed by the neighbors. Many projects entered my mind. At one period I thought of cutting the corpse into minute fragments, and destroying them by fire. At another, I resolved to dig a grave for it in the floor of the cellar. Again, I deliberated about casting it in the well in the yard—about packing it in a box, as if merchandize, with the usual arrangements, and so getting a porter to take it from the house. Finally I hit upon what I considered a far better expedient than either of these. I determined to wall it up in the cellar—as the monks of the middle ages are recorded to have walled up their victims.

For a purpose such as this the cellar was well adapted. Its walls were loosely constructed, and had lately been plastered throughout with a rough plaster, which the dampness of the atmosphere had prevented from hardening. Moreover, in one of the walls was a projection, caused by a false chimney, or fireplace, that had been filled up, and made to resemble the rest of the cellar. I made no doubt that I could readily displace the bricks at this point, insert the corpse, and wall the whole up as before, so that no eye could detect any thing suspicious.

And in this calculation I was not deceived. By means of a crow-bar I easily dislodged the bricks, and, having carefully deposited the body against the inner wall, I propped it in that position, while, with little trouble, I re-laid the whole structure as it originally stood. Having procured mortar, sand, and hair, with every possible precaution, I prepared a plaster which could not be distinguished from the old, and with this I very carefully went over the new brick-work. When I had finished, I felt satisfied that all was right. The wall did not present the slightest appearance of having been disturbed. The rubbish on the floor was picked up with the minutest care. I looked around triumphantly, and said to myself—'Here at least, then, my labor has not been in vain.'

My next step was to look for the beast which had been the cause of so much wretchedness; for I had, at length, firmly resolved to put it to death. Had I been able to meet with it, at the moment, there could have been no doubt of its fate; but it appeared that the crafty animal had been alarmed at the violence of my previous anger, and forebore to present itself in my present mood. It is impossible to describe, or to imagine, the deep, the blissful sense of relief which the absence of the detested creature occasioned in my bosom. It did not make its appearance during the night—and thus for one night at least, since its introduction into the house, I soundly and tranquilly slept; aye, slept even with the burden of murder upon my soul!

The second and the third day passed, and still my tormentor came not. Once again I breathed as a freeman. The monster, in terror, had fled the premises forever! I should behold it no more! My happiness was supreme! The guilt of my dark deed disturbed me but little. Some few inquiries had been made, but these had been readily answered. Even a search had been instituted—but of course nothing was to be discovered. I looked upon my future felicity as secured.

Upon the fourth day of the assassination, a party of the police came, very unexpectedly, into the house, and proceeded again to make rigorous investigation of the premises. Secure, however, in the inscrutability of my place of concealment, I felt no embarrassment whatever. The officers bade me accompany them in their search. They left no nook or corner unexplored. At length, for the third or fourth time, they descended into the cellar. I quivered not in a muscle. My heart beat calmly as that of one who slumbers in innocence. I walked the cellar from end to end. I folded my arms upon my bosom, and roamed easily to and fro. The police were thoroughly satisfied and prepared to depart. The glee at my heart was too strong to be restrained. I burned to say if but one word, by way of triumph, and to render doubly sure their assurance of my guiltlessness.

'Gentlemen,' I said at last, as the party ascended the steps, 'I delight to have allayed your suspicions. I wish you all health, and a little more courtesy. By the bye, gentlemen, this—this is a very well constructed house.' (In the rabid desire to say something easily, I scarcely knew what I uttered at all.)—'I may say an excellently well constructed house. These walls—are you going, gentlemen?—these walls are solidly put together;' and here, through the mere phrenzy of bravado, I rapped heavily, with a cane which I held in my hand, upon that very portion of the brick-work behind which stood the corpse of the wife of my bosom.

But may God shield and deliver me from the fangs of the Arch-Fiend! No sooner had the reverberation of my blows sunk into silence, than I was answered by a voice from within the tomb!—by a cry, at first muffled and broken, like the sobbing of a child, and then quickly swelling into one long, loud, and continuous scream, utterly anomalous and inhuman—a howl—a wailing shriek, half of horror and half of triumph, such as might have arisen only out of hell, conjointly from the throats of the dammed in their agony and of the demons that exult in the damnation.

Of my own thoughts it is folly to speak. Swooning, I staggered to the opposite wall. For one instant the party upon the stairs remained motionless, through extremity of terror and of awe. In the next, a dozen stout arms were toiling at the wall. It fell bodily. The corpse, already greatly decayed and clotted with gore, stood erect before the eyes of the spectators. Upon its head, with red extended mouth and solitary eye of fire, sat the hideous beast whose craft had seduced me into murder, and whose informing voice had consigned me to the hangman. I had walled the monster up within the tomb!

31

THE CRYSTAL EGG

H.G. Wells

There was, until a year ago, a little and very grimy-looking shop near Seven Dials, over which, in weather-worn yellow lettering, the name of 'C. Cave, Naturalist and Dealer in Antiquities,' was inscribed. The contents of its window were curiously variegated. They comprised some elephant tusks and an imperfect set of chessmen, beads and weapons, a box of eyes, two skulls of tigers and one human, several moth-eaten stuffed monkeys (one holding a lamp), an old-fashioned cabinet, a fly-blown ostrich egg or so, some fishing-tackle, and an extraordinarily dirty, empty glass fish-tank. There was also, at the moment the story begins, a mass of crystal, worked into the shape of an egg and brilliantly polished. And at that two people who stood outside the window were looking, one of them a tall, thin clergyman, the other a black-bearded young man of dusky complexion and unobtrusive costume. The dusky young man spoke with eager gesticulation, and seemed anxious for his companion to purchase the article.

While they were there, Mr. Cave came into his shop, his beard still wagging with the bread and butter of his tea. When he saw these men and the object of their regard, his countenance fell. He glanced guiltily over his shoulder, and softly shut the door. He was a little old man, with pale face and peculiar watery blue eyes; his hair was a dirty grey, and he wore a shabby blue frock-coat, an ancient silk hat, and carpet slippers very much down at heel. He remained watching the two men as they talked. The clergyman went deep into his trouser pocket, examined a handful of money, and showed his teeth in an agreeable smile. Mr. Cave seemed still more depressed when they came into the shop.

The clergyman, without any ceremony, asked the price of the crystal egg. Mr. Cave glanced nervously towards the door leading into the parlour, and said five pounds. The clergyman protested that the price was high, to his companion as well as to Mr. Cave—it was, indeed, very much more than Mr. Cave had intended to ask when he had stocked the article—and an attempt at bargaining ensued. Mr. Cave stepped to the shop door, and held it open. 'Five pounds is my price,' he said, as though he wished to save himself the trouble of unprofitable discussion. As he did so, the upper portion of a woman's face appeared above the blind in the glass upper panel of the door leading into the parlour, and stared curiously at the two customers. 'Five pounds is my price,' said Mr. Cave, with a quiver in his voice.

The swarthy young man had so far remained a spectator, watching Cave keenly. Now he spoke. 'Give him five pounds,' he said. The clergyman glanced at him to see if he were in earnest, and when he looked at Mr. Cave again, he saw that the latter's face was white. 'It's a lot of money,' said the clergyman, and, diving into his pocket, began counting his resources. He had little more than thirty shillings, and he appealed to his companion, with whom he seemed to be on terms of considerable intimacy. This gave Mr. Cave an opportunity of collecting his thoughts, and he began to explain in an agitated manner that the crystal was not, as a matter of fact, entirely free for sale. His two customers were naturally surprised at this, and inquired why he had not thought of that before he began to bargain. Mr. Cave became confused, but he stuck to his story, that the crystal was not in the market that afternoon, that a probable purchaser of it had already appeared. The two, treating this as an attempt to raise the price still further, made as if they would leave the shop. But at this point the parlour door opened, and the owner of the dark fringe and the little eyes appeared.

She was a coarse-featured, corpulent woman, younger and

very much larger than Mr. Cave; she walked heavily, and her face was flushed. 'That crystal *is* for sale,' she said. 'And five pounds is a good enough price for it. I can't think what you're about, Cave, not to take the gentleman's offer!'

Mr. Cave, greatly perturbed by the irruption, looked angrily at her over the rims of his spectacles, and, without excessive assurance, asserted his right to manage his business in his own way. An altercation began. The two customers watched the scene with interest and some amusement, occasionally assisting Mrs. Cave with suggestions. Mr. Cave, hard driven, persisted in a confused and impossible story of an inquiry for the crystal that morning, and his agitation became painful. But he stuck to his point with extraordinary persistence. It was the young Oriental who ended this curious controversy. He proposed that they should call again in the course of two days—so as to give the alleged inquirer a fair chance. 'And then we must insist,' said the clergyman. 'Five pounds.' Mrs. Cave took it on herself to apologise for her husband, explaining that he was sometimes 'a little odd,' and as the two customers left, the couple prepared for a free discussion of the incident in all its bearings.

Mrs. Cave talked to her husband with singular directness. The poor little man, quivering with emotion, muddled himself between his stories, maintaining on the one hand that he had another customer in view, and on the other asserting that the crystal was honestly worth ten guineas. 'Why did you ask five pounds?' said his wife. '*Do* let me manage my business my own way!' said Mr. Cave.

Mr. Cave had living with him a step-daughter and a step-son, and at supper that night the transaction was re-discussed. None of them had a high opinion of Mr. Cave's business methods, and this action seemed a culminating folly.

'It's my opinion he's refused that crystal before,' said the step-son, a loose-limbed lout of eighteen.

'But *Five Pounds*!' said the step-daughter, an argumentative young woman of six-and-twenty.

Mr. Cave's answers were wretched; he could only mumble

weak assertions that he knew his own business best. They drove him from his half-eaten supper into the shop, to close it for the night, his ears aflame and tears of vexation behind his spectacles. Why had he left the crystal in the window so long? The folly of it! That was the trouble closest in his mind. For a time he could see no way of evading sale.

After supper his step-daughter and step-son smartened themselves up and went out and his wife retired upstairs to reflect upon the business aspects of the crystal, over a little sugar and lemon and so forth in hot water. Mr. Cave went into the shop, and stayed there until late, ostensibly to make ornamental rockeries for gold-fish cases, but really for a private purpose that will be better explained later. The next day Mrs. Cave found that the crystal had been removed from the window, and was lying behind some second-hand books on angling. She replaced it in a conspicuous position. But she did not argue further about it, as a nervous headache disinclined her from debate. Mr. Cave was always disinclined. The day passed disagreeably. Mr. Cave was, if anything, more absent-minded than usual, and uncommonly irritable withal. In the afternoon, when his wife was taking her customary sleep, he removed the crystal from the window again.

The next day Mr. Cave had to deliver a consignment of dog-fish at one of the hospital schools, where they were needed for dissection. In his absence Mrs. Cave's mind reverted to the topic of the crystal, and the methods of expenditure suitable to a windfall of five pounds. She had already devised some very agreeable expedients, among others a dress of green silk for herself and a trip to Richmond, when a jangling of the front door bell summoned her into the shop. The customer was an examination coach who came to complain of the non-delivery of certain frogs asked for the previous day. Mrs. Cave did not approve of this particular branch of Mr. Cave's business, and the gentleman, who had called in a somewhat aggressive mood, retired after a brief exchange of words—entirely civil, so far as he was concerned. Mrs. Cave's eye then naturally turned to the window; for the sight of the crystal was an assurance of the five pounds and of her dreams. What was her surprise to find it gone!

She went to the place behind the locker on the counter, where she had discovered it the day before. It was not there; and she immediately began an eager search about the shop.

When Mr. Cave returned from his business with the dogfish, about a quarter to two in the afternoon, he found the shop in some confusion, and his wife, extremely exasperated and on her knees behind the counter, routing among his taxidermic material. Her face came up hot and angry over the counter, as the jangling bell announced his return, and she forthwith accused him of 'hiding it.'

'Hid *what*?' asked Mr. Cave.

'The crystal!'

At that Mr. Cave, apparently much surprised, rushed to the window. 'Isn't it here?' he said. 'Great Heavens! what has become of it?'

Just then Mr. Cave's step-son re-entered the shop from, the inner room—he had come home a minute or so before Mr. Cave—and he was blaspheming freely. He was apprenticed to a second-hand furniture dealer down the road, but he had his meals at home, and he was naturally annoyed to find no dinner ready.

But when he heard of the loss of the crystal, he forgot his meal, and his anger was diverted from his mother to his step-father. Their first idea, of course, was that he had hidden it. But Mr. Cave stoutly denied all knowledge of its fate, freely offering his bedabbled affidavit in the matter—and at last was worked up to the point of accusing, first, his wife and then his stepson of having taken it with a view to a private sale. So began an exceedingly acrimonious and emotional discussion, which ended for Mrs. Cave in a peculiar nervous condition midway between hysterics and amuck, and caused the step-son to be half-an-hour late at the furniture establishment in the afternoon. Mr. Cave took refuge from his wife's emotions in the shop.

In the evening the matter was resumed, with less passion and in a judicial spirit, under the presidency of the step-daughter. The supper passed unhappily and culminated in a painful scene. Mr. Cave gave way at last to extreme exasperation, and went out banging the front door violently. The rest of the family, having discussed him with the freedom his absence warranted, hunted the house from garret to cellar, hoping to light upon the crystal.

The next day the two customers called again. They were received by Mrs. Cave almost in tears. It transpired that no one could imagine all that she had stood from Cave at various times in her married pilgrimage...She also gave a garbled account of the disappearance. The clergyman and the Oriental laughed silently at one another, and said it was very extraordinary. As Mrs. Cave seemed disposed to give them the complete history of her life they made to leave the shop. Thereupon Mrs. Cave, still clinging to hope, asked for the clergyman's address, so that, if she could get anything out of Cave, she might communicate it. The address was duly given, but apparently was afterwards mislaid. Mrs. Cave can remember nothing about it.

In the evening of that day the Caves seem to have exhausted their emotions, and Mr. Cave, who had been out in the afternoon, supped in a gloomy isolation that contrasted pleasantly with the impassioned controversy of the previous days. For some time matters were very badly strained in the Cave household, but neither crystal nor customer reappeared.

Now, without mincing the matter, we must admit that Mr. Cave was a liar. He knew perfectly well where the crystal was. It was in the rooms of Mr. Jacoby Wace, Assistant Demonstrator at St. Catherine's Hospital, Westbourne Street. It stood on the sideboard partially covered by a black velvet cloth, and beside a decanter of American whisky. It is from Mr. Wace, indeed, that the particulars upon which this narrative is based were derived. Cave had taken off the thing to the hospital hidden in the dog-fish sack, and there had pressed the young investigator to keep it for him. Mr. Wace was a little dubious at first. His relationship to Cave was peculiar. He had a taste for singular characters, and he had more than once invited the old man to smoke and drink in his rooms, and to unfold his rather amusing views of life in general and of his wife in particular. Mr. Wace had encountered Mrs. Cave, too, on occasions when Mr. Cave was not at home to attend to him. He knew the constant interference to which Cave was subjected, and having weighed the story judicially, he decided to give the crystal a refuge. Mr. Cave promised to explain the reasons for his remarkable affection for the crystal more fully on a later occasion, but he spoke distinctly of seeing visions therein. He called on Mr. Wace the same evening.

He told a complicated story. The crystal he said had come into his possession with other oddments at the forced sale of another curiosity dealer's effects, and not knowing what its value might be, he had ticketed it at ten shillings. It had hung upon his hands at that price for some months, and he was thinking of 'reducing the figure,' when he made a singular discovery.

At that time his health was very bad—and it must be borne in mind that, throughout all this experience, his physical condition was one of ebb—and he was in considerable distress by reason of the negligence, the positive ill-treatment even, he received from his wife and step-children. His wife was vain, extravagant, unfeeling, and had a growing taste for private drinking; his step-daughter was mean and over-reaching; and his step-son had conceived a violent dislike for him, and lost no chance of showing it. The requirements of his business pressed heavily upon him, and Mr. Wace does not think that he was altogether free from occasional intemperance. He had begun life in a comfortable position, he was a man of fair education, and he suffered, for weeks at a stretch, from melancholia and insomnia. Afraid to disturb his family, he would slip quietly from his wife's side, when his thoughts became intolerable, and wander about the house. And about three o'clock one morning, late in August, chance directed him into the shop.

The dirty little place was impenetrably black except in one

spot, where he perceived an unusual glow of light. Approaching this, he discovered it to be the crystal egg, which was standing on the corner of the counter towards the window. A thin ray smote through a crack in the shutters, impinged upon the object, and seemed as it were to fill its entire interior.

It occurred to Mr. Cave that this was not in accordance with the laws of optics as he had known them in his younger days. He could understand the rays being refracted by the crystal and coming to a focus in its interior, but this diffusion jarred with his physical conceptions. He approached the crystal nearly, peering into it and round it, with a transient revival of the scientific curiosity that in his youth had determined his choice of a calling. He was surprised to find the light not steady, but writhing within the substance of the egg, as though that object was a hollow sphere of some luminous vapour. In moving about to get different points of view, he suddenly found that he had come between it and the ray, and that the crystal none the less remained luminous. Greatly astonished, he lifted it out of the light ray and carried it to the darkest part of the shop. It remained bright for some four or five minutes, when it slowly faded and went out. He placed it in the thin streak of daylight, and its luminousness was almost immediately restored.

So far, at least, Mr. Wace was able to verify the remarkable story of Mr. Cave. He has himself repeatedly held this crystal in a ray of light (which had to be of a less diameter than one millimetre). And in a perfect darkness, such as could be produced by velvet wrapping, the crystal did undoubtedly appear very faintly phosphorescent. It would seem, however, that the luminousness was of some exceptional sort, and not equally visible to all eyes; for Mr. Harbinger—whose name will be familiar to the scientific reader in connection with the Pasteur Institute—was quite unable to see any light whatever. And Mr. Wace's own capacity for its appreciation was out of comparison inferior to that of Mr. Cave's. Even with Mr. Cave the power varied very considerably: his vision was most vivid during states of extreme weakness and fatigue.

Now, from the outset, this light in the crystal exercised a curious fascination upon Mr. Cave. And it says more for his loneliness of soul than a volume of pathetic writing could do, that he told no human being of his curious observations. He seems to have been living in such an atmosphere of petty spite that to admit the existence of a pleasure would have been to risk the loss of it. He found that as the dawn advanced, and the amount of diffused light increased, the crystal became to all appearance non-luminous. And for some time he was unable to see anything in it, except at night-time, in dark corners of the shop.

But the use of an old velvet cloth, which he used as a background for a collection of minerals, occurred to him, and by doubling this, and putting it over his head and hands, he was able to get a sight of the luminous movement within the crystal even in the day-time. He was very cautious lest he should be thus discovered by his wife, and he practised this occupation only in the afternoons, while she was asleep upstairs, and then circumspectly in a hollow under the counter. And one day, turning the crystal about in his hands, he saw something. It came and went like a flash, but it gave him the impression that the object had for a moment opened to him the view of a wide and spacious and strange country; and turning it about, he did, just as the light faded, see the same vision again.

Now it would be tedious and unnecessary to state all the phases of Mr. Cave's discovery from this point. Suffice that the effect was this: the crystal, being peered into at an angle of about 137 degrees from the direction of the illuminating ray, gave a clear and consistent picture of a wide and peculiar country-side. It was not dream-like at all: it produced a definite impression of reality, and the better the light the more real and solid it seemed. It was a moving picture: that is to say, certain objects moved in it, but slowly in an orderly manner like real things, and, according as the direction of the lighting and vision changed, the picture changed also. It must, indeed, have been like looking through an oval glass at a view, and turning the glass about to get at different aspects.

Mr. Cave's statements, Mr. Wace assures me, were extremely circumstantial, and entirely free from any of that emotional quality that taints hallucinatory impressions. But it must be remembered that all the efforts of Mr. Wace to see any similar clarity in the faint opalescence of the crystal were wholly unsuccessful, try as he would. The difference in intensity of the impressions received by the two men was very great, and it is quite conceivable that what was a view to Mr. Cave was a mere blurred nebulosity to Mr. Wace.

The view, as Mr. Cave described it, was invariably of an extensive plain, and he seemed always to be looking at it from a considerable height, as if from a tower or a mast. To the east and to the west the plain was bounded at a remote distance by vast reddish cliffs, which reminded him of those he had seen in some picture; but what the picture was Mr. Wace was unable to ascertain. These cliffs passed north and south—he could tell the points of the compass by the stars that were visible of a night—receding in an almost illimitable perspective and fading into the mists of the distance before they met. He was nearer the eastern set of cliffs; on the occasion of his first vision the sun was rising over them, and black against the sunlight and pale against their shadow appeared a multitude of soaring forms that Mr. Cave regarded as birds. A vast range of buildings spread below him; he seemed to be looking down upon them; and as they approached the blurred and refracted edge of the picture they became indistinct. There were also trees curious in shape, and in colouring a deep mossy green and an exquisite grey, beside a wide and shining canal. And something great and brilliantly coloured flew across the picture. But the first time Mr. Cave saw these pictures he saw only in flashes, his hands shook, his head moved, the vision came and went, and grew foggy and indistinct. And at first he had the greatest difficulty in finding the picture again once the direction of it was lost.

His next clear vision, which came about a week after the first, the interval having yielded nothing but tantalising glimpses and some useful experience, showed him the view down the length of the valley. The view was different, but he had a curious persuasion, which his subsequent observations abundantly confirmed, that he was regarding the strange world from exactly the same spot, although he was looking in a different direction. The long façade of the great building, whose roof he had looked down upon before, was now receding in perspective. He recognised the roof. In the front of the façade was a terrace of massive proportions and extraordinary length, and down the middle of the terrace, at certain intervals, stood huge but very graceful masts, bearing small shiny objects which reflected the setting sun. The import of these small objects did not occur to Mr. Cave until some time after, as he was describing the scene to Mr. Wace. The terrace overhung a thicket of the most luxuriant and graceful vegetation, and beyond this was a wide grassy lawn on which certain broad creatures, in form like beetles but enormously larger, reposed. Beyond this again was a richly decorated causeway of pinkish stone; and beyond that, and lined with dense red weeds, and passing up the valley exactly parallel with the distant cliffs, was a broad and mirror-like expanse of water. The air seemed full of squadrons of great birds, manoeuvring in stately curves; and across the river was a multitude of splendid buildings, richly coloured and glittering with metallic tracery and facets, among a forest of moss-like and lichenous trees. And suddenly something flapped repeatedly across the vision, like the fluttering of a jewelled fan or the beating of a wing, and a face, or rather the upper part of a face with very large eyes, came as it were close to his own and as if on the other side of the crystal. Mr. Cave was so startled and so impressed by the absolute reality of these eyes that he drew his head back from the crystal to look behind it. He had become so absorbed in watching that he was quite surprised to find himself in the cool darkness of his little shop, with its familiar odour of methyl, mustiness, and decay. And as he blinked about him, the glowing crystal faded and went out.

Such were the first general impressions of Mr. Cave. The story is curiously direct and circumstantial. From the outset, when the valley first flashed momentarily on his senses, his imagination was strangely affected, and as he began to appreciate the details of the scene he saw, his wonder rose to the point of a passion. He went about his business listless and distraught, thinking only of the time when he should be able to return to his watching. And then a few weeks after his first sight of the valley came the two customers, the stress and excitement of their offer, and the narrow escape of the crystal from sale, as I have already told.

Now, while the thing was Mr. Cave's secret, it remained a mere wonder, a thing to creep to covertly and peep at, as a child might peep upon a forbidden garden. But Mr. Wace has, for a young scientific investigator, a particularly lucid and consecutive habit of mind. Directly the crystal and its story came to him, and he had satisfied himself, by seeing the phosphorescence with his own eyes, that there really was a certain evidence for Mr. Cave's statements, he proceeded to develop the matter systematically. Mr. Cave was only too eager to come and feast his eyes on this wonderland he saw, and he came every night from half-past eight until half-past ten, and sometimes, in Mr. Wace's absence, during the day. On Sunday afternoons, also, he came. From the outset Mr. Wace made copious notes, and it was due to his scientific method that the relation between the direction from which the initiating ray entered the crystal and the orientation of the picture were proved. And, by covering the crystal in a box perforated only with a small aperture to admit the exciting ray, and by substituting black holland for his buff blinds, he greatly improved the conditions of the observations; so that in a little while they were able to survey the valley in any direction they desired.

So having cleared the way, we may give a brief account of this visionary world within the crystal. The things were in all cases seen by Mr. Cave, and the method of working was invariably for him to watch the crystal and report what he saw, while Mr. Wace (who as a science student had learnt the trick of writing in the dark) wrote a brief note of his report. When the crystal faded, it was put into its box in the proper position and the electric light turned on. Mr. Wace asked questions, and suggested observations to clear up difficult points. Nothing, indeed, could have been less visionary and more matter-of-fact.

The attention of Mr. Cave had been speedily directed to the bird-like creatures he had seen so abundantly present in each of his earlier visions. His first impression was soon corrected, and he considered for a time that they might represent a diurnal species of bat. Then he thought, grotesquely enough, that they might be cherubs. Their heads were round and curiously human, and it was the eyes of one of them that had so startled him on his second observation. They had broad, silvery wings, not feathered, but glistening almost as brilliantly as new-killed fish and with the same subtle play of colour, and these wings were not built on the plan of bird-wing or bat, Mr. Wace learned, but supported by curved ribs radiating from the body. (A sort of butterfly wing with curved ribs seems best to express their appearance.) The body was small, but fitted with two bunches of prehensile organs, like long tentacles, immediately under the mouth. Incredible as it appeared to Mr. Wace, the persuasion at last became irresistible that it was these creatures which owned the great quasi-human buildings and the magnificent garden that made the broad valley so splendid. And Mr. Cave perceived that the buildings, with other peculiarities, had no doors, but that the great circular windows, which opened freely, gave the creatures egress and entrance. They would alight upon their tentacles, fold their wings to a smallness almost rod-like, and hop into the interior. But among them was a multitude of smaller-winged creatures, like great dragon-flies and moths and flying beetles, and across the greensward brilliantly-coloured gigantic ground-beetles crawled lazily to and fro. Moreover, on the causeways and terraces, large-headed creatures similar to the greater winged flies, but wingless, were visible, hopping busily upon their hand-like tangle of tentacles.

Allusion has already been made to the glittering objects upon masts that stood upon the terrace of the nearer building. It dawned upon Mr. Cave, after regarding one of these masts very fixedly on one particularly vivid day that the glittering object there was a crystal exactly like that into which he peered. And a still more careful scrutiny convinced him that each one in a vista of nearly twenty carried a similar object.

Occasionally one of the large flying creatures would flutter up to one, and folding its wings and coiling a number of its tentacles about the mast, would regard the crystal fixedly for a space—sometimes for as long as fifteen minutes. And a series of observations, made at the suggestion of Mr. Wace, convinced both watchers that, so far as this visionary world was concerned, the crystal into which they peered actually stood at the summit of the end-most mast on the terrace, and that on one occasion at least one of these inhabitants of this other world had looked into Mr. Cave's face while he was making these observations.

So much for the essential facts of this very singular story. Unless we dismiss it all as the ingenious fabrication of Mr. Wace, we have to believe one of two things: either that Mr. Cave's crystal was in two worlds at once, and that while it was carried about in one, it remained stationary in the other, which seems altogether absurd; or else that it had some peculiar relation of sympathy with another and exactly similar crystal in this other world, so that what was seen in the interior of the one in this world was, under suitable conditions, visible to an observer in the corresponding crystal in the other world; and vice versa. At present, indeed, we do not know of any way in which two crystals could so come en rapport, but nowadays we know enough to understand that the thing is not altogether impossible. This view of the crystals as en rapport was the supposition that occurred to Mr. Wace, and to me at least it seems extremely plausible...

And where was this other world? On this, also, the alert intelligence of Mr. Wace speedily threw light. After sunset, the sky darkened rapidly—there was a very brief twilight interval indeed—and the stars shone out. They were recognisably the same as those we see, arranged in the same constellations. Mr. Cave recognised the Bear, the Pleiades, Aldebaran, and Sirius; so that the other world must be somewhere in the solar system, and, at the utmost, only a few hundreds of millions of miles from our own. Following up this clue, Mr. Wace learned that the midnight sky was a darker blue even than our midwinter sky, and that the sun seemed a little smaller. And there were two small moons! 'like our moon but smaller, and quite differently marked,' one of which moved so rapidly that its motion was clearly visible as one regarded it. These moons were never high in the sky, but vanished as they rose: that is, every time they revolved they were eclipsed because they were so near their primary planet. And all this answers quite completely, although Mr. Cave did not know it, to what must be the condition of things on Mars.

Indeed, it seems an exceedingly plausible conclusion that peering into this crystal Mr. Cave did actually see the planet Mars and its inhabitants. And if that be the case, then the evening star that shone so brilliantly in the sky of that distant vision was neither more nor less than our own familiar earth.

For a time the Martians—if they were Martians—do not seem to have known of Mr. Cave's inspection. Once or twice one would come to peer, and go away very shortly to some other mast, as though the vision was unsatisfactory. During this time Mr. Cave was able to watch the proceedings of these winged people without being disturbed by their attentions, and although his report is necessarily vague and fragmentary, it is nevertheless very suggestive. Imagine the impression of humanity a Martian observer would get who, after a difficult process of preparation and with considerable fatigue to the eyes, was able to peer at London from the steeple of St. Martin's Church for stretches, at longest, of four minutes at a time. Mr. Cave was unable to ascertain if the winged Martians were the same as the Martians who hopped about the causeways and terraces, and if the latter could put on wings at will. He several times saw certain clumsy bipeds, dimly suggestive of apes, white and partially translucent, feeding among certain of the lichenous trees, and once some of these fled before one of the hopping, round-headed Martians. The latter caught one in its tentacles, and then the picture faded suddenly and left Mr. Cave most tantalisingly in the dark. On another occasion a vast thing, that Mr. Cave thought at first was some gigantic insect, appeared advancing along the causeway beside the canal with extraordinary rapidity. As this drew nearer Mr. Cave perceived that it was a mechanism of shining metals and of extraordinary complexity. And then, when he looked again, it had passed out of sight.

After a time Mr. Wace aspired to attract the attention of the Martians, and the next time that the strange eyes of one of them appeared close to the crystal Mr. Cave cried out and sprang away, and they immediately turned on the light and began to gesticulate in a manner suggestive of signalling. But when at last Mr. Cave examined the crystal again the Martian had departed.

Thus far these observations had progressed in early November, and then Mr. Cave, feeling that the suspicions of his family about the crystal were allayed, began to take it to and fro with him in order that, as occasion arose in the daytime or night, he might comfort himself with what was fast becoming the most real thing in his existence.

In December Mr. Wace's work in connection with a forthcoming examination became heavy, the sittings were reluctantly suspended for a week, and for ten or eleven days—he is not quite sure which—he saw nothing of Cave. He then grew anxious to resume these investigations, and, the stress of his seasonal labours being abated, he went down to Seven Dials. At the corner he noticed a shutter before a bird fancier's window, and then another at a cobbler's. Mr. Cave's shop was closed.

He rapped and the door was opened by the step-son in black. He at once called Mrs. Cave, who was, Mr. Wace could not but observe, in cheap but ample widow's weeds of the most imposing pattern. Without any very great surprise Mr. Wace learnt that Cave was dead and already buried. She was in tears, and her voice was a little thick. She had just returned from Highgate. Her mind seemed occupied with her own prospects and the honourable details of the obsequies, but Mr. Wace was at last able to learn the particulars of Cave's death. He had been found dead in his shop in the early morning, the day after his last visit to Mr. Wace, and the crystal had been clasped in his stone-cold hands. His face was smiling, said Mrs. Cave, and the velvet cloth from the minerals lay on the floor at his feet. He must have been dead five or six hours when he was found.

This came as a great shock to Wace, and he began to reproach himself bitterly for having neglected the plain symptoms of the old man's ill-health. But his chief thought was of the crystal. He approached that topic in a gingerly manner, because he knew Mrs. Cave's peculiarities. He was dumfounded to learn that it was sold.

Mrs. Cave's first impulse, directly Cave's body had been taken upstairs, had been to write to the mad clergyman who had offered five pounds for the crystal, informing him of its recovery; but after a violent hunt, in which her daughter joined her, they were convinced of the loss of his address. As they were without the means required to mourn and bury Cave in the elaborate style the dignity of an old Seven Dials inhabitant demands, they had appealed to a friendly fellow-tradesman in Great Portland Street. He had very kindly taken over a portion of the stock at a valuation. The valuation was his own, and the crystal egg was included in one of the lots. Mr. Wace, after a few suitable condolences, a little off-handedly proffered perhaps, hurried at once to Great Portland Street. But there he learned that the crystal egg had already been sold to a tall, dark man in grey. And there the material facts in this curious, and to me at least very suggestive, story come abruptly to an end. The Great Portland Street dealer did not know who the tall dark man in grey was, nor had he observed him with sufficient attention to describe him minutely. He did not even know which way this person had gone after leaving the shop. For a time Mr.

Wace remained in the shop, trying the dealer's patience with hopeless questions, venting his own exasperation. And at last, realising abruptly that the whole thing had passed out of his hands, had vanished like a vision of the night, he returned to his own rooms, a little astonished to find the notes he had made still tangible and visible upon, his untidy table.

His annoyance and disappointment were naturally very great. He made a second call (equally ineffectual) upon the Great Portland Street dealer, and he resorted to advertisements in such periodicals as were lively to come into the hands of a bric-a-brac collector. He also wrote letters to The Daily Chronicle and Nature, but both those periodicals, suspecting a hoax, asked him to reconsider his action before they printed, and he was advised that such a strange story, unfortunately so bare of supporting evidence, might imperil his reputation as an investigator. Moreover, the calls of his proper work were urgent. So that after a month or so, save for an occasional reminder to certain dealers, he had reluctantly to abandon the quest for the crystal egg, and from that day to this it remains undiscovered. Occasionally, however, he tells me, and I can quite believe him, he has bursts of zeal, in which he abandons his more urgent occupation and resumes the search.

Whether or not it will remain lost for ever, with the material and origin of it, are things equally speculative at the present time. If the present purchaser is a collector, one would have expected the enquiries of Mr. Wace to have reached him through the dealers. He has been able to discover Mr. Cave's clergyman and 'Oriental'—no other than the Rev. James Parker and the young Prince of Bosso-Kuni in Java. I am obliged to them for certain particulars. The object of the Prince was simply curiosity—and extravagance. He was so eager to buy because Cave was so oddly reluctant to sell. It is just as possible that the buyer in the second instance was simply a casual purchaser and not a collector at all, and the crystal egg, for all I know, may at the present moment be within a mile of me, decorating a drawing-room or serving as a paper-weight—its remarkable functions all unknown. Indeed, it is partly with the idea of such a possibility that I have thrown this narrative into a form that will give it a chance of being read by the ordinary consumer of fiction.

My own ideas in the matter are practically identical with those of Mr. Wace. I believe the crystal on the mast in Mars and the crystal egg of Mr. Cave's to be in some physical, but at present quite inexplicable, way en rapport, and we both believe further that the terrestrial crystal must have been—possibly at some remote date—sent hither from that planet, in order to give the Martians a near view of our affairs. Possibly the fellows to the crystals on the other masts are also on our globe. No theory of hallucination suffices for the facts.

32

THE BOARDED WINDOW

Ambrose Bierce

In 1830, only a few miles away from what is now the great city of Cincinnati, lay an immense and almost unbroken forest. The whole region was sparsely settled by people of the frontier—restless souls who no sooner had hewn fairly habitable homes out of the wilderness and attained to that degree of prosperity which to-day we should call indigence, than, impelled by some mysterious impulse of their nature, they abandoned all and pushed farther westward, to encounter new perils and privations in the effort to regain the meagre comforts which they had voluntarily renounced. Many of them had already forsaken that region for the remoter settlements, but among those remaining was one who had been of those first arriving. He lived alone in a house of logs surrounded on all sides by the great forest, of whose gloom and silence he seemed a part, for no one had ever known him to smile nor speak a needless word. His simple wants were supplied by the sale or barter of skins of wild animals in the river town, for not a thing did he grow upon the land which, if needful, he might have claimed by right of undisturbed possession. There were evidences of 'improvement'—a few acres of ground immediately about the house had once been cleared of its trees, the decayed stumps of which were half concealed by the new growth that had been suffered to repair the ravage wrought by the axe. Apparently the man's zeal for agriculture had burned with a failing flame, expiring in penitential ashes.

The little log house, with its chimney of sticks, its roof of warping clapboards weighted with traversing poles and its 'chinking' of clay, had a single door and, directly opposite, a window. The latter, however, was boarded up—nobody could remember a time when it was not. And none knew why it was so closed; certainly not because of the occupant's dislike of light and air, for on those rare occasions when a hunter had passed that lonely spot the recluse had commonly been seen sunning himself on his doorstep if heaven had provided sunshine for his need. I fancy there are few persons living to-day who ever knew the secret of that window, but I am one, as you shall see.

The man's name was said to be Murlock. He was apparently seventy years old, actually about fifty. Something besides years had had a hand in his ageing. His hair and long, full beard were white, his grey, lustreless eyes sunken, his face singularly seamed with wrinkles which appeared to belong to two intersecting systems. In figure he was tall and spare, with a stoop of the shoulders—a burden bearer. I never saw him; these particulars I learned from my grandfather, from whom also I got the man's story when I was a lad. He had known him when living near by in that early day.

One day Murlock was found in his cabin, dead. It was not a time and place for coroners and newspapers, and I suppose it was agreed that he had died from natural causes or I should have been told, and should remember. I know only that with what was probably a sense of the fitness of things the body was buried near the cabin, alongside the grave of his wife, who had preceded him by so many years that local tradition had retained hardly a hint of her existence. That closes the final chapter of this true story—excepting, indeed, the circumstance that many years afterward, in company with an equally intrepid spirit, I penetrated to the place and ventured near enough to the ruined cabin to throw a stone against it, and ran away to avoid the ghost which every well-informed boy thereabout knew haunted the spot. But there is an earlier chapter—that supplied by my grandfather.

When Murlock built his cabin and began laying sturdily about with his axe to hew out a farm—the rifle, meanwhile, his means of support—he was young, strong and full of hope. In that eastern country whence he came he had married, as was the fashion, a young woman in all ways worthy of his honest devotion, who shared the dangers and privations of his lot with a willing spirit and light heart. There is no known record of her name; of her charms of mind and person tradition is silent and the doubter is at liberty to entertain his doubt; but God forbid that I should share it! Of their affection and happiness there is abundant assurance in every added day of the man's widowed life; for what but the magnetism of a blessed memory could have chained that venturesome spirit to a lot like that?

One day Murlock returned from gunning in a distant part of the forest to find his wife prostrate with fever, and delirious. There was no physician within miles, no neighbour; nor was she in a condition to be left, to summon help. So he set about the task of nursing her back to health, but at the end of the third day she fell into unconsciousness and so passed away, apparently, with never a gleam of returning reason.

From what we know of a nature like his we may venture to sketch in some of the details of the outline picture drawn by my grandfather. When convinced that she was dead, Murlock had sense enough to remember that the dead must be prepared for burial. In performance of this sacred duty he blundered now and again, did certain things incorrectly, and others which he did correctly were done over and over. His occasional failures to accomplish some simple and ordinary act filled him with astonishment, like that of a drunken man who wonders at the suspension of familiar natural laws. He was surprised, too, that he did not weep—surprised and a little ashamed; surely it is unkind not to weep for the dead. 'To-morrow,' he said aloud, 'I shall have to make the coffin arid dig the grave; and then I shall miss her, when she is no longer in sight; but now—she is dead, of course, but it is all right—it must be all right, somehow. Things cannot be so bad as they seem.'

He stood over the body in the fading light, adjusting the hair and putting the finishing touches to the simple toilet, doing all mechanically, with soulless care. And still through his consciousness ran an undersense of conviction that all was right—that he should have her again as before, and everything explained. He had had no experience in grief; his capacity had not been enlarged by use. His heart could not contain it all, nor his imagination rightly conceive it. He did not know he was so hard struck; that knowledge would come later, and never go. Grief is an artist of powers as various as the instruments upon which he plays his dirges for the dead, evoking from some the sharpest, shrillest notes, from others the low, grave chords that throb recurrent like the slow beating of a distant drum. Some natures it startles; some it stupefies. To one it comes like the stroke of an arrow, stinging all the sensibilities to a keener life; to another as the blow of a bludgeon, which in crushing benumbs. We may conceive Murlock to have been that way affected, for (and here we are upon surer ground than that of conjecture) no sooner had he finished his pious work than, sinking into a chair by the side of the table upon which the body lay, and noting how white the profile showed in the deepening gloom, he laid his arms upon the table's edge, and dropped his face into them, tearless yet and unutterably weary. At that moment came in through the open window a long, wailing sound like the cry of a lost child in the far deeps of the darkening woods! But the man did not move. Again, and nearer than before, sounded that unearthly cry upon his failing sense. Perhaps it was a wild beast; perhaps it was a dream. For Murlock was asleep.

Some hours later, as it afterward appeared, this unfaithful watcher awoke and lifting his head from his arms intently listened—he knew not why. There in the black darkness by the side of the dead, recalling all without a shock, he strained his eyes to see—he knew not what. His senses were all alert, his breath was suspended, his blood had stilled its tides as if to assist the silence. Who—what had waked him, and where was it?

Suddenly the table shook beneath his arms, and at the same moment he heard, or fancied that he heard, a light, soft step—another—sounds as of bare feet upon the floor!

He was terrified beyond the power to cry out or move. Perforce he waited—waited there in the darkness through seeming centuries of such dread as one may know, yet live to tell. He tried vainly to speak the dead woman's name, vainly to stretch forth his hand across the table to learn if she were there. His throat was powerless, his arms and hands were like lead. Then occurred something most frightful. Some heavy body seemed hurled against the table with an impetus that pushed it against his breast so sharply as nearly to overthrow him, and at the same instant he heard and felt the fall of something upon the floor with so violent a thump that the whole house was shaken by the impact. A scuffling ensued, and a confusion of sounds impossible to describe. Murlock had risen to his feet. Fear had by excess forfeited control of his faculties. He flung his hands upon the table. Nothing was there!

There is a point at which terror may turn to madness; and madness incites to action. With no definite intent, from no motive but the wayward impulse of a madman, Murlock sprang to the wall, with a little groping seized his loaded rifle, and without aim discharged it. By the flash which lit up the room with a vivid illumination, he saw an enormous panther dragging the dead woman toward the window, its teeth fixed in her throat! Then there were darkness blacker than before, and silence; and when he returned to consciousness the sun was high and the wood vocal with songs of birds.

The body lay near the window, where the beast had left it when frightened away by the flash and report of the rifle. The clothing was deranged, the long hair in disorder, the limbs lay anyhow. From the throat, dreadfully lacerated, had issued a pool of blood not yet entirely coagulated. The ribbon with which he had bound the wrists was broken; the hands were tightly clenched. Between the teeth was a fragment of the animal's ear.

33

THE BET

Anton Chekov

It was a dark autumn night. The old banker was walking up and down his study and remembering how, fifteen years before, he had given a party one autumn evening. There had been many clever men there, and there had been interesting conversations. Among other things they had talked of capital punishment. The majority of the guests, among whom were many journalists and intellectual men, disapproved of the death penalty. They considered that form of punishment out of date, immoral, and unsuitable for Christian States. In the opinion of some of them the death penalty ought to be replaced everywhere by imprisonment for life. 'I don't agree with you,' said their host the banker. 'I have not tried either the death penalty or imprisonment for life, but if one may judge *a priori*, the death penalty is more moral and more humane than imprisonment for life. Capital punishment kills a man at once, but lifelong imprisonment kills him slowly. Which executioner is the more humane, he who kills you in a few minutes or he who drags the life out of you in the course of many years?'

'Both are equally immoral,' observed one of the guests, 'for they both have the same object—to take away life. The State is not God. It has not the right to take away what it cannot restore when it wants to.'

Among the guests was a young lawyer, a young man of five-and-twenty. When he was asked his opinion, he said:

'The death sentence and the life sentence are equally immoral, but if I had to choose between the death penalty and imprisonment for life, I would certainly choose the second. To live anyhow is better than not at all.'

A lively discussion arose. The banker, who was younger and more nervous in those days, was suddenly carried away by excitement; he struck the table with his fist and shouted at the young man:

'It's not true! I'll bet you two million you wouldn't stay in solitary confinement for five years.'

'If you mean that in earnest,' said the young man, 'I'll take the bet, but I would stay not five but fifteen years.'

'Fifteen? Done!' cried the banker. 'Gentlemen, I stake two million!'

'Agreed! You stake your millions and I stake my freedom!' said the young man.

And this wild, senseless bet was carried out! The banker, spoilt and frivolous, with millions beyond his reckoning, was delighted at the bet. At supper he made fun of the young man, and said:

'Think better of it, young man, while there is still time. To me two million is a trifle, but you are losing three or four of the best years of your life. I say three or four, because you won't stay longer. Don't forget either, you unhappy man, that voluntary confinement is a great deal harder to bear than compulsory. The thought that you have the right to step out in liberty at any moment will poison your whole existence in prison. I am sorry for you.'

And now the banker, walking to and fro, remembered all this, and asked himself: 'What was the object of that bet? What is the good of that man's losing fifteen years of his life and my throwing away two million? Can it prove that the death penalty is better or worse than imprisonment for life? No, no. It was all nonsensical and meaningless. On my part it was the caprice of a pampered man, and on his part simple greed for money...'

Then he remembered what followed that evening. It was decided that the young man should spend the years of his captivity under the strictest supervision in one of the lodges in the banker's garden. It was agreed that for fifteen years he should not be free to cross the threshold of the lodge, to see human beings, to hear the human voice, or to receive letters and newspapers. He was allowed to have a musical instrument and books, and was allowed to write letters, to drink wine, and to smoke. By the terms of the agreement, the only relations he could have with the outer world were by a little window made purposely for that object. He might have anything he wanted—books, music, wine, and so on—in any quantity he desired by writing an order, but could only receive them through the window. The agreement provided for every detail and every trifle that would make his imprisonment strictly solitary, and bound the young man to stay there *exactly* fifteen years, beginning from twelve o'clock of November 14, 1870, and ending at twelve o'clock of November 14, 1885. The slightest attempt on his part to break the conditions, if only two minutes before the end, released the banker from the obligation to pay him the two million.

For the first year of his confinement, as far as one could judge from his brief notes, the prisoner suffered severely from loneliness and depression. The sounds of the piano could be heard continually day and night from his lodge. He refused wine and tobacco. Wine, he wrote, excites the desires, and desires are the worst foes of the prisoner; and besides, nothing could be more dreary than drinking good wine and seeing no one. And tobacco spoilt the air of his room. In the first year the books he sent for were principally of a light character; novels with a complicated love plot, sensational and fantastic stories, and so on.

In the second year the piano was silent in the lodge, and the prisoner asked only for the classics. In the fifth year music was audible again, and the prisoner asked for wine. Those who watched him through the window said that all that year he spent doing nothing but eating and drinking and lying on his bed, frequently yawning and angrily talking to himself. He did not read books. Sometimes at night he would sit down to write; he would spend hours writing, and in the morning tear up all that he had written. More than once he could be heard crying.

In the second half of the sixth year the prisoner began zealously studying languages, philosophy, and history. He threw himself eagerly into these studies—so much so that the banker had enough to do to get him the books he ordered. In the course of four years some six hundred volumes were procured at his request. It was during this period that the banker received the following letter from his prisoner:

'My dear Jailer, I write you these lines in six languages. Show them to people who know the languages. Let them read them. If they find not one mistake I implore you to fire a shot in the garden. That shot will show me that my efforts have not been thrown away. The geniuses of all ages and of all lands speak different languages, but the same flame burns in them all. Oh, if you only knew what unearthly happiness my soul feels now from being able to understand them!' The prisoner's desire was fulfilled. The banker ordered two shots to be fired in the garden.

Then after the tenth year, the prisoner sat immovably at the table and read nothing but the Gospel. It seemed strange to the banker that a man who in four years had mastered six hundred learned volumes should waste nearly a year over one thin book easy of comprehension. Theology and histories of religion followed the Gospels.

In the last two years of his confinement the prisoner read an immense quantity of books quite indiscriminately. At one time he was busy with the natural sciences, then he would ask for Byron or Shakespeare. There were notes in which he demanded at the same time books on chemistry, and a manual of medicine, and a novel, and some treatise on philosophy or theology. His reading suggested a man swimming in the sea among the wreckage of his ship, and trying to save his life by greedily clutching first at one spar and then at another.

The old banker remembered all this, and thought:

'To-morrow at twelve o'clock he will regain his freedom. By our agreement I ought to pay him two million. If I do pay him, it is all over with me: I shall be utterly ruined.'

Fifteen years before, his millions had been beyond his reckoning; now he was afraid to ask himself which were greater, his debts or his assets. Desperate gambling on the Stock Exchange, wild speculation and the excitability which he could not get over even in advancing years, had by degrees led to the decline of his fortune and the proud, fearless, self-confident millionaire had become a banker of middling rank, trembling at every rise and fall in his investments. 'Cursed bet!' muttered the old man, clutching his head in despair 'Why didn't the man die? He is only forty now. He will take my last penny from me, he will marry, will enjoy life, will gamble on the Exchange; while I shall look at him with envy like a beggar, and hear from him every day the same sentence: "I am indebted to you for the happiness of my life, let me help you!" No, it is too much! The one means of being saved from bankruptcy and disgrace is the death of that man!'

It struck three o'clock, the banker listened; everyone was asleep in the house and nothing could be heard outside but the rustling of the chilled trees. Trying to make no noise, he took from a fireproof safe the key of the door which had not been opened for fifteen years, put on his overcoat, and went out of the house.

It was dark and cold in the garden. Rain was falling. A damp cutting wind was racing about the garden, howling and giving the trees no rest. The banker strained his eyes, but could see neither the earth nor the white statues, nor the lodge, nor the trees. Going to the spot where the lodge stood, he twice called the watchman. No answer followed. Evidently the watchman had sought shelter from the weather, and was now asleep somewhere either in the kitchen or in the greenhouse.

'If I had the pluck to carry out my intention,' thought the old man, 'Suspicion would fall first upon the watchman.'

He felt in the darkness for the steps and the door, and went into the entry of the lodge. Then he groped his way into a little passage and lighted a match. There was not a soul there. There was a bedstead with no bedding on it, and in the corner there was a dark cast-iron stove. The seals on the door leading to the prisoner's rooms were intact.

When the match went out the old man, trembling with emotion, peeped through the little window. A candle was burning dimly in the prisoner's room. He was sitting at the table. Nothing could be seen but his back, the hair on his head, and his hands. Open books were lying on the table, on the two easy-chairs, and on the carpet near the table.

Five minutes passed and the prisoner did not once stir. Fifteen years' imprisonment had taught him to sit still. The banker tapped at the window with his finger, and the prisoner made no movement whatever in response. Then the banker cautiously broke the seals off the door and put the key in the keyhole. The rusty lock gave a grating sound and the door creaked. The banker expected to hear at once footsteps and a cry of astonishment, but three minutes passed and it was as quiet as ever in the room. He made up his mind to go in.

At the table a man unlike ordinary people was sitting motionless. He was a skeleton with the skin drawn tight over his bones, with long curls like a woman's and a shaggy beard. His face was yellow with an earthy tint in it, his cheeks were hollow, his back long and narrow, and the hand on which his shaggy head was propped was so thin and delicate that it was dreadful to look at it. His hair was already streaked with silver, and seeing his emaciated, aged-looking face, no one would have believed that he was only forty. He was asleep... In front of his bowed head there lay on the table a sheet of paper on which there was something written in fine handwriting.

'Poor creature!' thought the banker, 'he is asleep and most likely dreaming of the millions. And I have only to take this half-dead man, throw him on the bed, stifle him a little with the pillow, and the most conscientious expert would find no sign of a violent death. But let us first read what he has written here...'

The banker took the page from the table and read as follows:

'To-morrow at twelve o'clock I regain my freedom and the right to associate with other men, but before I leave this room and see the sunshine, I think it necessary to say a few words to you. With a clear conscience I tell you, as before God, who beholds me, that I despise freedom and life and health, and all that in your books is called the good things of the world.

'For fifteen years I have been intently studying earthly life. It is true I have not seen the earth nor men, but in your books I have drunk fragrant wine, I have sung songs, I have hunted stags and wild boars in the forests, have loved women... Beauties as ethereal as clouds, created by the magic of your poets and geniuses, have visited me at night, and have whispered in my ears wonderful tales that have set my brain in a whirl. In your books I have climbed to the peaks of Elburz and Mont Blanc, and from there I have seen the sun rise and have watched it at evening flood the sky, the ocean, and the mountain-tops with gold and crimson. I have watched from there the lightning flashing over my head and cleaving the storm-clouds. I have seen green forests, fields, rivers, lakes, towns. I have heard the singing of the sirens, and the strains of the shepherds' pipes; I have touched the wings of comely devils who flew down to converse with me of God... In your books I have flung myself into the bottomless pit, performed miracles, slain, burned towns, preached new religions, conquered whole kingdoms...

'Your books have given me wisdom. All that the unresting thought of man has created in the ages is compressed into a small compass in my brain. I know that I am wiser than all of you.

'And I despise your books, I despise wisdom and the blessings of this world. It is all worthless, fleeting, illusory, and deceptive, like a mirage. You may be proud, wise, and fine, but death will wipe you off the face of the earth as though you were no more than mice burrowing under the floor, and your posterity, your history, your immortal geniuses will burn or freeze together with the earthly globe.

'You have lost your reason and taken the wrong path. You have taken lies for truth, and hideousness for beauty. You would marvel if, owing to strange events of some sorts, frogs and lizards suddenly grew on apple and orange trees instead of fruit, or if roses began to smell like a sweating horse; so I marvel at you who exchange heaven for earth. I don't want to understand you.

'To prove to you in action how I despise all that you live by, I renounce the two million of which I once dreamed as of paradise and which now I despise. To deprive myself of the right to the money I shall go out from here five hours before the time fixed, and so break the compact...'

When the banker had read this he laid the page on the table, kissed the strange man on the head, and went out of the lodge, weeping. At no other time, even when he had lost heavily on the Stock Exchange, had he felt so great a contempt for himself. When he got home he lay on his bed, but his tears and emotion kept him for hours from sleeping.

Next morning the watchmen ran in with pale faces, and told him they had seen the man who lived in the lodge climb out of the window into the garden, go to the gate, and disappear. The banker went at once with the servants to the lodge and made sure of the flight of his prisoner. To avoid arousing unnecessary talk, he took from the table the writing in which the millions were renounced, and when he got home locked it up in the fireproof safe.

34

A COWARD

Guy de Maupassant

Society called him 'Handsome Signoles'. His name was Viscount Gontran-Joseph de Signoles.

An orphan, and possessed of an adequate income, he cut a dash, as the saying is. He had a good figure and a good carriage, a sufficient flow of words to pass for wit, a certain natural grace, an air of nobility and pride, a gallant moustache and an eloquent eye, attributes which women like.

He was in demand in drawing-rooms, sought after for valses, and in men he inspired that smiling hostility which is reserved for vital and attractive rivals. He had been suspected of several love-affairs of a sort calculated to create a good opinion of a youngster. He lived a happy, care-free life, in the most complete well-being of body and mind. He was known to be a fine swordsman and a still finer shot with the pistol.

'When I come to fight a duel,' he would say, 'I shall choose pistols. With that weapon, I'm sure of killing my man.'

One evening, he went to the theatre with two ladies, quite young, friends of his, whose husbands were also of the party, and after the performance he invited them to take ices at Tortoni's.

They had been sitting there for a few minutes when he noticed a gentleman at a neighbouring table staring obstinately at one of the ladies of the party. She seemed embarrassed and ill at ease, and bent her head. At last she said to her husband:

'There's a man staring at me. I don't know him; do you?'

The husband, who had seen nothing, raised his eyes, but declared:

'No, not in the least.'

Half smiling, half in anger, she replied:

'It's very annoying; the creature's spoiling my ice.'

Her husband shrugged his shoulders.

'Deuce take him, don't appear to notice it. If we had to deal with all the discourteous people one meets, we'd never have done with them.'

But the Viscount had risen abruptly. He could not permit this stranger to spoil an ice of his giving. It was to him that the insult was addressed, since it was at his invitation and on his account that his friends had come to the café. The affair was no business of anyone but himself.

He went up to the man and said:

'You have a way of looking at those ladies, sir, which I cannot stomach. Please be so good as to set a limit to your persistence.'

'You hold your tongue,' replied the other.

'Take care, sir,' retorted the Viscount, clenching his teeth; 'you'll force me to overstep the bounds of common politeness.'

The gentleman replied with a single word, a vile word which rang across the café from one end to the other, and, like the release of a spring, jerked every person present into an abrupt movement. All those with their backs towards him turned round, all the rest raised their heads; three waiters spun round on their heels like tops; the two ladies behind the counter started, then the whole upper half of their bodies twisted round, as though they were a couple of automata worked by the same handle.

There was a profound silence. Then suddenly a sharp noise resounded in the air. The Viscount had boxed his adversary's ears. Every one rose to intervene. Cards were exchanged.

Back in his home, the Viscount walked for several minutes up and down his room with long quick strides. He was too excited to think. A solitary idea dominated his mind: 'a duel'; but as yet the idea stirred in him no emotion of any kind. He had done what he was compelled to do; he had shown himself to be what he ought to be. People would talk of it, would approve of him, congratulate him. He repeated aloud, speaking as a man speaks in severe mental distress:

'What a hound the fellow is!'

Then he sat down and began to reflect. In the morning he must find seconds. Whom should he choose? He searched his mind for the most important and celebrated names of his acquaintance. At last he decided on the Marquis de la Tour-Noire and Colonel Bourdin, an aristocrat and a soldier; they would do excellently. Their names would look well in the papers. He realised that he was thirsty, and drank three glasses of water one after the other; then he began to walk up and down again. He felt full of energy. If he played the gallant, showed himself determined, insisted on the most strict and dangerous arrangements, demanded a serious duel, a thoroughly serious duel, a positively terrible duel, his adversary would probably retire and apologize.

He took up once more the card which he had taken from his pocket and thrown down upon the table, and read it again as he had read it before, in the café, at a glance, and in the cab, by the light of each gas-lamp, on his way home.

'Georges Lamil, 51 rue Moncey.' Nothing more.

He examined the grouped letters; they seemed to him mysterious, full of confused meaning. Georges Lamil? Who was this man? What did he do? Why had he looked at the woman in that way? Was it not revolting that a stranger, an unknown man, could thus disturb a man's life, without warning, just because he chose to fix his insolent eyes upon a woman? Again the Viscount repeated aloud:

'What a hound!'

Then he remained standing stock-still, lost in thought, his eyes still fixed upon the card. A fury against this scrap of paper awoke in him, a fury of hatred in which was mingled a queer sensation of uneasiness. This sort of thing was so stupid! He took up an open knife which lay close at hand and thrust it through the middle of the printed name, as though he had stabbed a man.

So he must fight. Should he choose swords or pistols?—for he regarded himself as the insulted party. With swords there would be less risk, but with pistols there was a chance that his adversary might withdraw. It is very rare that a duel with swords is fatal, for mutual prudence is apt to restrain combatants from engaging at sufficiently close quarters for a point to penetrate deeply. With pistols he ran a grave risk of death; but he might also extricate himself from the affair with all the honours of the situation and without actually coming to a meeting.

'I must be firm,' he said. 'He will take flight.'

The sound of his voice set him trembling, and he looked round. He felt very nervous. He drank another glass of water, then began to undress for bed.

As soon as he was in bed, he blew out the light and closed his eyes.

'I've the whole of to-morrow,' he thought, 'in which to set my affairs in order. I'd better sleep now, so that I shall be quite calm.'

He was very warm in the blankets, but he could not manage to compose himself to sleep. He turned this way and that, lay for five minutes upon his back, turned on to his left side, then rolled over on to his right.

He was still thirsty. He got up to get a drink. A feeling of uneasiness crept over him:

'Is it possible that I'm afraid?'

Why did his heart beat madly at each familiar sound in his room? When the clock was about to strike, the faint squeak of the rising spring made him start; so shaken he was that for several seconds afterwards he had to open his mouth to get his breath.

He began to reason with himself on the possibility of his being afraid.

'Shall I be afraid?'

No, of course he would not be afraid, since he was resolved to see the matter through, and had duly made up his mind to fight and not to tremble. But he felt so profoundly distressed that he wondered:

'Can a man be afraid in spite of himself?'

He was attacked by this doubt, this uneasiness, this terror; suppose a force more powerful than himself, masterful, irresistible, overcame him, what would happen? Yes, what might not happen? Assuredly he would go to the place of the meeting, since he was quite ready to go. But supposing he trembled? Supposing he fainted? He thought of the scene, of his reputation, his good name.

There came upon him a strange need to get up and look at himself in the mirror. He relit his candle. When he saw his face reflected in the polished glass, he scarcely recognised it, it seemed to him as though he had never yet seen himself. His eyes looked to him enormous; and he was pale; yes, without doubt he was pale, very pale.

He remained standing in front of the mirror. He put out his tongue, as though to ascertain the state of his health, and abruptly the thought struck him like a bullet:

'The day after to-morrow, at this very hour, I may be dead.'

His heart began again its furious beating.

'The day after to-morrow, at this very hour, I may be dead. This person facing me, this me I see in the mirror, will be no more. Why, here I am, I look at myself, I feel myself alive, and in twenty-four hours I shall be lying in that bed, dead, my eyes closed, cold, inanimate, vanished.'

He turned back towards the bed, and distinctly saw himself lying on his back in the very sheets he had just left. He had the hollow face of a corpse, his hands had the slackness of hands that will never make another movement.

At that he was afraid of his bed, and, to get rid of the sight of it, went into the smoking-room. Mechanically he picked up a cigar, lit it, and began to walk up and down again. He was cold; he went to the bell to wake his valet; but he stopped, even as he raised his hand to the rope.

'He will see that I am afraid.'

He did not ring; he lit the fire. His hands shook a little, with a nervous tremor, whenever they touched anything. His brain whirled, his troubled thoughts became elusive, transitory, and gloomy; his mind suffered all the effects of intoxication, as though he were actually drunk.

Over and over again he thought:

'What shall I do? What is to become of me?'

His whole body trembled, seized with a jerky shuddering; he got up and, going to the window, drew back the curtains.

Dawn was at hand, a summer dawn. The rosy sky touched the town, its roofs and walls, with its own hue. A broad descending ray, like the caress of the rising sun, enveloped the awakened world; and with the light, hope—a gay, swift, fierce hope—filled the Viscount's heart! Was he mad, that he had allowed himself to be struck down by fear, before anything was settled even, before his seconds had seen those of this Georges Lamil, before he knew whether he was going to fight?

He washed, dressed, and walked out with a firm step.

He repeated to himself, as he walked:

'I must be energetic, very energetic. I must prove that I am not afraid.'

His seconds, the Marquis and the Colonel, placed themselves at his disposal, and after hearty handshakes discussed the conditions.

'You are anxious for a serious duel?' asked the Colonel.

'Yes, a very serious one,' replied the Viscount.

'You still insist on pistols?' said the Marquis.

'Yes.'

'You will leave us free to arrange the rest?'

In a dry, jerky voice the Viscount stated:

'Twenty paces; at the signal, raising the arm, and not lowering it. Exchange of shots till one is seriously wounded.'

'They are excellent conditions,' declared the Colonel in a tone of satisfaction. 'You shoot well, you have every chance.'

They departed. The Viscount went home to wait for them. His agitation, momentarily quietened, was now growing minute by minute. He felt a strange shivering, a ceaseless vibration, down his arms, down his legs, in his chest; he could not keep still in one place, neither seated nor standing. There was not the least moistening of saliva in his mouth, and at every instant he made a violent movement of his tongue, as though to prevent it sticking to his palate.

He was eager to have breakfast, but could not eat. Then the idea came to him to drink in order to give himself courage, and he sent for a decanter of rum, of which he swallowed six liqueur glasses full one after the other.

A burning warmth flooded through his body, followed immediately by a sudden dizziness of the mind and spirit.

'Now I know what to do,' he thought. 'Now it is all right.'

But by the end of an hour he had emptied the decanter, and his state of agitation had once more become intolerable. He was conscious of a wild need to roll on the ground, to scream, to bite. Night was falling.

The ringing of a bell gave him such a shock that he had not strength to rise and welcome his seconds.

He did not even dare to speak to them, to say 'Good evening' to them, to utter a single word, for fear they guessed the whole thing by the alteration in his voice.

'Everything is arranged in accordance with the conditions you fixed,' observed the Colonel. 'At first your adversary claimed the privileges of the insulted party, but he yielded almost at once, and has accepted everything. His seconds are two military men.'

'Thank you,' said the Viscount.

'Pardon us,' interposed the Marquis, 'if we merely come in and leave again immediately, but we have a thousand things to see to. We must have a good doctor, since the combat is not to end until a serious wound is inflicted, and you know that pistol bullets are no laughing-matter. We must appoint the ground, near a house to which we may carry the wounded man if necessary, etc. In fact, we shall be occupied for two or three hours arranging all that there is to arrange.'

'Thank you,' said the Viscount a second time.

'You are all right?' asked the Colonel. 'You are calm?'

'Yes, quite calm, thank you.'

The two men retired.

When he realised that he was once more alone, he thought that he was going mad. His servant had lit the lamps, and he sat down at the table to write letters. After tracing, at the head of a sheet: 'This is my will,' he rose shivering and walked away, feeling incapable of connecting two ideas, of taking a resolution, of making any decision whatever.

So he was going to fight! He could no longer avoid it. Then what was the matter with him? He wished to fight, he had absolutely decided upon this plan of action and taken his resolve, and he now felt clearly, in spite of every effort of mind and forcing of will, that he could not retain even the strength necessary to get him to the place of meeting. He tried to picture the duel, his own attitude and the bearing of his adversary.

From time to time his teeth chattered in his mouth with a slight clicking noise. He tried to read, and took down Chateauvillard's code of duelling. Then he wondered:

'Does my adversary go to shooting-galleries? Is he well known? Is he classified anywhere? How can I find out?'

He bethought himself of Baron Vaux's book on marksmen with the pistol, and ran through it from end to end. Georges Lamil was not mentioned in it. Yet if the man were not a good shot, he would surely not have promptly agreed to that dangerous weapon and those fatal conditions?

He opened, in passing, a case by Gastinne Renette standing on a small table, and took out one of the pistols, then placed himself as though to shoot and raised his arm. But he was trembling from head to foot and the barrel moved in every direction.

At that, he said to himself:

'It's impossible. I cannot fight in this state.'

He looked at the end of the barrel, at the little, black, deep hole that spits death; he thought of the disgrace, of the whispers at the club, of the laughter in drawing-rooms, of the contempt of women, of the allusions in the papers, of the insults which cowards would fling at him.

He was still looking at the weapon, and, raising the hammer, caught a glimpse of a cap gleaming beneath it like a tiny red flame. By good fortune or forgetfulness, the pistol had been left loaded. At the knowledge, he was filled with a confused inexplicable sense of joy.

If, when face to face with the other man, he did not show a proper gallantry and calm, he would be lost for ever. He would be sullied, branded with a mark of infamy, hounded out of society. And he would not be able to achieve that calm, that swaggering poise; he knew it, he felt it. Yet he was brave, since he wanted to fight. I... He was brave, since...

The thought which hovered in him did not even fulfil itself in his mind; but, opening his mouth wide, he thrust in the barrel of his pistol with savage gesture until it reached his throat, and pressed on the trigger.

When his valet ran in, at the sound of the report, he found him lying dead upon his back. A shower of blood had splashed the white paper on the table, and made a great red mark beneath these four words:

'This is my will.'

35

A CHILD'S DREAM OF A STAR

Charles Dickens

There was once a child, and he strolled about a good deal, and thought of a number of things. He had a sister, who was a child too, and his constant companion. These two used to wonder all day long. They wondered at the beauty of the flowers; they wondered at the height and blueness of the sky; they wondered at the depth of the bright water; they wondered at the goodness and the power of God, who made the lovely world.

They used to say to one another, sometimes, supposing all the children upon earth were to die, would the flowers and the water and the sky be sorry? They believed they would be sorry. For, said they, the buds are the children of the flowers, and the little playful streams that gambol down the hillsides are the children of the water; and the smallest bright specks playing at hide-and-seek in the sky all night must surely be the children of the stars; and they would all be grieved to see their playmates, the children of men, no more.

There was one clear shining star that used to come out in the sky before the rest, near the church-spire, above the graves. It was larger and more beautiful, they thought, than all the others, and every night they watched for it, standing hand in hand at a window. Whoever saw it first cried out, 'I see the star!' And often they cried out both together, knowing so well when it would rise and where. So they grew to be such friends with it, that, before lying down in their beds, they always looked out once again, to bid it good night; and when they were turning round to sleep, they used to say, 'God bless the star!'

But while she was still very young, O, very, very young,

the sister drooped, and came to be so weak that she could no longer stand in the window at night; and then the child looked sadly out by himself, and when he saw the star, turned round and said to the patient pale face on the bed, 'I see the star!' And then a smile would come upon the face, and a little weak voice used to say, 'God bless my brother and the star!'

And so the time came, all too soon! when the child looked out alone, and when there was no face on the bed; and when there was a little grave among the graves, not there before; and when the star made long rays down towards him, as he saw it through his tears.

Now, these rays were so bright, and they seemed to make such a shining way from earth to heaven, that when the child went to his solitary bed, he dreamed about the star; and dreamed that, lying where he was, he saw a train of people taken up that sparkling road by angels. And the star, opening, showed him a great world of light, where many more such angels waited to receive them.

All these angels, who were waiting, turned their beaming eyes upon the people who were carried up into the star; and some came out from the long rows in which they stood, and fell upon the people's necks, and kissed them tenderly, and went away with them down avenues of light, and were so happy in their company, that, lying in his bed, he wept for joy.

But there were many angels who did not go with them, and among them one he knew. The patient face that once had lain upon the bed was glorified and radiant, but his heart found out his sister among all the host.

His sister's angel lingered near the entrance of the star, and said to the leader among those who had brought the people thither, 'Is my brother come?'

And he said, 'No.'

She was turning hopefully away, when the child stretched out his arms, and cried, 'O sister, I am here! Take me!' And then she turned her beaming eyes upon him, and it was night; and the star was shining into the room, making long rays down towards him as he saw it through his tears.

From that hour forth, the child looked out upon the star as on the home he was to go to, when his time should come; and he thought that he did not belong to the earth alone, but to the star too, because of his sister's angel gone before.

There was a baby born to be a brother to the child; and while he was so little that he never yet had spoken word, he stretched his tiny form out on his bed, and died.

Again the child dreamed of the opened star, and of the company of angels, and the train of people, and the rows of angels with their beaming eyes all turned upon those people's faces.

Said his sister's angel to the leader, 'Is my brother come?'

And he said, 'Not that one, but another.'

As the child beheld his brother's angel in her arms, he cried, 'O sister, I am here! Take me!' And she turned and smiled upon him, and the star was shining.

He grew to be a young man, and was busy at his books when an old servant came to him and said, 'Thy mother is no more. I bring her blessing on her darling son!'

Again at night he saw the star, and all that former company. Said his sister's angel to the leader, 'Is my brother come?'

And he said, 'Thy mother!'

A mighty cry of joy went forth through all the star, because the mother was reunited to her two children. And he stretched out his arms and cried, 'O mother, sister, and brother, I am here! Take me!'

And they answered him, 'Not yet.' And the star was shining.

He grew to be a man, whose hair was turning gray; and he was sitting in his chair by the fireside, heavy with grief, and with his face bedewed with tears, when the star opened once again.

Said his sister's angel to the leader, 'Is my brother come?'

And he said, 'Nay, but his maiden daughter.'

And the man who had been the child saw his daughter, newly lost to him, a celestial creature among those three, and he said, 'My daughter's head is on my sister's bosom, and her arm is round my mother's neck, and at her feet there is the baby of old time, and I can bear the parting from her, God be praised!'

And the star was shining.

Thus the child came to be an old man, and his once smooth face was wrinkled, and his steps were slow and feeble, and his back was bent. And one night as he lay upon his bed, his children standing round, he cried, as he had cried so long ago, 'I see the star!'

They whispered one another, 'He is dying.'

And he said, 'I am. My age is falling from me like a garment, and I move towards the star as a child. And O my Father, now I thank thee that it has so often opened to receive those dear ones who await me!'

And the star was shining; and it shines upon his grave.

36

TRUST

Jack London

All lines had been cast off, and the Seattle No. 4 was pulling slowly out from the shore. Her decks were piled high with freight and baggage, and swarmed with a heterogeneous company of Indians, dogs, and dog-mushers, prospectors, traders, and homeward-bound gold-seekers. A goodly portion of Dawson was lined up on the bank, saying good-bye. As the gang-plank came in and the steamer nosed into the stream, the clamour of farewell became deafening. Also, in that eleventh moment, everybody began to remember final farewell messages and to shout them back and forth across the widening stretch of water. Louis Bondell, curling his yellow moustache with one hand and languidly waving the other hand to his friends on shore, suddenly remembered something and sprang to the rail.

'Oh, Fred!' he bawled. 'Oh, Fred!

The 'Fred' desired thrust a strapping pair of shoulders through the forefront of the crowd on the bank and tried to catch Louis Bondell's message. The latter grew red in the face with vain vociferation. Still the water widened between steamboat and shore.

'Hey, you, Captain Scott!' he yelled at the pilot-house. 'Stop the boat!'

The gongs clanged, and the big stern wheel reversed, then stopped. All hands on steamboat and on bank took advantage of this respite to exchange final, new, and imperative farewells. More futile than ever was Louis Bondell's effort to make himself heard. The Seattle No. 4 lost way and drifted down-stream, and Captain Scott had to go ahead and reverse a second time. His head disappeared inside the pilot-house, coming into view a moment later behind a big megaphone.

Now Captain Scott had a remarkable voice, and the 'Shut up!' he launched at the crowd on deck and on shore could have been heard at the top of Moosehide Mountain and as far as Klondike City. This official remonstrance from the pilot-house spread a film of silence over the tumult.

'Now, what do you want to say?' Captain Scott demanded.

'Tell Fred Churchill—he's on the bank there—tell him to go to Macdonald. It's in his safe—a small gripsack of mine. Tell him to get it and bring it out when he comes.'

In the silence Captain Scott bellowed the message ashore through the megaphone

'You, Fred Churchill, go to Macdonald—in his safe—small gripsack—belongs to Louis Bondell—important! Bring it out when you come! Got it!'

Churchill waved his hand in token that he had got it. In truth, had Macdonald, half a mile away, opened his window, he'd have got it, too. The tumult of farewell rose again, the gongs clanged, and the Seattle No. 4 went ahead, swung out into the stream, turned on her heel, and headed down the Yukon, Bondell and Churchill waving farewell and mutual affection to the last.

That was in midsummer. In the fall of the year, the W. H. Willis started up the Yukon with two hundred homeward-bound pilgrims on board. Among them was Churchill. In his state-room, in the middle of a clothes-bag, was Louis Bondell's grip. It was a small, stout leather affair, and its weight of forty pounds always made Churchill nervous when he wandered too far from it. The man in the adjoining state-room had a treasure of gold-dust hidden similarly in a clothes-bag, and the pair of them ultimately arranged to stand watch and watch. While one went down to eat, the other kept an eye on the two state-room doors. When Churchill wanted to take a hand at whist, the other man mounted guard, and when the other man wanted to relax his soul, Churchill read four-months' old newspapers on a camp stool between the two doors.

There were signs of an early winter, and the question that was discussed from dawn till dark, and far into the dark, was whether they would get out before the freeze-up or be compelled to abandon the steamboat and tramp out over the ice. There were irritating delays. Twice the engines broke down and had to be tinkered up, and each time there were snow flurries to warn them of the imminence of winter. Nine times the W.H. Willis essayed to ascend the Five-Finger Rapids with her impaired machinery, and when she succeeded, she was four days behind her very liberal schedule. The question that then arose was whether or not the steamboat Flora would wait for her above the Box Canon. The stretch of water between the head of the Box Canon and the foot of the White Horse Rapids was unnavigable for steamboats, and passengers were transhipped at that point, walking around the rapids from one steamboat to the other. There were no telephones in the country, hence no way of informing the waiting Flora that the Willis was four days late, but coming.

When the W. H. Willis pulled into White Horse, it was learned that the Flora had waited three days over the limit, and had departed only a few hours before. Also, it was learned that she would tie up at Tagish Post till nine o'clock, Sunday morning. It was then four o'clock, Saturday afternoon. The pilgrims called a meeting. On board was a large Peterborough canoe, consigned to the police post at the head of Lake Bennett. They agreed to be responsible for it and to deliver it. Next, they called for volunteers. Two men were needed to make a race for the Flora. A score of men volunteered on the instant. Among them was Churchill, such being his nature that he volunteered before he thought of Bondell's gripsack. When this thought came to him, he began to hope that he would not be selected; but a man who had made a name as captain of a college football eleven, as a president of an athletic club, as a dog-musher and a stampeder in the Yukon, and, moreover, who possessed such shoulders as he, had no right to avoid the honour. It was thrust upon him and upon a gigantic German, Nick Antonsen.

While a crowd of the pilgrims, the canoe on their shoulders, started on a trot over the portage, Churchill ran to his stateroom. He turned the contents of the clothes-bag on the floor and caught up the grip, with the intention of entrusting it to the man next door. Then the thought smote him that it was not his grip, and that he had no right to let it out of his possession. So he dashed ashore with it and ran up the portage changing it often from one hand to the other, and wondering if it really did not weigh more than forty pounds.

It was half-past four in the afternoon when the two men started. The current of the Thirty Mile River was so strong that rarely could they use the paddles. It was out on one bank with a tow-line over the shoulders, stumbling over the rocks, forcing a way through the underbrush, slipping at times and falling into the water, wading often up to the knees and waist; and then, when an insurmountable bluff was encountered, it was into the canoe, out paddles, and a wild and losing dash across the current to the other bank, in paddles, over the side, and out tow-line again. It was exhausting work. Antonsen toiled like the giant he was, uncomplaining, persistent, but driven to his utmost by the powerful body and indomitable brain of Churchill. They never paused for rest. It was go, go, and keep on going. A crisp wind blew down the river, freezing their hands and making it imperative, from time to time, to beat the blood back into the numbed fingers.

As night came on, they were compelled to trust to luck. They fell repeatedly on the untravelled banks and tore their clothing to sheds in the underbrush they could not see. Both men were badly scratched and bleeding. A dozen times, in their wild dashes from bank to bank, they struck snags and were capsized. The first time this happened, Churchill dived and groped in three feet of water for the gripsack. He lost half an hour in recovering it, and after that it was carried securely lashed to the canoe. As long as the canoe floated it was safe. Antonsen jeered at the grip, and toward morning began to curse it; but Churchill vouchsafed no explanations.

Their delays and mischances were endless. On one swift bend, around which poured a healthy young rapid, they lost two hours, making a score of attempts and capsizing twice. At this point, on both banks, were precipitous bluffs, rising out of deep water, and along which they could neither tow nor pole, while they could not gain with the paddles against the current. At each attempt they strained to the utmost with the paddles, and each time, with heads nigh to bursting from the effort, they were played out and swept back. They succeeded finally by an accident. In the swiftest current, near the end of another failure, a freak of the current sheered the canoe out of Churchill's control and flung it against the bluff. Churchill made a blind leap at the bluff and landed in a crevice. Holding on with one hand, he held the swamped canoe with the other till Antonsen dragged himself out of the water. Then they pulled the canoe out and rested. A fresh start at this crucial point took them by. They landed on the bank above and plunged immediately ashore and into the brush with the tow-line.

Daylight found them far below Tagish Post. At nine o'clock Sunday morning they could hear the Flora whistling her departure. And when, at ten o'clock, they dragged themselves in to the Post, they could barely see the Flora's smoke far to the southward. It was a pair of worn-out tatterdemalions that Captain Jones of the Mounted Police welcomed and fed, and he afterward averred that they possessed two of the most tremendous appetites he had ever observed. They lay down and slept in their wet rags by the stove. At the end of two hours Churchill got up, carried Bondell's grip, which he had used for a pillow, down to the canoe, kicked Antonsen awake, and started in pursuit of the Flora.

'There's no telling what might happen—machinery break down, or something,' was his reply to Captain Jones's expostulations. 'I'm going to catch that steamer and send her back for the boys.'

Tagish Lake was white with a fall gale that blew in their teeth. Big, swinging seas rushed upon the canoe, compelling one man to bale and leaving one man to paddle. Headway could not be made. They ran along the shallow shore and went overboard, one man ahead on the tow-line, the other shoving on the canoe. They fought the gale up to their waists in the icy water, often up to their necks, often over their heads and buried by the big, crested waves. There was no rest, never a moment's pause from the cheerless, heart-breaking battle. That night, at the head of Tagish Lake, in the thick of a driving snow-squall, they overhauled the Flora. Antonsen fell on board, lay where he had fallen, and snored. Churchill looked like a wild man. His clothes barely clung to him. His face was iced up and swollen from the protracted effort of twenty-four hours, while his hands were so swollen that he could not close the fingers. As for his feet, it was an agony to stand upon them.

The captain of the Flora was loth to go back to White Horse. Churchill was persistent and imperative; the captain was stubborn. He pointed out finally that nothing was to be gained by going back, because the only ocean steamer at Dyea, the Athenian, was to sail on Tuesday morning, and that he could not make the back trip to White Horse and bring up the stranded pilgrims in time to make the connection.

'What time does the Athenian sail?' Churchill demanded.

'Seven o'clock, Tuesday morning.'

'All right,' Churchill said, at the same time kicking a tattoo on the ribs of the snoring Antonsen. 'You go back to White Home. We'll go ahead and hold the Athenian.'

Antonsen, stupid with sleep, not yet clothed in his waking mind, was bundled into the canoe, and did not realize what had happened till he was drenched with the icy spray of a big sea, and heard Churchill snarling at him through the darkness:-

'Paddle, can't you! Do you want to be swamped?'

Daylight found them at Caribou Crossing, the wind dying down, and Antonsen too far gone to dip a paddle. Churchill grounded the canoe on a quiet beach, where they slept. He took the precaution of twisting his arm under the weight of his head. Every few minutes the pain of the pent circulation aroused him, whereupon he would look at his watch and twist the other arm under his head. At the end of two hours he fought with Antonsen to rouse him. Then they started. Lake Bennett, thirty miles in length, was like a millpond; but, half way across, a gale from the south smote them and turned the water white. Hour after hour they repeated the struggle on Tagish, over the side, pulling and shoving on the canoe, up to their waists and necks, and over their heads, in the icy water; toward the last the good-natured giant played completely out. Churchill drove him mercilessly; but when he pitched forward and bade fair to drown in three feet of water, the other dragged him into the canoe. After that, Churchill fought on alone, arriving at the police post at the head of Bennett in the early afternoon. He tried to help Antonsen out of the canoe, but failed. He listened to the exhausted man's heavy breathing, and envied him when he thought of what he himself had yet to undergo. Antonsen could lie there and sleep; but he, behind time, must go on over mighty Chilcoot and down to the sea. The real struggle lay before him, and he almost regretted the strength that resided in his frame because of the torment it could inflict upon that frame.

Churchill pulled the canoe up on the beach, seized Bondell's grip, and started on a limping dog-trot for the police post.

'There's a canoe down there, consigned to you from Dawson,' he hurled at the officer who answered his knock. 'And there's a man in it pretty near dead. Nothing serious; only played out. Take care of him. I've got to rush. Good-bye. Want to catch the Athenian.'

A mile portage connected Lake Bennett and Lake Linderman, and his last words he flung back after him as he resumed the trot. It was a very painful trot, but he clenched his teeth and kept on, forgetting his pain most of the time in the fervent heat with which he regarded the gripsack. It was a severe handicap. He swung it from one hand to the other, and back again. He tucked it under his arm. He threw one hand over the opposite shoulder, and the bag bumped and pounded on his back as he ran along. He could scarcely hold it in his bruised and swollen fingers, and several times he dropped it. Once, in changing from one hand to the other, it escaped his clutch and fell in front of him, tripped him up, and threw him violently to the ground.

At the far end of the portage he bought an old set of pack-straps for a dollar, and in them he swung the grip. Also, he chartered a launch to run him the six miles to the upper end of Lake Linderman, where he arrived at four in the afternoon. The Athenian was to sail from Dyea next morning at seven. Dyea was twenty-eight miles away, and between towered Chilcoot. He sat down to adjust his foot-gear for the long climb, and woke up. He had dozed the instant he sat down, though he had not slept thirty seconds. He was afraid his next doze might be longer, so he finished fixing his foot-gear standing up. Even then he was overpowered for a fleeting moment. He experienced the flash of unconsciousness; becoming aware of it, in mid-air, as his relaxed body was sinking to the ground and as he caught himself together, he stiffened his muscles with a spasmodic wrench, and escaped the fall. The sudden jerk back to consciousness left him sick and trembling. He beat his head with the heel of his hand, knocking wakefulness into the numbed brain.

Jack Burns's pack-train was starting back light for Crater Lake, and Churchill was invited to a mule. Burns wanted to put the gripsack on another animal, but Churchill held on to it, carrying it on his saddle-pommel. But he dozed, and the grip persisted in dropping off the pommel, one side or the other, each time wakening him with a sickening start. Then, in the early darkness, Churchill's mule brushed him against a projecting branch that laid his cheek open. To cap it, the mule blundered off the trail and fell, throwing rider and gripsack out upon the rocks. After that, Churchill walked, or stumbled rather, over the apology for a trail, leading the mule. Stray and awful odours, drifting from each side of the trail, told of the horses that had died in the rush for gold. But he did not mind. He was too sleepy. By the time Long Lake was reached, however, he had recovered from his sleepiness; and at Deep Lake he resigned the gripsack to Burns. But thereafter, by the light of the dim stars, he kept his eyes on Burns. There were not going to be any accidents with that bag.

At Crater Lake, the pack-train went into camp, and Churchill, slinging the grip on his back, started the steep climb for the summit. For the first time, on that precipitous wall, he realized how tired he was. He crept and crawled like a crab, burdened by the weight of his limbs. A distinct and painful effort of will was required each time he lifted a foot. An hallucination came to him that he was shod with lead, like a deep-sea diver, and it was all he could do to resist the desire to reach down and feel the lead. As for Bondell's gripsack, it was inconceivable that forty pounds could weigh so much. It pressed him down like a mountain, and he looked back with unbelief to the year before, when he had climbed that same pass with a hundred and fifty pounds on his back. If those loads had weighed a hundred and fifty pounds, then Bondell's grip weighed five hundred.

The first rise of the divide from Crater Lake was across a small glacier. Here was a well-defined trail. But above the glacier, which was also above timber-line, was naught but a chaos of naked rock and enormous boulders. There was no way of seeing the trail in the darkness, and he blundered on, paying thrice the ordinary exertion for all that he accomplished. He won the summit in the thick of howling wind and driving snow, providentially stumbling upon a small, deserted tent, into which he crawled. There he found and bolted some ancient fried potatoes and half a dozen raw eggs.

When the snow ceased and the wind eased down, he began the almost impossible descent. There was no trail, and he stumbled and blundered, often finding himself, at the last moment, on the edge of rocky walls and steep slopes the depth of which he had no way of judging. Part way down, the stars clouded over again, and in the consequent obscurity he slipped and rolled and slid for a hundred feet, landing bruised and bleeding on the bottom of a large shallow hole. From all about him arose the stench of dead horses. The hole was handy to the trail, and the packers had made a practice of tumbling into it their broken and dying animals. The stench overpowered him, making him deadly sick, and as in a nightmare he scrambled out. Half-way up, he recollected Bondell's gripsack. It had fallen into the hole with him; the pack-strap had evidently broken, and he had forgotten it. Back he went into the pestilential charnel-pit, where he crawled around on hands and knees and groped for half an hour. Altogether he encountered and counted seventeen dead horses (and one horse still alive that he shot with his revolver) before he found Bondell's grip. Looking back upon a life that had not been without valour and achievement, he unhesitatingly declared to himself that this return after the grip was the most heroic act he had ever performed. So heroic was it that he was twice on the verge of fainting before he crawled out of the hole.

By the time he had descended to the Scales, the steep pitch of Chilcoot was past, and the way became easier. Not that it was an easy way, however, in the best of places; but it became a really possible trail, along which he could have made good time if he had not been worn out, if he had had light with which to pick his steps, and if it had not been for Bondell's gripsack. To him, in his exhausted condition, it was the last straw. Having barely strength to carry himself along, the additional weight of the grip was sufficient to throw him nearly every time he tripped or stumbled. And when he escaped tripping, branches reached out in the darkness, hooked the grip between his shoulders, and held him back.

His mind was made up that if he missed the Athenian it would be the fault of the gripsack. In fact, only two things remained in his consciousness—Bondell's grip and the steamer. He knew only those two things, and they became identified, in a way, with some stern mission upon which he had journeyed and toiled for centuries. He walked and struggled on as in a dream. As part of the dream was his arrival at Sheep Camp. He stumbled into a saloon, slid his shoulders out of the straps, and started to deposit the grip at his feet. But it slipped from his fingers and struck the floor with a heavy thud that was not unnoticed by two men who were just leaving. Churchill drank a glass of whisky, told the barkeeper to call him in ten minutes, and sat down, his feet on the grip, his head on his knees.

So badly did his misused body stiffen, that when he was called it required another ten minutes and a second glass of whisky to unbend his joints and limber up the muscles.

'Hey not that way!' the barkeeper shouted, and then went after him and started him through the darkness toward Canyon City. Some little husk of inner consciousness told Churchill that the direction was right, and, still as in a dream, he took the canon trail. He did not know what warned him, but after what seemed several centuries of travelling, he sensed danger and drew his revolver. Still in the dream, he saw two men step out and heard them halt him. His revolver went off four times, and he saw the flashes and heard the explosions of their revolvers. Also, he was aware that he had been hit in the thigh. He saw one man go down, and, as the other came for him, he smashed him a straight blow with the heavy revolver full in the face. Then he turned and ran. He came from the dream shortly afterward, to find himself plunging down the trail at a limping lope. His first thought was for the gripsack. It was still on his back. He was convinced that what had happened was a dream till he felt for his revolver and found it gone. Next he became aware of a sharp stinging of his thigh, and after investigating, he found his hand warm with blood. It was a superficial wound, but it was incontestable. He became wider awake, and kept up the lumbering run to Canyon City.

He found a man, with a team of horses and a wagon, who got out of bed and harnessed up for twenty dollars. Churchill crawled in on the wagon-bed and slept, the gripsack still on his back. It was a rough ride, over water-washed boulders down the Dyea Valley; but he roused only when the wagon hit the highest places. Any altitude of his body above the wagon-bed of less than a foot did not faze him. The last mile was smooth going, and he slept soundly.

He came to in the grey dawn, the driver shaking him savagely and howling into his ear that the Athenian was gone. Churchill looked blankly at the deserted harbour.

'There's a smoke over at Skaguay,' the man said.

Churchill's eyes were too swollen to see that far, but he said: 'It's she. Get me a boat.'

The driver was obliging and found a skiff, and a man to row it for ten dollars, payment in advance. Churchill paid, and was helped into the skiff. It was beyond him to get in by himself. It was six miles to Skaguay, and he had a blissful thought of sleeping those six miles. But the man did not know how to row, and Churchill took the oars and toiled for a few more centuries. He never knew six longer and more excruciating miles. A snappy little breeze blew up the inlet and held him back. He had a gone feeling at the pit of the stomach, and suffered from faintness and numbness. At his command, the man took the baler and threw salt water into his face.

The Athenian's anchor was up-and-down when they came alongside, and Churchill was at the end of his last remnant of strength.

'Stop her! Stop her!' he shouted hoarsely.

'Important message! Stop her!'

Then he dropped his chin on his chest and slept. When half a dozen men started to carry him up the gang-plank, he awoke, reached for the grip, and clung to it like a drowning man.

On deck he became a centre of horror and curiosity. The clothing in which he had left White Horse was represented by a few rags, and he was as frayed as his clothing. He had travelled for fifty-five hours at the top notch of endurance. He had slept six hours in that time, and he was twenty pounds lighter than when he started. Face and hands and body were scratched and bruised, and he could scarcely see. He tried to stand up, but failed, sprawling out on the deck, hanging on to the gripsack, and delivering his message.

'Now, put me to bed,' he finished; 'I'll eat when I wake up.'

They did him honour, carrying him down in his rags and dirt and depositing him and Bondell's grip in the bridal chamber, which was the biggest and most luxurious state-room in the ship. Twice he slept the clock around, and he had bathed and shaved and eaten and was leaning over the rail smoking a cigar when the two hundred pilgrims from White Horse came alongside.

By the time the Athenian arrived in Seattle, Churchill had fully recuperated, and he went ashore with Bondell's grip in his hand. He felt proud of that grip. To him it stood for achievement and integrity and trust. 'I've delivered the goods,' was the way he expressed these various high terms to himself. It was early in the evening, and he went straight to Bondell's home. Louis Bondell was glad to see him, shaking hands with both hands at the same time and dragging him into the house.

'Oh, thanks, old man; it was good of you to bring it out,' Bondell said when he received the gripsack.

He tossed it carelessly upon a couch, and Churchill noted with an appreciative eye the rebound of its weight from the springs. Bondell was volleying him with questions.

'How did you make out? How're the boys? What became of Bill Smithers? Is Del Bishop still with Pierce? Did he sell my dogs? How did Sulphur Bottom show up? You're looking fine. What steamer did you come out on?'

To all of which Churchill gave answer, till half an hour had gone by and the first lull in the conversation had arrived.

'Hadn't you better take a look at it?' he suggested, nodding his head at the gripsack

'Oh, it's all right,' Bondell answered. 'Did Mitchell's dump turn out as much as he expected?'

'I think you'd better look at it,' Churchill insisted. 'When I deliver a thing, I want to be satisfied that it's all right. There's always the chance that somebody might have got into it when I was asleep, or something.'

'It's nothing important, old man,' Bondell answered, with a laugh.

'Nothing important,' Churchill echoed in a faint, small

voice. Then he spoke with decision: 'Louis, what's in that bag? I want to know.'

Louis looked at him curiously, then left the room and returned with a bunch of keys. He inserted his hand and drew out a heavy Colt's revolver. Next came out a few boxes of ammunition for the revolver and several boxes of Winchester cartridges.

Churchill took the gripsack and looked into it. Then he turned it upside down and shook it gently.

'The gun's all rusted,' Bondell said. 'Must have been out in the rain.'

'Yes,' Churchill answered. 'Too bad it got wet. I guess I was a bit careless.'

He got up and went outside. Ten minutes later Louis Bondell went out and found him on the steps, sitting down, elbows on knees and chin on hands, gazing steadfastly out into the darkness.

37

THE CURIOUS CASE OF BENJAMIN BUTTON

F. Scott Fitzgerald

1

As long ago as 1860 it was the proper thing to be born at home. At present, so I am told, the high gods of medicine have decreed that the first cries of the young shall be uttered upon the anaesthetic air of a hospital, preferably a fashionable one. So young Mr. and Mrs. Roger Button were fifty years ahead of style when they decided, one day in the summer of 1860, that their first baby should be born in a hospital. Whether this anachronism had any bearing upon the astonishing history I am about to set down will never be known.

I shall tell you what occurred, and let you judge for yourself.

The Roger Buttons held an enviable position, both social and financial, in Antebellum Baltimore. They were related to the This Family and the That Family, which, as every Southerner knew, entitled them to membership in that enormous peerage which largely populated the Confederacy. This was their first experience with the charming old custom of having babies—Mr. Button was naturally nervous. He hoped it would be a boy so that he could be sent to Yale College in Connecticut, at which institution Mr. Button himself had been known for four years by the somewhat obvious nickname of 'Cuff.'

On the September morning consecrated to the enormous event he arose nervously at six o'clock dressed himself, adjusted an impeccable stock, and hurried forth through the streets of Baltimore to the hospital, to determine whether the darkness of the night had borne in new life upon its bosom.

When he was approximately a hundred yards from the

Maryland Private Hospital for Ladies and Gentlemen he saw Doctor Keene, the family physician, descending the front steps, rubbing his hands together with a washing movement—as all doctors are required to do by the unwritten ethics of their profession.

Mr. Roger Button, the president of Roger Button & Co., Wholesale Hardware, began to run toward Doctor Keene with much less dignity than was expected from a Southern gentleman of that picturesque period. 'Doctor Keene!' he called. 'Oh, Doctor Keene!'

The doctor heard him, faced around, and stood waiting, a curious expression settling on his harsh, medicinal face as Mr. Button drew near.

'What happened?' demanded Mr. Button, as he came up in a gasping rush. 'What was it? How is she? A boy? Who is it? What—'

'Talk sense!' said Doctor Keene sharply, He appeared somewhat irritated.

'Is the child born?' begged Mr. Button.

Doctor Keene frowned. 'Why, yes, I suppose so—after a fashion.' Again he threw a curious glance at Mr. Button.

'Is my wife all right?'

'Yes.'

'Is it a boy or a girl?'

'Here now!' cried Doctor Keene in a perfect passion of irritation,' 'I'll ask you to go and see for yourself. Outrageous!' He snapped the last word out in almost one syllable, then he turned away muttering: 'Do you imagine a case like this will help my professional reputation? One more would ruin me—ruin anybody.'

'What's the matter?' demanded Mr. Button appalled. 'Triplets?'

'No, not triplets!' answered the doctor cuttingly. 'What's more, you can go and see for yourself. And get another doctor. I brought you into the world, young man, and I've been physician to your family for forty years, but I'm through with you! I don't want to see you or any of your relatives ever again! Good-bye!'

Then he turned sharply, and without another word climbed into his phaeton, which was waiting at the curbstone, and drove severely away.

Mr. Button stood there upon the sidewalk, stupefied and trembling from head to foot. What horrible mishap had occurred? He had suddenly lost all desire to go into the Maryland Private Hospital for Ladies and Gentlemen—it was with the greatest difficulty that, a moment later, he forced himself to mount the steps and enter the front door.

A nurse was sitting behind a desk in the opaque gloom of the hall. Swallowing his shame, Mr. Button approached her.

'Good-morning,' she remarked, looking up at him pleasantly.

'Good-morning. I—I am Mr. Button.'

At this a look of utter terror spread itself over girl's face. She rose to her feet and seemed about to fly from the hall, restraining herself only with the most apparent difficulty.

'I want to see my child,' said Mr. Button.

The nurse gave a little scream. 'Oh—of course!' she cried hysterically. 'Upstairs. Right upstairs. Go—up!'

She pointed the direction, and Mr. Button, bathed in cool perspiration, turned falteringly, and began to mount to the second floor. In the upper hall he addressed another nurse who approached him, basin in hand. 'I'm Mr. Button,' he managed to articulate. 'I want to see my—'

Clank! The basin clattered to the floor and rolled in the direction of the stairs. Clank! Clank! I began a methodical decent as if sharing in the general terror which this gentleman provoked.

'I want to see my child!' Mr. Button almost shrieked. He was on the verge of collapse.

Clank! The basin reached the first floor. The nurse regained control of herself, and threw Mr. Button a look of hearty contempt.

'All right, Mr. Button,' she agreed in a hushed voice. 'Very well! But if you knew what a state it's put us all in this morning!

It's perfectly outrageous! The hospital will never have a ghost of a reputation after—'

'Hurry!' he cried hoarsely. 'I can't stand this!'

'Come this way, then, Mr. Button.'

He dragged himself after her. At the end of a long hall they reached a room from which proceeded a variety of howls—indeed, a room which, in later parlance, would have been known as the 'crying-room.' They entered.

'Well,' gasped Mr. Button, 'which is mine?'

'There!' said the nurse.

Mr. Button's eyes followed her pointing finger, and this is what he saw. Wrapped in a voluminous white blanket, and partly crammed into one of the cribs, there sat an old man apparently about seventy years of age. His sparse hair was almost white, and from his chin dripped a long smoke-colored beard, which waved absurdly back and forth, fanned by the breeze coming in at the window. He looked up at Mr. Button with dim, faded eyes in which lurked a puzzled question.

'Am I mad?' thundered Mr. Button, his terror resolving into rage. 'Is this some ghastly hospital joke?

'It doesn't seem like a joke to us,' replied the nurse severely. 'And I don't know whether you're mad or not—but that is most certainly your child.'

The cool perspiration redoubled on Mr. Button's forehead. He closed his eyes, and then, opening them, looked again. There was no mistake—he was gazing at a man of threescore and ten—a baby of threescore and ten, a baby whose feet hung over the sides of the crib in which it was reposing.

The old man looked placidly from one to the other for a moment, and then suddenly spoke in a cracked and ancient voice. 'Are you my father?' he demanded.

Mr. Button and the nurse started violently.

'Because if you are,' went on the old man querulously, 'I wish you'd get me out of this place—or, at least, get them to put a comfortable rocker in here,'

'Where in God's name did you come from? Who are you?'

burst out Mr. Button frantically.

'I can't tell you exactly who I am,' replied the querulous whine, 'because I've only been born a few hours—but my last name is certainly Button.'

'You lie! You're an impostor!'

The old man turned wearily to the nurse. 'Nice way to welcome a new-born child,' he complained in a weak voice. 'Tell him he's wrong, why don't you?'

'You're wrong. Mr. Button,' said the nurse severely. 'This is your child, and you'll have to make the best of it. We're going to ask you to take him home with you as soon as possible-some time to-day.'

'Home?' repeated Mr. Button incredulously.

'Yes, we can't have him here. We really can't, you know?'

'I'm right glad of it,' whined the old man. 'This is a fine place to keep a youngster of quiet tastes. With all this yelling and howling, I haven't been able to get a wink of sleep. I asked for something to eat'—here his voice rose to a shrill note of protest—'and they brought me a bottle of milk!'

Mr. Button, sank down upon a chair near his son and concealed his face in his hands. 'My heavens!' he murmured, in an ecstasy of horror. 'What will people say? What must I do?'

'You'll have to take him home,' insisted the nurse—'immediately!'

A grotesque picture formed itself with dreadful clarity before the eyes of the tortured man—a picture of himself walking through the crowded streets of the city with this appalling apparition stalking by his side.

'I can't. I can't,' he moaned.

People would stop to speak to him, and what was he going to say? He would have to introduce this—this septuagenarian: 'This is my son, born early this morning.' And then the old man would gather his blanket around him and they would plod on, past the bustling stores, the slave market—for a dark instant Mr. Button wished passionately that his son was black—past the luxurious houses of the residential district, past the home for the aged...

'Come! Pull yourself together,' commanded the nurse.

'See here,' the old man announced suddenly, 'if you think I'm going to walk home in this blanket, you're entirely mistaken.'

'Babies always have blankets.'

With a malicious crackle the old man held up a small white swaddling garment. 'Look!' he quavered. 'This is what they had ready for me.'

'Babies always wear those,' said the nurse primly.

'Well,' said the old man, 'this baby's not going to wear anything in about two minutes. This blanket itches. They might at least have given me a sheet.'

'Keep it on! Keep it on!' said Mr. Button hurriedly. He turned to the nurse. 'What'll I do?'

'Go down town and buy your son some clothes.'

Mr. Button's son's voice followed him down into the hall: 'And a cane, father. I want to have a cane.'

Mr. Button banged the outer door savagely...

2

'Good-morning,' Mr. Button said nervously, to the clerk in the Chesapeake Dry Goods Company. 'I want to buy some clothes for my child.'

'How old is your child, sir?'

'About six hours,' answered Mr. Button, without due consideration.

'Babies' supply department in the rear.'

'Why, I don't think—I'm not sure that's what I want. It's—he's an unusually large-size child. Exceptionally—ah large.'

'They have the largest child's sizes.'

'Where is the boys' department?' inquired Mr. Button, shifting his ground desperately. He felt that the clerk must surely scent his shameful secret.

'Right here.'

'Well—' He hesitated. The notion of dressing his son in men's clothes was repugnant to him. If, say, he could only find a very large boy's suit, he might cut off that long and awful beard, dye the white hair brown, and thus manage to conceal the worst, and to retain something of his own self-respect—not to mention his position in Baltimore society.

But a frantic inspection of the boys' department revealed no suits to fit the new-born Button. He blamed the store, of course—in such cases it is the thing to blame the store.

'How old did you say that boy of yours was?' demanded the clerk curiously.

'He's—sixteen.'

'Oh, I beg your pardon. I thought you said six hours. You'll find the youths' department in the next aisle.'

Mr. Button turned miserably away. Then he stopped, brightened, and pointed his finger toward a dressed dummy in the window display. 'There!' he exclaimed. 'I'll take that suit, out there on the dummy.'

The clerk stared. 'Why,' he protested, 'that's not a child's suit. At least it is, but it's for fancy dress. You could wear it yourself!'

'Wrap it up,' insisted his customer nervously. 'That's what I want.'

The astonished clerk obeyed.

Back at the hospital Mr. Button entered the nursery and almost threw the package at his son. 'Here's your clothes,' he snapped out.

The old man untied the package and viewed the contents with a quizzical eye.

'They look sort of funny to me,' he complained, 'I don't want to be made a monkey of—'

'You've made a monkey of me!' retorted Mr. Button fiercely. 'Never you mind how funny you look. Put them on—or I'll—or I'll spank you.' He swallowed uneasily at the penultimate word, feeling nevertheless that it was the proper thing to say.

'All right, father'—this with a grotesque simulation of filial respect—'you've lived longer; you know best. Just as you say.'

As before, the sound of the word 'father' caused Mr. Button

to start violently.

'And hurry.'

'I'm hurrying, father.'

When his son was dressed Mr. Button regarded him with depression. The costume consisted of dotted socks, pink pants, and a belted blouse with a wide white collar. Over the latter waved the long whitish beard, drooping almost to the waist. The effect was not good.

'Wait!'

Mr. Button seized a hospital shears and with three quick snaps amputated a large section of the beard. But even with this improvement the ensemble fell far short of perfection. The remaining brush of scraggly hair, the watery eyes, the ancient teeth, seemed oddly out of tone with the gaiety of the costume. Mr. Button, however, was obdurate—he held out his hand. 'Come along!' he said sternly.

His son took the hand trustingly. 'What are you going to call me, dad?' he quavered as they walked from the nursery—'just "baby" for a while? Till you think of a better name?'

Mr. Button grunted. 'I don't know,' he answered harshly. 'I think we'll call you Methuselah.'

3

Even after the new addition to the Button family had had his hair cut short and then dyed to a sparse unnatural black, had had his face shaved so dose that it glistened, and had been attired in small-boy clothes made to order by a flabbergasted tailor, it was impossible for Button to ignore the fact that his son was a poor excuse for a first family baby. Despite his aged stoop, Benjamin Button—for it was by this name they called him instead of by the appropriate but invidious Methuselah—was five feet eight inches tall. His clothes did not conceal this, nor did the clipping and dyeing of his eyebrows disguise the fact that the eyes under—were faded and watery and tired. In fact, the baby-nurse who had been engaged in advance left the house after one look, in a state of considerable indignation.

But Mr. Button persisted in his unwavering purpose. Benjamin was a baby, and a baby he should remain. At first he declared that if Benjamin didn't like warm milk he could go without food altogether, but he was finally prevailed upon to allow his son bread and butter, and even oatmeal by way of a compromise. One day he brought home a rattle and, giving it to Benjamin, insisted in no uncertain terms that he should 'play with it,' whereupon the old man took it with—a weary expression and could be heard jingling it obediently at intervals throughout the day.

There can be no doubt, though, that the rattle bored him, and that he found other and more soothing amusements when he was left alone. For instance, Mr. Button discovered one day that during the preceding week be had smoked more cigars than ever before—a phenomenon, which was explained a few days later when, entering the nursery unexpectedly, he found the room full of faint blue haze and Benjamin, with a guilty expression on his face, trying to conceal the butt of a dark Havana. This, of course, called for a severe spanking, but Mr. Button found that he could not bring himself to administer it. He merely warned his son that he would 'stunt his growth.'

Nevertheless he persisted in his attitude. He brought home lead soldiers, he brought toy trains, he brought large pleasant animals made of cotton, and, to perfect the illusion which he was creating—for himself at least—he passionately demanded of the clerk in the toy-store whether 'the paint would come oft the pink duck if the baby put it in his mouth.' But, despite all his father's efforts, Benjamin refused to be interested. He would steal down the back stairs and return to the nursery with a volume of the Encyclopedia Britannica, over which he would pore through an afternoon, while his cotton cows and his Noah's ark were left neglected on the floor. Against such a stubbornness Mr. Button's efforts were of little avail.

The sensation created in Baltimore was, at first, prodigious. What the mishap would have cost the Buttons and their kinsfolk socially cannot be determined, for the outbreak of the Civil War drew the city's attention to other things. A few people who were unfailingly polite racked their brains for compliments to give to the parents—and finally hit upon the ingenious device of declaring that the baby resembled his grandfather, a fact which, due to the standard state of decay common to all men of seventy, could not be denied. Mr. and Mrs. Roger Button were not pleased, and Benjamin's grandfather was furiously insulted.

Benjamin, once he left the hospital, took life as he found it. Several small boys were brought to see him, and he spent a stiff-jointed afternoon trying to work up an interest in tops and marbles—he even managed, quite accidentally, to break a kitchen window with a stone from a sling shot, a feat which secretly delighted his father.

Thereafter Benjamin contrived to break something every day, but he did these things only because they were expected of him, and because he was by nature obliging.

When his grandfather's initial antagonism wore off, Benjamin and that gentleman took enormous pleasure in one another's company. They would sit for hours, these two, so far apart in age and experience, and, like old cronies, discuss with tireless monotony the slow events of the day. Benjamin felt more at ease in his grandfather's presence than in his parents'—they seemed always somewhat in awe of him and, despite the dictatorial authority they exercised over him, frequently addressed him as 'Mr.'

He was as puzzled as any one else at the apparently advanced age of his mind and body at birth. He read up on it in the medical journal, but found that no such case had been previously recorded. At his father's urging he made an honest attempt to play with other boys, and frequently he joined in the milder games—football shook him up too much, and he feared that in case of a fracture his ancient bones would refuse to knit.

When he was five he was sent to kindergarten, where he initiated into the art of pasting green paper on orange paper, of weaving colored maps and manufacturing eternal cardboard necklaces. He was inclined to drowse off to sleep in the middle of these tasks, a habit which both irritated and frightened his young teacher. To his relief she complained to his parents, and he was removed from the school. The Roger Buttons told their friends that they felt he was too young.

By the time he was twelve years old his parents had grown used to him. Indeed, so strong is the force of custom that they no longer felt that he was different from any other child—except when some curious anomaly reminded them of the fact. But one day a few weeks after his twelfth birthday, while looking in the mirror, Benjamin made, or thought he made, an astonishing discovery. Did his eyes deceive him, or had his hair turned in the dozen years of his life from white to iron-gray under its concealing dye? Was the network of wrinkles on his face becoming less pronounced? Was his skin healthier and firmer, with even a touch of ruddy winter color? He could not tell. He knew that he no longer stooped, and that his physical condition had improved since the early days of his life.

'Can it be—?' he thought to himself, or, rather, scarcely dared to think.

He went to his father. 'I am grown,' he announced determinedly. 'I want to put on long trousers.'

His father hesitated. 'Well,' he said finally, 'I don't know. Fourteen is the age for putting on long trousers—and you are only twelve.'

'But you'll have to admit,' protested Benjamin, 'that I'm big for my age.'

His father looked at him with illusory speculation. 'Oh, I'm not so sure of that,' he said. 'I was as big as you when I was twelve.'

This was not true—it was all part of Roger Button's silent agreement with himself to believe in his son's normality.

4

Finally a compromise was reached. Benjamin was to continue to dye his hair. He was to make a better attempt to play with boys of his own age. He was not to wear his spectacles or carry a cane in the street. In return for these concessions he was allowed his first suit of long trousers...

Of the life of Benjamin Button between his twelfth and twenty-first year I intend to say little. Suffice to record that they were years of normal ungrowth. When Benjamin was eighteen he was erect as a man of fifty; he had more hair and it was of a dark gray; his step was firm, his voice had lost its cracked quaver and descended to a healthy baritone. So his father sent him up to Connecticut to take examinations for entrance to Yale College. Benjamin passed his examination and became a member of the freshman class.

On the third day following his matriculation he received a notification from Mr. Hart, the college registrar, to call at his office and arrange his schedule. Benjamin, glancing in the mirror, decided that his hair needed a new application of its brown dye, but an anxious inspection of his bureau drawer disclosed that the dye bottle was not there. Then he remembered—he had emptied it the day before and thrown it away.

He was in a dilemma. He was due at the registrar's in five minutes. There seemed to be no help for it—he must go as he was. He did.

'Good-morning,' said the registrar politely. 'You've come to inquire about your son.'

'Why, as a matter of fact, my name's Button—,' began Benjamin, but Mr. Hart cut him off.

'I'm very glad to meet you, Mr. Button. I'm expecting your son here any minute.'

'That's me!' burst out Benjamin. 'I'm a freshman.'

'What!'

'I'm a freshman.'

'Surely you're joking.'

'Not at all.'

The registrar frowned and glanced at a card before him. 'Why, I have Mr. Benjamin Button's age down here as eighteen.'

'That's my age,' asserted Benjamin, flushing slightly.

The registrar eyed him wearily. 'Now surely, Mr. Button,

you don't expect me to believe that.'

Benjamin smiled wearily. 'I am eighteen,' he repeated.

The registrar pointed sternly to the door. 'Get out,' he said. 'Get out of college and get out of town. You are a dangerous lunatic.'

'I am eighteen.'

Mr. Hart opened the door. 'The idea!' he shouted. 'A man of your age trying to enter here as a freshman. Eighteen years old, are you? Well, I'll give you eighteen minutes to get out of town.'

Benjamin Button walked with dignity from the room, and half a dozen undergraduates, who were waiting in the hall, followed him curiously with their eyes. When he had gone a little way he turned around, faced the infuriated registrar, who was still standing in the door-way, and repeated in a firm voice: 'I am eighteen years old.'

To a chorus of titters which went up from the group of undergraduates, Benjamin walked away.

But he was not fated to escape so easily. On his melancholy walk to the railroad station he found that he was being followed by a group, then by a swarm, and finally by a dense mass of undergraduates. The word had gone around that a lunatic had passed the entrance examinations for Yale and attempted to palm himself off as a youth of eighteen. A fever of excitement permeated the college. Men ran hatless out of classes, the football team abandoned its practice and joined the mob, professors' wives with bonnets awry and bustles out of position, ran shouting after the procession, from which proceeded a continual succession of remarks aimed at the tender sensibilities of Benjamin Button.

'He must be the wandering Jew!'

'He ought to go to prep school at his age!'

'Look at the infant prodigy!' 'He thought this was the old men's home.'

'Go up to Harvard!'

Benjamin increased his gait, and soon he was running. He would show them! He would go to Harvard, and then they would regret these ill-considered taunts!

Safely on board the train for Baltimore, he put his head from the window. 'You'll regret this!' he shouted.

'Ha-ha!' the undergraduates laughed. 'Ha-ha-ha!' It was the biggest mistake that Yale College had ever made...

5

In 1880 Benjamin Button was twenty years old, and he signalized his birthday by going to work for his father in Roger Button & Co., Wholesale Hardware. It was in that same year that he began 'going out socially'—that is, his father insisted on taking him to several fashionable dances. Roger Button was now fifty, and he and his son were more and more companionable—in fact, since Benjamin had ceased to dye his hair (which was still grayish) they appeared about the same age, and could have passed for brothers.

One night in August they got into the phaeton attired in their full-dress suits and drove out to a dance at the Shevlins' country house, situated just outside of Baltimore. It was a gorgeous evening. A full moon drenched the road to the lusterless color of platinum, and late-blooming harvest flowers breathed into the motionless air aromas that were like low, half-heard laughter. The open country, carpeted for rods around with bright wheat, was translucent as in the day. It was almost impossible not to be affected by the sheer beauty of the sky—almost.

'There's a great future in the dry-goods business,' Roger Button was saying. He was not a spiritual man—his aesthetic sense was rudimentary.

'Old fellows like me can't learn new tricks,' he observed profoundly. 'It's you youngsters with energy and vitality that have the great future before you.'

Far up the road the lights of the Shevlins' country house drifted into view, and presently there was a sighing sound that crept persistently toward them—it might have been the fine plaint of violins or the rustle of the silver wheat under the moon.

They pulled up behind a handsome brougham whose

passengers were disembarking at the door. A lady got out, then an elderly gentleman, then another young lady, beautiful as sin. Benjamin started; an almost chemical change seemed to dissolve and recompose the very elements of his body. A rigor passed over him, blood rose into his cheeks, his forehead, and there was a steady thumping in his ears. It was first love.

The girl was slender and frail, with hair that was ashen under the moon and honey-colored under the sputtering gas-lamps of the porch. Over her shoulders was thrown a Spanish mantilla of softest yellow, butterflied in black; her feet were glittering buttons at the hem of her bustled dress.

Roger Button leaned over to his son. 'That,' he said, 'is young Hildegarde Moncrief, the daughter of General Moncrief.'

Benjamin nodded coldly. 'Pretty little thing,' he said indifferently. But when the Negro boy had led the buggy away, he added: 'Dad, you might introduce me to her.'

They approached a group, of which Miss Moncrief was the center. Reared in the old tradition, she curtsied low before Benjamin. Yes, he might have a dance. He thanked her and walked away—staggered away.

The interval until the time for his turn should arrive dragged itself out interminably. He stood close to the wall, silent, inscrutable, watching with murderous eyes the young bloods of Baltimore as they eddied around Hildegarde Moncrief, passionate admiration in their faces. How obnoxious they seemed to Benjamin; how intolerably rosy! Their curling brown whiskers aroused in him a feeling equivalent to indigestion.

But when his own time came, and he drifted with her out upon the changing floor to the music of the latest waltz from Paris, his jealousies and anxieties melted from him like a mantle of snow. Blind with enchantment, he felt that life was just beginning.

'You and your brother got here just as we did, didn't you?' asked Hildegarde, looking up at him with eyes that were like bright blue enamel.

Benjamin hesitated. If she took him for his father's brother, would it be best to enlighten her? He remembered his experience at Yale, so he decided against it. It would be rude to contradict a lady; it would be criminal to mar this exquisite occasion with the grotesque story of his origin. Later, perhaps. So he nodded, smiled, listened, was happy.

'I like men of your age,' Hildegarde told him. 'Young boys are so idiotic. They tell me how much champagne they drink at college, and how much money they lose playing cards. Men of your age know how to appreciate women.'

Benjamin felt himself on the verge of a proposal—with an effort he choked back the impulse. 'You're just the romantic age,' she continued—'fifty. Twenty-five is too wordly-wise; thirty is apt to be pale from overwork; forty is the age of long stories that take a whole cigar to tell; sixty is—oh, sixty is too near seventy; but fifty is the mellow age. I love fifty.'

Fifty seemed to Benjamin a glorious age. He longed passionately to be fifty.

'I've always said,' went on Hildegarde, 'that I'd rather marry a man of fifty and be taken care of than many a man of thirty and take care of him.'

For Benjamin the rest of the evening was bathed in a honey-colored mist. Hildegarde gave him two more dances, and they discovered that they were marvelously in accord on all the questions of the day. She was to go driving with him on the following Sunday, and then they would discuss all these questions further.

Going home in the phaeton just before the crack of dawn, when the first bees were humming and the fading moon glimmered in the cool dew, Benjamin knew vaguely that his father was discussing wholesale hardware.

'... And what do you think should merit our biggest attention after hammers and nails?' the elder Button was saying.

'Love,' replied Benjamin absent-mindedly.

'Lugs?' exclaimed Roger Button, 'Why, I've just covered the question of lugs.'

Benjamin regarded him with dazed eyes just as the eastern

sky was suddenly cracked with light, and an oriole yawned piercingly in the quickening trees...

6

When, six months later, the engagement of Miss Hildegarde Moncrief to Mr. Benjamin Button was made known (I say 'made known,' for General Moncrief declared he would rather fall upon his sword than announce it), the excitement in Baltimore society reached a feverish pitch. The almost forgotten story of Benjamin's birth was remembered and sent out upon the winds of scandal in picaresque and incredible forms. It was said that Benjamin was really the father of Roger Button, that he was his brother who had been in prison for forty years, that he was John Wilkes Booth in disguise—and, finally, that he had two small conical horns sprouting from his head.

The Sunday supplements of the New York papers played up the case with fascinating sketches which showed the head of Benjamin Button attached to a fish, to a snake, and, finally, to a body of solid brass. He became known, journalistically, as the Mystery Man of Maryland. But the true story, as is usually the case, had a very small circulation.

However, every one agreed with General Moncrief that it was 'criminal' for a lovely girl who could have married any beau in Baltimore to throw herself into the arms of a man who was assuredly fifty. In vain Mr. Roger Button published his son's birth certificate in large type in the *Baltimore Blaze*. No one believed it. You had only to look at Benjamin and see.

On the part of the two people most concerned there was no wavering. So many of the stories about her fiance were false that Hildegarde refused stubbornly to believe even the true one. In vain General Moncrief pointed out to her the high mortality among men of fifty—or, at least, among men who looked fifty; in vain he told her of the instability of the wholesale hardware business. Hildegarde had chosen to marry for mellowness, and marry she did...

7

In one particular, at least, the friends of Hildegarde Moncrief were mistaken. The wholesale hardware business prospered amazingly. In the fifteen years between Benjamin Button's marriage in 1880 and his father's retirement in 1895, the family fortune was doubled—and this was due largely to the younger member of the firm.

Needless to say, Baltimore eventually received the couple to its bosom. Even old General Moncrief became reconciled to his son-in-law when Benjamin gave him the money to bring out his *History of the Civil War* in twenty volumes, which had been refused by nine prominent publishers.

In Benjamin himself fifteen years had wrought many changes. It seemed to him that the blood flowed with new vigor through his veins. It began to be a pleasure to rise in the morning, to walk with an active step along the busy, sunny street, to work untiringly with his shipments of hammers and his cargoes of nails. It was in 1890 that he executed his famous business coup: he brought up the suggestion that *all nails used in nailing up the boxes in which nails are shipped are the property of the shippee*, a proposal which became a statute, was approved by Chief Justice Fossile, and saved Roger Button and Company, Wholesale Hardware, more than *six hundred nails every year*.

In addition, Benjamin discovered that he was becoming more and more attracted by the gay side of life. It was typical of his growing enthusiasm for pleasure that he was the first man in the city of Baltimore to own and run an automobile. Meeting him on the street, his contemporaries would stare enviously at the picture he made of health and vitality.

'He seems to grow younger every year,' they would remark. And if old Roger Button, now sixty-five years old, had failed at first to give a proper welcome to his son he atoned at last by bestowing on him what amounted to adulation.

And here we come to an unpleasant subject which it will be well to pass over as quickly as possible. There was only one thing that worried Benjamin Button; his wife had ceased to attract him.

At that time Hildegarde was a woman of thirty-five, with a son, Roscoe, fourteen years old. In the early days of their marriage Benjamin had worshipped her. But, as the years passed, her honey-colored hair became an unexciting brown, the blue enamel of her eyes assumed the aspect of cheap crockery—moreover, and, most of all, she had become too settled in her ways, too placid, too content, too anaemic in her excitements, and too sober in her taste. As a bride it been she who had 'dragged' Benjamin to dances and dinners—now conditions were reversed. She went out socially with him, but without enthusiasm, devoured already by that eternal inertia which comes to live with each of us one day and stays with us to the end.

Benjamin's discontent waxed stronger. At the outbreak of the Spanish-American War in 1898 his home had for him so little charm that he decided to join the army. With his business influence he obtained a commission as captain, and proved so adaptable to the work that he was made a major, and finally a lieutenant-colonel just in time to participate in the celebrated charge up San Juan Hill. He was slightly wounded, and received a medal.

Benjamin had become so attached to the activity and excitement of array life that he regretted to give it up, but his business required attention, so he resigned his commission and came home. He was met at the station by a brass band and escorted to his house.

8

Hildegarde, waving a large silk flag, greeted him on the porch, and even as he kissed her he felt with a sinking of the heart that these three years had taken their toll. She was a woman of forty now, with a faint skirmish line of gray hairs in her head. The sight depressed him.

Up in his room he saw his reflection in the familiar mirror—he went closer and examined his own face with anxiety, comparing it after a moment with a photograph of himself in uniform taken just before the war.

'Good Lord!' he said aloud. The process was continuing. There was no doubt of it—he looked now like a man of thirty. Instead of being delighted, he was uneasy—he was growing younger. He had hitherto hoped that once he reached a bodily age equivalent to his age in years, the grotesque phenomenon which had marked his birth would cease to function. He shuddered. His destiny seemed to him awful, incredible.

When he came downstairs Hildegarde was waiting for him. She appeared annoyed, and he wondered if she had at last discovered that there was something amiss. It was with an effort to relieve the tension between them that he broached the matter at dinner in what he considered a delicate way.

'Well,' he remarked lightly, 'everybody says I look younger than ever.'

Hildegarde regarded him with scorn. She sniffed. 'Do you think it's anything to boast about?'

'I'm not boasting,' he asserted uncomfortably. She sniffed again. 'The idea,' she said, and after a moment: 'I should think you'd have enough pride to stop it.'

'How can I?' he demanded.

'I'm not going to argue with you,' she retorted. 'But there's a right way of doing things and a wrong way. If you've made up your mind to be different from everybody else, I don't suppose I can stop you, but I really don't think it's very considerate.'

'But, Hildegarde, I can't help it.'

'You can too. You're simply stubborn. You think you don't want to be like anyone else. You always have been that way, and you always will be. But just think how it would be if every one else looked at things as you do—what would the world be like?'

As this was an inane and unanswerable argument Benjamin made no reply, and from that time on a chasm began to widen between them. He wondered what possible fascination she had ever exercised over him.

To add to the breach, he found, as the new century gathered

headway, that his thirst for gaiety grew stronger. Never a party of any kind in the city of Baltimore but he was there, dancing with the prettiest of the young married women, chatting with the most popular of the debutantes, and finding their company charming, while his wife, a dowager of evil omen, sat among the chaperons, now in haughty disapproval, and now following him with solemn, puzzled, and reproachful eyes.

'Look!' people would remark. 'What a pity! A young fellow that age tied to a woman of forty-five. He must be twenty years younger than his wife.' They had forgotten—as people inevitably forget—that back in 1880 their mammas and papas had also remarked about this same ill-matched pair.

Benjamin's growing unhappiness at home was compensated for by his many new interests. He took up golf and made a great success of it. He went in for dancing: in 1906 he was an expert at 'The Boston,' and in 1908 he was considered proficient at the 'Maxine,' while in 1909 his 'Castle Walk' was the envy of every young man in town.

His social activities, of course, interfered to some extent with his business, but then he had worked hard at wholesale hardware for twenty-five years and felt that he could soon hand it on to his son, Roscoe, who had recently graduated from Harvard.

He and his son were, in fact, often mistaken for each other. This pleased Benjamin—he soon forgot the insidious fear which had come over him on his return from the Spanish-American War, and grew to take a naive pleasure in his appearance. There was only one fly in the delicious ointment—he hated to appear in public with his wife. Hildegarde was almost fifty, and the sight of her made him feel absurd...

9

One September day in 1910—a few years after Roger Button & Co., Wholesale Hardware, had been handed over to young Roscoe Button—a man, apparently about twenty years old, entered himself as a freshman at Harvard University in Cambridge. He did not make the mistake of announcing that he would never see fifty again, nor did he mention the fact that his son had been graduated from the same institution ten years before.

He was admitted, and almost immediately attained a prominent position in the class, partly because he seemed a little older than the other freshmen, whose average age was about eighteen.

But his success was largely due to the fact that in the football game with Yale he played so brilliantly, with so much dash and with such a cold, remorseless anger that he scored seven touchdowns and fourteen field goals for Harvard, and caused one entire eleven of Yale men to be carried singly from the field, unconscious. He was the most celebrated man in college. Strange to say, in his third or junior year he was scarcely able to 'make' the team. The coaches said that he had lost weight, and it seemed to the more observant among them that he was not quite as tall as before. He made no touchdowns—indeed, he was retained on the team chiefly in hope that his enormous reputation would bring terror and disorganization to the Yale team. In his senior year he did not make the team at all. He had grown so slight and frail that one day he was taken by some sophomores for a freshman, an incident which humiliated him terribly. He became known as something of a prodigy—a senior who was surely no more than sixteen—and he was often shocked at the worldliness of some of his classmates. His studies seemed harder to him—he felt that they were too advanced. He had heard his classmates speak of St. Midas's, the famous preparatory school, at which so many of them had prepared for college, and he determined after his graduation to enter himself at St. Midas's, where the sheltered life among boys his own size would be more congenial to him.

Upon his graduation in 1914 he went home to Baltimore with his Harvard diploma in his pocket. Hildegarde was now residing in Italy, so Benjamin went to live with his son, Roscoe. But though he was welcomed in a general way there was obviously no heartiness in Roscoe's feeling toward him—there was even perceptible a tendency on his son's part to think that Benjamin, as he moped about the house in adolescent mooniness, was somewhat in the way. Roscoe was married now and prominent in Baltimore life, and he wanted no scandal to creep out in connection with his family.

Benjamin, no longer *persona grata* with the debutantes and younger college set, found himself left much done, except for the companionship of three or four fifteen-year-old boys in the neighborhood. His idea of going to St. Midas's school recurred to him.

'Say,' he said to Roscoe one day, 'I've told you over and over that I want to go to prep school.'

'Well, go, then,' replied Roscoe shortly. The matter was distasteful to him, and he wished to avoid a discussion.

'I can't go alone,' said Benjamin helplessly. 'You'll have to enter me and take me up there.'

'I haven't got time,' declared Roscoe abruptly. His eyes narrowed and he looked uneasily at his father. 'As a matter of fact,' he added, 'you'd better not go on with this business much longer. You better pull up short. You better—you better'—he paused and his face crimsoned as he sought for words—'you better turn right around and start back the other way. This has gone too far to be a joke. It isn't funny any longer. You—you behave yourself!'

Benjamin looked at him, on the verge of tears.

'And another thing,' continued Roscoe, 'when visitors are in the house I want you to call me "Uncle"—not "Roscoe," but "Uncle," do you understand? It looks absurd for a boy of fifteen to call me by my first name. Perhaps you'd better call me "Uncle" *all* the time, so you'll get used to it.'

With a harsh look at his father, Roscoe turned away...

10

At the termination of this interview, Benjamin wandered dismally upstairs and stared at himself in the mirror. He had not shaved for three months, but he could find nothing on his face but a faint white down with which it seemed unnecessary to meddle. When he had first come home from Harvard, Roscoe had approached him with the proposition that he should wear eye-glasses and imitation whiskers glued to his cheeks, and it had seemed for a moment that the farce of his early years was to be repeated. But whiskers had itched and made him ashamed. He wept and Roscoe had reluctantly relented.

Benjamin opened a book of boys' stories, *The Boy Scouts in Bimini Bay*, and began to read. But he found himself thinking persistently about the war. America had joined the Allied cause during the preceding month, and Benjamin wanted to enlist, but, alas, sixteen was the minimum age, and he did not look that old. His true age, which was fifty-seven, would have disqualified him, anyway.

There was a knock at his door, and the butler appeared with a letter bearing a large official legend in the corner and addressed to Mr.Benjamin Button. Benjamin tore it open eagerly, and read the enclosure with delight. It informed him that many reserve officers who had served in the Spanish-American War were being called back into service with a higher rank, and it enclosed his commission as brigadier-general in the United States army with orders to report immediately.

Benjamin jumped to his feet fairly quivering with enthusiasm. This was what he had wanted. He seized his cap, and ten minutes later he had entered a large tailoring establishment on Charles Street, and asked in his uncertain treble to be measured for a uniform.

'Want to play soldier, sonny?' demanded a clerk casually.

Benjamin flushed. 'Say! Never mind what I want!' he retorted angrily. 'My name's Button and I live on Mt. Vernon Place, so you know I'm good for it.'

'Well,' admitted the clerk hesitantly, 'if you're not, I guess your daddy is, all right.'

Benjamin was measured, and a week later his uniform was completed. He had difficulty in obtaining the proper general's insignia because the dealer kept insisting to Benjamin that a nice V.W.C.A. badge would look just as well and be much more fun to play with.

Saying nothing to Roscoe, he left the house one night and proceeded by train to Camp Mosby, in South Carolina, where he was to command an infantry brigade. On a sultry April day he approached the entrance to the camp, paid off the taxicab which had brought him from the station, and turned to the sentry on guard.

'Get some one to handle my luggage!' he said briskly.

The sentry eyed him reproachfully. 'Say,' he remarked, 'where you goin' with the general's duds, sonny?'

Benjamin, veteran of the Spanish-American War, whirled upon him with fire in his eye, but with, alas, a changing treble voice. 'Come to attention!' he tried to thunder; he paused for breath—then suddenly he saw the sentry snap his heels together and bring his rifle to the present. Benjamin concealed a smile of gratification, but when he glanced around his smile faded. It was not he who had inspired obedience, but an imposing artillery colonel who was approaching on horseback.

'Colonel!' called Benjamin shrilly.

The colonel came up, drew rein, and looked coolly down at him with a twinkle in his eyes. 'Whose little boy are you?' he demanded kindly. 'I'll soon darn well show you whose little boy I am!' retorted Benjamin in a ferocious voice. 'Get down off that horse!'

The colonel roared with laughter. 'You want him, eh, general?' 'Here!' cried Benjamin desperately. 'Read this.' And he thrust his commission toward the colonel. The colonel read it, his eyes popping from their sockets. 'Where'd you get this?' he demanded, slipping the document into his own pocket. 'I got it from the Government, as you'll soon find out!' 'You come along with me,' said the colonel with a peculiar look. 'We'll go up to headquarters and talk this over. Come along.' The colonel turned and began walking his horse in the direction of headquarters. There was nothing for Benjamin to do but follow with as much dignity as possible—meanwhile promising himself a stern revenge. But this revenge did not materialize. Two days later, however, his son Roscoe materialized from Baltimore, hot and cross from a hasty trip, and escorted the weeping general, sans uniform, back to his home.

11

In 1920 Roscoe Button's first child was born. During the attendant festivities, however, no one thought it 'the thing' to mention, that the little grubby boy, apparently about ten years of age who played around the house with lead soldiers and a miniature circus, was the new baby's own grandfather.

No one disliked the little boy whose fresh, cheerful face was crossed with just a hint of sadness, but to Roscoe Button his presence was a source of torment. In the idiom of his generation Roscoe did not consider the matter 'efficient.' It seemed to him that his father, in refusing to look sixty, had not behaved like a 'red-blooded he-man'—this was Roscoe's favorite expression—but in a curious and perverse manner. Indeed, to think about the matter for as much as a half an hour drove him to the edge of insanity. Roscoe believed that 'live wires' should keep young, but carrying it out on such a scale was—was—was inefficient. And there Roscoe rested.

Five years later Roscoe's little boy had grown old enough to play childish games with little Benjamin under the supervision of the same nurse. Roscoe took them both to kindergarten on the same day, and Benjamin found that playing with little strips of colored paper, making mats and chains and curious and beautiful designs, was the most fascinating game in the world. Once he was bad and had to stand in the corner—then he cried—but for the most part there were gay hours in the cheerful room, with the sunlight coming in the windows and Miss Bailey's kind hand resting for a moment now and then in his tousled hair.

Roscoe's son moved up into the first grade after a year, but Benjamin stayed on in the kindergarten. He was very happy. Sometimes when other tots talked about what they would do when they grew up a shadow would cross his little face as if in a dim, childish way he realized that those were things in which he was never to share.

The days flowed on in monotonous content. He went back a third year to the kindergarten, but he was too little now to understand what the bright shining strips of paper were for. He cried because the other boys were bigger than he, and he was afraid of them. The teacher talked to him, but though he tried to understand he could not understand at all.

He was taken from the kindergarten. His nurse, Nana, in her starched gingham dress, became the center of his tiny world. On bright days they walked in the park; Nana would point at a great gray monster and say 'elephant,' and Benjamin would say it after her, and when he was being undressed for bed that night he would say it over and over aloud to her: 'Elyphant, elyphant, elyphant.' Sometimes Nana let him jump on the bed, which was fun, because if you sat down exactly right it would bounce you up on your feet again, and if you said 'Ah' for a long time while you jumped you got a very pleasing broken vocal effect.

He loved to take a big cane from the hat-rack and go around hitting chairs and tables with it and saying: 'Fight, fight, fight.' When there were people there the old ladies would cluck at him, which interested him, and the young ladies would try to kiss him, which he submitted to with mild boredom. And when the long day was done at five o'clock he would go upstairs with Nana and be fed on oatmeal and nice soft mushy foods with a spoon.

There were no troublesome memories in his childish sleep; no token came to him of his brave days at college, of the glittering years when he flustered the hearts of many girls. There were only the white, safe walls of his crib and Nana and a man who came to see him sometimes, and a great big orange ball that Nana pointed at just before his twilight bed hour and called 'sun.' When the sun went his eyes were sleepy—there were no dreams, no dreams to haunt him.

The past—the wild charge at the head of his men up San Juan Hill; the first years of his marriage when he worked late into the summer dusk down in the busy city for young Hildegarde whom he loved; the days before that when he sat smoking far into the night in the gloomy old Button house on Monroe Street with his grandfather-all these had faded like unsubstantial dreams from his mind as though they had never been. He did not remember.

He did not remember clearly whether the milk was warm or cool at his last feeding or how the days passed—there was only his crib and Nana's familiar presence. And then he remembered nothing. When he was hungry he cried—that was all. Through the noons and nights he breathed and over him there were soft mumblings and murmurings that he scarcely heard, and faintly differentiated smells, and light and darkness. Then it was all dark, and his white crib and the dim faces that moved above him, and the warm sweet aroma of the milk, faded out altogether from his mind.

38

A RESUMED IDENTITY

Ambrose Bierce

The Review as a Form of Welcome

One summer night a man stood on a low hill overlooking a wide expanse of forest and field. By the full moon hanging low in the west he knew what he might not have known otherwise: that it was near the hour of dawn. A light mist lay along the earth, partly veiling the lower features of the landscape, but above it the taller trees showed in well-defined masses against a clear sky. Two or three farmhouses were visible through the haze, but in none of them, naturally, was a light. Nowhere, indeed, was any sign or suggestion of life except the barking of a distant dog, which, repeated with mechanical iteration, served rather to accentuate than dispel the loneliness of the scene.

The man looked curiously about him on all sides, as one who among familiar surroundings is unable to determine his exact place and part in the scheme of things. It is so, perhaps, that we shall act when, risen from the dead, we await the call to judgment.

A hundred yards away was a straight road, showing white in the moonlight. Endeavouring to orient himself, as a surveyor or navigator might say, the man moved his eyes slowly along its visible length and at a distance of a quarter-mile to the south of his station saw, dim and grey in the haze, a group of horsemen riding to the north. Behind them were men afoot, marching in column, with dimly gleaming rifles aslant above their shoulders. They moved slowly and in silence. Another group of horsemen, another regiment of infantry, another and another—all in unceasing motion toward the man's point of view, past it, and beyond. A battery of artillery followed, the cannoneers riding with folded arms on limber and caisson. And still the interminable procession came out of the obscurity to south and passed into the obscurity to north, with never a sound of voice, nor hoof, nor wheel.

The man could not rightly understand: he thought himself deaf; said so, and heard his own voice, although it had an unfamiliar quality that almost alarmed him; it disappointed his ear's expectancy in the matter of timbre and resonance. But he was not deaf, and that for the moment sufficed.

Then he remembered that there are natural phenomena to which some one has given the name 'acoustic shadows.' If you stand in an acoustic shadow there is one direction from which you will hear nothing. At the battle of Gaines's Mill, one of the fiercest conflicts of the Civil War, with a hundred guns in play, spectators a mile and a half away on the opposite side of the Chickahominy Valley heard nothing of what they clearly saw. The bombardment of Port Royal, heard and felt at St. Augustine, a hundred and fifty miles to the south, was inaudible two miles to the north in a still atmosphere. A few days before the surrender at Appomattox a thunderous engagement between the commands of Sheridan and Pickett was unknown to the latter commander, a mile in the rear of his own line.

These instances were not known to the man of whom we write, but less striking ones of the same character had not escaped his observation. He was profoundly disquieted, but for another reason than the uncanny silence of that moonlight march.

'Good Lord!' he said to himself—and again it was as if another had spoken his thought—'if those people are what I take them to be we have lost the battle and they are moving on Nashville!'

Then came a thought of self—an apprehension—a strong sense of personal peril, such as in another we call fear. He stepped quickly into the shadow of a tree. And still the silent battalions moved slowly forward in the haze.

The chill of a sudden breeze upon the back of his neck drew his attention to the quarter whence it came, and turning to the east he saw a faint grey light along the horizon—the first sign of returning day. This increased his apprehension.

'I must get away from here,' he thought, 'or I shall be discovered and taken.'

He moved out of the shadow, walking rapidly toward the greying east. From the safer seclusion of a clump of cedars he looked back. The entire column had passed out of sight: the straight white road lay bare and desolate in the moonlight!

Puzzled before, he was now inexpressibly astonished. So swift a passing of so slow an army!—he could not comprehend it. Minute after minute passed unnoted; he had lost his sense of time. He sought with a terrible earnestness a solution of the mystery, but sought in vain. When at last he roused himself from his abstraction the sun's rim was visible above the hills, but in the new conditions he found no other light than that of day; his understanding was involved as darkly in doubt as before.

On every side lay cultivated fields showing no sign of war and war's ravages. From the chimneys of the farmhouses thin ascensions of blue smoke signalled preparations for a day's peaceful toil. Having stilled its immemorial allocution to the moon, the watch-dog was assisting a negro who, prefixing a team of mules to the plough, was flatting and sharping contentedly at his task. The hero of this tale stared stupidly at the pastoral picture as if he had never seen such a thing in all his life; then he put his hand to his head, passed it through his hair and, withdrawing it, attentively considered the palm—a singular thing to do. Apparently reassured by the act, he walked confidently toward the road.

When You Have Lost Your Life Consult a Physician

Dr. Stilling Malson, of Murfreesboro, having visited a patient six or seven miles away, on the Nashville road, had remained with him all night. At daybreak he set out for home on horseback, as was the custom of doctors of the time and region. He had passed into the neighbourhood of Stone's River battlefield when a man approached him from the roadside and saluted in the military fashion, with a movement of the right hand to the hat-brim. But the hat was not a military hat, the man was not in uniform and had not a martial bearing. The doctor nodded civilly, half thinking that the stranger's uncommon greeting was perhaps in deference to the historic surroundings. As the stranger evidently desired speech with him he courteously reined in his horse and waited.

'Sir,' said the stranger, 'although a civilian, you are perhaps an enemy.'

'I am a physician,' was the non-committal reply.

'Thank you,' said the other. 'I am a lieutenant, of the staff of General Hazen.' He paused a moment and looked sharply at the person whom he was addressing, then added, 'Of the Federal army.' The physician merely nodded.

'Kindly tell me,' continued the other, 'what has happened here. Where are the armies? Which has won the battle?'

The physician regarded his questioner curiously with half-shut eyes. After a professional scrutiny, prolonged to the limit of politeness, 'Pardon me,' he said; 'one asking information should be willing to impart it. Are you wounded?' he added, smiling.

'Not seriously—it seems.'

The man removed the unmilitary hat, put his hand to his head, passed it through his hair and, withdrawing it, attentively considered the palm.

'I was struck by a bullet and have been unconscious. It must have been a light, glancing blow: I find no blood and feel no pain. I will not trouble you for treatment, but will you kindly direct me to my command—to any part of the Federal army—if you know?'

Again the doctor did not immediately reply: he was recalling much that is recorded in the books of his profession—something about lost identity and the effect of familiar scenes in restoring it. At length he looked the man in the face, smiled, and said:

'Lieutenant, you are not wearing the uniform of your rank

and service.'

At this the man glanced down at his civilian attire, lifted his eyes, and said with hesitation:

'That is true. I—I don't quite understand.'

Still regarding him sharply but not unsympathetically, the man of science bluntly inquired:

'How old are you?'

'Twenty-three—if that has anything to do with it.'

'You don't look it; I should hardly have guessed you to be just that.'

The man was growing impatient. 'We need not discuss that,' he said: 'I want to know about the army. Not two hours ago I saw a column of troops moving northward on this road. You must have met them. Be good enough to tell me the colour of their clothing, which I was unable to make out, and I'll trouble you no more.'

'You are quite sure that you saw them?'

'Sure? My God, sir, I could have counted them!'

'Why, really,' said the physician, with an amusing consciousness of his own resemblance to the loquacious barber of the Arabian Nights, 'this is very interesting. I met no troops.'

The man looked at him coldly, as if he had himself observed the likeness to the barber. 'It is plain,' he said, 'that you do not care to assist me. Sir, you may go to the devil!'

He turned and strode away, very much at random, across the dewy fields, his half-penitent tormentor quietly watching him from his point of vantage in the saddle till he disappeared beyond an array of trees.

The Danger of Looking into a Pool of Water

After leaving the road the man slackened his pace, and now went forward, rather deviously, with a distinct feeling of fatigue. He could not account for this, though truly the interminable loquacity of that country doctor offered itself in explanation. Seating himself upon a rock, he laid one hand upon his knee, back upward, and casually looked at it. It was lean and withered.

He lifted both hands to his face. It was seamed and furrowed; he could trace the lines with the tips of his fingers. How strange!—a mere bullet-stroke and a brief unconsciousness should not make one a physical wreck.

'I must have been a long time in hospital,' he said aloud. 'Why, what a fool I am! The battle was in December, and it is now summer!' He laughed. 'No wonder that fellow thought me an escaped lunatic. He was wrong: I am only an escaped patient.'

At a little distance a small plot of ground enclosed by a stone wall caught his attention. With no very definite intent he rose and went to it. In the centre was a square, solid monument of hewn stone. It was brown with age, weather-worn at the angles, spotted with moss and lichen. Between the massive blocks were strips of grass the leverage of whose roots had pushed them apart. In answer to the challenge of this ambitious structure Time had laid his destroying hand upon it, and it would soon be 'one with Nineveh and Tyre.' In an inscription on one side his eye caught a familiar name. Shaking with excitement, he craned his body across the wall and read:

HAZEN'S BRIGADE
to
The Memory of Its Soldiers
who fell at
Stone River, Dec. 31, 1862.

The man fell back from the wall, faint and sick. Almost within an arm's length was a little depression in the earth; it had been filled by a recent rain—a pool of clear water. He crept to it to revive himself, lifted the upper part of his body on his trembling arms, thrust forward his head and saw the reflection of his face, as in a mirror. He uttered a terrible cry. His arms gave way; he fell, face downward, into the pool and yielded up the life that had spanned another life.

39

A LITTLE CLOUD

James Joyce

Eight years before he had seen his friend off at the North Wall and wished him godspeed. Gallaher had got on. You could tell that at once by his travelled air, his well-cut tweed suit, and fearless accent. Few fellows had talents like his and fewer still could remain unspoiled by such success. Gallaher's heart was in the right place and he had deserved to win. It was something to have a friend like that.

Little Chandler's thoughts ever since lunch-time had been of his meeting with Gallaher, of Gallaher's invitation and of the great city London where Gallaher lived. He was called Little Chandler because, though he was but slightly under the average stature, he gave one the idea of being a little man. His hands were white and small, his frame was fragile, his voice was quiet and his manners were refined. He took the greatest care of his fair silken hair and moustache and used perfume discreetly on his handkerchief. The half-moons of his nails were perfect and when he smiled you caught a glimpse of a row of childish white teeth.

As he sat at his desk in the King's Inns he thought what changes those eight years had brought. The friend whom he had known under a shabby and necessitous guise had become a brilliant figure on the London Press. He turned often from his tiresome writing to gaze out of the office window. The glow of a late autumn sunset covered the grass plots and walks. It cast a shower of kindly golden dust on the untidy nurses and decrepit old men who drowsed on the benches; it flickered upon all the moving figures—on the children who ran screaming along the gravel paths and on everyone who passed through the gardens. He watched the scene and thought of life; and (as always happened when he thought of life) he became sad. A gentle melancholy took possession of him. He felt how useless it was to struggle against fortune, this being the burden of wisdom which the ages had bequeathed to him.

He remembered the books of poetry upon his shelves at home. He had bought them in his bachelor days and many an evening, as he sat in the little room off the hall, he had been tempted to take one down from the bookshelf and read out something to his wife. But shyness had always held him back; and so the books had remained on their shelves. At times he repeated lines to himself and this consoled him.

When his hour had struck he stood up and took leave of his desk and of his fellow-clerks punctiliously. He emerged from under the feudal arch of the King's Inns, a neat modest figure, and walked swiftly down Henrietta Street. The golden sunset was waning and the air had grown sharp. A horde of grimy children populated the street. They stood or ran in the roadway or crawled up the steps before the gaping doors or squatted like mice upon the thresholds. Little Chandler gave them no thought. He picked his way deftly through all that minute vermin-like life and under the shadow of the gaunt spectral mansions in which the old nobility of Dublin had roystered. No memory of the past touched him, for his mind was full of a present joy.

He had never been in Corless's but he knew the value of the name. He knew that people went there after the theatre to eat oysters and drink liqueurs; and he had heard that the waiters there spoke French and German. Walking swiftly by at night he had seen cabs drawn up before the door and richly dressed ladies, escorted by cavaliers, alight and enter quickly. They wore noisy dresses and many wraps. Their faces were powdered and they caught up their dresses, when they touched earth, like alarmed Atalantas. He had always passed without turning his head to look. It was his habit to walk swiftly in the street even by day and whenever he found himself in the city late at night he hurried on his way apprehensively and excitedly. Sometimes, however, he courted the causes of his fear. He chose the darkest and narrowest streets and, as he walked boldly forward, the silence that was spread about his footsteps troubled him, the wandering, silent figures troubled him; and at times a sound of low fugitive laughter made him tremble like a leaf.

He turned to the right towards Capel Street. Ignatius Gallaher on the London Press! Who would have thought it possible eight years before? Still, now that he reviewed the past, Little Chandler could remember many signs of future greatness in his friend. People used to say that Ignatius Gallaher was wild Of course, he did mix with a rakish set of fellows at that time. drank freely and borrowed money on all sides. In the end he had got mixed up in some shady affair, some money transaction: at least, that was one version of his flight. But nobody denied him talent. There was always a certain... something in Ignatius Gallaher that impressed you in spite of yourself. Even when he was out at elbows and at his wits' end for money he kept up a bold face. Little Chandler remembered (and the remembrance brought a slight flush of pride to his cheek) one of Ignatius Gallaher's sayings when he was in a tight corner:

'Half time now, boys,' he used to say light-heartedly. 'Where's my considering cap?'

That was Ignatius Gallaher all out; and, damn it, you couldn't but admire him for it.

Little Chandler quickened his pace. For the first time in his life he felt himself superior to the people he passed. For the first time his soul revolted against the dull inelegance of Capel Street. There was no doubt about it: if you wanted to succeed you had to go away. You could do nothing in Dublin. As he crossed Grattan Bridge he looked down the river towards the lower quays and pitied the poor stunted houses. They seemed to him a band of tramps, huddled together along the riverbanks, their old coats covered with dust and soot, stupefied by the panorama of sunset and waiting for the first chill of night bid them arise, shake themselves and begone. He wondered whether he could write a poem to express his idea. Perhaps Gallaher might be able to get it into some London paper for him. Could he write something original? He was not sure what idea he wished to express but the thought that a poetic moment had touched him took life within him like an infant hope. He stepped onward bravely.

Every step brought him nearer to London, farther from his own sober inartistic life. A light began to tremble on the horizon of his mind. He was not so old—thirty-two. His temperament might be said to be just at the point of maturity. There were so many different moods and impressions that he wished to express in verse. He felt them within him. He tried weigh his soul to see if it was a poet's soul. Melancholy was the dominant note of his temperament, he thought, but it was a melancholy tempered by recurrences of faith and resignation and simple joy. If he could give expression to it in a book of poems perhaps men would listen. He would never be popular: he saw that. He could not sway the crowd but he might appeal to a little circle of kindred minds. The English critics, perhaps, would recognise him as one of the Celtic school by reason of the melancholy tone of his poems; besides that, he would put in allusions. He began to invent sentences and phrases from the notice which his book would get. 'Mr. Chandler has the gift of easy and graceful verse.' ... 'wistful sadness pervades these poems.' ... 'The Celtic note.' It was a pity his name was not more Irish-looking. Perhaps it would be better to insert his mother's name before the surname: Thomas Malone Chandler, or better still: T. Malone Chandler. He would speak to Gallaher about it.

He pursued his revery so ardently that he passed his street and had to turn back. As he came near Corless's his former agitation began to overmaster him and he halted before the door in indecision. Finally he opened the door and entered.

The light and noise of the bar held him at the doorways for a few moments. He looked about him, but his sight was confused by the shining of many red and green wine-glasses

The bar seemed to him to be full of people and he felt that the people were observing him curiously. He glanced quickly to right and left (frowning slightly to make his errand appear serious), but when his sight cleared a little he saw that nobody had turned to look at him: and there, sure enough, was Ignatius Gallaher leaning with his back against the counter and his feet planted far apart.

'Hallo, Tommy, old hero, here you are! What is it to be? What will you have? I'm taking whisky: better stuff than we get across the water. Soda? Lithia? No mineral? I'm the same. Spoils the flavour... Here, garcon, bring us two halves of malt whisky, like a good fellow... Well, and how have you been pulling along since I saw you last? Dear God, how old we're getting! Do you see any signs of aging in me—eh, what? A little grey and thin on the top—what?'

Ignatius Gallaher took off his hat and displayed a large closely cropped head. His face was heavy, pale and cleanshaven. His eyes, which were of bluish slate-colour, relieved his unhealthy pallor and shone out plainly above the vivid orange tie he wore. Between these rival features the lips appeared very long and shapeless and colourless. He bent his head and felt with two sympathetic fingers the thin hair at the crown. Little Chandler shook his head as a denial. Ignatius Galaher put on his hat again.

'It pulls you down,' he said, 'Press life. Always hurry and scurry, looking for copy and sometimes not finding it: and then, always to have something new in your stuff. Damn proofs and printers, I say, for a few days. I'm deuced glad, I can tell you, to get back to the old country. Does a fellow good, a bit of a holiday. I feel a ton better since I landed again in dear dirty Dublin... Here you are, Tommy. Water? Say when.'

Little Chandler allowed his whisky to be very much diluted.

'You don't know what's good for you, my boy,' said Ignatius Gallaher. 'I drink mine neat.'

'I drink very little as a rule,' said Little Chandler modestly. 'An odd half-one or so when I meet any of the old crowd: that's all.'

'Ah well,' said Ignatius Gallaher, cheerfully, 'here's to us and to old times and old acquaintance.'

They clinked glasses and drank the toast.

'I met some of the old gang to-day,' said Ignatius Gallaher. 'O'Hara seems to be in a bad way. What's he doing?'

'Nothing, said Little Chandler. 'He's gone to the dogs.'

'But Hogan has a good sit, hasn't he?'

'Yes; he's in the Land Commission.'

'I met him one night in London and he seemed to be very flush... Poor O'Hara! Boose, I suppose?'

'Other things, too,' said Little Chandler shortly.

Ignatius Gallaher laughed.

'Tommy,' he said, 'I see you haven't changed an atom. You're the very same serious person that used to lecture me on Sunday mornings when I had a sore head and a fur on my tongue. You'd want to knock about a bit in the world. Have you never been anywhere even for a trip?'

'I've been to the Isle of Man,' said Little Chandler.

Ignatius Gallaher laughed.

'The Isle of Man!' he said. 'Go to London or Paris: Paris, for choice. That'd do you good.'

'Have you seen Paris?'

'I should think I have! I've knocked about there a little.'

'And is it really so beautiful as they say?' asked Little Chandler.

He sipped a little of his drink while Ignatius Gallaher finished his boldly.

'Beautiful?' said Ignatius Gallaher, pausing on the word and on the flavour of his drink. 'It's not so beautiful, you know. Of course, it is beautiful... But it's the life of Paris; that's the thing. Ah, there's no city like Paris for gaiety, movement, excitement...'

Little Chandler finished his whisky and, after some trouble, succeeded in catching the barman's eye. He ordered the same again.

'I've been to the Moulin Rouge,' Ignatius Gallaher continued when the barman had removed their glasses, 'and I've been to all the Bohemian cafes. Hot stuff! Not for a pious chap like you, Tommy.'

Little Chandler said nothing until the barman returned with two glasses: then he touched his friend's glass lightly and reciprocated the former toast. He was beginning to feel somewhat disillusioned. Gallaher's accent and way of expressing himself did not please him. There was something vulgar in his friend which he had not observed before. But perhaps it was only the result of living in London amid the bustle and competition of the Press. The old personal charm was still there under this new gaudy manner. And, after all, Gallaher had lived, he had seen the world. Little Chandler looked at his friend enviously.

'Everything in Paris is gay,' said Ignatius Gallaher. 'They believe in enjoying life—and don't you think they're right? If you want to enjoy yourself properly you must go to Paris. And, mind you, they've a great feeling for the Irish there. When they heard I was from Ireland they were ready to eat me, man.'

Little Chandler took four or five sips from his glass.

'Tell me,' he said, 'is it true that Paris is so...immoral as they say?'

Ignatius Gallaher made a catholic gesture with his right arm.

'Every place is immoral,' he said. 'Of course you do find spicy bits in Paris. Go to one of the students' balls, for instance. That's lively, if you like, when the cocottes begin to let themselves loose. You know what they are, I suppose?'

'I've heard of them,' said Little Chandler.

Ignatius Gallaher drank off his whisky and shook his had.

'Ah,' he said, 'you may say what you like. There's no woman like the Parisienne—for style, for go.'

'Then it is an immoral city,' said Little Chandler, with timid insistence—'I mean, compared with London or Dublin?'

'London!' said Ignatius Gallaher. 'It's six of one and half-a-dozen of the other. You ask Hogan, my boy. I showed him a bit about London when he was over there. He'd open your eye... I say, Tommy, don't make punch of that whisky: liquor up.'

'No, really...'

'O, come on, another one won't do you any harm. What is it? The same again, I suppose?'

'Well... all right.'

'Francois, the same again... Will you smoke, Tommy?'

Ignatius Gallaher produced his cigar-case. The two friends lit their cigars and puffed at them in silence until their drinks were served.

'I'll tell you my opinion,' said Ignatius Gallaher, emerging after some time from the clouds of smoke in which he had taken refuge, 'it's a rum world. Talk of immorality! I've heard of cases—what am I saying?—I've known them: cases of... immorality...'

Ignatius Gallaher puffed thoughtfully at his cigar and then, in a calm historian's tone, he proceeded to sketch for his friend some pictures of the corruption which was rife abroad. He summarised the vices of many capitals and seemed inclined to award the palm to Berlin. Some things he could not vouch for (his friends had told him), but of others he had had personal experience. He spared neither rank nor caste. He revealed many of the secrets of religious houses on the Continent and described some of the practices which were fashionable in high society and ended by telling, with details, a story about an English duchess—a story which he knew to be true. Little Chandler as astonished.

'Ah, well,' said Ignatius Gallaher, 'here we are in old jog-along Dublin where nothing is known of such things.'

'How dull you must find it,' said Little Chandler, 'after all the other places you've seen!'

Well,' said Ignatius Gallaher, 'it's a relaxation to come over here, you know. And, after all, it's the old country, as they say, isn't it? You can't help having a certain feeling for it. That's human nature... But tell me something about yourself. Hogan told me you had... tasted the joys of connubial bliss. Two years ago, wasn't it?'

Little Chandler blushed and smiled.

'Yes,' he said. 'I was married last May twelve months.'

'I hope it's not too late in the day to offer my best wishes,' said Ignatius Gallaher. 'I didn't know your address or I'd have done so at the time.'

He extended his hand, which Little Chandler took.

'Well, Tommy,' he said, 'I wish you and yours every joy in life, old chap, and tons of money, and may you never die till I shoot you. And that's the wish of a sincere friend, an old friend. You know that?'

'I know that,' said Little Chandler.

'Any youngsters?' said Ignatius Gallaher.

Little Chandler blushed again.

'We have one child,' he said.

'Son or daughter?'

'A little boy.'

Ignatius Gallaher slapped his friend sonorously on the back.

'Bravo,' he said, 'I wouldn't doubt you, Tommy.'

Little Chandler smiled, looked confusedly at his glass and bit his lower lip with three childishly white front teeth.

'I hope you'll spend an evening with us,' he said, 'before you go back. My wife will be delighted to meet you. We can have a little music and—'

'Thanks awfully, old chap,' said Ignatius Gallaher, 'I'm sorry we didn't meet earlier. But I must leave to-morrow night.'

'Tonight, perhaps...?'

'I'm awfully sorry, old man. You see I'm over here with another fellow, clever young chap he is too, and we arranged to go to a little card-party. Only for that...'

'O, in that case...'

'But who knows?' said Ignatius Gallaher considerately. 'Next year I may take a little skip over here now that I've broken the ice. It's only a pleasure deferred.'

'Very well,' said Little Chandler, 'the next time you come we must have an evening together. That's agreed now, isn't it?'

'Yes, that's agreed,' said Ignatius Gallaher. 'Next year if I come, parole d'honneur.'

'And to clinch the bargain,' said Little Chandler, 'we'll just have one more now.'

Ignatius Gallaher took out a large gold watch and looked a it.

'Is it to be the last?' he said. 'Because you know, I have an a.p.'

'O, yes, positively,' said Little Chandler.

'Very well, then,' said Ignatius Gallaher, 'let us have another one as a deoc an doruis—that's good vernacular for a small whisky, I believe.'

Little Chandler ordered the drinks. The blush which had risen to his face a few moments before was establishing itself. A trifle made him blush at any time: and now he felt warm and excited. Three small whiskies had gone to his head and Gallaher's strong cigar had confused his mind, for he was a delicate and abstinent person. The adventure of meeting Gallaher after eight years, of finding himself with Gallaher in Corless's surrounded by lights and noise, of listening to Gallaher's stories and of sharing for a brief space Gallaher's vagrant and triumphant life, upset the equipoise of his sensitive nature. He felt acutely the contrast between his own life and his friend's and it seemed to him unjust. Gallaher was his inferior in birth and education. He was sure that he could do something better than his friend had ever done, or could ever do, something higher than mere tawdry journalism if he only got the chance. What was it that stood in his way? His unfortunate timidity. He wished to vindicate himself in some way, to assert his manhood. He saw behind Gallaher's refusal of his invitation. Gallaher was only patronising him by his friendliness just as he was patronising Ireland by his visit.

The barman brought their drinks. Little Chandler pushed one glass towards his friend and took up the other boldly.

'Who knows?' he said, as they lifted their glasses. 'When you come next year I may have the pleasure of wishing long life and happiness to Mr. and Mrs. Ignatius Gallaher.'

Ignatius Gallaher in the act of drinking closed one eye expressively over the rim of his glass. When he had drunk he smacked his lips decisively, set down his glass and said:

'No blooming fear of that, my boy. I'm going to have my fling first and see a bit of life and the world before I put my head in the sack—if I ever do.'

'Some day you will,' said Little Chandler calmly.

Ignatius Gallaher turned his orange tie and slate-blue eyes full upon his friend.

'You think so?' he said.

'You'll put your head in the sack,' repeated Little Chandler stoutly, 'like everyone else if you can find the girl.'

He had slightly emphasised his tone and he was aware that he had betrayed himself; but, though the colour had heightened in his cheek, he did not flinch from his friend's gaze. Ignatius Gallaher watched him for a few moments and then said:

'If ever it occurs, you may bet your bottom dollar there'll be no mooning and spooning about it. I mean to marry money. She'll have a good fat account at the bank or she won't do for me.'

Little Chandler shook his head.

'Why, man alive,' said Ignatius Gallaher, vehemently, 'do you know what it is? I've only to say the word and to-morrow I can have the woman and the cash. You don't believe it? Well, I know it. There are hundreds—what am I saying?—thousands of rich Germans and Jews, rotten with money, that'd only be too glad... You wait a while my boy. See if I don't play my cards properly. When I go about a thing I mean business, I tell you. You just wait.'

He tossed his glass to his mouth, finished his drink and laughed loudly. Then he looked thoughtfully before him and said in a calmer tone:

'But I'm in no hurry. They can wait. I don't fancy tying myself up to one woman, you know.'

He imitated with his mouth the act of tasting and made a wry face.

'Must get a bit stale, I should think,' he said.

Little Chandler sat in the room off the hall, holding a child in his arms. To save money they kept no servant but Annie's young sister Monica came for an hour or so in the morning and an hour or so in the evening to help. But Monica had gone home long ago. It was a quarter to nine. Little Chandler had come home late for tea and, moreover, he had forgotten to bring Annie home the parcel of coffee from Bewley's. Of course she was in a bad humour and gave him short answers. She said she would do without any tea but when it came near the time at which the shop at the corner closed she decided to go out herself for a quarter of a pound of tea and two pounds of sugar. She put the sleeping child deftly in his arms and said:

'Here. Don't waken him.'

A little lamp with a white china shade stood upon the table and its light fell over a photograph which was enclosed in a frame of crumpled horn. It was Annie's photograph. Little Chandler looked at it, pausing at the thin tight lips. She wore the pale blue summer blouse which he had brought her home as a present one Saturday. It had cost him ten and elevenpence; but what an agony of nervousness it had cost him! How he had suffered that day, waiting at the shop door until the shop was empty, standing at the counter and trying to appear at his ease while the girl piled ladies' blouses before him, paying at the desk and forgetting to take up the odd penny of his change, being called back by the cashier, and finally, striving to hide his blushes as he left the shop by examining the parcel to see if it was securely tied. When he brought the blouse home Annie kissed him and said it was very pretty and stylish; but when she heard the price she threw the blouse on the table and said it was a regular swindle to charge ten and elevenpence for it. At first she wanted to take it back but when she tried it on she was delighted with it, especially with the make of the sleeves, and kissed him and said he was very good to think of her.

Hm!...

He looked coldly into the eyes of the photograph and they answered coldly. Certainly they were pretty and the face itself was pretty. But he found something mean in it. Why was it so unconscious and ladylike? The composure of the eyes irritated him. They repelled him and defied him: there was no passion in them, no rapture. He thought of what Gallaher had said about rich Jewesses. Those dark Oriental eyes, he thought, how full they are of passion, of voluptuous longing!... Why had he married the eyes in the photograph?

He caught himself up at the question and glanced nervously round the room. He found something mean in the pretty furniture which he had bought for his house on the hire system. Annie had chosen it herself and it reminded him of her. It too was prim and pretty. A dull resentment against his life awoke within him. Could he not escape from his little house? Was it too late for him to try to live bravely like Gallaher? Could he go to London? There was the furniture still to be paid for. If he could only write a book and get it published, that might open the way for him.

A volume of Byron's poems lay before him on the table. He opened it cautiously with his left hand lest he should waken the child and began to read the first poem in the book:

Hushed are the winds and still the evening gloom,
Not e'en a Zephyr wanders through the grove,
Whilst I return to view my Margaret's tomb
And scatter flowers on tbe dust I love.

He paused. He felt the rhythm of the verse about him in the room. How melancholy it was! Could he, too, write like that, express the melancholy of his soul in verse? There were so many things he wanted to describe: his sensation of a few hours before on Grattan Bridge, for example. If he could get back again into that mood...

The child awoke and began to cry. He turned from the page and tried to hush it: but it would not be hushed. He began to rock it to and fro in his arms but its wailing cry grew keener. He rocked it faster while his eyes began to read the second stanza:

Within this narrow cell reclines her clay,
That clay where once...

It was useless. He couldn't read. He couldn't do anything. The wailing of the child pierced the drum of his ear. It was useless, useless! He was a prisoner for life. His arms trembled with anger and suddenly bending to the child's face he shouted:

'Stop!'

The child stopped for an instant, had a spasm of fright and began to scream. He jumped up from his chair and walked hastily up and down the room with the child in his arms. It began to sob piteously, losing its breath for four or five seconds, and then bursting out anew. The thin walls of the room echoed the sound. He tried to soothe it but it sobbed more convulsively. He looked at the contracted and quivering face of the child and began to be alarmed. He counted seven sobs without a break between them and caught the child to his breast in fright. If it died!...

The door was burst open and a young woman ran in, panting.

'What is it? What is it?' she cried.

The child, hearing its mother's voice, broke out into a paroxysm of sobbing.

'It's nothing, Annie...it's nothing... He began to cry...'

She flung her parcels on the floor and snatched the child from him.

'What have you done to him?' she cried, glaring into his face.

Little Chandler sustained for one moment the gaze of her eyes and his heart closed together as he met the hatred in them. He began to stammer:

'It's nothing... He...he began to cry... I couldn't... I didn't do anything... What?'

Giving no heed to him she began to walk up and down the room, clasping the child tightly in her arms and murmuring:

'My little man! My little mannie! Was 'ou frightened, love?... There now, love! There now!... Lambabaun! Mamma's little lamb of the world!... There now!'

Little Chandler felt his cheeks suffused with shame and he stood back out of the lamplight. He listened while the paroxysm of the child's sobbing grew less and less; and tears of remorse started to his eyes.

40

DRACULA'S GUEST

Bram Stoker

When we started for our drive the sun was shining brightly on Munich, and the air was full of the joyousness of early summer. Just as we were about to depart, Herr Delbruck (the maitre d'hotel of the Quatre Saisons, where I was staying) came down bareheaded to the carriage and, after wishing me a pleasant drive, said to the coachman, still holding his hand on the handle of the carriage door, 'Remember you are back by nightfall. The sky looks bright but there is a shiver in the north wind that says there may be a sudden storm. But I am sure you will not be late.' Here he smiled and added, 'for you know what night it is.'

Johann answered with an emphatic, 'Ja, mein Herr,' and, touching his hat, drove off quickly. When we had cleared the town, I said, after signalling to him to stop:

'Tell me, Johann, what is tonight?'

He crossed himself, as he answered laconically: 'Walpurgis nacht.' Then he took out his watch, a great, old-fashioned German silver thing as big as a turnip and looked at it, with his eyebrows gathered together and a little impatient shrug of his shoulders. I realized that this was his way of respectfully protesting against the unnecessary delay and sank back in the carriage, merely motioning him to proceed. He started off rapidly, as if to make up for lost time. Every now and then the horses seemed to throw up their heads and sniff the air suspiciously. On such occasions I often looked round in alarm. The road was pretty bleak, for we were traversing a sort of high windswept plateau. As we drove, I saw a road that looked but little used and which seemed to dip through a little winding valley. It looked so inviting that, even at the risk of offending him, I called Johann to stop—and when he had pulled up, I told him I would like to drive down that road. He made all sorts of excuses and frequently crossed himself as he spoke. This somewhat piqued my curiosity, so I asked him various questions. He answered fencingly and repeatedly looked at his watch in protest.

Finally I said, 'Well, Johann, I want to go down this road. I shall not ask you to come unless you like; but tell me why you do not like to go, that is all I ask.' For answer he seemed to throw himself off the box, so quickly did he reach the ground. Then he stretched out his hands appealingly to me and implored me not to go. There was just enough of English mixed with the German for me to understand the drift of his talk. He seemed always just about to tell me something—the very idea of which evidently frightened him; but each time he pulled himself up saying, 'Walpurgis nacht!'

I tried to argue with him, but it was difficult to argue with a man when I did not know his language. The advantage certainly rested with him, for although he began to speak in English, of a very crude and broken kind, he always got excited and broke into his native tongue—and every time he did so, he looked at his watch. Then the horses became restless and sniffed the air. At this he grew very pale, and, looking around in a frightened way, he suddenly jumped forward, took them by the bridles, and led them on some twenty feet. I followed and asked why he had done this. For an answer he crossed himself, pointed to the spot we had left, and drew his carriage in the direction of the other road, indicating a cross, and said, first in German, then in English, 'Buried him—him what killed themselves.'

I remembered the old custom of burying suicides at cross roads: 'Ah! I see, a suicide. How interesting!' But for the life of me I could not make out why the horses were frightened.

Whilst we were talking, we heard a sort of sound between a yelp and a bark. It was far away; but the horses got very restless, and it took Johann all his time to quiet them. He was pale and said, 'It sounds like a wolf—but yet there are no wolves here now.'

'No?' I said, questioning him. 'Isn't it long since the wolves were so near the city?'

'Long, long,' he answered, 'in the spring and summer; but with the snow the wolves have been here not so long.'

Whilst he was petting the horses and trying to quiet them, dark clouds drifted rapidly across the sky. The sunshine passed away, and a breath of cold wind seemed to drift over us. It was only a breath, however, and more of a warning than a fact, for the sun came out brightly again.

Johann looked under his lifted hand at the horizon and said, 'The storm of snow, he comes before long time.' Then he looked at his watch again, and, straightway holding his reins firmly—for the horses were still pawing the ground restlessly and shaking their heads—he climbed to his box as though the time had come for proceeding on our journey.

I felt a little obstinate and did not at once get into the carriage.

'Tell me,' I said, 'about this place where the road leads,' and I pointed down.

Again he crossed himself and mumbled a prayer before he answered, 'It is unholy.'

'What is unholy?' I enquired.

'The village.'

'Then there is a village?'

'No, no. No one lives there hundreds of years.'

My curiosity was piqued, 'But you said there was a village.'

'There was.'

'Where is it now?'

Whereupon he burst out into a long story in German and English, so mixed up that I could not quite understand exactly what he said. Roughly I gathered that long ago, hundreds of years, men had died there and been buried in their graves; but sounds were heard under the clay, and when the graves were opened, men and women were found rosy with life and their mouths red with blood. And so, in haste to save their lives (aye, and their souls!—and here he crossed himself) those who were left fled away to other places, where the living lived and the dead were dead and not—not something. He was evidently afraid to speak the last words. As he proceeded with his narration, he grew more and more excited. It seemed as if his imagination had got hold of him, and he ended in a perfect paroxysm of fear—white-faced, perspiring, trembling, and looking round him as if expecting that some dreadful presence would manifest itself there in the bright sunshine on the open plain.

Finally, in an agony of desperation, he cried, 'Walpurgis nacht!' and pointed to the carriage for me to get in.

All my English blood rose at this, and standing back I said, 'You are afraid, Johann—you are afraid. Go home, I shall return alone, the walk will do me good.' The carriage door was open. I took from the seat my oak walking stick—which I always carry on my holiday excursions—and closed the door, pointing back to Munich, and said, 'Go home, Johann—Walpurgis nacht doesn't concern Englishmen.'

The horses were now more restive than ever, and Johann was trying to hold them in, while excitedly imploring me not to do anything so foolish. I pitied the poor fellow, he was so deeply in earnest; but all the same I could not help laughing. His English was quite gone now. In his anxiety he had forgotten that his only means of making me understand was to talk my language, so he jabbered away in his native German. It began to be a little tedious. After giving the direction, 'Home!' I turned to go down the cross road into the valley.

With a despairing gesture, Johann turned his horses towards Munich. I leaned on my stick and looked after him. He went slowly along the road for a while, then there came over the crest of the hill a man tall and thin. I could see so much in the distance. When he drew near the horses, they began to jump and kick about, then to scream with terror. Johann could not hold them in; they bolted down the road, running away madly. I watched them out of sight, then looked for the stranger; but

I found that he, too, was gone.

With a light heart I turned down the side road through the deepening valley to which Johann had objected. There was not the slightest reason, that I could see, for his objection; and I daresay I tramped for a couple of hours without thinking of time or distance and certainly without seeing a person or a house. So far as the place was concerned, it was desolation itself. But I did not notice this particularly till, on turning a bend in the road, I came upon a scattered fringe of wood; then I recognized that I had been impressed unconsciously by the desolation of the region through which I had passed.

I sat down to rest myself and began to look around. It struck me that it was considerably colder than it had been at the commencement of my walk—a sort of sighing sound seemed to be around me with, now and then, high overhead, a sort of muffled roar. Looking upwards I noticed that great thick clouds were drafting rapidly across the sky from north to south at a great height. There were signs of a coming storm in some lofty stratum of the air. I was a little chilly, and, thinking that it was the sitting still after the exercise of walking, I resumed my journey.

The ground I passed over was now much more picturesque. There were no striking objects that the eye might single out, but in all there was a charm of beauty. I took little heed of time, and it was only when the deepening twilight forced it self upon me that I began to think of how I should find my way home. The air was cold, and the drifting of clouds high overhead was more marked. They were accompanied by a sort of far away rushing sound, through which seemed to come at intervals that mysterious cry which the driver had said came from a wolf. For a while I hesitated. I had said I would see the deserted village, so on I went and presently came on a wide stretch of open country, shut in by hills all around. Their sides were covered with trees which spread down to the plain, dotting in clumps the gentler slopes and hollows which showed here and there. I followed with my eye the winding of the road and saw that it curved close to one of the densest of these clumps and was lost behind it.

As I looked there came a cold shiver in the air, and the snow began to fall. I thought of the miles and miles of bleak country I had passed, and then hurried on to seek shelter of the wood in front. Darker and darker grew the sky, and faster and heavier fell the snow, till the earth before and around me was a glistening white carpet the further edge of which was lost in misty vagueness. The road was here but crude, and when on the level its boundaries were not so marked as when it passed through the cuttings; and in a little while I found that I must have strayed from it, for I missed underfoot the hard surface, and my feet sank deeper in the grass and moss. Then the wind grew stronger and blew with ever increasing force, till I was fain to run before it. The air became icy-cold, and in spite of my exercise I began to suffer. The snow was now falling so thickly and whirling around me in such rapid eddies that I could hardly keep my eyes open. Every now and then the heavens were torn asunder by vivid lightning, and in the flashes I could see ahead of me a great mass of trees, chiefly yew and cypress all heavily coated with snow.

I was soon amongst the shelter of the trees, and there in comparative silence I could hear the rush of the wind high overhead. Presently the blackness of the storm had become merged in the darkness of the night. By-and-by the storm seemed to be passing away, it now only came in fierce puffs or blasts. At such moments the weird sound of the wolf appeared to be echoed by many similar sounds around me.

Now and again, through the black mass of drifting cloud, came a straggling ray of moonlight which lit up the expanse and showed me that I was at the edge of a dense mass of cypress and yew trees. As the snow had ceased to fall, I walked out from the shelter and began to investigate more closely. It appeared to me that, amongst so many old foundations as I had passed, there might be still standing a house in which, though in ruins, I could find some sort of shelter for a while. As I skirted the edge of the copse, I found that a low wall encircled it, and following this I presently found an opening. Here the cypresses formed an alley leading up to a square mass of some kind of building. Just as I caught sight of this, however, the drifting clouds obscured the moon, and I passed up the path in darkness. The wind must have grown colder, for I felt myself shiver as I walked; but there was hope of shelter, and I groped my way blindly on.

I stopped, for there was a sudden stillness. The storm had passed; and, perhaps in sympathy with nature's silence, my heart seemed to cease to beat. But this was only momentarily; for suddenly the moonlight broke through the clouds showing me that I was in a graveyard and that the square object before me was a great massive tomb of marble, as white as the snow that lay on and all around it. With the moonlight there came a fierce sigh of the storm which appeared to resume its course with a long, low howl, as of many dogs or wolves. I was awed and shocked, and I felt the cold perceptibly grow upon me till it seemed to grip me by the heart. Then while the flood of moonlight still fell on the marble tomb, the storm gave further evidence of renewing, as though it were returning on its track. Impelled by some sort of fascination, I approached the sepulchre to see what it was and why such a thing stood alone in such a place. I walked around it and read, over the Doric door, in German:

COUNTESS DOLINGEN OF GRATZ
IN STYRIA
SOUGHT AND FOUND DEATH
1801

On the top of the tomb, seemingly driven through the solid marble—for the structure was composed of a few vast blocks of stone—was a great iron spike or stake. On going to the back I saw, graven in great Russian letters:

'The dead travel fast.'

There was something so weird and uncanny about the

whole thing that it gave me a turn and made me feel quite faint. I began to wish, for the first time, that I had taken Johann's advice. Here a thought struck me, which came under almost mysterious circumstances and with a terrible shock. This was Walpurgis Night!

Walpurgis Night was when, according to the belief of mill ions of people, the devil was abroad—when the graves were opened and the dead came forth and walked. When all evil things of earth and air and water held revel. This very place the driver had specially shunned. This was the depopulated village of centuries ago. This was where the suicide lay; and this was the place where I was alone—unmanned, shivering with cold in a shroud of snow with a wild storm gathering again up on me! It took all my philosophy, all the religion I had been taught, all my courage, not to collapse in a paroxysm of fright.

And now a perfect tornado burst upon me. The ground shook as though thousands of horses thundered across it; and this time the storm bore on its icy wings, not snow, but great hailstones which drove with such violence that they might have come from the thongs of Balearic slingers—hailstones that beat down leaf and branch and made the shelter of the cypresses of no more avail than though their stems were standing corn. At the first I had rushed to the nearest tree; but I was soon fain to leave it and seek the only spot that seemed to afford refuge, the deep Doric doorway of the marble tomb. There, crouching against the massive bronze door, I gained a certain amount of protection from the beating of the hail stones, for now they only drove against me as they ricochetted from the ground and the side of the marble.

As I leaned against the door, it moved slightly and opened inwards. The shelter of even a tomb was welcome in that pitiless tempest and I was about to enter it when there came a flash of forked lightning that lit up the whole expanse of the heavens. In the instant, as I am a living man, I saw, as my eyes turned into the darkness of the tomb, a beautiful woman with rounded cheeks and red lips, seemingly sleeping on a bier. As the thunder broke overhead, I was grasped as by the hand of a giant and hurled out into the storm. The whole thing was so sudden that, before I could realize the shock, moral as well as physical, I found the hailstones beating me down. At the same time I had a strange, dominating feeling that I was not alone. I looked towards the tomb. Just then there came another blinding flash which seemed to strike the iron stake that surmounted the tomb and to pour through to the earth, blasting and crumbling the marble, as in a burst of flame. The dead woman rose for a moment of agony while she was lapped in the flame, and her bitter scream of pain was drowned in the thundercrash. The last thing I heard was this mingling of dreadful sound, as again I was seized in the giant grasp and dragged away, while the hailstones beat on me and the air around seemed reverberant with the howling of wolves. The last sight that I remembered was a vague, white, moving mass, as if all the graves around me had sent out the phantoms of their sheeted dead, and that they were closing in on me through the white cloudiness of the driving hail.

Gradually there came a sort of vague beginning of consciousness, then a sense of weariness that was dreadful. For a time I remembered nothing, but slowly my senses returned. My feet seemed positively racked with pain, yet I could not move them. They seemed to be numbed. There was an icy feeling at the back of my neck and all down my spine, and my ears, like my feet, were dead yet in torment; but there was in my breast a sense of warmth which was by comparison delicious. It was as a nightmare—a physical nightmare, if one may use such an expression; for some heavy weight on my chest made it difficult for me to breathe.

This period of semi-lethargy seemed to remain a long time, and as it faded away I must have slept or swooned. Then came a sort of loathing, like the first stage of seasickness, and a wild desire to be free of something—I knew not what. A vast stillness enveloped me, as though all the world were asleep or dead—only broken by the low panting as of some animal close to me. I felt a warm rasping at my throat, then came a consciousness of the awful truth which chilled me to the heart and sent the blood surging up through my brain. Some great animal was lying on me and now licking my throat. I feared to stir, for some instinct of prudence bade me lie still; but the brute seemed to realize that there was now some change in me, for it raised its head. Through my eyelashes I saw above me the two great flaming eyes of a gigantic wolf. Its sharp white teeth gleamed in the gaping red mouth, and I could feel its hot breath fierce and acrid upon me.

For another spell of time I remembered no more. Then I be came conscious of a low growl, followed by a yelp, renewed again and again. Then seemingly very far away, I heard a 'Holloa! holloa!' as of many voices calling in unison. Cautiously I raised my head and looked in the direction whence the sound came, but the cemetery blocked my view. The wolf still continued to yelp in a strange way, and a red glare began to move round the grove of cypresses, as though following the sound. As the voices drew closer, the wolf yelped faster and louder. I feared to make either sound or motion. Nearer came the red glow over the white pall which stretched into the darkness a round me. Then all at once from beyond the trees there came at a trot a troop of horsemen bearing torches. The wolf rose from my breast and made for the cemetery. I saw one of the horsemen (soldiers by their caps and their long military cloaks) raise his carbine and take aim. A companion knocked up his arm, and I heard the ball whiz over my head. He had evidently taken my body for that of the wolf. Another sighted the animal as it slunk away, and a shot followed. Then, at a gallop, the troop rode forward—some towards me, others following the wolf as it disappeared amongst the snow-clad cypresses.

As they drew nearer I tried to move but was powerless, although I could see and hear all that went on around me. Two or three of the soldiers jumped from their horses and knelt beside me. One of them raised my head and placed his hand over my heart.

'Good news, comrades!' he cried. 'His heart still beats!'

Then some brandy was poured down my throat; it put vigor into me, and I was able to open my eyes fully and look around. Lights and shadows were moving among the trees, and I heard men call to one another. They drew together, uttering frightened exclamations; and the lights flashed as the others came pouring out of the cemetery pell-mell, like men possessed. When the further ones came close to us, those who were around me asked them eagerly, 'Well, have you found him?'

The reply rang out hurriedly, 'No! no! Come away quick—quick! This is no place to stay, and on this of all nights!'

'What was it?' was the question, asked in all manner of keys. The answer came variously and all indefinitely as though the men were moved by some common impulse to speak yet were restrained by some common fear from giving their thoughts.

'It—it—indeed!' gibbered one, whose wits had plainly given out for the moment.

'A wolf—and yet not a wolf!' another put in shudderingly.

'No use trying for him without the sacred bullet,' a third remarked in a more ordinary manner.

'Serve us right for coming out on this night! Truly we have earned our thousand marks!' were the ejaculations of a fourth.

'There was blood on the broken marble,' another said after a pause, 'the lightning never brought that there. And for him—is he safe? Look at his throat! See comrades, the wolf has been lying on him and keeping his blood warm.'

The officer looked at my throat and replied, 'He is all right, the skin is not pierced. What does it all mean? We should never have found him but for the yelping of the wolf.'

'What became of it?' asked the man who was holding up my head and who seemed the least panic-stricken of the party, for his hands were steady and without tremor. On his sleeve was the chevron of a petty officer.

'It went home,' answered the man, whose long face was pallid and who actually shook with terror as he glanced around him fearfully. 'There are graves enough there in which it may lie.

Come, comrades—come quickly! Let us leave this cursed spot.'

The officer raised me to a sitting posture, as he uttered a word of command; then several men placed me upon a horse. He sprang to the saddle behind me, took me in his arms, gave the word to advance; and, turning our faces away from the cypresses, we rode away in swift military order.

As yet my tongue refused its office, and I was perforce silent. I must have fallen asleep; for the next thing I remembered was finding myself standing up, supported by a soldier on each side of me. It was almost broad daylight, and to the north a red streak of sunlight was reflected like a path of blood over the waste of snow. The officer was telling the men to say nothing of what they had seen, except that they found an English stranger, guarded by a large dog.

'Dog! that was no dog,' cut in the man who had exhibited such fear. 'I think I know a wolf when I see one.'

The young officer answered calmly, 'I said a dog.'

'Dog!' reiterated the other ironically. It was evident that his courage was rising with the sun; and, pointing to me, he said, 'Look at his throat. Is that the work of a dog, master?'

Instinctively I raised my hand to my throat, and as I touched it I cried out in pain. The men crowded round to look, some stooping down from their saddles; and again there came the calm voice of the young officer, 'A dog, as I said. If aught else were said we should only be laughed at.'

I was then mounted behind a trooper, and we rode on into the suburbs of Munich. Here we came across a stray carriage into which I was lifted, and it was driven off to the Quatre Saisons—the young officer accompanying me, whilst a trooper followed with his horse, and the others rode off to their barracks.

When we arrived, Herr Delbruck rushed so quickly down the steps to meet me, that it was apparent he had been watching within. Taking me by both hands he solicitously led me in. The officer saluted me and was turning to withdraw, when I recognized his purpose and insisted that he should come to my rooms. Over a glass of wine I warmly thanked him and his brave comrades for saving me. He replied simply that he was more than glad, and that Herr Delbruck had at the first taken steps to make all the searching party pleased; at which ambiguous utterance the maitre d'hotel smiled, while the officer pleaded duty and withdrew.

'But Herr Delbruck,' I enquired, 'how and why was it that the soldiers searched for me?'

He shrugged his shoulders, as if in depreciation of his own deed, as he replied, 'I was so fortunate as to obtain leave from the commander of the regiment in which I serve, to ask for volunteers.'

'But how did you know I was lost?' I asked.

'The driver came hither with the remains of his carriage, which had been upset when the horses ran away.'

'But surely you would not send a search party of soldiers merely on this account?'

'Oh, no!' he answered, 'but even before the coachman arrived, I had this telegram from the Boyar whose guest you are,' and he took from his pocket a telegram which he handed to me, and I read:

> Bistritz.
> Be careful of my guest—his safety is most precious to me. Should aught happen to him, or if he be missed, spare nothing to find him and ensure his safety. He is English and therefore adventurous. There are often dangers from snow and wolves and night. Lose not a moment if you suspect harm to him. I answer your zeal with my fortune.
> —Dracula.

As I held the telegram in my hand, the room seemed to whirl around me, and if the attentive maitre d'hotel had not caught me, I think I should have fallen. There was something so strange in all this, something so weird and impossible to imagine, that there grew on me a sense of my being in some way the sport of opposite forces—the mere vague idea of which seemed in a way to paralyse me. I was certainly under some form of mysterious protection. From a distant country had come, in the very nick of time, a message that took me out of the danger of the snow sleep and the jaws of the wolf.

41

AMY FOSTER

Joseph Conrad

Kennedy is a country doctor, and lives in Colebrook, on the shores of Eastbay. The high ground rising abruptly behind the red roofs of the little town crowds the quaint High Street against the wall which defends it from the sea. Beyond the sea-wall there curves for miles in a vast and regular sweep the barren beach of shingle, with the village of Brenzett standing out darkly across the water, a spire in a clump of trees; and still further out the perpendicular column of a lighthouse, looking in the distance no bigger than a lead pencil, marks the vanishing-point of the land. The country at the back of Brenzett is low and flat, but the bay is fairly well sheltered from the seas, and occasionally a big ship, windbound or through stress of weather, makes use of the anchoring ground a mile and a half due north from you as you stand at the back door of the 'Ship Inn' in Brenzett. A dilapidated windmill near by lifting its shattered arms from a mound no loftier than a rubbish heap, and a Martello tower squatting at the water's edge half a mile to the south of the Coastguard cottages, are familiar to the skippers of small craft. These are the official seamarks for the patch of trustworthy bottom represented on the Admiralty charts by an irregular oval of dots enclosing several figures six, with a tiny anchor engraved among them, and the legend 'mud and shells' over all.

The brow of the upland overtops the square tower of the Colebrook Church. The slope is green and looped by a white road. Ascending along this road, you open a valley broad and shallow, a wide green trough of pastures and hedges merging inland into a vista of purple tints and flowing lines closing the view.

In this valley down to Brenzett and Colebrook and up to Darnford, the market town fourteen miles away, lies the practice of my friend Kennedy. He had begun life as surgeon in the Navy, and afterwards had been the companion of a famous traveller, in the days when there were continents with unexplored interiors. His papers on the fauna and flora made him known to scientific societies. And now he had come to a country practice—from choice. The penetrating power of his mind, acting like a corrosive fluid, had destroyed his ambition, I fancy. His intelligence is of a scientific order, of an investigating habit, and of that unappeasable curiosity which believes that there is a particle of a general truth in every mystery.

A good many years ago now, on my return from abroad, he invited me to stay with him. I came readily enough, and as he could not neglect his patients to keep me company, he took me on his rounds—thirty miles or so of an afternoon, sometimes. I waited for him on the roads; the horse reached after the leafy twigs, and, sitting in the dogcart, I could hear Kennedy's laugh through the half-open door left open of some cottage. He had a big, hearty laugh that would have fitted a man twice his size, a brisk manner, a bronzed face, and a pair of grey, profoundly attentive eyes. He had the talent of making people talk to him freely, and an inexhaustible patience in listening to their tales.

One day, as we trotted out of a large village into a shady bit of road, I saw on our left hand a low, black cottage, with diamond panes in the windows, a creeper on the end wall, a roof of shingle, and some roses climbing on the rickety trellis-work of the tiny porch. Kennedy pulled up to a walk. A woman, in full sunlight, was throwing a dripping blanket over a line stretched between two old apple-trees. And as the bobtailed, long-necked chestnut, trying to get his head, jerked the left hand, covered by a thick dog-skin glove, the doctor raised his voice over the hedge: 'How's your child, Amy?'

I had the time to see her dull face, red, not with a mantling blush, but as if her flat cheeks had been vigorously slapped, and to take in the squat figure, the scanty, dusty brown hair drawn into a tight knot at the back of the head. She looked quite young. With a distinct catch in her breath, her voice sounded low and timid.

'He's well, thank you.'

We trotted again. 'A young patient of yours,' I said; and the doctor, flicking the chestnut absently, muttered, 'Her husband used to be.'

'She seems a dull creature,' I remarked listlessly.

'Precisely,' said Kennedy. 'She is very passive. It's enough to look at the red hands hanging at the end of those short arms, at those slow, prominent brown eyes, to know the inertness of her mind—an inertness that one would think made it everlastingly safe from all the surprises of imagination. And yet which of us is safe? At any rate, such as you see her, she had enough imagination to fall in love. She's the daughter of one Isaac Foster, who from a small farmer has sunk into a shepherd; the beginning of his misfortunes dating from his runaway marriage with the cook of his widowed father—a well-to-do, apoplectic grazier, who passionately struck his name off his will, and had been heard to utter threats against his life. But this old affair, scandalous enough to serve as a motive for a Greek tragedy, arose from the similarity of their characters. There are other tragedies, less scandalous and of a subtler poignancy, arising from irreconcilable differences and from that fear of the Incomprehensible that hangs over all our heads—over all our heads...'

The tired chestnut dropped into a walk; and the rim of the sun, all red in a speckless sky, touched familiarly the smooth top of a ploughed rise near the road as I had seen it times innumerable touch the distant horizon of the sea. The uniform brownness of the harrowed field glowed with a rosy tinge, as though the powdered clods had sweated out in minute pearls of blood the toil of uncounted ploughmen. From the edge of a copse a waggon with two horses was rolling gently along the ridge. Raised above our heads upon the sky-line, it loomed up against the red sun, triumphantly big, enormous, like a chariot of giants drawn by two slow-stepping steeds of legendary proportions. And the clumsy figure of the man plodding at the head of the leading horse projected itself on the background of the Infinite with a heroic uncouthness. The end of his carter's whip quivered high up in the blue. Kennedy discoursed.

'She's the eldest of a large family. At the age of fifteen they put her out to service at the New Barns Farm. I attended Mrs. Smith, the tenant's wife, and saw that girl there for the first time. Mrs. Smith, a genteel person with a sharp nose, made her put on a black dress every afternoon. I don't know what induced me to notice her at all. There are faces that call your attention by a curious want of definiteness in their whole aspect, as, walking in a mist, you peer attentively at a vague shape which, after all, may be nothing more curious or strange than a signpost. The only peculiarity I perceived in her was a slight hesitation in her utterance, a sort of preliminary stammer which passes away with the first word. When sharply spoken to, she was apt to lose her head at once; but her heart was of the kindest. She had never been heard to express a dislike for a single human being, and she was tender to every living creature. She was devoted to Mrs. Smith, to Mr. Smith, to their dogs, cats, canaries; and as to Mrs. Smith's grey parrot, its peculiarities exercised upon her a positive fascination. Nevertheless, when that outlandish bird, attacked by the cat, shrieked for help in human accents, she ran out into the yard stopping her ears, and did not prevent the crime. For Mrs. Smith this was another evidence of her stupidity; on the other hand, her want of charm, in view of Smith's well-known frivolousness, was a great recommendation. Her short-sighted eyes would swim with pity for a poor mouse in a trap, and she had been seen once by some boys on her knees in the wet grass helping a toad in difficulties. If it's true, as some German fellow has said, that without phosphorus there is no thought, it is still more true that there is no kindness of heart without a certain amount of imagination. She had some. She had even more than is necessary to understand suffering and to be moved by pity. She fell in love under circumstances that leave no room for doubt in the matter; for you need imagination to form a notion of beauty at all, and still more to discover your ideal in an unfamiliar shape.

'How this aptitude came to her, what it did feed upon, is an inscrutable mystery. She was born in the village, and had never been further away from it than Colebrook or perhaps Darnford. She lived for four years with the Smiths. New Barns is an isolated farmhouse a mile away from the road, and she was content to look day after day at the same fields, hollows, rises; at the trees and the hedgerows; at the faces of the four men about the farm, always the same—day after day, month after month, year after year. She never showed a desire for conversation, and, as it seemed to me, she did not know how to smile. Sometimes of a fine Sunday afternoon she would put on her best dress, a pair of stout boots, a large grey hat trimmed with a black feather (I've seen her in that finery), seize an absurdly slender parasol, climb over two stiles, tramp over three fields and along two hundred yards of road—never further. There stood Foster's cottage. She would help her mother to give their tea to the younger children, wash up the crockery, kiss the little ones, and go back to the farm. That was all. All the rest, all the change, all the relaxation. She never seemed to wish for anything more. And then she fell in love. She fell in love silently, obstinately—perhaps helplessly. It came slowly, but when it came it worked like a powerful spell; it was love as the Ancients understood it: an irresistible and fateful impulse—a possession! Yes, it was in her to become haunted and possessed by a face, by a presence, fatally, as though she had been a pagan worshipper of form under a joyous sky—and to be awakened at last from that mysterious forgetfulness of self, from that enchantment, from that transport, by a fear resembling the unaccountable terror of a brute...'

With the sun hanging low on its western limit, the expanse of the grass-lands framed in the counter-scarps of the rising ground took on a gorgeous and sombre aspect. A sense of penetrating sadness, like that inspired by a grave strain of music, disengaged itself from the silence of the fields. The men we met walked past slow, unsmiling, with downcast eyes, as if the melancholy of an over-burdened earth had weighted their feet, bowed their shoulders, borne down their glances.

'Yes,' said the doctor to my remark, 'one would think the earth is under a curse, since of all her children these that cling to her the closest are uncouth in body and as leaden of gait as if their very hearts were loaded with chains. But here on this same road you might have seen amongst these heavy men a being lithe, supple, and long-limbed, straight like a pine with something striving upwards in his appearance as though the heart within him had been buoyant. Perhaps it was only the force of the contrast, but when he was passing one of these villagers here, the soles of his feet did not seem to me to touch the dust of the road. He vaulted over the stiles, paced these slopes with a long elastic stride that made him noticeable at a great distance, and had lustrous black eyes. He was so different from the mankind around that, with his freedom of movement, his soft—a little startled, glance, his olive complexion and graceful bearing, his humanity suggested to me the nature of a woodland creature. He came from there.'

The doctor pointed with his whip, and from the summit of the descent seen over the rolling tops of the trees in a park by the side of the road, appeared the level sea far below us, like the floor of an immense edifice inlaid with bands of dark ripple, with still trails of glitter, ending in a belt of glassy water at the foot of the sky. The light blur of smoke, from an invisible steamer, faded on the great clearness of the horizon like the mist of a breath on a mirror; and, inshore, the white sails of a coaster, with the appearance of disentangling themselves slowly from under the branches, floated clear of the foliage of the trees.

'Shipwrecked in the bay?' I said.

'Yes; he was a castaway. A poor emigrant from Central Europe bound to America and washed ashore here in a storm.

And for him, who knew nothing of the earth, England was an undiscovered country. It was some time before he learned its name; and for all I know he might have expected to find wild beasts or wild men here, when, crawling in the dark over the sea-wall, he rolled down the other side into a dyke, where it was another miracle he didn't get drowned. But he struggled instinctively like an animal under a net, and this blind struggle threw him out into a field. He must have been, indeed, of a tougher fibre than he looked to withstand without expiring such buffetings, the violence of his exertions, and so much fear. Later on, in his broken English that resembled curiously the speech of a young child, he told me himself that he put his trust in God, believing he was no longer in this world. And truly—he would add—how was he to know? He fought his way against the rain and the gale on all fours, and crawled at last among some sheep huddled close under the lee of a hedge. They ran off in all directions, bleating in the darkness, and he welcomed the first familiar sound he heard on these shores. It must have been two in the morning then. And this is all we know of the manner of his landing, though he did not arrive unattended by any means. Only his grisly company did not begin to come ashore till much later in the day...'

The doctor gathered the reins, clicked his tongue; we trotted down the hill. Then turning, almost directly, a sharp corner into the High Street, we rattled over the stones and were home.

Late in the evening Kennedy, breaking a spell of moodiness that had come over him, returned to the story. Smoking his pipe, he paced the long room from end to end. A reading-lamp concentrated all its light upon the papers on his desk; and, sitting by the open window, I saw, after the windless, scorching day, the frigid splendour of a hazy sea lying motionless under the moon. Not a whisper, not a splash, not a stir of the shingle, not a footstep, not a sigh came up from the earth below—never a sign of life but the scent of climbing jasmine; and Kennedy's voice, speaking behind me, passed through the wide casement, to vanish outside in a chill and sumptuous stillness.

'...The relations of shipwrecks in the olden time tell us of much suffering. Often the castaways were only saved from drowning to die miserably from starvation on a barren coast; others suffered violent death or else slavery, passing through years of precarious existence with people to whom their strangeness was an object of suspicion, dislike or fear. We read about these things, and they are very pitiful. It is indeed hard upon a man to find himself a lost stranger, helpless, incomprehensible, and of a mysterious origin, in some obscure corner of the earth. Yet amongst all the adventurers shipwrecked in all the wild parts of the world there is not one, it seems to me, that ever had to suffer a fate so simply tragic as the man I am speaking of, the most innocent of adventurers cast out by the sea in the bight of this bay, almost within sight from this very window.

'He did not know the name of his ship. Indeed, in the course of time we discovered he did not even know that ships had names—"like Christian people"'; and when, one day, from the top of the Talfourd Hill, he beheld the sea lying open to his view, his eyes roamed afar, lost in an air of wild surprise, as though he had never seen such a sight before. And probably he had not. As far as I could make out, he had been hustled together with many others on board an emigrant-ship lying at the mouth of the Elbe, too bewildered to take note of his surroundings, too weary to see anything, too anxious to care. They were driven below into the 'tweendeck and battened down from the very start. It was a low timber dwelling—he would say—with wooden beams overhead, like the houses in his country, but you went into it down a ladder. It was very large, very cold, damp and sombre, with places in the manner of wooden boxes where people had to sleep, one above another, and it kept on rocking all ways at once all the time. He crept into one of these boxes and laid down there in the clothes in which he had left his home many days before, keeping his bundle and his stick by his side. People groaned, children cried, water dripped, the lights went out, the walls of the place creaked, and everything was being shaken so that in one's little box one dared not lift one's head. He had lost touch with his only companion (a young man from the same valley, he said), and all the time a great noise of wind went on outside and heavy blows fell—boom! boom! An awful sickness overcame him, even to the point of making him neglect his prayers. Besides, one could not tell whether it was morning or evening. It seemed always to be night in that place.

'Before that he had been travelling a long, long time on the iron track. He looked out of the window, which had a wonderfully clear glass in it, and the trees, the houses, the fields, and the long roads seemed to fly round and round about him till his head swam. He gave me to understand that he had on his passage beheld uncounted multitudes of people—whole nations—all dressed in such clothes as the rich wear. Once he was made to get out of the carriage, and slept through a night on a bench in a house of bricks with his bundle under his head; and once for many hours he had to sit on a floor of flat stones dozing, with his knees up and with his bundle between his feet. There was a roof over him, which seemed made of glass, and was so high that the tallest mountain-pine he had ever seen would have had room to grow under it. Steam-machines rolled in at one end and out at the other. People swarmed more than you can see on a feast-day round the miraculous Holy Image in the yard of the Carmelite Convent down in the plains where, before he left his home, he drove his mother in a wooden cart—a pious old woman who wanted to offer prayers and make a vow for his safety. He could not give me an idea of how large and lofty and full of noise and smoke and gloom, and clang of iron, the place was, but some one had told him it was called Berlin. Then they rang a bell, and another steam-machine came in, and again he was taken on and on through a land that wearied his eyes by its flatness without a single bit of a hill to be seen anywhere. One more night he spent shut up in a building like a good stable with a litter of straw on the floor, guarding his bundle amongst a lot of men, of whom not one could understand a single word he said. In the morning they were all led down to the stony shores of an extremely broad muddy river, flowing not between hills but between houses that seemed immense. There was a steam-machine that went on the water, and they all stood upon it packed tight, only now there were with them many women and children who made much noise. A cold rain fell, the wind blew in his face; he was wet through, and his teeth chattered. He and the young man from the same valley took each other by the hand.

'They thought they were being taken to America straight away, but suddenly the steam-machine bumped against the side of a thing like a house on the water. The walls were smooth and black, and there uprose, growing from the roof as it were, bare trees in the shape of crosses, extremely high. That's how it appeared to him then, for he had never seen a ship before. This was the ship that was going to swim all the way to America. Voices shouted, everything swayed; there was a ladder dipping up and down. He went up on his hands and knees in mortal fear of falling into the water below, which made a great splashing. He got separated from his companion, and when he descended into the bottom of that ship his heart seemed to melt suddenly within him.

'It was then also, as he told me, that he lost contact for good and all with one of those three men who the summer before had been going about through all the little towns in the foothills of his country. They would arrive on market days driving in a peasant's cart, and would set up an office in an inn or some other Jew's house. There were three of them, of whom one with a long beard looked venerable; and they had red cloth collars round their necks and gold lace on their sleeves like Government officials. They sat proudly behind a long table; and in the next room, so that the common people shouldn't hear, they kept a cunning telegraph machine, through which they could talk to the Emperor of America. The fathers hung about the door, but the young men of the mountains would crowd up to the table asking many questions, for there was work to be got all the year round at three dollars a day in America, and no military service to do.

'But the American Kaiser would not take everybody. Oh, no! He himself had a great difficulty in getting accepted, and the venerable man in uniform had to go out of the room several times to work the telegraph on his behalf. The American Kaiser engaged him at last at three dollars, he being young and strong. However, many able young men backed out, afraid of the great distance; besides, those only who had some money could be taken. There were some who sold their huts and their land because it cost a lot of money to get to America; but then, once there, you had three dollars a day, and if you were clever you could find places where true gold could be picked up on the ground. His father's house was getting over full. Two of his brothers were married and had children. He promised to send money home from America by post twice a year. His father sold an old cow, a pair of piebald mountain ponies of his own raising, and a cleared plot of fair pasture land on the sunny slope of a pine-clad pass to a Jew inn-keeper in order to pay the people of the ship that took men to America to get rich in a short time.

'He must have been a real adventurer at heart, for how many of the greatest enterprises in the conquest of the earth had for their beginning just such a bargaining away of the paternal cow for the mirage or true gold far away! I have been telling you more or less in my own words what I learned fragmentarily in the course of two or three years, during which I seldom missed an opportunity of a friendly chat with him. He told me this story of his adventure with many flashes of white teeth and lively glances of black eyes, at first in a sort of anxious baby-talk, then, as he acquired the language, with great fluency, but always with that singing, soft, and at the same time vibrating intonation that instilled a strangely penetrating power into the sound of the most familiar English words, as if they had been the words of an unearthly language. And he always would come to an end, with many emphatic shakes of his head, upon that awful sensation of his heart melting within him directly he set foot on board that ship. Afterwards there seemed to come for him a period of blank ignorance, at any rate as to facts. No doubt he must have been abominably sea-sick and abominably unhappy—this soft and passionate adventurer, taken thus out of his knowledge, and feeling bitterly as he lay in his emigrant bunk his utter loneliness; for his was a highly sensitive nature. The next thing we know of him for certain is that he had been hiding in Hammond's pig-pound by the side of the road to Norton six miles, as the crow flies, from the sea. Of these experiences he was unwilling to speak: they seemed to have seared into his soul a sombre sort of wonder and indignation. Through the rumours of the country-side, which lasted for a good many days after his arrival, we know that the fishermen of West Colebrook had been disturbed and startled by heavy knocks against the walls of weatherboard cottages, and by a voice crying piercingly strange words in the night. Several of them turned out even, but, no doubt, he had fled in sudden alarm at their rough angry tones hailing each other in the darkness. A sort of frenzy must have helped him up the steep Norton hill. It was he, no doubt, who early the following morning had been seen lying (in a swoon, I should say) on the roadside grass by the Brenzett carrier, who actually got down to have a nearer look, but drew back, intimidated by the perfect immobility, and by something queer in the aspect of that tramp, sleeping so still under the showers. As the day advanced, some children came dashing into school at Norton in such a fright that the schoolmistress went out and spoke indignantly to a "horrid-looking man" on the road. He edged away, hanging his head, for a few steps, and then suddenly ran off with extraordinary fleetness. The driver of Mr. Bradley's milk-cart made no secret of it that he had lashed with his whip at a hairy sort of gipsy fellow who, jumping up at a turn of the road by the Vents, made a snatch at the pony's bridle. And he caught him a good one too, right over the face, he said, that made him drop down in the mud a jolly sight quicker than he had jumped up; but it was a good half-a-mile before he could stop the pony. Maybe that in his desperate endeavours to get help, and in his need to get in touch with some one, the poor devil had tried to stop the cart. Also three boys confessed afterwards to throwing stones at a funny tramp, knocking about all wet and muddy, and, it seemed, very drunk, in the narrow deep lane by the limekilns. All this was the talk of three villages for days; but we have Mrs. Finn's (the wife of Smith's waggoner) unimpeachable testimony that she saw him get over the low wall of Hammond's pig-pound and lurch straight at her, babbling aloud in a voice that was enough to make one die of fright. Having the baby with her in a perambulator, Mrs. Finn called out to him to go away, and as he persisted in coming nearer, she hit him courageously with her umbrella over the head and, without once looking back, ran like the wind with the perambulator as far as the first house in the village. She stopped then, out of breath, and spoke to old Lewis, hammering there at a heap of stones; and the old chap, taking off his immense black wire goggles, got up on his shaky legs to look where she pointed. Together they followed with their eyes the figure of the man running over a field; they saw him fall down, pick himself up, and run on again, staggering and waving his long arms above his head, in the direction of the New Barns Farm. From that moment he is plainly in the toils of his obscure and touching destiny. There is no doubt after this of what happened to him. All is certain now: Mrs. Smith's intense terror; Amy Foster's stolid conviction held against the other's nervous attack, that the man "meant no harm"; Smith's exasperation (on his return from Darnford Market) at finding the dog barking himself into a fit, the back-door locked, his wife in hysterics; and all for an unfortunate dirty tramp, supposed to be even then lurking in his stackyard. Was he? He would teach him to frighten women.

'Smith is notoriously hot-tempered, but the sight of some nondescript and miry creature sitting cross-legged amongst a lot of loose straw, and swinging itself to and fro like a bear in a cage, made him pause. Then this tramp stood up silently before him, one mass of mud and filth from head to foot.

Smith, alone amongst his stacks with this apparition, in the stormy twilight ringing with the infuriated barking of the dog, felt the dread of an inexplicable strangeness. But when that being, parting with his black hands the long matted locks that hung before his face, as you part the two halves of a curtain, looked out at him with glistening, wild, black-and-white eyes, the weirdness of this silent encounter fairly staggered him. He had admitted since (for the story has been a legitimate subject of conversation about here for years) that he made more than one step backwards. Then a sudden burst of rapid, senseless speech persuaded him at once that he had to do with an escaped lunatic. In fact, that impression never wore off completely. Smith has not in his heart given up his secret conviction of the man's essential insanity to this very day.

'As the creature approached him, jabbering in a most discomposing manner, Smith (unaware that he was being addressed as "gracious lord," and adjured in God's name to afford food and shelter) kept on speaking firmly but gently to it, and retreating all the time into the other yard. At last, watching his chance, by a sudden charge he bundled him headlong into the wood-lodge, and instantly shot the bolt. Thereupon he wiped his brow, though the day was cold. He had done his duty to the community by shutting up a wandering and probably dangerous maniac. Smith isn't a hard man at all, but he had room in his brain only for that one idea of lunacy. He was not imaginative enough to ask himself whether the man might not be perishing with cold and hunger. Meantime, at first, the maniac made a great deal of noise in the lodge. Mrs. Smith was screaming upstairs, where she had locked herself in her bedroom; but Amy Foster sobbed piteously at the kitchen door, wringing her hands and muttering, "Don't! don't!" I daresay Smith had a rough time of it that evening with one noise and another, and this insane, disturbing voice crying obstinately through the door only added to his irritation. He couldn't possibly have connected this troublesome lunatic with the sinking of a ship in Eastbay, of which there had been a rumour in the Darnford marketplace. And I daresay the man inside had been very near to insanity on that night. Before his excitement collapsed and he became unconscious he was throwing himself violently about in the dark, rolling on some dirty sacks, and biting his fists with rage, cold, hunger, amazement, and despair.

'He was a mountaineer of the eastern range of the Carpathians, and the vessel sunk the night before in Eastbay was the Hamburg emigrant-ship *Herzogin Sophia-Dorothea*, of appalling memory.

'A few months later we could read in the papers the accounts of the bogus "Emigration Agencies" among the Sclavonian peasantry in the more remote provinces of Austria. The object of these scoundrels was to get hold of the poor ignorant people's homesteads, and they were in league with the local usurers. They exported their victims through Hamburg mostly. As to the ship, I had watched her out of this very window, reaching close-hauled under short canvas into the bay on a dark, threatening afternoon. She came to an anchor, correctly by the chart, off the Brenzett Coastguard station. I remember before the night fell looking out again at the outlines of her spars and rigging that stood out dark and pointed on a background of ragged, slaty clouds like another and a slighter spire to the left of the Brenzett church-tower. In the evening the wind rose. At midnight I could hear in my bed the terrific gusts and the sounds of a driving deluge.

'About that time the Coastguardmen thought they saw the lights of a steamer over the anchoring-ground. In a moment they vanished; but it is clear that another vessel of some sort had tried for shelter in the bay on that awful, blind night, had rammed the German ship amidships (a breach—as one of the divers told me afterwards—"that you could sail a Thames barge through"), and then had gone out either scathless or damaged, who shall say; but had gone out, unknown, unseen, and fatal, to perish mysteriously at sea. Of her nothing ever came to light, and yet the hue and cry that was raised all over the world would have found her out if she had been in existence anywhere on the face of the waters.

'A completeness without a clue, and a stealthy silence as of a neatly executed crime, characterise this murderous disaster, which, as you may remember, had its gruesome celebrity. The wind would have prevented the loudest outcries from reaching the shore; there had been evidently no time for signals of distress. It was death without any sort of fuss. The Hamburg ship, filling all at once, capsized as she sank, and at daylight there was not even the end of a spar to be seen above water. She was missed, of course, and at first the Coastguardmen surmised that she had either dragged her anchor or parted her cable some time during the night, and had been blown out to sea. Then, after the tide turned, the wreck must have shifted a little and released some of the bodies, because a child—a little fair-haired child in a red frock—came ashore abreast of the Martello tower. By the afternoon you could see along three miles of beach dark figures with bare legs dashing in and out of the tumbling foam, and rough-looking men, women with hard faces, children, mostly fair-haired, were being carried, stiff and dripping, on stretchers, on wattles, on ladders, in a long procession past the door of the "Ship Inn," to be laid out in a row under the north wall of the Brenzett Church.

'Officially, the body of the little girl in the red frock is the first thing that came ashore from that ship. But I have patients amongst the seafaring population of West Colebrook, and, unofficially, I am informed that very early that morning two brothers, who went down to look after their cobble hauled up on the beach, found, a good way from Brenzett, an ordinary ship's hencoop lying high and dry on the shore, with eleven drowned ducks inside. Their families ate the birds, and the hencoop was split into firewood with a hatchet. It is possible that a man (supposing he happened to be on deck at the time of the accident) might have floated ashore on that hencoop. He might. I admit it is improbable, but there was the man—and for days, nay, for weeks—it didn't enter our heads that we had amongst us the only living soul that had escaped from that disaster. The man himself, even when he learned to speak intelligibly, could tell us very little. He remembered he had felt better (after the ship had anchored, I suppose), and that the darkness, the wind, and the rain took his breath away. This looks as if he had been on deck some time during that night. But we mustn't forget he had been taken out of his knowledge, that he had been seasick and battened down below for four days, that he had no general notion of a ship or of the sea, and therefore could have no definite idea of what was happening to him. The rain, the wind, the darkness he knew; he understood the bleating of the sheep, and he remembered the pain of his wretchedness and misery, his heartbroken astonishment that it was neither seen nor understood, his dismay at finding all the men angry and all the women fierce. He had approached them as a beggar, it is true, he said; but in his country, even if they gave nothing, they spoke gently to beggars. The children in his country were not taught to throw stones at those who asked for compassion. Smith's strategy overcame him completely. The wood-lodge presented the horrible aspect of a dungeon. What would be done to him next?... No wonder that Amy Foster appeared to his eyes with the aureole of an angel of light. The girl had not been able to sleep for thinking of the poor man, and in the morning, before the Smiths were up, she slipped out across the back yard. Holding the door of the wood-lodge ajar, she looked in and extended to him half a loaf of white bread—"such bread as the rich eat in my country," he used to say.

'At this he got up slowly from amongst all sorts of rubbish, stiff, hungry, trembling, miserable, and doubtful. "Can you eat this?" she asked in her soft and timid voice. He must have taken her for a "gracious lady." He devoured ferociously, and tears were falling on the crust. Suddenly he dropped the bread, seized her wrist, and imprinted a kiss on her hand. She was not frightened. Through his forlorn condition she had observed that he was good-looking. She shut the door and walked back slowly to the kitchen. Much later on, she told Mrs. Smith, who shuddered at the bare idea of being touched by that creature.

'Through this act of impulsive pity he was brought back again within the pale of human relations with his new surroundings. He never forgot it—never.

'That very same morning old Mr. Swaffer (Smith's nearest neighbour) came over to give his advice, and ended by carrying him off. He stood, unsteady on his legs, meek, and caked over in half-dried mud, while the two men talked around him in an incomprehensible tongue. Mrs. Smith had refused to come downstairs till the madman was off the premises; Amy Foster, far from within the dark kitchen, watched through the open back door; and he obeyed the signs that were made to him to the best of his ability. But Smith was full of mistrust. "Mind, sir! It may be all his cunning," he cried repeatedly in a tone of warning. When Mr. Swaffer started the mare, the deplorable being sitting humbly by his side, through weakness, nearly fell out over the back of the high two-wheeled cart. Swaffer took him straight home. And it is then that I come upon the scene.

'I was called in by the simple process of the old man beckoning to me with his forefinger over the gate of his house as I happened to be driving past. I got down, of course.

'"I've got something here," he mumbled, leading the way to an outhouse at a little distance from his other farm-buildings.

'It was there that I saw him first, in a long low room taken upon the space of that sort of coach-house. It was bare and whitewashed, with a small square aperture glazed with one cracked, dusty pane at its further end. He was lying on his back upon a straw pallet; they had given him a couple of horse-blankets, and he seemed to have spent the remainder of his strength in the exertion of cleaning himself. He was almost speechless; his quick breathing under the blankets pulled up to his chin, his glittering, restless black eyes reminded me of a wild bird caught in a snare. While I was examining him, old Swaffer stood silently by the door, passing the tips of his fingers along his shaven upper lip. I gave some directions, promised to send a bottle of medicine, and naturally made some inquiries.

'"Smith caught him in the stackyard at New Barns," said

the old chap in his deliberate, unmoved manner, and as if the other had been indeed a sort of wild animal. "That's how I came by him. Quite a curiosity, isn't he? Now tell me, doctor—you've been all over the world—don't you think that's a bit of a Hindoo we've got hold of here."

'I was greatly surprised. His long black hair scattered over the straw bolster contrasted with the olive pallor of his face. It occurred to me he might be a Basque. It didn't necessarily follow that he should understand Spanish; but I tried him with the few words I know, and also with some French. The whispered sounds I caught by bending my ear to his lips puzzled me utterly. That afternoon the young ladies from the Rectory (one of them read Goethe with a dictionary, and the other had struggled with Dante for years), coming to see Miss Swaffer, tried their German and Italian on him from the doorway. They retreated, just the least bit scared by the flood of passionate speech which, turning on his pallet, he let out at them. They admitted that the sound was pleasant, soft, musical—but, in conjunction with his looks perhaps, it was startling—so excitable, so utterly unlike anything one had ever heard. The village boys climbed up the bank to have a peep through the little square aperture. Everybody was wondering what Mr. Swaffer would do with him.

'He simply kept him.

'Swaffer would be called eccentric were he not so much respected. They will tell you that Mr. Swaffer sits up as late as ten o'clock at night to read books, and they will tell you also that he can write a cheque for two hundred pounds without thinking twice about it. He himself would tell you that the Swaffers had owned land between this and Darnford for these three hundred years. He must be eighty-five to-day, but he does not look a bit older than when I first came here. He is a great breeder of sheep, and deals extensively in cattle. He attends market days for miles around in every sort of weather, and drives sitting bowed low over the reins, his lank grey hair curling over the collar of his warm coat, and with a green plaid rug round his legs. The calmness of advanced age gives a solemnity to his manner. He is clean-shaved; his lips are thin and sensitive; something rigid and monarchal in the set of his features lends a certain elevation to the character of his face. He has been known to drive miles in the rain to see a new kind of rose in somebody's garden, or a monstrous cabbage grown by a cottager. He loves to hear tell of or to be shown something that he calls "outlandish." Perhaps it was just that outlandishness of the man which influenced old Swaffer. Perhaps it was only an inexplicable caprice. All I know is that at the end of three weeks I caught sight of Smith's lunatic digging in Swaffer's kitchen garden. They had found out he could use a spade. He dug barefooted.

'His black hair flowed over his shoulders. I suppose it was Swaffer who had given him the striped old cotton shirt; but he wore still the national brown cloth trousers (in which he had been washed ashore) fitting to the leg almost like tights; was belted with a broad leathern belt studded with little brass discs; and had never yet ventured into the village. The land he looked upon seemed to him kept neatly, like the grounds round a landowner's house; the size of the cart-horses struck him with astonishment; the roads resembled garden walks, and the aspect of the people, especially on Sundays, spoke of opulence. He wondered what made them so hardhearted and their children so bold. He got his food at the back door, carried it in both hands carefully to his outhouse, and, sitting alone on his pallet, would make the sign of the cross before he began. Beside the same pallet, kneeling in the early darkness of the short days, he recited aloud the Lord's Prayer before he slept. Whenever he saw old Swaffer he would bow with veneration from the waist, and stand erect while the old man, with his fingers over his upper lip, surveyed him silently. He bowed also to Miss Swaffer, who kept house frugally for her father—a broad-shouldered, big-boned woman of forty-five, with the pocket of her dress full of keys, and a grey, steady eye. She was Church—as people said (while her father was one of the trustees of the Baptist Chapel)—and wore a little steel cross at her waist. She dressed severely in black, in memory of one of the innumerable Bradleys of the neighbourhood, to whom she had been engaged some twenty-five years ago—a young farmer who broke his neck out hunting on the eve of the wedding day. She had the unmoved countenance of the deaf, spoke very seldom, and her lips, thin like her father's, astonished one sometimes by a mysteriously ironic curl.

'These were the people to whom he owed allegiance, and an overwhelming loneliness seemed to fall from the leaden sky of that winter without sunshine. All the faces were sad. He could talk to no one, and had no hope of ever understanding anybody. It was as if these had been the faces of people from the other world—dead people—he used to tell me years afterwards. Upon my word, I wonder he did not go mad. He didn't know where he was. Somewhere very far from his mountains—somewhere over the water. Was this America, he wondered?

'If it hadn't been for the steel cross at Miss Swaffer's belt he would not, he confessed, have known whether he was in a Christian country at all. He used to cast stealthy glances at it, and feel comforted. There was nothing here the same as in his country! The earth and the water were different; there were no images of the Redeemer by the roadside. The very grass was different, and the trees. All the trees but the three old Norway pines on the bit of lawn before Swaffer's house, and these reminded him of his country. He had been detected once, after dusk, with his forehead against the trunk of one of them, sobbing, and talking to himself. They had been like brothers to him at that time, he affirmed. Everything else was strange. Conceive you the kind of an existence overshadowed, oppressed, by the everyday material appearances, as if by the visions of a nightmare. At night, when he could not sleep, he kept on thinking of the girl who gave him the first piece of bread he had eaten in this foreign land. She had been neither fierce nor angry, nor frightened. Her face he remembered as the only comprehensible face amongst all these faces that were as closed, as mysterious, and as mute as the faces of the dead who are possessed of a knowledge beyond the comprehension of the living. I wonder whether the memory of her compassion prevented him from cutting his throat. But there! I suppose I am an old sentimentalist, and forget the instinctive love of life which it takes all the strength of an uncommon despair to overcome.

'He did the work which was given him with an intelligence which surprised old Swaffer. By-and-by it was discovered that he could help at the ploughing, could milk the cows, feed the bullocks in the cattle-yard, and was of some use with the sheep. He began to pick up words, too, very fast; and suddenly, one fine morning in spring, he rescued from an untimely death a grand-child of old Swaffer.

'Swaffer's younger daughter is married to Willcox, a solicitor and the Town Clerk of Colebrook. Regularly twice a year they come to stay with the old man for a few days. Their only child, a little girl not three years old at the time, ran out of the house alone in her little white pinafore, and, toddling across the grass of a terraced garden, pitched herself over a low wall head first into the horse-pond in the yard below.

'Our man was out with the waggoner and the plough in the field nearest to the house, and as he was leading the team round to begin a fresh furrow, he saw, through the gap of the gate, what for anybody else would have been a mere flutter of something white. But he had straight-glancing, quick, far-reaching eyes, that only seemed to flinch and lose their amazing power before the immensity of the sea. He was barefooted, and looking as outlandish as the heart of Swaffer could desire. Leaving the horses on the turn, to the inexpressible disgust of the waggoner he bounded off, going over the ploughed ground in long leaps, and suddenly appeared before the mother, thrust the child into her arms, and strode away.

'The pond was not very deep; but still, if he had not had such good eyes, the child would have perished—miserably suffocated in the foot or so of sticky mud at the bottom. Old

Swaffer walked out slowly into the field, waited till the plough came over to his side, had a good look at him, and without saying a word went back to the house. But from that time they laid out his meals on the kitchen table; and at first, Miss Swaffer, all in black and with an inscrutable face, would come and stand in the doorway of the living-room to see him make a big sign of the cross before he fell to. I believe that from that day, too, Swaffer began to pay him regular wages.

'I can't follow step by step his development. He cut his hair short, was seen in the village and along the road going to and fro to his work like any other man. Children ceased to shout after him. He became aware of social differences, but remained for a long time surprised at the bare poverty of the churches among so much wealth. He couldn't understand either why they were kept shut up on week days. There was nothing to steal in them. Was it to keep people from praying too often? The rectory took much notice of him about that time, and I believe the young ladies attempted to prepare the ground for his conversion. They could not, however, break him of his habit of crossing himself, but he went so far as to take off the string with a couple of brass medals the size of a sixpence, a tiny metal cross, and a square sort of scapulary which he wore round his neck. He hung them on the wall by the side of his bed, and he was still to be heard every evening reciting the Lord's Prayer, in incomprehensible words and in a slow, fervent tone, as he had heard his old father do at the head of all the kneeling family, big and little, on every evening of his life. And though he wore corduroys at work, and a slop-made pepper-and-salt suit on Sundays, strangers would turn round to look after him on the road. His foreignness had a peculiar and indelible stamp. At last people became used to see him. But they never became used to him. His rapid, skimming walk; his swarthy complexion; his hat cocked on the left ear; his habit, on warm evenings, of wearing his coat over one shoulder, like a hussar's dolman; his manner of leaping over the stiles, not as a feat of agility, but in the ordinary course of progression—all these peculiarities were, as one may say, so many causes of scorn and offence to the inhabitants of the village. *They* wouldn't in their dinner hour lie flat on their backs on the grass to stare at the sky. Neither did they go about the fields screaming dismal tunes. Many times have I heard his high-pitched voice from behind the ridge of some sloping sheep-walk, a voice light and soaring, like a lark's, but with a melancholy human note, over our fields that hear only the song of birds. And I should be startled myself. Ah! He was different: innocent of heart, and full of good will, which nobody wanted, this castaway, that, like a man transplanted into another planet, was separated by an immense space from his past and by an immense ignorance from his future. His quick, fervent utterance positively shocked everybody. "An excitable devil," they called him. One evening, in the tap-room of the Coach and Horses (having drunk some whisky), he upset them all by singing a love song of his country. They hooted him down, and he was pained; but Preble, the lame wheelwright, and Vincent, the fat blacksmith, and the other notables too, wanted to drink their evening beer in peace. On another occasion he tried to show them how to dance. The dust rose in clouds from the sanded floor; he leaped straight up amongst the deal tables, struck his heels together, squatted on one heel in front of old Preble, shooting out the other leg, uttered wild and exulting cries, jumped up to whirl on one foot, snapping his fingers above his head—and a strange carter who was having a drink in there began to swear, and cleared out with his half-pint in his hand into the bar. But when suddenly he sprang upon a table and continued to dance among the glasses, the landlord interfered. He didn't want any "acrobat tricks in the taproom." They laid their hands on him. Having had a glass or two, Mr. Swaffer's foreigner tried to expostulate: was ejected forcibly: got a black eye.

'I believe he felt the hostility of his human surroundings. But he was tough—tough in spirit, too, as well as in body. Only the memory of the sea frightened him, with that vague terror that is left by a bad dream. His home was far away; and he did not want now to go to America. I had often explained to him that there is no place on earth where true gold can be found lying ready and to be got for the trouble of the picking up. How then, he asked, could he ever return home with empty hands when there had been sold a cow, two ponies, and a bit of land to pay for his going? His eyes would fill with tears, and, averting them from the immense shimmer of the sea, he would throw himself face down on the grass. But sometimes, cocking his hat with a little conquering air, he would defy my wisdom. He had found his bit of true gold. That was Amy Foster's heart; which was "a golden heart, and soft to people's misery," he would say in the accents of overwhelming conviction.

'He was called Yanko. He had explained that this meant little John; but as he would also repeat very often that he was a mountaineer (some word sounding in the dialect of his country like Goorall) he got it for his surname. And this is the only trace of him that the succeeding ages may find in the marriage register of the parish. There it stands—Yanko Goorall—in the rector's handwriting. The crooked cross made by the castaway, a cross whose tracing no doubt seemed to him the most solemn part of the whole ceremony, is all that remains now to perpetuate the memory of his name.

'His courtship had lasted some time—ever since he got his precarious footing in the community. It began by his buying for Amy Foster a green satin ribbon in Darnford. This was what you did in his country. You bought a ribbon at a Jew's stall on a fair-day. I don't suppose the girl knew what to do with it, but he seemed to think that his honourable intentions could not be mistaken.

'It was only when he declared his purpose to get married that I fully understood how, for a hundred futile and inappreciable reasons, how—shall I say odious?—he was to all the countryside. Every old woman in the village was up in arms. Smith, coming upon him near the farm, promised to break his head for him if he found him about again. But he twisted his little black moustache with such a bellicose air and rolled such big, black fierce eyes at Smith that this promise came to nothing. Smith, however, told the girl that she must be mad to take up with a man who was surely wrong in his head. All the same, when she heard him in the gloaming whistle from beyond the orchard a couple of bars of a weird and mournful tune, she would drop whatever she had in her hand—she would leave Mrs. Smith in the middle of a sentence—and she would run out to his call. Mrs. Smith called her a shameless hussy. She answered nothing. She said nothing at all to anybody, and went on her way as if she had been deaf. She and I alone all in the land, I fancy, could see his very real beauty. He was very good-looking, and most graceful in his bearing, with that something wild as of a woodland creature in his aspect. Her mother moaned over her dismally whenever the girl came to see her on her day out. The father was surly, but pretended not to know; and Mrs. Finn once told her plainly that "this man, my dear, will do you some harm some day yet." And so it went on. They could be seen on the roads, she tramping stolidly in her finery—grey dress, black feather, stout boots, prominent white cotton gloves that caught your eye a hundred yards away; and he, his coat slung picturesquely over one shoulder, pacing by her side, gallant of bearing and casting tender glances upon the girl with the golden heart. I wonder whether he saw how plain she was. Perhaps among types so different from what he had ever seen, he had not the power to judge; or perhaps he was seduced by the divine quality of her pity.

'Yanko was in great trouble meantime. In his country you get an old man for an ambassador in marriage affairs. He did not know how to proceed. However, one day in the midst of sheep in a field (he was now Swaffer's under-shepherd with Foster) he took off his hat to the father and declared himself humbly. "I daresay she's fool enough to marry you," was all Foster said. "And then," he used to relate, "he puts his hat on his head, looks black at me as if he wanted to cut my throat, whistles the dog, and off he goes, leaving me to do the work."

The Fosters, of course, didn't like to lose the wages the girl earned: Amy used to give all her money to her mother. But there was in Foster a very genuine aversion to that match. He contended that the fellow was very good with sheep, but was not fit for any girl to marry. For one thing, he used to go along the hedges muttering to himself like a dam' fool; and then, these foreigners behave very queerly to women sometimes. And perhaps he would want to carry her off somewhere—or run off himself. It was not safe. He preached it to his daughter that the fellow might ill-use her in some way. She made no answer. It was, they said in the village, as if the man had done something to her. People discussed the matter. It was quite an excitement, and the two went on "walking out" together in the face of opposition. Then something unexpected happened.

'I don't know whether old Swaffer ever understood how much he was regarded in the light of a father by his foreign retainer. Anyway the relation was curiously feudal. So when Yanko asked formally for an interview—"and the Miss too" (he called the severe, deaf Miss Swaffer simply *Miss*)—it was to obtain their permission to marry. Swaffer heard him unmoved, dismissed him by a nod, and then shouted the intelligence into Miss Swaffer's best ear. She showed no surprise, and only remarked grimly, in a veiled blank voice, "He certainly won't get any other girl to marry him."

'It is Miss Swaffer who has all the credit of the munificence: but in a very few days it came out that Mr. Swaffer had presented Yanko with a cottage (the cottage you've seen this morning) and something like an acre of ground—had made it over to him in absolute property. Willcox expedited the deed, and I remember him telling me he had a great pleasure in making it ready. It recited: "In consideration of saving the life of my beloved grandchild, Bertha Willcox."

'Of course, after that no power on earth could prevent them from getting married.

'Her infatuation endured. People saw her going out to meet him in the evening. She stared with unblinking, fascinated eyes up the road where he was expected to appear, walking freely, with a swing from the hip, and humming one of the love-tunes of his country. When the boy was born, he got elevated at the "Coach and Horses," essayed again a song and a dance, and was again ejected. People expressed their commiseration for a woman married to that Jack-in-the-box. He didn't care. There was a man now (he told me boastfully) to whom he could sing and talk in the language of his country, and show how to dance by-and-by.

'But I don't know. To me he appeared to have grown less springy of step, heavier in body, less keen of eye. Imagination, no doubt; but it seems to me now as if the net of fate had been drawn closer round him already.

'One day I met him on the footpath over the Talfourd Hill. He told me that "women were funny." I had heard already of domestic differences. People were saying that Amy Foster was beginning to find out what sort of man she had married. He looked upon the sea with indifferent, unseeing eyes. His wife had snatched the child out of his arms one day as he sat on the doorstep crooning to it a song such as the mothers sing to babies in his mountains. She seemed to think he was doing it some harm. Women are funny. And she had objected to him praying aloud in the evening. Why? He expected the boy to repeat the prayer aloud after him by-and-by, as he used to do after his old father when he was a child—in his own country. And I discovered he longed for their boy to grow up so that he could have a man to talk with in that language that to our ears sounded so disturbing, so passionate, and so bizarre. Why his wife should dislike the idea he couldn't tell. But that would pass, he said. And tilting his head knowingly, he tapped his breastbone to indicate that she had a good heart: not hard, not fierce, open to compassion, charitable to the poor!

'I walked away thoughtfully; I wondered whether his difference, his strangeness, were not penetrating with repulsion that dull nature they had begun by irresistibly attracting. I wondered...'

The Doctor came to the window and looked out at the frigid splendour of the sea, immense in the haze, as if enclosing all the earth with all the hearts lost among the passions of love and fear.

'Physiologically, now,' he said, turning away abruptly, 'it was possible. It was possible.'

He remained silent. Then went on—'At all events, the next time I saw him he was ill—lung trouble. He was tough, but I daresay he was not acclimatised as well as I had supposed. It was a bad winter; and, of course, these mountaineers do get fits of home sickness; and a state of depression would make him vulnerable. He was lying half dressed on a couch downstairs.

'A table covered with a dark oilcloth took up all the middle of the little room. There was a wicker cradle on the floor, a kettle spouting steam on the hob, and some child's linen lay drying on the fender. The room was warm, but the door opens right into the garden, as you noticed perhaps.

'He was very feverish, and kept on muttering to himself. She sat on a chair and looked at him fixedly across the table with her brown, blurred eyes. "Why don't you have him upstairs?" I asked. With a start and a confused stammer she said, "Oh! ah! I couldn't sit with him upstairs, Sir."

'I gave her certain directions; and going outside, I said again that he ought to be in bed upstairs. She wrung her hands. "I couldn't. I couldn't. He keeps on saying something—I don't know what." With the memory of all the talk against the man that had been dinned into her ears, I looked at her narrowly. I looked into her shortsighted eyes, at her dumb eyes that once in her life had seen an enticing shape, but seemed, staring at me, to see nothing at all now. But I saw she was uneasy.

'"What's the matter with him?" she asked in a sort of vacant trepidation. "He doesn't look very ill. I never did see anybody look like this before..."

'"Do you think," I asked indignantly, "he is shamming?"

'"I can't help it, sir," she said stolidly. And suddenly she clapped her hands and looked right and left. "And there's the baby. I am so frightened. He wanted me just now to give him the baby. I can't understand what he says to it."

'"Can't you ask a neighbour to come in tonight?" I asked.

'"Please, sir, nobody seems to care to come," she muttered, dully resigned all at once.

'I impressed upon her the necessity of the greatest care, and then had to go. There was a good deal of sickness that winter. "Oh, I hope he won't talk!" she exclaimed softly just as I was going away.

'I don't know how it is I did not see—but I didn't. And yet, turning in my trap, I saw her lingering before the door, very still, and as if meditating a flight up the miry road.

'Towards the night his fever increased.

'He tossed, moaned, and now and then muttered a complaint. And she sat with the table between her and the couch, watching every movement and every sound, with the terror, the unreasonable terror, of that man she could not understand creeping over her. She had drawn the wicker cradle close to her feet. There was nothing in her now but the maternal instinct and that unaccountable fear.

'Suddenly coming to himself, parched, he demanded a drink of water. She did not move. She had not understood, though he may have thought he was speaking in English. He waited, looking at her, burning with fever, amazed at her silence and immobility, and then he shouted impatiently, "Water! Give me water!"

'She jumped to her feet, snatched up the child, and stood still. He spoke to her, and his passionate remonstrances only increased her fear of that strange man. I believe he spoke to her for a long time, entreating, wondering, pleading, ordering, I suppose. She says she bore it as long as she could. And then a gust of rage came over him.

'He sat up and called out terribly one word—some word. Then he got up as though he hadn't been ill at all, she says. And as in fevered dismay, indignation, and wonder he tried to get to her round the table, she simply opened the door and ran out with the child in her arms. She heard him call twice after her down the road in a terrible voice—and fled... Ah! but you should have seen stirring behind the dull, blurred glance of these eyes the spectre of the fear which had hunted her on that night three miles and a half to the door of Foster's cottage! I did the next day.

'And it was I who found him lying face down and his body in a puddle, just outside the little wicket-gate.

'I had been called out that night to an urgent case in the village, and on my way home at daybreak passed by the cottage. The door stood open. My man helped me to carry him in. We laid him on the couch. The lamp smoked, the fire was out, the chill of the stormy night oozed from the cheerless yellow paper on the wall. "Amy!" I called aloud, and my voice seemed to lose itself in the emptiness of this tiny house as if I had cried in a desert. He opened his eyes. "Gone!" he said distinctly. "I had only asked for water—only for a little water..."

'He was muddy. I covered him up and stood waiting in silence, catching a painfully gasped word now and then. They were no longer in his own language. The fever had left him, taking with it the heat of life. And with his panting breast and lustrous eyes he reminded me again of a wild creature under the net; of a bird caught in a snare. She had left him. She had left him—sick—helpless—thirsty. The spear of the hunter had entered his very soul. "Why?" he cried in the penetrating and indignant voice of a man calling to a responsible Maker. A gust of wind and a swish of rain answered.

'And as I turned away to shut the door he pronounced the word "Merciful!" and expired.

'Eventually I certified heart-failure as the immediate cause of death. His heart must have indeed failed him, or else he might have stood this night of storm and exposure, too. I closed his eyes and drove away. Not very far from the cottage I met Foster walking sturdily between the dripping hedges with his collie at his heels.

'"Do you know where your daughter is?" I asked.

'"Don't I!" he cried. "I am going to talk to him a bit. Frightening a poor woman like this."

'"He won't frighten her any more," I said. "He is dead."

'He struck with his stick at the mud.

'"And there's the child."

'Then, after thinking deeply for a while—' "I don't know that it isn't for the best."

'That's what he said. And she says nothing at all now. Not a word of him. Never. Is his image as utterly gone from her mind as his lithe and striding figure, his carolling voice are gone from our fields? He is no longer before her eyes to excite her imagination into a passion of love or fear; and his memory seems to have vanished from her dull brain as a shadow passes away upon a white screen. She lives in the cottage and works for Miss Swaffer. She is Amy Foster for everybody, and the child is "Amy Foster's boy." She calls him Johnny—which means Little John.

'It is impossible to say whether this name recalls anything to her. Does she ever think of the past? I have seen her hanging over the boy's cot in a very passion of maternal tenderness. The little fellow was lying on his back, a little frightened at me, but very still, with his big black eyes, with his fluttered air of a bird in a snare. And looking at him I seemed to see again the other one—the father, cast out mysteriously by the sea to perish in the supreme disaster of loneliness and despair.'

42

THE MAN WHO COULD WORK MIRACLES

H.G. Wells

It is doubtful whether the gift was innate. For my own part, I think it came to him suddenly. Indeed, until he was thirty he was a sceptic, and did not believe in miraculous powers. And here, since it is the most convenient place, I must mention that he was a little man, and had eyes of a hot brown, very erect red hair, a moustache with ends that he twisted up, and freckles. His name was George McWhirter Fotheringay—not the sort of name by any means to lead to any expectation of miracles—and he was clerk at Gomshott's. He was greatly addicted to assertive argument. It was while he was asserting the impossibility of miracles that he had his first intimation of his extraordinary powers. This particular argument was being held in the bar of the Long Dragon, and Toddy Beamish was conducting the opposition by a monotonous but effective 'So you say,' that drove Mr. Fotheringay to the very limit of his patience.

There were present, besides these two, a very dusty cyclist, landlord Cox, and Miss Maybridge, the perfectly respectable and rather portly barmaid of the Dragon. Miss Maybridge was standing with her back to Mr. Fotheringay, washing glasses; the others were watching him, more or less amused by the present ineffectiveness of the assertive method. Goaded by the Torres Vedras tactics of Mr. Beamish, Mr. Fotheringay determined to make an unusual rhetorical effort. 'Looky here, Mr. Beamish,' said Mr. Fotheringay. 'Let us clearly understand what a miracle is. It's something contrariwise to the course of nature done by power of Will, something what couldn't happen without being specially willed.'

'So you say,' said Mr. Beamish, repulsing him.

Mr. Fotheringay appealed to the cyclist, who had hitherto been a silent auditor, and received his assent—given with a hesitating cough and a glance at Mr. Beamish. The landlord would express no opinion, and Mr. Fotheringay, returning to Mr. Beamish, received the unexpected concession of a qualified assent to his definition of a miracle.

'For instance,' said Mr. Fotheringay, greatly encouraged. 'Here would be a miracle. That lamp, in the natural course of nature, couldn't burn like that upsy-down, could it, Beamish?'

'You say it couldn't,' said Beamish.

'And you?' said Fotheringay. 'You don't mean to say—eh?'

'No,' said Beamish reluctantly. 'No, it couldn't.'

'Very well,' said Mr. Fotheringay. 'Then here comes someone, as it might be me, along here, and stands as it might be here, and says to that lamp, as I might do, collecting all my will—Turn upsy-down without breaking, and go on burning steady, and—Hullo!'

It was enough to make anyone say 'Hullo!' The impossible, the incredible, was visible to them all. The lamp hung inverted in the air, burning quietly with its flame pointing down. It was as solid, as indisputable as ever a lamp was, the prosaic common lamp of the Long Dragon bar.

Mr. Fotheringay stood with an extended forefinger and the knitted brows of one anticipating a catastrophic smash. The cyclist, who was sitting next the lamp, ducked and jumped across the bar. Everybody jumped, more or less. Miss Maybridge turned and screamed. For nearly three seconds the lamp remained still. A faint cry of mental distress came from Mr. Fotheringay. 'I can't keep it up,' he said, 'any longer.' He staggered back, and the inverted lamp suddenly flared, fell against the corner of the bar, bounced aside, smashed upon the floor, and went out.

It was lucky it had a metal receiver, or the whole place would have been in a blaze. Mr. Cox was the first to speak, and his remark, shorn of needless excrescences, was to the effect that Fotheringay was a fool. Fotheringay was beyond disputing even so fundamental a proposition as that! He was astonished beyond measure at the thing that had occurred. The subsequent conversation threw absolutely no light on the matter so far as Fotheringay was concerned; the general opinion not only followed Mr. Cox very closely but very vehemently. Everyone accused Fotheringay of a silly trick, and presented him to himself as a foolish destroyer of comfort and security. His mind was in a tornado of perplexity, he was himself inclined to agree with them, and he made a remarkably ineffectual opposition to the proposal of his departure.

He went home flushed and heated, coat-collar crumpled, eyes smarting and ears red. He watched each of the ten street lamps nervously as he passed it. It was only when he found himself alone in his little bed-room in Church Row that he was able to grapple seriously with his memories of the occurrence, and ask, 'What on earth happened?'

He had removed his coat and boots, and was sitting on the bed with his hands in his pockets repeating the text of his defence for the seventeenth time, 'I didn't want the confounded thing to upset,' when it occurred to him that at the precise moment he had said the commanding words he had inadvertently willed the thing he said, and that when he had seen the lamp in the air he had felt it depended on him to maintain it there without being clear how this was to be done. He had not a particularly complex mind, or he might have stuck for a time at that 'inadvertently willed,' embracing, as it does, the abstrusest problems of voluntary action; but as it was, the idea came to him with a quite acceptable haziness. And from that, following, as I must admit, no clear logical path, he came to the test of experiment.

He pointed resolutely to his candle and collected his mind, though he felt he did a foolish thing. 'Be raised up,' he said. But in a second that feeling vanished. The candle was raised, hung in the air one giddy moment, and as Mr. Fotheringay gasped, fell with a smash on his toilet-table, leaving him in darkness save for the expiring glow of its wick.

For a time Mr. Fotheringay sat in the darkness, perfectly still. 'It did happen, after all,' he said. 'And 'ow I'm to explain it I don't know.' He sighed heavily, and began feeling in his pockets for a match. He could find none, and he rose and groped about the toilet-table. 'I wish I had a match,' he said. He resorted to his coat, and there was none there, and then it dawned upon him that miracles were possible even with matches. He extended a hand and scowled at it in the dark. 'Let there be a match in that hand,' he said. He felt some light object fall across his palm, and his fingers closed upon a match.

After several ineffectual attempts to light this, he discovered it was a safety-match. He threw it down, and then it occurred to him that he might have willed it lit. He did, and perceived it burning in the midst of his toilet-table mat. He caught it up hastily, and it went out. His perception of possibilities enlarged, and he felt for and replaced the candle in its candlestick. 'Here! you be lit,' said Mr. Fotheringay, and forthwith the candle was flaring, and he saw a little black hole in the toilet-cover, with a wisp of smoke rising from it. For a time he stared from this to the little flame and back, and then looked up and met his own gaze in the looking glass. By this help he communed with himself in silence for a time.

'How about miracles now?' said Mr. Fotheringay at last, addressing his reflection.

The subsequent meditations of Mr. Fotheringay were of a severe but confused description. So far, he could see it was a case of pure willing with him. The nature of his experiences so far disinclined him for any further experiments, at least until he had reconsidered them. But he lifted a sheet of paper, and turned a glass of water pink and then green, and he created a snail, which he miraculously annihilated, and got himself a miraculous new tooth-brush. Somewhen in the small hours he had reached the fact that his will-power must be of a particularly rare and pungent quality, a fact of which he had certainly had inklings before, but no certain assurance. The scare and perplexity of his first discovery was now qualified by pride in this evidence of singularity and by vague intimations of advantage. He became aware that the church clock was striking one, and as it did not occur to him that his daily duties at Gomshott's might be miraculously dispensed with, he resumed undressing, in order to get to bed without further delay. As he struggled to get his shirt over his head, he was struck with a brilliant idea. 'Let me be in bed,' he said, and found himself so. 'Undressed,' he stipulated; and, finding the sheets cold, added hastily, 'and in my nightshirt—no, in a nice soft woollen nightshirt. Ah!' he said with immense enjoyment. 'And now let me be comfortably asleep...'

He awoke at his usual hour and was pensive all through breakfast-time, wondering whether his overnight experience might not be a particularly vivid dream. At length his mind turned again to cautious experiments. For instance, he had three eggs for breakfast; two his landlady had supplied, good, but shoppy, and one was a delicious fresh goose-egg, laid, cooked, and served by his extraordinary will. He hurried off to Gomshott's in a state of profound but carefully concealed excitement, and only remembered the shell of the third egg when his landlady spoke of it that night. All day he could do no work because of this astonishingly new self-knowledge, but this caused him no inconvenience, because he made up for it miraculously in his last ten minutes.

As the day wore on his state of mind passed from wonder to elation, albeit the circumstances of his dismissal from the Long Dragon were still disagreeable to recall, and a garbled account of the matter that had reached his colleagues led to some badinage. It was evident he must be careful how he lifted frangible articles, but in other ways his gift promised more and more as he turned it over in his mind.

He intended among other things to increase his personal property by unostentatious acts of creation. He called into existence a pair of very splendid diamond studs, and hastily annihilated them again as young Gomshott came across the counting-house to his desk. He was afraid young Gomshott might wonder how he had come by them. He saw quite clearly the gift required caution and watchfulness in its exercise, but so far as he could judge the difficulties attending its mastery would be no greater than those he had already faced in the study of cycling. It was that analogy, perhaps, quite as much as the feeling that he would be unwelcome in the Long Dragon, that drove him out after supper into the lane beyond the gas-works, to rehearse a few miracles in private.

There was possibly a certain want of originality in his attempts, for apart from his will-power Mr. Fotheringay was not a very exceptional man. The miracle of Moses' rod came to his mind, but the night was dark and unfavourable to the proper control of large miraculous snakes. Then he recollected the story of 'Tannhauser' that he had read on the back of the Philharmonic programme. That seemed to him singularly attractive and harmless. He stuck his walking-stick—a very nice Poona-Penang lawyer—into the turf that edged the footpath, and commanded the dry wood to blossom. The air was immediately full of the scent of roses, and by means of a match he saw for himself that this beautiful miracle was indeed accomplished. His satisfaction was ended by advancing footsteps. Afraid of a premature discovery of his powers, he addressed the blossoming stick hastily: 'Go back.' What he meant was 'Change back;' but of course he was confused. The stick receded at a considerable velocity, and incontinently came a cry of anger and a bad word from the approaching person. 'Who are you throwing brambles at, you fool?' cried a voice. 'That got me on the shin.'

'I'm sorry, old chap,' said Mr. Fotheringay, and then realising the awkward nature of the explanation, caught nervously at his moustache. He saw Winch, one of the three Immering constables, advancing.

'What d'yer mean by it?' asked the constable. 'Hullo! it's you, is it? The gent that broke the lamp at the Long Dragon!'

'I don't mean anything by it,' said Mr. Fotheringay. 'Nothing at all.'

'What d'yer do it for then?'

'Oh, bother!' said Mr. Fotheringay.

'Bother indeed! D'yer know that stick hurt? What d'yer do it for, eh?'

For the moment Mr. Fotheringay could not think what he had done it for. His silence seemed to irritate Mr. Winch. 'You've been assaulting the police, young man, this time. That's what you done.'

'Look here, Mr. Winch,' said Mr. Fotheringay, annoyed and confused, 'I'm very sorry. The fact is—'

'Well?'

He could think of no way but the truth. 'I was working a miracle.' He tried to speak in an off-hand way, but try as he would he couldn't.

'Working a—! 'Ere, don't you talk rot. Working a miracle, indeed! Miracle! Well, that's downright funny! Why, you's the chap that don't believe in miracles... Fact is, this is another of your silly conjuring tricks—that's what this is. Now, I tell you—'

But Mr. Fotheringay never heard what Mr. Winch was going to tell him. He realised he had given himself away, flung his valuable secret to all the winds of heaven. A violent gust of irritation swept him to action. He turned on the constable swiftly and fiercely. 'Here,' he said, 'I've had enough of this, I have! I'll show you a silly conjuring trick, I will! Go to Hades! Go, now!'

He was alone!

Mr. Fotheringay performed no more miracles that night nor did he trouble to see what had become of his flowering stick. He returned to the town, scared and very quiet, and went to his bed-room. 'Lord!' he said, 'it's a powerful gift—an extremely powerful gift. I didn't hardly mean as much as that. Not really... I wonder what Hades is like!'

He sat on the bed taking off his boots. Struck by a happy thought he transferred the constable to San Francisco, and without any more interference with normal causation went soberly to bed. In the night he dreamt of the anger of Winch.

The next day Mr. Fotheringay heard two interesting items

of news. Someone had planted a most beautiful climbing rose against the elder Mr. Gomshott's private house in the Lullaborough Road, and the river as far as Rawling's Mill was to be dragged for Constable Winch.

Mr. Fotheringay was abstracted and thoughtful all that day, and performed no miracles except certain provisions for Winch, and the miracle of completing his day's work with punctual perfection in spite of all the bee-swarm of thoughts that hummed through his mind. And the extraordinary abstraction and meekness of his manner was remarked by several people, and made a matter for jesting. For the most part he was thinking of Winch.

On Sunday evening he went to chapel and oddly enough, Mr. Maydig, who took a certain interest in occult matters, preached about 'things that are not lawful.' Mr. Fotheringay was not a regular chapel goer, but the system of assertive scepticism, to which I have already alluded, was now very much shaken. The tenor of the sermon threw an entirely new light on these novel gifts, and he suddenly decided to consult Mr. Maydig immediately after the service. So soon as that was determined, he found himself wondering why he had not done so before.

Mr. Maydig, a lean, excitable man with quite remarkably long wrists and neck, was gratified at a request for a private conversation from a young man whose carelessness in religious matters was a subject for general remark in the town. After a few necessary delays, he conducted him to the study of the Manse, which was contiguous to the chapel, seated him comfortably, and, standing in front of a cheerful fire—his legs threw a Rhodian arch of shadow on the opposite wall—requested Mr. Fotheringay to state his business.

At first Mr. Fotheringay was a little abashed, and found some difficulty in opening the matter. 'You will scarcely believe me, Mr. Maydig, I am afraid'—and so forth for some time. He tried a question at last, and asked Mr. Maydig his opinion of miracles.

Mr. Maydig was still saying 'Well' in an extremely judicial tone, when Mr. Fotheringay interrupted again: 'You don't believe,

I suppose, that some common sort of person—like myself, for instance—as it might be sitting here now, might have some sort of twist inside him that made him able to do things by his will.'

'It's possible,' said Mr. Maydig. 'Something of the sort, perhaps, is possible.'

'If I might make free with something here, I think I might show you by a sort of experiment,' said Mr. Fotheringay. 'Now, take that tobacco-jar on the table, for instance. What I want to know is whether what I am going to do with it is a miracle or not. Just half a minute, Mr. Maydig, please.'

He knitted his brows, pointed to the tobacco-jar and said: 'Be a bowl of violets.'

The tobacco-jar did as it was ordered.

Mr. Maydig started violently at the change, and stood looking from the thaumaturgist to the bowl of flowers. He said nothing. Presently he ventured to lean over the table and smell the violets; they were fresh-picked and very fine ones. Then he stared at Mr. Fotheringay again.

'How did you do that?' he asked.

Mr. Fotheringay pulled his moustache. 'Just told it—and there you are. Is that a miracle, or is it black art, or what is it? And what do you think's the matter with me? That's what I want to ask.'

'It's a most extraordinary occurrence.'

'And this day last week I knew no more that I could do things like that than you did. It came quite sudden. It's something odd about my will, I suppose, and that's as far as I can see.'

'Is that—the only thing? Could you do other things besides that?'

'Lord, yes! said Mr. Fotheringay. 'Just anything.' He thought, and suddenly recalled a conjuring entertainment he had seen. 'Here!' He pointed. 'Change into a bowl of fish—no, not that—change into a glass bowl full of water with goldfish swimming in it. That's better! You see that, Mr. Maydig?'

'It's astonishing. It's incredible. You are either a most extraordinary...But no—'

'I could change it into anything,' said Mr. Fotheringay. 'Just anything. Here! be a pigeon, will you?'

In another moment a blue pigeon was fluttering round the room and making Mr. Maydig duck every time it came near him. 'Stop there, will you,' said Mr. Fotheringay; and the pigeon hung motionless in the air. 'I could change it back to a bowl of flowers,' he said, and after replacing the pigeon on the table worked that miracle. 'I expect you will want your pipe in a bit,' he said, and restored the tobacco-jar.

Mr. Maydig had followed all these later changes in a sort of ejaculatory silence. He stared at Mr. Fotheringay and, in a very gingerly manner, picked up the tobacco-jar, examined it, replaced it on the table. 'Well!' was the only expression of his feelings.

'Now, after that it's easier to explain what I came about,' said Mr. Fotheringay; and proceeded to a lengthy and involved narrative of his strange experiences, beginning with the affair of the lamp in the Long Dragon and complicated by persistent allusions to Winch. As he went on, the transient pride Mr. Maydig's consternation had caused passed away; he became the very ordinary Mr. Fotheringay of everyday intercourse again. Mr. Maydig listened intently, the tobacco-jar in his hand, and his bearing changed also with the course of the narrative. Presently, while Mr. Fotheringay was dealing with the miracle of the third egg, the minister interrupted with a fluttering extended hand—

'It is possible,' he said. 'It is credible. It is amazing, of course, but it reconciles a number of amazing difficulties. The power to work miracles is a gift—a peculiar quality like genius or second sight—hitherto it has come very rarely and to exceptional people. But in this case...I have always wondered at the miracles of Mahomet, and at Yogi's miracles, and the miracles of Madame Blavatsky. But, of course! Yes, it is simply a gift! It carries out so beautifully the arguments of that great thinker'—Mr. Maydig's voice sank—'his Grace the Duke of Argyll. Here we plumb some profounder law—deeper than the ordinary laws of nature. Yes—yes. Go on. Go on!'

Mr. Fotheringay proceeded to tell of his misadventure with Winch, and Mr. Maydig, no longer overawed or scared, began to jerk his limbs about and interject astonishment. 'It's this what troubled me most,' proceeded Mr. Fotheringay; 'it's this I'm most mijitly in want of advice for; of course he's at San Francisco—wherever San Francisco may be—but of course it's awkward for both of us, as you'll see, Mr. Maydig. I don't see how he can understand what has happened, and I daresay he's scared and exasperated something tremendous, and trying to get at me. I daresay he keeps on starting off to come here. I send him back, by a miracle, every few hours, when I think of it. And of course, that's a thing he won't be able to understand, and it's bound to annoy him; and, of course, if he takes a ticket every time it will cost him a lot of money. I done the best I could for him, but of course it's difficult for him to put himself in my place. I thought afterwards that his clothes might have got scorched, you know—if Hades is all it's supposed to be—before I shifted him. In that case I suppose they'd have locked him up in San Francisco. Of course I willed him a new suit of clothes on him directly I thought of it. But, you see, I'm already in a deuce of a tangle—'

Mr. Maydig looked serious. 'I see you are in a tangle. Yes, it's a difficult position. How you are to end it...' He became diffuse and inconclusive.

'However, we'll leave Winch for a little and discuss the larger question. I don't think this is a case of the black art or anything of the sort. I don't think there is any taint of criminality about it at all, Mr. Fotheringay—none whatever, unless you are suppressing material facts. No, it's miracles—pure miracles—miracles, if I may say so, of the very highest class.'

He began to pace the hearthrug and gesticulate, while Mr. Fotheringay sat with his arm on the table and his head on his arm, looking worried. 'I don't see how I'm to manage about Winch,' he said.

'A gift of working miracles—apparently a very powerful

gift,' said Mr. Maydig, 'will find a way about Winch—never fear. My dear Sir, you are a most important man—a man of the most astonishing possibilities. As evidence, for example! And—in other ways, the things you may do...'

'Yes, I've thought of a thing or two,' said Mr. Fotheringay. 'But—some of the things came a bit twisty. You saw that fish at first? Wrong sort of bowl and wrong sort of fish. And I thought I'd ask someone.'

'A proper course,' said Mr. Maydig, 'a very proper course—altogether the proper course.' He stopped and looked at Mr. Fotheringay. 'It's practically an unlimited gift. Let us test your powers, for instance. If they really are... If they really are all they seem to be.'

And so, incredible as it may seem, in the study of the little house behind the Congregational Chapel, on the evening of Sunday, Nov. 10, 1896, Mr. Fotheringay, egged on and inspired by Mr. Maydig, began to work miracles. The reader's attention is specially and definitely called to the date. He will object, probably has already objected, that certain points in this story are improbable, that if any things of the sort already described had indeed occurred, they would have been in all the papers a year ago. The details immediately following he will find particularly hard to accept, because among other things they involve the conclusion that he or she, the reader in question, must have been killed in a violent and unprecedented manner more than a year ago. Now a miracle is nothing if not improbable, and as a matter of fact the reader was killed in a violent and unprecedented manner a year ago. In the subsequent course of this story that will become perfectly clear and credible, as every right-minded and reasonable reader will admit. But this is not the place for the end of the story, being but little beyond the hither side of the middle. And at first the miracles worked by Mr. Fotheringay were timid little miracles—little things with the cups and parlour fitments—as feeble as the miracles of Theosophists, and, feeble as they were, they were received with awe by his collaborator. He would have preferred to settle the Winch business out of hand, but Mr. Maydig would not let him. But after they had worked a dozen of these domestic trivialities, their sense of power grew, their imagination began to show signs of stimulation, and their ambition enlarged. Their first larger enterprise was due to hunger and the negligence of Mrs. Minchin, Mr. Maydig's housekeeper. The meal to which the minister conducted Mr. Fotheringay was certainly ill-laid and uninviting as refreshment for two industrious miracle-workers; but they were seated, and Mr. Maydig was descanting in sorrow rather than in anger upon his housekeeper's shortcomings, before it occurred to Mr. Fotheringay that an opportunity lay before him. 'Don't you think, Mr. Maydig,' he said; 'if it isn't a liberty, I—'

'My dear Mr. Fotheringay! Of course! No—I didn't think.'

Mr. Fotheringay waved his hand. 'What shall we have?' he said, in a large, inclusive spirit, and, at Mr. Maydig's order, revised the supper very thoroughly. 'As for me,' he said, eyeing Mr. Maydig's selection, 'I am always particularly fond of a tankard of stout and a nice Welsh rarebit, and I'll order that. I ain't much given to Burgundy,' and forthwith stout and Welsh rarebit promptly appeared at his command. They sat long at their supper, talking like equals, as Mr. Fotheringay presently perceived, with a glow of surprise and gratification, of all the miracles they would presently do. 'And, by the bye, Mr. Maydig,' said Mr. Fotheringay, 'I might perhaps be able to help you—in a domestic way.'

'Don't quite follow,' said Mr. Maydig pouring out a glass of miraculous old Burgundy.

Mr. Fotheringay helped himself to a second Welsh rarebit out of vacancy, and took a mouthful. 'I was thinking,' he said, 'I might be able (chum, chum) to work (chum, chum) a miracle with Mrs. Minchin (chum, chum)—make her a better woman.'

Mr. Maydig put down the glass and looked doubtful. 'She's—She strongly objects to interference, you know, Mr. Fotheringay. And—as a matter of fact—it's well past eleven and she's probably in bed and asleep. Do you think, on the whole—'

Mr. Fotheringay considered these objections. 'I don't see that it shouldn't be done in her sleep.'

For a time Mr. Maydig opposed the idea, and then he yielded. Mr. Fotheringay issued his orders, and a little less at their ease, perhaps, the two gentlemen proceeded with their repast. Mr. Maydig was enlarging on the changes he might expect in his housekeeper next day, with an optimism that seemed even to Mr. Fotheringay's supper senses a little forced and hectic, when a series of confused noises from upstairs began. Their eyes exchanged interrogations, and Mr. Maydig left the room hastily. Mr. Fotheringay heard him calling up to his housekeeper and then his footsteps going softly up to her.

In a minute or so the minister returned, his step light, his face radiant. 'Wonderful!' he said, 'and touching! Most touching!'

He began pacing the hearthrug. 'A repentance—a most touching repentance—through the crack of the door. Poor woman! A most wonderful change! She had got up. She must have got up at once. She had got up out of her sleep to smash a private bottle of brandy in her box. And to confess it too!... But this gives us—it opens—a most amazing vista of possibilities. If we can work this miraculous change in her...'

'The thing's unlimited seemingly,' said Mr. Fotheringay. 'And about Mr. Winch—'

'Altogether unlimited.' And from the hearthrug Mr. Maydig, waving the Winch difficulty aside, unfolded a series of wonderful proposals—proposals he invented as he went along.

Now what those proposals were does not concern the essentials of this story. Suffice it that they were designed in a spirit of infinite benevolence, the sort of benevolence that used to be called post-prandial. Suffice it, too, that the problem of Winch remained unsolved. Nor is it necessary to describe how far that series got to its fulfilment. There were astonishing changes. The small hours found Mr. Maydig and Mr. Fotheringay careering across the chilly market-square under the still moon, in a sort of ecstasy of thaumaturgy, Mr. Maydig all flap and gesture, Mr. Fotheringay short and bristling, and no longer abashed at his greatness. They had reformed every drunkard in the Parliamentary division, changed all the beer and alcohol to water (Mr. Maydig had overruled Mr. Fotheringay on this point); they had, further, greatly improved the railway communication of the place, drained Flinder's swamp, improved the soil of One Tree Hill, and cured the Vicar's wart. And they were going to see what could be done with the injured pier at South Bridge. 'The place,' gasped Mr. Maydig, 'won't be the same place tomorrow. How surprised and thankful everyone will be!' And just at that moment the church clock struck three.

'I say,' said Mr. Fotheringay, 'that's three o'clock! I must be getting back. I've got to be at business by eight. And besides, Mrs. Wimms—'

'We're only beginning,' said Mr. Maydig, full of the sweetness of unlimited power. 'We're only beginning. Think of all the good we're doing. When people wake—'

'But—' said Mr. Fotheringay.

Mr. Maydig gripped his arm suddenly. His eyes were bright and wild. 'My dear chap,' he said, 'there's no hurry. 'Look'—he pointed to the moon at the zenith—'Joshua!'

'Joshua?' said Mr. Fotheringay.

'Joshua,' said Mr. Maydig. 'Why not? Stop it.'

Mr. Fotheringay looked at the moon.

'That's a bit tall,' he said after a pause.

'Why not?' said Mr. Maydig. 'Of course it doesn't stop. You stop the rotation of the earth, you know. Time stops. It isn't as if we were doing harm.'

'H'm!' said Mr. Fotheringay. 'Well.' He sighed. 'I'll try. Here—'

He buttoned up his jacket and addressed himself to the habitable globe, with as good an assumption of confidence as lay in his power. 'Jest stop rotating, will you,' said Mr. Fotheringay.

Incontinently he was flying head over heels through the air at the rate of dozens of miles a minute. In spite of the innumerable circles he was describing per second, he thought; for thought is wonderful—sometimes as sluggish as flowing pitch, sometimes as instantaneous as light. He thought in a second, and willed. 'Let me come down safe and sound. Whatever else happens, let me down safe and sound.'

He willed it only just in time, for his clothes, heated by his rapid flight through the air, were already beginning to singe. He came down with a forcible, but by no means injurious bump in what appeared to be a mound of fresh-turned earth. A large mass of metal and masonry, extraordinarily like the clock-tower in the middle of the market-square, hit the earth near him, ricochetted over him, and flew into stonework, bricks, and masonry, like a bursting bomb. A hurtling cow hit one of the larger blocks and smashed like an egg. There was a crash that made all the most violent crashes of his past life seem like the sound of falling dust, and this was followed by a descending series of lesser crashes. A vast wind roared throughout earth and heaven' so that he could scarcely lift his head to look. For a while he was too breathless and astonished even to see where he was or what had happened. And his first movement was to feel his head and reassure himself that his streaming hair was still his own.

'Lord!' gasped Mr. Fotheringay, scarce able to speak for the gale, 'I've had a squeak! What's gone wrong? Storms and thunder. And only a minute ago a fine night. It's Maydig set me on to this sort of thing. What a wind! If I go on fooling in this way I'm bound to have a thundering accident!...

'Where's Maydig?

'What a confounded mess everything's in!'

He looked about him so far as his flapping jacket would permit. The appearance of things was really extremely strange. 'The sky's all right anyhow,' said Mr. Fotheringay. 'And that's about all that is all right. And even there it looks like a terrific gale coming up. But there's the moon overhead just as it was just now. Bright as midday. But as for the rest—Where's the village? Where's—where's anything? And what on earth set this wind a-blowing? I didn't order no wind.'

Mr. Fotheringay struggled to get to his feet in vain, and after one failure, remained on all fours, holding on. He surveyed the moonlit world to leeward, with the tails of his jacket streaming over his head. 'There's something seriously wrong,' said Mr. Fotheringay. 'And what it is—goodness knows.'

Far and wide nothing was visible in the white glare through the haze of dust that drove before a screaming gale but tumbled masses of earth and heaps of inchoate ruins, no trees, no houses, no familiar shapes, only a wilderness of disorder vanishing at last into the darkness beneath the whirling columns and streamers, the lightnings and thunderings of a swiftly rising storm. Near him in the livid glare was something that might once have been an elm-tree, a smashed mass of splinters, shivered from boughs to base, and further a twisted mass of iron girders—only too evidently the viaduct—rose out of the piled confusion.

You see when Mr. Fotheringay had arrested the rotation of the solid globe, he had made no stipulation concerning the trifling movables upon its surface. And the earth spins so fast that the surface at its equator is travelling at rather more than a thousand miles an hour, and in these latitudes at more than half that pace. So that the village, and Mr. Maydig, and Mr. Fotheringay, and everybody and everything had been jerked violently forward at about nine miles per second—that is to say, much more violently than if they had been fired out of a cannon. And every human being, every living creature, every house, and every tree—all the world as we know it—had been so jerked and smashed and utterly destroyed. That was all.

These things Mr. Fotheringay did not, of course, fully appreciate. But he perceived that his miracle had miscarried, and with that a great disgust of miracles came upon him. He was in darkness now, for the clouds had swept together and blotted out his momentary glimpse of the moon, and the air was full of fitful struggling tortured wraiths of hail. A great roaring of wind and waters filled earth and sky, and, peering under his hand through the dust and sleet to windward, he saw by the play of the lightnings a vast wall of water pouring towards him.

'Maydig!' screamed Mr. Fotheringay's feeble voice amid the

elemental uproar. 'Here!—Maydig!'

'Stop!' cried Mr. Fotheringay to the advancing water. 'Oh, for goodness' sake, stop!'

'Just a moment,' said Mr. Fotheringay to the lightnings and thunder. 'Stop jest a moment while I collect my thoughts.... And now what shall I do?' he said. 'What shall I do? Lord! I wish Maydig was about.'

'I know,' said Mr. Fotheringay. 'And for goodness' sake let's have it right this time.'

He remained on all fours, leaning against the wind, very intent to have everything right.

'Ah!' he said. 'Let nothing what I'm going to order happen until I say "Off!"...Lord! I wish I'd thought of that before!'

He lifted his little voice against the whirlwind, shouting louder and louder in the vain desire to hear himself speak. 'Now then!—here goes! Mind about that what I said just now. In the first place, when all I've got to say is done, let me lose my miraculous power, let my will become just like anybody else's will, and all these dangerous miracles be stopped. I don't like them. I'd rather I didn't work 'em. Ever so much. That's the first thing. And the second is—let me be back just before the miracles begin; let everything be just as it was before that blessed lamp turned up. It's a big job, but it's the last. Have you got it? No more miracles, everything as it was—me back in the Long Dragon just before I drank my half-pint. That's it! Yes.'

He dug his fingers into the mould, closed his eyes, and said 'Off!'

Everything became perfectly still. He perceived that he was standing erect.

'So you say,' said a voice.

He opened his eyes. He was in the bar of the Long Dragon, arguing about miracles with Toddy Beamish. He had a vague sense of some great thing forgotten that instantaneously passed. You see, except for the loss of his miraculous powers, everything was back as it had been; his mind and memory therefore were now just as they had been at the time when this story began. So that he knew absolutely nothing of all that is told here, knows nothing of all that is told here to this day. And among other things, of course, he still did not believe in miracles.

'I tell you that miracles, properly speaking, can't possibly happen,' he said, 'whatever you like to hold. And I'm prepared to prove it up to the hilt.'

'That's what you think,' said Toddy Beamish, and 'Prove it if you can.'

'Looky here, Mr. Beamish,' said Mr. Fotheringay. 'Let us clearly understand what a miracle is. It's something contrariwise to the course of nature done by power of Will...'

43

A TERRIBLY STRANGE BED

Wilkie Collins

Shortly after my education at college was finished, I happened to be staying at Paris with an English friend. We were both young men then, and lived, I am afraid, rather a wild life, in the delightful city of our sojourn. One night we were idling about the neighbourhood of the Palais Royal, doubtful to what amusement we should next betake ourselves. My friend proposed a visit to Frascati's; but his suggestion was not to my taste. I knew Frascati's, as the French saying is, by heart; had lost and won plenty of five-franc pieces there, merely for amusement's sake, until it was amusement no longer, and was thoroughly tired, in fact, of all the ghastly respectabilities of such a social anomaly as a respectable gambling-house. 'For Heaven's sake,' said I to my friend, 'let us go somewhere where we can see a little genuine, blackguard, poverty-stricken gaming with no false gingerbread glitter thrown over it all. Let us get away from fashionable Frascati's, to a house where they don't mind letting in a man with a ragged coat, or a man with no coat, ragged or otherwise.' 'Very well,' said my friend, 'we needn't go out of the Palais Royal to find the sort of company you want. Here's the place just before us; as blackguard a place, by all report, as you could possibly wish to see.' In another minute we arrived at the door and entered the house.

When we got upstairs, and had left our hats and sticks with the doorkeeper, we were admitted into the chief gambling-room. We did not find many people assembled there. But, few as the men were who looked up at us on our entrance, they were all types—lamentably true types—of their respective classes.

We had come to see blackguards; but these men were

something worse. There is a comic side, more or less appreciable, in all blackguardism—here there was nothing but tragedy—mute, weird tragedy. The quiet in the room was horrible. The thin, haggard, long-haired young man, whose sunken eyes fiercely watched the turning up of the cards, never spoke; the flabby, fat-faced, pimply player, who pricked his piece of pasteboard perseveringly, to register how often black won, and how often red—never spoke; the dirty, wrinkled old man, with the vulture eyes and the darned great-coat, who had lost his last sou, and still looked on desperately, after he could play no longer—never spoke. Even the voice of the croupier sounded as if it were strangely dulled and thickened in the atmosphere of the room. I had entered the place to laugh, but the spectacle before me was something to weep over. I soon found it necessary to take refuge in excitement from the depression of spirits which was fast stealing on me. Unfortunately I sought the nearest excitement, by going to the table and beginning to play. Still more unfortunately, as the event will show, I won—won prodigiously; won incredibly; won at such a rate that the regular players at the table crowded round me; and staring at my stakes with hungry, superstitious eyes, whispered to one another that the English stranger was going to break the bank.

The game was Rouge et Noir. I had played at it in every city in Europe, without, however, the care or the wish to study the Theory of Chances—that philosopher's stone of all gamblers! And a gambler, in the strict sense of the word, I had never been. I was heart-whole from the corroding passion for play. My gaming was a mere idle amusement. I never resorted to it by necessity, because I never knew what it was to want money. I never practised it so incessantly as to lose more than I could afford, or to gain more than I could coolly pocket without being thrown off my balance by my good luck. In short, I had hitherto frequented gambling-tables—just as I frequented ball-rooms and opera-houses—because they amused me, and because I had nothing better to do with my leisure hours.

But on this occasion it was very different—now, for the first time in my life, I felt what the passion for play really was. My success first bewildered, and then, in the most literal meaning of the word, intoxicated me. Incredible as it may appear, it is nevertheless true, that I only lost when I attempted to estimate chances, and played according to previous calculation. If I left everything to luck, and staked without any care or consideration, I was sure to win—to win in the face of every recognized probability in favour of the bank. At first some of the men present ventured their money safely enough on my colour; but I speedily increased my stakes to sums which they dared not risk. One after another they left off playing, and breathlessly looked on at my game.

Still, time after time, I staked higher and higher, and still won. The excitement in the room rose to fever pitch. The silence was interrupted by a deep-muttered chorus of oaths and exclamations in different languages, every time the gold was shovelled across to my side of the table—even the imperturbable croupier dashed his rake on the floor in a (French) fury of astonishment at my success. But one man present preserved his self-possession, and that man was my friend. He came to my side, and whispering in English, begged me to leave the place, satisfied with what I had already gained. I must do him the justice to say that he repeated his warnings and entreaties several times, and only left me and went away after I had rejected his advice (I was to all intents and purposes gambling drunk) in terms which rendered it impossible for him to address me again that night.

Shortly after he had gone, a hoarse voice behind me cried: 'Permit me, my dear sir—permit me to restore to their proper place two napoleons which you have dropped. Wonderful luck, sir! I pledge you my word of honour, as an old soldier, in the course of my long experience in this sort of thing, I never saw such luck as yours—never! Go on, sir—Sacre mille bombes! Go on boldly, and break the bank!'

I turned round and saw, nodding and smiling at me with inveterate civility, a tall man, dressed in a frogged and braided surtout.

If I had been in my senses, I should have considered him, personally, as being rather a suspicious specimen of an old soldier. He had goggling bloodshot eyes, mangy moustaches, and a broken nose. His voice betrayed a barrack-room intonation of the worst order, and he had the dirtiest pair of hands I ever saw—even in France. These little personal peculiarities exercised, however, no repelling influence on me. In the mad excitement, the reckless triumph of that moment, I was ready to 'fraternize' with anybody who encouraged me in my game. I accepted the old soldier's offered pinch of snuff; clapped him on the back, and swore he was the honestest fellow in the world—the most glorious relic of the Grand Army that I had ever met with. 'Go on!' cried my military friend, snapping his fingers in ecstasy—'Go on, and win! Break the bank—Mille tonnerres! my gallant English comrade, break the bank!'

And I did go on—went on at such a rate, that in another quarter of an hour the croupier called out, 'Gentlemen, the bank has discontinued for to-night.' All the notes, and all the gold in that 'bank', now lay in a heap under my hands; the whole floating capital of the gambling-house was waiting to pour into my pockets!

'Tie up the money in your pocket-handkerchief, my worthy sir,' said the old soldier, as I wildly plunged my hands into my heap of gold. 'Tie it up, as we used to tie up a bit of dinner in the Grand Army; your winnings are too heavy for any breeches-pockets that ever were sewed. There! that's it—shovel them in, notes and all! Credie! what luck! Stop! another napoleon on the floor! Ah! sacre petit polisson de Napoleon! have I found thee at last? Now then, sir—two tight double knots each way with your honourable permission, and the money's safe. Feel it! feel it, fortunate sir! hard and round as a cannon-ball—Ah, bah! if they had only fired such cannon-balls at us at Austerlitz—nom d'une pipe! if they only had! And now, as an ancient grenadier, as an ex-brave of the French army, what remains for me to do? I ask what? Simply this: to entreat my valued English friend to drink a bottle of champagne with me, and toast the goddess Fortune in foaming goblets before we part!'

'Excellent ex-brave! Convivial ancient grenadier! Champagne by all means! An English cheer for an old soldier! Hurrah! hurrah! Another English cheer for the goddess Fortune! Hurrah! hurrah! hurrah!'

'Bravo! the Englishman; the amiable, gracious Englishman, in whose veins circulates the vivacious blood of France! Another glass? Ah, bah!—the bottle is empty! Never mind! Vive le vin! I, the old soldier, order another bottle, and half a pound of bonbons with it!'

'No, no, ex-brave; never—ancient grenadier! Your bottle last time; my bottle this. Behold it! Toast away! The French Army! the great Napoleon! the present company! the croupier! the honest croupier's wife and daughters—if he has any! the Ladies generally! everybody in the world!'

By the time the second bottle of champagne was emptied, I felt as if I had been drinking liquid fire—my brain seemed all aflame. No excess in wine had ever had this effect on me before in my life. Was it the result of a stimulant acting upon my system when I was in a highly excited state? Was my stomach in a particularly disordered condition? Or was the champagne amazingly strong?

'Ex-brave of the French Army!' cried I, in a mad state of exhilaration, 'I am on fire! how are you? You have set me on fire. Do you hear, my hero of Austerlitz? Let us have a third bottle of champagne to put the flame out!'

The old soldier wagged his head, rolled his goggle-eyes, until I expected to see them slip out of their sockets; placed his dirty forefinger by the side of his broken nose; solemnly ejaculated 'Coffee!' and immediately ran off into an inner room.

The word pronounced by the eccentric veteran seemed to have a magical effect on the rest of the company present. With one accord they all rose to depart. Probably they had expected to profit by my intoxication; but finding that my new friend was benevolently bent on preventing me from getting dead drunk, had now abandoned all hope of thriving pleasantly on my winnings. Whatever their motive might be, at any rate they went away in a body. When the old soldier returned, and sat down again opposite to me at the table, we had the room to ourselves. I could see the croupier, in a sort of vestibule which opened out of it, eating his supper in solitude. The silence was now deeper than ever.

A sudden change, too, had come over the 'ex-brave'. He assumed a portentously solemn look; and when he spoke to me again, his speech was ornamented by no oaths, enforced by no finger-snapping, enlivened by no apostrophes or exclamations.

'Listen, my dear sir,' said he, in mysteriously confidential tones—'listen to an old soldier's advice. I have been to the mistress of the house (a very charming woman, with a genius for cookery!) to impress on her the necessity of making us some particularly strong and good coffee. You must drink this coffee in order to get rid of your little amiable exaltation of spirits before you think of going home—you must, my good and gracious friend! With all that money to take home to-night, it is a sacred duty to yourself to have your wits about you. You are known to be a winner to an enormous extent by several gentlemen present to-night, who, in a certain point of view, are very worthy and excellent fellows; but they are mortal men, my dear sir, and they have their amiable weaknesses. Need I say more? Ah, no, no! you understand me! Now, this is what you must do—send for a cabriolet when you feel quite well again—draw up all the windows when you get into it—and tell the driver to take you home only through the large and well-lighted thoroughfares. Do this; and you and your money will be safe. Do this; and to-morrow you will thank an old soldier for giving you a word of honest advice.'

Just as the ex-brave ended his oration in very lachrymose tones, the coffee came in, ready poured out in two cups. My attentive friend handed me one of the cups with a bow. I was parched with thirst, and drank it off at a draught. Almost instantly afterwards, I was seized with a fit of giddiness, and felt more completely intoxicated than ever. The room whirled round and round furiously; the old soldier seemed to be regularly bobbing up and down before me like the piston of a steam-engine. I was half deafened by a violent singing in my ears; a feeling of utter bewilderment, helplessness, idiocy, overcame me. I rose from my chair, holding on by the table to keep my balance; and stammered out that I felt dreadfully unwell—so unwell that I did not know how I was to get home.

'My dear friend,' answered the old soldier—and even his voice seemed to be bobbing up and down as he spoke—'my dear friend, it would be madness to go home in your state; you would be sure to lose your money; you might be robbed and murdered with the greatest ease. I am going to sleep here; do you sleep here, too—they make up capital beds in this house—take one; sleep off the effects of the wine, and go home safely with your winnings to-morrow—to-morrow, in broad daylight.'

I had but two ideas left: one, that I must never let go hold of my handkerchief full of money; the other, that I must lie down somewhere immediately, and fall off into a comfortable sleep. So I agreed to the proposal about the bed, and took the offered arm of the old soldier, carrying my money with my disengaged hand. Preceded by the croupier, we passed along some passages and up a flight of stairs into the bedroom which I was to occupy. The ex-brave shook me warmly by the hand, proposed that we should breakfast together, and then, followed by the croupier, left me for the night.

I ran to the wash-hand stand; drank some of the water in my jug; poured the rest out, and plunged my face into it; then sat down in a chair and tried to compose myself. I soon felt better. The change for my lungs, from the fetid atmosphere of the gambling-room to the cool air of the apartment I now occupied, the almost equally refreshing change for my eyes, from the glaring gaslights of the 'salon' to the dim, quiet flicker of one bedroom-candle, aided wonderfully the restorative effects of cold water. The giddiness left me, and I began to feel a little like a reasonable being again. My first thought was of the risk of sleeping all night in a gambling-house; my second, of the still greater risk of trying to get out after the house was closed, and of going home alone at night through the streets of Paris with a large sum of money about me. I had slept in worse places than this on my travels; so I determined to lock, bolt, and barricade my door, and take my chance till the next morning.

Accordingly, I secured myself against all intrusion; looked under the bed, and into the cupboard; tried the fastening of the window; and then, satisfied that I had taken every proper precaution, pulled off my upper clothing, put my light, which was a dim one, on the hearth among a feathery litter of wood-ashes, and got into bed, with the handkerchief full of money under my pillow.

I soon felt not only that I could not go to sleep, but that I could not even close my eyes. I was wide awake, and in a high fever. Every nerve in my body trembled—every one of my senses seemed to be preternaturally sharpened. I tossed and rolled, and tried every kind of position, and perseveringly sought out the cold corners of the bed, and all to no purpose. Now I thrust my arms over the clothes; now I poked them under the clothes; now I violently shot my legs straight out down to the bottom of the bed; now I convulsively coiled them up as near my chin as they would go; now I shook out my crumpled pillow, changed it to the cool side, patted it flat, and lay down quietly on my back; now I fiercely doubled it in two, set it up on end, thrust it against the board of the bed, and tried a sitting posture. Every effort was in vain; I groaned with vexation as I felt that I was in for a sleepless night.

What could I do? I had no book to read. And yet, unless I found out some method of diverting my mind, I felt certain that I was in the condition to imagine all sorts of horrors; to rack my brain with forebodings of every possible and impossible danger; in short, to pass the night in suffering all conceivable varieties of nervous terror.

I raised myself on my elbow, and looked about the room—which was brightened by a lovely moonlight pouring straight through the window—to see if it contained any pictures or ornaments that I could at all clearly distinguish. While my eyes wandered from wall to wall, a remembrance of Le Maistre's delightful little book, Voyage autour de ma Chambre, occurred to me. I resolved to imitate the French author, and find occupation and amusement enough to relieve the tedium of my wakefulness, by making a mental inventory of every article of furniture I could see, and by following up to their sources the multitude of associations which even a chair, a table, or a wash-hand stand may be made to call forth.

In the nervous unsettled state of my mind at that moment, I found it much easier to make my inventory than to make my reflections, and thereupon soon gave up all hope of thinking in Le Maistre's fanciful track—or, indeed, of thinking at all. I looked about the room at the different articles of furniture, and did nothing more.

There was, first, the bed I was lying in; a four-post bed, of all things in the world to meet with in Paris—yes, a thorough clumsy British four-poster, with the regular top lined with chintz—the regular fringed valance all round—the regular stifling, unwholesome curtains, which I remembered having mechanically drawn back against the posts without particularly noticing the bed when I first got into the room. Then there was the marble-topped wash-hand stand, from which the water I had spilled, in my hurry to pour it out, was still dripping, slowly and more slowly, on to the brick floor. Then two small chairs, with my coat, waistcoat, and trousers flung on them. Then a large elbow-chair covered with dirty-white dimity, with my cravat and shirt collar thrown over the back. Then a chest of drawers with two of the brass handles off, and a tawdry, broken china inkstand placed on it by way of ornament for the top. Then the dressing-table, adorned by a very small looking-glass, and a very large pincushion. Then the window—an unusually large window. Then a dark old picture, which the feeble candle dimly showed me. It was a picture of a fellow in a high Spanish hat, crowned with a plume of towering feathers. A swarthy, sinister ruffian, looking upward, shading his eyes with his hand, and looking intently upward—it might be at some tall gallows at which he was going to be hanged. At any rate, he had the appearance of thoroughly deserving it.

This picture put a kind of constraint upon me to look upward too—at the top of the bed. It was a gloomy and not an interesting object, and I looked back at the picture. I counted the feathers in the man's hat—they stood out in relief—three white, two green. I observed the crown of his hat, which was of conical shape, according to the fashion supposed to have been favoured by Guido Fawkes. I wondered what he was looking up at. It couldn't be at the stars; such a desperado was neither astrologer nor astronomer. It must be at the high gallows, and he was going to be hanged presently. Would the executioner come into possession of his conical crowned hat and plume of feathers? I counted the feathers again—three white, two green.

While I still lingered over this very improving and intellectual employment, my thoughts insensibly began to wander. The moonlight shining into the room reminded me of a certain moonlight night in England—the night after a picnic party in a Welsh valley. Every incident of the drive homeward, through lovely scenery, which the moonlight made lovelier than ever, came back to my remembrance, though I had never given the picnic a thought for years; though, if I had tried to recollect it, I could certainly have recalled little or nothing of that scene long past. Of all the wonderful faculties that help to tell us we are immortal, which speaks the sublime truth more eloquently than memory? Here was I, in a strange house of the most suspicious character, in a situation of uncertainty, and even of peril, which might seem to make the cool exercise of my recollection almost out of the question; nevertheless, remembering, quite involuntarily, places, people, conversations, minute circumstances of every kind, which I had thought forgotten for ever; which I could not possibly have recalled at will, even under the most favourable auspices. And what cause had produced in a moment the whole of this strange, complicated, mysterious effect? Nothing but some rays of moonlight shining in at my bedroom window.

I was still thinking of the picnic—of our merriment on the drive home—of the sentimental young lady who would quote 'Childe Harold' because it was moonlight. I was absorbed by these past scenes and past amusements, when, in an instant, the thread on which my memories hung snapped asunder; my attention immediately came back to present things more vividly than ever, and I found myself, I neither knew why nor wherefore, looking hard at the picture again.

Looking for what?

Good God! the man had pulled his hat down on his brows! No! the hat itself was gone! Where was the conical crown? Where the feathers—three white, two green? Not there! In place of the hat and feathers, what dusky object was it that now hid his forehead, his eyes, his shading hand?

Was the bed moving?

I turned on my back and looked up. Was I mad? drunk? dreaming? giddy again? or was the top of the bed really moving down—sinking slowly, regularly, silently, horribly, right down throughout the whole of its length and breadth—right down upon me, as I lay underneath?

My blood seemed to stand still. A deadly paralysing coldness stole all over me as I turned my head round on the pillow and determined to test whether the bed-top was really moving or not, by keeping my eye on the man in the picture.

The next look in that direction was enough. The dull, black, frowzy outline of the valance above me was within an inch of being parallel with his waist. I still looked breathlessly. And steadily and slowly—very slowly—I saw the figure, and the line of frame below the figure, vanish, as the valance moved down before it.

I am, constitutionally, anything but timid. I have been on more than one occasion in peril of my life, and have not lost my self-possession for an instant; but when the conviction first settled on my mind that the bed-top was really moving, was steadily and continuously sinking down upon me, I looked up shuddering, helpless, panic-stricken, beneath the hideous machinery for murder, which was advancing closer and closer to suffocate me where I lay.

I looked up, motionless, speechless, breathless. The candle, fully spent, went out; but the moonlight still brightened the room. Down and down, without pausing and without sounding, came the bed-top, and still my panic-terror seemed to bind me faster and faster to the mattress on which I lay—down and down it sank, till the dusty odour from the lining of the canopy came stealing into my nostrils.

At that final moment the instinct of self-preservation startled me out of my trance, and I moved at last. There was just room for me to roll myself sidewise off the bed. As I dropped noiselessly to the floor, the edge of the murderous canopy touched me on the shoulder.

Without stopping to draw my breath, without wiping the cold sweat from my face, I rose instantly on my knees to watch the bed-top. I was literally spellbound by it. If I had heard footsteps behind me, I could not have turned round; if a means of escape had been miraculously provided for me, I could not have moved to take advantage of it. The whole life in me was, at that moment, concentrated in my eyes.

It descended—the whole canopy, with the fringe round it, came down—down—close down; so close that there was not room now to squeeze my finger between the bed-top and the bed. I felt at the sides, and discovered that what had appeared to me from beneath to be the ordinary light canopy of a four-post bed was in reality a thick, broad mattress, the substance of which was concealed by the valance and its fringe. I looked up and saw the four posts rising hideously bare. In the middle of the bed-top was a huge wooden screw that had evidently worked it down through a hole in the ceiling, just as ordinary presses are worked down on the substance selected for compression. The frightful apparatus moved without making the faintest noise. There had been no creaking as it came down; there was now not the faintest sound from the room above. Amid a dead and awful silence I beheld before me—in the nineteenth century, and in the civilized capital of France—such a machine for secret murder by suffocation as might have existed in the worst days of the Inquisition, in the lonely inns among the Hartz Mountains, in the mysterious tribunals of Westphalia! Still, as I looked on it, I could not move, I could hardly breathe, but I began to recover the power of thinking, and in a moment I discovered the murderous conspiracy framed against me in all its horror.

My cup of coffee had been drugged, and drugged too strongly. I had been saved from being smothered by having taken an overdose of some narcotic. How I had chafed and fretted at the fever-fit which had preserved my life by keeping me awake! How recklessly I had confided myself to the two wretches who had led me into this room, determined, for the sake of my winnings, to kill me in my sleep by the surest and most horrible contrivance for secretly accomplishing my destruction! How many men, winners like me, had slept, as I had proposed to sleep, in that bed, and had never been seen or heard of more! I shuddered at the bare idea of it.

But, ere long, all thought was again suspended by the sight of the murderous canopy moving once more. After it had remained on the bed—as nearly as I could guess—about ten minutes, it began to move up again. The villains who worked it from above evidently believed that their purpose was now accomplished. Slowly and silently, as it had descended, that horrible bed-top rose towards its former place. When it reached the upper extremities of the four posts, it reached the ceiling, too. Neither hole nor screw could be seen; the bed became in appearance an ordinary bed again—the canopy an ordinary canopy—even to the most suspicious eyes.

Now, for the first time, I was able to move—to rise from my knees—to dress myself in my upper clothing—and to consider of how I should escape. If I betrayed by the smallest noise that the attempt to suffocate me had failed, I was certain to be murdered. Had I made any noise already? I listened intently, looking towards the door.

No! no footsteps in the passage outside—no sound of a tread, light or heavy, in the room above—absolute silence everywhere. Besides locking and bolting my door, I had moved an old wooden chest against it, which I had found under the bed. To remove this chest (my blood ran cold as I thought of what its contents might be!) without making some disturbance was impossible; and, moreover, to think of escaping through the house, now barred up for the night, was sheer insanity. Only one chance was left me—the window. I stole to it on tiptoe.

My bedroom was on the first floor, above an entresol, and looked into a back street. I raised my hand to open the window, knowing that on that action hung, by the merest hair-breadth, my chance of safety. They keep vigilant watch in a House of Murder. If any part of the frame cracked, if the hinge creaked, I was a lost man! It must have occupied me at least five minutes, reckoning by time—five hours, reckoning by suspense—to open that window. I succeeded in doing it silently—in doing it with all the dexterity of a house-breaker—and then looked down into the street. To leap the distance beneath me would be almost certain destruction! Next, I looked round at the sides of the house. Down the left side ran a thick water-pipe—it passed close by the outer edge of the window. The moment I saw the pipe I knew I was saved. My breath came and went freely for the first time since I had seen the canopy of the bed moving down upon me!

To some men the means of escape which I had discovered might have seemed difficult and dangerous enough—to me the prospect of slipping down the pipe into the street did not suggest even a thought of peril. I had always been accustomed, by the practice of gymnastics, to keep up my schoolboy powers as a daring and expert climber; and knew that my head, hands, and feet would serve me faithfully in any hazards of ascent or descent. I had already got one leg over the window-sill, when I remembered the handkerchief filled with money under my pillow. I could well have afforded to leave it behind me, but I was revengefully determined that the miscreants of the gambling-house should miss their plunder as well as their victim. So I went back to the bed and tied the heavy handkerchief at my back by my cravat.

Just as I had made it tight and fixed it in a comfortable place, I thought I heard a sound of breathing outside the door. The chill feeling of horror ran through me again as I listened. No! dead silence still in the passage—I had only heard the night air blowing softly into the room. The next moment I was on the window-sill—and the next I had a firm grip on the water-pipe with my hands and knees.

I slid down into the street easily and quietly, as I thought I should, and immediately set off at the top of my speed to a branch 'Prefecture' of Police, which I knew was situated in the immediate neighbourhood. A 'Sub-prefect', and several picked men among his subordinates, happened to be up, maturing, I believe, some scheme for discovering the perpetrator of a mysterious murder which all Paris was talking of just then. When I began my story, in a breathless hurry and in very bad French, I could see that the Sub-prefect suspected me of being a drunken Englishman who had robbed somebody; but he soon altered his opinion as I went on, and before I had anything like concluded, he shoved all the papers before him into a drawer, put on his hat, supplied me with another (for I was bareheaded), ordered a file of soldiers, desired his expert followers to get ready all sorts of tools for breaking open doors and ripping up brick flooring, and took my arm, in the most friendly and familiar manner possible, to lead me with him out of the house. I will venture to say that when the Sub-prefect was a little boy, and was taken for the first time to the play, he was not half as much pleased as he was now at the job in prospect for him at the gambling-house!

Away we went through the streets, the Sub-prefect cross-examining and congratulating me in the same breath as we marched at the head of our formidable posse comitatus. Sentinels were placed at the back and front of the house the moment we got to it; a tremendous battery of knocks was directed against the door; a light appeared at a window; I was told to conceal myself behind the police—then came more knocks and a cry of 'Open in the name of the law!' At that terrible summons bolts and locks gave way before an invisible hand, and the moment after the Sub-prefect was in the passage, confronting a waiter half-dressed and ghastly pale. This was the short dialogue which immediately took place:

'We want to see the Englishman who is sleeping in this house?'

'He went away hours ago.'

'He did no such thing. His friend went away; he remained. Show us to his bedroom!'

'I swear to you, Monsieur le Sous-prefect, he is not here! he—'

'I swear to you, Monsieur le Garcon, he is. He slept here—he didn't find your bed comfortable he came to us to complain of it—here he is among my men—and here am I ready to look for a flea or two in his bedstead. Renaudin!' calling to one of the subordinates, and pointing to the waiter—'collar that man and tie his hands behind him. Now, then, gentlemen, let us walk upstairs!'

Every man and woman in the house was secured—the 'Old Soldier' the first. Then I identified the bed in which I had slept, and then we went into the room above.

No object that was at all extraordinary appeared in any part of it. The Sub-prefect looked round the place, commanded everybody to be silent, stamped twice on the floor, called for a candle, looked attentively at the spot he had stamped on, and ordered the flooring there to be carefully taken up. This was done in no time. Lights were produced, and we saw a deep raftered cavity between the floor of this room and the ceiling of the room beneath. Through this cavity there ran perpendicularly a sort of case of iron thickly greased; and inside the case appeared the screw, which communicated with the bed-top below. Extra lengths of screw, freshly oiled; levers covered with felt; all the complete upper works of a heavy press—constructed with infernal ingenuity so as to join the fixtures below, and when taken to pieces again, to go into the smallest possible compass—were next discovered and pulled out on the floor. After some little difficulty the Sub-prefect succeeded in putting the machinery together, and, leaving his men to work it, descended with me to the bedroom. The smothering canopy was then lowered, but not so noiselessly as I had seen it lowered. When I mentioned this to the Sub-prefect, his answer, simple as it was, had a terrible significance. 'My men,' said he, 'are working down the bed-top for the first time—the men whose money you won were in better practice.'

We left the house in the sole possession of two police agents—every one of the inmates being removed to prison on the spot. The Sub-prefect, after taking down my proces verbal in his office, returned with me to my hotel to get my passport. 'Do you think,' I asked, as I gave it to him, 'that any men have really been smothered in that bed, as they tried to smother me?'

'I have seen dozens of drowned men laid out at the Morgue,' answered the Sub-prefect, 'in whose pocketbooks were found letters stating that they had committed suicide in the Seine, because they had lost everything at the gaming table. Do I know how many of those men entered the same gambling-house that you entered? won as you won? took that bed as you took it? slept in it? were smothered in it? and were privately thrown into the river, with a letter of explanation written by the murderers and placed in their pocket-books? No man can say how many or how few have suffered the fate from which you have escaped. The people of the gambling-house kept their bedstead machinery a secret from us—even from the police! The dead kept the rest of the secret for them. Good night, or rather good morning, Monsieur Faulkner! Be at my office again at nine o'clock—in the meantime, au revoir!'

The rest of my story is soon told. I was examined and re-examined; the gambling-house was strictly searched all through from top to bottom; the prisoners were separately interrogated;

and two of the less guilty among them made a confession. I discovered that the Old Soldier was the master of the gambling-house—justice discovered that he had been drummed out of the army as a vagabond years ago; that he had been guilty of all sorts of villainies since; that he was in possession of stolen property, which the owners identified; and that he, the croupier, another accomplice, and the woman who had made my cup of coffee, were all in the secret of the bedstead. There appeared some reason to doubt whether the inferior persons attached to the house knew anything of the suffocating machinery; and they received the benefit of that doubt, by being treated simply as thieves and vagabonds. As for the Old Soldier and his two head myrmidons, they went to the galleys; the woman who had drugged my coffee was imprisoned for I forget how many years; the regular attendants at the gambling-house were considered 'suspicious' and placed under 'surveillance'; and I became, for one whole week (which is a long time) the head 'lion' in Parisian society. My adventure was dramatized by three illustrious playmakers, but never saw theatrical daylight; for the censorship forbade the introduction on the stage of a correct copy of the gambling-house bedstead.

One good result was produced by my adventure, which any censorship must have approved: it cured me of ever again trying Rouge et Noir as an amusement. The sight of a green cloth, with packs of cards and heaps of money on it, will henceforth be for ever associated in my mind with the sight of a bed canopy descending to suffocate me in the silence and darkness of the night.

44

A SCHOOL STORY

M.R. James

TWO men in a smoking-room were talking of their private-school days. 'At *our* school,' said A., 'we had a ghost's footmark on the staircase. What was it like? Oh, very unconvincing. Just the shape of a shoe, with a square toe, if I remember right. The staircase was a stone one. I never heard any story about the thing. That seems odd, when you come to think of it. Why didn't somebody invent one, I wonder?'

'You never can tell with little boys. They have a mythology of their own. There's a subject for you, by the way—"The Folklore of Private Schools."'

'Yes; the crop is rather scanty, though. I imagine, if you were to investigate the cycle of ghost stories, for instance, which the boys at private schools tell each other, they would all turn out to be highly-compressed versions of stories out of books.'

'Nowadays the *Strand* and *Pearson's*, and so on, would be extensively drawn upon.'

'No doubt: they weren't born or thought of in *my* time. Let's see. I wonder if I can remember the staple ones that I was told. First, there was the house with a room in which a series of people insisted on passing a night; and each of them in the morning was found kneeling in a corner, and had just time to say, "I've seen it," and died.'

'Wasn't that the house in Berkeley Square?'

'I dare say it was. Then there was the man who heard a noise in the passage at night, opened his door, and saw someone crawling towards him on all fours with his eye hanging out on his cheek. There was besides, let me think—Yes! the room where a man was found dead in bed with a horseshoe mark on his forehead, and the floor under the bed was covered with marks of horseshoes also; I don't know why. Also there was the lady who, on locking her bedroom door in a strange house, heard a thin voice among the bed-curtains say, "Now we're shut in for the night." None of those had any explanation or sequel. I wonder if they go on still, those stories.'

'Oh, likely enough—with additions from the magazines, as I said. You never heard, did you, of a real ghost at a private school? I thought not, nobody has that ever I came across.'

'From the way in which you said that, I gather that *you* have.'

'I really don't know, but this is what was in my mind. It happened at my private school thirty odd years ago, and I haven't any explanation of it.

'The school I mean was near London. It was established in a large and fairly old house—a great white building with very fine grounds about it; there were large cedars in the garden, as there are in so many of the older gardens in the Thames valley, and ancient elms in the three or four fields which we used for our games. I think probably it was quite an attractive place, but boys seldom allow that their schools possess any tolerable features.

'I came to the school in a September, soon after the year 1870; and among the boys who arrived on the same day was one whom I took to: a Highland boy, whom I will call McLeod. I needn't spend time in describing him: the main thing is that I got to know him very well. He was not an exceptional boy in any way—not particularly good at books or games—but he suited me.

'The school was a large one: there must have been from 120 to 130 boys there as a rule, and so a considerable staff of masters was required, and there were rather frequent changes among them.

'One term—perhaps it was my third or fourth—a new master made his appearance. His name was Sampson. He was a tallish, stoutish, pale, black-bearded man. I think we liked him: he had travelled a good deal, and had stories which amused us on our school walks, so that there was some competition among us to get within earshot of him. I remember too—dear me, I have hardly thought of it since then—that he had a charm on his watch-chain that attracted my attention one day, and he let me examine it. It was, I now suppose, a gold Byzantine coin; there was an effigy of some absurd emperor on one side; the other side had been worn practically smooth, and he had had cut on it—rather barbarously—his own initials, G.W.S., and a date, 24 July, 1865. Yes, I can see it now: he told me he had picked it up in Constantinople: it was about the size of a florin, perhaps rather smaller.

'Well, the first odd thing that happened was this. Sampson was doing Latin grammar with us. One of his favourite methods—perhaps it is rather a good one—was to make us construct sentences out of our own heads to illustrate the rules he was trying to make us learn. Of course that is a thing which gives a silly boy a chance of being impertinent: there are lots of school stories in which that happens—or any-how there might be. But Sampson was too good a disciplinarian for us to think of trying that on with him. Now, on this occasion he was telling us how to express *remembering* in Latin: and he ordered us each to make a sentence bringing in the verb *memini*, "I remember." Well, most of us made up some ordinary sentence such as "I remember my father," or "He remembers his book," or something equally uninteresting: and I dare say a good many put down *memino librum meum*, and so forth: but the boy I mentioned—McLeod—was evidently thinking of something more elaborate than that. The rest of us wanted to have our sentences passed, and get on to something else, so some kicked him under the desk, and I, who was next to him, poked him and whispered to him to look sharp. But he didn't seem to attend. I looked at his paper and saw he had put down nothing at all. So I jogged him again harder than before and upbraided him sharply for keeping us all waiting. That did have some effect. He started and seemed to wake up, and then very quickly he scribbled about a couple of lines on his paper, and showed it up with the rest. As it was the last, or nearly the last, to come in, and as Sampson had a good deal to say to the boys who had written *meminiscimus patri meo* and the rest of it, it turned out that the clock struck twelve before he had got to McLeod, and McLeod had to wait afterwards to have his sentence corrected. There was nothing much going on outside when I got out, so I waited for him to come. He came very slowly when he did arrive, and I guessed there had been some sort of trouble. "Well," I said, "what did you get?" "Oh, I don't know," said McLeod, "nothing much: but I think Sampson's rather sick with me." "Why, did you show him up some rot?" "No fear," he said. "It was all right as far as I could see: it was like this: *Memento*—that's right enough for remember, and it takes a genitive,—*memento putei inter quatuor taxos*." "What silly rot!" I said. "What made you shove that down? What does it mean?" "That's the funny part," said McLeod. "I'm not quite sure what it does mean. All I know is, it just came into my head and I corked it down. I know what I *think* it means, because just before I wrote it down I had a sort of picture of it in my head: I believe it means 'Remember the well among the four'—what are those dark sort of trees that have red berries on them?" "Mountain ashes, I s'pose you mean." "I never heard of them," said McLeod; "no, *I'll* tell you—yews." "Well, and what did Sampson say?" "Why, he was jolly odd about it. When he read it he got up and went to the mantel-piece and stopped quite a long time without saying anything, with his back to me. And then he said, without turning round, and rather quiet, 'What do you suppose that means?' I told him what I thought; only I couldn't remember the name of the silly tree: and then he wanted to know why I put it down, and I had to say something or other. And after that he left off talking about it, and asked me how long I'd been here, and where my people lived, and things like that: and then I came away: but he wasn't looking a bit well."

'I don't remember any more that was said by either of us about this. Next day McLeod took to his bed with a chill or something of the kind, and it was a week or more before he was in school again. And as much as a month went by without anything happening that was noticeable. Whether or not Mr. Sampson was really startled, as McLeod had thought, he didn't show it. I am pretty sure, of course, now, that there was something very curious in his past history, but I'm not going to pretend that we boys were sharp enough to guess any such thing.

'There was one other incident of the same kind as the last which I told you. Several times since that day we had had to make up examples in school to illustrate different rules, but there had never been any row except when we did them wrong. At last there came a day when we were going through those dismal things which people call Conditional Sentences, and we were told to make a conditional sentence, expressing a future consequence. We did it, right or wrong, and showed up our bits of paper, and Sampson began looking through them. All at once he got up, made some odd sort of noise in his throat, and rushed out by a door that was just by his desk. We sat there for a minute or two, and then—I suppose it was incorrect—but we went up, I and one or two others, to look at the papers on his desk. Of course I thought someone must have put down some nonsense or other, and Sampson had gone off to report him. All the same, I noticed that he hadn't taken any of the papers with him when he ran out. Well, the top paper on the desk was written in red ink—which no one used—and it wasn't in anyone's hand who was in the class. They all looked at it—McLeod and all—and took their dying oaths that it wasn't theirs. Then I thought of counting the bits of paper. And of this I made quite certain: that there were seventeen bits of paper on the desk, and sixteen boys in the form. Well, I bagged the extra paper, and kept it, and I believe I have it now. And now you will want to know what was written on it. It was simple enough, and harmless enough, I should have said.

'"*Si tu non veneris ad me, ego veniam ad te*," which means, I suppose, "If you don't come to me, I'll come to you."'

'Could you show me the paper?' interrupted the listener.

'Yes, I could: but there's another odd thing about it. That same afternoon I took it out of my locker—I know for certain it was the same bit, for I made a finger-mark on it and no single trace of writing of any kind was there on it. I kept it, as I said, and since that time I have tried various experiments to see whether sympathetic ink had been used, but absolutely without result.

'So much for that. After about half an hour Sampson looked in again: said he had felt very unwell, and told us we might go. He came rather gingerly to his desk, and gave just one look at the uppermost paper: and I suppose he thought he must have been dreaming: anyhow, he asked no questions.

'That day was a half-holiday, and next day Sampson was in school again, much as usual. That night the third and last incident in my story happened.

'We—McLeod and I—slept in a dormitory at right angles to the main building. Sampson slept in the main building on the first floor. There was a very bright full moon. At an hour which I can't tell exactly, but some time between one and two, I was woken up by somebody shaking me. It was McLeod, and a nice state of mind he seemed to be in. "Come," he said,—"come there's a burglar getting in through Sampson's window." As soon as I could speak, I said, "Well, why not call out and wake everybody up?" "No, no," he said, "I'm not sure who it is: don't make a row: come and look." Naturally I came and looked, and naturally there was no one there. I was cross enough, and should have called McLeod plenty of names: only—I couldn't tell why—it seemed to me that there *was* something wrong—something that made me very glad I wasn't alone to face it. We were still at the window looking out, and as soon as I could, I asked him what he had heard or seen. "I didn't *hear* anything at all," he said, "but about five minutes before I woke you, I found myself looking out of this window here, and there was a man sitting or kneeling on Sampson's window-sill, and looking in, and I thought he was beckoning." "What sort of man?" McLeod wriggled. "I don't know," he said, "but I can tell you one thing—he was beastly thin: and he looked as if he was wet all over: and," he said, looking round and whispering as if he hardly liked to hear himself, "I'm not at all sure that he was alive."

'We went on talking in whispers some time longer, and eventually crept back to bed. No one else in the room woke or stirred the whole time. I believe we did sleep a bit afterwards, but we were very cheap next day.

'And next day Mr. Sampson was gone: not to be found: and I believe no trace of him has ever come to light since. In thinking it over, one of the oddest things about it all has seemed to me to be the fact that neither McLeod nor I ever mentioned what we had seen to any third person whatever. Of course no questions were asked on the subject, and if they had been, I am inclined to believe that we could not have made any answer: we seemed unable to speak about it.

'That is my story,' said the narrator. 'The only approach to a ghost story connected with a school that I know, but still, I think, an approach to such a thing.'

◆

The sequel to this may perhaps be reckoned highly conventional; but a sequel there is, and so it must be produced. There had been more than one listener to the story, and, in the latter part of that same year, or of the next, one such listener was staying at a country house in Ireland.

One evening his host was turning over a drawer full of odds and ends in the smoking-room. Suddenly he put his hand upon a little box. 'Now,' he said, 'you know about old things; tell me what that is.' My friend opened the little box, and found in it a thin gold chain with an object attached to it. He glanced at the object and then took off his spectacles to examine it more narrowly. 'What's the history of this?' he asked. 'Odd enough,' was the answer. 'You know the yew thicket in the shrubbery: well, a year or two back we were cleaning out the old well that used to be in the clearing here, and what do you suppose we found?'

'Is it possible that you found a body?' said the visitor, with an odd feeling of nervousness.

'We did that: but what's more, in every sense of the word, we found two.'

'Good Heavens! Two? Was there anything to show how they got there? Was this thing found with them?'

'It was. Amongst the rags of the clothes that were on one of the bodies. A bad business, whatever the story of it may have been. One body had the arms tight round the other. They must have been there thirty years or more—long enough before we came to this place. You may judge we filled the well up fast enough. Do you make anything of what's cut on that gold coin you have there?'

'I think I can,' said my friend, holding it to the light (but he read it without much difficulty); 'it seems to be G.W.S., 24 July, 1865.'

45

THE DANCING PARTNER

Jerome K. Jerome

'This story,' commenced MacShaugnassy, 'comes from Furtwangen, a small town in the Black Forest. There lived there a very wonderful old fellow named Nicholaus Geibel. His business was the making of mechanical toys, at which work he had acquired an almost European reputation. He made rabbits that would emerge from the heart of a cabbage, flop their ears, smooth their whiskers, and disappear again; cats that would wash their faces, and mew so naturally that dogs would mistake them for real cats and fly at them; dolls with phonographs concealed within them, that would raise their hats and say, "Good morning; how do you do?" and some that would even sing a song.

'But, he was something more than a mere mechanic; he was an artist. His work was with him a hobby, almost a passion. His shop was filled with all manner of strange things that never would, or could, be sold—things he had made for the pure love of making them. He had contrived a mechanical donkey that would trot for two hours by means of stored electricity, and trot, too, much faster than the live article, and with less need for exertion on the part of the driver, a bird that would shoot up into the air, fly round and round in a circle, and drop to earth at the exact spot from where it started; a skeleton that, supported by an upright iron bar, would dance a hornpipe, a life-size lady doll that could play the fiddle, and a gentleman with a hollow inside who could smoke a pipe and drink more lager beer than any three average German students put together, which is saying much.

'Indeed, it was the belief of the town that old Geibel could make a man capable of doing everything that a respectable man need want to do. One day he made a man who did too much, and it came about in this way:

'Young Doctor Follen had a baby, and the baby had a birthday. Its first birthday put Doctor Follen's household into somewhat of a flurry, but on the occasion of its second birthday, Mrs. Doctor Follen gave a ball in honour of the event. Old Geibel and his daughter Olga were among the guests.

'During the afternoon of the next day some three or four of Olga's bosom friends, who had also been present at the ball, dropped in to have a chat about it. They naturally fell to discussing the men, and to criticizing their dancing. Old Geibel was in the room, but he appeared to be absorbed in his newspaper, and the girls took no notice of him.

'"There seem to be fewer men who can dance at every ball you go to," said one of the girls.

'"Yes, and don't the ones who can give themselves airs," said another; "they make quite a favor of asking you."'

'"And how stupidly they talk," added a third. "They always say exactly the same things: 'How charming you are looking tonight.' 'Do you often go to Vienna? Oh, you should, it's delightful.' 'What a charming dress you have on.' 'What a warm day it has been.' 'Do you like Wagner?' I do wish they'd think of something new."

'"Oh, I never mind how they talk," said a fourth. "If a man dances well he may be a fool for all I care."

'"He generally is," slipped in a thin girl, rather spitefully.

'"I go to a ball to dance," continued the previous speaker, not noticing the interruption. "All I ask is that he shall hold me firmly, take me round steadily, and not get tired before I do."

'"A clockwork figure would be the thing for you," said the girl who had interrupted.

'"Bravo!" cried one of the others, clapping her hands, "what a capital idea!"

'"What's a capital idea?" they asked.

'"Why, a clockwork dancer, or, better still, one that would

go by electricity and never run down."

'The girls took up the idea with enthusiasm.

'"Oh, what a lovely partner he would make," said one; "he would never kick you, or tread on your toes."

'"Or tear your dress," said another.

'"Or get out of step."

'"Or get giddy and lean on you."

'"And he would never want to mop his face with his handkerchief. I do hate to see a man do that after every dance."

'"And wouldn't want to spend the whole evening in the supper-room."

'"Why, with a phonograph inside him to grind out all the stock remarks, you would not be able to tell him from a real man," said the girl who had first suggested the idea.

'"Oh yes, you would," said the thin girl, "he would be so much nicer."

'Old Geibel had laid down his paper, and was listening with both his ears. On one of the girls glancing in his direction, however, he hurriedly hid himself again behind it.

'After the girls were gone, he went into his workshop, where Olga heard him walking up and down, and every now and then chuckling to himself; and that night he talked to her a good deal about dancing and dancing men—asked what dances were most popular—what steps were gone through, with many other questions bearing on the subject.

'Then for a couple of weeks he kept much to his factory, and was very thoughtful and busy, though prone at unexpected moments to break into a quiet low laugh, as if enjoying a joke that nobody else knew of.

'A month later another ball took place in Furtwangen. On this occasion it was given by old Wenzel, the wealthy timber merchant, to celebrate his niece's betrothal, and Geibel and his daughter were again among the invited.

'When the hour arrived to set out, Olga sought her father. Not finding him in the house, she tapped at the door of his workshop. He appeared in his shirt-sleeves, looking hot but radiant.

'"Don't wait for me," he said, "you go on, I'll follow you. I've got something to finish."

'As she turned to obey he called after her, "Tell them I'm going to bring a young man with me—such a nice young man, and an excellent dancer. All the girls will like him." Then he laughed and closed the door.

'Her father generally kept his doings secret from everybody, but she had a pretty shrewd suspicion of what he had been planning, and so, to a certain extent, was able to prepare the guests for what was coming. Anticipation ran high, and the arrival of the famous mechanist was eagerly awaited.

'At length the sound of wheels was heard outside, followed by a great commotion in the passage, and old Wenzel himself, his jolly face red with excitement and suppressed laughter, burst into the room and announced in stentorian tones:

'"Herr Geibel—and a friend."

'Herr Geibel and his "friend" entered, greeted with shouts of laughter and applause, and advanced to the centre of the room.

'"Allow me, ladies and gentlemen," said Herr Geibel, "to introduce you to my friend, Lieutenant Fritz. Fritz, my dear fellow, bow to the ladies and gentlemen."

'Geibel placed his hand encouragingly on Fritz's shoulder, and the Lieutenant bowed low, accompanying the action with a harsh clicking noise in his throat, unpleasantly suggestive of a death-rattle. But that was only a detail.

'"He walks a little stiffly" (old Geibel took his arm and walked him forward a few steps. He certainly did walk stiffly), "but then, walking is not his forte. He is essentially a dancing man. I have only been able to teach him the waltz as yet, but at that he is faultless. Come, which of you ladies may I introduce him to as a partner? He keeps perfect time; he never gets tired; he won't kick you or tread on your dress; he will hold you as firmly as you like, and go as quickly or a slowly as you please; he never gets giddy; and he is full of conversation. Come, speak up for yourself, my boy."

'The old gentleman twisted one of the buttons at the back of his coat, and immediately Fritz opened his mouth, and in thin tones that appeared to proceed from the back of his head, remarked suddenly, "May I have the pleasure?" and then shut his mouth again with a snap.

'That Lieutenant Fritz had made a strong impression on the company was undoubted, yet none of the girls seemed inclined to dance with him. They looked askance at his waxen face, with its staring eyes and fixed smile, and shuddered. At last old Geibel came to the girl who had conceived the idea.

'"It is your own suggestion, carried out to the letter," said Geibel, "an electric dancer. You owe it to the gentleman to give him a trial."

'She was a bright, saucy little girl, fond of a frolic. Her host added his entreaties, and she consented.

'Herr Geibel fixed the figure to her. Its right arm was screwed round her waist, and held her firmly; its delicately jointed left hand was made to fasten upon her right. The old toymaker showed her how to regulate its speed, and how to stop it, and release herself.

'"It will take you round in a complete circle," he explained; "be careful that no one knocks against you, and alters its course."

'The music struck up. Old Geibel put the current in motion, and Annette and her strange partner began to dance.

'For a while everyone stood watching them. The figure performed its purpose admirably. Keeping perfect time and step, and holding its little partner tight clasped in an unyielding embrace, it revolved steadily, pouring forth at the same time a constant flow of squeaky conversation, broken by brief intervals of grinding silence. '"How charming you are looking tonight," it remarked in its thin, far-away voice. "What a lovely day it has been. Do you like dancing? How well our steps agree. You will give me another, won't you? Oh, don't be so cruel. What a charming gown you have on. Isn't waltzing delightful? I could go on dancing for ever—with you. Have you had supper?"

'As she grew more familiar with the uncanny creature, the girl's nervousness wore off, and she entered into the fun of the thing.

'"Oh, he's just lovely," she cried, laughing; "I could go on dancing with him all my life."

'Couple after couple now joined them, and soon all the dancers in the room were whirling round behind them. Nicholaus Geibel stood looking on, beaming with childish delight at his success.

'Old Wenzel approached him, and whispered something in his ear. Geibel laughed and nodded, and the two worked their way quietly towards the door.

'"This is the young people's house to-night," said Wenzel, as soon as they were outside; "you and I will have a quiet pipe and glass of hock, over in the counting-house."

'Meanwhile the dancing grew more fast and furious. Little Annette loosened the screw regulating her partner's rate of progress, and the figure flew round with her swifter and swifter. Couple after couple dropped out exhausted, but they only went the faster, till at length they remained dancing alone.

'Madder and madder became the waltz. The music lagged behind: the musicians, unable to keep pace, ceased, and sat staring. The younger guests applauded, but the older faces began to grow anxious.

'"Hadn't you better stop, dear," said one of the women, "you'll make yourself so tired."

'But Annette did not answer.

'"I believe she's fainted," cried out a girl who had caught sight of her face as it was swept by.

'One of the men sprang forward and clutched at the figure, but its impetus threw him down on to the floor, where its steel-cased feet laid bare his cheek. The thing evidently did not intend to part with its prize so easily.

'Had any one retained a cool head, the figure, one cannot help thinking, might easily have been stopped. Two or three men acting in concert might have lifted it bodily off the floor, or have jammed it into a corner. But few human heads are capable of remaining cool under excitement. Those who are not present think how stupid must have been those who were; those who are reflect afterwards how simple it would have been to do this, that, or the other, if only they had thought of it at the time.

'The women grew hysterical. The men shouted contradictory directions to one another. Two of them made a bungling rush at the figure, which had the end result of forcing it out of its orbit at the centre of the room, and sending it crashing against the walls and furniture. A stream of blood showed itself down the girl's white frock, and followed her along the floor. The affair was becoming horrible. The women rushed screaming from the room. The men followed them.

'One sensible suggestion was made: "Find Geibel—fetch Geibel."

'No one had noticed him leave the room, no one knew where he was. A party went in search of him. The others, too unnerved to go back into the ballroom, crowded outside the door and listened. They could hear the steady whir of the wheels upon the polished floor as the thing spun round and round; the dull thud as every now and again it dashed itself and its burden against some opposing object and ricocheted off in a new direction.

'And everlastingly it talked in that thin ghostly voice, repeating over and over the same formula: "How charming you look to-night. What a lovely day it has been. Oh, don't be so cruel. I could go on dancing for ever—with you. Have you had supper?"

'Of course they sought Geibel everywhere but where he was. They looked in every room in the house, then they rushed off in a body to his own place, and spent precious minutes waking up his deaf old housekeeper. At last it occurred to one of the party that Wenzel was missing also, and then the idea of the counting-house across the yard presented itself to them, and there they found him.

'He rose up, very pale, and followed them; and he and old Wenzel forced their way through the crowd of guests gathered outside, and entered the room, and locked the door behind them.

'From within there came the muffled sound of low voices and quick steps, followed by a confused scuffling noise, then silence, then the low voices again.

'After a time the door opened, and those near it pressed forward to enter, but old Wenzel's broad head and shoulders barred the way.

"I want you—and you, Bekler," he said, addressing a couple of the elder men. His voice was calm, but his face was deadly white. "The rest of you, please go—get the women away as quickly as you can."

'From that day old Nicholaus Geibel confined himself to the making of mechanical rabbits, and cats that mewed and washed their faces.'

46

RAIN

W. Somerset Maugham

It was nearly bed-time and when they awoke next morning land would be in sight. Dr. Macphail lit his pipe and, leaning over the rail, searched the heavens for the Southern Cross. After two years at the front and a wound that had taken longer to heal than it should, he was glad to settle down quietly at Apia for twelve months at least, and he felt already better for the journey. Since some of the passengers were leaving the ship next day at Pago-Pago they had had a little dance that evening and in his ears hammered still the harsh notes of the mechanical piano. But the deck was quiet at last. A little way off he saw his wife in a long chair talking with the Davidsons, and he strolled over to her. When he sat down under the light and took off his hat you saw that he had very red hair, with a bald patch on the crown, and the red, freckled skin which accompanies red hair; he was a man of forty, thin, with a pinched face, precise and rather pedantic; and he spoke with a Scots accent in a very low, quiet voice.

Between the Macphails and the Davidsons, who were missionaries, there had arisen the intimacy of shipboard, which is due to propinquity rather than to any community of taste. Their chief tie was the disapproval they shared of the men who spent their days and nights in the smoking-room playing poker or bridge and drinking. Mrs. Macphail was not a little flattered to think that she and her husband were the only people on board with whom the Davidsons were willing to associate, and even the doctor, shy but no fool, half unconsciously acknowledged the compliment. It was only because he was of an argumentative mind that in their cabin at night he permitted himself to carp.

'Mrs. Davidson was saying she didn't know how they'd have got through the journey if it hadn't been for us,' said Mrs. Macphail, as she neatly brushed out her transformation. 'She said we were really the only people on the ship they cared to know.'

'I shouldn't have thought a missionary was such a big bug that he could afford to put on frills.'

'It's not frills. I quite understand what she means. It wouldn't have been very nice for the Davidsons to have to mix with all that rough lot in the smoking-room.'

'The founder of their religion wasn't so exclusive,' said Dr. Macphail with a chuckle.

'I've asked you over and over again not to joke about religion,' answered his wife. 'I shouldn't like to have a nature like yours, Alec. You never look for the best in people.'

He gave her a sidelong glance with his pale, blue eyes, but did not reply. After many years of married life he had learned that it was more conducive to peace to leave his wife with the last word. He was undressed before she was, and climbing into the upper bunk he settled down to read himself to sleep.

When he came on deck next morning they were close to land. He looked at it with greedy eyes. There was a thin strip of silver beach rising quickly to hills covered to the top with luxuriant vegetation. The coconut trees, thick and green, came nearly to the water's edge, and among them you saw the grass houses of the Samoaris; and here and there, gleaming white, a little church. Mrs. Davidson came and stood beside him. She was dressed in black, and wore round her neck a gold chain, from which dangled a small cross. She was a little woman, with brown, dull hair very elaborately arranged, and she had prominent blue eyes behind invisible *pince-nez*. Her face was long, like a sheep's, but she gave no impression of foolishness, rather of extreme alertness; she had the quick movements of a bird. The most remarkable thing about her was her voice, high, metallic, and without inflection; it fell on the ear with a hard monotony, irritating to the nerves like the pitiless clamour of the pneumatic drill.

'This must seem like home to you,' said Dr. Macphail, with his thin, difficult smile.

'Ours are low islands, you know, not like these. Coral. These are volcanic. We've got another ten days' journey to reach them.'

'In these parts that's almost like being in the next street at home,' said Dr. Macphail facetiously.

'Well, that's rather an exaggerated way of putting it, but one does look at distances differently in the South Seas. So far you're right.'

Dr. Macphail sighed faintly.

'I'm glad we're not stationed here,' she went on. 'They say this is a terribly difficult place to work in. The steamers' touching makes the people unsettled; and then there's the naval station; that's bad for the natives. In our district we don't have difficulties like that to contend with. There are one or two traders, of course, but we take care to make them behave, and if they don't we make the place so hot for them they're glad to go.'

Fixing the glasses on her nose she looked at the green island with a ruthless stare.

'It's almost a hopeless task for the missionaries here. I can never be sufficiently thankful to God that we are at least spared that.'

Davidson's district consisted of a group of islands to the North of Samoa; they were widely separated and he had frequently to go long distances by canoe. At these times his wife remained at their headquarters and managed the mission. Dr. Macphail felt his heart sink when he considered the efficiency with which she certainly managed it. She spoke of the depravity of the natives in a voice which nothing could hush, but with a vehemently unctuous horror. Her sense of delicacy was singular. Early in their acquaintance she had said to him:

'You know, their marriage customs when we first settled in the islands were so shocking that I couldn't possibly describe them to you. But I'll tell Mrs. Macphail and she'll tell you.'

Then he had seen his wife and Mrs. Davidson, their deck-chairs close together, in earnest conversation for about two hours. As he walked past them backwards and forwards for the sake of exercise, he had heard Mrs. Davidson's agitated whisper, like the distant flow of a mountain torrent, and he saw by his wife's open mouth and pale face that she was enjoying an alarming experience. At night in their cabin she repeated to him with bated breath all she had heard.

'Well, what did I say to you?' cried Mrs. Davidson, exultant, next morning. 'Did you ever hear anything more dreadful? You don't wonder that I couldn't tell you myself, do you? Even though you are a doctor.'

Mrs. Davidson scanned his face. She had a dramatic eagerness to see that she had achieved the desired effect.

'Can you wonder that when we first went there our hearts sank? You'll hardly believe me when I tell you it was impossible to find a single good girl in any of the villages.'

She used the word *good* in a severely technical manner.

'Mr. Davidson and I talked it over, and we made up our minds the first thing to do was to put down the dancing. The natives were crazy about dancing.'

'I was not averse to it myself when I was a young man,' said Dr. Macphail.

'I guessed as much when I heard you ask Mrs. Macphail to have a turn with you last night. I don't think there's any real harm if a man dances with his wife, but I was relieved that she wouldn't. Under the circumstances I thought it better that we should keep ourselves to ourselves.'

'Under what circumstances? '

Mrs. Davidson gave him a quick look through her *pince-nez*, but did not answer his question.

'But among white people it's not quite the same,' she went on, 'though I must say I agree with Mr. Davidson, who says he can't understand how a husband can stand by and see his wife in another man's arms, and as far as I'm concerned I've never danced a step since I married. But the native dancing is quite another matter. It's not only immoral in itself, but it distinctly leads to immorality. However, I'm thankful to God that we stamped it out, and I don't think I'm wrong in saying that no one has danced in our district for eight years.'

But now they came to the mouth of the harbour and Mrs. Macphail joined them. The ship turned sharply and steamed slowly in. It was a great landlocked harbour big enough to hold a fleet of battleships; and all around it rose, high and steep, the green hills. Near the entrance, getting such breeze as blew from the sea, stood the governor's house in a garden. The Stars and Stripes dangled languidly from a flagstaff. They passed two or three trim bungalows, and a tennis court, and then they came to the quay with its warehouses. Mrs. Davidson pointed out the schooner, moored two or three hundred yards from the side, which was to take them to Apia. There was a crowd of eager, noisy, and good-humoured natives come from all parts of the island, some from curiosity, others to barter with the travellers on their way to Sydney; and they brought pineapples and huge bunches of bananas, *tapa* cloths, necklaces of shells or sharks' teeth, *kava*-bowls, and models of war canoes. American sailors, neat and trim, clean-shaven and frank effeace, sauntered among them, and there was a little group of officials. While their luggage was being landed the Macphails and Mrs. Davidson watched the crowd. Dr. Macphail looked at the yaws from which most of the children and the young boys seemed to suffer, disfiguring sores like torpid ulcers, and his professional eyes glistened when he saw for the first time in his experience cases of elephantiasis, men going about with a huge, heavy arm or dragging along a grossly disfigured leg. Men and women wore the *lava-lava*.

'It's a very indecent costume,' said Mrs. Davidson. 'Mr. Davidson thinks it should be prohibited by law. How can you expect people to be moral when they wear nothing but a strip of red cotton round their loins?'

'It's suitable enough to the climate,' said the doctor, wiping the sweat off his head.

Now that they were on land the heat, though it was so early in the morning, was already oppressive. Closed in by its hills, not a breath of air came in to Pago-Pago.

'In our islands,' Mrs. Davidson went on in her high-pitched tones, 'we've practically eradicated the *lava-lava*. A few old men still continue to wear it, but that's all. The women have all taken to the Mother Hubbard, and the men wear trousers and singlets. At the very beginning of our stay Mr. Davidson said in one of his reports: the inhabitants of these islands will never be thoroughly Christianised till every boy of more than ten years is made to wear a pair of trousers.'

But Mrs. Davidson had given two or three of her birdlike glances at heavy grey clouds that came floating over the mouth of the harbour. A few drops began to fall.

'We'd better take shelter,' she said.

They made their way with all the crowd to a great shed of corrugated iron, and the rain began to fall in torrents. They stood there for some time and then were joined by Mr. Davidson. He had been polite enough to the Macphails during the journey, but he had not his wife's sociability, and had spent much of his time reading. He was a silent, rather sullen man, and you felt that his affability was a duty that he imposed upon himself Christianly; he was by nature reserved and even morose. His appearance was singular. He was very tall and thin, with long limbs loosely jointed; hollow cheeks and curiously high cheek-bones; he had so cadaverous an air that it surprised you to notice how full and sensual were his lips. He wore his hair very long. His dark eyes, set deep in their sockets, were large and tragic; and his hands with their big, long fingers, were finely shaped; they gave him a look of great strength. But the most striking thing about him was the feeling he gave you of suppressed fire. It was impressive and vaguely troubling. He was not a man with whom any intimacy was possible.

He brought now unwelcome news. There was an epidemic of measles, a serious and often fatal disease among the Kanakas, on the island, and a case had developed among the crew of the schooner which was to take them on their journey. The sick man had been brought ashore and put in hospital on the quarantine station, but telegraphic instructions had been sent from Apia to say that the schooner would not be allowed to enter the harbour till it was certain no other member of the crew was affected.

'It means we shall have to stay here for ten days at least.'

'But I'm urgently needed at Apia,' said Dr. Macphail.

'That can't be helped. If no more cases develop on board, the schooner will be allowed to sail with white passengers, but all native traffic is prohibited for three months.'

'Is there a hotel here?' asked Mrs. Macphail.

Davidson gave a low chuckle.

'There's not.'

'What shall we do then?'

'I've been talking to the governor. There's a trader along the front who has rooms that he rents, and my proposition is that as soon as the rain lets up we should go along there and see what we can do. Don't expect comfort. You've just got to be thankful if we get a bed to sleep on and a roof over our heads.'

But the rain showed no sign of stopping, and at length with umbrellas and waterproofs they set out. There was no town, but merely a group of official buildings, a store or two, and at the back, among the coconut trees and plantains, a few native dwellings. The house they sought was about five minutes' walk from the wharf. It was a frame house of two storeys, with broad verandahs on both floors and a roof of corrugated iron. The owner was a half-caste named Horn, with a native wife surrounded by little brown children, and on the ground-floor he had a store where he sold canned goods and cottons. The rooms he showed them were almost bare of furniture. In the Macphails' there was nothing but a poor, worn bed with a ragged mosquito net, a rickety chair, and a washstand. They looked round with dismay. The rain poured down without ceasing.

'I'm not going to unpack more than we actually need,' said

Mrs. Macphail.

Mrs. Davidson came into the room as she was unlocking a portmanteau. She was very brisk and alert. The cheerless surroundings had no effect on her.

'If you'll take my advice you'll get a needle and cotton and start right in to mend the mosquito net, she said, or you'll not be able to get a wink of sleep tonight.'

'Will they be very bad?' asked Dr. Macphail.

'This is the season for them. When you're asked to a party at Government House at Apia you'll notice that all the ladies are given a pillow-slip to put their—their lower extremities in.'

'I wish the rain would stop for a moment,' said Mrs. Macphail. 'I could try to make the place comfortable with more heart if the sun were shining.'

'Oh, if you wait for that, you'll wait a long time. Pago-Pago is about the rainiest place in the Pacific. You see, the hills, and that bay, they attract the water, and one expects rain at this time of year anyway.'

She looked from Macphail to his wife, standing helplessly in different parts of the room, like lost souls, and she pursed her lips. She saw that she must take them in hand. Feckless people like that made her impatient, but her hands itched to put everything in the order which came so naturally to her.

'Here, you give me a needle and cotton and I'll mend that net of yours, while you go on with your unpacking. Dinner's at one. Dr. Macphail, you'd better go down to the wharf and see that your heavy luggage has been put in a dry place. You know what these natives are, they're quite capable of storing it where the rain will beat in on it all the time.'

The doctor put on his waterproof again and went downstairs. At the door Mr. Horn was standing in conversation with the quartermaster of the ship they had just arrived in and a second-class passenger whom Dr. Macphail had seen several times on board. The quartermaster, a little, shrivelled man, extremely dirty, nodded to him as he passed.

'This is a bad job about the measles, doc,' he said. 'I see you've fixed yourself up already.'

Dr. Macphail thought he was rather familiar, but he was a timid man and he did not take offence easily.

'Yes, we've got a room upstairs.'

'Miss Thompson was sailing with you to Apia, so I've brought her along here.'

The quartermaster pointed with his thumb to the woman standing by his side. She was twenty-seven perhaps, plump, and in a coarse fashion pretty. She wore a white dress and a large white hat. Her fat calves in white cotton stockings bulged over the tops of long white boots in glace kid. She gave Macphail an ingratiating smile.

'The feller's tryin' to soak me a dollar and a half a day for the meanest sized room,' she said in a hoarse voice.

'I tell you she's a friend of mine, Jo,' said the quartermaster. 'She can't pay more than a dollar, and you've sure got to take her for that.'

The trader was fat and smooth and quietly smiling. 'Well, if you put it like that, Mr. Swan, I'll see what I can do about it. I'll talk to Mrs. Horn and if we think we can make a reduction we will.'

'Don't try to pull that stuff with me,' said Miss Thompson. 'We'll settle this right now. You get a dollar a day for the room and not one bean more.'

Dr. Macphail smiled. He admired the effrontery with which she bargained. He was the sort of man who always paid what he was asked. He preferred to be over-charged than to haggle. The trader sighed.

'Well, to oblige Mr. Swan I'll take it.'

'That's the goods,' said Miss Thompson. 'Come right in and have a shot of hooch. I've got some real good rye in that grip if you'll bring it' along, Mr. Swan. You come along too, doctor.'

'Oh, I don't think I will, thank you,' he answered. 'I'm just going down to see that our luggage is all right.'

He stepped out into the rain. It swept in from the opening of the harbour in sheets and the opposite shore was all blurred. He passed two or three natives clad in nothing but the *lava-lava*, with huge umbrellas over them. They walked finely, with leisurely movements, very upright; and they smiled and greeted him in a strange tongue as they went by.

It was nearly dinner-time when he got back, and their meal was laid in the trader's parlour. It was a room designed not to live in but for purposes of prestige, and it had a musty, melancholy air. A suite of stamped plush was arranged neatly round the walls, and from the middle of the ceiling, protected from the flies by yellow tissue paper, hung a gilt chandelier. Davidson did not come.

'I know he went to call on the governor,' said Mrs. Davidson, 'and I guess he's kept him to dinner.'

A little native girl brought them a dish of hamburger steak, and after a while the trader came up to see that they had everything they wanted.

'I see we have a fellow lodger, Mr. Horn.' said Dr. Macphail.

'She's taken a room, that's all,' answered the trader. 'She's getting her own board.'

He looked at the two ladies with an obsequious air.

'I put her downstairs so she shouldn't be in the way. She won't be any trouble to you.'

'Is it someone who was on the boat?' asked Mrs. Macphail.

'Yes, ma'am, she was in the second cabin. She was going to Apia. She has a position as cashier waiting for her.'

'Oh!'

When the trader was gone Macphail said:

'I shouldn't think she'd find it exactly cheerful having her meals in her room.'

'If she was in the second cabin I guess she'd rather,' answered Mrs. Davidson. 'I don't exactly know who it can be.'

'I happened to be there when the quartermaster brought her along. Her name's Thompson.'

'It's not the woman who was dancing with the quartermaster

last night? ' asked Mrs. Davidson.

'That's who it must be,' said Mrs. Macphail. 'I wondered at the time what she was. She looked rather fast to me.'

'Not good style at all,' said Mrs. Davidson.

They began to talk of other things, and after dinner, tired with their early rise, they separated and slept. When they awoke, though the sky was still grey and the clouds hung low, it was not raining, and they went for a walk on the high road which the Americans had built along the bay.

On their return they found that Davidson had just come in.

'We may be here for a fortnight,' he said irritably. 'I've argued it out with the governor, but he says there is nothing to be done.'

'Mr. Davidson's just longing to get back to his work,' said his wife, with an anxious glance at him.

'We've been away for a year,' he said, walking up and down the verandah. 'The mission has been in charge of native missionaries and I'm terribly nervous that they've let things slide. They're good men, I'm not saying a word against them, God-fearing, devout, and truly Christian men—their Christianity would put many so-called Christians at home to the blush—but they're pitifully lacking in energy, They can make a stand once, they can make a stand twice, but they can't make a stand all the time. If you leave a mission in charge of a native missionary, no matter how trust-worthy he seems, in course of time you'll find he's let abuses creep in.'

Mr. Davidson stood still. With his tall, spare form, and his great eyes flashing out of his pale face, he was an impressive figure. His sincerity was obvious in the fire of his gestures and in his deep, ringing voice.

'I expect to have my work cut out for me. I shall act and I shall act promptly. If the tree is rotten it shall be cut down and cast into the flames.'

And in the evening after the high tea which was their last meal, while they sat in the stiff parlour, the ladies working and Dr. Macphail smoking his pipe, the missionary told them of his work in the islands.

'When we went there they had no sense of sin at all,' he said. 'They broke the commandments one after the other and never knew they were doing wrong. And I think that was the most difficult part of my work, to instil into the natives the sense of sin.'

The Macphails knew already that Davidson had worked in the Solomons for five years before he met his wife. She had been a missionary in China, and they had become acquainted in Boston, where they were both spending part of their leave to attend a missionary congress. On their marriage they had been appointed to the islands in which they had laboured ever since.

In the course of all the conversations they had had with Mr. Davidson one thing had shone out clearly and that was the man's unflinching courage. He was a medical missionary, and he was liable to be called at any time to one or other of the islands in the group. Even the whaleboat is not so very safe a conveyance in the stormy pacific of the wet season, but often he would be sent for in a canoe, and then the danger was great. In cases of illness or accident he never hesitated. A dozen times he had spent the whole night baling for his life, and more than once Mrs. Davidson had given him up for lost.

'I'd beg him not to go sometimes,' she said, 'or at least to wait till the weather was more settled, but he'd never listen. He's obstinate, and when he's once made up his mind, nothing can move him.'

'How can I ask the natives to put their trust in the Lord if I am afraid to do so myself?' cried Davidson. 'And I'm not, I'm not. They know that if they send for me in their trouble I'll come if it's humanly possible. And do you think the Lord is going to abandon me when I am on his business? The wind blows at his bidding and the waves toss and rage at his word.'

Dr. Macphail was a timid man. He had never been able to get used to the hurtling of the shells over the trenches, and when he was operating in an advanced dressing-station the sweat poured from his brow and dimmed his spectacles in the effort he made to control his unsteady hand. He shuddered a little as he looked at the missionary.

'I wish I could say that I've never been afraid,' he said.

'I wish you could say that you believed in God,' retorted the other.

But for some reason, that evening the missionary's thoughts travelled back to the early days he and his wife had spent on the islands.

'Sometimes Mrs. Davidson and I would look at one another and the tears would stream down our cheeks. We worked without ceasing, day and night, and we seemed to make no progress. I don't know what I should have done without her then. When I felt my heart sink, when I was very near despair, she gave me courage and hope.'

Mrs. Davidson looked down at her work, and a slight colour rose to her thin cheeks. Her hands trembled a little. She did not trust herself to speak.

'We had no one to help us. We were alone, thousands of miles from any of our own people, surrounded by darkness. When I was broken and weary she would put her work aside and take the Bible and read to me till peace came and settled upon me like sleep upon the eyelids of a child, and when at last she closed the book she'd say: "We'll save them in spite of themselves." And I felt strong again in the Lord, and I answered: "Yes, with God's help I'll save them. I must save them."'

He came over to the table and stood in front of it as though it were a lectern.

'You see, they were so naturally depraved that they couldn't be brought to see their wickedness. We had to make sins out of what they thought were natural actions. We had to make it a sin, not only to commit adultery and to lie and thieve, but to expose their bodies, and to dance and not to come to church. I made it a sin for a girl to show her bosom and a sin for a man not to wear trousers.'

'How?' asked Dr. Macphail, not without surprise.

'I instituted fines. Obviously the only way to make people

realise that an action is sinful is to punish them if they commit it. I fined them if they didn't come to church, and I fined them if they danced. I fined them if they were improperly dressed. I had a tariff, and every sin had to be paid for either in money or work. And at last I made them understand.'

'But did they never refuse to pay?'

'How could they?' asked the missionary.

'It would be a brave man who tried to stand up against Mr. Davidson,' said his wife, tightening her lips.

Dr. Macphail looked at Davidson with troubled eyes. What he heard shocked him, but he hesitated to express his disapproval.

'You must remember that in the last resort I could expel them from their church membership."

'Did they mind that?'

Davidson smiled a little and gently rubbed his hands.

'They couldn't sell their copra. When the men fished they got no share of the catch. It meant something very like starvation. Yes, they minded quite a lot.'

'Tell him about Fred Ohlson,' said Mrs. Davidson.

The missionary fixed his fiery eyes on Dr. Macphail.

'Fred Ohlson was a Danish trader who had been in the islands a good many years. He was a pretty rich man as traders go and he wasn't very pleased when we came. You see, he'd had things very much his own way. He paid the natives what he liked for their copra, and he paid in goods and whiskey. He had a native wife, but he was flagrantly unfaithful to her. He was a drunkard. I gave him a chance to mend his ways, but he wouldn't take it. He laughed at me.'

Davidson's voice fell to a deep bass as he said the last words, and he was silent for a minute or two. The silence was heavy with menace.

'In two years he was a ruined man. He'd lost everything he'd saved in a quarter of a century. I broke him, and at last he was forced to come to me like a beggar and beseech me to give him a passage back to Sydney.'

'I wish you could have seen him when he came to see

Mr. Davidson,' said the missionary's wife.

'He had been a fine, powerful man, with a lot of fat on him, and he had a great big voice, but now he was half the size, and he was shaking all over. He'd suddenly become an old man.'

With abstracted gaze Davidson looked out into the night. The rain was falling again.

Suddenly from below came a sound, and Davidson turned and looked questioningly at his wife. It was the sound of a gramophone, harsh and loud, wheezing out a syncopated tune.

'What's that?' he asked.

Mrs. Davidson fixed her *pince-nez* more firmly on her nose.

'One of the second-class passengers has a room in the house. I guess it comes from there.'

They listened in silence, and presently they heard the sound of dancing. Then the music stopped, and they heard the popping of corks and voices raised in animated conversation.

'I daresay she's giving a farewell party to her friends on board,' said Dr. Macphail. 'The ship sails at twelve, doesn't it?'

Davidson made no remark, but he looked at his watch.

'Are you ready?' he asked his wife.

She got up and folded her work.

'Yes, I guess I am,' she answered.

'It's early to go to bed yet, isn't it?' said the doctor.

'We have a good deal of reading to do,' explained Mrs. Davidson. 'Wherever we are, we read a chapter of the Bible before retiring for the night and we study it with the commentaries, you know, and discuss it thoroughly. It's a wonderful training for the mind.'

The two couples bade one another good night. Dr. and Mrs. Macphail were left alone. For two or three minutes they did not speak.

'I think I'll go and fetch the cards,' the doctor said at last.

Mrs. Macphail looked at him doubtfully. Her conversation with the Davidsons had left her a little uneasy, but she did not like to say that she thought they had better not play cards when the Davidsons might come in at any moment.

Dr. Macphail brought them and she watched him, though with a vague sense of guilt, while he laid out his patience. Below the sound of revelry continued.

It was fine enough next day, and the Macphails, condemned to spend a fortnight of idleness at Pago-Pago, set about making the best of things. They went down to the quay and got out of their boxes a number of books. The doctor called on the chief surgeon of the naval hospital and went round the beds with him. They left cards on the governor. They passed Miss Thompson on the road. The doctor took off his hat, and she gave him a 'Good morning, doc,' in a loud, cheerful voice. She was dressed as on the day before, in a white frock, and her shiny white boots with their high heels, her fat legs bulging over the tops of them, were strange things on that exotic scene.

'I don't think she's very suitably dressed, I must say,' said Mrs. Macphail. 'She looks extremely common to me.'

When they got back to their house, she was on the verandah playing with one of the trader's dark children.

'Say a word to her,' Dr. Macphail whispered to his wife. 'She's all alone here, and it seems rather unkind to ignore her.'

Mrs. Macphail was shy, but she was in the habit of doing what her husband bade her.

'I think we're fellow lodgers here,' she said rather foolishly.

'Terrible, ain't it, bein' cooped up in a one-horse burg like this?' answered Miss Thompson. 'And they tell me I'm lucky to have gotten a room. I don't see myself livin' in a native house, and that's what some have to do. I don't know why they don't have a hotel.'

They exchanged a few more words. Miss Thompson, loud-voiced and garrulous, was evidently quite willing to gossip, but Mrs. Macphail had a poor stock of small talk and presently she said:

'Well, I think we must go upstairs.'

In the evening when they sat down to their high tea Davidson on coming in said:

'I see that woman downstairs has a couple of sailors sitting there. I wonder how she's gotten acquainted with them.'

'She can't be very particular,' said Mrs. Davidson.

They were all rather tired after the idle, aimless day.

'If there's going to be a fortnight of this I don't know what we shall feel like at the end of it,' said Dr. Macphail.

'The only thing to do is to portion out the day to different activities,' answered the missionary. 'I shall set aside a certain number of hours to study and a certain number to exercise, rain or fine—in the wet season you can't afford to pay any attention to the rain—and a certain number to recreation.'

Dr. Macphail looked at his companion with misgiving. Davidson's programme oppressed him. They were eating Hamburger steak again. It seemed the only dish the cook knew how to make. Then below the gramophone began. Davidson started nervously when he heard it, but said nothing. Men's voices floated up. Miss Thompson's guests were joining in a well-known song and presently they heard her voice too, hoarse and loud. There was a good deal of shouting and laughing. The four people upstairs, trying to make conversation, listened despite themselves to the clink of glasses and the scrape of chairs. More people had evidently come. Miss Thompson was giving a party.

'I wonder how she gets them all in,' said Mrs. Macphail, suddenly breaking into a medical conversation between the missionary and her husband.

It showed whither her thoughts were wandering. The twitch of Davidson's face proved that, though he spoke of scientific things, his mind was busy in the same direction. Suddenly, while the doctor was giving some experience of practice on the Flanders front, rather prosily, he sprang to his feet with a cry.

'What's the matter, Alfred?' asked Mrs. Davidson.

'Of course! It never occurred to me. She's out of Iwelei.'

'She can't be.'

'She came on board at Honolulu. It's obvious. And she's carrying on her trade here. Here.'

He uttered the last word with a passion of indignation.

'What's Iwelei?' asked Mrs. Macphail.

He turned his gloomy eyes on her and his voice trembled with horror.

'The plague spot of Honolulu. The Red Light district. It was a blot on our civilisation.'

Iwelei was on the edge of the city. You went down side streets by the harbour, in the darkness, across a rickety bridge, till you came to a deserted road, all ruts and holes, and then suddenly you came out into the light. There was parking room for motors on each side of the road, and there were saloons, tawdry and bright, each one noisy with its mechanical piano, and there were barbers' shops and tobacconists. There was a stir in the air and a sense of expectant gaiety. You turned down a narrow alley, either to the right or to the left, for the road divided Iwelei into two parts, and you found yourself in the district. There were rows of little bungalows, trim and neatly painted in green, and the pathway between them was broad and straight. It was laid out like a garden-city. In its respectable regularity, its order and spruceness, it gave an impression of sardonic horror; for never can the search for love have been so systematised and ordered. The pathways were lit by a rare lamp, but they would have been dark except for the lights that came from the open windows of the bungalows. Men wandered about, looking at the women who sat at their windows, reading or sewing, for the most part taking no notice of the passers-by; and like the women they were of all nationalities. There were Americans, sailors from the ships in port, enlisted men off the gunboats, sombrely drunk, and soldiers from the regiments, white and black, quartered on the island; there were Japanese, walking in twos and threes; Hawaiians, Chinese in long robes, and Filipinos in preposterous hats. They were silent and as it were oppressed. Desire is sad.

'It was the most crying scandal of the Pacific,' exclaimed Davidson vehemently. 'The missionaries had been agitating against it for years, and at last the local press took it up. The police refused to stir. You know their argument. They say that vice is inevitable and consequently the best thing is to localise and control it. The truth is, they were paid. Paid. They were paid by the saloon-keepers, paid by the bullies, paid by the women themselves. At last they were forced to move.'

'I read about it in the papers that came on board in Honolulu,' said Dr. Macphail.

'Iwelei, with its sin and shame, ceased to exist on the very day we arrived. The whole population was brought before the justices. I don't know why I didn't understand at once what that woman was.'

'Now you come to speak of it,' said Mrs. Macphail, 'I remember seeing her come on board only a few minutes before the boat sailed. I remember thinking at the time she was cutting it rather fine.'

'How dare she come here!' cried Davidson indignantly. 'I'm not going to allow it.'

He strode towards the door.

'What are you going to do?' asked Macphail.

'What do you expect me to do? I'm going to stop it. I'm not going to have this house turned into—into...'

He sought for a word that should not offend the ladies' ears. His eyes were flashing and his pale face was paler still in his emotion.

'It sounds as though there were three or four men down there,' said the doctor. 'Don't you think it's rather rash to go in just now?'

The missionary gave him a contemptuous look and without a word flung out of the room.

'You know Mr. Davidson very little if you think the fear of personal danger can stop him in the performance of his duty,' said his wife.

She sat with her hands nervously clasped, a spot of colour on her high cheek bones, listening to what was about to happen below. They all listened. They heard him clatter down the wooden stairs and throw open the door. The singing stopped suddenly, but the gramophone continued to bray out its vulgar tune. They heard Davidson's voice and then the noise of something heavy falling. The music stopped. He had hurled the gramophone on the floor. Then again they heard Davidson's voice, they could not make out the words, then Miss Thompson's, loud and shrill, then a confused clamour as though several people were shouting together at the top of their lungs. Mrs. Davidson gave a little gasp, and she clenched her hands more tightly. Dr. Macphail looked uncertainly from her to his wife. He did not want to go down, but he wondered if they expected him to. Then there was something that sounded like a scuffle. The noise now was more distinct. It might be that Davidson was being thrown out of the room. The door was slammed. There was a moment's silence and they heard Davidson come up the stairs again. He went to his room.

'I think I'll go to him,' said Mrs. Davidson.

She got up and went out.

'If you want me, just call,' said Mrs. Macphail, and then when the other was gone: 'I hope he isn't hurt.'

'Why couldn't he mind his own business?' said Dr. Macphail.

They sat in silence for a minute or two and then they both started, for the gramophone began to play once more, defiantly, and mocking voices shouted hoarsely the words of an obscene song.

Next day Mrs. Davidson was pale and tired. She complained of headache, and she looked old and wizened. She told Mrs. Macphail that the missionary had not slept at all; he had passed the night in a state of frightful agitation and at five had got up and gone out. A glass of beer had been thrown over him and his clothes were stained and stinking. But a sombre fire glowed in Mrs. Davidson's eyes when she spoke of Miss Thompson.

'She'll bitterly rue the day when she flouted Mr. Davidson,' she said. 'Mr. Davidson has a wonderful heart and no one who is in trouble has ever gone to I him without being comforted, but he has no mercy for sin, and when his righteous wrath is excited he's terrible.'

'Why, what will he do?' asked Mrs. Macphail.

'I don't know, but I wouldn't stand in that creature's shoes for anything in the world.'

Mrs. Macphail shuddered. There was something positively alarming in the triumphant assurance of the little woman's manner. They were going out together that morning, and they went down the stairs side by side. Miss Thompson's door was open, and they saw her in a bedraggled dressing-gown, cooking something in a chafing-dish.

'Good morning,' she called. 'Is Mrs. Davidson better this morning?'

They passed her in silence, with their noses in the air, as if she did not exist. They flushed, however, when she burst into a shout of derisive laughter. Mrs. Davidson turned on her suddenly. 'Don't you dare to speak to me,' she screamed. 'If you insult me I shall have you turned out of here.'

'Say, did I ask Mr. Davidson to visit with me?'

'Don't answer her,' whispered Mrs. Macphail hurriedly.

They walked on till they were out of earshot.

'She's brazen, brazen,' burst from Mrs. Davidson.

Her anger almost suffocated her.

And on their way home they met her strolling towards the quay. She had all her finery on. Her great white hat with its vulgar, showy flowers was an affront. She called out cheerily to them as she went by, and a couple of American sailors who were standing there grinned as the ladies set their faces to an icy stare. They got in just before the rain began to fall again.

'I guess she'll get her fine clothes spoilt,' said Mrs. Davidson with a bitter sneer.

Davidson did not come in till they were half way through dinner. He was wet through, but he would not change. He sat, morose and silent, refusing to eat more than a mouthful, and he stared at the slanting rain. When Mrs. Davidson told him of their two encounters with Miss Thompson he did not answer. His deepening frown alone showed that he had heard.

'Don't you think we ought to make Mr. Horn turn her out of here?' asked Mrs. Davidson. 'We can't allow her to insult us.'

'There doesn't seem to be any other place for her to go,' said Macphail.

'She can live with one of the natives.'

'In weather like this a native hut must be a rather uncomfortable place to live in.'

'I lived in one for years,' said the missionary.

When the little native girl brought in the fried bananas which formed the sweet they had every day, Davidson turned to her.

'Ask Miss Thompson when it would be convenient for me to see her,' he said.

The girl nodded shyly and went out.

'What do you want to see her for, Alfred?' asked his wife.

'It's my duty to see her. I won't act till I've given her every chance.'

'You don't know what she is. She'll insult you.'

'Let her insult me. Let her spit on me. She has an immortal soul, and I must do all that is in my power to save it.'

Mrs. Davidson's ears rang still with the harlot's mocking laughter.

'She's gone too far.'

'Too far for the mercy of God?' His eyes lit up suddenly and his voice grew mellow and soft.

'Never. The sinner may be deeper in sin than the depth of hell itself, but the love of the Lord Jesus can reach him still.'

The girl came back with the message.

'Miss Thompson's compliments and as long as Rev. Davidson don't come in business hours she'll be glad to see him any time.'

The party received it in stony silence, and Dr. Macphail quickly effaced from his lips the smile which had come upon them. He knew his wife would be vexed with him if he found Miss Thompson's effrontery amusing.

They finished the meal in silence. When it was over the two ladies got up and took their work, Mrs. Macphail was making another of the innumerable comforters which she had turned out since the beginning of the war, and the doctor lit his pipe. But Davidson remained in his chair and with abstracted eyes stared at the table. At last he got up and without a word went out of the room. They heard him go down and they heard Miss Thompson's defiant 'Come in' when he knocked at the door. He remained with her for an hour. And Dr. Macphail watched the rain. It was beginning to get on his nerves. It was not like our soft English rain that drops gently on the earth; it was unmerciful and somehow terrible; you felt in it the malignancy of the primitive powers of nature. It did not pour, it flowed. It was like a deluge from heaven, and it rattled on the roof of corrugated iron with a steady persistence that was maddening. It seemed to have a fury of its own. And sometimes you felt that you must scream if it did not stop, and then suddenly you felt powerless, as though your bones had suddenly become soft; and you were miserable and hopeless.

Macphail turned his head when the missionary came back. The two women looked up.

'I've given her every chance. I have exhorted her to repent. She is an evil woman.'

He paused, and Dr. Macphail saw his eyes darken and his pale face grow hard and stern.

'Now I shall take the whips with which the Lord Jesus drove the usurers and the money changers out of the Temple of the Most High.'

He walked up and down the room. His mouth was close set, and his black brows were frowning.

'If she fled to the uttermost parts of the earth I should pursue her.'

With a sudden movement he turned round and strode out of the room. They heard him go downstairs again.

'What is he going to do?' asked Mrs. Macphail.

'I don't know.' Mrs. Davidson took off her *pince-nez* and wiped them. 'When he is on the Lord's work I never ask him questions.'

She sighed a little.

'What is the matter?'

'He'll wear himself out. He doesn't know what it is to

spare himself.'

Dr. Macphail learnt the first results of the missionary's activity from the half-caste trader in whose house they lodged. He stopped the doctor when he passed the store 'and came out to speak to him on the stoop. His fat face was worried.

'The Rev. Davidson has been at me for letting Miss Thompson have a room here,' he said, 'but I didn't know what she was when I rented it to her. When people come and ask if I can rent them a room all I want to know is if they've the money to pay for it. And she paid me for hers a week in advance.'

Dr. Macphail did not want to commit himself. 'When all's said and done it's your house. We're very much obliged to you for taking us in at all.'

Horn looked at him doubtfully. He was not certain yet how definitely Macphail stood on the missionary's side.

'The missionaries are in with one another,' he said, hesitatingly olf they get it in for a trader he may just as well shut up his store and quit.'

'Did he want you to turn her out?'

'No, he said so long as she behaved herself he couldn't ask me to do that. He said he wanted to be just to me. I promised she shouldn't have no more visitors. I've just been and told her.

'How did she take it?'

'She gave me Hell.'

The trader squirmed in his old ducks. He had found Miss Thompson a rough customer.

'Oh, well, I daresay she'll get out. I don't suppose she wants to stay here if she can't have anyone in.'

'There's nowhere she can go, only a native house, and no native'll take her now, not now that the missionaries have got their knife in her.'

Dr. Macphail looked at the falling rain.

'Well, I don't suppose it's any good waiting for it to clear up.'

In the evening when they sat in the parlour Davidson talked to them of his early days at college. He had had no means and had worked his way through by doing odd jobs during the vacations.

There was silence downstairs. Miss Thompson was sitting in her little room alone. But suddenly the gramophone began to play. She had set it on in defiance, to cheat her loneliness, but there was no one to sing, and it had a melancholy note. It was like a cry for help Davidson took no notice. He was in the middle of a long anecdote and without change of expression went on. The gramophone continued. Miss Thompson put on one reel after another. It looked as though the silence of the night were getting on her nerves. It was breathless and sultry. When the Macphails went to bed they could not sleep. They lay side by side with their eyes wide open, listening to the cruel singing of the mosquitoes outside their curtain.

'What's that?' whispered Mrs. Macphail at last.

They heard a voice, Davidson's voice, through the wooden partition. It went on with a monotonous, earnest insistence. He was praying aloud. He was praying for the soul of Miss Thompson.

Two or three days went by. Now when they passed Miss Thompson on the road she did not greet them with ironic cordiality or smile; she passed with her nose in the air, a sulky look on her painted face, frowning, as though she did not see them. The trader told Macphail that she had tried to get lodging elsewhere, but had failed. In the evening she played through the various reels of her gramophone, but the pretence of mirth was obvious now. The ragtime had a cracked, heart-broken rhythm as though it were a one-step of despair. When she began to play on Sunday Davidson sent Horn to beg her to stop at once since it was the Lord's day. The reel was taken off and the house was silent except for the steady pattering of the rain on the iron roof.

'I think she's getting a bit worked up,' said the trader next day to Macphail. 'She don't know what Mr. Davidson's up to and it makes her scared.'

Macphail had caught a glimpse of her that morning and it struck him that her arrogant expression had changed. There was in her face a hunted look. The half-caste gave him a sidelong glance.

'I suppose you don't know what Mr. Davidson is doing about it?' he hazarded.

'No, I don't.'

It was singular that Horn should ask him that question, for he also had the idea that the misssionary was mysteriously at work. He had an impression that he was weaving a net around the woman, carefully, systematically, and suddenly, when everything was ready, would pull the strings tight.

'He told me to tell her,' said the trader, 'that if at any time she wanted him she only had to send and he'd come.'

'What did she say when you told her that?'

'She didn't say nothing. I didn't stop. I just said what he said I was to and then I beat it. I thought she might be going to start weepin'.'

'I have no doubt the loneliness is getting on her nerves,' said the doctor. 'And the rain—that's enough to make anyone jumpy,' he continued irritably. 'Doesn't it ever stop in this confounded place?'

'It goes on pretty steady in the rainy season. We have three hundred inches in the year. You see, it's the shape of the bay. It seems to attract the rain from all over the Pacific.'

'Damn the shape of the bay,' said the doctor.

He scratched his mosquito bites. He felt very short-tempered. When the rain stopped and the sun shone, it was like a hothouse, seething, humid, sultry, breathless, and you had a strange feeling that everything was growing with a savage violence. The natives, blithe and childlike by reputation, seemed then, with their tattooing an their dyed hair, to have something sinister in their appearance; and when they pattered along at your heels with their naked feet you looked back instinctively. You felt they might at any moment come behind you swiftly and thrust long knife between your shoulder blades. You could not tell what dark thoughts lurked behind their wide-set eyes. They had a little the look of ancient Egyptians painted on a temple wall, and there was about them the terror of what is immeasurably old.

The missionary came and went. He was busy, but the Macphails did not know what he was doing. Horn told the doctor that he saw the governor every day, and once Davidson mentioned him.

'He looks as if he had plenty of determination,' he said, 'but when you come down to brass tacks he has no backbone.'

'I suppose that means he won't do exactly what you want,' suggested the doctor facetiously.

The missionary did not smile.

'I want him to do what's right. It shouldn't be necessary to persuade a man to do that.'

'But there may be differences of opinion about what is right.'

'If a man had a gangrenous foot would you have patience with anyone who hesitated to amputate it?'

'Gangrene is a matter of fact.'

'And Evil?'

What Davidson had done soon appeared. The four of them had just finished their midday meal, and they had not yet separated for the siesta which the heat imposed on the ladies and on the doctor. Davidson had little patience with the slothful habit. The door was suddenly flung open and Miss Thompson came in. She looked round the room and then went up to Davidson.

'You low-down skunk, what have you been saying about me to the governor?'

She was spluttering with rage. There was a moment's pause. Then the missionary drew forward a chair.

'Won't you be seated, Miss Thompson? I've been hoping to have another talk with you.'

'You poor low-life bastard.'

She burst into a torrent of insult, foul and insolent. Davidson kept his grave eyes on her.

'I'm indifferent to the abuse you think fit to heap on me, Miss Thompson,' he said, 'but I must beg you to remember that ladies are present.'

Tears by now were struggling with her anger. Her face was red and swollen as though she were choking.

'What has happened?' asked Dr. Macphail.

'A feller's just been in here and he says I gotter beat it on the next boat.'

Was there a gleam in the missionary's eyes? His face remained impassive.

'You could hardly expect the governor to let you stay here under the circumstances.'

'You done it,' she shrieked. 'You can't kid me. You done it.'

'I don't want to deceive you. I urged the governor to take the only possible step consistent with his obligations.'

'Why couldn't you leave me be? I wasn't doin' you no harm.'

'You may be sure that if you had I should be the last man to resent it.'

'Do you think I want to stay on in this poor imitation of a burg? I don't look no busher, do I?'

'In that case I don't see what cause of complaint you have,' he answered.

She gave an inarticulate cry of rage and flung out of the room. There was a short silence.

'It's a relief to know that the governor has acted at last,' said Davidson finally. 'He's a weak man and he shilly-shallied. He said she was only here for a fortnight anyway, and if she went on to Apia that was under British jurisdiction and had nothing to do with him.'

The missionary sprang to his feet and strode across the room.

'It's terrible the way the men who are in authority seek to evade their responsibility. They speak as though evil that was out of sight ceased to be evil. The very existence of that woman is a scandal and it does not help matters to shift it to another of the islands. In the end I had to speak straight from the shoulder.'

Davidson's brow lowered, and he protruded his firm chin. He looked fierce and determined.

'What do you mean by that?'

'Our mission is not entirely without influence at Washington. I pointed out to the governor that it wouldn't do him any good if there was a complaint about the way he managed things here.'

'When has she got to go?' asked the doctor, after a pause.

'The San Francisco boat is due here from Sydney next Tuesday. She's to sail on that.'

That was in five days' time. It was next day, when he was coining back from the hospital where for want of something better to do Macphail spent most of his mornings, that the half-caste stopped him as he was going upstairs.

'Excuse me, Dr. Macphail, Miss Thompson's sick. Will you have a look at her.'

'Certainly.'

Horn led him to her room. She was sitting in a chair idly, neither reading nor sewing, staring in front of her. She wore her white dress and the large hat with the flowers on it. Macphail noticed that her skin was yellow and muddy under her powder, and her eyes were heavy.

'I'm sorry to hear you're not well,' he said.

'Oh, I ain't sick really. I just said that, because I just had to see you. I've got to clear on a boat that's going to 'Frisco.'

She looked at him and he saw that her eyes were suddenly startled. She opened and clenched her hands spasmodically. The trader stood at the door, listening.

'So I understand,' said the doctor.

She gave a little gulp

'I guess it ain't very convenient for me to go to Frisco just now. I went to see the governor yesterday afternoon, but I couldn't get to him. I saw the secretary, and he told me I'd got to take that boat and that was all there was to it. I just had to see the governor, so I waited outside his house this morning, and when he come out I spoke to him. He didn't want to speak to me, I'll say, but I wouldn't let him shake me off, and at last he said he hadn't no objection to my staying here till the next boat to Sydney if the Rev. Davidson will stand for it.'

She stopped and looked at Dr. Macphail anxiously.

'I don't know exactly what I can do,' he said.

'Well, I thought maybe you wouldn't mind asking him. I swear to God I won't start anything here if he'll just only let me stay. I won't go out of the house if that'll suit him. It's no more'n a fortnight.'

'I'll ask him.'

'He won't stand for it,' said Horn. 'He'll have you out on Tuesday, so you may as well make up your mind to it.'

'Tell him I can get work in Sydney, straight stuff, I mean. Tain't asking very much.'

'I'll do what I can.'

'And come and tell me right away, will you? I can't set down to a thing till I get the dope one way or the other.'

It was not an errand that much pleased the doctor, and, characteristically perhaps, he went about it indirectly. He told his wife what Miss Thompson had said to him and asked her to speak to Mrs. Davidson. The missionary's attitude seemed rather arbitrary and it could do no harm if the girl were allowed to stay in Pago-Pago another fortnight. But he was not prepared for the result of his diplomacy. The missionary came to him straightway.

'Mrs. Davidson tells me that Thompson has been speaking to you.'

Dr. Macphail, thus directly tackled, had the shy man's resentment at being forced out into the open. He felt his temper rising, and he flushed.

'I don't see that it can make any difference if she goes to Sydney rather than to San Francisco, and so long as she promises to behave while she's here it's dashed hard to persecute her.'

The missionary fixed him with his stern eyes. 'Why is she unwilling to go back to San Francisco?'

'I didn't inquire,' answered the doctor with some asperity. 'And I think one does better to mind one's own business.'

Perhaps it was not a very tactful answer.

'The governor has ordered her to be deported by the first boat that leaves the island. He's only done his duty and I will not interfere. Her presence is a peril here.'

'I think you're very harsh and tyrannical.'

The two ladies looked up at the doctor with some alarm, but they need not have feared a quarrel, for the missionary smiled gently.

'I'm terribly sorry you should think that of me Dr. Macphail. Believe me, my heart bleeds for the unfortunate woman, but I'm only trying to do my duty.'

The doctor made no answer. He looked out of the window sullenly. For once it was not raining and across the bay you saw nestling among the trees the huts of a native village.

'I think I'll take advantage of the rain stopping to go out,' he said.

'Please don't bear me malice because I can't accede to your wish,' said Davidson, with a melancholy smile. 'I respect you very much, doctor, and I should be sorry if you thought ill of me.'

'I have no doubt you have a sufficiently good opinion of yourself to bear mine with equanimity,' he retorted.

'That's one on me,' chuckled Davidson.

When Dr. Macphail, vexed with himself because he had been uncivil to no purpose, went downstairs, Miss Thompson was waiting for him with her door ajar.

'Well,' she said, 'have you spoken to him?'

'Yes, I'm sorry, he won't do anything,' he answered, not looking at her in his embarrassment.

But then he gave her a quick glance, for a sob broke from her. He saw that her face was white with fear. It gave him a shock of dismay. And suddenly he had an idea.

'But don't give up hope yet. I think it's a shame the way they're treating you and I'm going to see the governor myself.'

'Now?'

He nodded. Her face brightened.

'Say, that's real good of you. I'm sure he'll let me stay if you speak for me. I just won't do a thing I didn't ought all the time I'm here.'

Dr. Macphail hardly knew why he had made up his mind to appeal to the governor. He was perfectly indifferent to Miss Thompson's affairs, the missionary had irritated him, and with him temper was a smouldering thing. He found the governor at home. He was a large, handsome man, a sailor, with a grey toothbrush moustache; and he wore a spotless uniform of white drill.

'I've come to see you about a woman who's lodging in the same house as we are,' he said. 'Her name's Thompson.'

'I guess I've heard nearly enough about her, Dr. Macphail,' said the governor, smiling. 'I've given her the order to get out next Tuesday and that's all I can do.'

'I wanted to ask you if you couldn't stretch a point and let her stay here till the boat comes in from San Francisco so that she can go to Sydney. I will guarantee her good behaviour.'

The governor continued to smile, but his eyes grew small and serious.

'I'd be very glad to oblige you, Dr. Macphail, but I've given the order and it must stand.'

The doctor put the case as reasonably as he could, but now the governor ceased to smile at all. He listened sullenly, with averted gaze. Macphail saw that he was making no impression.

'I'm sorry to cause any lady inconvenience, but she'll have to sail on Tuesday and that's all there is to it.'

'But what difference can it make?'

'Pardon me, doctor, but I don't feel called upon to explain my official actions except to the, proper authorities.'

Macphail looked at him shrewdly. He remembered Davidson's hint that he had used threats, and in the governor's attitude he read a singular embarrassment.

'Davidson's a damned busybody,' he said hotly.

'Between ourselves, Dr. Macphail, I don't say that I have formed a very favourable opinion of Mr. Davidson, but I am bound to confess that he was within his rights in pointing out to me the danger that the presence of a woman of Miss Thompson's character was to a place like this where a number of enlisted men are stationed among a native population.'

He got up and Dr. Macphail was obliged to do so too.

'I must ask you to excuse me. I have an engagement. Please give my respects to Mrs. Macphail.'

The doctor left him crest-fallen. He knew that Miss Thompson would be waiting for him, and unwilling to tell her himself that he had failed, he went into the house by the back door and sneaked up the stairs as though he had something to hide.

At supper he was silent and ill-at-ease, but the missionary was jovial and animated. Dr. Macphail thought his eyes rested on him now and then with triumphant good-humour. It struck him suddenly that Davidson knew of his visit to the governor and of its ill success. But how on earth could he have heard of it? There was something sinister about the power of that man. After supper he saw Horn on the verandah and, as though to have a casual word with him, went out.

'She wants to know if you've seen the governor,' the trader whispered.

'Yes. He wouldn't do anything. I'm awfully sorry, I can't do anything more.'

'I knew he wouldn't. They daren't go against the missionaries.'

'What are you talking about?' said Davidson affably, corning out to join them.

'I was just saying there was no chance of your getting over to Apia for at least another week,' said the trader glibly.

He left them, and the two men returned into the parlour. Mr. Davidson devoted one hour after each meal to recreation. Presently a timid knock was heard at the door.

'Come in,' said Mrs. Davidson, in her sharp voice.

The door was not opened. She got up and opened it. They saw Miss Thompson standing at the threshold. But the change in her appearance was extraordinary. This was no longer the flaunting hussy who had jeered at them in the road, but a broken, frightened woman. Her hair, as a rule so elaborately arranged, was tumbling untidily over her neck. She wore bedroom slippers and a skirt and blouse. They were unfresh and bedraggled. She stood at the door with the tears streaming down her face and did not dare to enter.

'What do you want?' said Mrs. Davidson harshly.

'May I speak to Mr. Davidson?' she said in a choking voice.

The missionary rose and went towards her.

'Come right in, Miss Thompson,' he said in cordial tones. 'What can I do for you?'

She entered the room.

'Say, I'm sorry for what I said to you the other day an' for—for everythin' else. I guess I was a bit lit up. I beg pardon.'

'Oh, it was nothing. I guess my back's broad enough to bear a few hard words.'

She stepped towards him with a movement that was horribly cringing.

'You've got me beat. I'm all in. You won't make me go back to 'Frisco?'

His genial manner vanished and his voice grew on a sudden hard and stern.

'Why don't you want to go back there?'

She cowered before him.

'I guess my people live there. I don't want them to see me like this. I'll go anywhere else you say.'

'Why don't you want to go back to San Francisco?'

'I've told you.'

He leaned forward, staring at her, and his great, shining eyes seemed to try to bore into her soul. He gave a sudden gasp.

'The penitentiary.'

She screamed, and then she fell at his feet, clasping his legs.

'Don't send me back there. I swear to you before God I'll be a good woman. I'll give all this up.'

She burst into a torrent of confused supplication and the tears coursed down her painted cheeks. He leaned over her and, lifting her face, forced her to look at him.

'Is that it, the penitentiary?'

'I beat it before they could get me,' she gasped. 'If the bulls grab me it's three years for mine.'

He let go his hold of her and she fell in a heap on the floor, sobbing bitterly. Dr. Macphail stood up.

'This alters the whole thing,' he said. 'You can't make her go back when you know this. Give her another chance. She wants to turn over a new leaf.'

'I'm going to give her the finest chance she's ever had. If she repents let her accept her punishment.'

She misunderstood the words and looked up. There was a gleam of hope in her heavy eyes.

'You'll let me go?'

'No. You shall sail for San Francisco on Tuesday.'

She gave a groan of horror and then burst into low, hoarse shrieks which sounded hardly human, and she beat her head passionately on the ground. Dr. Macphail sprang to her and lifted her up:

'Come on, you mustn't do that. You'd better go to your room and lie down. I'll get you something.'

He raised her to her feet and partly dragging her, partly carrying her, got her downstairs. He was furious with Mrs. Davidson and with his wife because they made no effort to help. The half-caste was standing on the landing and with his assistanc he managed to get her on the bed. She was moaning and crying. She was almost insensible. He gave her a hypodermic injection. He was hot and exhausted when he went upstairs again.

'I've got her to lie down.'

The two women and Davidson were in the same, positions as when he had left them. They could not have moved or spoken since he went.

'I was waiting for you,' said Davidson, in a strange, distant voice. 'I want you all to pray with me for the soul of our erring sister.'

He took the Bible off a shelf, and sat down at the table at which they had supped. It had not been cleared, and he pushed the tea-pot out of the way. In a powerful voice, resonant and deep, he read to them the chapter in which is narrated the meeting of Jesus Christ with the woman taken in adultery.

'Now kneel with me and let us pray for the soul of our dear sister, Sadie Thompson.'

He burst into a long, passionate prayer in which he implored God to have mercy on the sinful woman. Mrs. Macphail and Mrs. Davidson knelt with covered eyes. The doctor, taken by surprise, awkward and sheepish, knelt too. The missionary's prayer had a savage eloquence. He was extraordinarily moved, and as he spoke the tears ran down his cheeks. Outside, the pitiless rain fell, fell steadily, with a fierce malignity that was all too human.

At last he stopped. He paused for a moment and said:

'We will now repeat the Lord's prayer.'

They said it and then, following him, they rose from their knees. Mrs. Davidson's face was pale and restful. She was comforted and at peace, but the Macphails felt suddenly bashful. They did not know which way to look.

'I'll just go down and see how she is now,' said Dr. Macphail.

When he knocked at her door it was opened for him by Horn. Miss Thompson was in a rocking-chair, sobbing quietly.

'What are you doing there?' exclaimed Macphail. ' I told you to lie down.'

'I can't lie down. I want to see Mr. Davidson.'

'My poor child, what do you think is the good of it? You'll never move him.'

'He said he'd come if I sent for him.'

Macphail motioned to the trader.

'Go and fetch him.'

He waited with her in silence while the trader went upstairs. Davidson came in.

'Excuse me for asking you to come here,' she said, looking at him sombrely.

'I was expecting you to send for me. I knew the Lord would answer my prayer.'

They stared at one another for a moment and then she

looked away. She kept her eyes averted when she spoke.

'I've been a bad woman. I want to repent.'

'Thank God! Thank God! He has heard our prayers.'

He turned to the two men.

'Leave me alone with her. Tell Mrs. Davidson that our prayers have been answered.'

They went out and closed the door behind them.

'Gee whizz,' said the trader.

That night Dr. Macphail could not get to sleep till late, and when he heard the missionary come upstairs he looked at his watch. It was two o'clock. But even then he did not go to bed at once, for through the wooden partition that separated their rooms he heard him praying aloud, till he himself, exhausted, fell asleep.

When he saw him next morning he was surprised at his appearance. He was paler than ever, tired, but his eyes shone with an inhuman fire. It looked as though he were filled with an overwhelming joy.

'I want you to go down presently and see Sadie,' he said. 'I can't hope that her body is better, but her soul—her soul is transformed.'

The doctor was feeling wan and nervous.

'You were with her very late last night,' he said.

'Yes, she couldn't bear to have me leave her.'

'You look as pleased as punch,' the doctor said irritably.

Davidson's eyes shone with ecstasy.

'A great mercy has been vouchsafed me. Last night I was privileged to bring a lost soul to the loving arms of Jesus.'

Miss Thompson was again in the rocking-chair. The bed had not been made. The room was in disorder. She had not troubled to dress herself, but wore a dirty dressing-gown, and her hair was tied in a sluttish knot. She had given her face a dab with a wet towel, but it was all swollen and creased with crying. She looked a drab.

She raised her eyes dully when the doctor came in. She was cowed and broken.

'Where's Mr. Davidson?' she asked;

'He'll come presently if you want him,' answered Macphail acidly. 'I came here to see how you were.'

'Oh, I guess I'm OK. You needn't worry about that.'

'Have you had anything to eat?'

'Horn brought me some coffee.'

She looked anxiously at the door.

'D'you think he'll come down soon? I feel as if it wasn't so terrible when he's with me.'

'Are you still going on Tuesday?'

'Yes, he says I've got to go. Please tell him to come right along. You can't do me any good. He's the only one as can help me now.'

'Very well,' said Dr. Macphail.

During the next three days the missionary spent almost all his time with Sadie Thompson. He joined the others only to have his meals. Dr. Macphail noticed that he hardly ate.

'He's wearing himself out,' said Mrs. Davidson pitifully. 'He'll have a breakdown if he doesn't take care, but he won't spare himself.'

She herself was white and pale. She told Mrs. Macphail that she had no sleep. When the missionary came upstairs from Miss Thompson he prayed till he was exhausted, but even then he did not sleep for long. After an hour or two he got up and dressed himself, and went for a tramp along the bay. He had strange dreams.

'This morning he told me that he'd been dreaming about the mountains of Nebraska,' said Mrs. Davidson.

'That's curious,' said Dr. Macphail.

He remembered seeing them from the windows of the train when he crossed America. They were like huge mole-hills, rounded and smooth, an they rose from the plain abruptly. Dr. Macphail remembered how it struck him that they were like a woman's breasts.

Davidson's restlessness was intolerable even to himself. But he was buoyed up by a wonderful exhilaration. He was tearing out by the roots the last vestiges of sin that lurked in the hidden corners of that poor woman's heart. He read with her and prayed with her.

'It's wonderful,' he said to them one day at supper. 'It's a true rebirth. Her soul, which was black as night, is now pure and white like the new-fallen snow. I am humble and afraid. Her remorse for all her sins is beautiful. I am not worthy to touch the hem of her garment.'

'Have you the heart to send her back to San Francisco?' said the doctor. 'Three years in an American prison. I should have thought you might have saved her from that.'

'Ah, but don't you see? It's necessary. Do you think my heart doesn't bleed for her? I love her as I love my wife and my sister. All the time that she is in prison I shall suffer all the pain that she suffers.'

'Bunkum,' cried the doctor impatiently.

'You don't understand because you're blind. She's sinned, and she must suffer. I know what she'll endure. She'll be starved and tortured and humiliated. I want her to accept the punishment of man as a sacrifice to God. I want her to accept it joyfully. She has an opportunity which is offered to very few of us. God is very good and very merciful.'

Davidson's voice trembled with excitement. He could hardly articulate the words that tumbled passionately from his lips.

'All day I pray with her and when I leave her I pray again, I pray with all my might and main, so that Jesus may grant her this great mercy. I want to put in her heart the passionate desire to be punished so that at the end, even if I offered to let her go, she would refuse. I want her to feel that the bitter punishment of prison is the thank-offering that she places at the feet of our Blessed Lord, who gave his life for her.'

The days passed slowly. The whole household, intent on the wretched, tortured woman down-stairs, lived in a state of unnatural excitement. She was like a victim that was being prepared for the savage rites of a bloody idolatry. Her terror numbed her. She could not bear to let Davidson out of her sight; it was only when he was with her that she had courage, and she hung upon him with a slavish dependence. She cried a great deal, and she read the Bible, and prayed. Sometimes she was exhausted and apathetic. Then she did indeed look forward to her ordeal, for it seemed to offer an escape, direct and concrete, from the anguish she was enduring. She could not bear much longer the vague terrors which now assailed her. With her sins she had put aside all personal vanity, and she slopped about her room, unkempt and dishevelled, in her tawdry dressing-gown. She had not taken off her nightdress for four days, nor put on stockings. Her room was littered and untidy. Meanwhile the rain fell with a cruel persistence. You felt that the heavens must at last be empty of water, but still it poured down, straight and heavy, with a maddening iteration, on the iron roof. Everything was damp and clammy. There was mildew on the wail and on the boots that stood on the floor. Through the sleepless nights the mosquitoes droned their angry chant.

'If it would only stop raining for a single day it wouldn't be so bad,' said Dr. Macphail.

They all looked forward to the Tuesday when the boat for San Francisco was to arrive from Sydney. The strain was intolerable. So far as Dr. Macphail was concerned, his pity and his resentment were alike extinguished by his desire to be rid of the unfortunate woman. The inevitable must be accepted. He felt he would breathe more freely when the ship had sailed. Sadie Thompson was to be escorted on board by a clerk in the governor's office. This person called on the Monday evening and told Miss Thompson to be prepared at eleven in the morning. Davidson was with her.

'I'll see that everything is ready. I mean to come on board with her myself.'

Miss Thompson did not speak.

When Dr. Macphail blew out his candle and crawled cautiously under his mosquito curtains, he gave a sigh of relief.

'Well, thank God that's over. By this time to-morrow she'll

be gone.'

'Mrs. Davidson will be glad too. She says he's wearing himself to a shadow,' said Mrs. Macphail. 'She's a different woman.'

'Who?'

'Sadie, I should never have thought it possible. It makes one humble.'

Dr. Macphail did not answer, and presently he fell asleep. He was tired out, and he slept more soundly than usual.

He was awakened in the morning by a hand placed on his arm, and, starting up, saw Horn by the side of his bed. The trader put his finger on his mouth to prevent any exclamation from Dr. Macphail and beckoned to him to come. As a rule he wore shabby ducks, but now he was barefoot and wore only the *lava-lava* of the natives. He looked suddenly savage, and Dr. Macphail, getting out of bed, saw that he was heavily tattooed. Horn made him a sign to come on to the verandah. Dr. Macphail got out of bed and followed the trader out.

'Don't make a noise,' he whispered. 'You're wanted. Put on a coat and some shoes. Quick.'

Dr. Macphail's first thought was that something had happened to Miss Thompson.

'What is it? Shall I bring my instruments?'

'Hurry, please, hurry.'

Dr. Macphail crept back into the bedroom, put on a waterproof over his pyjamas, and a pair of rubber-soled shoes. He rejoined the trader, and together they tiptoed down the stairs. The door leading out to the road was open and at it were standing half a dozen natives.

'What is it?' repeated the doctor.

'Come along with me,' said Horn.

He walked out and the doctor followed him. The natives came after them in a little bunch. They crossed the road and came on to the beach. The doctor saw a group of natives standing round some object at the water's edge. They hurried along, a couple of dozen yards perhaps, and the natives opened out as the doctor came up. The trader pushed him forwards.

Then he saw, lying half in the water and half out, a dreadful object, the body of Davidson. Dr. Macphail bent down—he was not a man to lose his head in an emergency—and turned the body over. The throat was cut from ear to ear, and in the right hand was still the razor with which the deed was done.

'He's quite cold,' said the doctor. 'He must have been dead some time.'

'One of the boys saw him lying there on his way to work just now and came and told me. Do you think he did it himself?'

'Yes. Someone ought to go for the police.'

Horn said something in the native tongue, and two youths started off.

'We must leave him here till they come,' said the doctor.

'They mustn't take him into my house. I won't have him in my house.'

'You'll do what the authorities say,' replied the doctor sharply. 'In point of fact I expect they'll take him to the mortuary.'

They stood waiting where they were. The trader took a cigarette from a fold in his *lava-lava* and gave one to Dr. Macphail. They smoked while they stared at the corpse. Dr. Macphail could not understand.

'Why do you think he did it?' asked Horn.

The doctor shrugged his shoulders. In a little while native police came along, under the charge of a marine, with a stretcher, and immediately afterwards a couple of naval officers and a naval doctor. They managed everything in businesslike manner.

'What about the wife.' said one of the officers.

'Now that you've come I'll go back to the house and get some things on. I'll see that it's broken to her. She'd better not see him till he's been fixed up a little.'

'I guess that's right,' said the naval doctor. When Dr. Macphail went back he found his wife nearly dressed.

'Mrs. Davidson's in a dreadful state about her husband,' she said to him as soon as he appeared. 'He hasn't been to bed all night. She heard him leave Miss Thompson's room at two, but he went out. If he's been walking about since then he'll be absolutely dead.'

Dr. Macphail told her what had happened and asked her to break the news to Mrs. Davidson.

'But why did he do it?' she asked, horror-stricken.

'I don't know.'

'But I can't. I can't.'

'You must.'

She gave him a frightened look and went out. He heard her go into Mrs. Davidson's room. He waited a minute to gather himself together and then began to shave and wash. When he was dressed he sat down on the bed and waited for his wife. At last she came.

'She wants to see him,' she said.

'They've taken him to the mortuary. We'd better go down with her. How did she take it?'

'I think she's stunned. She didn't cry. But she's trembling like a leaf.'

'We'd better go at once.'

When they knocked at her door Mrs. Davidson came out. She was very pale, but dry-eyed. To the doctor she seemed unnaturally composed. No word was exchanged, and they set out in silence down the road. When they arrived at the mortuary Mrs. Davidson spoke.

'Let me go in and see him alone.'

They stood aside. A native opened a door for her and closed it behind her. They sat down and waited. One or two white men came and talked to them in undertones. Dr. Macphail told them again what he knew of the tragedy. At last the door was quietly opened and Mrs. Davidson came out. Silence fell upon them.

'I'm ready to go back now,' she said.

Her voice was hard and steady. Dr. Macphail could not understand the look in her eyes. Her pale face was very stern. They walked back slowly, never saying a word, and at last they came round the bend on the other side of which stood the ir house. Mrs. Davidson gave a gasp, and for moment they stopped still. An incredible sound assaulted their ears. The gramophone which had been silent for so long was playing, playing ragtime loud and harsh.

'What's that?' cried Mrs. Macphail with horror.

'Let's go on,' said Mrs. Davidson.

They walked up the steps and entered the hall. Miss Thompson was standing at her door, chatting with a sailor. A sudden change had taken place in her. She was no longer the cowed drudge of the last days. She was dressed in all her finery, in her white dress, with the high shiny boots over which her fat legs bulged in their cotton stockings; her hair was elaborately arranged; and she wore that enormous hat covered with gaudy flowers. Her face was painted, her eyebrows were boldly black, and her lips were scarlet. She held herself erect. She was the flaunting quean that they had known at first. As they came in she broke into a loud, jeering laugh; and then, when Mrs. Davidson involuntarily stopped, she collected the spittle in her mouth and spat. Mrs. Davidson cowered back, and two red spots rose suddenly to her cheeks. Then, covering her face with her hands, she broke away and ran quickly up the stairs. Dr. Macphail was outraged. He pushed past the woman into her room.

'What the devil are you doing?' he cried. 'Stop that, damned machine.'

He went up to it and tore the record off. She turned on him.

'Say, doc, you can that stuff with me. What the hell are you doin' in my room?'

'What do you mean?' he cried. 'What d'you mean?'

She gathered herself together. No one could describe the scorn of her expression or the contemptuous hatred she put into her answer.

'You men! You filthy, dirty pigs! You're all the same, all of you. Pigs! Pigs!'

Dr. Macphail gasped. He understood.

47

A HAUNTED HOUSE

Virginia Woolf

Whatever hour you woke there was a door shunting. From room to room they went, hand in hand, lifting here, opening there, making sure—a ghostly couple.

'Here we left it,' she said. And he added, 'Oh, but here too!' 'It's upstairs,' she murmured. 'And in the garden,' he whispered 'Quietly,' they said, 'or we shall wake them.'

But it wasn't that you woke us. Oh, no. They're looking for it; they're drawing the curtain, one might say, and so read on a page or two. 'Now they've found it,' one would be certain, stopping the pencil on the margin. And then, tired of reading, one might rise and see for oneself, the house all empty, the doors standing open, only the wood pigeons bubbling with content and the hum of the threshing machine sounding from the farm. 'What did I come in here for? What did I want to find?' My hands were empty. 'Perhaps it's upstairs then?' The apples were in the loft. And so down again, the garden still as ever, only the book had slipped into the grass.

But they had found it in the drawing room. Not that one could ever see them. The window panes reflected apples, reflected roses; all the leaves were green in the glass. If they moved in the drawing room, the apple only turned its yellow side. Yet, the moment after, if the door was opened, spread about the floor, hung upon the walls, pendant from the ceiling—what? My hands were empty. The shadow of a thrush crossed the carpet; from the deepest wells of silence the wood pigeon drew its bubble of sound. 'Safe, safe, safe,' the pulse of the house beat softly. 'The treasure buried; the room...' the pulse stopped short. Oh, was that the buried treasure?

A moment later the light had faded. Out in the garden then? But the trees spun darkness for a wandering beam of sun. So fine, so rare, coolly sunk beneath the surface the beam I sought always burnt behind the glass. Death was the glass; death was between us; coming to the woman first, hundreds of years ago, leaving the house, sealing all the windows; the rooms were darkened. He left it, left her, went North, went East, saw the stars turned in the Southern sky; sought the house, found it dropped beneath the Downs. 'Safe, safe, safe,' the pulse of the house beat gladly. 'The Treasure yours.'

The wind roars up the avenue. Trees stoop and bend this way and that. Moonbeams splash and spill wildly in the rain. But the beam of the lamp falls straight from the window. The candle burns stiff and still. Wandering through the house, opening the windows, whispering not to wake us, the ghostly couple seek their joy.

'Here we slept,' she says. And he adds, 'Kisses without number.' 'Waking in the morning—' 'Silver between the trees—' 'Upstairs—' 'In the garden—' 'When summer came—' 'In winter snowtime—' The doors go shutting far in the distance, gently knocking like the pulse of a heart.

Nearer they come; cease at the doorway. The wind falls, the rain slides silver down the glass. Our eyes darken; we hear no steps beside us; we see no lady spread her ghostly cloak. His hands shield the lantern. 'Look,' he breathes. 'Sound asleep. Love upon their lips.'

Stooping, holding their silver lamp above us, long they look and deeply. Long they pause. The wind drives straightly; the flame stoops slightly. Wild beams of moonlight cross both floor and wall, and, meeting, stain the faces bent; the faces pondering; the faces that search the sleepers and seek their hidden joy.

'Safe, safe, safe,' the heart of the house beats proudly. 'Long years—' he sighs. 'Again you found me.' 'Here,' she murmurs, 'sleeping; in the garden reading; laughing, rolling apples in the loft. Here we left our treasure—' Stooping, their light lifts the lids upon my eyes. 'Safe! safe! safe!' the pulse of the house beats wildly. Waking, I cry 'Oh, is this your buried treasure? The light in the heart.'

48

MY OWN TRUE GHOST STORY

Rudyard Kipling

As I came through the Desert thus it was—
As I came through the Desert.

—The City of Dreadful Night.

Somewhere in the Other World, where there are books and pictures and plays and shop-windows to look at, and thousands of men who spend their lives in building up all four, lives a gentleman who writes real stories about the real insides of people; and his name is Mr. Walter Besant. But he will insist upon treating his ghosts—he has published half a workshopful of them—with levity. He makes his ghost-seers talk familiarly, and, in some cases, flirt outrageously, with the phantoms. You may treat anything, from a Viceroy to a Vernacular Paper, with levity; but you must behave reverently toward a ghost, and particularly an Indian one.

There are, in this land, ghosts who take the form of fat, cold, pobby corpses, and hide in trees near the roadside till a traveler passes. Then they drop upon his neck and remain. There are also terrible ghosts of women who have died in child-bed. These wander along the pathways at dusk, or hide in the crops near a village, and call seductively. But to answer their call is death in this world and the next. Their feet are turned backward that all sober men may recognize them. There are ghosts of little children who have been thrown into wells. These haunt well-curbs and the fringes of jungles, and wail under the stars, or catch women by the wrist and beg to be taken up and carried. These and the corpse-ghosts, however, are only vernacular articles and do not attack Sahibs. No native ghost has yet been authentically reported to have frightened an Englishman; but many English ghosts have scared the life out of both white and black.

Nearly every other Station owns a ghost. There are said to be two at Simla, not counting the woman who blows the bellows at Syree dâk-bungalow on the Old Road; Mussoorie has a house haunted of a very lively Thing; a White Lady is supposed to do night-watchman round a house in Lahore; Dalhousie says that one of her houses 'repeats' on autumn evenings all the incidents of a horrible horse-and-precipice accident; Murree has a merry ghost, and, now that she has been swept by cholera, will have room for a sorrowful one; there are Officers Quarters in Mian Mir whose doors open without reason, and whose furniture is guaranteed to creak, not with the heat of June but with the weight of Invisibles who come to lounge in the chair; Peshawur possesses houses that none will willingly rent; and there is something—not fever—wrong with a big bungalow in Allahabad. The older Provinces simply bristle with haunted houses, and march phantom armies along their main thoroughfares.

Some of the dâk-bungalows on the Grand Trunk Road have handy little cemeteries in their compound—witnesses to the 'changes and chances of this mortal life' in the days when men drove from Calcutta to the Northwest. These bungalows are objectionable places to put up in. They are generally very old, always dirty, while the *khansamah* is as ancient as the bungalow. He either chatters senilely, or falls into the long trances of age. In both moods he is useless. If you get angry with him, he refers to some Sahib dead and buried these thirty years, and says that when he was in that Sahib's service not a *khansamah* in the Province could touch him. Then he jabbers and mows and trembles and fidgets among the dishes, and you repent of your irritation.

In these dâk-bungalows, ghosts are most likely to be found, and when found, they should be made a note of. Not long ago it was my business to live in dâk-bungalows. I never inhabited the same house for three nights running, and grew to be learned in the breed. I lived in Government-built ones with red brick walls and rail ceilings, an inventory of the furniture posted in every room, and an excited snake at the threshold to give welcome. I lived in 'converted' ones—old houses officiating as dâk-bungalows—where nothing was in its proper place and there wasn't even a fowl for dinner. I lived in second-hand palaces where the wind blew through open-work marble tracery just as uncomfortably as through a broken pane. I lived in dâk-bungalows where the last entry in the visitors' book was fifteen months old, and where they slashed off the curry-kid's head with a sword. It was my good-luck to meet all sorts of men, from sober traveling missionaries and deserters flying from British Regiments, to drunken loafers who threw whiskey bottles at all who passed; and my still greater good-fortune just to escape a maternity case. Seeing that a fair proportion of the tragedy of our lives out here acted itself in dâk-bungalows, I wondered that I had met no ghosts. A ghost that would voluntarily hang about a dâk-bungalow would be mad of course; but so many men have died mad in dâk-bungalows that there must be a fair percentage of lunatic ghosts.

In due time I found my ghost, or ghosts rather, for there were two of them. Up till that hour I had sympathized with Mr. Besant's method of handling them, as shown in 'The Strange Case of Mr. Lucraft and other Stories.' I am now in the Opposition.

We will call the bungalow Katmal dâk-bungalow. But that was the smallest part of the horror. A man with a sensitive hide has no right to sleep in dâk-bungalows. He should marry. Katmal dâk-bungalow was old and rotten and unrepaired. The floor was of worn brick, the walls were filthy, and the windows were nearly black with grime. It stood on a bypath largely used by native Sub-Deputy Assistants of all kinds, from Finance to Forests; but real Sahibs were rare. The *khansamah*, who was nearly bent double with old age, said so.

When I arrived, there was a fitful, undecided rain on the face of the land, accompanied by a restless wind, and every gust made a noise like the rattling of dry bones in the stiff toddy-palms outside. The *khansamah* completely lost his head on my arrival. He had served a Sahib once. Did I know that Sahib? He gave me the name of a well-known man who has been buried for more than a quarter of a century, and showed me an ancient daguerreotype of that man in his prehistoric youth. I had seen a steel engraving of him at the head of a double volume of Memoirs a month before, and I felt ancient beyond telling.

The day shut in and the *khansamah* went to get me food. He did not go through the pretence of calling it '*khana*'—man's victuals. He said '*ratub*,' and that means, among other things, 'grub'—dog's rations. There was no insult in his choice of the term. He had forgotten the other word, I suppose.

While he was cutting up the dead bodies of animals, I settled myself down, after exploring the dâk-bungalow. There were three rooms, beside my own, which was a corner kennel, each giving into the other through dingy white doors fastened with long iron bars. The bungalow was a very solid one, but the partition-walls of the rooms were almost jerry-built in their flimsiness. Every step or bang of a trunk echoed from my room down the other three, and every footfall came back tremulously from the far walls. For this reason I shut the door. There were no lamps—only candles in long glass shades. An oil wick was set in the bath-room.

For bleak, unadulterated misery that dâk-bungalow was the worst of the many that I had ever set foot in. There was no fireplace, and the windows would not open; so a brazier of charcoal would have been useless. The rain and the wind splashed and gurgled and moaned round the house, and the toddy-palms rattled and roared. Half a dozen jackals went through the compound singing, and a hyena stood afar off and mocked them. A hyena would convince a Sadducee of the Resurrection of the Dead—the worst sort of Dead. Then came the *ratub*—a curious meal, half native and half English in composition—with the old *khansamah* babbling behind my chair about dead and gone English people, and the wind-blown candles playing shadow-bo-peep with the bed and the mosquito-curtains. It was just the sort of dinner and evening to make a man think of every single one of his past sins, and of all the others that he intended to commit if he lived.

Sleep, for several hundred reasons, was not easy. The lamp in the bath-room threw the most absurd shadows into the room, and the wind was beginning to talk nonsense.

Just when the reasons were drowsy with blood-sucking I heard the regular—'Let-us-take-and-heave-him-over' grunt of doolie-bearers in the compound. First one doolie came in, then a second, and then a third. I heard the doolies dumped on the ground, and the shutter in front of my door shook. 'That's some one trying to come in,' I said. But no one spoke, and I persuaded myself that it was the gusty wind. The shutter of the room next to mine was attacked, flung back, and the inner door opened, 'That's some Sub-Deputy Assistant,' I said, 'and he has brought his friends with him. Now they'll talk and spit and smoke for an hour.'

But there were no voices and no footsteps, No one was putting his luggage into the next room. The door shut, and I thanked Providence that I was to be left in peace. But I was curious to know where the doolies had gone. I got out of bed and looked into the darkness. There was never a sign of a doolie. Just as I was getting into bed again, I heard, in the next room, the sound that no man in his senses can possibly mistake—the whir of a billiard ball down the length of the slates when the striker is stringing for break. No other sound is like it. A minute afterward there was another whir, and I got into bed. I was not frightened—indeed I was not. I was very curious to know what had become of the doolies. I jumped into bed for that reason.

Next minute I heard the double click of a cannon and my hair sat up. It is a mistake to say that hair stands up. The skin of the head tightens and you can feel a faint, prickly bristling all ever the scalp. That is the hair sitting up.

There was a whir and a click, and both sounds could only

have been made by one thing—a billiard ball. I argued the matter out at great length with myself; and the more I argued the less probable it seemed that one bed, one table, and two chairs—all the furniture of the room next to mine—could so exactly duplicate the sounds of a game of billiards. After another cannon, a three-cushion one to judge by the whir, I argued no more. I had found my ghost and would have given worlds to have escaped from that dâk-bungalow. I listened, and with each listen the game grew clearer. There was whir on whir and click on click. Sometimes there was a double click and a whir and another click. Beyond any sort of doubt, people were playing billiards in the next room. And the next room was not big enough to hold a billiard table!

Between the pauses of the wind I heard the game go forward—stroke after stroke. I tried to believe that I could not hear voices; but that attempt was a failure.

Do you know what fear is? Not ordinary fear of insult, injury or death, but abject, quivering dread of something that you cannot see—fear that dries the inside of the mouth and half of the throat—fear that makes you sweat on the palms of the hands, and gulp in order to keep the uvula at work? This is a fine Fear—a great cowardice, and must be felt to be appreciated. The very improbability of billiards in a dâk-bungalow proved the reality of the thing. No man—drunk or sober—could imagine a game a billiards, or invent the spitting crack of a 'screw-cannon.'

A severe course of dâk-bungalows has this disadvantage—it breeds infinite credulity. If a man said to a confirmed dâk-bungalow-haunter:—'There is a corpse in the next room, and there's a mad girl in the next but one, and the woman and man on that camel have just eloped from a place sixty miles away,' the hearer would not disbelieve because he would know that nothing is too wild, grotesque, or horrible to happen in a dâk-bungalow.

This credulity, unfortunately extends to ghosts. A rational person fresh from his own house would have turned on his side and slept. I did not. So surely as I was given up as a bad carcass by the scores of things in the bed because the bulk of my blood was in my heart, so surely did I hear every stroke of a long game at billiards played in the echoing room behind the iron-barred door. My dominant fear was that the players might want a marker. It was an absurd fear; because creatures who could play in the dark would be above such superfluities. I only know that that was my terror; and it was real.

After a long long while, the game stopped, and the door banged, I slept because I was dead tired. Otherwise I should have preferred to have kept awake. Not for everything in Asia would I have dropped the door-bar and peered into the dark of the next room.

When the morning came, I considered that I had done well and wisely, and inquired for the means of departure.

'By the way, *khansamah*,' I said, 'what were those three doolies doing in my compound in the night?'

'There were no doolies,' said the *khansamah*.

I went into the next room and the daylight streamed through the open door. I was immensely brave. I would, at that hour, have played Black Pool with the owner of the big Black Pool down below.

'Has this place always been a dâk-bungalow?' I asked.

'No,' said the *khansamah*. 'Ten or twenty years ago, I have forgotten how long, it was a billiard-room.'

'A how much?'

'A billiard-room for the Sahibs who built the Railway. I was *khansamah* then in the big house where all the Railway-Sahibs lived, and I used to come across with brandy-*shrab*. These three rooms were all one, and they held a big table on which the Sahibs played every evening. But the Sahibs are all dead now, and the Railway runs, you say, nearly to Kabul.'

'Do you remember anything about the Sahibs?'

'It is long ago, but I remember that one Sahib, a fat man and always angry, was playing here one night, and he said to me:—'Mangal Khan, brandy-*pani* do,' and I filled the glass, and he bent over the table to strike, and his head fell lower and lower till it hit the table, and his spectacles came off, and when we—the Sahibs and I myself—ran to lift him he was dead. I helped to carry him out. Aha, he was a strong Sahib! But he is dead and I, old Mangal Khan, am still living, by your favor.'

That was more than enough! I had my ghost—a first-hand, authenticated article. I would write to the Society for Psychical Research—I would paralyze the Empire with the news! But I would, first of all, put eighty miles of assessed crop-land between myself and that dâk-bungalow before nightfall. The Society might send their regular agent to investigate later on.

I went into my own room and prepared to pack after noting down the facts of the case. As I smoked I heard the game begin again—with a miss in balk this time, for the whir was a short one.

The door was open and I could see into the room. *Click-click*! That was a cannon. I entered the room without fear, for there was sunlight within and a fresh breeze without. The unseen game was going on at a tremendous rate. And well it might, when a restless little rat was running to and fro inside the dingy ceiling-cloth, and a piece of loose window-sash was making fifty breaks off the window-bolt as it shook in the breeze!

Impossible to mistake the sound of billiard balls! Impossible to mistake the whir of a ball over the slate! But I was to be excused. Even when I shut my enlightened eyes the sound was marvelously like that of a fast game.

Entered angrily the faithful partner of my sorrows, Kadir Baksh.

'This bungalow is very bad and low-caste! No wonder the Presence was disturbed and is speckled. Three sets of doolie-bearers came to the bungalow late last night when I was sleeping outside, and said that it was their custom to rest in the rooms set apart for the English people! What honor has the *khansamah*? They tried to enter, but I told them to go. No wonder, if these *Oorias* have been here, that the Presence is sorely spotted. It is shame, and the work of a dirty man!'

Kadir Baksh did not say that he had taken from each gang two annas for rent in advance, and then, beyond my earshot, had beaten them with the big green umbrella whose use I could never before divine. But Kadir Baksh has no notions of morality.

There was an interview with the *khansamah*, but as he promptly lost his head, wrath gave place to pity, and pity led to a long conversation, in the course of which he put the fat Engineer-Sahib's tragic death in three separate stations—two of them fifty miles away. The third shift was to Calcutta, and there the Sahib died while driving a dog-cart.

If I had encouraged him the *khansamah* would have wandered all through Bengal with his corpse.

I did not go away as soon as I intended. I stayed for the night, while the wind and the rat and the sash and the window-bolt played a ding-dong 'hundred and fifty up.' Then the wind ran out and the billiards stopped, and I felt that I had ruined my one genuine, hall-marked ghost story.

Had I only stopped at the proper time, I could have made *anything* out of it.

That was the bitterest thought of all!

49

THE HORLA

Guy de Maupassant

May 8. What a lovely day! I have spent all the morning lying on the grass in front of my house, under the enormous plantain tree which covers and shades and shelters the whole of it. I like this part of the country; I am fond of living here because I am attached to it by deep roots, the profound and delicate roots which attach a man to the soil on which his ancestors were born and died, to their traditions, their usages, their food, the local expressions, the peculiar language of the peasants, the smell of the soil, the hamlets, and to the atmosphere itself.

I love the house in which I grew up. From my windows I can see the Seine, which flows by the side of my garden, on the other side of the road, almost through my grounds, the great and wide Seine, which goes to Rouen and Havre, and which is covered with boats passing to and fro.

On the left, down yonder, lies Rouen, populous Rouen with its blue roofs massing under pointed, Gothic towers. Innumerable are they, delicate or broad, dominated by the spire of the cathedral, full of bells which sound through the blue air on fine mornings, sending their sweet and distant iron clang to me, their metallic sounds, now stronger and now weaker, according as the wind is strong or light.

What a delicious morning it was! About eleven o'clock, a long line of boats drawn by a steam-tug, as big a fly, and which scarcely puffed while emitting its thick smoke, passed my gate.

After two English schooners, whose red flags fluttered toward the sky, there came a magnificent Brazilian three-master; it was perfectly white and wonderfully clean and shining. I saluted it, I hardly know why, except that the sight of the vessel gave me great pleasure.

May 12. I have had a slight feverish attack for the last few days, and I feel ill, or rather I feel low-spirited.

Whence come those mysterious influences which change our happiness into discouragement, and our self-confidence into diffidence? One might almost say that the air, the invisible air, is full of unknowable Forces, whose mysterious presence we have to endure. I wake up in the best of spirits, with an inclination to sing in my heart. Why? I go down by the side of the water, and suddenly, after walking a short distance, I return home wretched, as if some misfortune were awaiting me there. Why? Is it a cold shiver which, passing over my skin, has upset my nerves and given me a fit of low spirits? Is it the form of the clouds, or the tints of the sky, or the colors of the surrounding objects which are so changeable, which have troubled my thoughts as they passed before my eyes? Who can tell? Everything that surrounds us, everything that we see without looking at it, everything that we touch without knowing it, everything that we handle without feeling it, everything that we meet without clearly distinguishing it, has a rapid, surprising, and inexplicable effect upon us and upon our organs, and through them on our ideas and on our being itself.

How profound that mystery of the Invisible is! We cannot fathom it with our miserable senses: our eyes are unable to perceive what is either too small or too great, too near to or too far from us; we can see neither the inhabitants of a star nor of a drop of water; our ears deceive us, for they transmit to us the vibrations of the air in sonorous notes. Our senses are fairies who work the miracle of changing that movement into noise, and by that metamorphosis give birth to music, which makes the mute agitation of nature a harmony. So with our sense of smell, which is weaker than that of a dog, and so with our sense of taste, which can scarcely distinguish the age of a wine!

Oh! If we only had other organs which could work other miracles in our favor, what a number of fresh things we might discover around us!

May 16. I am ill, decidedly! I was so well last month! I am feverish, horribly feverish, or rather I am in a state of feverish enervation, which makes my mind suffer as much as my body. I have without ceasing the horrible sensation of some danger threatening me, the apprehension of some coming misfortune or of approaching death, a presentiment which is no doubt, an attack of some illness still unnamed, which germinates in the flesh and in the blood.

May 18. I have just come from consulting my medical man, for I can no longer get any sleep. He found that my pulse was high, my eyes dilated, my nerves highly strung, but no alarming symptoms. I must have a course of shower baths and of bromide of potassium.

May 25. No change! My state is really very peculiar. As the evening comes on, an incomprehensible feeling of disquietude seizes me, just as if night concealed some terrible menace toward me. I dine quickly, and then try to read, but I do not understand the words, and can scarcely distinguish the letters. Then I walk up and down my drawing-room, oppressed by a feeling of confused and irresistible fear, a fear of sleep and a fear of my bed.

About ten o'clock I go up to my room. As soon as I have entered I lock and bolt the door. I am frightened—of what? Up till the present time I have been frightened of nothing. I open my cupboards, and look under my bed; I listen—I listen—to what? How strange it is that a simple feeling of discomfort, of impeded or heightened circulation, perhaps the irritation of a nervous center, a slight congestion, a small disturbance in the imperfect and delicate functions of our living machinery, can turn the most light-hearted of men into a melancholy one, and make a coward of the bravest? Then, I go to bed, and I wait for sleep as a man might wait for the executioner. I wait for its coming with dread, and my heart beats and my legs tremble, while my whole body shivers beneath the warmth of the bedclothes, until the moment when I suddenly fall asleep, as a man throws himself into a pool of stagnant water in order to drown. I do not feel this perfidious sleep coming over me as I used to, but a sleep which is close to me and watching me, which is going to seize me by the head, to close my eyes and annihilate me.

I sleep—a long time—two or three hours perhaps—then a dream—no—a nightmare lays hold on me. I feel that I am in bed and asleep—I feel it and I know it—and I feel also that somebody is coming close to me, is looking at me, touching me, is getting on to my bed, is kneeling on my chest, is taking my neck between his hands and squeezing it—squeezing it with all his might in order to strangle me.

I struggle, bound by that terrible powerlessness which paralyzes us in our dreams; I try to cry out—but I cannot; I want to move—I cannot; I try, with the most violent efforts and out of breath, to turn over and throw off this being which is crushing and suffocating me—I cannot!

And then suddenly I wake up, shaken and bathed in perspiration; I light a candle and find that I am alone, and after that crisis, which occurs every night, I at length fall asleep and slumber tranquilly till morning.

June 2. My state has grown worse. What is the matter with me? The bromide does me no good, and the shower-baths have no effect whatever. Sometimes, in order to tire myself out, though I am fatigued enough already, I go for a walk in the forest of Roumare. I used to think at first that the fresh light and soft air, impregnated with the odor of herbs and leaves, would instill new life into my veins and impart fresh energy to my heart. One day I turned into a broad ride in the wood, and then I diverged toward La Bouille, through a narrow path, between two rows of exceedingly tall trees, which placed a thick, green, almost black roof between the sky and me.

A sudden shiver ran through me, not a cold shiver, but a shiver of agony, and so I hastened my steps, uneasy at being alone in the wood, frightened stupidly and without reason, at the profound solitude. Suddenly it seemed as if I were being followed, that somebody was walking at my heels, close, quite close to me, near enough to touch me.

I turned round suddenly, but I was alone. I saw nothing behind me except the straight, broad ride, empty and bordered by high trees, horribly empty; on the other side also it extended until it was lost in the distance, and looked just the same—terrible.

I closed my eyes. Why? And then I began to turn round on one heel very quickly, just like a top. I nearly fell down, and opened my eyes; the trees were dancing round me and the earth heaved; I was obliged to sit down. Then, ah! I no longer remembered how I had come! What a strange idea! What a strange, strange idea! I did not the least know. I started off to the right, and got back into the avenue which had led me into the middle of the forest.

June 3. I have had a terrible night. I shall go away for a few weeks, for no doubt a journey will set me up again.

July 2. I have come back, quite cured, and have had a most delightful trip into the bargain. I have been to Mont Saint-Michel, which I had not seen before.

What a sight, when one arrives as I did, at Avranches toward the end of the day! The town stands on a hill, and I was taken into the public garden at the extremity of the town. I uttered a cry of astonishment. An extraordinarily large bay lay extended before me, as far as my eyes could reach, between two hills which were lost to sight in the mist; and in the middle of this immense yellow bay, under a clear, golden sky, a peculiar hill rose up, somber and pointed in the midst of the sand. The sun had just disappeared, and under the still flaming sky stood out the outline of that fantastic rock which bears on its summit a picturesque monument.

At daybreak I went to it. The tide was low, as it had been the night before, and I saw that wonderful abbey rise up before me as I approached it. After several hours' walking, I reached the enormous mass of rock which supports the little town, dominated by the great church. Having climbed the steep and narrow street, I entered the most wonderful Gothic building that has ever been erected to God on earth, large as a town, and full of low rooms which seem buried beneath vaulted roofs, and of lofty galleries supported by delicate columns.

I entered this gigantic granite jewel, which is as light in its effect as a bit of lace and is covered with towers, with slender belfries to which spiral staircases ascend. The flying buttresses raise strange heads that bristle with chimeras, with devils, with fantastic animals, with monstrous flowers, are joined together by finely carved arches, to the blue sky by day, and to the black sky by night.

When I had reached the summit. I said to the monk who accompanied me: 'Father, how happy you must be here!' And he replied: 'It is very windy, Monsieur'; and so we began to talk while watching the rising tide, which ran over the sand and covered it with a steel cuirass.

And then the monk told me stories, all the old stories belonging to the place—legends, nothing but legends.

One of them struck me forcibly. The country people, those belonging to the Mornet, declare that at night one can hear talking going on in the sand, and also that two goats bleat, one with a strong, the other with a weak voice. Incredulous people declare that it is nothing but the screaming of the sea birds, which occasionally resembles bleatings, and occasionally human lamentations; but belated fishermen swear that they have met an old shepherd, whose cloak covered head they can never see, wandering on the sand, between two tides, round the little town placed so far out of the world. They declare he is guiding and walking before a he-goat with a man's face and a she-goat with a woman's face, both with white hair, who talk incessantly, quarreling in a strange language, and then suddenly cease talking in order to bleat with all their might.

'Do you believe it?' I asked the monk. 'I scarcely know,' he replied; and I continued: 'If there are other beings besides ourselves on this earth, how comes it that we have not known it for so long a time, or why have you not seen them? How is it that I have not seen them?'

He replied: 'Do we see the hundred-thousandth part of what exists? Look here; there is the wind, which is the strongest force in nature. It knocks down men, and blows down buildings, uproots trees, raises the sea into mountains of water, destroys cliffs and casts great ships on to the breakers; it kills, it whistles, it sighs, it roars. But have you ever seen it, and can you see it? Yet it exists for all that.'

I was silent before this simple reasoning. That man was a philosopher, or perhaps a fool; I could not say which exactly, so I held my tongue. What he had said had often been in my own thoughts.

July 3. I have slept badly; certainly there is some feverish influence here, for my coachman is suffering in the same way as I am. When I went back home yesterday, I noticed his singular paleness, and I asked him: 'What is the matter with you, Jean?'

'The matter is that I never get any rest, and my nights devour my days. Since your departure, Monsieur, there has been a spell over me.'

However, the other servants are all well, but I am very frightened of having another attack, myself.

July 4. I am decidedly taken again; for my old nightmares have returned. Last night I felt somebody leaning on me who was sucking my life from between my lips with his mouth. Yes, he was sucking it out of my neck like a leech would have done. Then he got up, satiated, and I woke up, so beaten, crushed, and annihilated that I could not move. If this continues for a few days, I shall certainly go away again.

July 5. Have I lost my reason? What has happened? What I saw last night is so strange that my head wanders when I think of it!

As I do now every evening, I had locked my door; then, being thirsty, I drank half a glass of water, and I accidentally noticed that the water-bottle was full up to the cut-glass stopper.

Then I went to bed and fell into one of my terrible sleeps,

from which I was aroused in about two hours by a still more terrible shock.

Picture to yourself a sleeping man who is being murdered, who wakes up with a knife in his chest, a gurgling in his throat, is covered with blood, can no longer breathe, is going to die and does not understand anything at all about it—there you have it.

Having recovered my senses, I was thirsty again, so I lighted a candle and went to the table on which my water-bottle was. I lifted it up and tilted it over my glass, but nothing came out. It was empty! It was completely empty! At first I could not understand it at all; then suddenly I was seized by such a terrible feeling that I had to sit down, or rather fall into a chair! Then I sprang up with a bound to look about me; then I sat down again, overcome by astonishment and fear, in front of the transparent crystal bottle! I looked at it with fixed eyes, trying to solve the puzzle, and my hands trembled! Somebody had drunk the water, but who? I? I without any doubt. It could surely only be I? In that case I was a somnambulist—was living, without knowing it, that double, mysterious life which makes us doubt whether there are not two beings in us—whether a strange, unknowable, and invisible being does not, during our moments of mental and physical torpor, animate the inert body, forcing it to a more willing obedience than it yields to ourselves.

Oh! Who will understand my horrible agony? Who will understand the emotion of a man sound in mind, wide-awake, full of sense, who looks in horror at the disappearance of a little water while he was asleep, through the glass of a water-bottle! And I remained sitting until it was daylight, without venturing to go to bed again.

July 6. I am going mad. Again all the contents of my water-bottle have been drunk during the night; or rather I have drunk it!

But is it I? Is it I? Who could it be? Who? Oh! God! Am I going mad? Who will save me?

July 10. I have just been through some surprising ordeals. Undoubtedly I must be mad! And yet!

On July 6, before going to bed, I put some wine, milk, water, bread, and strawberries on my table. Somebody drank—I drank—all the water and a little of the milk, but neither the wine, nor the bread, nor the strawberries were touched.

On the seventh of July I renewed the same experiment, with the same results, and on July 8 I left out the water and the milk and nothing was touched.

Lastly, on July 9 I put only water and milk on my table, taking care to wrap up the bottles in white muslin and to tie down the stoppers. Then I rubbed my lips, my beard, and my hands with pencil lead, and went to bed.

Deep slumber seized me, soon followed by a terrible awakening. I had not moved, and my sheets were not marked. I rushed to the table. The muslin round the bottles remained intact; I undid the string, trembling with fear. All the water had been drunk, and so had the milk! Ah! Great God! I must start for Paris immediately.

July 12. Paris. I must have lost my head during the last few days! I must be the plaything of my enervated imagination, unless I am really a somnambulist, or I have been brought under the power of one of those influences—hypnotic suggestion, for example—which are known to exist, but have hitherto been inexplicable. In any case, my mental state bordered on madness, and twenty-four hours of Paris sufficed to restore me to my equilibrium.

Yesterday after doing some business and paying some visits, which instilled fresh and invigorating mental air into me, I wound up my evening at the Theatre Francais. A drama by Alexander Dumas the Younger was being acted, and his brilliant and powerful play completed my cure. Certainly solitude is dangerous for active minds. We need men who can think and can talk, around us. When we are alone for a long time, we people space with phantoms.

I returned along the boulevards to my hotel in excellent spirits. Amid the jostling of the crowd I thought, not without irony, of my terrors and surmises of the previous week, because

I believed, yes, I believed, that an invisible being lived beneath my roof. How weak our mind is; how quickly it is terrified and unbalanced as soon as we are confronted with a small, incomprehensible fact. Instead of dismissing the problem with: 'We do not understand because we cannot find the cause,' we immediately imagine terrible mysteries and supernatural powers.

July 14. Fete of the Republic. I walked through the streets, and the crackers and flags amused me like a child. Still, it is very foolish to make merry on a set date, by Government decree. People are like a flock of sheep, now steadily patient, now in ferocious revolt. Say to it: 'Amuse yourself,' and it amuses itself. Say to it: 'Go and fight with your neighbor,' and it goes and fights. Say to it: 'Vote for the Emperor,' and it votes for the Emperor; then say to it: 'Vote for the Republic,' and it votes for the Republic.

Those who direct it are stupid, too; but instead of obeying men they obey principles, a course which can only be foolish, ineffective, and false, for the very reason that principles are ideas which are considered as certain and unchangeable, whereas in this world one is certain of nothing, since light is an illusion and noise is deception.

July 16. I saw some things yesterday that troubled me very much. I was dining at my cousin's, Madame Sable, whose husband is colonel of the Seventy-sixth Chasseurs at Limoges. There were two young women there, one of whom had married a medical man, Dr. Parent, who devotes himself a great deal to nervous diseases and to the extraordinary manifestations which just now experiments in hypnotism and suggestion are producing.

He related to us at some length the enormous results obtained by English scientists and the doctors of the medical school at Nancy, and the facts which he adduced appeared to me so strange, that I declared that I was altogether incredulous.

'We are,' he declared, 'on the point of discovering one of the most important secrets of nature, I mean to say, one of its most important secrets on this earth, for assuredly there are some up in the stars, yonder, of a different kind of importance. Ever since man has thought, since he has been able to express and write down his thoughts, he has felt himself close to a mystery which is impenetrable to his coarse and imperfect senses, and he endeavors to supplement the feeble penetration of his organs by the efforts of his intellect. As long as that intellect remained in its elementary stage, this intercourse with invisible spirits assumed forms which were commonplace though terrifying. Thence sprang the popular belief in the supernatural, the legends of wandering spirits, of fairies, of gnomes, of ghosts, I might even say the conception of God, for our ideas of the Workman-Creator, from whatever religion they may have come down to us, are certainly the most mediocre, the stupidest, and the most unacceptable inventions that ever sprang from the frightened brain of any human creature. Nothing is truer than what Voltaire says: "If God made man in His own image, man has certainly paid Him back again."

'But for rather more than a century, men seem to have had a presentiment of something new. Mesmer and some others have put us on an unexpected track, and within the last two or three years especially, we have arrived at results really surprising.'

My cousin, who is also very incredulous, smiled, and Dr. Parent said to her: 'Would you like me to try and send you to sleep, Madame?'

'Yes, certainly.'

She sat down in an easy-chair, and he began to look at her fixedly, as if to fascinate her. I suddenly felt myself somewhat discomposed; my heart beat rapidly and I had a choking feeling in my throat. I saw that Madame Sable's eyes were growing heavy, her mouth twitched, and her bosom heaved, and at the end of ten minutes she was asleep.

'Go behind her,' the doctor said to me; so I took a seat behind her. He put a visiting-card into her hands, and said to her: 'This is a looking-glass; what do you see in it?'

She replied: 'I see my cousin.'

'What is he doing?'

'He is twisting his mustache.'

'And now?'

'He is taking a photograph out of his pocket.'

'Whose photograph is it?'

'His own.'

That was true, for the photograph had been given me that same evening at the hotel.

'What is his attitude in this portrait?'

'He is standing up with his hat in his hand.'

She saw these things in that card, in that piece of white pasteboard, as if she had seen them in a looking-glass.

The young women were frightened, and exclaimed: 'That is quite enough! Quite, quite enough!'

But the doctor said to her authoritatively: 'You will get up at eight o'clock to-morrow morning; then you will go and call on your cousin at his hotel and ask him to lend you the five thousand francs which your husband asks of you, and which he will ask for when he sets out on his coming journey.'

Then he woke her up.

On returning to my hotel, I thought over this curious *seance* and I was assailed by doubts, not as to my cousin's absolute and undoubted good faith, for I had known her as well as if she had been my own sister ever since she was a child, but as to a possible trick on the doctor's part. Had not he, perhaps, kept a glass hidden in his hand, which he showed to the young woman in her sleep at the same time as he did the card? Professional conjurers do things which are just as singular.

However, I went to bed, and this morning, at about half past eight, I was awakened by my footman, who said to me: 'Madame Sable has asked to see you immediately, Monsieur.' I dressed hastily and went to her.

She sat down in some agitation, with her eyes on the floor, and without raising her veil said to me: 'My dear cousin, I am going to ask a great favor of you.'

'What is it, cousin?'

'I do not like to tell you, and yet I must. I am in absolute want of five thousand francs.'

'What, you?'

'Yes, I, or rather my husband, who has asked me to procure them for him.'

I was so stupefied that I hesitated to answer. I asked myself whether she had not really been making fun of me with Dr. Parent, if it were not merely a very well-acted farce which had been got up beforehand. On looking at her attentively, however, my doubts disappeared. She was trembling with grief, so painful was this step to her, and I was sure that her throat was full of sobs.

I knew that she was very rich and so I continued: 'What! Has not your husband five thousand francs at his disposal? Come, think. Are you sure that he commissioned you to ask me for them?'

She hesitated for a few seconds, as if she were making a great effort to search her memory, and then she replied: 'Yes—yes, I am quite sure of it.'

'He has written to you?'

She hesitated again and reflected, and I guessed the torture of her thoughts. She did not know. She only knew that she was to borrow five thousand francs of me for her husband. So she told a lie.

'Yes, he has written to me.'

'When, pray? You did not mention it to me yesterday.'

'I received his letter this morning.'

'Can you show it to me?'

'No; no—no—it contained private matters, things too personal to ourselves. I burned it.'

'So your husband runs into debt?'

She hesitated again, and then murmured: 'I do not know.'

Thereupon I said bluntly: 'I have not five thousand francs at my disposal at this moment, my dear cousin.'

She uttered a cry, as if she were in pair; and said: 'Oh! oh! I beseech you, I beseech you to get them for me.'

She got excited and clasped her hands as if she were praying to me! I heard her voice change its tone; she wept and sobbed, harassed and dominated by the irresistible order that she had received.

'Oh! oh! I beg you to—if you knew what I am suffering—I want them to-day.'

I had pity on her: 'You shall have them by and by, I swear to you.'

'Oh! thank you! thank you! How kind you are.'

I continued: 'Do you remember what took place at your house last night?'

'Yes.'

'Do you remember that Dr. Parent sent you to sleep?'

'Yes.'

'Oh! Very well then; he ordered you to come to me this morning to borrow five thousand francs, and at this moment you are obeying that suggestion.'

She considered for a few moments, and then replied: 'But as it is my husband who wants them—'

For a whole hour I tried to convince her, but could not succeed, and when she had gone I went to the doctor. He was just going out, and he listened to me with a smile, and said: 'Do you believe now?'

'Yes, I cannot help it.'

'Let us go to your cousin's.'

She was already resting on a couch, overcome with fatigue. The doctor felt her pulse, looked at her for some time with one hand raised toward her eyes, which she closed by degrees under the irresistible power of this magnetic influence. When she was asleep, he said:

'Your husband does not require the five thousand francs any longer! You must, therefore, forget that you asked your cousin to lend them to you, and, if he speaks to you about it, you will not understand him.'

Then he woke her up, and I took out a pocket-book and said: 'Here is what you asked me for this morning, my dear cousin.' But she was so surprised, that I did not venture to persist; nevertheless, I tried to recall the circumstance to her, but she denied it vigorously, thought that I was making fun of her, and in the end, very nearly lost her temper.

There! I have just come back, and I have not been able to eat any lunch, for this experiment has altogether upset me.

July 19. Many people to whom I have told the adventure have laughed at me. I no longer know what to think. The wise man says: Perhaps?

July 21. I dined at Bougival, and then I spent the evening at a boatmen's ball. Decidedly everything depends on place and surroundings. It would be the height of folly to believe in the supernatural on the *ile de la Grenouilliere*. But on the top of Mont Saint-Michel or in India, we are terribly under the influence of our surroundings. I shall return home next week.

July 30. I came back to my own house yesterday. Everything is going on well.

August 2. Nothing fresh; it is splendid weather, and I spend my days in watching the Seine flow past.

August 4. Quarrels among my servants. They declare that the glasses are broken in the cupboards at night. The footman accuses the cook, she accuses the needlewoman, and the latter accuses the other two. Who is the culprit? It would take a clever person to tell.

August 6. This time, I am not mad. I have seen—I have seen—I have seen!—I can doubt no longer—I have seen it!

I was walking at two o'clock among my rose-trees, in the full sunlight—in the walk bordered by autumn roses which are beginning to fall. As I stopped to look at a *Geant de Bataille*, which had three splendid blooms, I distinctly saw the stalk of one of the roses bend close to me, as if an invisible hand had bent it, and then break, as if that hand had picked it! Then the flower raised itself, following the curve which a hand would have described in carrying it toward a mouth, and remained suspended in the transparent air, alone and motionless, a terrible red spot, three yards from my eyes. In desperation I rushed at it to take it! I found nothing; it had disappeared. Then I was seized with furious rage against myself, for it is not wholesome for a reasonable and serious man to have such hallucinations.

But was it a hallucination? I turned to look for the stalk, and I found it immediately under the bush, freshly broken, between the two other roses which remained on the branch. I returned home, then, with a much disturbed mind; for I am certain now, certain as I am of the alternation of day and night, that there exists close to me an invisible being who lives on milk and on water, who can touch objects, take them and change their places; who is, consequently, endowed with a material nature, although imperceptible to sense, and who lives as I do, under my roof.

August 7. I slept tranquilly. He drank the water out of my decanter, but did not disturb my sleep.

I ask myself whether I am mad. As I was walking just now in the sun by the riverside, doubts as to my own sanity arose in me; not vague doubts such as I have had hitherto, but precise and absolute doubts. I have seen mad people, and I have known some who were quite intelligent, lucid, even clear-sighted in every concern of life, except on one point. They could speak clearly, readily, profoundly on everything; till their thoughts were caught in the breakers of their delusions and went to pieces there, were dispersed and swamped in that furious and terrible sea of fogs and squalls which is called *madness*.

I certainly should think that I was mad, absolutely mad, if I were not conscious that I knew my state, if I could not fathom it and analyze it with the most complete lucidity. I should, in fact, be a reasonable man laboring under a hallucination. Some unknown disturbance must have been excited in my brain, one of those disturbances which physiologists of the present day try to note and to fix precisely, and that disturbance must have caused a profound gulf in my mind and in the order and logic of my ideas. Similar phenomena occur in dreams, and lead us through the most unlikely phantasmagoria, without causing us any surprise, because our verifying apparatus and our sense of control have gone to sleep, while our imaginative faculty wakes and works. Was it not possible that one of the imperceptible keys of the cerebral finger-board had been paralyzed in me? Some men lose the recollection of proper names, or of verbs, or of numbers, or merely of dates, in consequence of an accident. The localization of all the avenues of thought has been accomplished nowadays; what, then, would there be surprising in the fact that my faculty of controlling the unreality of certain hallucinations should be destroyed for the time being?

I thought of all this as I walked by the side of the water. The sun was shining brightly on the river and made earth delightful, while it filled me with love for life, for the swallows, whose swift agility is always delightful in my eyes, for the plants by the riverside, whose rustling is a pleasure to my ears.

By degrees, however, an inexplicable feeling of discomfort seized me. It seemed to me as if some unknown force were numbing and stopping me, were preventing me from going further and were calling me back. I felt that painful wish to return which comes on you when you have left a beloved invalid at home, and are seized by a presentiment that he is worse.

I, therefore, returned despite of myself, feeling certain that I should find some bad news awaiting me, a letter or a telegram. There was nothing, however, and I was surprised and uneasy, more so than if I had had another fantastic vision.

August 8. I spent a terrible evening, yesterday. He does not show himself any more, but I feel that He is near me, watching me, looking at me, penetrating me, dominating me, and more terrible to me when He hides himself thus than if He were to manifest his constant and invisible presence by supernatural phenomena. However, I slept.

August 9. Nothing, but I am afraid.

August 10. Nothing; but what will happen to-morrow?

August 11. Still nothing. I cannot stop at home with this fear hanging over me and these thoughts in my mind; I shall go away.

August 12. Ten o'clock at night. All day long I have been trying to get away, and have not been able. I contemplated a simple and easy act of liberty, a carriage ride to Rouen—and I have not been able to do it. What is the reason?

August 13. When one is attacked by certain maladies, the springs of our physical being seem broken, our energies destroyed, our muscles relaxed, our bones to be as soft as our flesh, and our blood as liquid as water. I am experiencing the same in my moral being, in a strange and distressing manner. I have no longer any strength, any courage, any self-control, nor even any power to set my own will in motion. I have no power left to *will* anything, but some one does it for me and I obey.

August 14. I am lost! Somebody possesses my soul and governs it! Somebody orders all my acts, all my movements, all my thoughts. I am no longer master of myself, nothing except an enslaved and terrified spectator of the things which I do. I wish to go out; I cannot. *He* does not wish to; and so I remain, trembling and distracted in the armchair in which he keeps me sitting. I merely wish to get up and to rouse myself, so as to think that I am still master of myself: I cannot! I am riveted to my chair, and my chair adheres to the floor in such a manner that no force of mine can move us.

Then suddenly, I must, I *must* go to the foot of my garden to pick some strawberries and eat them—and I go there. I pick the strawberries and I eat them! Oh! my God! my God! Is there a God? If there be one, deliver me! save me! succor me! Pardon! Pity! Mercy! Save me! Oh! what sufferings! what torture! what horror!

August 15. Certainly this is the way in which my poor cousin was possessed and swayed, when she came to borrow five thousand francs of me. She was under the power of a strange will which had entered into her, like another soul, a parasitic and ruling soul. Is the world coming to an end?

But who is he, this invisible being that rules me, this unknowable being, this rover of a supernatural race?

Invisible beings exist, then! How is it, then, that since the beginning of the world they have never manifested themselves in such a manner as they do to me? I have never read anything that resembles what goes on in my house. Oh! If I could only leave it, if I could only go away and flee, and never return, I should be saved; but I cannot.

August 16. I managed to escape to-day for two hours, like a prisoner who finds the door of his dungeon accidentally open. I suddenly felt that I was free and that He was far away, and so I gave orders to put the horses in as quickly as possible, and I drove to Rouen. Oh! how delightful to be able to say to my coachman: 'Go to Rouen!'

I made him pull up before the library, and I begged them to lend me Dr. Herrmann Herestauss's treatise on the unknown inhabitants of the ancient and modern world.

Then, as I was getting into my carriage, I intended to say: 'To the railway station!' but instead of this I shouted—I did not speak; but I shouted—in such a loud voice that all the passers-by turned round: 'Home!' and I fell back on to the cushion of my carriage, overcome by mental agony. He had found me out and regained possession of me.

August 17. Oh! What a night! What a night! And yet it seems to me that I ought to rejoice. I read until one o'clock in the morning! Herestauss, Doctor of Philosophy and Theogony, wrote the history and the manifestation of all those invisible beings which hover around man, or of whom he dreams. He describes their origin, their domains, their power; but none of them resembles the one which haunts me. One might say that man, ever since he has thought, has had a foreboding and a fear of a new being, stronger than himself, his successor in this world, and that, feeling him near, and not being able to foretell the nature of the unseen one, he has, in his terror, created the whole race of hidden beings, vague phantoms born of fear.

Having, therefore, read until one o'clock in the morning, I went and sat down at the open window, in order to cool my forehead and my thoughts in the calm night air. It was very pleasant and warm! How I should have enjoyed such a night formerly!

There was no moon, but the stars darted out their rays in the dark heavens. Who inhabits those worlds? What forms, what living beings, what animals are there yonder? Do those who are thinkers in those distant worlds know more than we do? What can they do more than we? What do they see which we do not? Will not one of them, some day or other, traversing space, appear on our earth to conquer it, just as formerly the Norsemen crossed the sea in order to subjugate nations feebler than themselves?

We are so weak, so powerless, so ignorant, so small—we who live on this particle of mud which revolves in liquid air.

I fell asleep, dreaming thus in the cool night air, and then, having slept for about three quarters of an hour, I opened my eyes without moving, awakened by an indescribably confused and strange sensation. At first I saw nothing, and then suddenly it appeared to me as if a page of the book, which had remained open on my table, turned over of its own accord. Not a breath of air had come in at my window, and I was surprised and waited. In about four minutes, I saw, I saw—yes I saw with my own eyes—another page lift itself up and fall down on the others, as if a finger had turned it over. My armchair was empty, appeared empty, but I knew that He was there, He, and sitting in my place, and that He was reading. With a furious bound, the bound of an enraged wild beast that wishes to disembowel its tamer, I crossed my room to seize him, to strangle him, to kill him! But before I could reach it, my chair fell over as if somebody had run away from me. My table rocked, my lamp fell and went out, and my window closed as if some thief had been surprised and had fled out into the night, shutting it behind him.

So He had run away; He had been afraid; He, afraid of me!

So to-morrow, or later—some day or other, I should be able to hold him in my clutches and crush him against the ground! Do not dogs occasionally bite and strangle their masters?

August 18. I have been thinking the whole day long. Oh! yes, I will obey Him, follow His impulses, fulfill all His wishes, show myself humble, submissive, a coward. He is the stronger; but an hour will come.

August 19. I know, I know, I know all! I have just read the following in the *Revue du Monde Scientifique*: 'A curious piece of news comes to us from Rio de Janeiro. Madness, an epidemic of madness, which may be compared to that contagious madness which attacked the people of Europe in the Middle Ages, is at this moment raging in the Province of San-Paulo. The frightened inhabitants are leaving their houses, deserting their villages, abandoning their land, saying that they are pursued, possessed, governed like human cattle by invisible, though tangible beings, by a species of vampire, which feeds on their life while they are asleep, and which, besides, drinks water and milk without appearing to touch any other nourishment.

'Professor Don Pedro Henriques, accompanied by several medical savants, has gone to the Province of San-Paulo, in order to study the origin and the manifestations of this surprising madness on the spot, and to propose such measures to the Emperor as may appear to him to be most fitted to restore the mad population to reason.'

Ah! Ah! I remember now that fine Brazilian three-master which passed in front of my windows as it was going up the Seine, on the eighth of last May! I thought it looked so pretty, so white and bright! That Being was on board of her, coming from there, where its race sprang from. And it saw me! It saw my house, which was also white, and He sprang from the ship on to the land. Oh! Good heavens!

Now I know, I can divine. The reign of man is over, and he has come. He whom disquieted priests exorcised, whom sorcerers evoked on dark nights, without seeing him appear, He to whom the imaginations of the transient masters of the world lent all the monstrous or graceful forms of gnomes, spirits, genii, fairies, and familiar spirits. After the coarse conceptions of primitive fear, men more enlightened gave him a truer form. Mesmer divined him, and ten years ago physicians accurately discovered the nature of his power, even before He exercised it himself. They played with that weapon of their new Lord, the sway of a mysterious will over the human soul, which had become enslaved. They called it mesmerism, hypnotism, suggestion, I know not what? I have seen them diverting themselves like rash children with this horrible power! Woe to us! Woe to man! He has come, the—the—what does He call himself—the—I fancy that he is shouting out his name to me and I do not hear him—the—yes—He is shouting it out—I am listening—I cannot—repeat—it—Horla—I have heard—the Horla—it is He—the Horla—He has come!

Ah! The vulture has eaten the pigeon; the wolf has eaten the lamb; the lion has devoured the sharp-horned buffalo; man has killed the lion with an arrow, with a spear, with gunpowder; but the Horla will make of man what man has made of the horse and of the ox: his chattel, his slave, and his food, by the mere power of his will. Woe to us!

But, nevertheless, sometimes the animal rebels and kills the man who has subjugated it. I should also like—I shall be able to—but I must know Him, touch Him, see Him! Learned men say that eyes of animals, as they differ from ours, do not distinguish as ours do. And my eye cannot distinguish this newcomer who is oppressing me.

Why? Oh! Now I remember the words of the monk at Mont Saint-Michel: 'Can we see the hundred-thousandth part of what exists? Listen; there is the wind which is the strongest force in nature; it knocks men down, blows down buildings, uproots trees, raises the sea into mountains of water, destroys cliffs, and casts great ships on to the breakers; it kills, it whistles, it sighs, it roars,—have you ever seen it, and can you see it? It exists for all that, however!'

And I went on thinking: my eyes are so weak, so imperfect, that they do not even distinguish hard bodies, if they are as transparent as glass! If a glass without quicksilver behind it were to bar my way, I should run into it, just like a bird which has flown into a room breaks its head against the windowpanes. A thousand things, moreover, deceive a man and lead him astray. How then is it surprising that he cannot perceive a new body which is penetrated and pervaded by the light?

A new being! Why not? It was assuredly bound to come! Why should we be the last? We do not distinguish it, like all the others created before us? The reason is, that its nature is more delicate, its body finer and more finished than ours. Our makeup is so weak, so awkwardly conceived; our body is encumbered with organs that are always tired, always being strained like locks that are too complicated; it lives like a plant and like an animal nourishing itself with difficulty on air, herbs, and flesh; it is a brute machine which is a prey to maladies, to malformations, to decay; it is broken-winded, badly regulated, simple and eccentric, ingeniously yet badly made, a coarse and yet a delicate mechanism, in brief, the outline of a being which might become intelligent and great.

There are only a few—so few—stages of development in this world, from the oyster up to man. Why should there not be one more, when once that period is accomplished which separates the successive products one from the other?

Why not one more? Why not, also, other trees with immense, splendid flowers, perfuming whole regions? Why not other elements beside fire, air, earth, and water? There are four, only four, nursing fathers of various beings! What a pity! Why should not there be forty, four hundred, four thousand! How poor everything is, how mean and wretched—grudgingly given, poorly invented, clumsily made! Ah! the elephant and the hippopotamus, what power! And the camel, what suppleness!

But the butterfly, you will say, a flying flower! I dream of one that should be as large as a hundred worlds, with wings whose shape, beauty, colors, and motion I cannot even express. But I see it—it flutters from star to star, refreshing them and perfuming them with the light and harmonious breath of its flight! And the people up there gaze at it as it passes in an ecstasy of delight!

What is the matter with me? It is He, the Horla who haunts me, and who makes me think of these foolish things! He is within me, He is becoming my soul; I shall kill him!

August 20. I shall kill Him. I have seen Him! Yesterday I

sat down at my table and pretended to write very assiduously. I knew quite well that He would come prowling round me, quite close to me, so close that I might perhaps be able to touch him, to seize him. And then—then I should have the strength of desperation; I should have my hands, my knees, my chest, my forehead, my teeth to strangle him, to crush him, to bite him, to tear him to pieces. And I watched for him with all my overexcited nerves.

I had lighted my two lamps and the eight wax candles on my mantelpiece, as if, by this light I should discover Him.

My bed, my old oak bed with its columns, was opposite to me; on my right was the fireplace; on my left the door, which was carefully closed, after I had left it open for some time, in order to attract Him; behind me was a very high wardrobe with a looking-glass in it, which served me to dress by every day, and in which I was in the habit of inspecting myself from head to foot every time I passed it.

So I pretended to be writing in order to deceive Him, for He also was watching me, and suddenly I felt, I was certain, that He was reading over my shoulder, that He was there, almost touching my ear.

I got up so quickly, with my hands extended, that I almost fell. Horror! It was as bright as at midday, but I did not see myself in the glass! It was empty, clear, profound, full of light! But my figure was not reflected in it—and I, I was opposite to it! I saw the large, clear glass from top to bottom, and I looked at it with unsteady eyes. I did not dare advance; I did not venture to make a movement; feeling certain, nevertheless, that He was there, but that He would escape me again, He whose imperceptible body had absorbed my reflection.

How frightened I was! And then suddenly I began to see myself through a mist in the depths of the looking-glass, in a mist as it were, or through a veil of water; and it seemed to me as if this water were flowing slowly from left to right, and making my figure clearer every moment. It was like the end of an eclipse. Whatever hid me did not appear to possess any clearly defined outlines, but was a sort of opaque transparency, which gradually grew clearer.

At last I was able to distinguish myself completely, as I do every day when I look at myself.

I had seen Him! And the horror of it remained with me, and makes me shudder even now.

August 21. How could I kill Him, since I could not get hold of Him? Poison? But He would see me mix it with the water; and then, would our poisons have any effect on His impalpable body? No—no—no doubt about the matter. Then?—then?

August 22. I sent for a blacksmith from Rouen and ordered iron shutters of him for my room, such as some private hotels in Paris have on the ground floor, for fear of thieves, and he is going to make me a similar door as well. I have made myself out a coward, but I do not care about that!

September 10. Rouen, Hotel Continental. It is done; it is done—but is He dead? My mind is thoroughly upset by what I have seen.

Well then, yesterday, the locksmith having put on the iron shutters and door, I left everything open until midnight, although it was getting cold.

Suddenly I felt that He was there, and joy, mad joy took possession of me. I got up softly, and I walked to the right and left for some time, so that He might not guess anything; then I took off my boots and put on my slippers carelessly; then I fastened the iron shutters and going back to the door quickly I double-locked it with a padlock, putting the key into my pocket.

Suddenly I noticed that He was moving restlessly round me, that in his turn He was frightened and was ordering me to let Him out. I nearly yielded, though I did not quite, but putting my back to the door, I half opened it, just enough to allow me to go out backward, and as I am very tall, my head touched the lintel. I was sure that He had not been able to escape, and I shut Him up quite alone, quite alone. What happiness! I had Him fast. Then I ran downstairs into the drawing-room which was under my bedroom. I took the two lamps and poured all the oil on to the carpet, the furniture, everywhere; then I set fire to it and made my escape, after having carefully double locked the door.

I went and hid myself at the bottom of the garden, in a clump of laurel bushes. How long it was! how long it was! Everything was dark, silent, motionless, not a breath of air and not a star, but heavy banks of clouds which one could not see, but which weighed, oh! so heavily on my soul.

I looked at my house and waited. How long it was! I already began to think that the fire had gone out of its own accord, or that He had extinguished it, when one of the lower windows gave way under the violence of the flames, and a long, soft, caressing sheet of red flame mounted up the white wall, and kissed it as high as the roof. The light fell on to the trees, the branches, and the leaves, and a shiver of fear pervaded them also! The birds awoke; a dog began to howl, and it seemed to me as if the day were breaking! Almost immediately two other windows flew into fragments, and I saw that the whole of the lower part of my house was nothing but a terrible furnace. But a cry, a horrible, shrill, heart-rending cry, a woman's cry, sounded through the night, and two garret windows were opened! I had forgotten the servants! I saw the terror-struck faces, and the frantic waving of their arms!

Then, overwhelmed with horror, I ran off to the village, shouting: 'Help! help! fire! fire!' Meeting some people who were already coming on to the scene, I went back with them to see!

By this time the house was nothing but a horrible and magnificent funeral pile, a monstrous pyre which lit up the whole country, a pyre where men were burning, and where He was burning also, He, He, my prisoner, that new Being, the new Master, the Horla!

Suddenly the whole roof fell in between the walls, and a volcano of flames darted up to the sky. Through all the windows which opened on to that furnace, I saw the flames darting, and I reflected that He was there, in that kiln, dead.

Dead? Perhaps? His body? Was not his body, which was

transparent, indestructible by such means as would kill ours?

If He were not dead? Perhaps time alone has power over that Invisible and Redoubtable Being. Why this transparent, unrecognizable body, this body belonging to a spirit, if it also had to fear ills, infirmities, and premature destruction?

Premature destruction? All human terror springs from that! After man the Horla. After him who can die every day, at any hour, at any moment, by any accident, He came, He who was only to die at his own proper hour and minute, because He had touched the limits of his existence!

No—no—there is no doubt about it—He is not dead. Then—then—I suppose I must kill myself!

50

THE BODY SNATCHER

Robert Louis Stevenson

Every night in the year, four of us sat in the small parlour of the George at Debenham—the undertaker, and the landlord, and Fettes, and myself. Sometimes there would be more; but blow high, blow low, come rain or snow or frost, we four would be each planted in his own particular arm-chair. Fettes was an old drunken Scotchman, a man of education obviously, and a man of some property, since he lived in idleness. He had come to Debenham years ago, while still young, and by a mere continuance of living had grown to be an adopted townsman. His blue camlet cloak was a local antiquity, like the church-spire. His place in the parlour at the George, his absence from church, his old, crapulous, disreputable vices, were all things of course in Debenham. He had some vague Radical opinions and some fleeting infidelities, which he would now and again set forth and emphasise with tottering slaps upon the table. He drank rum—five glasses regularly every evening; and for the greater portion of his nightly visit to the George sat, with his glass in his right hand, in a state of melancholy alcoholic saturation. We called him the Doctor, for he was supposed to have some special knowledge of medicine, and had been known, upon a pinch, to set a fracture or reduce a dislocation; but beyond these slight particulars, we had no knowledge of his character and antecedents.

One dark winter night—it had struck nine some time before the landlord joined us—there was a sick man in the George, a great neighbouring proprietor suddenly struck down with apoplexy on his way to Parliament; and the great man's still greater London doctor had been telegraphed to his bedside. It was the first time that such a thing had happened in Debenham, for the railway was but newly open, and we were all proportionately moved by the occurrence.

'He's come,' said the landlord, after he had filled and lighted his pipe.

'He?' said I. 'Who?—not the doctor?'

'Himself,' replied our host.

'What is his name?'

'Dr. Macfarlane,' said the landlord.

Fettes was far through his third tumblers stupidly fuddled, now nodding over, now staring mazily around him; but at the last word he seemed to awaken, and repeated the name 'Macfarlane' twice, quietly enough the first time, but with sudden emotion at the second.

'Yes,' said the landlord, 'that's his name, Doctor Wolfe Macfarlane.'

Fettes became instantly sober; his eyes awoke, his voice became clear, loud, and steady, his language forcible and earnest. We were all startled by the transformation, as if a man had risen from the dead.

'I beg your pardon,' he said. 'I am afraid I have not been paying much attention to your talk. Who is this Wolfe Macfarlane?' And then, when he had heard the landlord out, 'It cannot be, it cannot be,' he added; 'and yet I would like well to see him face to face.'

'Do you know him, Doctor?' asked the undertaker, with a gasp.

'God forbid!' was the reply. 'And yet the name is a strange one; it were too much to fancy two. Tell me, landlord, is he old?'

'Well,' said the host, 'he's not a young man, to be sure, and his hair is white; but he looks younger than you.'

'He is older, though; years older. But,' with a slap upon the table, 'it's the rum you see in my face—rum and sin. This man, perhaps, may have an easy conscience and a good digestion. Conscience! Hear me speak. You would think I was some good, old, decent Christian, would you not? But no, not I; I never canted. Voltaire might have canted if he'd stood in my shoes; but the brains'—with a rattling fillip on his bald head—'the brains were clear and active, and I saw and made no deductions.'

'If you know this doctor,' I ventured to remark, after a somewhat awful pause, 'I should gather that you do not share the landlord's good opinion.'

Fettes paid no regard to me.

'Yes,' he said, with sudden decision, 'I must see him face to face.'

There was another pause, and then a door was closed rather sharply on the first floor, and a step was heard upon the stair.

'That's the doctor,' cried the landlord. 'Look sharp, and you can catch him.'

It was but two steps from the small parlour to the door of the old George Inn; the wide oak staircase landed almost in the street; there was room for a Turkey rug and nothing more between the threshold and the last round of the descent; but this little space was every evening brilliantly lit up, not only by the light upon the stair and the great signal-lamp below the sign, but by the warm radiance of the barroom window. The George thus brightly advertised itself to passers-by in the cold street. Fettes walked steadily to the spot, and we, who were hanging behind, beheld the two men meet, as one of them had phrased it, face to face. Dr. Macfarlane was alert and vigorous. His white hair set off his pale and placid, although energetic, countenance. He was richly dressed in the finest of broadcloth and the whitest of linen, with a great gold watch-chain, and studs and spectacles of the same precious material. He wore a broad-folded tie, white and speckled with lilac, and he carried on his arm a comfortable driving-coat of fur. There was no doubt but he became his years, breathing, as he did, of wealth and consideration; and it was a surprising contrast to see our parlour sot—bald, dirty, pimpled, and robed in his old camlet cloak—confront him at the bottom of the stairs.

'Macfarlane!' he said somewhat loudly, more like a herald than a friend.

The great doctor pulled up short on the fourth step, as though the familiarity of the address surprised and somewhat shocked his dignity.

'Toddy Macfarlane!' repeated Fettes.

The London man almost staggered. He stared for the swiftest of seconds at the man before him, glanced behind him with a sort of scare, and then in a startled whisper 'Fettes!' he said, 'you!'

'Ay,' said the other, 'me! Did you think I was dead too? We are not so easy shut of our acquaintance.'

'Hush, hush!' exclaimed the doctor. 'Hush, hush! this meeting is so unexpected—I can see you are unmanned. I hardly knew you, I confess, at first; but I am overjoyed—overjoyed to have this opportunity. For the present it must be how-d'ye-do and good-by in one, for my fly is waiting, and I must not fail the train; but you shall—let me see—yes—you shall give me your address, and you can count on early news of me. We must do something for you, Fettes. I fear you are out at elbows; but we must see to that for auld lang syne, as once we sang at suppers.'

'Money!' cried Fettes; 'money from you! The money that I had from you is lying where I cast it in the rain.'

Dr. Macfarlane had talked himself into some measure of superiority and confidence, but the uncommon energy of this refusal cast him back into his first confusion.

A horrible, ugly look came and went across his almost venerable countenance. 'My dear fellow,' he said, 'be it as you please; my last thought is to offend you. I would intrude on none. I will leave you my address however—'

'I do not wish it—I do not wish to know the roof that shelters you,' interrupted the other. 'I heard your name; I feared it might be you; I wished to know if, after all, there were a God; I know now that there is none. Begone!'

He still stood in the middle of the rug, between the stair and doorway; and the great London physician, in order to escape, would be forced to step to one side. It was plain that he hesitated before the thought of this humiliation. White as he was, there was a dangerous glitter in his spectacles; but while he still paused uncertain, he became aware that the driver of his fly was peering in from the street at this unusual scene, and caught a glimpse at the same time of our little body from the parlour, huddled by the corner of the bar. The presence of so many witnesses decided him at once to flee. He crouched together, brushing on the wainscot, and made a dart like a serpent, striking for the door. But his tribulation was not yet entirely at an end, for even as he was passing Fettes clutched him by the arm and these words came in a whisper, and yet painfully distinct, 'Have you seen it again?'

The great rich London doctor cried out aloud with a sharp, throttling cry; he dashed his questioner across the open space, and, with his hands over his head, fled out of the door like a detected thief. Before it had occurred to one of us to make a movement the fly was already rattling toward the station. The scene was over like a dream, but the dream had left proofs and traces of its passage. Next day the servant found the fine gold spectacles broken on the threshold, and that very night we were all standing breathless by the barroom window, and Fettes at our side, sober, pale and resolute in look.

'God protect us, Mr. Fettes!' said the landlord, coming first into possession of his customary senses. 'What in the universe is all this? These are strange things you have been saying.'

Fettes turned toward us; he looked us each in succession in the face. 'See if you can hold your tongues,' said he. 'That man Macfarlane is not safe to cross; those that have done so already have repented it too late.'

And then, without so much as finishing his third glass, far less waiting for the other two, he bade us good-by and went forth, under the lamp of the hotel, into the black night.

We three turned to our places in the parlour, with the big red fire and four clear candles; and as we recapitulated what had passed the first chill of our surprise soon changed into a glow of curiosity. We sat late; it was the latest session I have known in the old George. Each man, before we parted, had his theory that he was bound to prove; and none of us had any nearer business in this world than to track out the past of our condemned companion, and surprise the secret that he shared with the great London doctor. It is no great boast, but I believe I was a better hand at worming out a story than either of my fellows at the George; and perhaps there is now no other man alive who could narrate to you the following foul and unnatural events.

In his young days Fettes studied medicine in the schools of Edinburgh. He had talent of a kind, the talent that picks up swiftly what it hears and readily retails it for its own. He worked little at home; but he was civil, attentive, and intelligent in the presence of his masters. They soon picked him out as a lad who listened closely and remembered well; nay, strange as it seemed to me when I first heard it, he was in those days well favoured, and pleased by his exterior. There was, at that period, a certain extramural teacher of anatomy, whom I shall here designate by the letter K. His name was subsequently too well known. The man who bore it skulked through the streets of Edinburgh in disguise, while the mob that applauded at the execution of Burke called loudly for the blood of his employer. But Mr. K— was then at the top of his vogue; he enjoyed a popularity due partly to his own talent and address, partly to the incapacity of his rival, the university professor. The students, at least, swore by his name, and Fettes believed himself, and was believed by others, to have laid the foundations of success when he had acquired the favour of this meteorically famous man. Mr. K— was a *bon vivant* as well as an accomplished teacher; he liked a sly allusion no less than a careful preparation. In both capacities Fettes enjoyed and deserved his notice, and by the second year of his attendance he held the half-regular position of second demonstrator or sub-assistant in his class.

In this capacity, the charge of the theatre and lecturerdom devolved in particular upon his shoulders. He had to answer for the cleanliness of the premises and the conduct of the other students, and it was a part of his duty to supply, receive, and divide the various subjects. It was with a view to this last—at that time very delicate—affair that he was lodged by Mr. K— in the same wynd, and at last in the same building, with the dissecting-room. Here, after a night of turbulent pleasures, his hand still tottering, his sight still misty and confused, he would be called out of bed in the black hours before the winter dawn by the unclean and desperate interlopers who supplied the table. He would open the door to these men, since infamous throughout the land. He would help them with their tragic burden, pay them their sordid price, and remain alone, when they were gone, with the unfriendly relics of humanity. From such a scene he would return to snatch another hour or two of slumber, to repair the abuses of the night, and refresh himself for the labours of the day.

Few lads could have been more insensible to the impressions of a life thus passed among the ensigns of mortality. His mind was closed against all general considerations. He was incapable of interest in the fate and fortunes of another, the slave of his own desires and low ambitions. Cold, light, and selfish in the last resort, he had that modicum of prudence, miscalled morality, which keeps a man from inconvenient drunkenness or punishable theft. He coveted, besides, a measure of consideration from his masters and his fellow-pupils, and he had no desire to fail conspicuously in the external parts of life. Thus he made it his pleasure to gain some distinction in his studies, and day after day rendered unimpeachable eye-service to his employer, Mr. K—. For his day of work he indemnified himself by nights of roaring, blackguardly enjoyment; and when that balance had been struck, the organ that he called his conscience declared itself content.

The supply of subjects was a continual trouble to him as well as to his master. In that large and busy class, the raw material of the anatomists kept perpetually running out; and the business thus rendered necessary was not only unpleasant in itself, but threatened dangerous consequences to all who were concerned. It was the policy of Mr. K— to ask no questions in his dealings with the trade. 'They bring the body, and we pay the price,' he used to say, dwelling on the alliteration—'quid pro quo.' And again, and somewhat profanely, 'Ask no questions,' he would tell his assistants, 'for conscience sake.' There was no understanding that the subjects were provided by the crime of murder. Had that idea been broached to him in words, he would have recoiled in horror; but the lightness of his speech upon so grave a matter was, in itself, an offence against good manners, and a temptation to the men with whom he dealt. Fettes, for instance, had often remarked to himself upon the singular freshness of the bodies. He had been struck again and again by the hang-dog, abominable looks of the ruffians who came to him before the dawn; and putting things together clearly in his private thoughts, he perhaps attributed a meaning too immoral and too categorical to the unguarded counsels of his master. He understood his duty, in short, to have three branches: to take what was brought, to pay the price, and to avert the eye from any evidence of crime.

One November morning this policy of silence was put sharply to the test. He had been awake all night with a racking toothache—pacing his room like a caged beast or throwing himself in fury on his bed—and had fallen at last into that profound, uneasy slumber that so often follows on a night of pain, when he was awakened by the third or fourth angry repetition of the concerted signal. There was a thin, bright moonshine; it was bitter cold, windy, and frosty; the town had not yet awakened, but an indefinable stir already preluded the noise and business of the day. The ghouls had come later than usual, and they seemed more than usually eager to be gone. Fettes, sick with sleep, lighted them upstairs. He heard their grumbling Irish voices through a dream; and as they stripped the sack from their sad merchandise he leaned dozing, with his shoulder propped against the wall; he had to shake himself to find the men their money. As he did so his eyes lighted on the dead face. He started; he took two steps nearer, with the candle raised.

'God Almighty!' he cried. 'That is Jane Galbraith!' The men answered nothing, but they shuffled nearer the door.

'I know her, I tell you,' he continued. 'She was alive and hearty yesterday. It's impossible she can be dead; it's impossible you should have got this body fairly.'

'Sure, sir, you're mistaken entirely,' said one of the men.

But the other looked Fettes darkly in the eyes, and demanded the money on the spot.

It was impossible to misconceive the threat or to exaggerate the danger. The lad's heart failed him. He stammered some excuses, counted out the sum, and saw his hateful visitors depart. No sooner were they gone than he hastened to confirm his doubts. By a dozen unquestionable marks he identified the girl he had jested with the day before. He saw, with horror, marks upon her body that might well betoken violence. A panic seized him, and he took refuge in his room. There he reflected at length over the discovery that he had made; considered soberly the bearing of Mr. K—'s instructions and the danger to himself of interference in so serious a business, and at last, in sore perplexity, determined to wait for the advice of his immediate superior, the class assistant.

This was a young doctor, Wolfe Macfarlane, a high favourite among all the reckless students, clever, dissipated, and unscrupulous to the last degree. He had travelled and studied abroad. His manners were agreeable and a little forward. He was an authority on the stage, skilful on the ice or the links with skate or golf-club; he dressed with nice audacity, and, to put the finishing touch upon his glory, he kept a gig and a strong trotting-horse. With Fettes he was on terms of intimacy; indeed, their relative positions called for some community of life; and when subjects were scarce the pair would drive far into the country in Macfarlane's gig, visit and desecrate some lonely graveyard, and return before dawn with their booty to the door of the dissecting-room.

On that particular morning Macfarlane arrived somewhat earlier than his wont. Fettes heard him, and met him on the stairs, told him his story, and showed him the cause of his alarm. Macfarlane examined the marks on her body.

'Yes,' he said with a nod, 'it looks fishy.'

'Well, what should I do? ' asked Fettes.

'Do?' repeated the other. 'Do you want to do anything? Least said soonest mended, I should say.'

'Some one else might recognise her,' objected Fettes. 'She was as well known as the Castle Rock.'

'We'll hope not,' said Macfarlane, 'and if anybody does—well, you didn't, don't you see, and there's an end. The fact is, this has been going on too long. Stir up the mud, and you'll get K— into the most unholy trouble; you'll be in a shocking box yourself. So will I, if you come to that. I should like to know how any one of us would look, or what the devil we should have to say for ourselves in any Christian witness-box. For me, you know there's one thing certain—that, practically speaking, all our subjects have been murdered.'

'Macfarlane!' cried Fettes.

'Come now!' sneered the other. 'As if you hadn't suspected it yourself!'

'Suspecting is one thing—'

'And proof another. Yes, I know; and I'm as sorry as you are this should have come here,' tapping the body with his cane. 'The next best thing for me is not to recognise it; and,' he added coolly, 'I don't. You may, if you please. I don't dictate, but I think a man of the world would do as I do; and I may add, I fancy that is what K— would look for at our hands. The question is, why did he choose us two for his assistants? And I answer, because he didn't want old wives.'

This was the tone of all others to affect the mind of a lad like Fettes. He agreed to imitate Macfarlane. The body of the unfortunate girl was duly dissected, and no one remarked or appeared to recognize her.

One afternoon, when his day's work was over, Fettes dropped into a popular tavern and found Macfarlane sitting with a stranger. This was a small man, very pale and dark, with coal-black eyes. The cut of his features gave a promise of intellect and refinement which was but feebly realised in his manners, for he proved, upon a nearer acquaintance, coarse, vulgar, and stupid. He exercised, however, a very remarkable control over Macfarlane; issued orders like the Great Bashaw; became inflamed at the least discussion or delay, and commented rudely on the servility with which he was obeyed. This most offensive person took a fancy to Fettes on the spot, plied him with drinks, and honoured him with unusual confidences on his past career. If a tenth part of what he confessed were true, he was a very loathsome rogue; and the lad's vanity was tickled by the attention of so experienced a man.

'I'm a pretty bad fellow myself,' the stranger remarked, 'but Macfarlane is the boy—Toddy Macfarlane, I call him. Toddy, order your friend another glass.' Or it might be, 'Toddy, you jump up and shut the door.' 'Toddy hates me,' he said again. 'Oh, yes, Toddy, you do!'

'Don't you call me that confounded name,' growled Macfarlane.

'Hear him! Did you ever see the lads play knife? He would like to do that all over my body,' remarked the stranger.

'We medicals have a better way than that,' said Fettes. 'When we dislike a dead friend of ours, we dissect him.'

Macfarlane looked up sharply, as though this jest was scarcely to his mind.

The afternoon passed. Gray, for that was the stranger's name, invited Fettes to join them at dinner, ordered a feast so sumptuous that the tavern was thrown in commotion, and when all was done commanded Macfarlane to settle the bill. It was late before they separated; the man Gray was incapably drunk. Macfarlane, sobered by his fury, chewed the cud of the money he had been forced to squander and the slights he had been obliged to swallow. Fettes, with various liquors singing in his head, returned home with devious footsteps and a mind entirely in abeyance. Next day Macfarlane was absent from the class, and Fettes smiled to himself as he imagined him still squiring the intolerable Gray from tavern to tavern. As soon as the hour of liberty had struck he posted from place to place in quest of his last night's companions. He could find them, however, nowhere; so returned early to his rooms, went early to bed, and slept the sleep of the just.

At four in the morning he was awakened by the well-known signal. Descending to the door, he was filled with astonishment to find Macfarlane with his gig, and in the gig one of those long and ghastly packages with which he was so well acquainted.

'What?' he cried. 'Have you been out alone? How did you manage?'

But Macfarlane silenced him roughly, bidding him turn to business. When they had got the body upstairs and laid it on the table, Macfarlane made at first as if he were going away. Then he paused and seemed to hesitate; and then, 'You had better look at the face,' said he, in tones of some constraint. 'You had better,' he repeated, as Fettes only stared at him in wonder.

'But where, and how, and when did you come by it?' cried the other.

'Look at the face,' was the only answer.

Fettes was staggered; strange doubts assailed him. He looked from the young doctor to the body, and then back again. At last, with a start, he did as he was bidden. He had almost expected the sight that met his eyes, and yet the shock was cruel. To see, fixed in the rigidity of death and naked on that coarse layer of sackcloth, the man whom he had left well clad and full of meat and sin upon the threshold of a tavern, awoke, even in the thoughtless Fettes, some of the terrors of the conscience. It was a *cras tibi* which re-echoed in his soul, that two whom he had known should have come to lie upon these icy tables. Yet these were only secondary thoughts. His first concern regarded Wolfe. Unprepared for a challenge so momentous, he knew not how to look his comrade in the face. He durst not meet his eye, and he had neither words nor voice at his command.

It was Macfarlane himself who made the first advance. He came up quietly behind and laid his hand gently but firmly on the other's shoulder.

'Richardson,' said he, 'may have the head.'

Now Richardson was a student who had long been anxious for that portion of the human subject to dissect. There was no answer, and the murderer resumed: 'Talking of business, you must pay me; your accounts, you see, must tally.'

Fettes found a voice, the ghost of his own: 'Pay you!' he cried. 'Pay you for that?'

'Why, yes, of course you must. By all means and on every possible account, you must,' returned the other. 'I dare not give it for nothing, you dare not take it for nothing; it would compromise us both. This is another case like Jane Galbraith's. The more things are wrong the more we must act as if all were right. Where does old K— keep his money?'

'There,' answered Fettes hoarsely, pointing to a cupboard in the corner.

'Give me the key, then,' said the other, calmly, holding out his hand.

There was an instant's hesitation, and the die was cast. Macfarlane could not suppress a nervous twitch, the infinitesimal mark of an immense relief, as he felt the key between his fingers. He opened the cupboard, brought out pen and ink and a paper-book that stood in one compartment, and separated from the funds in a drawer a sum suitable to the occasion.

'Now, look here,' he said, 'there is the payment made—first proof of your good faith: first step to your security. You have now to clinch it by a second. Enter the payment in your book, and then you for your part may defy the devil.'

The next few seconds were for Fettes an agony of thought; but in balancing his terrors it was the most immediate that triumphed. Any future difficulty seemed almost welcome if he could avoid a present quarrel with Macfarlane. He set down the candle which he had been carrying all this time, and with a steady hand entered the date, the nature, and the amount of the transaction.

'And now,' said Macfarlane, 'it's only fair that you should pocket the lucre. I've had my share already. By the bye, when a man of the world falls into a bit of luck, has a few shillings extra in his pocket—I'm ashamed to speak of it, but there's a rule of conduct in the case. No treating, no purchase of expensive class-books, no squaring of old debts; borrow, don't lend.'

'Macfarlane,' began Fettes, still somewhat hoarsely, 'I have put my neck in a halter to oblige you.'

'To oblige me?' cried Wolfe. 'Oh, come! You did, as near as I can see the matter; what you downright had to do in self-defence. Suppose I got into trouble, where would you be? This second little matter flows clearly from the first. Mr. Gray is the continuation of Miss Galbraith. You can't begin and then stop. If you begin, you must keep on beginning; that's the truth. No rest for the wicked.'

A horrible sense of blackness and the treachery of fate seized hold upon the soul of the unhappy student.

'My God!' he cried, 'but what have I done? and when did I begin? To be made a class assistant—in the name of reason, where's the harm in that? Service wanted the position; Service might have got it. Would *he* have been where I am now?'

'My dear fellow,' said Macfarlane, 'what a boy you are! What harm *has* come to you? What harm *can* come to you if you hold your tongue? Why, man, do you know what this life is? There are two squads of us—the lions, and the lambs. If you're a lamb, you'll come to lie upon these tables like Gray or Jane Galbraith; if you're a lion, you'll live and drive a horse like me, like K—, like all the world with any wit or courage. You're staggered at the first. But look at K—! My dear fellow, you're clever, you have pluck. I like you, and K— likes you. You were born to lead the hunt; and I tell you, on my honour and my experience of life, three days from now you'll laugh at all these scarecrows like a high-school boy at a farce.'

And with that Macfarlane took his departure and drove off up the wynd in his gig to get under cover before daylight.

Fettes was thus left alone with his regrets. He saw the miserable peril in which he stood involved. He saw, with inexpressible dismay, that there was no limit to his weakness, and that, from concession to concession, he had fallen from the arbiter of Macfarlane's destiny to his paid and helpless accomplice. He would have given the world to have been a little braver at the time, but it did not occur to him that he might still be brave. The secret of Jane Galbraith and the cursed entry in the daybook closed his mouth.

Hours passes; the class began to arrive; the members of the unhappy Gray were dealt out to one and to another, and received without remark. Richardson was made happy with the head; and before the hour of freedom rang Fettes trembled with exultation to perceive how far they had already gone toward safety.

For two days he continued to watch, with increasing joy, the dreadful process of disguise.

On the third day Macfarlane made his appearance. He had been ill, he said; but he made up for lost time by the energy with which he directed the students. To Richardson in particular he extended the most valuable assistance and advice, and that student, encouraged by the praise of the demonstrator, burned high with ambitious hopes, and saw the medal already in his grasp.

Before the week was out Macfarlane's prophecy had been fulfilled. Fettes had outlived his terrors and had forgotten his baseness. He began to plume himself upon his courage, and had so arranged the story in his mind that he could look back on these events with an unhealthy pride. Of his accomplice he saw but little. They met, of course, in the business of the class; they received their orders together from Mr. K—. At times they had a word or two in private, and Macfarlane was from first to last particularly kind and jovial. But it was plain that he avoided any reference to their common secret; and even when Fettes whispered to him that he had cast in his lot with the lions and forsworn the lambs, he only signed to him smilingly to hold his peace.

At length an occasion arose which threw the pair once more into a closer union. Mr. K— was again short of subjects; pupils were eager, and it was a part of this teacher's pretensions to be always well supplied. At the same time there came the news of a burial in the rustic graveyard of Glencorse. Time has little changed the place in question. It stood then, as now, upon a cross road, out of call of human habitations, and buried fathoms deep in the foliage of six cedar trees. The cries of the sheep upon the neighbouring hills, the streamlets upon either hand, one loudly singing among pebbles, the other dripping furtively from pond to pond, the stir of the wind in mountainous old flowering chestnuts, and once in seven days the voice of the bell and the old tunes of the precentor, were the only sounds that disturbed the silence around the rural church. The Resurrection Man—to use a byname of the period—was not to be deterred by any of the sanctities of customary piety. It was part of his trade to despise and desecrate the scrolls and trumpets of old tombs, the paths worn by the feet of worshippers and mourners, and the offerings and the inscriptions of bereaved affection. To rustic neighbourhoods, where love is more than commonly tenacious, and where some bonds of blood or fellowship unite the entire society of a parish, the body-snatcher, far from being repelled by natural respect, was attracted by the ease and safety of the task. To bodies that had been laid in earth, in joyful expectation of a far different awakening, there came that hasty, lamp-lit, terror-haunted resurrection of the spade and mattock. The coffin was forced, the cerements torn, and the melancholy relics, clad in sackcloth, after being rattled for hours on moonless byways, were at length exposed to uttermost indignities before a class of gaping boys.

Somewhat as two vultures may swoop upon a dying lamb, Fettes and Macfarlane were to be let loose upon a grave in that green and quiet resting-place. The wife of a farmer, a woman who had lived for sixty years, and been known for nothing but good butter and a godly conversation, was to be rooted from her grave at midnight and carried, dead and naked to that far-away city that she had always honoured with her Sunday's best; the place beside her family was to be empty till the crack of doom; her innocent and almost venerable members to be exposed to that last curiosity of the anatomist.

Late one afternoon the pair set forth, well wrapped in cloaks and furnished with a formidable bottle. It rained without remission—a cold, dense, lashing rain. Now and again there blew a puff of wind, but these sheets of falling water kept it down. Bottle and all, it was a sad and silent drive as far as Penicuik, where they were to spend the evening. They stopped once, to hide their implements in a thick bush not far from the churchyard, and once again at the Fisher's Tryst, to have a toast before the kitchen fire and vary their nips of whisky with a glass of ale. When they reached their journey's end the gig was housed, the horse was fed and comforted, and the two young doctors in a private room sat down to the best dinner and the best wine the house afforded. The lights, the fire, the beating rain upon the window, the cold, incongruous work that lay before them, added zest to their enjoyment of the meal. With every glass their cordiality increased. Soon Macfarlane handed a little pile of gold to his companion.

'A compliment,' he said. 'Between friends these little d—d accommodations ought to fly like pipe-lights.'

Fettes pocketed the money, and applauded the sentiment to the echo. 'You are a philosopher,' he cried. 'I was an ass till I knew you. You and K— between you, by the Lord Harry! but you'll make a man of me.'

'Of course, we shall,' applauded Macfarlane. 'A man? I tell you, it required a man to back me up the other morning. There are some big, brawling, forty-year-old cowards who would have turned sick at the look of the d—d thing; but not you—you kept your head. I watched you.'

'Well, and why not?' Fettes thus vaunted himself.

'It was no affair of mine. There was nothing to gain on the one side but disturbance, and on the other I could count on your gratitude, don't you see?' And he slapped his pocket till the gold pieces rang.

Macfarlane somehow felt a certain touch of alarm at these unpleasant words. He may have regretted that he had taught his young companion so successfully, but he had no time to interfere, for the other noisily continued in this boastful strain:

'The great thing is not to be afraid. Now, between you and me, I don't want to hang—that's practical; but for all cant, Macfarlane, I was born with a contempt. Hell, God, Devil, right, wrong, sin, crime, and all the old gallery of curiosities—they may frighten boys, but men of the world, like you and me, despise them. Here's to the memory of Gray!'

It was by this time growing somewhat late. The gig, according to order, was brought round to the door with both lamps brightly shining, and the young men had to pay their bill and take the road. They announced that they were bound for Peebles, and drove in that direction till they were clear of the last houses of the town; then, extinguishing the lamps, returned upon their course, and followed a by-road toward Glencorse. There was no sound but that of their own passage, and the incessant, strident pouring of the rain. It was pitch dark; here and there a white gate or a white stone in the wall guided them for a short space across the night; but for the most part it was at a foot pace, and almost groping, that they picked their way through that resonant blackness to their solemn and isolated destination. In the sunken woods that traverse the neighbourhood of the burying-ground the last glimmer failed them, and it became necessary to kindle a match and reillumine one of the lanterns of the gig. Thus, under the dripping trees, and environed by huge and moving shadows, they reached the scene of their unhallowed labours.

They were both experienced in such affairs, and powerful with the spade; and they had scarce been twenty minutes at their task before they were rewarded by a dull rattle on the coffin lid. At the same moment Macfarlane, having hurt his hand upon a stone, flung it carelessly above his head. The grave, in which they now stood almost to the shoulders, was close to the edge of the plateau of the graveyard; and the gig lamp had been propped, the better to illuminate their labours, against a tree, and on the immediate verge of the steep bank descending to the stream. Chance had taken a sure aim with the stone. Then came a clang of broken glass; night fell upon them; sounds alternately dull and ringing announced the bounding of the lantern down the bank, and its occasional collision with the trees. A stone or two, which it had dislodged in its descent, rattled behind it into the profundities of the glen; and then silence, like night, resumed its sway; and they might bend their hearing to its utmost pitch, but naught was to be heard except the rain, now marching to the wind, now steadily falling over miles of open country.

They were so nearly at an end of their abhorred task that they judged it wisest to complete it in the dark. The coffin was exhumed and broken open; the body inserted in the dripping sack and carried between them to the gig; one mounted to keep it in its place, and the other, taking the horse by the mouth, groped along by wall and bush until they reached the wider road by the Fisher's Tryst. Here was a faint, diffused radiancy, which they hailed like daylight; by that they pushed the horse to a good pace and began to rattle along merrily in the direction of the town.

They had both been wetted to the skin during their operations, and now, as the gig jumped among the deep ruts, the thing that stood propped between them fell now upon one and now upon the other. At every repetition of the horrid contact each instinctively repelled it with the greater haste; and the process, natural although it was, began to tell upon the nerves of the companions. Macfarlane made some ill-favoured jest about the farmer's wife, but it came hollowly from his lips, and was allowed to drop in silence. Still their unnatural burden bumped from side to side; and now the head would be laid, as if in confidence, upon their shoulders, and now the drenching sackcloth would flap icily about their faces. A creeping chill began to possess the soul of Fettes. He peered at the bundle, and it seemed somehow larger than at first. All over the countryside, and from every degree of distance, the farm dogs accompanied their passage with tragic ululations; and it grew and grew upon his mind that some unnatural miracle had been accomplished, that some nameless change had befallen the dead body, and that it was in fear of their unholy burden that the dogs were howling.

'For God's sake,' said he, making a great effort to arrive at speech, 'for God's sake, let's have a light!'

Seemingly Macfarlane was affected in the same direction; for, though he made no reply, he stopped the horse, passed the reins to his companion, got down, and proceeded to kindle the remaining lamp. They had by that time got no farther than the cross-road down to Auchenclinny. The rain still poured as though the deluge were returning, and it was no easy matter to make a light in such a world of wet and darkness. When at last the flickering blue flame had been transferred to the wick and began to expand and clarify, and shed a wide circle of misty brightness round the gig, it became possible for the two young men to see each other and the thing they had along with them. The rain had moulded the rough sacking to the outlines of the body underneath; the head was distinct from the trunk, the shoulders plainly modelled; something at once spectral and human riveted their eyes upon the ghastly comrade of their drive.

For some time Macfarlane stood motionless, holding up the lamp. A nameless dread was swathed, like a wet sheet, about the body, and tightened the white skin upon the face of Fettes; a fear that was meaningless, a horror of what could not be, kept mounting to his brain. Another beat of the watch, and he had spoken. But his comrade forestalled him.

'That is not a woman,' said Macfarlane in a hushed voice.

'It was a woman when we put her in,' whispered Fettes.

'Hold that lamp,' said the other. 'I must see her face.'

And as Fettes took the lamp his companion untied the

fastenings of the sack and drew down the cover from the head. The light fell very clear upon the dark, well-moulded features and smooth-shaven cheeks of a too familiar countenance, often beheld in dreams of both of these young men. A wild yell rang up into the night; each leaped from his own side into the roadway; the lamp fell, broke and was extinguished; and the horse, terrified by this unusual commotion, bounded and went off toward Edinburgh at a gallop, bearing along with it, sole occupant of the gig, the body of the dead and long-dissected Gray.

ABOUT THE AUTHORS

Oscar Wilde: An Irish writer and poet, Oscar Fingal O'Flahertie Wills Wilde (16 October 1854–30 November 1900) was known for the sharp wit and flamboyant elegance of his writing.

Katherine Mansfield: Katherine Mansfield Beauchamp Murry (14 October 1888–9 January 1923) was a modernist writer of short fiction. Born and brought up in colonial New Zealand, Mansfield spent much of her adult life in London.

Ambrose Bierce: Ambrose Gwinnett Bierce (24 June 1842–circa 1914), was an American journalist, short-story writer and satirist. A searing critic and cynic in his writing, he came to be known by the nickname 'Bitter Bierce'.

O. Henry: William Sydney Porter (11 September 1862–5 June 1910), known by his pen name O. Henry, was an American writer whose writing was marked by wit, warmth and humanity.

Anton Chekov: Anton Pavlovich Chekov (29 January 1860–15 July 1904) was a Russian physician and author who is considered one of the greatest short-story writers of all time.

Kate Chopin: Born Katherine O'Flaherty (8 February 1850–22 August 1904), Kate Chopin was an American author of short stories and novels.

Rudyard Kipling: Joseph Rudyard Kipling (30 December 1865–18 January 1936) was an English writer and poet. One of the most popular writers in England in the late nineteenth and early twentieth centuries, Kipling was known for his innovativeness in the short-story format.

D.H. Lawrence: David Herbert Richards Lawrence (11 September 1885–2 March 1930) was an English novelist, poet and painter. His work often explored the dehumanizing effects of industrialization.

H.G. Wells: Best remembered today for his science fiction, English writer Herbert George Wells (21 September 1866–

13 August 1946) wrote in his time in many genres, including the novel, history and political and social commentary.

Saki: Hector Hugh Munro (18 December 1870–14 November 1916), better known by his pen name Saki and also frequently as H.H. Munro, was a British writer often regarded as a master of the short story.

Frank Stockton: Frank Richard Stockton (5 April 1834–20 April 1902) was an American writer and humorist, who is remembered today for his innovative fairy tales for children.

W.W. Jacobs: William Wymark Jacobs (8 September 1863–1 September 1943) was an English writer of short stories and novels. He is best known for his horror story 'The Monkey's Paw' but more often wrote humorous tales, frequently about life at sea.

Edgar Allan Poe: Born Edgar Poe (19 January 1809–7 October 1849), Edgar Allan Poe was an American author, poet, editor and literary critic. Widely acknowledged as the inventor of the detective fiction, Poe was one of the earliest American short-story writers.

Jack London: Born John Griffith Chaney (12 January 1876–22 November 1916), Jack London was an American author, journalist and social activist. A pioneer of magazine fiction, he was one of the most popular writers of his time.

Stephen Leacock: Stephen P. H. Butler Leacock, FRSC (30 December 1869–28 March 1944), was a Canadian teacher, political scientist and writer. His writings, known for their light humour and criticism of human follies, were widely read.

H. Rider Haggard: Sir Henry Rider Haggard, KBE (22 June 1856–14 May 1925), was an English writer of tales of swashbuckling adventure set in exotic locations, predominantly Africa.

Guy de Maupassant: Henri René Albert Guy de Maupassant (5 August 1850–6 July 1893) is generally considered the greatest French short-story writer and one of the finest exponents of the form.

Herman Melville: Herman Melville (1 August 1819–28 September 1891) was an American novelist, short-story writer and poet. Best known for his whaling adventure *Moby Dick,* Melville had mixed success as a writer during his lifetime but his work saw a later revival.

Charles Dickens: Charles John Huffam Dickens (7 February 1812–9 June 1870) was an English writer and social critic. He created some of the world's best-known fictional characters and by the twentieth century had been recognized by critics and scholars as a literary genius. His short stories and novels enjoy enduring popularity.

F. Scott Fitzgerald: Francis Scott Key Fitzgerald (24 September 1896–21 December 1940) was an American writer whose work accurately, if somewhat cynically, documented the Jazz Age.

James Joyce: James Augustine Aloysius Joyce (2 February 1882—13 January 1941) was an Irish novelist and poet, considered one of the most influential writers of the twentieth century. His stream of consciousness and interior monologue writing brought about the avant-garde movement in literature.

Bram Stoker: Abraham 'Bram' Stoker (8 November 1847–20 April 1912) was an Irish author best known for his Gothic novel *Dracula*. His understanding of vampire folklore has shaped the depiction of vampires in fiction and film.

Joseph Conrad: Born Józef Teodor Konrad Korzeniowski (3 December 1857–3 August 1924), Joseph Conrad was a Polish author who wrote in English after settling in England. He is one of the most acclaimed novelists in English literature.

M. R. James: Montague Rhodes James (1 August 1862–12 June 1936) was an English author and medievalist scholar, best remembered for his ghost stories.

Jerome K. Jerome: Jerome Klapka Jerome (2 May 1859–14 June 1927) was an English writer and humorist. While his comic travelogue *Three Men in a Boat* (1889) remains immensely popular to this day, his shorter fiction explores genres ranging from humorous to eerie, thoughtful and sombre.

W. Somerset Maugham: William Somerset Maugham (25 January 1874–16 December 1965) was an immensely successful British playwright, novelist and short-story writer of his time, whose work enjoys lasting popularity.

Virginia Woolf: Adeline Virginia Woolf (née Stephen; 25 January 1882–28 March 1941) was an English novelist and essayist and was one of the foremost literary figures of the modernist movement of the twentieth century.

Robert Louis Stevenson: Robert Louis Balfour Stevenson (13 November 1850–3 December 1894) was a Scottish novelist, poet, essayist and travel writer. His *Treasure Island*, *Kidnapped* and *Strange Case of Dr Jekyll and Mr Hyde* are widely read even today.

ABOUT TERRY O'BRIEN

Terry O'Brien is an academic with three decades of experience in teaching language and communication skills in India and abroad. He also headed a college under the auspices of the University of Delhi.

A prolific writer, with several books to his credit, Terry O'Brien is a reputed professional motivational speaker and a quizmaster.